A DURABLE FIRE

Barbara and Stephanie Keating grew up in Kenya. One sister now lives in France and the other in Dublin. Their first novel was the bestselling *To My Daughter in France*, which was followed by the acclaimed novel *Blood Sisters*.

BARBARA & STEPHANIE KEATING

A Durable Fire

VINTAGE BOOKS
London

Published by Vintage 2007

6 8 10 9 7 5

First published in Great Britain in 2006 by Harvill Secker

Vintage
Random House, 20 Vauxhall Bridge Road,
London SW1V 2SA

www.vintage-books.co.uk

Addresses for companies within The Random House Group Limited
can be found at: www.randomhouse.co.uk/offices.htm

The Random House Group Limited Reg. No. 954009

A CIP catalogue record for this book
is available from the British Library

ISBN 9780099501695

The Random House Group Limited supports The Forest Stewardship
Council (FSC), the leading international forest certification organisation.
All our titles that are printed on Greenpeace approved FSC certified paper
carry the FSC logo. Our paper procurement policy can be found at:
www.rbooks.co.uk/environment

Mixed Sources
Product group from well-managed
forests and other controlled sources
www.fsc.org Cert no. TT-COC-2139
© 1996 Forest Stewardship Council
FSC

Typeset by SX Composing DTP, Rayleigh, Essex
Printed and bound in Great Britain by
CPI Cox & Wyman, Reading, RG1 8EX

FOR CHRISTOPHER

But true love is a durable fire,
In the mind ever burning,
Never sick, never old, never dead,
From itself never turning.
Walter Raleigh

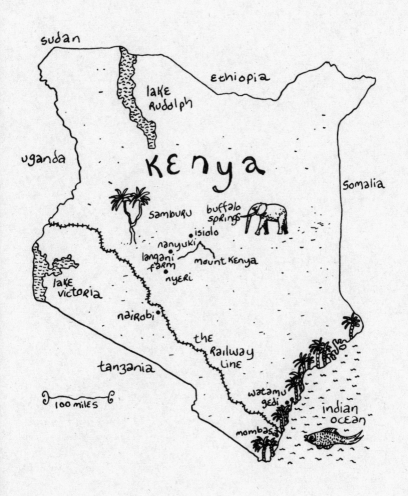

Prologue

Kenya, September 1970

She would never go back. That was the promise she had made to herself, but now she could not quell her excitement as the plane began plunging through layers of cloud towards the parched earth. She closed her eyes and turned her head away from the window in case it might distort, in some way, her first view of the land. Then she felt the thud of impact, and later Edward reached out his hand to help her up from her seat. There was a clunking sound as the heavy door swung open and Camilla took the first deliberate breath, savouring the unmistakable scent of Africa, dragging the familiar taste into her mouth and lungs.

The runway was like a mirage in the shimmering heat. Before them sprawled the glass and concrete of Nairobi's airport buildings, but she barely noticed them. Her gaze devoured the bleached plains beyond the security fence, the empty blue of the morning sky, the flat tops of thorn trees, the swirl of dust as a truck made its way across a dirt track to reach the main road into the city. Tears blurred her vision as she followed Edward down the aircraft steps, placing her feet deliberately and slowly, like a pilgrim, on to the Kenyan soil. It had been so long, each year a kind of lifetime. And now she was returning for the wrong reasons, but it didn't matter because she was here.

They had arranged with the airline that there would be no press interviews, and she was grateful when they were escorted across the tarmac into a private lounge. The handling of formalities had not changed. She could sense Edward's irritation as he stood waiting for their passports to be stamped, shifting his weight from one leg to another. He hated bureaucracy. The immigration officer seemed bored and surly as he read the passports from cover to cover, making Camilla feel like a criminal. Or a fugitive whose disguise must be penetrated. She looked at him, deeply

I

weary and a little afraid. Her head was aching and she tried to ignore the anxious fluttering in her stomach. The man's brow wrinkled in a frown, nostrils flaring for a moment in the broad nose as he glanced up at her and then went back to the slow turning of pages. Eventually he lifted a rubber stamp from its pad and banged it down, on to the visa forms. She had begun to turn away when suddenly he smiled at her, his black face breaking into a flash of white teeth and humorous eyes.

'Welcome to Nairobi, madam. Sir. Enjoy your stay.'

A porter appeared with their bags and they followed him to the customs area. An Indian couple stood beside an inspection bench, the woman stoical and silent, the husband arguing volubly. His gums and teeth were stained red from chewing betel nut and a speck of foam appeared at the corner of his mouth. His wife sighed and pulled her sari over her long hair. The customs official was turning out all their possessions, refusing to meet their gaze or to heed their pleading explanations. With five suitcases they were going to be there for a while. That evidently hadn't changed much either. Camilla felt a rush of sympathy for them as a member of the airport staff arrived to usher her away. She felt Edward's hand beneath her elbow as they passed through a side door marked 'Staff Only' and found themselves outside in a private car park.

She saw Sarah at once. They ran towards one another and embraced in silence, moved apart to study each other and then hugged again.

'I'm so sorry.' Sarah tucked a strand of unruly hair behind her ear. 'It shouldn't have taken this to bring you back.'

Camilla nodded, raising a hand to brush away tears of a different origin. They walked the short distance to the waiting car with Edward close behind them. Already the outsider. There was nothing he could say. On the twenty-minute drive into the city, a deluge of humanity spilled from houses, buses and cars. Hundreds of schoolchildren clogged the dusty paths. Office workers in crisp, starched clothes clutched briefcases and plastic bags. Older women, wrapped in brightly printed *kitenge* cloth, still carried bundles of sticks on their backs, the leather straps that bound the wood pressing deep into their foreheads. A herdsman in a scarlet *shuka* guided scrawny cattle across a ditch, tapping them with a long stick, whistling his commands. Young men swerved close on bicycles and ramshackle cars belched poisonous fumes. Uniformed drivers slid past in Mercedes cars bearing perfectly groomed black men and women.

Politicians, probably; Camilla had rarely seen an African woman riding in the back of a Mercedes or even driving a car. Tilting buses overtook them, careering past at breakneck speed, packed with people, topped with a swaying cargo of sacks and bales roped on to the sagging roofs.

'So many people! I didn't expect so many people.' Her voice was choked, and she found herself slightly breathless. 'All these houses and shacks in every direction. My God, where have they all sprung from?'

'You'll see it everywhere, and you'll feel it too,' Sarah said.

Camilla turned to Edward. 'All this space used to be empty, remember? Beautiful, empty Africa. I saw lions on the edge of this road once. And plenty of plains game, always.'

'It's called progress.' Sarah's tone was resigned.

Camilla shivered, unable to come to terms with the daunting glut and press of bodies. She had been steeling herself to accept whatever changes she might find. So much had happened since the night she had fled the land of her childhood. It had taken a long time for Edward to draw her out of the protective shell she had built around herself, but he had been patient. When the phone call had come, out of the blue, she had initially been torn apart by grief, then filled with guilt and foreboding.

'You must go back now, darling. I know that,' Edward had said, holding her steady in a world that was spinning away. 'But I could take a few days off and come with you. Would that help?'

Camilla had been surprised by his offer. He seldom set aside any time for himself. It was something she had never learned to deal with well, this dedication that excluded everything and everybody when he was working. She had never believed he would get away until the moment of leaving for the airport last night. But here they were in Kenya, the land of her earliest memories, her childhood dreams and later failures.

They came to a halt outside the Norfolk Hotel and she stepped out of the Land Rover. The manager was waiting for them, all smooth assurances. They could fill in the registration cards later, he said, and he had banished the press for the time being. Camilla shut her eyes for a moment and took a deep breath, before walking through the lobby and into her past. She had stood in this courtyard so many times. As a child gazing at the brilliant plumage of the birds in the aviary, as a teenager in her first ball gown, as a young woman in the throes of her first love affair. She looked at the twisted trunk of the bougainvillea that still clung to these same walls, showering the balconies with purple splendour. There were weaver birds nesting in the acacia tree and a sunbird hovered, iridescent, over the hibiscus flowers.

'I'll find a table for breakfast,' Sarah said, and disappeared in the direction of the dining room.

Camilla followed Edward into their cottage suite. The room smelled of floor polish and there was a large vase of roses with a card. She read the note and placed it face down on the sideboard. Not yet, she told herself. You don't need to deal with this now. She unlocked her suitcase, tossed a layer of clothes on to the bed and found a clean shirt and slacks. The black dress was near the top and she lifted it out and held it for a few moments, wondering if she was in the middle of a bad dream. Then she shook her head and put it on a hanger in the wardrobe. Her hand luggage was on the chest of drawers and she snapped open the locks, searching for the basics that would help her to freshen up for breakfast.

'*Hodi! Hodi,* memsahib?'

The soft call was both comforting and familiar and she smiled a greeting at the room boy. They weren't called room boys any more, of course, and Camilla wondered what the correct term was these days. She asked him to take the black dress away for pressing and to turn down the bed. It was a moment or two before she realised she was addressing him in Swahili, as though she had never left. Edward emerged from the bathroom.

'Good God! I wondered who was out here, chattering away,' he said. 'You haven't forgotten, then.'

'I thought I had, but it was just waiting to be reawakened,' she said. 'I must say it's very irritating, the way you always manage to look like that after a long flight. As if you'd come from some grand hotel where they press your suit and polish your shoes every hour. Give me a moment before we join Sarah. I need strong Kenyan coffee and a wedge of pawpaw with lime. In fact, why don't you go on ahead to the dining room, and I'll follow in a few minutes.'

In the bathroom mirror her reflection was not encouraging. 'The red-eye, dead-eye look of overnight travel,' she said aloud. 'And my hair – full of static, like dried twigs. I hope I don't see anyone I know.'

She washed her face and combed her hair back, twisting it into a smooth, pale gold knot on the nape of her neck. There was an outsize pair of dark glasses in her handbag and she put them on. Then she crossed the courtyard in the bright sunlight and picked her way through the morning frenzy of the lobby. A large man was standing close to the reception desk, uncomfortable and self-conscious in a bush jacket that was new and shiny. His perfectly coiffed wife watched and counted, pointing with manicured fingertips as their baggage was loaded into a safari vehicle. Camilla smiled. Soon the lacquered hair would become a helmet of trapped dust. New travelling companions introduced them-selves, outwardly courteous but already vying for the best places in the safari cars. Drivers revved engines and tour guides checked their lists. Husbands chided wives lingering in the boutique, riffling through displays of shirts and hats and African jewellery. Camilla moved on. Too many reminders here.

In the comparative quiet of the dining room, Sarah and Edward were already working their way through coffee, tea and bacon and eggs. Sarah was smiling, her face open and friendly, green eyes shining as she leaned forward, explaining something with enthusiasm. She looked well, Camilla thought. Tanned and full of energy. Her brown hair was streaked with sunshine and her nose was a little burnt and beginning to peel, just as it had always been when they were children. Camilla glanced around the room. No familiar faces, thank God, and no one had recognised her.

'Did you order for me? I'm rather hungry.' She did not want to talk about the days ahead. It was too raw, and she needed time to compose herself.

'You didn't eat anything on the plane, so I've ordered you the works,' Edward said, pouring coffee. 'Then you'll need to rest. Tomorrow will be long and demanding. I suggest we stay here today, and choose somewhere quiet for dinner this evening.'

'No.' She looked at him a little wildly, her distress evident. 'I can't lie around all day, doing nothing. I want to spend time with Sarah. This evening too. It's been so long. And I haven't seen Hannah since – well, since another age.'

'She hasn't changed. She's very anxious to get here,' Sarah said.

'Is she, really?' Camilla saw that Edward had registered the anxiety in her voice.

'Those were bad days for all of us. Full of confusion. And fear. We were too young for what happened. None of us could have been prepared.'

Sarah reached out a hand. 'Of course we can spend the day together. I'm here only for you.'

'We were unbelievably close, weren't we?' Camilla twisted the gold bangle on her wrist and tried to smile. Sarah was so straightforward, so guileless. Totally unlike everyone in her London circle. It had taken her some time to navigate the loaded sentences of apparently innocent conversations, searching for a give-away inflection to guide her to the real meaning behind every line. 'We're older now, and maybe wiser,' she said. 'Less idealistic at any rate.'

'When is Hannah coming into Nairobi?' Edward said.

'Maybe this afternoon, if she can get away. Otherwise first thing tomorrow. She said she'd ring when she got here.' Sarah tried to sound casual, but she had noticed Camilla's tight grip on her knife and fork and the apprehension in her eyes.

Camilla stared at the glistening eggs on her plate. So yellow, the yolks here. She wasn't hungry any more and she wished Edward had not ordered such a large breakfast. Her stomach was churning and her courage had evaporated. She was not ready for Hannah. For any of it. She wondered if she would ever be ready to pick up the threads that had never quite broken, in spite of the years and the miles that had stretched the distances between them. They had been inseparable once, the three of them, in spite of their different backgrounds and the diverse paths they had followed since leaving school. They had believed then that nothing could destroy the bond between them. At least Sarah would be here when they were finally reunited. That would smooth over the first, difficult steps towards understanding and forgiveness.

'How about a little shut-eye, darling? Even an hour would be good for you.' Edward's voice sounded very loud, crashing through her thoughts.

'No, thank you. I told you, I don't want to sleep.' She was aware that she sounded shrill, that the tension between them was obvious. 'I thought Sarah could take me to the hospital this morning,' she said. Her heart had begun to jump, and she put down her cup to hide the tremor in her hands.

'I don't think you should do that right away.' Edward was frowning as he signed for breakfast and rose from the table. 'You've been through enough, and there are going to be so many people you'll have to talk to tomorrow. You need to give yourself time, Camilla. Prepare for what will be pretty gruelling.'

'I want to go to the hospital this morning,' she said, her voice cracking.

'Camilla – there's something you should know.' Sarah was sitting very straight in her chair, her body tense. 'Before you see him.'

'What is it?' Camilla's perfect skin had turned chalky. 'He's not going to die, is he? Is that what you're going to tell me?' She could hear her heart thumping, loud and much too fast. Her limbs weakened with relief as Sarah shook her head. 'What is it, then? What's happened that I don't—'

'Excuse me, madam,' the head waiter spoke softly, 'there is someone to see you. She says she is your friend. Your *rafiki ya zamani*.'

Camilla turned, unable to control the apprehension that was closing her throat. There was no doubt in her mind that it would be Hannah. She had not had time to think this through, to search for the right words. She looked around for Edward. He was standing a little apart and she resented his expression, the way that he allowed his curiosity to result in slightly raised eyebrows. She shouldn't have come with him. It was her own journey into the past, her own all-consuming sadness, and he had no place there until she could make sense of it.

Hannah had reached the table. She stood very still, her face unreadable as she gazed at her childhood friend, her eyes level, a slight tilt to her chin. Then she reached out towards Camilla with both hands. The gesture seemed to freeze for a moment in the air between them, before they took the first steps across the scarred landscape of their past.

Chapter 1

Buffalo Springs, June 1966

It was the sound of cackling beyond the compound fence that unnerved her and brought back the nightmare's full force. From the edge of sleep Sarah could hear the hyena's maniacal laughter, the *whup whup* of its calling. The dream flooded her mind and she was up on the ridge once more. She could see the warrior with his feathered headdress, poised and motionless with arm raised, spear point glinting in the cold wash of moonlight. And then the hyena, crouching on the outcrop above her. Suddenly she was falling. Falling down the side of the hill with the sound of rocks tumbling after her, and she could hear screaming.

She opened her mouth to cry out in fear and pain but no sound came and she found herself awake, sitting bolt upright in her bed. There was a furtive rustling in the thatched roof and the night was all around her, smothering her in its blackness. Her hands were trembling as she struck a match and lit the kerosene lamp, keeping the flame low in case Dan or Allie were still awake and might notice her light. Sarah did not want to answer their knock on her door, or hear the kindness and concern in their voices. She sat on the edge of the bed trying to regain control of her shaking limbs, forcing herself to take long, slow breaths that might help to banish the horror in her head.

The images would gradually fade, Dr Markham had told her. Her father had said the same thing during their telephone conversations. But several months had passed and the dreams continued, always vivid and terrifying. She had refused sleeping pills and tranquillisers, rejected her parents' urgings to come back to Ireland where she could distance herself from the pain. Finally, Raphael and Betty Mackay had travelled to Buffalo Springs, arriving unannounced at the research camp where their daughter lived and worked.

It was a modest compound, rather like a *manyatta*, with a thorn fence surrounding the rondavels in which they lived and ate. The Briggses had set up their office in the largest building. The main room was protected from rain and heat by a woven thatched roof, and the large windows had shutters that were almost always open, to allow every possible hint of breeze into the area. The furniture was old and chipped, but Allie had spread colourful *kangas* over the chairs to disguise their lumpy upholstery. The inside dining table doubled as her desk, and one end of it was piled with notes written in her neat hand. The back wall served as a giant notice-board on which Dan had pinned up a series of charts, showing the numbers and movements of the elephant herds they were studying. He updated them each day, moving the coloured pins that indicated the size, age and sex of the members in each family group. Before dinner each evening he would type up the day's observations on an ancient typewriter which made a high-pitched pinging sound each time he pushed the carriage return. A good deal of the floor space was taken up with boxes of reference papers and piles of books. Their bedroom was on one side of the living room, and they relied on the low thatch to keep out the heat and also the rain.

Sarah had been allocated her own rondavel which contained a wooden bed set beneath a cloud of mosquito netting, a roughly made desk and chair, and a cupboard with some hanging space and shelves. On the other side of the compound was a mud and wattle building that housed the kitchen and stores, and provided rooms for the staff. Two simple enclosures contained showers, with big canvas buckets hanging from overhead branches, the dangling chains ready to release hot, wood-scented water that washed away dust and sand and sweat, and always made Sarah feel newborn. The tents enclosing the long-drops were discreetly situated to one side of the sleeping huts. There was a second rondavel for the occasional guests, and Allie had planted a few hardy flowers and shrubs outside the modest buildings, adding a splash of colour to the dusty surroundings. Some three hundred yards away, the Uaso Nyiro River flowed past them, sometimes blue and silver, more often muddy and turgid in the dry heat. At night Sarah could hear the sound of hippos snorting and wallowing in the cool hours of darkness. From the day of her arrival she had loved her simple home, and her research work with Dan and Allie Briggs was the fulfilment of her childhood dreams.

9

After the tragedy she had returned to the camp, flayed by loss and grief but sure that her only chance of sanity lay in her work. She had been sitting under a tree, reading through her notes for the day, when the cloud of dust announced the arrival of a car. It was late afternoon and a light breeze riffled her papers, scattering several pages on the dusty ground. She bent to retrieve them, half listening to voices that were oddly familiar. Then the wooden gate creaked open and she found herself staring in amazement at her parents. On that first night she had poured out the whole story as they sat on camp chairs around the fire. She was grateful for the comfort of their presence, although there was really nothing they could say to alleviate her suffering. It was only a year since Raphael's health problems had forced him to leave Kenya, and he was plainly overjoyed to be back in the country. But Betty was anxious about the risk of his contracting malaria again — something they all knew would be fatal. It was clear to Sarah that they had made the journey with the express purpose of persuading her to come home.

They remained in camp for a week, going out in the Land Rover each day, learning about Sarah's work as she followed her group of elephants. She was glad that they could see her here, know that she was safe and well looked after, that this was the best place for her to be right now. But on the night before their departure, she saw that she had failed to convince them of her certainty. Betty pleaded with her to return to Ireland, to spend time at the family home in Sligo, and Raphael tried his own gentle form of persuasion.

'We're going to Mombasa for ten days now,' he said. 'We'll visit old friends and walk the beach and swim, before heading back to Sligo. And we'd like you to come back with us when we leave for Ireland. Come home, for a while.'

Sarah shook her head. 'I can't leave here now,' she said. 'It isn't the right time, Dad.'

'It's peaceful there,' he said. 'A good place to think. A healing place, with the sound of the sea and the strand, and the green fields and hills around you. We'll all be there to get you through any bad patch, especially Tim. You've always been close to your brother.'

But after that first recounting of the horror, Sarah's nightmares had redoubled and she did not want to talk about it any more. She knew that in Ireland she would be unable to deal with their continuing compassion, their hushed sympathy. Nor could she cope with the questions, the bewildered sorrow in the faces of relatives and friends. On the morning of their departure for the coast, Raphael and Betty finally accepted that she would not come back with them to Sligo. Dan and Allie had supported her decision, sitting up late into the night with the Mackays, trying to put their minds at ease, promising to watch over their daughter and to send her home if they thought it had all become too much. As they said their goodbyes, Sarah was torn between the longing to have them near and the need to escape into her own world. She was sure that total immersion in her work would prove the best way towards healing, towards filling the bottomless void of loss.

She had watched with tears in her eyes as their small aircraft vanished into the piercing blue of the afternoon, and then headed back to the camp. Driving through the bush in the ancient Land Rover, watching the spin and flash of an eagle in the bleached-out sky, following the herds of game through the coarse, yellow grasslands, she knew that this was the way to navigate her altered life with some sense of purpose. But the nights still lay in wait for her. Her once-welcoming hut had become a place of menacing shadows, filling her with dread each time she closed the door on another day.

Alone now, in the flicker of lamplight, Sarah heard the hyena call again and she shivered in spite of the heat in the night air. There was no point in trying to sleep. She pushed her feet into her sandals and lifted the mosquito net. Her hand was not quite steady as she picked up the lantern and went to the jumble of research papers on her desk. A folder of her most recent photographs lay on the top of the pile and she took the pictures out one by one to look at the elephants, hoping to draw strength from their ancient wisdom.

She found her work completely satisfying, thinking of it more as a vocation, relishing each new experience as she recorded the behaviour of the great creatures, in her notebooks and with her camera. And she had been more than fortunate in her employers. The Briggses had taken her on as a raw recruit, a newly qualified graduate with no experience outside of a dissecting dish in the laboratory of her Dublin college. But they had decided to give her a chance because she had spent her childhood in Kenya, already spoke fluent Swahili and was an exceptional photographer. They paid her very little, but she had a place to live and they supplied food, and she had the use of a battered Land Rover and unlimited supplies of film. Since she spent almost all of her time in the area around Buffalo Springs and the adjacent Samburu Game Reserve, Sarah had little need for money and the arrangement suited her perfectly.

During the past eight months Dan and Allie had taught her the science of observing their fascinating subjects, shown her how to write up her notes with scientific discipline, and helped her to devise a system of cataloguing her pictures. From Erope, her Samburu tracker and trusted friend, she had learned to follow the herds without intruding, and to anticipate the direction in which they might travel next in search of food and water. Slowly she had begun to understand their actions, to respect their intentions and to admire the order of their family and social structures. The team worked well together, and Sarah was proud of the fact that her talent for photography had become a new and valuable part of the project.

She sat down at her desk and began to put yesterday's notes in order. Her eyes prickled with exhaustion and she blinked away the sensation of grit and burning, determined to focus on her papers, to obliterate the nightmare. But after half an hour she abandoned any attempt at concentration and went back to bed, turning down the lamp until it was barely a flicker, lying stiffly under the mosquito net, eyes still open. Her alarm clock told her that the dawn would not come to her rescue for another three hours. She wished that she could pray, but her childhood faith in a merciful God had been extinguished during that one, terrible night, and now she could only clutch at the sheet with anxious fingers and count out the minutes until a fractured form of sleep enveloped her.

Sarah joined Dan and Allie at the breakfast table under the acacia tree, squinting in the bright light and pulling her chair into a puddle of shade. She was too tired to eat more than the slice of pawpaw on her plate, and she crumbled some toast into small pieces and fed it to the noisy starlings strutting at her feet, waiting for any offerings and quarrelling over the spoils.

'We need to talk about our presentation in Nairobi next week.' Allie had noticed the shadows beneath Sarah's eyes and the jerky movements of her strung-out body. 'It's shaping up to be extremely important. We're going to put forward our budget for next year as planned, and Dan is pretty sure the African Wildlife Federation will back us for the same amount as before. But we have to expand the study now, and we badly need a new vehicle. That rattletrap you're driving will collapse one of these days, Sarah, and land you in big trouble. You and Erope will end up trekking through the *bundu* past a few very unfriendly creatures, just to get back into camp.'

'You've put in for more money, haven't you?' Sarah said.

'We have. Although the A.W.F. aren't too encouraging,' Allie said, but her eyes were bright with excitement. 'Dan has had another letter from the Smithsonian, and they're going to have one of their chaps at the meeting. If they like what they see and hear, he may come up here afterwards.'

'They've hinted that they're willing to offer us *some* funding, at last,' Dan said.

'A published paper would bring Dan the recognition he deserves,' Allie said, looking at her husband with pride. 'And that's not all. There will be press people there, including someone interested in doing a feature on us for a London paper. Plus they'll see your photographs, Sarah. It would be fantastic if they were willing to use some of those with an article.'

'This is our plan,' Dan said. 'We're going to present our annual report as usual. But the A.W.F. has invited a couple of Nairobi-based journalists to the second half of the meeting. Guys that write articles for *Time* magazine and one of the British newspapers. So, after our budget discussions, we want to show some of your slides. Pictures which will catch the interest of the press, and which are not aimed only at a bunch of dry old scientists and committee members.'

'In fact, we'd like you to make the presentation,' Allie said. 'You have that native gift of the gab, Sarah. No, it's much more than that. You have a poetic turn of phrase that fires people's imagination, makes things come alive. I've seen it when you talk to tourists and other visitors who come here. And since we're using your pictures, you should be the one to talk about them.'

'That's right,' Dan said. 'Allie and I – we're real good at what we do, wandering around after our elephants, writing things into our notebooks and all. But we don't cut much ice on the public platform. So I reckon you could put together a slide show that gives a general picture of things up here. Something that will have a wider appeal than our usual facts and figures.'

'Oh, I don't think so. I've never done anything like that.' Sarah was alarmed.

'And on the way back from Nairobi you could stop off at Langani for a couple of days,' Allie said. 'Take a break. See how Hannah's coming along now, especially with the baby so close. What do you say?'

Sarah looked down at her plate, furiously concentrating on spreading jam on a slice of toast that she could not eat. She did not want them to recognise the panic that had begun to dry up her mouth. They were offering her a valuable opportunity to show her photographs to influential people and she was moved by their confidence, by their kindness. She owed them so much, Dan and Allie. From the beginning they had been ideal employers, and now they had become steadfast friends. But her mind and body still felt perilously close to a breakdown. Each sentence she spoke required effort, even at Buffalo Springs where she was with people who understood. She did not think she was ready to face any gathering of strangers or make a speech. Someone in the audience would be bound to know who she was, and if anyone raised the subject of the events at Langani Farm, she would fall apart.

In addition, she did not feel ready to return to Langani. It was more than three months since the wedding and she had not been able to go back, in spite of several invitations. Lately Hannah had stopped asking, and the possibility of even a weekend visit had been dropped from letters and conversations on the radio telephone. Sarah felt guilty. She knew that it would mean a great deal to her dearest friend if she drove down to the farm, but she could not bring herself to do it. On the other hand, this presentation in Nairobi was a professional matter, and it was vital to Dan and Allie. Funding for the coming year depended largely upon its success, and Sarah wanted to contribute. But if she went to pieces in the middle of it and lost them a sponsorship, she would not be able to forgive herself.

'You know how grateful I am to both of you.' She looked away, attempting to hide the welling of tears. 'You've been so generous, and I'm touched by your faith in my powers of communication. But I can't do it. Not yet. I could ruin things for you if I broke down, or something stupid.'

'I can see it would be hard at first.' Dan patted her arm. 'But sooner or later, kid, you have to leave your sanctuary. It's been a boon to have the bush and the elephants as a retreat. You've needed that during these past months. It's not possible, though, to stay up here in isolation for ever. Otherwise I'd do it myself, for different reasons.'

'I know that. And I will try soon to take a few days and—'

'You'll be among people who are working with us to protect the wildlife,' Dan said. 'And your fine pictures could bring us in a raft of money for the project. Allie and I are sure of that. So don't give it the thumbs down just yet. Mull it over for a day or two. Because I do believe you're a heck of a lot stronger than you think.'

Allie said nothing, but Sarah could read the appeal in her eyes. Even the prospect of being in the busy hum of Nairobi made her feel nauseous. Unwilling to let her friends see the depth of her fear, she mumbled that she would think things over and rose from the table with an excuse about collecting her gear for the morning's work.

Inside her hut she remembered those first days after her return from Langani. It had been Allie who had stayed with her late into the nights, setting the lantern where it would give maximum light, making no comment when Sarah jumped at every sound and followed the room's shifting shadows with frightened eyes. Allie, with her down-to-earth support and understanding, had allowed Sarah to make her slow adjustments and to deal with her nightmares without having to speak about the things she longed to forget. Allie and Dan had given her time to grieve, had made no demands on her since she had returned to work. Now they were asking her to do this one thing for them and she would have to refuse. It was absolutely out of the question, and in any case they could manage perfectly well on their own. After all, what had they done before she came along?

She sat down at her desk and began to sift through her slides and photographs, picking out the best shots to illustrate each aspect of their present work programme. She would write a script and Dan could read it as he showed her slides. That would have to do. But she realised that without more sponsorship for the Briggses, she herself might even be out of work and she would have to leave Buffalo Springs. To allow the research project to fail when it was so vital to the survival of the elephants she had come to love and admire – that was too awful to contemplate. For an hour she wrestled with the sentences, turning them over in her mind, trying to recapture her own awed delight as the individual characters of the herd had emerged.

She had come to know each family group, watching the huge beasts each day as they followed each other to the river with silent tread, using their trunks to drink and spray the water, digging with their tusks in the sand, rumbling to one another in conversation or trumpeting messages of warning or alarm. She had all her working notes, recorded in the precise, scientific terms that Allie had taught her to use. But they did not convey the excitement she had felt as her knowledge grew, and she had begun to understand fully the importance of protecting the magnificent animals. Finally she threw down her pen in frustration.

The idea came to her suddenly and she suppressed it at once. She knew where to find the right words, but the source was too painful to contemplate. Yet, against her will, she reached into the drawer of her desk and took out the letters. She had written them to Piet, when she had first come to Buffalo Springs and the world was a place of joy and unlimited possibilities. But she had never sent them, because she was not sure then that he loved her. Instead she had put them away, hoping that one day she might read them aloud to him. When he asked her to marry him she had decided to make the letters and her drawings and photographs into a book, and give them to him for a wedding gift.

She was barely able to read the first sentences, but as she forced herself to turn the pages, she understood what Allie had been saying. When she described the elephants, wrote about their lives and their surroundings, she did have a real gift for bringing to life a variety of stories and incidents in their daily experiences. Tears fell on to the pages she had written, blurring the power of the words she had set down for the man she had loved. Still loved. And she knew that neither Dan nor Allie could read them out on her behalf, knew she would have to find the courage to stand up and say them herself. Say them loud and clear, for the elephants, for her friends, and for the memory of a time when Piet's image was a bright, shining hope in her life. She would have to steel herself. When she had folded the letters away she climbed into her narrow camp bed although the day had barely begun, and turned her face to the wall. Swallowing the sounds of her mourning, she lay curled into a ball, her fists clenched together until at last she slept.

A knock on the door jolted her into consciousness. The immediate sense of loss that always attended her wakening hurtled forward to invade her brain, and the noonday light was tainted with the darkness of her mind's eye.

'Lunch is ready, Memsahib Sarah.' Ahmed, the camp cook, was carrying a tray with a cold Tusker beer and a tall glass. He peered in at her with concern. 'I have made your best favourite. It will give you plenty of *nguvu* for the rest of the day. And Bwana Dan has sent you a Tusker.'

She took her place at the table that had been pushed further into the mottled shade. Even the birds were silent in the heat of the early afternoon and there was no hint of a breeze in the heavy air.

'Thanks for the beer, Dan,' she said. 'I fell by the wayside this morning. Sorry.'

'Come on now, kid,' Dan said. 'We have to look after you. Keep you in good shape for all our sakes. Finish up all that chow on your plate, and go find some elephants. I'll drive with you this afternoon.'

She smiled at his gruff tone, aware of the underlying protectiveness that he offered, although he made valiant attempts to conceal it.

'Look, there's something I want to say.' She rushed the words so that she would not be tempted to go back on her resolution. 'You are both right. I have to face the world at some stage, and this is as good a time as any. I'll put together a slide show for next week. And thanks for your faith in me. I'll try to live up to it.'

In the days that followed Sarah whittled down her elephant portraits and shots of the dry, northern region, choosing her most dramatic pictures of the terrain and vegetation and then discarding them in favour of sharper images. When darkness swallowed the surrounding bush, she started up her projector and with Dan and Allie she studied and put aside her best slides, laughing over recollections of vehicles stuck in the sand, of narrow escapes from angry animals, of cameras and notebooks thrown aside as a young elephant rushed at the Land Rover, or times when clothing and notes were drenched through an open roof hatch by unexpected downpours.

It was important to create a balance. This was a scientific study, not a tourist promotion. But Sarah wanted her audience to feel the power and majesty of the elephants and their habitat, to immerse themselves in the complex structure of the reserve, to understand the reasons for the study and the way that Dan's project could fill in the jigsaw of the region's wildlife and its structure. There was a natural harmony in her wilderness, but there was ugliness too. Weaklings were left behind by the herds and died; drought brought starvation. Elephants and rhinos were decimated by poachers with lorries and guns. There was no place in the Briggses' camp for a research assistant who used knowledge to hide reality. She remembered Dan's stern challenge after she had witnessed the slaughter of several elephants by Shifta bandits. Seeing a fallen elephant, left to die after the tusks had been hacked from its majestic head, she had wept. Dan had asked her, on that day, if she was strong enough to live and work in Africa. She would learn that strength, she had told him wholeheartedly, little knowing that she would soon be put to the limits of endurance, to the edge of sanity. And today she still wanted to keep that resolve, to stay on, to contribute something to a world she had loved from childhood.

On the day before their departure for Nairobi, Allie asked her what she planned to wear.

'Wear? I hadn't given it a thought.' Now that the question had arisen, Sarah realised that she had spent the last six months in faded khaki trousers and bush shirts, with a canvas hat pulled down over her eyes to shade her from the sun and prevent her nose from peeling.

'I'll bet you have something really good that Camilla gave you,' Allie said. 'This is one of the times when it's handy to have a fashion model for a best friend.'

They settled on a linen skirt with a woven leather belt, and a cream silk blouse that showed up Sarah's tanned complexion.

'You can add some Samburu beads,' Allie said. 'The ones Erope had made for you. And you need to do something with your hair. It's a beautiful warm colour, but it needs shaping. Maybe I can trim it. Come on, I can see you don't trust my hairdressing skills, but I can do a great job on you. Sit out there under the tree, and I'll get my scissors. You've seen me giving Dan a haircut, and he doesn't look too bad.'

The result was surprisingly professional, and Sarah was taken aback when she looked into the small mirror on the wall of her hut. She rarely took stock of her appearance. Her face was thinner than it had been six months ago, but she was suntanned with a smattering of freckles on her cheeks, and her green eyes were bright. She had shampooed her hair and brushed it vigorously while it was still wet, so that it framed her features in a sun-streaked mass. Sarah smiled. It seemed amazing that she could look so vibrant and still feel a cold void of loss in the pit of her stomach. An emptiness that she could not afford to dwell on, lest her determination to function normally should be derailed.

She was nervous when she arrived at the headquarters of the African Wildlife Federation. Dan and Allie were in the boardroom testing the microphone, running a tray of slides through the projector, adjusting the screen. A long table and chairs stretched down the centre of the room. Thirty chairs. Each place had a folder containing the project report; a financial statement showed their expenditure to date, and a budget estimate for the following year. Dan had been told to expect someone from *National Geographic*, and he was on the lookout for a director from the Research Department of the Smithsonian Institute. These were the men who decided on grants that would keep the Briggses' research alive, and hopefully allow expansion. Sarah had never addressed a meeting through a microphone before. Her mouth felt uncomfortably dry and she looked around for something to drink. On a side table stood trays of refreshments, and the smell of the coffee was comforting. She poured herself a cup and within minutes she was anxiously searching for a bathroom.

'Oh God,' she muttered to Allie, 'I didn't realise this would be so nerve-wracking. I hope I won't let you down. You've heard me rehearse it, and you could still take my place.'

'Rubbish,' Allie said. 'You're going to be fine. Just speak from your heart. Speak out for the elephants. This is not about you or me, or Dan. It's about them. Keep that in mind and you'll be grand. And don't drink any more coffee, or you'll be wanting to pee. Take small sips of water if it's really necessary.'

Introductions were made. People gathered around the table, smoking cigarettes or pipes, and discussing conservation and politics, corruption and greed and international aid funds. Sarah began to feel more confident as she talked to Dan and Allie's sponsors, who were openly enthusiastic and impressed by the year's results. The man from the Smithsonian Institute was more formal, and Dan took him aside to engage him in a more detailed conversation. Allie concentrated on a rumpled man who chain-smoked and had yellow fingers. He was from *The Times* in London and Sarah talked to him at length, hoping that something she said would persuade him to write a feature about the elephants. She was startled when Dan suddenly asked everyone to be seated and launched into his introduction.

'Last year we took on an extra researcher to help with our work,' he said. 'I'd like you all to meet Sarah Mackay. She's a great addition to our team, and she's going to show you some of her own photographs which will illustrate the behaviour of the herds we're studying. Through these observations you will see the delicate and essential balance that has to be maintained between the elephants and their environment. And you will understand the all-important role of the Samburu people who share the same land, and in whose hands its future protection must lie.'

Sarah stood up beside Dan, her palms clammy, her mouth dry again. But as the blinds were drawn and her photographs appeared on the large screen, she knew that the power of the pictures had captured her audience. There were slides of the river, sometimes brown and slow and lazy, sometimes rushing over shining boulders under a rain-laden sky. She showed portraits of Samburu tribesmen in their scarlet *shuka*s and pictures of their scrawny, hump-backed cattle and flocks of ravenous goats whose images glowed through the ever-present halo of dust. She had captured the fragility of feathery grasses and wild flowers bathed in the gold light of evening, and silhouettes of baobab trees with giant trunks and spidery arms reaching into a blue, cloudless emptiness.

But more than these, there were the photographs of the elephants themselves. Their gigantic heads filled the screen, wise and silent. Power loomed in their scale, in their great feet and the bulk of thick, cross-hatched skin, in the enormous flapping ears and the raised trunk of a charging male. But she had caught their vulnerability too, with shots of a calf huddled and protected between its mother's legs, and a series of family pictures that showed the delicacy of a caress, the joyous splashing of a mud bath, the tiny jewel of an eye set into a massive head, the glitter of water caught on an eyelash, a small mouth curved in a smile.

Finally she described the extraordinary scene she had filmed when the group she was studying had been decimated by poachers. After the ambush, when the bandits had hacked the ivory from the dead animals, she and Erope had been separated from their vehicle by the unpredictable movements of the panicked herd. Forced to hide in the thick scrub, they had stayed there all through the dark hours of that night, watching in awe as the surviving elephants emerged like ghosts from the surrounding trees, using their feet and trunks to build a cairn from stones and branches to cover their fallen comrades, keeping a vigil over the graves they had constructed until the rising sun sent them away, in search of shade and water. The rapt attention of her audience and their gasps of astonishment indicated to Sarah the impact of the pictures taken on that fateful night. When she had finished the presentation there was a brief and total silence, and then sustained applause.

Her work was inspiring and fresh the Smithsonian director said afterwards, smiling and shaking her hand. He was impressed with the Briggses and what they had accomplished so far, and her contribution had made a real impact. He had decided to visit the camp, and would drive up with Dan and Allie in a couple of days.

'Miss Mackay, may I have a few words?'

Sarah turned to see a tall Indian man who had been in the audience. He was regarding her with interest, and holding a notebook and pencil.

'I'm Rabindrah Singh. I do freelance work for a number of papers and magazines around East Africa,' he said. 'And I'm a stringer for *Newsweek* and the *Daily Telegraph*. Congratulations on a brilliant presentation. The Briggses are lucky to have such a talented colleague.'

His voice was cultured, suggesting a British education. There was a faintly perfumed aura around him which Sarah found odd in a man, but his face was full of intelligence. He did not take his eyes off her as he questioned her about her work, and after a few moments she began to feel uncomfortable beneath the intensity of his gaze. He obviously had a clear grasp of the Briggses' work and the difficulty of balancing wildlife conservation and human needs in an area where arid land and patchy rainfall created frequent clashes between nomadic tribesmen and the wild animals that shared their terrain.

'I'm interested in this problem of land,' he said. 'It's one of the key issues that the Kenya Government has to deal with, and so far their efforts have been less than impressive. I know there has been heavy poaching up there. Armed Somalis from over the border, and local officials turning a blind eye while holding out their hands.'

'Unfortunately, yes,' she said. 'But there are Samburu people coming up in wildlife management and local government, people who are determined to make things better. Like my tracker, Erope. He believes that—'

'So how do you, as a single woman, cope with living up there alone and in such rough terrain?' He switched abruptly to a more personal line of enquiry. 'What sort of motivation makes a young woman put aside the issue of personal safety? It must be dangerous sometimes. And lonely.'

'I live in a compound with the Briggses, and we have plenty of visitors.' She was annoyed at herself for sounding defensive. 'There's no time to be lonely. And you have to travel further north and east to get into trouble with bandits.'

'Still, it's different for them as a couple,' he said. 'You, on the other hand, are an attractive, single woman living in the *bundu* for weeks or months at a time. I'd like to write about you, as well as the elephants. A personal twist to the article will get it more attention. How do you deal with the isolation, stay in touch with friends and family, with what's happening in the outside world?'

'There's a radio in the camp, so we're not without communications,' she said.

'Do you come down to Nairobi regularly? Do you make up for your days in the bush when you're in town? Do you have a boyfriend down here? Or up there, perhaps? What are your interests when you're not tracking down elephants and taking remarkable photographs?'

Sarah glanced around, looking for an escape. This was what she had dreaded, and she felt that the Indian was insensitive to be leading their conversation in this direction. Pushy. He must know who she was. Her name had been in the papers often enough.

'When did you first start working up there, in Buffalo Springs?' he went on. 'With all these Shifta raids your life must be at risk occasionally, if not on a daily basis. Like the incident of the ambush that you've just shown us. Aren't you afraid of being hacked to pieces one dark night?'

A look of desolation had come over Sarah and she reached out with one hand to grip the back of a chair as her knees weakened. She stared at him in silence, her face drained of colour. When she finally answered her voice sounded distant, although she was standing so close to him that she could feel his breath in the air between them.

'Danger doesn't confine itself to any specific place,' she said. 'It's a random thing that can strike anywhere. The Briggses' project is not going to be derailed by threats of violence from the Shifta. That simply makes our work more necessary.'

From across the room Dan had seen the change in her expression. He came swiftly to her side and nodded to the journalist. 'I hope you'll forgive me, but it's time to leave – our sponsors have arranged dinner. I hope you enjoyed the presentation enough to write something about our project.'

'Thank you for your interest, Mr Singh.' Sarah recovered herself and shook his hand. 'By the way, there's information about donations in the press file, in case you feel like making a personal contribution. Every little helps. Goodnight.'

She turned and walked away with Dan, conscious that the journalist was still watching her as she climbed into the waiting car. At the Norfolk Hotel, Allie drew her aside.

'Well done, girl! Dan is delighted with the way things went. That was quite a conquest you made among the scientists and accountants.'

Sarah smiled, relaxing into the crowd, answering questions about her work, enjoying the company of influential people from organisations she had always revered. She was relieved that no one had referred to the tragic events that had marred her past. Here, at least, she was not the subject of the hushed pity she had come to dread. Instead, the table talk focused on conservation issues, on the elephants and the various means of tracking and identifying them, and on the contentious problems of land shared by man and beast. But as coffee was served and orders were taken for port and brandy, she felt drained.

'Would you mind if I crept away now?' she whispered to Allie, and was grateful for the discreet nod. She left the table and made her way towards the foyer. On a sudden whim she had decided to splurge and book a room at the Norfolk Hotel for the night. She had not spent a farthing of her salary for weeks, and she was also aware that it would be good for Dan and Allie to have some time to themselves, without having to look out for her. She would feel safe at the hotel, and she might find it easier to sleep. As she took her room key from the desk a voice hailed her, and she was dismayed to see the Indian journalist striding towards her. He had not been at dinner with the sponsors and she wondered how he had found her.

'Miss Mackay! I tracked you down because I wanted to ask you something.' He hesitated, cleared his throat. 'I wondered if you have a portfolio that you use to show your work? Any photographs that you would sell? Outside of your work at Buffalo Springs, I mean. I'm pretty sure there are magazines that would publish them. In fact, I might be able to use them myself, for the article I'm writing. If you're interested, and it doesn't clash with what you're doing for the Briggses.'

'I hadn't thought about selling any of my pictures,' she said. 'I only use them for my research work. But if you're going to write something about our project I can send you a few slides, or black and white prints.'

'I could pick them up in Buffalo Springs,' he said. 'I'm thinking of driving up to spend a few days in Samburu, and then going on to visit George Adamson further north.'

'I'm afraid I won't be there for a while,' she said. 'I'm taking some time off. But I can forward the pictures to you, if you give me an address.'

'Fine.' He held out his business card. 'Are you around tomorrow, by the way? Maybe we could have lunch. Or a drink. Discuss some possibilities.'

Sarah's only wish was to get away, to take refuge in her hotel bedroom. The evening had been a tremendous effort, and she could not deal with more socialising or questions.

'I'm leaving early in the morning,' she said. 'To stay with friends. Thanks anyway. And I'll look forward to reading your article.'

'Ah.' He wondered if she was distancing herself because she did not accept invitations from Indians. '*Au revoir*, then. Good meeting you. And congratulations once again on your pictures.'

'Thank you. Goodnight.'

Sarah knew that she sounded abrupt, but she had to escape. She shook his hand briskly, and fled. She had survived the whole evening, and had even enjoyed some of it. Her portfolio was lying on a table and she began to leaf through it, considering which pictures and slides she might send to the Indian reporter. She only hoped that he would not mention her personal history in his article, if he wrote one at all. There were no guarantees with the press.

The sky was grey and the morning air chilly as she headed north. The Land Rover wheezed and sputtered, climbing through the glassy green of coffee plantations, and the patches of maize and vegetables and bananas that were the favoured crops of the Kikuyu tribe. There was a fluttering sensation in Sarah's stomach, a curdled mixture of sadness and anticipation in her heart as she drove through the rich, fertile terrain. Children waved from the roadside, women toiled up steep, red paths between the *shambas*, bending forward under the crippling loads of firewood strapped on to their backs. The summit of the great mountain was hidden in a band of cloud, and the mood of the land felt heavy and sullen. At the entrance to Langani Farm she stopped and tried to compose herself. She had spoken to Hannah before leaving Nairobi, and heard the excitement in her friend's voice.

'You'll never believe how large I am,' Hannah had said. 'Lars says he'll have to take the doors off their hinges if I spread any further. But Dr Markham swears it's not twins. Ach, Sarah, I'm so happy you're coming home at last. I'm so glad.'

But it wasn't home. Langani would never be home now, because Piet was not there and the life that they had planned together was gone, along with all the joy and love that had filled her heart for a brief, glorious moment in time. He would not be waiting for her on the steps of the house, he would not put his arms around her and swing her off her feet, laughing and kissing and teasing her, telling her that he loved her. He would never be waiting for her again.

Sarah turned the key in the ignition and drove through the gates and up the driveway. Her heart was hammering and she could taste grief in her mouth. She stepped out of the car, struggling to suppress the wall of sorrow that threatened to overcome her. It was Lottie's garden that came to her rescue. Lottie who had been like a mother to her during the years at boarding school, and who was now an exile, thousands of miles away from the oasis of calm and order she had created out of the voracious bush. As Sarah turned, a band of sunlight broke through the thick belly of cloud to give the lawn a luminous, velvet quality. The sight of the flower beds, the curves of glorious colour that shaped and bordered the old house, brought back the love she had felt for this place since the first day she had come here as a child. The dogs appeared on the verandah and ran to her, barking hysterically, tails waving, as Hannah came down the steps, her arms outstretched, her broad face wreathed in smiles. Their embrace was silent and fierce, and they hugged one another for a long time before Sarah stood back and put her hand gently on her friend's swollen stomach.

'You look wonderful.'

'I look heavy.' Hannah was laughing. 'I feel heavy. Lars keeps telling me to take a rest in the afternoons, but I try to go walking with the dogs instead. Otherwise I soon won't be able to move at all. I don't think any woman would have a baby if this went on for a day longer than nine months.' She was interrupted by the arrival of Lars who tramped up the verandah steps, leaving a rifle propped against the rail.

'Sarah. Good to have you back. No punctures, no crisis on the way?'

He put his arms around her and she hugged him very hard. What a good man he was, Hannah's big husband. What a good, kind, lovely man.

'No problems at all.' She looked up at him with affection and then glanced at the gun. A small fissure of alarm opened in her mind. 'Is everything all right here?'

He smiled. 'That was for dinner. I've been out hunting for the pot. Everything is quiet. No troubles, no *shauri*s at all. Except for your friend here, who refuses to take things easy. Maybe you can do something about that while you're around.' He touched Hannah's braid of yellow hair and then leaned forward to kiss her forehead. 'I have a couple of things to see to before lunch. I'll join you in a while.'

'I'll take you to your room,' Hannah said. 'And here's Mwangi with some coffee.'

The old houseboy greeted Sarah with pleasure, pressing her hands between his own, murmuring his Kikuyu words of welcome. Then he went out to collect her suitcase from the Land Rover, making fussing sounds as he smoothed down the already-perfect bed and twitched the curtains back to let in the sunlight. When he was gone Hannah sat down on a chair beside the window.

'You've brought the first sunshine we've had in days,' she said. 'It's been overcast and gloomy all week. Depressing. How was the presentation in Nairobi? How long can you stay?'

'Three or four days. Then I need to head back,' Sarah said. 'Everything went well in Nairobi. We got a renewal of funding for the next year, and there's a strong possibility that there will be some extra money from the Smithsonian Institute. There was some interest from the press, too. Dan and Allie are optimistic.'

'So you're all set to continue in Buffalo Springs?'

'Yes. And Han, I met a journalist who thought he might be able to use some of my photographs. Pay for them, I mean. At first I didn't feel right about it, but now I see that it can only help the Briggses' efforts. And give me some pocket money at the same time. I don't know if he's serious, but it would be amazing to see my work in *Time* or *Newsweek*. Or anywhere!'

'You deserve it,' Hannah said. 'Your pictures *are* extraordinary. That's great news.'

'Well, it's encouraging, anyway. Now tell me about you.'

'There's not much to tell. I'm glad you're here. I need someone to talk to right now. It's probably the weather, but I feel uneasy. Anxious. Everything is quiet on the farm, but . . . I don't know. I suppose it's natural to be nervous, now that the baby's so close. It's hard to sleep, and I keep thinking about Lars. About how he really feels.'

'He feels good, Hannah. I could see it in the way he spoke to you, kissed you just now.'

'But we never discuss it.' Hannah was looking out of the window and up towards the ridge. Piet's ridge.

'Never discuss what?' Sarah did not want to look at the ridge, to think about loss. She did not know how she would be able to sleep tonight in this house. In this room.

'We never talk about the baby. About whether it might be a boy or a girl. Think about names. The baby that is a result of my stupid affair. The baby that is not my husband's child, but will be part of our lives very soon.'

'Maybe that's the best way for Lars. And for you too. It's your child, Han, and you know he loves you and that he'll love the baby too. Because it's a part of you, growing inside you and protected by his love. Perhaps that's all you need to think about.'

'You're a hopeless romantic. And it's hard to believe that he feels that way all the time. That he doesn't ever bring up my affair with Viktor, or resent the coming of this baby.'

'He doesn't look like a man filled with resentment,' Sarah said. 'I honestly believe he loves you as he's always loved you, and he wants to look after you and everything that is a part of you. The baby, the house, the farm. They're all things that you're building together. Don't be scared, Han. He's strong and so are you, and you love each other. It will be fine.'

Hannah nodded, silent. Then she stood up.

'I need to go to the kitchen and organise a few things with Kamau. I'll see you at lunchtime.' She smiled. 'I'm OK, really. It's just that I get

27

twitchy sometimes, and I long for someone to talk to. You or Ma. But you're both so far away.'

'What's the news from your mother? I thought of Lottie the moment the garden came into view.' Sarah tried to bury the feeling of guilt that Hannah's words had awakened. She should not have stayed away so long.

'It's rough down there,' Hannah said, leaning against the door frame and looking out over her mother's garden. 'They made a mistake, leaving Kenya. I hated the tobacco farm, the whole country. When I ran away and made my way back here, I did feel guilty at leaving Ma in that awful place, with no one to comfort her or help her out. But all I thought about was coming home to Langani and working alongside Piet. At first he treated me like the little sister, the runaway nuisance who would cause nothing but trouble. But when I took over the office work and started to pull my weight, it all worked out fine.'

'You worked so well together,' Sarah said, her stomach turning at the sound of his name.

'Yes we did,' Hannah said. 'And I'm so grateful that I was with him for a time, before we all lost him. As for Ma and Pa, Rhodesia is a bad place to be right now, and they hate the tobacco farm. Pa isn't drinking so much, apparently, but it's grim being a hired hand on someone else's land. Kobus is a brute. They may be related, but he treats Pa like a labourer, not a cousin. And there are raids all the time. The rebels are getting arms from Russia and China. There are more of them and they're better organised. I know Ma would like to come home to Langani, but Pa won't consider it.'

'That's miserable for her.'

'Yes.' Hannah was frowning. 'But having been away for three years it would be difficult for Lars if my parents suddenly came back and took over the farm again. It was Pa's decision to up stakes and leave without warning, just before Independence. And even though it's still his land, I don't know how we would cope if he announced that he was coming back. It would be tricky with him here. He'd be wandering around the place, drinking too much and thinking about Piet not being here, and maybe trying to take over the management again. What would Lars do then? What would we do, Sarah? I feel guilty about saying this, but I don't know how it would work if they came back now. Anyway, I'd better go and talk to Kamau about the vegetables that are ready to be picked, before the bush pigs or the buffalo get at them.'

After lunch Sarah sat down on the verandah outside her bedroom, absorbing the quiet of the afternoon, glad that she had persuaded Hannah to rest. On either side of her chair the dogs lay, feigning sleep, the twitching of their furry eyebrows betraying their interest in the biscuit she was eating. Only Piet's dog was missing. Piet was missing. He would never call out to her again, never appear beside her, full of dreams and hope and great plans for the future. Their future. She began to cry, her body shaking as she tried not to let her desolation unravel her precarious self-control. The dogs looked up, whining softly, licking at her hand. Stroking their smooth heads and speaking to them helped dilute her anguish.

'Interested in a stroll?' Lars had come to find her.

'I'd love it.' She looked away, hoping he would not see that she had been weeping. 'Hannah still asleep?'

'Yes.' He was smiling as they set out. 'I don't know how you did that. I've been trying for weeks.'

'She looks good, though.'

'Physically she's doing well, ja. But she's edgy.' Lars jabbed his thick walking stick into the ground. 'She retreats, sometimes for days, into a place where I can't reach her. Perhaps it is the baby, and the fact that women become more emotional when they're about to give birth. But she insists on working such long hours. Far too long, I think.'

'If she's feeling good, then there's no reason to stop working.'

'That's what Dr Markham says. But she's not at ease with the *watu*, not like she used to be. She doesn't listen to them any more, and she's often angry with them for no reason. They sense that she suspects them of being involved in what happened to Piet, and that's not good. It's as if she has forgotten their loyalty, down through all the years that went before. She doesn't remember that they are mourning too.'

'Being angry has always been her way of getting over obstacles,' Sarah said. 'We can only help by being patient.'

'You know, everyone thinks of me as a big, slow, patient Norwegian,' Lars said. 'But I am angry too. Often raging. And even the most beautiful day here is contaminated with mourning for me, although I am trying to make Langani a place of peace again. A good place for a family. But I cannot do it alone, and sometimes I wonder if I can do it at all.'

Sarah saw that his eyes were starred. He looked away from her quickly and she was struck by the realisation that the loss of his friend Piet had devastated him too. No one had acknowledged that sufficiently. She thought of his generosity, his faithfulness, his love for Hannah that had led him to marry her and accept her child as his own. Lars the practical one, the one who kept everything going, the voice of reason and balance. She felt ashamed that she had not asked him how he felt.

'I know it affects your life as much as anyone's,' she said. 'This terrible hole that seems to get deeper.'

He looked back at her in silence and she saw that he was struggling to control his emotion, to remain steady for them all.

'Well, it is over now,' he said, at last. 'And we are left to go on with our lives as best we can. I suppose it will get better with time, and when the baby brings new life to Langani. Look at the mountain Sarah, in this evening light. It has come out of the clouds to remind us of its beauty.'

They talked about the workings of the farm and Sarah's research at Buffalo Springs. As they reached the part of the driveway where the dairy was visible, Hannah was waving to them. They looked in on the milking cows that were her pride and joy and then strolled back towards the house together.

'So, you did well in Nairobi,' Lars said. 'It must have been difficult, standing up in front of a bunch of scientists and other people, with so much riding on your presentation.'

'It was hard,' Sarah acknowledged. 'But I'm glad Dan and Allie pushed me into it. I hope at least one of the press people will write up the project. We could do with some hefty donations. And one of the journalists might use my pictures.'

'And pay for them,' Hannah reminded her, delighted. 'Make you rich and famous.'

'Yes, and if he does we'll celebrate by going to Nairobi for the weekend,' Sarah said. 'And I'll treat you to dinner and dancing at the New Stanley Grill.'

'It had better be after the baby comes.' Hannah was chuckling. 'Right now Lars wouldn't be able to get his arms around me.'

'They might not take hayseeds like us in the Grill.' Lars joined in the laughter. 'Even under the wing of the rich and famous.'

'Speaking of the rich and famous, I heard from Camilla about two weeks ago. She said she was trying to get here by the end of September. Have you heard anything since then?' Sarah asked.

'Same as you,' Hannah said. 'She's stuck in London. Her agent says she can't get out of her contract in New York, and she's also locked into doing pictures for a new French perfume. She can't come back until that's over. But she sent us some money.'

'Money?' Sarah was puzzled.

'She's determined to start a business, making clothes and bags and such. Here at Langani, I mean. Lars is going to fix up the manager's cottage so she can turn it into a workroom.'

'She needs a fairly big space for sewing and cutting,' Lars said. 'She said she would live in the cottage, too. But Hannah thinks she'd be better off staying in the house, to start with. In case she would be nervous once she gets here.'

'It's brave of her to try and start a business here,' Sarah said. 'But I imagine she's right about there being a market for clothes made from exotic materials, and decorated with African beading and so on. Like the fabulous wedding dress she made for you, Han.'

'I hope she won't miss London too much, once she gets here,' Lars said. 'Langani is pretty remote, and even Nairobi is like a sleepy village compared to where she's been.'

'I bought an English magazine yesterday and there she was, staring at me from the cover, more beautiful and luminous than ever,' Sarah said. 'But her letter was glum. She really does want to get out of there, and come back to Kenya.'

'She wants to be wherever Anthony is,' Hannah said.

'Yes. But she's scared of him now,' Sarah said. 'She's keeping a little distance, waiting to see whether he's ready.'

'A big distance,' Hannah said. 'She's thousands of miles away, and he's here on his own. The great white hunter and guide. A target for rich American ladies on safari, buying into his world of big game and camp fires and lions roaring in the moonlight. He's glamorous and single, and apparently irresistible to all of them.'

'Well, that's the test, I suppose.' Sarah's expression was doubtful. 'Whether he can stay faithful to Camilla in spite of all that. I hope he won't throw away a second chance. She loves him, and they would make a terrific couple.'

'She'd be an asset to his business, being so famous and glamorous,' Hannah said. 'And she could add the missing feminine touch to his camps, put some variety into the menus, not to mention the way the food is presented. Camilla could look after his guests in Nairobi, too. Take them shopping and all that. He hates doing those things, but the clients expect it. He brought a couple of Americans to Langani for lunch a few weeks ago. They were nice people, but very put out that he had left them to their own devices in the city. Even refused their invitation to dinner. That hadn't gone down well at all.'

They had reached the house and Lars left them, driving away with one of the farm workers to inspect a fence that had been trampled yet again by buffalo.

'Sarah, there's something I'd like to do,' Hannah said.

'I don't know, Han.' Sarah knew at once what it was. 'The last part of the track is steep. If you slipped—'

'I won't slip. You'll help me over the tough parts. And I haven't been there recently, because Lars made me promise not to go up on my own. Please, Sarah. Let's go together and visit Piet, up on the ridge. In the place he loved the best. It may be my last time before the baby comes.'

They took Sarah's Land Rover and started out across the gold expanse of the veldt with the peak of the mountain dominating the horizon. Sarah drove in silence, her heart racing. Like a young woman going to meet her lover. But Piet would never be her lover again except in the lonely maze of her dreams when she saw him, distant and inaccessible, tearing at her heart, so that she woke in the night filled with the pain of his absence. They parked the vehicle at the foot of the steep track and began to walk up, picking their way slowly towards the summit. At the top they stood close together, looking at the smooth stones that they had used to build the cairn. From the centre of the mound a tortillis tree rose in solitary beauty, its wide branches reaching into the pale air. Birdsong drifted on the wind and beneath them lay the wheat fields and the open plains and dark green forest that made up Langani Farm. The sun had set fire to the sky, touching the trees and rocks with a gold and crimson wash that spread slowly over the land, ancient and benign and voluptuous in the evening light.

Sarah sat down at the edge of the cairn, in the place that Piet had always loved, overlooking the place where they had planned to live their lives.

She put her hand on the warm stones, breathing in the memory of him, the sound of his voice, his laughter, the touch of his fingers.

'It's so calm.' Hannah's voice was choked. 'Do you think he's really at peace up here, my beautiful brother?'

'I think so.' Sarah reached out and took her friend's hand. 'I think this is where he would want to be, and where we can always find him. His favourite place.'

'Will we ever feel less pain?' Hannah asked. 'I keep waiting for it to be less deep. Less shattering. For that awful, twisting sensation to be dulled in some way. But it doesn't happen.'

'They say it's all about time,' Sarah said. 'But I don't know, Han. I just don't know at all. Look – there's a cheetah down there.'

Below them on the wide open plain the cat walked slowly, head just above the feathered tops of the grasses, eyes locked on its prey, muscles stretched and sinewy as she stalked a young gazelle at the edge of a small herd. But some undetected sound caused the grazing animals to scatter and they bounded away, across the veldt and into the protective cover of thick bush. The cheetah, recognising the futility of any further effort, positioned herself on a low mound from which she could survey the plains in search of an alternative target.

Turning her head, Sarah could see the kopje and the outline of the lodge that Piet had built with such vision and enthusiasm. It was abandoned now, hidden and silent among the surrounding trees and rocks. Only Lars visited regularly, cutting back the creepers, chasing monkeys and baboons away, putting salt down at the waterhole for the elephants and buffalo and the smaller game that still visited the place, heedless of the tragedy that had been played out there.

'I'm going to open the lodge after the baby is born,' Hannah said. 'As soon as I have a good routine going and a reliable ayah to help me. Then I'll open it, for Piet. It will be something to do, something he would have wanted me to do. And it will bring visitors to Langani, help with our plan to turn part of the farm into a game reserve. Boost our cash flow, too. Piet put almost all the money we had into the building, and it's been idle since—' Her voice faded and she pressed her knuckles against her mouth. 'It hasn't been easy lately,' she said finally. 'I don't know how Lars has managed to keep everything going. He's wonderful beyond belief.'

Sarah nodded and rose to her feet. It was time to leave Piet, his spirit abroad in the pink dusk, at one with the environment he had cherished and guarded all his life. She made a silent request for peace, begging him to help her, to show her how to live without his loving presence.

'I think we should start back now,' she said. 'It's getting dark, and Lars will be anxious.'

They moved carefully down the path, clutching at small branches to steady themselves. In the brief moment of African twilight the land seemed to be holding its breath, still and suspenseful as the night approached with its own strange sounds and rustlings beneath the mask of darkness. Lars was on the verandah when they reached the house, relieved when he saw the swing of the car lights on the trees and shrubs along the driveway.

'I was getting worried about you,' he said. 'Did you go to the ridge?'

'I thought it best to drive up there while Sarah was with me.' Hannah leaned into his large frame, her head resting on his shoulder. 'Let's get ready for dinner, Lars. And you can tell me how Juma managed to overturn the trailer this morning, and how he proposes to pay for the damage.'

After dinner they sat round the crackle of the log fire, but Sarah's body was chilled in spite of its warmth. She was reluctant to go to bed, afraid of the dreams, but she realised that she was keeping Lars and Hannah up and that they would have to rise early and be out on the farm first thing in the morning.

'Bedtime,' she said, with an attempt at a smile that did not reach her eyes.

They hugged her tightly and then she took a kerosene lamp and walked along the verandah towards her bedroom. She saw the night watchman on the lawn, his old army greatcoat pulled close around him, a woollen hat covering most of his face. He raised his stick in a salute as Sarah passed, and she wondered what protection it offered against the weapons that had ravaged the peace and security of Langani. She lingered in the bathroom and dawdled over putting her clothes away, but finally there was nothing more to do and she got into bed and turned out the lamp. The sounds of the night pressed in on her as she listened to the creaks and shifts of the house that she had once loved and now feared. She knew that she could not stay at the farm any longer than was necessary. Even Hannah's friendship and needs, and Lars's strength, were insufficient props to shore up the ruins of her own life. She sat up and lit the kerosene lantern again, her nerves jangling as she saw the shadows loom in the hissing light. The chill of the night and her own loneliness struck her with a force that made her suck in her breath. She wanted Piet, needed to hear his voice and see his face, feel his arms wound tight around her, loving and protective. She went to stand by the window with her eyes closed, reliving him, imagining, gripping her ribcage with her own arms, lifting her face into the empty darkness to feel his kiss once more. Then she was back on the ridge and she cried out and clapped her hand over her mouth, afraid that she would be heard in the black menace of the night where all comfort had left her and only ghosts shared her solitary path.

High on the ridge, the old Kikuyu stood looking down on the farm spread out before him in the moonlight. The lights of the house glowed in the distance, a beacon in the dark landscape, and his eyes narrowed as he watched. His grizzled head was covered in a woollen hat and his long earlobes were decorated with beads and copper wire. He wore a leather cloak wrapped around his shoulders to protect him from the cold of the night wind. The silvery wash of the moon threw his face into relief against the shadows of the rocks among which he was standing, lighting the long scar that he had won in battle. He had been waiting, watching here, for three days. Behind him, hidden from view in the scree, was a makeshift shelter fashioned from branches and thorn bushes. Within its confines he had built a small charcoal fire over a shallow pit. The cover afforded by the crossed boughs prevented the smoke being observed by anyone below him, at the lodge or out on the plain.

He left his vantage point and returned to the fire, crouching in front of it and taking a small leather bag from his belt. He placed a pinch of powder on his tongue and inhaled some of it. Then he began to hum, making a hypnotic sound in the back of his throat, and sprinkling the rest of the fine particles on the glowing embers. They hissed and crackled, giving off a pungent smell like pulverised bone. He reached out and lifted a gourd filled with blood, and poured half of the viscous liquid over the sputtering flames. His voice began to rise and fall in waves of wordless sound, and from a bag on the ground he drew some pieces of raw flesh and the scrotum of a young goat, adding them to the conflagration. Taking a knife, he removed the charred meat and genitals of the animal from the fire and ate them slowly, before draining the contents of the gourd. With gnarled fingertips he wiped his lips, streaking his face with smears of blood, chanting softly and rocking back and forth on his heels, his eyes on the homestead far below him, his teeth bared in a rictus of hate.

After a time he scooped up several handfuls of sand and spread them over the fire, covering every part of it so that it was extinguished, and all trace concealed. He rose and walked to the edge of the ridge again to gaze across the silent plain at the house. His curse would drive them all into eternal darkness. Soon. The land would not be *wazungu* land any longer. It would revert to the Kikuyu tribe. It would be his land. He spat into the rising wind, gathered his leather cloak around him, and melted into the thorn and scrub that covered the slopes of the ridge. Beneath the sand his hidden fire scorched its way into the thirsty earth, leaving it marked for death.

Chapter 2

Kenya, July 1966

Rabindrah Singh leaned back in his chair and stretched his arms above his head. His fingers ached from typing all afternoon, and he needed a new ribbon, but he was trying to get the last vestiges of ink out of the existing one before opening another spool. A new typewriter would be even better, but that was not something he could afford as yet. His top priority was a flat of his own. Uncle Indar's house was an orderly and welcoming place, but he could not bring his friends there. His aunt watched over him with a keen eye and produced a stream of suitable Sikh girls of a marriageable age for his approval. They came with their mothers, or their sisters, flashing dark eyes at him, making no secret of the fact that they considered him a good catch. After each visit there would be a post-mortem, with Kuldip Auntie pointing out the particularly attractive features of each girl, looking at him for a sign that one of her choices had at last found favour. But Rabindrah was not interested in a traditional Sikh marriage. He had lived in England for several years and had grown used to freedom between the sexes. His taste now was for the foreign girls he met in Nairobi's bars and cafés. They were generous with their favours and demanded little in return. He was meeting a blonde Swedish girl tonight, an air hostess with china-blue eyes and luscious breasts. She had a flat in Lavington, and he smiled at the prospect of the evening ahead. Another hour's work and he would be free to indulge himself.

He began to pound at the keys again, frowning as he tried to find the most emotive words to describe the elephants and their environment. When he had finished he knew that the piece carried a powerful message, especially with the pictures the Irish girl had sent him. She was a fine photographer. The local paper had already printed a drastically edited version of his story about the Briggses and their research, but now the

Daily Telegraph had agreed to publish the whole piece, and Rabindrah realised that Sarah Mackay's photographs had tipped the balance. He had submitted six or seven articles to London newspapers since his return from England, but they had all been turned down.

'Maybe I'm being blacklisted,' he had said to his uncle.

'You were very outspoken in the Manchester newspaper,' Indar Singh said. 'The whole question of full British passports for Indians became your cause and they don't like that kind of clarity there. Not when it concerns British policy in the dying colonies that they are deserting. But I don't think that would be held against you by a London paper, now that you are submitting articles about saving the wildlife of Africa. They may not give a damn about their citizens, but the British are always kind-hearted and sentimental when it comes to four-footed creatures.'

Indar Uncle had been right, it seemed. Rabindrah was about to see his name in an international broadsheet. After that, other publications might begin to take him seriously. East Africa correspondent for *The Economist* or *The Times*. An occasional article in *Newsweek*. Those were his targets. Taking a strong stand on conservation could be an ideal vehicle to bring him recognition. It was an emotive subject and one that was easy to research and write about. The illegal slaughter of Kenya's wildlife was becoming an increasing scandal, and the government's lethargy in dealing with the issue of poachers was well known. There would be no shortage of ready material, much of it sensational. The international community was already up in arms about the uncontrolled killing of elephants and rhinos, and he had placed an article in an American magazine only last month that was well received.

At first the girl had seemed reluctant to let him use her pictures. But then the envelope landed on his desk, and she had not even asked about her fee. Perhaps she was so truly bound up in the lives of the elephants that she thought only about the potential benefit to her research project. Actually, he could not get her out of his mind. There was something about the way she had looked at him that evening. Some fleeting expression of anguish, and then wariness tinged with fear. It was a startling contrast to her polished slide presentation. He had meant to ask someone about her, but his focus over the past few days had been exclusively on his writing and his precarious toehold on the ladder of international journalism. The telephone interrupted his train of thought.

'That was a good piece about the elephants. I wonder if you'd do an interview for me?' Gordon Hedley was the editor of the *Daily News*. An old Africa hand and a damn good journalist, he had been non-committal about a staff job or any regular input from Rabindrah. 'You're a good writer, but you're very outspoken,' he said. 'We're walking through a minefield here, my friend. You and I can be deported without notice for writing stories that these new politicians don't like. You've got to learn how to frame things so that the message comes over, without seeming to attack individual officials.'

'This whole country will come to a grinding halt if someone doesn't put a stop to the rampant corruption and thuggery that's become rife since Independence.'

'It will take time for things to settle down.' Gordon was resigned. 'Three or four generations, in my view. But don't ever quote me. In the meantime, there's a new director of the International Wildlife Fund. A fellow called Broughton-Smith. He lived here for years before *Uhuru* — used to be in the British Foreign Office. He was involved with the purchase and distribution of land before Independence. Canny fellow, very able. Anyhow, he's back in Kenya as of yesterday. His new outfit seems to have plenty of money and support from Europe and America, but I don't know if they have any teeth. Could you find out what he hopes to do initially? Get details of their long-term plan. All that general stuff.'

Rabindrah scribbled down the name. 'Where do I find him?'

'Haven't a clue. Try the Wildlife Ministry — or the A.W.F. They're bound to know where he means to set up shop. And see if he would be willing to make some comment on hunting in Kenya, and the corruption that allows the government to turn a blind eye to all the poaching that's going on. I'd like a piece for Thursday's paper.'

George Broughton-Smith was staying at Muthaiga Club. Not a particularly welcoming place for an Indian journalist, even one with a British passport. It was only recently that people of dark complexion had been allowed through the doors at all, except as cooks and waiters or cleaners. They settled on tea in the Lord Delamere Bar at the Norfolk Hotel.

George turned out to be a tall, distinguished-looking man with silver hair, and the benefit of a good tailor to disguise the beginnings of corpulence. Rabindrah immediately recognised the British public school, Oxbridge product. The man might have been considered arrogant but for the diffidence and self-deprecating humour typical of his class. Affable was the word that came to mind, but with overtones of shrewdness.

'Are you particularly involved in conservation issues, Mr Singh?'

Rabindrah decided on the truth. 'It's a recent thing for me, because it's very current. And it's at the heart of this country's development, with its impact on land allocation, and the issues of tourism and foreign revenue. The whole world is curious to see how an independent Kenya will deal with the problems of demand for agricultural land vis-à-vis national parks and game reserves. It's a political hot potato in the context of such a fast-growing population.'

'The government has a good man in Johnson Kiberu, who is now responsible for environmental and wildlife policy. That includes the use of private land, as well as the protection of existing conservation areas. We're going to be working together on these issues. You probably know him already.'

'I've met him briefly. But I haven't been around long. Four months. I'm still trying to make my way through the maze of government ministries and new departments. But I'll go and see Mr Kiberu as soon as I can.'

'Where have you been?' George asked. 'Apart from England, which I can hear in your speech of course.'

'Mine is a common story. I was born here. My Sikh grandfather arrived in 1898, brought in by the British as a policeman. Brothers and wives and cousins followed, and eventually set up as millet and sugar-cane farmers around Kericho and Kisii. Now we're all over the place.' Rabindrah shrugged. 'My parents left before Independence, clutching their British passports and heading for their rightful place in the UK. I have uncles in Canada too, and extended family still here and in Uganda.'

'But you left too, for a time at least?' George asked.

'I was packed off to university in the UK, and I've spent the last four years working on provincial newspapers there. A regional hack, I suppose you'd call it. But it has been a good grounding.'

'Have you decided to stay on permanently?' George wondered why the young man would have abandoned the security of Britain for the upheavals of the African continent.

'Yes, I have.' Rabindrah realised that the tables had been rather charmingly turned and that *he* was now being interviewed. He was reluctantly flattered by the Englishman's interest. 'To tell the truth, I resigned from my paper in Manchester. I got tired of writing articles about Asians being denied British passports and the right to live in jolly old England. And the editors got tired of reading them. So I've come back to Nairobi. I like it better in Kenya anyway. There's more scope for me here, and it's a challenging time to be around.'

'It may prove too challenging for some.'

'I'm up to it. I had no desire to stay in England with my parents. Fade into the ex-colonial Indian community. The older members of that particular club are mired in memories of the past, and many of the younger ones have developed giant chips on their shoulders. They spend a lot of time commiserating with one another over their losses, and the grim reality of settling down in British suburbia. And the less fortunate Indians have a major struggle ahead of them, in terms of economic security and acceptance in the local communities. Not for me.'

'In that case I hope you'll do great things in Kenya. Now, what is it you want to know?'

The interview covered a wide range of issues. George Broughton-Smith was not afraid to speak his mind, although he did so in language that was carefully phrased. He stressed on several occasions the need for local involvement in conservation issues.

'We'll never be able to protect the wildlife in this country, unless the ordinary citizen can see an immediate benefit from it,' he said. 'Money from game parks and reserves must be put back into local communities, and not frittered away by politicians in Nairobi. Our funding policy insists on there being a quid pro quo for money given. Helping small farmers to fence in their *shambas* is a good example. You can't expect a Kikuyu to support the protection of animals that wreck his patch of maize or attack his family. Like the elephants and buffalo that walk through these small-holdings in the Nyeri and Nanyuki areas and destroy everything in their wake.'

'What about the Maasai and the Samburu? You can't fence *them* in.'

'We're not in the business of trying to change lifestyles. If we're going to make rules about their use of designated wildlife areas, then we have to spend money on alternatives. Like mobile veterinary services and watering facilities for their animals. And we have to try and convince them that owning a smaller number of cattle and goats in good condition is preferable to overgrazing the land.'

'They'll never come round to that idea,' Rabindrah said. 'Their wealth and social standing has always been measured by livestock. That's not going to change.'

'Not in my lifetime, I suspect,' George said. 'But we have to make a start, and education is the key. We need to train teachers from within their own tribes. People they already know and trust. Younger men and women who will try to guide them towards a modern approach to land use. Because their traditional grazing will turn into desert if they continue to run these increasingly large herds.'

'So you're going to be based here in Nairobi, full time?' Rabindrah said.

'Yes. It gives me a better grasp of what's really going on, and more time to listen.'

'That's an improvement,' Rabindrah said. 'The place is swarming with consultants who fly in for a few days and pronounce on every kind of policy in reports that no one reads. Then they're gone and nothing is resolved. Parasites, most of them. Or do-gooders, and they are even more dangerous.'

'I trust that your printed words are less opinionated than your spoken comments,' George said, enjoying the refreshingly brash and open attitude of the young man. 'But even the so-called two-year wonders come up with some good ideas. Look at things from a fresh perspective. Now, let me outline what I hope to achieve over the next twelve months or so. I've brought a summary of the main tasks, in case you might go astray. Or invent an agenda of your own!'

At the end of an hour, Rabindrah was genuinely impressed by George Broughton-Smith, and by the practical ideas that were the basis of his plan.

'I think that's enough about conservation,' George said finally. 'Too much talking doesn't necessarily give you a clearer picture, and it makes you extremely thirsty. Can I offer you a drink?'

'I'd like a Scotch, please. With water.' Rabindrah saw George's raised eyebrows and smiled. 'I'm not a traditional Sikh, as you can see. No turban or beard, and a fondness for good whisky makes me even less exemplary. My father likes his whisky too, although my mother would never touch alcohol and doesn't allow it in the house. She hasn't discovered that I've taken to the bottle, and she still chastises my father in a resigned sort of manner. It's just as well that she's thousands of miles away.'

'I read your article about the Briggses' project in Buffalo Springs,' George said, and was amused by the Indian's surprise. 'I like to know something about a journalist who is interviewing me. What they've written lately. Where they're coming from. Whether they have a particular axe to grind. That was a good piece. The Briggses are admirable people, and of course Sarah Mackay's photographs are magnificent. She's a terrific young woman.'

'She seems dedicated. But a little reclusive.'

'That's hardly surprising, after what she's been through. She's a close friend of my daughter, Camilla.'

'The London model?' Rabindrah gave an appreciative whistle. 'She's your daughter? My goodness. Unobservant of me not to have made the connection.'

'They were at school together, here in Kenya,' George said. 'Since then, I'm sorry to say, they've seen far too much sadness. Sarah in particular.'

'In what regard?'

'She was engaged to a young Afrikaans farmer, Piet van der Beer. He was murdered last year by one of his Kikuyu workers, a bright boy called Simon Githiri, with no apparent motive. In an odd twist of fate, Githiri himself died fleeing the scene of his crime. It's a wonder that poor girl is able to function at all.'

'The murder was reported in the British papers at the time,' Rabindrah said. 'But the article was more concerned with a white Kenyan settler being killed by an African, than with any other aspect. There was nothing about family or friends. The Indians living in the UK all shook their heads and said it boded ill for Kenya's minority communities. A new Mau Mau-type movement, designed to rid the country of the last white settlers, they thought. What happened to the farm? Was it a political thing?'

'It's now run by Piet van der Beer's sister and her husband. They're trying to turn part of the property into a wildlife reserve. A plan that I support wholeheartedly. But I don't know if young Hannah will be strong enough to stay on, with that appalling tragedy hanging over her. Now if you'll excuse me, I have a dinner appointment. I trust you've got what you needed out of this interview. You can ring me if there's anything vital missing. I hope we'll meet again, to work towards better things for man and beast.'

On the following morning Rabindrah went to the offices of the *Daily News* and sat down in the room that was the archive for the paper's back issues. It did not take him long to find the reports about Piet van der Beer's death on Langani Farm. The murder resembled a ritual killing like those carried out by the Mau Mau during the fifties, when some of the Kikuyu tribe had conducted a campaign of terror against white settlers and those of their own people who would not take an oath of allegiance to support the movement. It was Sarah Mackay and Hannah, the murdered man's sister, who had found the body. Rabindrah shuddered as he thought of his own sisters, and the lifelong effect that such an incident might have had on them. There seemed to be no real motive for the crime, although Piet's father had fought against the Mau Mau during the Emergency years, along with many of the white farming community. The victim was in his late twenties, however, and would have been a teenager at that time. It was hard to believe that the killing was connected with that cause.

Chief Inspector Jeremy Hardy had closed the case when his officers found the recent remains of a man in the forest that bordered the farm. He had been attacked and for the most part eaten, probably by hyenas, Hardy stated at the time. It was almost certain that the bones were Simon Githiri's, because a tribal headdress and ornaments he had worn on the night of the killing had been found close to his body. Rabindrah frowned as he reread the file, puzzled by the barbaric nature of the killing and the seeming lack of reason behind it. Maybe Githiri had some grudge against his employer. The Afrikaans farmers were reputed to be tough on their *watu*. But if the police believed the murder to be the result of a grudge, or connected with the days of the Emergency, it was strange that they had abandoned the case so early. They must have considered the possibility of similar incidents following on from it.

Rabindrah made some notes about the case, folded them neatly into his briefcase and went back to the cramped office he had rented near his uncle's garage. If the surviving sister was still planning to turn the property into some kind of game reserve, there might be a story in it. '*Murdered man's sister turns his land into a wildlife refuge, creating a memorial to his ideals, soldiering on in spite of the brutal killing.*' That would make for good copy. It might also be worth talking to the policeman who had handled the case. Or paying a visit to the sister at the farm. And to

Sarah Mackay who had lost her fiancé, but stayed on in Kenya to save elephants. He could turn this into a poignant, uplifting story for one of the English tabloids. He lifted the telephone and rang Police Headquarters to track down his second cousin, Inspector Laxman Singh.

'Can you get me the police report on the murder at Langani Farm last year?' Rabindrah asked.

'No, I can't. It's probably still up in Nyeri, and I'm sure it's confidential anyway. Why are you interested in that?' Laxman sounded annoyed. It was not the first time that he had been asked to do a little private research for Rabindrah.

'I met Piet van der Beer's fiancée. I'm writing a story about the elephant research project she's working on. But scientists are as plentiful as flies round here at the moment. Everyone's doing a study of something. I want to base the story on this girl's personality and how inspiring she is. So brave to keep going, up in the wilds of the Northern Frontier. All that sentimental stuff that people like. I'd be grateful for the chance to read the report on the murder. See if the man in charge had any ideas about motive. It seemed like a senseless killing.'

'Probably a grudge. Someone they sacked. These Afrikaans farmers are tough, you know. It wouldn't surprise me if van der Beer beat his *watu*. And paid the price.'

'What about the inspector on the case?' Rabindrah asked. 'Is he any good, or was this an investigation that never went anywhere?'

'Are you stupid, cousin? The whole country was agog with the story, and the police were under maximum pressure to come up with a culprit. White farmer, brutal killing, resurrection of the Mau Mau and all that. I have worked with Hardy a few times. He's thorough and fair. A typical old-school British policeman. If he didn't find anything, then there's nothing more to be found.'

'Still, I'd like to read the file.'

'It's not possible, I'm telling you.' Laxman had lost patience.

'Maybe I can set up a date for you with that Italian girl.' Rabindrah's voice turned silky. 'She seemed quite keen on you. Even though you're such a duffer. I might be able to persuade her that you have some redeeming qualities.'

'Give me a couple of days, then,' Laxman said, laughing. 'But don't ask me for any more favours.'

'Good man. I'll round her up and we can meet at the Sombrero Club around nine. You'd better spend the interim practising your Italian.'

It was three days before Rabindrah received a copy of the police transcript in an anonymous brown envelope. There was little to be gleaned from the pages. No one could understand why Simon Githiri, unremarkable Kikuyu orphan, model student, promising employee, had suddenly turned brutal murderer. At the Consolata Mission in Nyeri, where he had spent most of his life, the priests pronounced themselves mystified by the boy's dramatic transformation. No one remembered anything unusual about the young man. There was a note on the file stating that the police had not been able to interview one of Githiri's teachers who was in hospital. But he was an elderly priest, seriously ill and already forgetful. Rabindrah read the report twice, made a note of the old man's name and then shook his head. It was one of those tragic incidents that would almost certainly remain unexplained. But he was interested in the story, and the lack of apparent motive. He decided to drive up to Nyeri and talk to Chief Inspector Jeremy Hardy in person. Then he would go to Langani Farm and visit the dead man's sister. He had often been sent out by the paper in Manchester to interview relatives whose nearest and dearest had come to a gritty end. It was surprising what people said under duress, without realising that they were contributing something new or different. And maybe he would go on to Buffalo Springs afterwards, and talk to Sarah Mackay about her photographs.

His aunt was waiting for him when he went home at lunchtime. Kuldip Kaur Singh was a gracious woman whose household ran like clockwork. Her sitting room served as a meeting place for her many friends with sons and daughters whose futures needed to be arranged. She moved with a regal, swaying motion that was at once purposeful and sensuous, and in the days of her youth she had been considered a great beauty and a fine match for her husband.

'I'm going to Nyeri this afternoon,' Rabindrah said. 'And then on to Nanyuki to follow up a story. I'll probably stay at the Sportsman's Arms for the night. Back tomorrow.'

'I was hoping you'd be here this evening, my boy,' she said, her eyes reproachful. 'I've prepared a special dinner with your favourite dishes.

And the Manjit Singhs are coming with their family to join us. Anoop will be here.'

'Oh come now, Kuldip Auntie.' Rabindrah put his arms around her, laughing. 'You know I don't see anything in that poor girl. And even you must admit Anoop is not an ideal name for her. She's very pleasant and no doubt virtuous, but she's not the "matchless beauty" of her name.'

'Beauty is not merely physical.' Kuldip frowned with pretended severity.

'I'm sure her soul is matchless, yes,' Rabindrah said, smiling. 'But she's not a match for me. I'm a prime catch in Nairobi, so you don't need to sell me short. Besides, I hear she likes one of Patel's sons from across the road.'

'He's not suitable for her at all.' Kuldip snorted her disapproval. 'That family has no standing, even in their own community. The father was suspected of embezzlement, you know. That's why they let him go from the railway.'

'Well, unless I keep my career on track I won't be able to take care of any of your lovely girls,' Rabindrah said. 'And for now I think I will play the role of the struggling journalist, not reliable or stable enough for a well-brought-up girl. Not a good specimen at all. You might end up ashamed of me, if you push me into an early marriage. That would be bad for your match-making reputation.'

'You are a spoiled, arrogant boy,' she said, laughing and cuffing him lightly on the ear. 'I'm glad your mother isn't here to see how you are carrying on. Don't think I was asleep when you came in at four o'clock this morning. You need to get home at a reasonable hour sometimes, and save your money for a wife and a family, instead of spending it in these fast places. You are thirty years old now. Time to settle down.' But she was still chuckling and rolling her eyes at him as he drove away.

Chief Inspector Hardy drummed his fingers on the desktop, irritated by the Indian journalist. He had no desire to discuss Piet van der Beer's murder with this belligerent young hack from Nairobi whom he had not met before. But the Sikh persisted with his questions and he had obviously read all the reports. Done his homework.

'It was a bad case,' Hardy was forced to admit. 'Not least because those two young girls were the ones who found the body. I don't know how they stayed sane after what they saw that night. May I ask why you're interested in this now?'

'I'm writing a story about Sarah Mackay and the elephant study at Buffalo Springs. I believe people will be more interested in her work if I fill in some of the personal background. Show how brave she is to continue after such a tragedy. And the sister too, staying on at the farm and so on. You closed the case after a short time.'

'We closed the case because we had all the evidence required to do so. Githiri was finished off by hyena. To put it bluntly, he probably had blood on him, and he was eaten when he fled from the crime. We found his headdress and other odds and ends in the forest, beside his bones. A strange kind of natural justice allowed us to put away the file.' The policeman shrugged, reached for his baton and stood up, clearly wanting to end the interview. 'It was a blessing, really.'

'But what was his motive?' Rabindrah asked, remaining seated. 'And were the police not afraid that there would be other killings like this?'

'There weren't any other killings.' Hardy was frowning, his eyes flinty. 'Because Githiri was dead. And the earlier incidents were directed only at Langani. No one else in the area was affected. So it was reasonable to assume that they were carried out by the same man.'

'What earlier incidents?'

'There was an armed raid on the place a few months before. And some of their cattle were slaughtered.'

'Was Piet van der Beer a rough fellow, then?' Rabindrah was scribbling in his notebook. 'Violent with his *watu*? His murder had the marks of a ritual. Or a kind of revenge killing, perhaps.'

'Piet was one of the finest young men I've ever come across.' Hardy's words carried a hint of outrage. 'The kind of man this country needs, if people of all races are to work together. I've known the van der Beer family for years. Decent, honest people who were always fair to their workers and respected by their neighbours.'

'What about the father?' Rabindrah said. 'I understand he was in the King's African Rifles and fought the Mau Mau. And that he went to Rhodesia around the time of Independence. Is that right?'

'He was one of many farmers who left shortly before or after Independence.' The inspector made no attempt to hide his rising anger. His face had reddened and he walked over to his office door and opened it. 'I'm afraid there's nothing else I can tell you. And I have two *askaris* waiting outside with work to do.'

'I was wondering if you had a note of the priests who taught Simon Githiri at the mission school, and where they are now?' Rabindrah stood up, but his notebook was still in his hand.

'Look here, I don't think another sensational story is called for. The survivors would be deeply distressed by it. There's been enough grief already. The thing is over now.' Hardy did not offer a handshake. 'Goodbye, Mr Singh.'

Rabindrah stopped at a roadside *duka* an hour later, to ask for directions to Langani. He had never visited an Afrikaans farm, and in fact it was unusual to find one in this area. Most of them were further west and north, up on the flat Uasin Gishu plateau with its endless fields of wheat and lines of gum trees that he had always considered gloomy. Like the Boers who had planted them. Driving across the van der Beers' land he was struck by its beauty and diversity, and by the sight of Mount Kenya's glistening peaks rising out of the wheat in their awesome and remote beauty. He stopped for a moment to watch a herd of giraffe lope away from him. Further along the way a troupe of baboons scampered across the dusty road, the largest male pausing to open his mouth and display the ferocity of long, pointed teeth. Rabindrah shuddered. He had always disliked monkeys, even feared them. As a child he had seen baboons swarming across the windscreen of his father's car in Nairobi National Park, and while his sisters and parents had shrieked with laughter at their antics, he had cowered in the back seat willing them to go away.

He rounded a bend in the track and was suddenly confronted by a clipped hedge and a low stone building surrounded by a sumptuous lawn. The land had been transformed into a place of orderly and meticulous beauty, with curving flower beds and shrubs of every colour and shape. It was almost impossible to see the roof of the house, or the posts that held it up. The entire structure was covered with a tumble of honeysuckle and bougainvillea, and other climbing plants that he did not recognise. When he turned off the engine and stepped out of the car he found himself in a place where the wind sang through the trees, and for a moment the chatter of birds was the only other sound. And then there was a frenzy of barking and three huge dogs appeared on the verandah, hackles up. Rabindrah froze. The sun disappeared without warning behind a passing cloud, and the place felt cold and threatening.

'Can I help you?' The woman was young and blonde and heavily pregnant, and her voice carried the flat cadences of an Afrikaner. 'Don't worry about the dogs. They won't hurt you.'

She whistled for the great beasts and they stopped in their tracks, but they were still making small growling sounds at the backs of their throats. Rabindrah remained in the same spot, standing very still.

'I'm looking for Hannah van der Beer.'

'That's me. I'm Mrs Olsen, in fact. Have you come about the seed we ordered? Or are you from the sawmill?'

'Neither, I'm afraid. I'm a journalist and I wondered if I could talk to you.'

'What about?' Hannah stiffened and remained standing on the top step of the verandah, looking down at him. She did not indicate that he should come into the house and he felt at a disadvantage. It was infuriating how these white farmers could still make him feel somehow inferior.

'I read about your brother.' He saw her face tighten. 'I'm very sorry. And I met Sarah Mackay recently in Nairobi. In fact, she sent me some of her photographs and I've used them for an article about her research. So we have been working together, in a manner of speaking. I understand that you want to turn part of your farm into a wildlife reserve. To carry on your brother's work. Very courageous. So I wondered—'

'If you know this already, then I don't understand what you're doing here,' Hannah said. 'Right now my husband and I are trying to run a farm, like everyone else in this area. And yes, we hope to open a small game lodge one day, but not right now. I really don't have anything to say to a newspaper.'

'Well, you've probably seen more than enough of journalists, and under terrible circumstances. But it seems that the reasons for your brother's murder are still unresolved. I mean, the motive was never discovered and—'

'My brother's death was investigated by the police.' She moved forward, negotiating the steps slowly, her movements clumsy. But her eyes were blazing with pain and anger. 'The killer was found. He was a madman and he's dead. And I don't wish to discuss the subject with you. Or with anyone else from any newspaper, ever again.'

He saw her clasp her hands together to keep them from trembling.

Before he had a chance to respond, or to try and calm her, a tall man appeared further along the verandah.

'What's the matter, Han?' he asked, coming to her side. 'What does this fellow want?' He listened to her explanation for a moment, putting his arm around her shoulders. Then he turned to Rabindrah.

'I have no idea why you've come here. But my wife is pregnant, as you can see, and I don't want her upset. We have nothing to say about her brother's death or about our lives. So I'd like you to leave now, if you don't mind.'

'I thought Mrs Olsen might be glad to talk about the farm as a wildlife sanctuary,' Rabindrah said. 'I didn't mean to cause any distress.'

'What else could you have caused?' Hannah said. 'Do you think my brother's murder is an appropriate topic for an afternoon visit? Were you expecting tea, and a chat about his life and times and his hacked-up body?' Her voice rose and he could see her fingers digging into the sleeve of her husband's bush jacket.

'You'd better leave now,' Lars repeated. Two veins stood out on his neck and his eyes were angry. 'And there's no reason for you to return here, or to bother us again.'

'I'm sorry you feel that way,' Rabindrah said, 'because I'm writing a series of articles about conservation, and I know you're transforming part of the farm into a wildlife reserve. I might even be of help to you.'

But Lars had turned away. He took his wife's arm and walked her back into the house, leaving Rabindrah alone with the dogs in the driveway. The afternoon sun pushed its way through the cloud cover to illuminate the rambling building, its honeyed light pouring into the deep recess of the verandah. He saw her then, the Irish girl. She was standing at a window watching him, her arms folded, her face tense. When she realised that he had spotted her she raised her arms and pulled the curtains closed.

'If you change your mind, Miss Mackay has my number,' Rabindrah called out to Lars's retreating figure. But as soon as he had said the words he regretted them. He did not want to alienate the girl. She would still be a good subject for a story. And another idea had begun to form in his head.

Hannah stopped for a moment and looked back over her shoulder, white with rage. Then she continued into the house. The dogs were still standing beside the steps, watching Rabindrah's every movement. He spun on his heel and climbed into his car, seething at the way he had been treated. There was a crunching sound as he accelerated on the gravel, and then he drove away, leaving in his wake a trail of dust and unease.

'Did you know that Hindi reporter was coming here?' Hannah asked at dinner. 'He said you were working together, Sarah.'

'I never dreamed he would turn up at Langani,' Sarah said, resenting the suggestion that she was responsible for the visit. 'And we're not working together. I sent him some photographs to use for his article about Dan's and Allie's research, that's all.'

'Did he ask you about Piet?' Hannah said. 'When you met him in Nairobi, did he want to know about the – about Piet's death?'

'He never mentioned it,' Sarah said, troubled. 'I didn't think he'd connected me with Piet at all. I was just someone doing elephant research at Buffalo Springs.'

'He must have come here because of you, though,' Hannah said accusingly. 'He mentioned your name. And what did he mean – unresolved? Piet's dead, and that bloody savage who killed him is dead. What more is there to resolve, except the fact that our lives are torn to shreds and will never be the same again?'

'Journalists are always trying to create some new twist to a story, Han.' Lars reached out to stroke her arm. 'That's what this fellow was doing, I'm sure.'

'But there must have been something behind the question. Something you said to him in Nairobi, Sarah, that brought him here.'

'That's not fair at all.' Sarah's face was flushed with resentment. 'I'd never encourage anyone to come to Langani and start asking questions about Piet. Or pry into our lives. Piet was never mentioned in Nairobi. I don't know why the man came here, but it was absolutely not my doing. Oh God, I knew I shouldn't have gone to that presentation. I had a feeling something would go wrong.'

'You had a feeling about Simon Githiri, too,' Hannah said. 'You thought you would have known if he had died out there in the forest. That you would have felt it in some way, and it would have helped to close off the horror of it all. And now it's all being dug up again.'

'Don't allow yourself to get upset, Han,' Lars said. 'It's not good for you right now. Sarah had nothing to do with this fellow turning up here. You know that.'

Hannah stared at them for a moment and then began to cry. 'Oh God. Oh God, why doesn't it ever go away? When will it all fade and let us live with a little peace, a few good memories of the happy times?' She leaned forward, her hands spread across her belly, her body convulsed with weeping. 'You know, sometimes I feel we should move away. Leave Langani. I think that nothing really good can happen here now, and we're living the wrong lives. Maybe we should find somewhere else, and begin again.'

'Come, my dear,' Lars said. 'Let's go and sit by the fire, and Mwangi will bring you a hot drink. And then we'll go to bed early, and everything will look better in the morning.'

For a short time they sat together in front of the log fire, each one trying to regain their fragile hold on hope. It was Hannah who broke the silence with an apology.

'Lars is right. I have to go to bed. My back's really aching and I feel very tired. And so heavy. I'm going to drop unless I lie down. 'Night, Sarah.' She leaned over and kissed her friend, taking her hand. 'I'm sorry I've been so stupid and out of sorts. I'll be fine tomorrow.'

Lars rose to help her and they left the room together. Mwangi moved back and forth, clearing plates, subdued and silent. In the shadows of the room, Sarah could feel the ghosts gathering, and she began to wish that she had gone straight back to Buffalo Springs. Then she heard the sound of hurrying feet and Lars rushed into the room.

'I think we have a problem,' he said. 'Hannah's bleeding. I'm going to ring Dr Markham now. I reckon we need to get her to the hospital. That bloody journalist is responsible for this.'

'I'll pack a few things she might need,' Sarah said. 'I can sit with her in the back of the Land Rover, and you can drive.'

'Mwangi, we'll need you to help carry her to the car,' Lars said, his face white. 'She shouldn't walk anywhere.'

There was no time for any further discussion. A loud wailing sound came from the bedroom and Sarah rushed into the room to find Hannah curled on the bed, her mouth open as she tried to breathe away the first pains.

'She's in labour. Her waters have broken,' Sarah said, grasping Lars's large clammy hand. 'You'll have to try and get Dr Markham to come over. I think it's too risky to take her to the hospital now. This baby is going to be born right here, at Langani.' She leaned over and placed her hand on Hannah's forehead. 'You'll be fine, Han. We're here to help you. Don't worry now. Just breathe. Take big, deep gulps of air and get ready for all that pushing.'

'Do you know anything about delivering babies?' Hannah looked up, her eyes wide with fear. 'Did they teach you that when you were at the university?'

'Of course they did.' The lie rolled off Sarah's tongue as she tried to subdue a rising sense of panic. Nothing had prepared her for this. 'Lars, tell Mwangi to get his wife Agnes. She's delivered dozens of babies on the labour lines and in Lottie's clinic. And we'll need warm water and lots of towels and cotton wool. Now breathe, Han. Take big, deep breaths. I'm going to wash my hands and get ready for the big event.'

Outside the bedroom she found Lars, like a statue and transfixed with fear. 'My God, I can't get through this,' he said. 'I don't know what to do for her. When she cries out like that I don't know what to do. This is a terrible thing.'

'Nonsense,' Sarah said briskly. 'Pull yourself together, Lars. You must have delivered plenty of calves in your time. And now you know why. They were practice runs. Practice for the arrival of your son or daughter. But we may be in for a long night. Did you get hold of Dr Markham?'

'I spoke to his wife. He's with old Mrs Hudson. She's had a bad asthma attack and she needed oxygen and maybe a transfer to the hospital. He'll be here as soon as possible, but he can't say when. The Hudsons are twenty miles away and their road is in terrible shape.'

'Sarah?' Hannah was calling. 'Sarah, will you stay here beside me, from now on?' Her face was beaded with sweat, and she was clutching at the sheet that covered her. 'I'm so scared. And now that it's happening I don't know if this can work. I don't know if Lars can really love us, love this baby that isn't his own. And it hasn't even got a name. We've never talked about a name. Oh God. This is awful. I didn't ever imagine it would be like this.'

'Hannah, I do have a name.' Lars loomed in the doorway, and then crossed the room to sit on the edge of the bed and take her hand. 'If we have a son then we're going to call him Piet, after my best friend. But if it's a girl, Han, then I want her to have a Norwegian name. I want to call my daughter Suniva. She was an Irish princess, you know. Like Sarah here. She came to Norway and everyone loved her, and her name meant "gift from the sun". So that is what our daughter will be called. Suniva, yes.'

Hannah looked up at him and smiled, and then her face screwed up as the next wave of pain hit her and she writhed on the bed, her fingers clutching at Sarah's arm. Lars hovered to one side, awkward and out of place. His usual calm had deserted him. Mwangi brought tea for Sarah, and after a swift glance at Lars he disappeared to return with a large snifter of brandy. His wife arrived with the maddeningly cheerful smile of a woman who has seen the birth of many children.

'Eeeehhh, Bwana Lars. You will soon have a fine child to help you on the *shamba*,' Agnes said, shunting him firmly to one side. 'Now, you leave the women to their work. *Sukuma*, Memsahib Hannah. It is good, now that the day has come. *Sukuma, Mama!* Push.'

And all past tragedies were forgotten as they exhorted Hannah to breathe, or push, or to rest. Through the next hours their reassurances mingled with her cries of pain, with Lars's groans of alarm, and with the age-old instructions of the Kikuyu midwife.

Finally Sarah caught the first glimpse of the baby's head and then, with one last ferocious push from Hannah, the child slid into the world. Sarah lifted it and watched as Agnes wiped the blood and mucus from its tiny face. Then she laid it, with the cord still pulsing, on Hannah's breast.

'You have a little girl, Hannah. A beautiful little girl.' Sarah's voice was shaking. 'Lars is going to cut the cord in a minute. Well done, Han.'

She stood with Lars, watching his fingers tremble as he made the separation between mother and child, heard the baby cry for the first time. His eyes were filled with tears of relief as he marvelled at the perfect little creature. The baby's eyes opened, and she looked at him with a solemn, violet gaze. He stared down at her, almost lost in his big hands, and then her fingers closed over one of his, and with a small snuffling sigh, she slept. Lars looked at Hannah, lying in the sweat and blood of her labour, her hair damp and dishevelled, and then down at the infant who rested in his arms. And he said to Sarah, 'I have never seen any two people so beautiful in all my life.'

Chapter 3

London, August 1966

'You can't bloody walk away from your career, on the off-chance that this cock-eyed scheme in Kenya will turn out well.' Tom Bartlett was angry. 'It's a reckless idea that can ruin you.'

'Ruin me how?' Camilla's expression was calm.

'Have you conveniently forgotten what happened last summer?' He was incredulous. 'You were the world's most perfect face when you left here, and six weeks later you walked into this office with your head sliced open by a bloody great panga.' He brushed the hair from her forehead. 'What about this scar? Five men with knives barged into the van der Beer farm one evening and attacked you. Shot your farmer friend, Lars. And almost ruined your face. You were a nervous wreck for months afterwards. You're only just back to normal. Christ Almighty, you could have been killed. And now you're going back to the very place where it happened. That doesn't seem very clever. Not well thought out at all. But I'm just a simple boy from the East End, so what would I know?'

'That was an isolated incident. A robbery.' Her smile was all sweetness. 'I could just as easily have been attacked on a dark street in London, or in the souk in Tangier while we were doing the *Tatler* pictures.'

'Don't be bloody daft,' he said. 'The kind of danger we're talking about is—'

'Besides, I've been back to Kenya since then,' she interrupted him, knowing how feeble her argument was. 'And everything was peaceful at Langani.'

'Oh yes? So, how come one of your closest friends was murdered there a few months ago?' he said brutally. 'It's a bloody dangerous country, Camilla.'

'I don't agree.' Camilla stared past him at a framed poster of herself on his office wall. 'A madman killed Piet van der Beer. A young Kikuyu who might have been drugged, or part of a cult, or simply off his rocker. Piet who was part of my life since my childhood. He was Hannah's adored, only brother, and Sarah's fiancé. And of course none of us will ever truly recover from that.' She bit her lip, trying to compose herself. 'God knows why these things happen. But it's no different from some lunatic pushing an unsuspecting commuter under a train for no apparent reason. Anyway, the man who killed Piet is dead. There's no threat to anyone at Langani now.'

'Doesn't *anything* make an impression on you?' Tom leaned back in his chair and put his feet up on to the desk. 'You're the most famous beauty in Europe, and soon you'll conquer the States as well. You're at parties with the Beatles and the Stones, you're on the front of every magazine, and you've appeared on every television show worth being seen on. You've been photographed by Donovan and Bailey and John French. In fact, everybody wants to photograph you, write something about you, pretend they have a connection with you. And you want to chuck it all in for some fucking fairy tale.'

'I need to live another life,' she said, leaning across the desk so that her eyes were level with his. 'I've had it with studios and cameras and silly clothes, and layers of paint on my face. I'm tired of being stopped in the street and doing guest appearances on *Ready Steady Go*, and having flash-bulbs popping in my face. It seems so trivial, somehow.'

'As opposed to doing something really worthwhile, like squatting over a smoking fire in a mud hut, cooking a leg of buffalo for the returning hunter. Huhhh! Huhhh! Huhhh!' He made grunting noises and scratched his armpits. 'Where will you get your legs waxed, darling?'

'You're so bloody myopic, Tom,' she said, furious. 'This isn't the only place where there's life. I won't cease to exist just because I'm out of London. Out of your dismal little orbit. There are other worlds, you know. I've had enough of being a high-priced clothes horse. This idea I have, this workshop in Kenya, *is* something really worthwhile.'

'Don't waste time trying to draw me into your fantasy.' Tom lit a cigarette and blew the smoke out slowly, making a smoke-screen between them. 'I know the real reason you're going back, and it's even more daft than the scheme itself.'

'I'm going back to start a business.'

'You're already in business, in case you haven't noticed. We're in business together, darling, and doing rather well at it. Making bags of money. Saul Greenberg has put your name on all his fancy frocks, and now you're going to get a nice little bonus every time somebody's secretary buys one in the futile hope of looking like you. New York is going to be awash with pictures of you in the next few weeks, and that poor besotted sod, Greenberg, wants to name a line of underwear and cosmetics after you. How many more businesses do you need?'

'I want to create my own clothes and bags, and jewellery. Things with an African theme, limited in number and completely different. Designed by me.'

'Great idea. I can find you studio space this very minute and you can set up your little project this afternoon. There's an ideal spot three doors down from here. Honest.'

'You're making fun of me, which is patronising and insulting. I'm going to do this in Kenya, because it's where I want to be.' She stopped, aware that she needed to sound calm and reasonable. It was so hard to explain to someone who did not know the force and pull of Africa, impossible to rationalise the way in which the essence of the place had long ago buried itself deep in her psyche. She could barely understand it herself. 'I may be pale and blonde, but I'm rooted in Africa. I know you'll never figure that out, any more than you can understand the connection between Hannah and Sarah and me. They were my lifeline all through the years of growing up. The sisters I never had. I was an only child, mostly left to my own devices in a cold, unhappy household. It was only at Langani that I ever felt a real sense of home and family. I felt safe there with my two friends, and we promised then that we'd always stick together. We cut our hands and mingled the blood and made the vow. I love that farm, and the country, and the wildlife that Sarah is working to preserve. I want to go back and contribute something myself. It's where I really belong, Tom.'

'Sounds like a truckload of sentimental bollocks to me,' he said.

'I'll still make plenty of money, and you'll still be my agent,' she said, ignoring his scorn. 'I'm going to start with jackets and bags and belts, all embroidered with tribal beads and feathers and semi-precious stones and crystals. Like the things I sold in London earlier this year. They'll have the same quality as the wedding dress I made for Hannah. You said you loved that. And Saul has promised to use whatever I can produce. He's mad about the whole idea.'

'He's mad about you, that's all.' Tom made a lewd gesture. 'Anything you say is music to his ears, no matter how ludicrous it is. People may want to go round looking like Maasai maidens for a moment or two, I grant you that. But after one season you'll be stuck with an inventory that's last year's fad. What then?'

'I'll create new designs, like every other manufacturer,' she said impatiently. 'A limited number of items each year. And I'm willing to do selected fashion shoots when I have time.'

'Selected fashion shoots!' He snorted with derision. 'You don't really believe you'll still be in the running for the best jobs, when you're thousands of miles away in Africa, mooning over Jungle Jim. Jean Shrimpton is available and right here. To say nothing of Twiggy, who can do no wrong for the time being, and Penelope Tree. He's not worth it, Camilla.'

'That's not why I'm going,' she said, defensively. 'I won't be in Nairobi. I'm planning to stay at Langani for the first few months. The local women I'm taking on need to be trained. And supervised full-time to start with, otherwise I'll never get the quality I need. Besides, Anthony's mostly out on safari.'

'You've been taken in, darling, hook, line and sinker. Is this chap aware of what you're giving up for him? Because so far he's only succeeded in making you unhappy, behaving like the self-centred Lothario he is.'

'This is not about him, I tell you.' She thumped her fist on his desk, spilling coffee on to the stack of photos and papers littering the surface. 'I do have a brain, you know. I can plan and think for myself.'

'Look, Camilla, we've worked together since the day you started in this racket,' Tom said. 'I've always felt we were friends, as well as being involved in business together.'

'We *are* friends,' she said. 'And you've done great things for me.'

'You have brains and extraordinary good looks, darling.' He lit another cigarette and studied her, as she leaned towards him with her huge blue eyes pleading for understanding. She had moved closer and perched herself on the front of his desk, the miniskirt riding up to show off impossibly long and perfect legs. He was surprised that her beauty could still make him catch his breath. 'But it's a combination you're not using to your best advantage right now.'

'I know what I'm doing,' she said stubbornly.

'I don't care what you say.' Tom was weary of the argument. 'This yearning for Africa is all about the white hunter, Camilla. And nothing I've heard about him tells me he's worth it. Has it also slipped your mind that I've just got you the cover of *Vogue*? They've chosen you as one of only three models for the Paris collections. And you're doing all of Mary Quant's new dresses for next summer. This is on top of your existing agreement with Saul. You mustn't walk away. You can't be that stupid.'

'I'd have to have my face done for the *Vogue* pictures. Get the scar removed.' She stood up and went to look out of the window.

'Yes, you would. That was the deal, and thanks to my efforts and incomparable charm, they're willing to believe it will be a total success.' He looked at her with growing suspicion. 'I thought you were going to have the scar taken care of in November, so you'd be ready for work early in the new year. That's what Edward said, and he's the expert.'

'I don't want Edward mixed up in this.'

'Look, you rushed off to Africa for Hannah's wedding against his advice, and he was pissed off. You had a lovers' tiff.' Tom sighed. 'He'll forgive you. The man's in love with you, poor bastard. Edward is a decent bloke who'll take proper care of you. He'll give you security and a good life. He's not like this unreliable character out of some adventure comic, with nothing to offer except uncertainty.'

'Edward and I – well, we're not together any more. You know that. I broke it off when I went away. It wouldn't be fair to—'

'To go back to the best plastic surgeon in London as agreed, and get your face fixed,' he interrupted, the last of his patience gone. 'Oh, for God's sake, darling, grow up. You have to get rid of that scar to land the best jobs.'

'I'm doing the best jobs now.'

'You've scraped by for a few months with fringes and hats over your forehead, because people were sympathetic after your horrible experience. But you've got to get rid of the scar and move on. Get a new look. *Vogue* is talking about outside shots, hair blown away from the face. And for the jewellery pictures they want a combed-back, sleek look. It's Donovan who's taking the pictures, and he's talking about doing the diamond necklace draped over your forehead, instead of around your neck.'

'He can line it up with the scar, then,' she said, trying to lighten his mood.

'You'll have to get in touch with Edward, because he is what you need,' Tom said. 'And that's all there is to it. What does George have to say about your decamping to Nairobi, by the way?'

'I haven't told him.' She did not meet his gaze. 'He wouldn't care anyway.'

'He's living there, for God's sake. He's your father, Camilla. If you're dead set on this mad notion, then you could at least stay with him while you get organised. He must have a posh residence with bags of room.'

'I don't want to live with him. And if he was such a good father, he wouldn't have run off with his lover-boy directly after Mother's death.'

'I thought you'd accepted the boyfriend,' Tom said. 'You were all pals together last time I saw you with George.'

'I've had to come to terms with the fact that he's – well, with his lifestyle. So I invited them to dinner. Once. But then my darling daddy skipped off on holiday with Giles, when the earth had barely settled on Mother's grave. That's not a sign of love, Tom.'

'People do weird things in moments of grief,' he said. 'George loved your mother, in his way. You've said so yourself. They stayed together in spite of all their problems, and he was with Marina most of the time while she was ill. They were very close.'

'Yes.' She admitted it grudgingly. 'But she's gone, and it's different now. He's left all that behind. Left me behind.'

'He loves you, Camilla,' Tom insisted. 'You know that.'

'No, I don't know it,' she said. 'And what I hate is that I have to make such an effort to try and believe it. Love shouldn't be like that. It should be something deep and certain. It should be someone you can rely on. When I was a child I thought he was the only person I could trust, because my mother was so remote and unpredictable. But then I found that my father's life was a lie, and that I couldn't trust him at all.'

'He's a victim of hypocrisy at a high level,' Tom said. 'If public figures like him are honest and admit they're homosexual, they're considered a liability. Disgraced and hounded and laughed at. They could be put in jail until recently. So they marry and try and live the way that society demands. But they almost always fail, because it's unnatural for them. It's sad, really.'

'I'm tired of sad,' she said. 'I'm twenty-one years old, Tom, and I've been far too sad all my life. My mother's dead, and my father's queer. I had a love affair in Africa that brought me nothing but misery. My two best friends are thousands of miles away, and we've lost someone we all loved very much, in a revolting and primitive killing. I can't cope with any more sadness.'

'You're also phenomenally successful and wealthy and beautiful,' he said. 'You can go anywhere. Do anything you want.'

'That's what I've been trying to tell you.' She was exasperated by his glib response. 'You don't seem to have heard a word I said. I want to go back to Kenya. Do something to help Hannah and maybe raise money for Sarah's elephant study, too. Those are the things I really want. Out there I can live a life that will make a real difference to other people. And I don't understand why you're hell-bent on talking me out of it.'

'Why are you so altruistic all of a sudden?' Tom was unconvinced. 'Is it something you've eaten? If so, it's a dish I need to avoid.'

'You're poking fun at me again,' she said bitterly. 'I've worked like a donkey here in London, but I'm tired of it. I'm sick of the whole shallow business, of putting on three sets of eyelashes and trunkloads of impossible clothes, and pretending to millions of people that they can go out and buy them and look just like me. I want to do something worthwhile, and I don't think you should be so contemptuous about it.'

He left his desk and came to stand beside her, placing his arm around her shoulder and pulling her round to face him. In the end, she always won him over. He'd given up hoping that she might one day think of him as more than her agent and look at him in a different way.

'I'm sorry,' he said, genuinely contrite. 'You've been through a lot in the last year, and I know you have this thing about Africa being your true home. So take a couple of months off, and go back. If you're determined to do this design thing, then start really small. That way you won't plough too much money into the scheme at the beginning. And if it goes wrong, you can chalk it up to experience and come back to what you do so well. Or you can live both lives – spend part of the year in Kenya and the rest in London and Paris, or even New York.'

'You've just told me that won't work,' she pointed out. 'But it doesn't matter, because I won't be coming back, Tom. Except to sell the things I make out there. I'll be as good a designer as I was a model.'

'That remains to be seen.' He was wise enough not to pursue the issue. 'Meanwhile, you're booked for the Biba pictures next week, and the perfume and jewellery campaigns, and this great trip to New York. You've got to get through those before you take off in pursuit of your jungle hunk. In fact, you should have your face fixed too. Hide out in Kenya while it heals, and then come back to do the collections. But for God's sake don't rush out to Africa and put up buildings, or buy expensive machines and materials that will suck up all your capital. Kenya's not safe these days, Camilla. It's not the place of your childhood with British rule and protection for people like you.'

'You still don't get it, do you?' She wanted him to understand. 'Hannah's going to give me a place to stay and to work – the old manager's cottage on the farm. Lars has already started to convert the building, with some money I wired out there last month. My workshop will bring jobs and revenue to Langani. They're really struggling. The wheat and dairy production is doing fine, but all their cash is tied up in the lodge Piet built. And Hannah can't open it right now, because she's busy with the baby. She's going to help me teach the local women to sew and do the beading and embroidery. And I've told her we'll share the income.'

'Now I know for sure that you've lost your marbles.' Tom shook his head in disbelief. 'But you're determined to learn the hard way. As far as I'm concerned, the only certainty about this wild idea is that you'll be back in London very soon, darling, and crying out for work.'

'If I am, then you'd better have plenty of contracts lined up.' Camilla tried to sound amused, but she was hurt by his lack of faith in her judgement.

'I might add that you haven't even considered what will happen to me. As your agent I stand to lose a great deal of money if you insist on buggering off into the jungle.'

'You're always telling me there are more dolly birds on the way up, just waiting to topple me off my pedestal.'

'You're impossible, Camilla,' he said. 'What about dinner tonight?'

'No thanks. I'll be wiped out after the studio session this afternoon.'

'Go ahead and punish me, then, just for caring about you and giving you sound advice. But you'd better kiss and make up with Edward Carradine soon,' Tom said. 'Because whatever happens, you need to get rid of that line on your forehead. Now get out of here. Joe Blandford is waiting with his big camera, and he doesn't like models who are late.'

She left him, half laughing and half exasperated at his inability to grasp the seriousness of her dreams. Blandford's studio was overheated and dusty, and she started the afternoon with a fit of coughing that left her red-eyed and limp.

'I want you to wear this dress, to emphasise your eyes.' Joe held out a scrap of blue silk. 'And this long scarf thing with the feathers. I want you to look as though you're going to jump over the moon – mouth wide open, laughing, arms all over the place. Shake your head so your hair flies out. Look like you're floating.'

The shoot did not go well. Camilla tried to forget Tom's comments, the disparaging remarks he had made about Anthony, the self-doubt he had planted in her mind. But she could not transform herself into the light-hearted creature that Joe demanded for the camera. He became exasperated, shouting commands at her, ordering his assistant to move the large lights around the studio so that the planes and shadows of her face would change with every frame, swearing when her smile seemed false and her body stiff.

'What's the matter with you, for God's sake? You look like you're going to a bloody funeral. You look like you're going to cry. Joy is what I need to see. I want fucking joy! This is for *Vanity Fair*, Camilla. You've got to cheer up, doll. I don't want you bringing your troubles into my studio, whatever they are. You'll have to do better than this.'

'I'm sad,' she said, hiding her face in her hands. An idea came into her head as she spoke the words. 'Let's do it sad, Joe. A blue dress for a blue mood. Wait – I'll show you.'

She rummaged in her tote bag, took out make-up and brushes and headed for the large mirror at the back of the room. Ten minutes later she stood in front of him, her hair tousled, eyes rimmed with dark kohl, painted mouth drooping. She stared into the camera, one arm over her head, dangling down to frame her face, her fingers grasping a torn envelope. With her other hand she pulled down the neck of the dress to expose collarbones and the curve of her breasts. Tears formed in her eyes and slid slowly down her cheek.

'Well, fuck me! That's it! Beautiful. Open your mouth just a little. Now keep still, darling. Still, still, still. You're the best, Camilla. The bloody best there is. There's no one like you in this business. What about dinner tonight? There's a new place with—'

'I'm going home to read a book and watch television. I need a quiet night.' She smiled as he shrugged off the put-down with theatrical bad grace.

When she left the studio her mood was still dark, and the splash of her footsteps on the rain-soaked pavements dragged her deeper into the hole of her depression. People pushed past her on the crowded street, hats and scarves and umbrellas covering their faces. A heedless crush of humanity whose troubles were probably far greater than her own. The realisation did not comfort her at all.

Back in her flat, she threw her bag on to the bed and ran a bath, pouring an entire bottle of expensive oil into the water. She lay back and closed her eyes to seal off the day, to empty her mind of anxiety. But Anthony Chapman immediately filled the void she had created, his face tanned and freckled and laughing, gingery hair curling over the back of his shirt collar, long legs planted apart, arms folded across his chest so that she could see the nomad's bracelets that adorned his wrist. Once, she had thought he loved her, but she did not want to wind back the spool of memory which had ended in rejection. She had managed to remain cool towards him at Hannah's wedding, to keep her head, to distance herself from his determined advances. But it had been hard. She stepped out of the bath and dried herself quickly, pulled on a pair of suede trousers and a sweater, and twisted her hair, still damp with steam, into a knot at the back of her neck. Moments later she was in a taxi on her way to the cinema.

'One for *Torn Curtain*, please,' she said, glancing at the poster. 'Tears you apart with suspense,' it proclaimed, in bold letters. It was exactly what she needed. A pleasurable escape for an hour or two, a view of the world through the blue, blue eyes of Paul Newman. She bought a bar of chocolate and made her way into the darkened auditorium, slipping off her coat and hat, bending to lay her umbrella on the floor at her feet. She saw Edward as she straightened, guiding his companion along the aisle and into their seats two rows in front of her. The woman reached up, smiling, and touched his face as she settled herself. Camilla slid down in her seat, praying he would not see her. She was relieved when the newsreel started, blaring out the world's latest disasters and the high drama of coming attractions. When the lights went up at the interval she was trying to decide whether it would be best to leave. But it was too late. Something made Edward turn around and their eyes locked. Camilla lifted her hand in a small wave. He nodded an acknowledgement, looked as though he was going to stand up, appeared to change his mind, and then returned his gaze to the screen. During the performance Camilla saw the woman lean her head sideways towards his shoulder, but he made a small, shrugging gesture and created a distance between them.

'How are you, Camilla?' He was waiting outside when the film ended. 'This is Juliette Dawson. You've probably met.'

In the bright light of the foyer Camilla recognised the American woman. She was in her late thirties and would need a lucky break if she was to make it past a supporting role, but she was a competent actress. Edward was probably doing her face. Or her breasts. Or both.

'I loved your last film,' Camilla said. 'I thought you deserved an Oscar.'

'I thought so too.' Juliette pasted on a dazzling smile, displaying impeccable dental work. 'Edward is hoping you'll join us for a drink.' Her tone was less than enthusiastic.

'Or dinner,' he said. 'Do you realise it's about five months since I last saw you? I'd love to hear about your visit to Kenya.'

'Sweet of you to ask, but I have an early shoot tomorrow,' Camilla said. 'Lovely to see you both. Bye now.'

She did not sleep well, and was already awake and inexplicably anxious when the telephone rang early in the morning.

'I wanted to catch you before you left for your session.' Edward tried to sound casual. 'I thought perhaps we could have dinner tonight.'

'I don't think so,' Camilla said. 'I'm going to—'

'I made a mistake.' His voice changed. 'I was angry when you went back to Nairobi for Hannah's wedding, and that was foolish of me. Of course you had to be there. I had no right to suggest otherwise, and you had every right to ignore my advice and go. I saw your picture in the paper last week, and I've been trying to summon up the courage to ring and apologise. I'd like to see you, Camilla, now that you're back.'

'I'm not back for long.'

There was a brief silence. 'All the more reason, then,' he said. 'What about tonight?'

'No. I don't want a disagreement with you, Edward. Or with anyone. I'm going back to Kenya to live, and I'm sure you'll try to talk me out of it. But I'm not going to change my mind, and I don't have the energy or the inclination to argue all evening.'

'I have no intention of arguing with you,' he said equably. 'Suppose I pick you up at eight? We'll go somewhere quiet, and you can tell me all about the wedding and how it felt to be back at Langani.'

She had forgotten how easy it was to confide in him. Edward the Confessor, she had called him once. He was a good listener, and there was sympathy in his expression as she described the wedding at the farm.

'It was beautiful. Very moving, to be standing there in Lottie's garden, listening to Lars and Hannah make their promises. But I felt such pain for Sarah, because she and Piet should have been married there too. She was so brave and generous to be at that ceremony, and she even sang for them. It was heartbreaking. I only hope that the joy of their marriage will cancel out part of the tragedy. Begin to reconcile something that is irreconcilable in all our hearts.'

'What a tragic mix of memories,' Edward said.

'Yes, it was. I could feel Piet's presence everywhere. Sometimes I thought I could hear him, even smell him. I don't know how they cope with it on a day-to-day basis, knowing he will never walk out on to the lawn again to look up at the mountain, or whistle for the dogs, or answer the phone.' She stopped and swallowed hard. 'I can never think of him now, without that awful pain in my heart. So I try not to think of him at all. And I regret that especially, because I want to remember all the lovely things he was.'

'At least it's over,' he said. 'And Hannah's child will bring new life to Langani.'

'I suppose it's over.' Her voice wavered. 'But it would have been easier to close the door on it all if Simon Githiri had been brought to justice. Although it would have been terrible to sit in a courtroom for days or weeks on end, listening to the ghastly evidence, thinking of Piet dying on the ridge.' She shuddered, and for a few moments she was silent. 'The truth is that it will never be over,' she said finally.

'What are your plans now?' Edward looked down into his glass, not wanting her to see the hope he could barely conceal. She had always had this absurd effect on him, making him behave like a teenage boy on a first date rather than a mature, successful man of forty-two.

'I'm going back. As soon as I can.'

She had already told him this on the telephone, but hearing it from her lips made him feel as though someone had punched him in the stomach. Taken his breath away. He managed to smile at her, however, and drank what remained of his wine as she outlined her plans.

'I've decided to start a business there, making clothes under my own name. I think I can sell them here, and even in America.' Camilla was surprised that he did not immediately try to dissuade her or express doubts about her idea. 'I can't go right away because I'm committed to a whole series of shoots, and Saul Greenberg is about to launch the dress range he's named after me. I have to fly to New York next week to do the pictures for that. But I'd like to leave for Kenya before Christmas, if it's possible.'

Edward nodded, still wary of making a comment. He could not let her slide away out of his life again, and now he saw that he had a few weeks during which he might change her mind. If he was careful and subtle he might persuade her to run her Kenya business from London, suggest that she find and train a local manager in Nairobi, and fly out for occasional supervision. Perhaps Hannah could even take over the operation once it was up and running. He did not think it would be a long-term project. In the meantime, there was the excitement of her first visit to New York with all the glamour and adulation that would accompany it. It was impossible to believe that she would give all this up and go to Kenya, presumably because she was still smitten with the white hunter fellow.

'I think it's awfully brave of you to consider going back there to live,' he said. 'After Piet's death, and your own experience at Langani. Your face looks fine, by the way.'

'Yes, it does. Thanks to you. But the line on my forehead shows in close-ups, and I have to get rid of it.' She paused. 'I wondered if you would still be willing to take care of that.'

'Of course I would,' he said without hesitation. 'Whenever you're ready. You won't be able to work for a while afterwards, though.' He had visions of taking her away on holiday to an exotic island, or spending time with her in the English countryside, perhaps staying in the cottage in the Cotswolds that her mother had left her.

'I can hide out in Kenya until after the new year,' she said. 'I'll have to come back and do the *Vogue* pictures in Paris, and the job for Quant, because I don't want to let Tom down. Besides, I need to keep making money as a model until my new business is established. But Langani will be a good place for my face to heal.'

'I hear George has moved to Nairobi,' he said. 'How does he like it? Did Giles Hannington go with him?'

'I've no idea.' She made it clear that she did not want to discuss her father.

'I'd like to see you over the weekend.' He changed the subject in favour of something more hopeful.

'Look, Edward,' Camilla said. 'It's been lovely having dinner with you. But I can't go back to where we were, and I don't want to . . . to hurt you. We shouldn't start seeing each other regularly, because it can never come to anything.'

'We're still friends, aren't we?' He smiled at her. 'I certainly hope so. I won't pretend that I feel any less strongly about you, Camilla. But I have my career, which is extremely important to me, and time-consuming. You've often told me that it's my first passion. And I respect what you're saying about the past. So I don't see any reason why we shouldn't enjoy one another's company on that basis. What do you say?'

She hesitated, studying the dessert menu as if it were an inspirational text, a vital rule book for the rest of her life. Edward had always been generous. A good friend. They had become lovers almost by accident, at a time when she had needed someone to soothe and comfort her. At the moment she had learned of Piet's death. Afterwards they had drifted along together comfortably enough, until the quarrel over her return to Kenya. She was relieved at how easily he had accepted that things could no longer be the same between them. And it was true that his work was his passion – an obsession, almost. Camilla had often spent days alone in her flat while he stayed with a patient in a critical condition. Sometimes he was called away to some distant place to operate on a child disfigured at birth, or to repair a body damaged in a fire or an accident. Then he might be away for days or even weeks. But when they were together he had always been amusing and clever. Good company. She had missed him during the past few months.

'If you're really happy with a friendship, then I suppose we could see each other occasionally,' she said. 'But—'

'No "buts".' He was delighted. 'Why don't we find somewhere

pleasant for lunch on Sunday? You still haven't told me about the dress you made for Hannah, or where they went on their honeymoon.'

'I can't see you this weekend,' Camilla said.

He cursed himself for asking too much too soon. But to his relief she began to laugh.

'I'm flying to New York on Monday morning,' she said. 'My first visit, and I have to admit that I'm excited about it. So you'll have to wait until I come back. And then I'd like to hear about you, too. The most recent stories of your surgical skills bringing triumph and hope over despair.' She made a small grimace. 'I still feel guilty about that dreadful article in the paper.'

'I rather liked it,' he said, smiling. 'It had all the qualities of the "penny dreadfuls", as my mother used to call them. "Older man saves beautiful girl from permanent disfigurement, and falls in love." A modern day Beauty and the Beast fairy tale that appealed to everyone. Even I was fooled by it for a short while.' He saw her flush with embarrassment and genuine distress. 'I know you didn't have anything to do with it, Camilla, but I'll wager that Tom Bartlett let it slip to one of his journalist cronies. And then it was only a matter of time before they were on to us. It wasn't important, though. Not at all.' He was anxious to avoid any subject that might sour the evening. 'Where will you stay in New York? And what are you going to do apart from be photographed?'

'I want to go to the top of the Empire State Building and look for Cary Grant,' she said. 'I must see the Statue of Liberty from the Staten Island Ferry, and go shopping on Fifth Avenue, and eat hot dogs and pretzels from a street vendor. Since this is my first visit, I won't be recognised everywhere I go. It won't be like London where everyone knows me and I have to go round wearing a wig or a scarf, and looking like a charlady.'

He saw her home, made no attempt to come in, but kissed her on the cheek and wished her well in New York. Camilla was smiling as she prepared for bed, and still smiling when she picked up the telephone on the second ring.

'What's your news?' Anthony Chapman's voice shattered the fragile veneer of tranquillity. 'I thought you'd be back here by now. I've just had dinner with your father, and we decided to ring and find out what you're up to. Lars and Hannah are christening the baby next week, and we thought you might try and get here.'

'I'll be in New York.' Camilla's heart had jumped into her throat and was threatening to choke her. 'I'm going on Monday. It's something I can't get out of.'

'You are still planning to come, though? Soon. I'd like it to be very soon, Camilla.'

'Yes. I'll try and be there by mid-September,' she said, scarcely daring to believe the note of pleading in his voice.

'That's what I wanted to hear,' he said. 'I suppose I can last till then, but only just. Now I'll put you on to your dad. He's doing great things, and I'm delighted to be working with him on a couple of conservation issues. You'll see when you get here. *Salaams.*'

Camilla barely heard her father's words of greeting, his suggestion that she should stay with him when she arrived, his assurance that he would be there to meet her, that she could use his car and driver. He was anxious to let her know that he would help her in every way. But his words made little impression. Anthony had telephoned. He wanted her to come back. She was going to New York where she would make a fortune in a matter of a few days. As soon as she returned to London she would arrange for Edward to deal with the scar, and then she would go home to Kenya. To everyone and everything she loved and valued most. Kenya, where Anthony was waiting and her new life would be wonderful.

She would never forget her first sight of the New York skyline, the thrill of the soaring buildings on the horizon, at once powerful and delicate, the curved tracery of bridges and the slow boats along the Hudson River, the glittering stream of cars, on roads six lanes wide, passing to and from the fabled island of Manhattan.

The press and the public were waiting in hordes, and more people than she could have imagined. They screamed unintelligible questions and the flashbulbs were blinding, causing her to stumble as she tried to negotiate a graceful passage down the aircraft steps. She grabbed at Tom's arm and tried to move through the excited throng.

'Camilla! Camilla, what do you like best about New York?'

'Camilla, where do you like to eat? Where are you staying?'

'Camilla, what do you think of beer and hamburgers?'

'What's the thing you like most about the USA?'

'When did you last see the Beatles?'

The crowd pressed closer, their arms reaching out in a crazed frenzy to pull at her clothes and touch her hair. Hysterical voices formed a cacophony louder than anything she had heard in her life. It was Saul Greenberg who came to her rescue, taking her elbow, pushing her past the mob, shouting above the din as he helped her into the waiting helicopter.

'Get in. We're going straight to the centre of Manhattan. Landing on the PanAm building, a couple of blocks from my apartment. There's a limousine waiting for us there. No more screaming fans until tomorrow.'

'God! Oh God, I never expected anything as wild as this,' she said, limp with relief.

'In that case, you're very naive,' Saul said. 'Ever since the Beatles set foot on our soil the American public has been screaming for everything British. You're a famous part of cool, swinging London. Your picture has been in newspapers and magazines, hobnobbing with everyone from the Rolling Stones to royalty. And now you're going to be the Queen of New York.'

'A helicopter just for me! This is amazing,' she said, kissing him on his plump cheek. 'I could never have dreamed of such a thing. You're a genius, Mr Greenberg darling.'

Saul's apartment floated high above Park Avenue, a vast cube of glass and steel that absorbed and reflected the surrounding lights and sounds of the city. Camilla stood transfixed at her bedroom window, opening it a little to look down on the slow crawl of buses and long, streamlined cars and yellow taxicabs, and to hear the strident sound of police sirens as they crawled through the traffic-clogged grid of streets below. A dark river of people surged along the sidewalks to gather briefly in knots at pedestrian crossings. A traffic cop raised his shrill whistle and blew, long and loud. She longed to be a part of the milling crowd, to feel the urgency of it within herself, and she pulled on a jacket and slipped out of the apartment. The elevator made a rushing sound and deposited her within seconds on the ground floor, leaving her stomach thirty storeys up. A smiling doorman tipped his hat as she traversed the marble foyer and stepped out to become part of the great metropolis.

She crossed the street and made her way to Fifth Avenue where she was swept along with the evening crowds, left a little breathless by the unaccustomed speed at which they moved. The energy of the city entered her body like an electric jolt, pushing her forward, filling her with a wild excitement she had never experienced before. Steam hissed and curled up from beneath the pavements, as though the city's foundations rested on a fierce, depthless source of heat that might erupt and envelop the streets at any moment. In a diner she gave her order to a jaded waiter who could not understand her accent. She sat for a while, sipping her coffee and gazing at the customers in the small, steamy space, listening to their New York voices, their abrupt sentences, the slang she had heard in movies that was now a gritty, living sound in her ears. Men in expensive suits bought huge sandwiches and coffee to take away, jostling for attention at the counter, joking with the short-order cooks, sharing the day's news with shuffling old ladies and loud girls with fake eyelashes and high hopes of discovery. Two blocks away Camilla passed a stand selling hot dogs and stopped to buy one, smothering the sausage and the roll with sauerkraut, mustard and ketchup that spilled out on to her fingers and down her chin as she bit into it with relish. For a long while she stood at the Rockefeller Center, gazing upward, awestruck by the beauty and authority of the buildings, and the unceasing sounds that ricocheted within the narrow canyons of the streets. She had seen it all before, in books, in films, on television. But the brash, glorious reality of it was larger, brighter, more vivid than anything she could have imagined and she was enchanted by its magic.

She walked uptown, and found herself on 59th Street and the entrance to Bloomingdales. Inside, she wandered through the aisles, delighted by the glitter and variety on display, the exuberance of it so different from the decorum of an English department store. The unexpected shove and the insistent nasal twang broke into her reverie.

'Autograph?'

She turned in surprise to find a woman behind her, holding out a piece of white card.

'I think you've made a mistake,' Camilla said, but she realised immediately that the error had been her own. On a large panel only ten yards away she saw the photograph that had been taken in Paris two months before. She was wearing a minidress made from silver tiles and discs, her legs were long and bare, and her face stared out across the aisle, seductive and unmistakable.

'Look, I'm on a private holiday,' she said. 'I'd be awfully grateful if you would—'

It was too late. Within seconds she was surrounded by people, calling out to her, thrusting paper and pens into her hands, shouting questions, pushing and shoving to get closer. She tried to fight her way out, holding up her arms to protect herself from the excitement she had created, searching desperately for an escape route. But there was nowhere she could go. Panic rose in her as the numbers grew, and she felt the world closing around her in the shrinking, airless space. Her breath came in short gasps, and she backed into one of the sales booths. She began to cry silently, make-up running down her cheeks in dark runnels as the crowd swelled and pressed closer. Her lungs felt as though they would burst as she collapsed on to a small chair. It was the burly floor manager who took her arm and half carried her into the seclusion of his office. He handed her a paper cup of iced water and watched as she gulped it down. She summoned a smile, expecting sympathy.

'Don't you have a bodyguard with you?' he asked, unexpectedly hostile. 'We don't like scenes like that in here. Another ten minutes and we would have had to close off half the floor. You'd better call someone to come and take you away.'

She stared at him, shocked. 'I don't have anyone to call,' she said. 'I'm sorry. I never expected anything like this to happen.'

'Your picture is all over this store, ma'am,' he said, irritated. 'You're public property here. You must have known you'd cause a ruckus, coming in here during the rush hour for shoppers. We nearly had a riot on our hands out there. Do you have a car outside? A limo? There must be someone I can call?'

She was lost for words, embarrassed by her own naivety. She dabbed at her face, wiping the mascara off her cheeks and trying to regain her dignity and poise. 'I'm staying with friends on Park Avenue,' she said. 'I'm really sorry about all this.'

'My name's Walter Jackman. I'll get you a coffee,' he said, in a more kindly tone. 'If you give me the number where you're staying, I'll call them.'

'I don't have the phone number,' she said, feeling even more foolish. 'But I do know the address. So if you could find me a taxi . . .'

He stared at her in disbelief and then began to laugh, his large belly wobbling as he leaned back in his chair. 'Goddam, Miss Camilla,' he said, shaking his head. 'I sure have heard it all now. Come on. We'll make our escape together. But you'll have to give me your autograph for sure. Jeez, my wife and kids are never gonna believe this. Oh man, this is something else again!'

She held his hand as he led her through a second door and into a service elevator. In the basement of the building he shouted for someone called Joe.

'This here's Camilla, the English model girl. Friend of the Beatles and all. Believe it or not she's lost, and I want you to take her home before she gets in any more trouble.' He handed Joe a scrap of paper with the Park Avenue address. 'Don't let her out of your sight until she's safely in the door of that building. You hear me?'

'OK, ma'am.' Joe was grinning. 'Just follow me. But I'd sure like to have your autograph for my girlfriend. Hell, for me too.'

Camilla turned to Jackman. 'I'm really grateful to you,' she said. 'Is there some way I can thank you? Something I can do for—'

'Just stay out of Bloomies during busy hours,' he said. 'And have a good time in New York.'

'Look,' she said, 'I'm going to be on television tomorrow. At around eight-thirty in the morning on CBS. And I'll make a sign, just for you and your family. To say thank you. I'll just bring my finger up to my lips like this and tap twice. Just for you.'

She kissed him on the cheek and left him, still tapping his lips as she stepped into Joe's delivery van and sped away. At the Park Avenue apartment she received an unsympathetic reception.

'Where the hell have you been?' Tom was shouting at her as she came into the drawing room. 'You disappeared without a bloody word. No message, nothing. I've been going out of my mind worrying that you'd been run over in the street. Saul was about to start phoning round the hospitals. You can't just fucking vanish like that, Camilla.'

'Hey, let's get the girl a drink,' Saul said. 'Let's calm down and hear where she's been. I'll mix us some Martinis.'

She sat down in an overstuffed armchair and stared out at the glitter of New York, at the long tail of evening traffic and the scurrying masses in the streets far below her.

'I've had quite an adventure,' she said, launching into a description of

75

the incident in Bloomingdales. 'I was rather naive, I'm afraid. Actually I'd be quite happy to stay in this amazing apartment and never go out again. Thank God we're not in a hotel where anyone else might recognise me.'

'You can stay here for ever, as far as I'm concerned.' Her host was beaming as he rattled his cocktail shaker then poured carefully.

'Here's your drink, darling,' Tom said, handing her the frosted glass. 'But you'd better take it to your bath. We're going out to dinner and you have thirty minutes to get ready.'

They were shown to the best table at the 21 Club, where the glances in her direction were more discreet. But Camilla was aware that even here, where celebrities dined all the time, the entire room was watching her every movement. She was tired after the flight and the frightening experience earlier in the evening, and she could not eat. When she had drunk her second glass of champagne her head began to spin.

'I must be more tired than I'd imagined,' she said. 'This is exhausting, with everyone staring at me.'

'They do the same thing in London,' Saul said. 'It's no different here. And your arrival is in the evening papers.'

'It is different, though,' Camilla said. 'In London people would never dream of grabbing at me in public, or blocking my way. The best restaurants are full of people who don't want to be gawped at. And the less famous guests don't stare for long, because they'd never be given a table again.'

'Here it comes with the territory, kid. But you'll have a bodyguard from tomorrow. I have a great guy who'll be around all the time. You'll like him, I know.'

'A bodyguard sounds sinister,' she said, alarmed.

'It's the norm,' Saul assured her. 'Half the people in this room have one of those guys waiting outside for them. Yours is called Harold. He's built like a brick shit-house, he's pushing six foot six, and no one is going to mess with him or come near you while he's around. A good guy. Now let's talk about tomorrow and the rest of the week. We have the television thing in the morning. They want us at the studio around seven to get you ready. You'll be out and about for the rest of the day. Weather forecast is fine. The camera crew will follow you along Fifth Avenue and we'll shoot there first. Then it will be the Empire State Building, and finally uptown to Central Park for the horse and buggy ride. There'll be a support team in the van that brings the clothes, including the hairdresser and make-up girl. And the caterers. You'll be great. The whole thing will be a breeze.'

'But I'll be recognised on the street, like this evening. Especially with cameras and so on.' Camilla felt her stomach knot.

'Sure, you'll be recognised. But the back-up guys will be with you, and Harold will take care of any little problems that may arise.' Saul had ordered another bottle of champagne. 'While you were out, Tom and I went over your contract. Made a couple of small changes. So you can look over it when we get back to the apartment and sign it tonight or in the morning. Then we have all the paperwork taken care of.'

'What changes?' Camilla asked, irritated by the prospect of having to discuss their business arrangements when she was so tired.

'I was doubtful when you made me put those African-style dresses in my new catalogue, but I can see that they're selling just fine.' Saul saw her face light up. 'So I want to do an extra session with the camera guys for a spread in *Bazaar*. That will take another couple of days. Three or four, maybe, by the time we have it set up. Tom knows a guy who has a tame leopard and—'

'It's a cheetah,' Tom said, raising his eyebrows and lighting a cigarette.

'One of those spotted things,' Saul waved his hand vaguely. 'Anyways, it's like a puppy dog if you give it a few pounds of meat before bringing it into town. The photographer wants to shoot in the Plaza Hotel, have you strolling around with this animal on a diamond collar and leash. And you'll wear the beaded skirts and boots and feathers. We have a black guy who'll dress up and be part of the scenery. The make-up girl thinks it might be good to cover him with oil and put some kind of scary, tribal-looking paint on his face. It'll be great. Cause a riot. S-e-x-y!'

'I don't want to cause any more riots,' Camilla said, smiling. 'And I'm not staying for more than ten days, because I've made an appointment to get my face done as soon as I get back to London. I don't want to cancel that.'

She was mildly surprised at how easily Tom swallowed the lie. But she would put it right tomorrow by telephoning Edward and asking if he would fit her in as a favour. And then she could go home to Kenya. To Hannah and Sarah. To Anthony.

*

The days in New York rolled across her consciousness like a surreal movie. Photographers and interviewers and make-up artists and hairdressers came and went in an unceasing procession. Once she stepped outside the well-guarded privacy of Saul's apartment she was a source of frantic adulation that bordered on hysteria. Famous television hosts fawned over her, designers gave her clothes to wear for public events and to keep afterwards. In several restaurants other diners rose to their feet and applauded when she came into the room. After a week she wanted to hide. Her spare moments were spent curled up in Saul's apartment, reading or immersing herself in the novelty of daytime television. She was the toast of New York, the darling of the press, the refined, ethereal British beauty beyond compare. She was exhausted.

Harold accompanied her everywhere, guiding her, shielding her from the press of people who reached out to her. Tom was constantly by her side, enjoying her amazement when she found herself sitting beside Frank Sinatra and Peter Sellers at a dinner party, dancing with Gene Kelly at a charity event, visiting Andy Warhol at The Factory. The days stretched out, longer and longer, each one increasing the momentum of her fame.

Greenberg puffed on his cigars and smiled. He had found the most beautiful, classy broad in the world, and he intended to hang on to her for as long as he could. The dresses he had manufactured under Camilla's name were bringing in more orders than he had anticipated in his most avaricious dreams, and his machines were running overtime to produce enough stock for the coming season. Camilla's every move was reported and photographed for the daily newspapers. Business had never been so good. He asked her what she would like to do on her last day, wanting to arrange something for her that was special, that would stay in her memory and bring her back again.

'I can't take any more smart restaurants, or "intimate" dinner parties with dozens of strangers,' she said, her face drawn and pale. 'I'm so tired, Saul. I need a day when I do things that ordinary people do. Or, better still, a day when I do nothing at all. Otherwise I'll be flying out of here in a long, narrow box.' She sat upright in her chair suddenly. 'You can't possibly live like this all the time, Saul. So I'll tell you what I'd like to do next. I'd like to go to a good movie. And then I'd like you to take me somewhere that you like to eat when you're not on parade. Somewhere that you used to go as a child, for example.'

He took her to a comedy with Jack Lemmon and then to his favourite Jewish deli in the Village. They lined up at the long counter and he showed her what to order, proudly presenting her to the owner, the people behind the counter and the waiters that he had known since he was a boy. Camilla ordered a corned-beef sandwich on rye and it came with a couple of fat, shiny pickles, a portion of coleslaw and a cold beer.

'I've never seen such huge amounts of food,' she said, astonished by the sheer volume of it on her plate. 'This sandwich is the size of an apartment building. How can anyone get a thing this big into their mouth? People don't eat this much every day, do they?'

But she ate it all, laughing and joking with the staff, imitating their New York accents, learning Yiddish words from Saul, teaching the waiters cockney slang and upper-class English expressions that made them laugh and slap her on the back, and try to persuade her to eat the cheesecake and apple pie and ice cream on offer. She left with an invitation to come back at breakfast time for bagels and cream cheese and lox.

'This was my best day in New York,' she said. 'The very best.'

'You could stay on a few more days,' he said hopefully. 'I could take you to Coney Island and—'

'We're done, Saul. It's time to go.' Tom was affable but firm. 'She's worn out, and there are things pending in London and Paris. We'll see you on the other side of the pond.'

For two days after her arrival back in London Camilla lay in bed, or stretched out on the sofa in her flat.

'I can't talk to anyone,' she told Tom. 'I need a few days to myself, so don't suggest anything that would take me out of the house. And don't tell a soul I'm here, because I haven't the strength to say a word, let alone smile or perform.'

'You were magnificent in New York and you deserve a break,' he said. 'What a triumph. And your bank manager will want to set up a special vault for all that loot you've brought back. I can't see you languishing in Africa after this, darling. You'd miss it all too much. You were born to be a star, Camilla. And the money isn't bad either.'

'Don't start that conversation, Tom,' she said. 'And don't take on any new jobs without ringing me first.'

But Tom's publicity machine was already up and running, and the next morning's newspapers announced that she had returned home to London, in spite of being toasted as the darling of New York. Edward called in the afternoon and she took advantage of his obvious pleasure at her return.

'I'll have dinner with you,' she said. 'I need to set a date for finishing the work on my face. But we'll eat here, because I can't face going out. And don't ask me to describe New York. I need time to stand back from it all and recover.'

The surgery was scheduled for the following week. Although she did not like hospitals, Camilla's brief stay in the hushed atmosphere of the clinic made her feel rested.

'The stitches can come out in ten days,' Edward said, inspecting his handiwork. 'And in a few months the line will have vanished altogether. Along with the last memories of that dreadful night. In the meantime, I wondered if you'd like to spend a few days in Scotland. I have friends with a handsome old pile outside Edinburgh, and you could stay up there in total privacy. I'd come up at the weekend, if you could bear the thought, and we could drive around the countryside and enjoy the moors and the heather and the whisky. What do you say?'

'I'll think about it,' she said. 'I'm so grateful, Edward. Your skill and care have made it possible for me to continue working. When I came back from Kenya last year with my face slashed, I could have lost my livelihood. But you've made me as good as new, and I'm acutely aware of it.'

He could not resist putting his arms around her, then and there, in his consulting rooms. He knew he should not be doing it, that it was unprofessional behaviour, and it was too soon to woo her. And he was aware of the difference in their ages, painfully conscious of the fact that she did not share the feelings that fired his every private, conscious moment. But she trusted him, she was grateful to him. He began to make a plan in his head, mapping out a way in which he could help her to start up her business in Kenya, foolish though that was. He would fly out to Nairobi with her, stay for a few days while she was there, help her to find a manager for her enterprise. His presence would protect her from any risk of being hurt by the white hunter she had fallen for in the past. It would not take long for her to realise that her future lay in London with a man she could rely on. Everything else would be a pleasant hobby.

'I'll telephone you tomorrow, my dear,' he said, as she disengaged herself from his embrace. 'Perhaps we could have dinner somewhere, if you feel like going out.'

But when he rang her on the following afternoon she was gone, had flown away far beyond the safe borders he had constructed for her in his dreams.

Chapter 4

Buffalo Springs, September 1966

Sarah edged the Land Rover slowly down a steep, rutted track and turned on to a wider dirt road at the bottom of the hill, picking up speed across the plain in the direction of Buffalo Springs. Night was rushing down, silhouetting the shaggy outlines of doum palms and the filigree of acacia trees. A fading palette of rose-gold washed the setting sun from the sky, and flocks of francolin scattered in front of the car, flapping out of the dust to roost in the thorn-spiked thickets beyond the beam of the headlights. From time to time, a set of eyes would glow and vanish as the car bounced past on the corrugated surface of the track.

The day had been eventful and she had scribbled the last of her afternoon's observations in the margins of her notebook as her group of elephants headed for a bend in the river, intent on joining the main herd for the night. She and Erope watched as they greeted each other, rumbling and trumpeting and touching trunks, and the younger ones began to spar and play chasing games. Even the adults took to this frivolous behaviour at times, and Sarah laughed as huge matrons galloped like teenagers, swinging their trunks and flapping their ears, barging into their companions like giant dodgems in a funfair. There was something utterly endearing about such enormous, stately creatures abandoning themselves to the exuberance of life, and she was still smiling as she turned the vehicle away from them and headed for home.

They had been out since dawn, leaving the Land Rover parked in the scant shade of an acacia tree and following the herd on foot, but keeping a safe distance from a slow-moving family unit. Erope led the way, completely attuned to his surroundings and the wild creatures with whom he had always shared his world. She relied completely on his timeless, inherited knowledge of the area. Although he was officially her assistant she had come to think of him as an invaluable partner and a trusted friend. She was also impressed by his ability to discard the trappings of his Western training and garb, put on a *shuka*, and transform himself instantly into a feral inhabitant of the bush. He was like a snake shedding its skin, slipping effortlessly from one life to another.

Most young men of his age would have considered clerical work in the big city far more prestigious than being out in the bush, and Erope had the education for such a job. But he chaffed at the idea of being shut in, surrounded by typewriters and filing cabinets and reports. He had encountered Dan Briggs at the National Park Headquarters. When he learned that the American was based in the Samburu area, he had begged for a job, claiming that he could be of service as a guide and as a contact with the local tribes in his home territory. Dan always said that taking him on was one of the best decisions he had ever made.

Whenever they were away from the vehicle, Sarah kept close behind the Samburu. He walked with an easy, loping grace, making no sound, moving with stealth, smelling the wind, looking at the way a twig had broken off, scanning the dry earth for spoor, the depth of an indentation giving him the age and weight of his quarry. Sometimes he would crumble a piece of dung to gauge its texture and moistness, so that he knew how long ago the animal had passed. They did not want an unexpected encounter with buffalo. When she tried to emulate him she would invariably tread on a dry branch, and the snap would make her freeze, one foot still raised for the next step, her eyes rolling in mute apology for her clumsiness.

Erope never mentioned Piet. But occasionally, when Sarah was assailed by grief, he would nod and touch her hand and she felt comforted. The work was her salvation, the only part of her life that brought her peace of mind, helped her to bury the memories of the past. And she had begun to allow a vision of Piet into her mind, an image that was vibrant and golden, a memory that might eventually replace her last dreadful sight of him lying lifeless on the ground. She could feel close to him out here. His absence was not as unbearable as it had been at Langani, perhaps because his spirit seemed free in the wilderness that she loved. The long hours spent outdoors, and the time she allocated at night to writing her notes, made sleep a more natural possibility and her dreams slowly became less troubled.

A large animal suddenly darted out of the scrub, jerking her back to the present. She clutched at the wheel as the car lurched sideways, spun on a patch of loose earth and came to a halt. Erope clung to the back of the seat to brace himself, and it took a few seconds before the dust settled and she realised how close they had come to rolling over.

'Sorry,' she said. 'I was distracted for a moment. Was that a bushbuck?'

'*Ndio*,' he said. 'I think you are beginning to drive like Mama Allie.'

'I'd say I did very well.' She was laughing with relief. 'I managed to avoid the buck and stay upright. Of course, if I'd hit it we could have had dinner for everybody tonight.'

'But you would not eat it,' Erope said, with a grin. 'You would be crying for the dead buck.'

'I suppose you're right.' Sarah was chuckling as she reached out to start the vehicle. 'Let's get back before we have any more mishaps.'

There was a grating sound, almost like a cough, as she turned the key in the ignition. Then silence. She tried again, but this time there was no noise at all. Erope made a soft grunt of dismay.

'Broken,' he said. 'Dan said it would happen.'

'What now?' Sarah looked at the darkening bowl of the sky where the first stars had begun to appear. 'There are buffalo around, and we saw lions earlier. It's not the best time for a stroll. We must be three or four miles from the camp.'

'We will try to fix the *gari*,' Erope said. 'And if we cannot make it go, then we will walk.'

It took him almost an hour to start the Land Rover, and Sarah realised in that brief space of time that she knew next to nothing about engines. Without Erope's rudimentary knowledge they would have been obliged to spend the night in the vehicle, or make an attempt to walk along the track with only a spear and a torch to defend themselves from lions or buffalo, or the smaller hunters that knew how to take full advantage of the dark. Once, they heard a deep grunting sound close by and Sarah froze. Erope was lying underneath the chassis, wrestling with some part of its elderly anatomy. But he, too, had heard the noise. His lean body slid out and was standing upright and in front of her within seconds, spear in hand, ready to protect her from a direct attack. When he turned the torch in a wide arc they saw the lioness. For a timeless moment she stared at them, her tail lashing from one side to the other, and then she whirled away into the long grass.

'Get into the *gari*, Sarah. It will start now, I think.' Erope loped around to the passenger door and climbed in beside her.

Sarah took a deep breath and turned the key, rejoicing in the sputtering, groaning response of the engine as they started slowly down the rutted track. As she drove into the camp, her mind was fixed on the pleasing prospect of a shower and a cold beer, and a description of her adventure. She pulled up in her usual parking spot and immediately noticed a grey Peugeot outside the main living area. Visitors. She shrugged inwardly, wondering who they were. Erope left her with a wave, and she envied him for not being obliged to socialise. But even unannounced guests might be important. Some were fellow scientists who brought research notes that could be shared, and tourists had been known to give generous donations.

'We were beginning to worry about you.' Allie appeared from the main hut. 'I'm glad you're safe and sound. We have a visitor, by the way. It's the journalist who wrote up our presentation. Rabindrah Singh.'

Sarah frowned. What was he doing here? She searched for an excuse to avoid him, to retire for her shower and remain in her hut until he was gone. But Allie's next words ruined her plan.

'He's brought the article that came out in the *Daily Telegraph*. Someone arrived on the plane from London yesterday with copies for us all. It's a good piece, great publicity, and your photographs look splendid. I must say he researched it very well. Used our annual report as a basis, and got all the facts right. Come and join us, Sarah. You look like you could do with a cold beer.'

'The Land Rover broke down,' Sarah said. 'Erope fixed it, but a curious lioness came to watch his efforts. It was a little alarming for a moment or two. I think I'll have a shower, and then write up my notes. Today was exceptional, even before the car died on us.'

'Don't be ridiculous,' Allie said briskly. 'Have your shower by all means. It's been a scorcher of a day. Then you must come and tell us about the breakdown. But be quick. This Rabindrah has been here all afternoon, talking to Dan. He's come with an interesting proposal and I can't wait for you to hear it. We've asked him to stay the night so you can talk to him and make a decision.'

'A decision? Why me?' Sarah was desperate to avoid the man who had caused such distress at Langani. 'You're the ones who make the decisions around here. I just write notes and take pictures.'

'You're very *kali* this evening,' Allie said, eyebrows raised. 'I thought you had a good day.' She reached out and patted Sarah on the shoulder. 'Come on now, you're a vital member of this team and a part of every decision we make these days. You can't shut yourself away when we have guests. So go and spruce yourself up for our visitor. The hot water is ready, and I'll send over a cold Tusker to help you along.'

Rabindrah was sitting in a canvas chair under the acacia tree, with Dan and Allie on either side of him. He looked well turned out in a striped shirt with precisely rolled-up sleeves, and neatly pressed safari slacks. Sleek was the word that came to Sarah's mind. A man who clearly expended a good deal of trouble on his appearance. She could smell expensive aftershave. He looked at her directly and held out a smooth, manicured hand and she noticed that he was wearing a steel bracelet on his wrist. She was unsure of the meaning in his slight smile. Sardonic? Amused? Or just polite? She turned away as the red flush in her cheeks betrayed her discomfort. He must know that he had caused her embarrassment, if not pain, by visiting Langani. Probably journalists did not care about such things.

'Miss Mackay. It is good to see you again, and this time on your own territory.'

'My own territory?' She felt foolish, repeating his words. He was still staring at her, and she thought the directness of his gaze bordered on rudeness.

'I meant that here, in this wild landscape and among the elephants, you are in your true element. No one could take photographs like yours if they did not feel at one with their surroundings.'

His voice was pitched low and she found herself leaning forward to listen, although his words were perfectly audible. A clever ruse for keeping the attention of his audience. Or his quarry. His remark was too personal, and she found it strange that this Indian reporter should have seen that in her work. She could still see him standing on the lawn at Langani, asking provocative questions that had brought distress, raising the spectre of Piet's death. He was a typical hack, a scavenger living off the miseries of hapless people. Certainly unscrupulous. She could not imagine what had brought him to Buffalo Springs. Dan handed her a drink, and gestured towards the table where he worked on his reports.

'There are copies of the paper there, Sarah. Half a page in the *Daily*

Telegraph. Take a look. It will bring us a good deal of support, I'd say. And there's a cheque for your photos, too. Good for you, kid.' He patted her on the shoulder. 'I hear that old crate finally broke down on you. We'll have to get you something safer to drive around in. And soon.'

Sarah had to admit that the article was compulsive. She made a point of saying how good she thought it was, of thanking him for including her images. His pleasure at her reaction came as a surprise. She had taken him for a hard-boiled reporter, someone who would publish any story, regardless of its effect. But perhaps she had been a little harsh. He began to outline his idea, leaning towards her, his eyes lit with enthusiasm.

'I'm glad you like the piece,' he said. 'Because I've had an idea in my head for a while, and when I saw your slides in Nairobi I realised that I'd found the perfect photographer to collaborate with me.'

'Collaborate with you?' Sarah cursed herself for sounding like a parrot.

'Now, wait until you hear this, Sarah.' Allie smiled at her and then glanced knowingly at Rabindrah.

'What I had in mind was a book on the elephants in this area,' the Indian said. 'A book with fine-quality colour plates of your pictures. Plus my text. It would describe Dan's research project in a form that would make it accessible to the general public, while still getting the message across. I know I can write the story well. But your pictures would guarantee its success.'

She could see that it would be a wonderful opportunity, to have her photographs published in a book and to gain recognition for the Briggses. But she did not trust him. He was certainly a smooth talker, but what chance did he have of finding a publisher? She knew a number of people involved in worthy causes who dreamed of getting into print, but very few achieved it. She might spend months of valuable time preparing photographs for a book, only to face rejection.

'You're doubtful that I can find a publisher,' he said, as though he had read her mind. 'I've been lucky in that respect. I submitted an outline, with some of the pictures you sent me, to a man called John Sinclair. Ah! I see that you know of him. Dan and Allie agree that he publishes the best wildlife books available. Sinclair & Lewis was started by his grandfather. I met John while I was in university, and then I ran across him again while I was working as a journalist in Manchester. He remembered I was from

Kenya, and he asked me to look over an introduction to a book on the East African coast. When you sent me your photos, I took the liberty of posting him a selection, and now he's prepared to go a stage further if you are willing to work with me.'

'But – what form would the book take? I mean, how would you find the material for the text?'

'Rabindrah has suggested that he spends a period of time up here at Buffalo Springs.' Allie was plainly in favour of the idea. 'He would go out with Dan and me, and with you and Erope, every day for a couple of months or however long it takes. Dan would vet the text, ensure that the observations are scientifically valid and so on.'

'And your photographs speak for themselves,' Rabindrah said. 'Dan and Allie are pretty gung-ho on the idea.'

Sarah noticed with irritation that the man was already on first-name terms with the Briggses. He was smiling broadly, his teeth very white and even in his burnished face. She saw now that he had a hooked nose and that his eyes were flecked with gold, and she thought he looked like a bird of prey that had made a perfect swoop on its victim.

'I would not get in the way of the work you are doing here, I can assure you,' he said. 'I am familiar with the role of discreet observer. In any case, I would have to commute between here and Nairobi, where I earn my living as an ordinary hack. So I wouldn't be in your hair all the time, you see.'

Sarah was at a loss as to how she should respond. She looked to Dan for support, but he was studiously filling his pipe and Allie was busy opening a second bottle of wine.

'As regards money, I expect you want to know what the situation would be.' Rabindrah sensed that he must keep the initiative. 'So I would suggest that we share the proceeds equally? I can imagine that funds might be tight on a project like this. I thought the extra income would be very welcome for the research, and for you personally, and—'

She bristled, and he hurried on, realising that he would never understand the British middle class and their reluctance to talk about money. 'I had a look at the old vehicle you've been driving and I agree with Dan that it's a miracle it hasn't fallen apart long ago. In fact, I'm wondering if I can get my uncle, Indar Singh, to donate or sponsor a vehicle.'

'That sounds like a long shot to me.' Sarah was now sure that the journalist was trying to impress Dan for some obscure reason that she could not figure out.

'My uncle owns a large garage, and is a leading pillar of the Sikh community,' Rabindrah continued smoothly. 'He might be happy to have his name featured in connection with a worthy research programme. And he could be mentioned in the elephant book.'

'The idea seems a little far-fetched to me.' Sarah was openly sceptical.

'He has given money to a variety of causes.' Rabindrah needed another hook to ensure the girl's collaboration, an incentive she would not be able to turn down. There was some special empathy she seemed to have with the elephants, which was exceptional. The publisher had recognised it immediately and been amazed by the quality of her work.

'I think the book is the most important thing here.' Dan had heard the animosity in Sarah's voice and he steered the conversation back to the main topic.

'You know, Miss Mackay, the best thing about getting this book into print is the publicity it will generate for your research,' Rabindrah said, trying another tack. Without her pictures, he knew he had no chance of seeing his name on such a prestigious publication. 'I would like to suggest that we give a percentage of the royalties to Dan and Allie here. If you agree. In that way everyone would benefit, including your elephants.'

He was smiling broadly, his expression almost triumphant. Sarah felt a stir of annoyance, even resentment. He had been very clever. She did not really want to work with him, but his offer was too good to refuse, for her own career and for the Briggses and their work. And he knew it. He was manipulative and she did not like him at all. But she owed it to Dan and Allie to agree, and she was forced to acknowledge a level of excitement over the possible publication of her photographs. If she had to put up with Rabindrah Singh for a few weeks, then she could manage that. After all, it couldn't take all that long for him to put his basic text together, especially if Dan was helping him. Once the groundwork had been put in place at Buffalo Springs he would have to return to Nairobi to do all the conservation research. It might even prove to be an enjoyable experience, as long as he understood that any reference to her personal life was off limits.

'Well, Mr Singh, what can I say to that?' She gave him a tight smile. 'Let's shake hands on the plan, and prepare to tell the world about the elephants of Buffalo Springs.'

'Now that is excellent!' Allie said, raising her glass. 'Here's to you both, and a grand collaboration.'

'If you're going to give this a try, then you may as well start by taking your co-author out with you in the morning, Sarah. See how you get along together.' Dan looked at Rabindrah. 'I hope you like to get started early in the day, my friend. Because this kid sure is a crack-of-dawn person.'

Sarah had opened her mouth to protest. She didn't like going out with strangers. She had no doubt that Rabindrah's presence would interfere with the work, and she did not want to change the rhythm of her days with Erope and the elephants. But Dan was her employer, and she had now committed herself to the book. If the journalist wanted to start tomorrow, she was hardly in a position to cause a delay.

'I leave at first light. You'll have to be prepared for a long hot day.' Her tone was brisk.

'I'll be ready whenever you say.' Rabindrah had visions of a broken-down Land Rover, of fleeing a stampede of wild animals in the wilderness, but he had got this far and there was no turning back. 'And while I'm here, perhaps we can start looking over your existing photographs. John Sinclair will need about five hundred slides, from which he will probably select about one hundred and fifty of the best quality. I hope you can manage that, Sarah.'

He had slipped into first-name terms with her now, and she could hardly insist on formality. It was not the Briggses' way.

'Fine,' she said stiffly. 'I'll start sorting them tomorrow.'

'What about some fine old single malt, young man?' Dan was taking out his best bottle of Scotch.

Sarah saw that he was in for one of his long nights of talk and philosophising, with plenty of good alcohol to fuel the discussion. Rabindrah Singh would have to have a strong head to survive this initiation and still be up early in the morning. She grinned at Allie, and slipped away to her own hut to begin writing up her daily report. Some time later there was a knock on her door.

'*Hodi*. Can I come in?' Allie said. 'I brought some tea.'

'Thanks. Here – I'll move this pile of papers on to the floor. Put the mugs on the chest of drawers. No room on the table I'm afraid.'

They sat companionably, sipping their tea and going over the happenings of the day.

'So, what's the problem with Mr Singh?' Allie switched the topic of conversation suddenly. 'I've rarely seen you so prickly. The man has come up with an interesting proposal, Sarah, if he's on the level. It's a chance in a lifetime, and I thought you were rather cool about it.'

Sarah sat back and sighed. She had not told Allie about the journalist's visit to Langani, or his questions about Piet's death, but she realised now that she would have to explain her behaviour. She described the incident at the farm, and her belief that his questions had precipitated the arrival of Hannah's baby.

'Thank God, there were no complications,' she said. 'But this Rabindrah had already started asking questions about my personal life when we met in Nairobi, and then he turned up without warning and started sniffing around at Langani. So I got a horrible fright when you said he was here. I was afraid he had come here to bring up the subject of Piet's death again.'

'I see,' said Allie. 'If it's any consolation he didn't mention either Piet or Langani before you got back this evening.'

'Lars told me that Jeremy Hardy sent him off with a flea in his ear. That's why I was so rattled. I'm sorry I overreacted. He's here for a valid reason. I can see that now.'

'If he does raise the issue of Piet again, you just let me know and I'll give him more than a flea in his ear,' Allie said. 'In the meantime I do think you should take him out with you tomorrow. See how you get on. If he bothers you, he can come with me the next day. By the way, we want you to take our vehicle in the morning, so that Dan can try and patch up yours. He's worried about it, but he thinks it will last a little while longer. Replacing it will have to be on top of the list when we get our new grant although it will blow a big hole in the budget. But we have no choice, unless Rabindrah's uncle turns into a fairy godfather.'

'What nonsense that was,' Sarah said. 'But thanks, Allie. And I'll do the very best I can. Don't worry.'

Rabindrah was ready and waiting when she appeared in the morning. He showed no sign of a hangover, and Sarah thought he must have a strong constitution. They drank mugs of tea and climbed into the Land Rover where Erope had stowed a food basket, a thermos and three large water bottles. Sarah made the introductions, and the men shook hands.

'Erope leads when we're walking in the bush,' Sarah said. 'You follow in silence, and do whatever he tells you. We don't carry any rifles, so we're dependent on him to keep us out of trouble.'

Rabindrah nodded, and they set off in search of the herd. Dan had insisted that they take the better Land Rover, and he had decided to spend the morning checking the other vehicle. Sarah drove in silence for a while, irritated by the feeling of tension that was corroding her morning. The Sikh seemed quite at ease, asking occasional questions of Erope about the countryside, about his tribe, and what had brought him to work for the Briggses. He did not ask Sarah anything at all and she found herself faintly annoyed at being excluded from the conversation. Finally, she asked a question of her own.

'Why us?' she asked. 'Why did you pick the Briggses? Have you worked in the field of conservation before?'

'No, I haven't. Although it's a big issue nowadays. Something people want to read about, particularly in Europe and the United States.' He paused to look at her as she leaned forward over the steering wheel, squinting into the morning sun and looking for her elephants. 'Actually, I wasn't especially interested in the subject until I was sent to report on the Briggses' presentation. I found the whole thing inspiring, worth following up, you see. And then there was a strong reaction from the *Telegraph*, and from John Sinclair. So it all started with you.'

'You'll have to be very careful with the text,' she said.

'That's why I'm here. I can't write with any conviction about an issue like this unless I have researched it thoroughly. I do understand that your work is important in a global sense.'

She was flattered in spite of herself and she began to relax and to explain to him how the project worked.

'We've divided up certain tasks over the last few weeks, so that we can widen our area of research,' she said. 'Allie has been following three family sets, focusing on recording the lives of the females, while Dan is concentrating on the bulls who have left the family to become part of an all-male club. I've been allocated a number of calves, with the idea that I should follow them from birth, if that's possible, and record the patterns of feeding, care and development in their family unit. I've never actually seen a calf being born, but Erope pointed out a young, pregnant female last week, and he says she is near her term. In fact, we thought it might happen

92

yesterday. There may even be a new calf waiting for our inspection this morning.'

'I would certainly like to see that,' Rabindrah said, as Sarah applied her brakes and skidded to a dusty halt. 'Oh, my God,' he said. 'That is one huge buffalo. Aren't we too close? Should we shut the windows? Sarah?'

'Sssshhh! We've come across him before,' she said in a low voice. 'He's mean and unpredictable. Look at that huge boss, and the curve of his horns. He could kill you in the blink of an eye, that old *mbogo*.'

'What happens now?' Rabindrah asked, unable to hide his alarm.

'I'm going to back up,' she said. 'But I'm not very good at it.'

'*Kweli*. This is true,' Erope added unhelpfully.

He was clearly put out by the idea that the journalist from Nairobi would be in the Land Rover every day. His brother had worked for an Indian *duka wallah* once. They were not known for treating their African staff well.

'Sarah can turn the car over easily,' he said, pleased with the effect his words were having on Rabindrah. 'Just like Allie.'

The buffalo was moving towards them, massive head lowered, the vehicle in his sights. Rabindrah closed his eyes, waiting for the sound of horn ripping into metal. But when he was within six feet of them the old bull turned without warning, snorted loudly, and crashed away into the bush.

'You can open your eyes now,' Sarah said. 'He's gone and you don't have to worry about my reversing. For the time being.'

'My God,' Rabindrah said again. 'In all my years here I never came that close to any dangerous animal. I was not that aware of them, actually, except as a tourist attraction. Going on safari was not the kind of thing my parents ever did. Wild animals were legendary creatures that had eaten our great uncle who was building the railways.'

'You said you studied and worked in England,' Sarah said. 'What brought you back here?'

He shrugged. 'It's my home, I suppose. Where I grew up. I could have stayed in the UK. My parents live there now, and my sisters. But I got sick of door-stepping.'

'What's that?'

'You know, knocking at people's doors, asking some widow how she felt when her husband had died in a fire at the factory, or got crushed by a truck, or some such.'

'Just like asking people if they think about their murdered brothers,'

Sarah said and was pleased to see him flinch. 'Sounds soul-destroying. That can't be all you did, though.'

'I wrote pieces about the Asian community in England, mainly on the question of passports and full British citizenship. But I felt I was being drawn into a campaign, pressured into spouting an exclusively Asian point of view. I didn't want to get typecast as the Indian journalist who only writes about Indians. And you meet with considerable hostility when you go digging into subjects people want to suppress . . .' He saw her knuckles whiten on the steering wheel. 'I mean, like bigotry and racism, and resentment about Asians getting what local English people felt was theirs.'

'Why not be involved? As a voice for your own people?'

'I wanted more variety in my work. I wanted a good life. There's no money in being a provincial hack and I couldn't get a job in London. Also, the weather in England is less than enticing.'

'I would agree with that. I thought I'd never dry out after three years of living in Ireland,' Sarah said.

'So I came back. And so far I'm enjoying life here. I like the freedom to do as I please, to be what I want.'

'But you didn't come back for love of Kenya and its future?'

'I'm afraid it was nothing so noble,' he said. 'I'm here to carve out a career and make a decent living. I have an instinct for a meaty story and I write well. You don't have to be a devotee to tell a powerful tale. Sometimes it's better to be outside of the issue – you can see things that the people in the middle miss if you can remain objective.'

They had arrived at the place where Sarah had last seen the herds on the previous night. She gestured for silence and stopped downwind of the great beasts, shutting off the engine. After a few minutes of watching, Erope pointed out their particular unit. The leading matriarch was an imperious old dame with tattered ears and tusks that almost crossed one another. Sarah had named her Hippolyte, after the Amazonian queen, because she was a fearless warrior, always ready to take on any foe that threatened her family. She was standing at the edge of the waterhole, spraying herself all over until her whole body turned a rich terracotta red. As the mud dried, it formed a delicate tracery of cracks, giving the impression that she was wearing a layer of heavy lace over her grey, wrinkled hide. There were four younger matrons in her group, including the pregnant one that Sarah had mentioned.

'There she is – the one that's about to give birth,' Sarah said. 'I call her Lily, and we'll be concentrating on her for the next few days. Normally, when they are going to drop a calf they move away from the main herd, with a couple of attendant females. When that happens, we may have to follow on foot which can be dangerous. If the elephants think we're a threat to the new baby they can turn aggressive in seconds.'

'In those circumstances I may stay in the car,' Rabindrah said. 'Keep a low profile and let the experienced scientists do the walking.'

'You certainly cannot stay in the car on your own,' Sarah said crisply. 'Unless you want to take a chance on becoming target practice for some fresh young bull. Now that you're here, your only option is to stick with Erope and me.'

Within the hour Hippolyte and her immediate family had separated from the main part of the herd. Erope and Sarah slid out of the car with Rabindrah reluctantly close behind them. Lily seemed restless, wandering away from the other females and then running back to them, rumbling and calling. By midday the heat was unbearable, and the group had travelled a considerable way. Finally, they came to a halt and Rabindrah leaned into the shelter of a fig tree, wiping the sweat from his face and neck. Sarah realised he was uneasy about the distance between himself and the vehicle, and about the proximity of her bulky subjects.

'The only thing I know about African elephants is that they're dangerous and unpredictable.' He was frowning as he spoke, rubbing his arms where the skin had been torn by scrub and whistling thorns as they walked through the bush. 'And right now, this is too close for comfort.'

'They're fine as long as they don't feel threatened,' Sarah said. 'And we are upwind of them. Don't worry.'

He nodded, unconvinced, and she watched him unscrew his water bottle and peer at the scant remains. He had drunk the contents too quickly, and now he would have to conserve what little remained. Sarah allowed herself a small grin, acknowledging to herself that she was mean. It had been a punishing morning, and Rabindrah had endured it well for a greenhorn, making no sound of protest or complaint, following Erope's signals without question. She considered offering him some of her own water, then decided against it. He would have to learn to eke out his own supply. If he became dehydrated she would give him a few sips from her flask. He was the one who had come back to Kenya looking for the good life. Let him thirst for it! Erope was on the other side of the tree, balanced, stork-like, on one leg as was his tribal custom, unaffected by the heat or the harshness of their surroundings. He looked as if he were asleep, but then Sarah saw him signal for them to move forward again.

They crouched behind an outcrop of rocks, watching the flurry of activity among the elephants. Sarah raised her camera as Lily tried to deliver her calf. She stood apart, flapping her ears, moving from foot to foot and rumbling anxiously, until at last the little creature slid from her and on to the ground. But he was trapped in the membrane sac, and his mother did not seem to know how to open it. Within a few minutes the other females surrounded her, pushing gently with their trunks and feet until the calf was free. Then Lily used her own trunk and her foreleg to hoist him on to his legs. Sarah glanced at Rabindrah, and saw that he was enthralled. The newborn calf was trying to stand. His head was covered in a thatch of fuzzy, black hair and his eyes were rimmed with red as though he had been on a heavy binge. He staggered, fell several times, and eventually managed a few wobbly steps. He fed almost immediately from his mother, his trunk whiffling inexpertly around her until he found her teats and began to suckle. The other females stood around Lily, touching her with their trunks, caressing the baby. The noises they made drew the attention of several younger bulls.

'Lie down.' Erope hissed the order as the elephants headed towards them. 'The big mama is going to chase the bulls away, and they may come in this direction.'

Sarah flattened herself on the thorny ground and dragged Rabindrah down beside her. He covered his head with his arms and lay prone in the dust, waiting to be trampled to death. All around them they could hear rumbling noises and the crackle of branches as the elephants pushed their way through the scrub, moving closer, bearing down on the three prone figures. Then there was the sound of trumpeting and the ground vibrated beneath them. The air was thick with dust and Sarah heard Rabindrah give a small exclamation of terror. She turned her head and saw him press his lips together and look at her, perhaps hoping for a sign of reassurance that did not materialise. His eyes were closed when she finally shook him by the arm and spoke to him.

'The bulls have moved away,' she said. 'You can get up now.'

'You're smiling! You must be insane. I almost died in abject terror on the ground and you are smiling. My heart was beating so fast, and there was dust in my nose. I thought I was going to sneeze and be trampled to death. I didn't dare to blink, and I can't believe the noise of my fear, pounding in my head.'

But Sarah was already on her feet, using her camera again and again, anxious in case the click of the shutter would draw attention to their position, but unable to resist the opportunity to record such an amazing event. After a time one of the senior bulls came to investigate the new arrival. The calf went to him and was touched on the head by the elder's trunk, in what resembled a ceremony of blessing. He spent the remainder of the day sheltered beneath his mother's legs, until Hippolyte began to lead her family back to the safety of the main herd for the night. Rabindrah watched, oblivious to his recent fear and discomfort, entranced by the ceremonials that had surrounded the birth. Sarah raised her eyebrows and smiled at Erope. It was clear that they had a convert.

The late afternoon shadows had begun to stretch into soft, umber patterns on the sandy soil when they finally left the herd, walking back through the thorny landscape to the Land Rover. The inside of the vehicle was like an oven and their sandwiches had been reduced to a soggy mess. But there was coffee in the thermos and they wolfed down a packet of biscuits, elation overcoming all other considerations.

They were back among the elephants at sun-up the next morning, and this time, as they drove, there was a sense of ease between them. The birth had made a profound impression on Rabindrah. Yesterday, Sarah had felt that he was there purely to obtain recognition for himself through the proposed book, and to make money. Now he was eager to locate the herd, to see the small elephant again and to note its progress. She hoped that his experience would transform his writing into something inspirational, create text that would bring the lives of the elephants and their needs to a wide audience. As they drove in search of Lily and her baby she began to hum an Irish air, and was surprised when he took up the tune, and even knew the words.

'Half the journalists I worked with in Manchester were Irish,' he said. 'A savage lot they were, too. They made me an honorary Paddy, you

97

know. Saw me as a rebel like themselves, always asking awkward questions about the activities of the British on the world stage. That's where I learned how to put away a good quantity of whisky in one sitting. And to this day, I prefer Irish to Scotch – but don't tell that to Dan!'

She laughed and glanced at him. At least he had a sense of humour. That might make it easier to work with him over the coming months. He sat beside her in silence as she drove, breathing in the dusty air, listening to the call of hornbills and the chatter of weaver birds, looking through the hot light in the hopes of spotting a cheetah, or even a lion, before the tracker saw it. The passive role he had been allocated did not come easily to Rabindrah, and he was aware that both Sarah and Erope considered him a hanger-on, irrelevant to their everyday work.

They found the elephants travelling slowly in the direction of the river. The water was low, and the short rains would not begin for several weeks, if they came at all. The dry grass crackled, yellow-brown and prickly, and several members of the herd were digging into the soil with their tusks or feet, forcing the hard ground to yield a slow ooze of muddy liquid – barely enough to sustain the group or to keep them cool in the sweltering sun. After an hour the heat had invaded the Land Rover and flies buzzed and settled on Rabindrah's skin and clothing, so that he was forever slapping them away. When they moved the vehicle to position themselves ahead of the herd, the wheels slithered and spun in the thick sand of the track and he had visions of being stuck in this scorching place for hours or days on end. Ahead of them the animals trudged on, snapping off twigs and bark as they went. The new calf was struggling to keep up with its mother, and the family stopped regularly, turning to watch his progress and to wait for him when necessary, encouraging him with rumblings and nudges, and caresses from their trunks.

They followed the same group for ten days. Sarah photographed the small elephant as he tried to work out what to do with his trunk, and they listened to his cries of protest when his mother did not let him feed. He squealed when he became entangled in a thicket, or when he could not negotiate a large branch in his path, and then one or more of the females would amble over to help him. As the days passed they were surprised at how quickly he became stronger and more adventurous.

'I'm handing this little unit over to Dan and Allie tomorrow,' Sarah said to Rabindrah as they sat in the Land Rover, surrounded by the herd.

'You'll be leaving for Nairobi, and it's my turn to pick up the mail in Isiolo and take care of regular chores in camp. So take a careful look at young Louis here, because he will be an awful lot larger next time you visit.'

She was opening a thermos of coffee when the baby elephant came over to the vehicle, and she froze. He felt all around the fenders with his trunk. Then he approached the driver's door, and looked in at Sarah from his bright eye. She sat very still, her skin prickling with fear and excitement. There was no way to predict what his mother and the other matrons might do, if they thought he was in danger. His soft trunk wound into the window and touched her hair, followed the contours of her face and then ran down her arm to her hand. Slowly she turned her palm up, and let her fingers caress the bristly skin, feeling his light breath as he puffed at her. Then he stretched out his trunk again, and ran it across her face once more. Lily was making agitated noises, but she did not approach. Her companions milled around, fretful and waiting for her signal. Rabindrah was afraid to breathe, convinced that they would all be crushed by the herd. Even Erope did not move a muscle. After a few minutes the calf turned, and with a flourish of his trunk and a first attempt at trumpeting he rejoined his family. For a long time Sarah sat in a haze of delight, sniffing the sharp scent where he had fleetingly gripped her hand, reliving every instant of the encounter.

'My God! We could have been killed!' Rabindrah broke the silence. 'By the mother in particular. And the largest one with the crossed tusks – she could have crushed us in seconds. What a risk to take! You are mad, Sarah. I cannot think of any other word.'

'I was hardly in a position to drive off,' Sarah pointed out, but she, too, was shaken. 'Anyway, we can't beat that today. Or any day ever again, I imagine. Let's head back to camp.'

She spent the evening selecting and packing slides and prints for Rabindrah to take with him. It would be several weeks before he returned, but in the meantime he would send the first chapters of his text, together with a synopsis and her pictures, to London. He seemed sure that a publishing contract would be the result, and Sarah found his enthusiasm infectious.

Dan and Allie were the first to leave the camp on the following morning, driving out in search of Lily and her calf. Sarah shook hands with Rabindrah, relieved that things would now return to the comfortable pattern she shared with Erope.

'Goodbye,' she said. 'I'll look forward to seeing your first chapters.'

'You'll have them soon,' Rabindrah said. 'But before I leave, I owe you an apology.'

'An apology?'

'I know we got off on the wrong foot when we first met,' he said. 'I had no idea what had happened in your life. And I'm sorry I upset your friends at Langani. You all shared a terrible loss, and I should have respected your privacy.'

'Yes, you should,' she said. 'We're not fodder for another sensational story, you know. We're ordinary human beings and we've had enough of inquiries and investigations and grief. I hear you even went to see Chief Inspector Hardy in Nyeri.'

He looked at her for a moment, wanting to ask whether she had any ideas as to the motive behind the killing of her fiancé. But her face was tight, her eyes cold with anger, and he was afraid that if he alienated her now she might still put a stop to the book project. In any case, he no longer needed to base his story on her personal tragedy. He had seen all her photographs, watched her at work, heard from Dan Briggs that *National Geographic* might be interested in backing their research. If he wrote the text of a book about the Briggses and their elephants, there was a chance that the magazine might also offer him work. Everything was weighted in his favour and he had no intention of making any false moves.

'I'm really sorry,' he said. 'I suppose I was looking for holes in the police investigation. Following up for the sake of it. It's a common characteristic in all journalists. So I hope you'll accept my apology, and that we can put my insensitive blunder behind us.'

'I have no wish to dwell on it,' she said. 'And by the way, I appreciate your proposal to give a percentage of the royalties to Dan and Allie.'

'It's an honour to be working with all of you,' he said, with genuine respect.

When he had gone Sarah set out for Isiolo where she collected a bundle of mail, packed the Land Rover with crates and cartons of supplies, and sat in the shade of a tree to open her own letters. On the thickest envelope she recognised her brother's spidery hand, and she slit it open first and read his news with mixed feelings. Then she made her way to the small government office and asked to make a phone call.

'I want to make a call to Ireland,' she told the clerk, smiling at his doubtful reaction. 'Don't worry, it's just next to England and it will be the same thing to book a call there. The operator will tell us afterwards how much money I owe you.'

There was a great deal of discussion with the operator before Tim came on the line.

'You've set the date, then,' she said.

'You've got to be here, Sarah,' he shouted. 'Look, we could even put it off again. For a month or so. Deirdre said she wouldn't mind.'

Sarah was caught in the ache of her own loss. They had already put back the date twice and it would be unfair to expect them to wait any longer. But the thought of going to a wedding so close to the anniversary of Piet's death made her feel ill. She found her voice.

'I'm so happy for you, Tim. You know I am. And Mum and Dad must be thrilled too. I haven't got to their letter yet – I wanted to phone you as soon as I read yours. It's wonderful, it really is. But don't put it off any longer. Don't wait for me. I can't—'

'We're going to have the wedding at home,' Tim interrupted her. 'It will be a small affair, and there aren't many of her family coming. Actually, she'd like you to be her maid of honour. She's really keen on that.' He didn't seem to know how to continue, and there was an uneasy silence while he waited for her consent. Then he started again. 'I understand how hard this must be. God – it should have been you and Piet. And I know it's asking a lot, but please, please be there with us all. It's so important to me.'

'Tim, of course I'd love to be with you for your big day.' She was having trouble keeping her voice steady. This was turning out to be much harder than she had anticipated. 'I'm touched that Deirdre wants me to play a role. But I'm at a vital stage of my research, and you know how much time I was given off after . . .' She found she could not finish the sentence. 'Anyway, it would be very bad form to ask the Briggses if I could go away again. I'm their one and only assistant, and they need me. I'm sorry, Tim, I really am.'

'I can't believe you're saying this.' His tone changed. 'After all, you went to Hannah's wedding, didn't you? She needed you, and you were there. I'm only asking you to do the same for me. And you must know how much Mum and Dad would like you to be there – what it means to us all.'

'I do know,' Sarah said. 'But Hannah lives a few hours down the road. I don't think I can leave here and come all the way to Ireland. Not even for you.'

She registered the disappointment and the anger in his voice as he said goodbye, and handed over the phone to Betty. But although her parents made no concerted effort to change her mind, Sarah put down the telephone, aware that she had upset them all. Tim would probably think that she was not coming because she had always had reservations about Deirdre. The girl was bossy and clingy all at once. Her background was different from theirs, and her view of the world was narrow. Sarah suspected that the maid of honour thing had probably been Tim's idea, to make her feel a part of the celebration. But she could not go to Ireland. The thought of this wedding, or any celebration, made her shrivel inside. Perhaps if she wrote to him again, tried to explain it a little better, he would see how impossible it was. The phone was hopeless for that sort of thing. Emotion and distance made it hard to express the realities. You could do it better on paper, go over the words till they sounded right. She stepped out into the blinding sun, her mind still troubled by her dilemma, and bumped into Anthony Chapman.

'I thought I recognised that beat-up thing you drive,' he said, hugging her. 'You've got to do something about that car before it dies beneath you, out in the *bundu*. I'm on my way back from Samburu. Sent the clients to Nairobi by plane. I thought I'd drop in on you in Buffalo Springs, and here you are, waiting to guide me to the nearest cold beer.'

She was pleased to see him, to put her own troubles aside. Anthony always made her laugh, with his descriptions of awkward or happy clients and the antics of his camp staff.

'Are you coming to stay with us for a day or two?' she asked.

'I am not,' he said. 'I'm in a hurry to get back to Nairobi. Tonight, if possible.'

'You hate Nairobi,' she said. 'What's going on? Have you got another safari right away?'

'I'm going to Nairobi because Camilla is arriving the day after tomorrow.' He gave her a sideways glance, half smiling, half questioning. 'And I'm going to ask her to marry me.'

Chapter 5

Kenya, December 1966

'I'm driving up tomorrow.' Camilla's slightly breathless voice sounded cheerful. 'The agent has managed to clear all my parcels and they're stowed in the back of the car. Can I bring a guest?'

'Of course you can,' Hannah said. 'Is it Anthony?'

'Actually, it's my father. He'd love to see the workshop, and talk to you and Lars about your game rangers. He's going to stay with friends in Nyeri for New Year, so it would be lovely if he could be with us for Christmas. Is that all right?'

'It's fine,' Hannah said. 'I've been meaning to phone him, but the baby takes up so much time and everything else gets put on the long finger.'

'See you tomorrow, then,' Camilla said. 'Is there anything you want from the big city? I'm going to do some last-minute shopping this afternoon.'

'I tried to get sultanas from old Patel today. For the Christmas pudding. But he had bags of things that were covered in dust and looked like dried ants. I think they've been in the shop since the first settlers arrived. Did Sarah get you yesterday? She was on the radio.'

'She did. I'm picking up her prints first thing in the morning, and a block of text from her writer. Our friend the famous photographer,' Camilla said with satisfaction. 'It's wonderful that she's coming down to join us.'

'I despaired of ever seeing her back here,' Hannah said. 'After Suniva was born I hoped she would come often, but that didn't happen. Allie must have forcibly turfed her out for Christmas. They're probably afraid that she'll grow a trunk if she stays up there much longer. What about Anthony?'

*

Anthony. He had been waiting at the airport when Camilla arrived from London. She had stayed with her father for a week, and on the second evening, when George had gone to an obligatory reception, Anthony drove her up into the Ngong Hills to watch the sunset, bringing a rug and cushions and chilled champagne. He took her hand and led her through the bush and out on to a flat, rocky area from which they could see the plains speckled with grazing herds of zebra and gazelle and kongoni. A lone giraffe stood gazing at the outline of the city from his lofty viewpoint, and in the middle distance the sun caught the glint of a spear and the red *shuka* of a Maasai herdsman, guiding his cattle and goats into the *manyatta* for the night.

'Welcome home,' Anthony said.

She drew in her breath, inhaling the smell of dust in the air, savouring the space and glory of the raw land, the sense of danger that was Africa.

'This continent reduces you to your proper size,' she said. 'Tells you how insignificant you are in the overall plan of the universe. I was right, this feels like home.'

'I've been a fool,' he said. 'I let you go. Out of my life and much too far away. And now I want to say something to you that I've never said before. I love you, Camilla.' She did not reply, and as the silence lengthened between them he started to speak and stopped.

He searched for a way to tell her how much she meant to him, realising that he had never before bared his soul to anyone and that he had never been as vulnerable as he was at this moment. He put his arms around her, catching her at the waist and lifting her face to kiss her mouth. She closed her eyes and felt a rush of love and desire so strong that she could barely stand. He guided her down on to the rug and knelt beside her, smoothing back her hair to run his finger along the thin red line that was still visible on her forehead. Her shirt had small silver buttons down the front and he began to unfasten them slowly, kissing each inch of skin as it was revealed, awed and humbled by the perfection of her. They made love as though it was the first and the last time, and the intensity of it made her cry.

'I want to marry you,' he said afterwards, lying beside her, face to face, their fingers locked, limbs touching. 'Everything I've done, every thought I've had during the last few months has been leading to the realisation that I love you. And everything in my life makes sense now that I understand that. Marry me, Camilla, please.'

She could feel the breeze, cool and light on her skin. But a current of heat ran through her and her heart was fluttering like a trapped bird inside her body. She lifted one hand to touch his face.

'No,' she said.

'But I love you.' He was staring at her in disbelief. 'We're crazy about each other. Meant to be together. You know it, and I know it too. Don't play games, Camilla. I want you to marry me.'

'No,' she said again.

'Is there someone else?' he asked. 'Is it something to do with the man who fixed your face?'

'There's no one else,' she said. 'But I made a mistake before about our feelings for each other. So this time we have to go more carefully and see what—'

'I was the one who made the mistake,' he said. 'And now you're going to make me pay for it. Or am I not sophisticated and worldly enough for the most beautiful creature on earth?'

'I want us both to be sure,' she said 'I want you to be certain that you'll love me enough to be faithful to me. And I need time to be sure that I can live here and make a success of it. That I have the guts to do that.'

'You're famous and successful all over the world,' he said. 'Everything you've done has turned into a huge triumph.'

'It hasn't really been like that,' she said, putting her fingers against his lips to prevent him from saying more. 'I drifted into my modelling career by accident. It wasn't something I worked for, or achieved against all odds. When I was rejected for drama school I simply gave up the idea of acting, and I was presented with an easy alternative. And it was the same when you rejected me before. I gave up and went back to what I knew. Took the path of least resistance.'

'I should have come to get you,' he said.

'But you didn't. And I wasn't brave enough to stay here, like Sarah or Hannah. I turned tail and left.'

'You're here now,' he said, kissing her again. 'We're here together.'

'True, but I need to prove to myself that I'm up to the challenge. I want to make a success of the workshop at Langani. I need to know that I can deal with whatever problems come my way, and not run away at the first sign of trouble, as everyone thinks I will.'

'Who thinks that?' he asked.

'I want you to give me six months,' she said, ignoring his question. 'To live up at Langani and get my business established. I have to go back to London in the new year, to finish a couple of contracts I've signed up for, and to sell the things I've made at the farm. Then we'll see whether the two of us are made of strong enough stuff to think about marriage.'

He turned away from her, his face dark with disappointment. 'That's a crazy idea,' he said. 'Six months for each of us to prove something we already know. It sounds like a plot from a Hollywood film. Haven't I seen a film like that?'

'You probably have,' she said, smiling and reaching for her clothes. 'And it ended happily ever after. But our story will finish up in Nairobi Hospital if we don't get back into the car. Now that the sun has gone down I'm rather cold. Suffering from exposure to the elements.'

'You might be more malleable if you were strapped to a hospital bed,' he said, sulking. 'We'll head back into town, but I'm pretty upset because I was going to present myself to George tonight as his future son-in-law. And you've scuppered my plan.'

Two days later he left on safari and Camilla had made a determined effort to set aside the thoughts of his proposal. For three months she focused her attention on the workshop. Now Christmas was only a few days away, and she was not sure if Anthony would be around to share it with her. She had hoped he might ask her to join him in one of his camps, if his clients decided to stay there. But so far there had been no such suggestion.

'Anthony's in the Mara,' she said, in answer to Hannah's question. 'I think he'll be there over Christmas. But the clients might go to Nairobi or the Mount Kenya Safari Club for New Year, in which case he'll turn up at Langani.'

'Fine,' Hannah said. 'I'll see you tomorrow, then. By the way, Suniva has another tooth, and I have a lunch date. So I must fly.'

'Lunch with whom?' Camilla was curious. Hannah had barely left the farm since her daughter's birth.

'A tall, dark stranger,' Hannah said, laughing. 'I like contrast, you know.'

'Sounds interesting and dangerous,' Camilla said. 'I'll see you tomorrow.'

An hour later Hannah checked her shopping list for the last time, repeated a litany of instructions for Suniva's routine and then looked uncertainly at Lars.

'Go,' he said, grinning at her. 'Suniva and I have plenty to do, and you're late. We're off to look at the wheat and to talk about things that girls can only discuss with their fathers.'

'Like what?' Hannah said. 'She knows more about the dairy than the state of the wheat.'

'Exactly,' Lars said. 'So we are going to put that right today, the two of us. Now go, Hannah. Esther is here, we have all the bottles ready and nappies and so forth. I'll see you in Nanyuki at four. We haven't played tennis for a long time, and I'm looking forward to it.'

'Don't forget her rug,' Hannah said, taking a last look at her daughter.

'Go!' Lars thundered.

She drove away from the farm, a little nervous at leaving the baby for the first time. But she was grateful for Barbie Murray's insistence that they have lunch together. The Murrays were good neighbours. They had been discreetly kind and supportive since Piet's death, and they had welcomed Lars on his return to the farm. During the planting season they had come to help, and when the tractor broke down at a key moment, Bill Murray had lent Lars his new Massey Ferguson. Barbie had recommended the ayah for Suniva too, a comforting, reliable woman called Esther who had taken care of the Murray children when they were small.

Hannah was humming as she parked the car outside Patel's *duka* to leave her shopping list, and to haggle with the Indian owner over the price of nails and kerosene. She would collect her order in the afternoon and hope there were no vital goods missing. Her tennis would be terrible after so long although she was generally in good shape, fit from the long walks she took each day, pushing Suniva in her pram with the dogs at her heels. Yesterday she had arranged a picnic and Lars had put the baby's carrycot into the back of the truck and headed for the river. By the time they parked, the sun had lodged itself at its zenith. Even in the shade of the wild fig tree it was breathlessly hot.

'Swimming,' Lars announced. 'Time this young lady learned to swim.'

'You can't put a small child into that icy river,' Hannah said. 'It will be too much of a shock, and she might hate the water for ever after.'

But Lars had already discarded his shorts and shirt. He picked up Suniva and slid down the bank to sit on a half-submerged tree trunk, dangling the baby's feet in the rushing water. She looked up at him with an air of amazement and then returned her focus to her feet, wriggling and splashing with her fat little legs, waving her arms in delighted discovery.

'Come and join us.' Lars beckoned to his wife.

Hannah stood up, stripped off all her clothes and plunged into the swimming hole, gasping at the shock of the cold water. Lars looked at her and fell in love with her all over again, and when she came to float beside him he held the baby in his lap and reached out with one hand to caress her full, beautiful breasts and her soft stomach and strong legs.

'I love you, Han.'

'I love you,' she said, and her eyes were bright with joy. She rose out of the water shivering a little, and he kissed her and helped her up the bank, with Suniva tucked in the crook of his other arm. She turned to hand him his shorts and at that moment she saw the generosity in his broad face, the blonde hair that was receding a little, the crinkling at the corners of his grey-green eyes, and all the strength and love and kindness in him. And she thought that he was perfect.

Sitting in her armchair on the verandah of the club now, she blushed at the memory of the lovemaking that had followed. Barbie Murray eyed her with approval.

'You look wonderful, my dear,' she said. 'Glowing and beautiful. The tennis will be fun. Doubles are never that exacting, so it's a good way to start up again.'

'I was thinking of a curry for lunch,' Hannah said. 'But that might finish off any chance of playing well.'

They ordered their food and were about to move into the dining room when a loud, thickly accented voice hailed them.

'Two beautiful women alone. I cannot see such a thing without coming to the rescue.'

Viktor Szustak strolled across the room and grasped Barbie's hand, bowing low over it. His black hair was thick and wild, his smile predatory. When he straightened, he looked for a long moment at Hannah before wrapping his arms around her, and whispering something deliberately unintelligible in her ear. She stiffened in his embrace, inhaling the familiar cigar smoke on his clothes, the scent of gin on his breath. He had been her lover, but now she felt something close to revulsion at the feel and smell of him.

'You are as glorious as ever,' he said, releasing her and stepping back. 'Unchanged. Still the magnificent warrior queen.' His voice dropped and his expression was genuinely sad for a moment. 'I am so sorry about Piet. The finest of men and my good friend.'

Hannah stood like Lot's wife, silent and unmoving. She had not seen him for a year. Not since she had found him in bed with an African woman in Nairobi. Viktor who had seduced her, and then walked out when he had tired of their affair. Viktor who had been Piet's friend, architect of the lodge that now lay abandoned at Langani. Viktor, the father of her child.

'You haven't changed either,' Barbie was saying, with a wide smile. 'You look more villainous than ever, and your skin is practically black, for God's sake. Where have you been?'

'In Tanzania.' Viktor waved his cigar. 'I am building a magnificent lodge down in the south. In Ruaha. It is pristine territory, and it has taken me the best part of a year to finish the design and get the materials in place. I rented a house in Dar es Salaam and I spent my free time by the sea. On the beach. I have become a man of the ocean and the trade winds, a master of willing slaves that cater to my every desire.' His black eyes were gleaming as he put his arm around Barbie's shoulder. 'Are you having lunch? I will join you.'

Hannah's eyes widened in dismay and Barbie caught the expression. There had been gossip about Hannah and Viktor during the previous year, talk about an affair. But he had disappeared from the local scene and then Piet had died. His reappearance was obviously conjuring up unhappy memories.

'Hannah has a day off from the farm and the husband and the baby,' Barbie said. 'We're having a hen party. No men allowed. But if you're around for a day or two, come and have a drink. Bill would love to see you.'

'I heard you were married.' Viktor's eyes bored into Hannah. 'Congratulations to the big Viking farmer. And now Barbie has said there is a baby, too?'

He was smiling at her, expecting a proud response, when he saw a flicker of something in her eyes. He could not define it but he thought it might be fear. His skin prickled.

'Do you have a son or a daughter?' His tone was different and she heard the change.

'A daughter,' she said, her chin tilted in the way he remembered. Defiant.

He nodded. 'Double congratulations,' he said. 'And many happy years. Barbie, I will come to see you tomorrow evening, if it is good for you and Bill. I am here for two days to discuss the possibility of a new viewing lodge on Mount Kenya. Deep in the forest where they hope to see bongo and leopard at night. It is only a proposal for the moment, but it looks interesting.'

'Sounds great,' Barbie said, pleased with the prospect of his company. 'Come on, Hannah, we need to have some breathing space between eating and tennis.'

'I am crushed by your rejection,' Viktor said. 'I will return to the bar and drown my sorrows with gin, and you will be responsible for my downfall. Expect me, then, Barbie. And I will bring a decent bottle of whisky for Bill.'

'He's a rogue, that man.' Barbie was chuckling as they ate their lunch. 'A charmer, but not to be trusted for a second.' She had noticed the way Hannah picked at the food, her expression sombre. 'My dear,' she said. 'Old flames are always a bit of a nuisance when they show up again without warning. But you must not worry about someone like Viktor. He doesn't think about women as a permanent fixture – he's not the kind of man who wants to go back.'

'You're right,' Hannah said, attempting a smile. 'We had a brief fling, and then I came to my senses. But I hope Lars doesn't run into him – he can't stand the sight of Viktor.'

'Of course he can't.' Barbie was laughing outright. 'I remember Bill coming across an old boyfriend of mine at a dance in Nyeri one night. And my gentle, kind-hearted husband suddenly became a raging beast, all set for a fight. It was rather flattering, though, because we'd been married for ten years or more and we had become rather dull and set in our ways. Did us good, in fact. Now tell me about your famous house-guest and the new workshop. The whole farming community is talking about it.'

'Camilla has really settled in, and we're beginning to see a glimmer of understanding from the *bibis* that are working there.'

'I met her in the *duka* in Nanyuki last week, like a beam of light dancing in that dusty old place. It struck me that I'd never seen a more beautiful girl. There's something quite ethereal about her, the delicate, perfect skin and the cornflower-blue eyes and pale, silvery hair. She looks as though she might drift away at any moment, disappear into the clouds like a heavenly apparition. And she's clever with it.'

'She's been in Nairobi for the last few days,' Hannah said. 'She's trying to clear some new fabric through customs, and it's driving her nuts even though she has an agent to help. I don't think she expected such lethargy and corruption.'

'Us old hands can't believe what's going on,' Barbie said. 'Corruption is rampant wherever you look. I can't figure out how it took hold so quickly. Before Independence we always used to pride ourselves on the fact that Kenya was a pretty fair society. Not like the West African countries where you can't turn around without a handout.'

'It's bad, yes,' Hannah said. 'I've been giving one of our *watu* driving lessons and he's done very well. But when he went for his test last week, the examiner demanded three hundred shillings to pass him because he was from another tribe. If they'd both been Luos then it would have cost less. Anyhow, he's still riding round on his bicycle as a result.'

'Some minor official in the Agricultural Department tried to get at Bill the other day,' Barbie said. 'Threatened to deport him, for sacking one of our men. Or Bill could cough up five hundred shillings. Blatant bribery. The fellow had been drunk for a week or more, and hadn't come to work. And he'd made off with a whole set of tools owned by the Indian mechanic who services the harvester.'

'So what happened?'

'The old Hindi went looking for him, and made him sign a statement saying he'd pinched the tools. Of course he didn't get them back – they'd already been sold, probably for a tenth of what they're worth. The piece of paper saved Bill from any more trouble, but they'll remember next time he wants a permit for something. How are things at Langani?'

'Fine,' Hannah said. 'The wheat looks good, the cows are healthy, and our game patrols seem to have deterred the poachers for the moment.'

'I'm glad for you, my dear. And you have a great man in Lars. Bill and I are so fond of him.'

'I feel pretty good with him around,' Hannah said, her face soft. 'We took on an extra night watchman last month, just to be sure that our security is tight. We've begun to feel relaxed again. And Camilla is training five *bibis* in the workshop.'

'Are these things really going to be sent to London and even New York?' Barbie was openly impressed.

'Most of them,' Hannah said. 'But she might do a fashion show in Nairobi, in conjunction with one of the dress shops. Camilla thinks we should try and develop a small local market and I agree. But her main objective is to sell the things we make in England, and even America.'

'I hear her main objective is much closer to home,' Barbie said knowingly.

'She's playing that one carefully,' Hannah said. 'Anthony's been at Langani a couple of times since she arrived, and she sees him in Nairobi when he's not out in the *bundu* with clients. But she's aware of how these hunters and safari people carry on, and she's wary.'

'Smart girl. He's an attractive man. She'll need to reel him in slowly and keep the line tight. Keep him guessing, too. That's what gets them, every time. Pudding? I'm having pudding.'

The afternoon tennis proved enjoyable enough. But Hannah found herself looking over her shoulder at the club and later in the town, as she and Lars collected their supplies from Mr Patel. There was no sign of Viktor, however, and she felt dizzy with relief as they left Nanyuki and headed home.

A flurry of excitement erupted on the following day, when both Sarah and Camilla converged on the farm at the same time. The dogs set up a frenzy of barking, Mwangi and Kamau appeared from the kitchen beaming their welcome, and Hannah was all smiles as everyone cooed over the baby. George Broughton-Smith stood a little apart, feeling somewhat excluded from the noise and chatter of the three young women, relieved when Lars came striding across the lawn to join them.

'Good to see you here,' Lars said, after the handshakes.

'I hear things are going well. No poaching, that is,' George said.

'That's right. I can drive you round the farm this afternoon, if you like.

Show you how we've set up our game patrols,' Lars said. 'They seem to be working well.'

'Let's leave everything in the car for the moment,' Camilla said. 'I want to take Daddy and Sarah to see the workshop.'

'Where's Anthony right now?' Sarah took Camilla's arm as they walked across the lawn to the building Lars had converted.

'He's out with a party of Americans from Seattle, all retired and desperately earnest and dull. The "jet-set medicare" brigade. They can't make up their minds if they want to stay in camp for Christmas, or go and live it up with a mob of other people. We might have New Year's Eve together.' She looked at Sarah, her eyes a little sad. 'I'm glad I'm here with Lars and Hannah,' she said. 'And that I have Daddy in Nairobi when I go down there. Otherwise it would be awfully lonely. But the workshop is coming on, and the women are learning.'

The former manager's cottage was several hundred yards from the main house, and it had been transformed into a small factory. Lars had knocked down a couple of dividing walls and created an airy space with polished floors and large windows. Down the centre of the room was a trestle table that was used for laying out patterns and cutting fabric. There were several wooden storage chests set against the walls, and four electric sewing machines stood at the far end of the room, two for straight stitching, one for overlocking seams, and a heavy-duty model for sewing skin and hide. Shelves and cupboards against the back wall were stacked with bolts of silk, canvas cloth, leather and soft suede, all neatly rolled on to cardboard tubes.

'It will take time to get everything working smoothly,' Camilla said to her father. 'Things around here don't move at quite the same speed as in London.'

She had found the first two months taxing in the extreme. After Anthony left on safari she had spent long, frustrating hours in Nairobi, going from one government department to another to arrange for her work permit and business licence. The machines she had ordered were not delivered on the date promised, and when they did arrive one of them was badly damaged. There was additional import duty to pay on everything she had brought into the country. At the Customs Department a newly appointed inspector pored over the forms she had filled in, and handed her another sheaf of paperwork. He rummaged through her boxes and parcels, rolling out yards of delicate textiles and pale suede over the grubby surface of his work bench, marking them beyond repair. He was high-handed and surly – a small official with a big vision of his own importance, clearly enjoying the novel experience of delaying a white memsahib. He obviously expected a bribe which Camilla refused to acknowledge. In the Immigration Department she ran up against the same problem.

'I'm setting up a business,' she said to an impassive official. 'I sent in my application for a permit weeks ago. I sent it registered mail from England. I'm giving employment to several people, bringing foreign currency into the country, making things for export that will help Kenyans.'

'We cannot find your application. You must fill out new forms,' he said, closing her file in dismissal.

She was determined not to offer bribes, although she found the officials she dealt with obstructive and even threatening. After four days she had sat down with her father, exhausted and close to tears.

'Everything is like this now,' he said. 'You need someone with connections who will see that your permit is processed, and your business licence issued. I'll have a word with Johnson Kiberu and get things sorted out.'

'Johnson Kiberu. I met him once in London.' Camilla frowned at the memory. The man had tried to seduce her and she had fled his clumsy advances.

'He's an able politician,' George said. 'Dedicated and tough. Determined to exercise real control in the management of the national parks and reserves. I wouldn't be able to achieve much without his support. He'll recommend someone in customs and immigration that you can deal with. Don't worry, darling. I'll help you to get a system going. In the meantime I suggest you head up to Langani and get settled in.'

'But I have all this material in customs,' she said. 'It will probably disappear if I don't clear it.'

'You need a shipping agent to clear things for you,' George said. 'There's a young Indian journalist I met recently who's bound to have a relative in that business. It will cost you a few bob extra, but at least you won't have to spend your time tearing your hair out in government offices.'

At Langani, Lars and Hannah insisted that she stay with them in the main house.

'You can have your old room at the end of the verandah,' Hannah said. 'We'll feel happier if you're with us. And I'll be glad of your company when Lars has to go to Nairobi.'

Camilla had noticed a second night watchman at the house, and the guns in the drinks cabinet. Lars and Hannah also had revolvers in the office and the bedroom. But there had been no trouble at the farm since the tragedy of Piet's death, almost a year ago. With the wildlife conservation fund that George's organisation had given them, Hannah had bought a Land Rover and taken on four rangers for anti-poaching patrols. Lars drilled them for weeks and set up a series of patrol routes that covered most of their land. During the last few months there had been no wild animals snared or slaughtered on the farm.

On her first afternoon back at Langani Camilla had settled into her room and then gone to take a first look at her future workspace. When she returned to the main house there was an ancient Land Rover parked in the driveway.

'Surprise!' Sarah ran down the steps, her arms stretched out, her smile as wide as the sky. 'I had to come down for a night to make sure that you were really back.'

'Here we are, the three of us, together again.' Hannah was beaming. 'And that is *lekker*, I'd say.'

They spent a contented evening, taking turns to play with the baby and reminiscing over their schooldays, until the talk turned to Anthony and his marriage proposal.

'I love him,' Camilla said. 'I truly do. But I need to know that I can carve out a life that will occupy me while he's out in the bush for weeks at a time. I'm glad he's not here though, because if he walked into this room right now and asked me again, I don't know how strong my resolve would be.'

'You shouldn't discuss him when he's not here,' Lars said, but he was grinning. 'It's a terrible thing to be at the mercy of three women, let alone one, and not have a chance to say a word in your own defence.'

At dinner there was a silence as they thought of Piet and remembered the many nights when Jan and Lottie had presided over this same table, full of optimism for the family's future at Langani. Lars felt the sadness creep into the room. He did his best to distract them with stories of his first visit to Kenya as a boy when he had learned the workings of his uncle's coffee plantation, and longed to stay.

In the room they had shared during their childhood Sarah and Camilla smiled at one another as they lay in bed, listening for the chug of the generator to slow down, waiting for the verandah lights to fade and to be replaced by the starred velvet of the African night. Camilla reached across the space between their beds and found Sarah's hand.

'I love you,' she said. 'Goodnight.'

'Love you too,' Sarah said. And for the first time since Piet's going, she fell asleep at Langani with a smile on her lips.

'We're riding this morning,' Hannah announced the next day at the breakfast table. 'I haven't been out much since Suniva was born, and this will be special.'

They set out across the veldt, following the herds of plains game, stopping to watch a family of warthogs rolling in a mud bath. In the short grass a secretary bird attacked a snake with unyielding ferocity, swallowed it, and then continued his walk with precise, mincing steps, resplendent in his trim black and grey and white plumage as though he were going to his club. They dismounted on the bank of the river and let the horses loose to graze. As they stood beside the clear rush of the mountain stream they all knew why Hannah had brought them there.

'We made our promise here four years ago,' she said. 'Cut our hands and took a blood oath to look after each other always. Piet was here as our witness. And now that Camilla is back, I thought we could renew that promise. We don't have to start gouging holes in our palms again, but we could say the words. And I know that Piet can still hear them, and that he's with us today too.'

'I promise never to forget, always to stay true to our friendship, always to be there for my sisters.' Sarah had remembered the words exactly, as if she had spoken them yesterday. They joined hands as Hannah and Camilla repeated the vow, and then they stood with their arms around each other, under the fig tree where Piet had tethered his horse and witnessed the original promise. On a bright day that now seemed like another lifetime.

*

High above them on the ridge, the old man looked at the figures of the three white memsahibs and cursed them softly. They were standing very close together, holding hands as if they were part of a ritual. Then they put their arms around each other, embraced and stepped apart. He spat on the ground. Soon afterwards they mounted the horses, and he watched them ride across the plains with the wind singing its ancient song through the long grass, passing the herds of wild animals and the edge of the golden wheat until they reached the place where the cows and the maize and vegetables were. The place that would soon be his.

The following afternoon, Sarah had returned to her elephants, while Camilla set out to establish the workshop. She had interviewed women that Hannah recommended from the Langani labour lines, examining their native beadwork, and trying to judge their sewing skills. But operating an electric machine did not come easily. There had been shrieks of alarm when someone pressed the foot pedal down too hard, and the needle flew into overdrive, gobbling up the cloth in a pattern of zig-zag stitching. Camilla sat with the women for days, unpicking tangles and trying to salvage some of the torn fabric. They could not grasp the method of inserting the spool thread in the correct order of loops, and they wailed with frustration when the machine refused to sew, or broke the yarn. A significant amount of expensive silk and suede was lost as they learned their craft. There had been pilfering, too. The *bibis* were like magpies, drawn to the brightest and shiniest beads and decorations, and not above pocketing a selection to adorn their own garments and homes. Camilla consulted Lars, and he arranged for the farm carpenter to install padlocks on all the cupboards and drawers.

On several occasions she had driven down to Nairobi to stay with Anthony, in between safaris. They had spent their precious evenings in his cottage, talking over their recent experiences in the bush and on the farm, lying close together at night, making love with a sweetness that left them sated but longing for more. Camilla bought embroidered sheets and pillowcases, new table linen and cushions, glass and silver candlesticks and vases. She was rewarded by his surprise and pleasure at the transformation of his bachelor quarters into a romantic retreat. Her table settings also took the houseboy by surprise.

'The bwana can see very well at the table.' Joshua pointed at the overhead lamp and the wall lights as Camilla arranged candles throughout the room. 'He does not need these things, Memsahib Camilla, and they will drop their mess all over the sideboard.'

'This is a special kind of dinner for the bwana, and we will do it like this when I am here,' she said. 'Now, Joshua, I want you to take this napkin and fold it in two. Then in four. Well done. Now take these corners . . .'

She enjoyed seeing his expression as he learned to created flower shapes from the starched pieces of cloth, and gradually she taught him new ways to set the table, to arrange the roses and dahlias she cut in the garden, and to put the candles in place. On each visit she brought boxes of clothes and accessories she had made in the workshop at Langani, and after the first month she showed samples to one of the leading boutiques in Nairobi and immediately signed a contract to supply them.

'I don't want my creations to be available everywhere,' she explained to Anthony. 'I think one shop in Nairobi is enough. I'll go to the Mount Kenya Safari Club next month, and see if they would like some pieces. And maybe one of the smart hotels at the coast. But they should be exclusive. Besides, I have a big order to fill for Saul Greenberg, so I can't set aside too much stock for local sales.'

At Langani, Camilla spent every day in the workshop. At the end of the first month, when she had paid the women for the hours they had worked, only two of them returned to the machines on the following Monday morning. Makena, her best seamstress, spread out her hands in a fatalistic gesture, explaining that the husbands of the missing three had bought seed or got drunk on the wages, and sent their wives back to work on the family *shambas*. For the first six weeks she had felt as though she was taking two steps back for every three forward and on many nights she lay awake and thought about Tom Bartlett and his dire warnings. But his conviction that she would come crawling back to London, begging for assignments, finally served to strengthen her determination to succeed.

At last she saw that her Kikuyu *bibis* were beginning to grasp what was required of them. And the women were justly proud of their efforts. She liked to listen to them chattering as they worked, their sing-song voices and raucous laughter making her wish that she understood their tribal language. Her knowledge of Swahili was good, but she could not follow the Kikuyu dialect except for a few phrases she had recently picked up. Hannah helped to pack the finished goods in layers of tissue paper, and box them up for local sales and for dispatch to London and New York.

Sarah was disappointed that neither of her friends had found the time to visit Buffalo Springs in the weeks before Christmas, and she was uneasy about the prospect of spending the holiday period at Langani. She did not want to speculate on how they would all feel on the anniversary of her engagement to Piet, and the appalling days that had followed. But in the end she went out of love and loyalty, and because she could not imagine suffering through the memories by herself. She was pleased when she saw that George had joined them. He would be good company for Lars. He was obviously impressed by what Camilla had achieved. He caught her eye frequently as they explored the workshop, making the thumbs up sign, his expression one of paternal pride.

'I met your journalist friend in Nairobi,' he said to Sarah. 'Rabindrah Singh.'

'He's hardly a friend,' she said.

'Well, he's a bright chap, and ambitious,' George said. 'He's been very helpful to me, placing articles about our fund in the local papers and magazines. What's the situation on your book?'

'He's coming back to Buffalo Springs early in the new year,' Sarah said. 'We've been over what he's written so far and Dan has corrected it. It looks good, but we are still waiting for the final go-ahead from the publisher. I've had an encouraging letter from John Sinclair, though, saying that he is impressed by what we have sent so far.'

After lunch George set out to tour the farm, and to meet the game rangers Hannah had taken on with the money he had allocated to Langani. Lars lined them up for inspection outside the office, smartly dressed in khaki uniforms with wool berets rolled into the tabs on their shoulders, and heavy jackets for night patrols. They stood to attention proudly as George greeted them, and then climbed into the back of the Land Rover to accompany him. A fence had been built around part of the area set aside as a wildlife reserve, and Lars stopped in two places where elephants or buffalo had recently broken through the wire. The conservation area was spread out across flat, yellow plains and bordered by the line of trees along the river and a few acres of thick forest. A male ostrich raced away from the vehicle, stepping high, his plumage black and glittering. In the cloudless expanse of sky a Bateleur eagle made effortless circles, and a pair of dik diks skittered into a thicket on tiny, fragile legs. Towards the end of the afternoon Lars turned the Land Rover up the track to the place where Piet had built his lodge.

'It can't be easy to come up here, even now,' George said.

'No. But I do it regularly,' Lars said, 'to keep the bush from swallowing up the building, and to see that the inside is maintained. Hannah is talking about opening it in the new year. At first she couldn't even think about the place, but now she's started to see it as a kind of shrine to Piet. She feels she has a duty to open it. So I bring a couple of *watu* up here every week, and we clean the rooms and cut back the *bundu* and put salt down to keep the game coming in.'

They stood on the viewing platform and looked out at the tranquil afternoon. There was a solitary warthog at the waterhole and he looked up for a moment before returning to the business of drinking. Otherwise there was no sound except birdsong. In the distance George could see a small herd of elephants making their way out of the forest, heading for the *kopje*.

'The patrol comes up here most nights, but we change the route and the time regularly so that potential poachers never know when we might suddenly appear, or where. It seems to be working so far.'

'It's hard to think of this beautiful spot as the setting for such a foul deed,' George said. 'I'm full of admiration for those three young women, and for the way that you have supported them. And I'm very glad that the money from my organisation has helped with your security.'

When they returned to the house, George decided on a siesta and Lars made his way to the office. He was about to open the door when he heard Hannah on the telephone. Her tone was angry, the words clipped.

'You don't need to come up here at any time. I have nothing to say to you, except goodbye.' She slammed the telephone on to its cradle and stormed from the room, bumping straight into her husband.

'Hey, who was that you were talking to?' he asked in surprise.

'Ach, it was a stupid man trying to sell us something,' she replied. 'I couldn't get him off the phone.'

'What was he selling?' Lars was puzzled by her flustered manner and the anger blazing in her eyes.

'Are you going to start pressing me too?' she demanded. 'Do I have to report every word I say to some stupid salesman?'

'Hannah, what is the matter with you?' He put his arms around her and held her close.

'I'm sorry,' she said, at last. 'I'm a little jumpy this afternoon. Maybe I'm tired. Suniva woke me up twice last night, and I've been running around like a crazy woman all day getting everything ready.'

'I think you should have a siesta, like George,' he said. 'Esther has taken the baby out, so you should get an hour to yourself. Go on.'

Hannah nodded and walked down the verandah to the room shared by Sarah and Camilla.

'Hello,' she said, putting her head round the door.

Sarah looked up from a folder of typed manuscript and smiled. 'I'm halfway through Rabindrah's draft and I have to admit that he writes well,' she said. 'Better than I thought he would. Especially when you consider he was only up there a short time. But the style is strong and he's got the facts right, thanks to Dan's editing. It makes you want to know about the elephants, without going all sentimental over them. I don't say too much, though, because he is quite cocky about his work. It would be all too easy to give him a swelled head.'

'I met Viktor in Nanyuki yesterday,' Hannah blurted out. 'He wants to come up here. I think he wants to see Suniva.'

'Oh my God!' Sarah stared at her with dismay. 'What was he doing in Nanyuki? Allie told me he was working in Tanzania. Surely he doesn't suspect—'

'I don't know,' Hannah said miserably. 'But I'm scared. He phoned just now and I think Lars heard me talking to him. So I lied about who was on the line.'

'You'd better tell Lars exactly what's happened,' Sarah said. 'Han, it would be better if you faced this together.'

'I can't talk to Lars about this.' Hannah shook her head vehemently. 'I just can't.'

'How long will Viktor be around?' Sarah asked.

'I don't know. A couple of days, he said to Barbie Murray. But he might be asked to design a new lodge here.'

'Then you absolutely have to tell Lars,' Sarah said.

'Tell Lars what?' Camilla appeared in the doorway. She sat down on her bed and listened to the story. 'Viktor's a coward,' she said at last. 'He's not the sort of person who would want the responsibility of a child tying him down. He didn't want anything to do with you, Hannah, once he thought you could become a permanent fixture. I don't believe he'd come up here and make trouble.'

'I don't know.' Sarah was doubtful. 'Some men don't care much about their girlfriends or wives, but they feel quite differently about a child. We have to keep him away from here. Get rid of him somehow.'

'Short of pushing him down a ravine, I'm not sure how,' Camilla said.

'I have a bad feeling about this.' Hannah's eyes were clouded with fear. 'I've been feeling bad altogether today. I keep thinking that it's nearly a year ago since Piet was killed. I didn't want to talk about it, but I feel rotten right now. I miss him so much every day. And I'm dreading Christmas and the day he died.' She put her head in her hands and began to cry.

Sarah stood up and went to the window with its view of the ridge. She had tried not to think about the anniversary but now that Hannah had brought it up she felt sick with apprehension. The old grief swept through her, eating into her tenuous hold on buried emotions. She had not been able to pray since the night of his death, had not set foot in a church, did not want to celebrate Christmas with it songs of joy and hope and birth.

'We're going to see this through together.' Camilla went to stand beside her. 'I don't think Viktor would want a row with Lars, and that's what would happen if he came up here.'

'Besides, Han, when it comes down to it, Suniva is a carbon copy of you,' Sarah said. 'I know this is a terribly emotional thing you're facing. But your daughter is blonde and blue-eyed. She looks far more like you and Lars than Viktor.'

Hannah turned away, her arms folded tight in front of her, her face stony. For a moment she wanted to strike out at Sarah, resenting her blunt statement. Then her face changed and she began to laugh. 'Only you would say something as plain and sensible as that,' she said, putting her arms around her friend. 'But I hope this isn't going to become a problem. Because Lars and I are so happy with each other and with the baby, and I drove in to Nanyuki thinking I was the most fortunate girl in the entire world.'

*

They began their Christmas preparations the next day. Hannah spent the morning in the kitchen with Kamau. The old cook was more than capable of recreating Lottie's recipes without help, but he listened with love and patience to the instructions and asked for advice that he did not need. George offered to drive into Nanyuki to collect last-minute items from the shops, and in the sitting room Camilla and Sarah took out the large box of Christmas decorations and began to hang them on the tree that had been delivered after breakfast. But a pall of memory soured their efforts, and the house fell silent as they worked. The sound of a vehicle brought them out on to the verandah, and they gazed in dismay at Viktor as he stepped out of his car. Sarah held her breath as she heard the door of the office open. Lars looked down at the visitor for a long moment before striding down the steps.

'You're not welcome here,' he said.

'I was a close friend of Piet, long before your arrival,' Viktor said. 'My congratulations, by the way. I met your wife in Nanyuki and I hear you have a fine daughter. So I thought it would be good for me to meet her.'

Hannah had been alerted by Mwangi, and she came from the kitchen, her face pale with shock. 'What do you want, Viktor?' she said. 'I told you not to come here.'

'Did you, Hannah?' Lars looked at her and then directed his attention back to Viktor. 'You have thirty seconds to get into your car and leave our property,' he said. 'Starting from now.'

Viktor stood his ground, his eyes black and mocking, his fleshy mouth turned down in a sardonic smile. Then he threw back his head and laughed loudly. Lars moved like lightning across the space that separated them, his right arm coming forward from nowhere to land beneath Viktor's chin. Viktor staggered and fell, and for a moment there was a heavy silence. Then he took a handkerchief from his pocket and dabbed at the trickle of blood on his lip. He scrambled to his feet and raised a fist, but Lars charged towards him and he thought better of prolonging the fight.

'You have not seen the last of me,' he said, and his arm waved from the car window as he drove away in a cloud of dust, tyres squealing as he rounded the bend in the driveway and was lost from sight.

'You didn't tell me you'd seen Viktor. In fact you lied to me,' Lars said as Hannah stared at him, mute with dismay, shocked by the cold rage she saw in his face. 'I'll be out for the rest of the day,' he said, as he walked away.

It was almost dark when he returned. Hannah was waiting on the verandah, pacing up and down with Suniva in her arms. The baby had sensed the tension and she was fractious and tearful.

'I'm sorry,' Hannah said. 'I'm so sorry, Lars. I should have told you, but I was so shocked when I saw him at the club. And scared. I was just scared.'

But he passed her without a word and she heard the door of the office slam. She walked up to the window and tapped lightly on it, but he did not look up and after a few minutes she went away.

An hour later she was slumped in a chair in the sitting room when she heard the sound of a car engine. And froze.

'My clients decided to spend Christmas at the Mount Kenya Safari Club.' Anthony was bounding up the steps of the verandah, grinning broadly. 'Where is everybody? I have a Christmas surprise for you all.'

Hannah flung herself into his arms, hiding her face in his bush jacket, clinging on to him. He hugged her and then prised her fingers from his arm, waiting for a greeting, listening as she explained in short, tangled sentences what had happened.

'The man's a halfwit. A royal shit,' Anthony said. 'I'm sure he only came up here to amuse himself. Viktor would never want to claim a child and all the responsibilities that go with it. He has a string of women stashed away all over the country, and halfway round Tanzania as well. Don't worry, Han. He won't come back.'

'He says he might design a lodge near here,' Hannah said. 'And Lars is so angry I think he . . . I don't know what he is going to do.'

'He's going to join George and me for a whisky and soda,' Anthony said. 'Have you got a bed for me?'

'I think you'd better sleep in my grandparents' old room.' Hannah was smiling a little. 'There's a double bed in there, and I suspect Sarah's going to lose her room-mate.'

The mood of the household changed with Anthony's arrival, and the prospect of Christmas took on a brighter aspect.

'I have a plan,' he told them that evening at dinner. 'There are big problems with rhinos in the Nyeri area. They're trampling *shambas* and attacking people as the settlements increase around the edge of the forest.

Some of them need to be moved elsewhere if they're to survive, and George is thinking of funding the plan. So I've sent the camp staff up to my favourite spot in the Aberdares, and I suggest we all leave in the morning and head up there for Christmas.'

'I can't walk off the farm tomorrow,' Lars said. He had hardly spoken during the evening and he was in no mood to consider anything of a frivolous nature.

'It's only for a couple of days,' Anthony said. 'There's a beautiful girl here who deserves a holiday, and I'll be delighted to take Suniva on safari for the first time. Afterwards, I thought we could all come back here. For – for the anniversary. So we can go up to the ridge together and make our *salaams* to Piet.'

'Yes,' said Hannah. 'Yes, that's what we should do, Lars. We could be away for a short time. Juma can take care of things for a couple of days, and Mwangi and Kamau can sleep up here, at the house. I'll tell the Murrays, and if there's a problem they can get us on the radio. We'll only be a couple of hours away. Look, we haven't had a holiday at all, since I don't know when.'

'Seems like a sound idea, Lars, old chap,' George said. 'I'll stay with you in the camp, and afterwards I'll go and spend New Year with chums in Nyeri.'

The camp was set in a glade, and as they drove up through the forest they stopped to admire the colobus monkeys, their black and white coats spread out like wings as they sprang through the tracery of branches. A male waterbuck was standing just outside the clearing, his eyes liquid and glowing in the dappled sunlight, heart-shaped nose moist, luxuriant coat soft and shaggy. Anthony's staff stood beside the mess tent, and there were wide smiles and applause as he helped Camilla down from his Land Rover. They ate their lunch under the trees, surrounded by the rustle and call of birds and the flash of scarlet wings as a pair of turacos clucked and shuttled through the branches in search of food.

In the afternoon they took two vehicles and set out on a game drive, following a little-used track through the forest which climbed up towards the open moors. All around them were thick stands of bamboo, the stalks rising from the dark, loamy earth, their leaves feathering out into the welcoming sunshine. Ferns and wild flowers nestled in the rich soil and Anthony stopped the car frequently, pointing out specimens of groundsel and lobelia more than six feet high, giant mutations of tiny alpine plants. Further up the track the vegetation was hung with lichen, ghostly green and drifting in the misty light. On the moorland they breathed in the thin air and stopped to admire a plunging waterfall, and to watch as a herd of elephants made their way towards the sparkle of a mountain stream.

It was on their way back to the camp that they encountered the buffalo. As they rounded the corner on the track, several young bulls appeared on the road in front of the two cars, blocking the way, sniffing the air aggressively, their small black eyes glinting with suspicion. Camilla was sitting in front beside Anthony, but Hannah had climbed up to sit on the roof of the vehicle, leaving the baby asleep in a basket on the seat below. She turned around to see if it was possible to reverse, and gasped in alarm as the remainder of the herd emerged on to the track to surround the cars.

'We're caught,' she whispered, slithering down on to the back seat. 'And there are several young ones, separated from the main part of the group. They're right behind Lars and George. Even Sarah has climbed down into the Land Rover.'

The animals began to mill closer, pushing and snorting and tossing their heavy bossed heads up and down, agitated but unsure of what to do. Anthony's hand was on the gear lever and Hannah noticed that his knuckles were white, although his face was calm. She saw Lars signal to her from the other car, his expression tense. But there was nothing he could do. They were trapped between the two groups. An older female began to paw the ground, her massive chest and bulky body advancing closer so that they could hear the wheeze of her breathing. Her curved horns were large, the tips pointed and lethal, ready to hook the bumper and strong enough to topple them. They sat still, waiting for the impact. Then, without warning, an ancient tattered bull exploded out of the bush further up the track, crashing through the branches, snorting fiercely and scattering the herd before galloping for cover, vanishing as abruptly as he had appeared. The rest of the group dispersed in every direction, blundering through the forest on both sides of the road until there was an eerie silence, and even the birds had ceased to sing.

'That was a little close,' Anthony said, seeing Hannah's ashen complexion in the driving mirror and reaching for Camilla's hand. 'Let's make for home and a stiff drink round the fire.'

They drove back to the camp, and when Hannah opened the door and jumped down from the vehicle Lars was instantly at her side, lifting the baby down and taking his wife by the hand.

'You're the most precious thing in my world,' he murmured into her ear as he held her. 'You and Suniva. My own precious girls whom I love. And that's all that matters.'

Christmas morning dawned, clear and pristine. There had been a light shower during the night and the forest was adorned with raindrops that glittered on stalks of grass and glassy leaves. The sky was washed and clear blue. Above the tree line, the snow-capped peak of Kirinyaga rose in lofty domination. Sarah stood outside her tent, mesmerised by the beauty of the world. For a moment she thought of going to one of the African churches on the Kinangop, but then her mind fastened on her memory of Christmas a year ago. She had knelt beside Lottie in the church, singing out the carols, thanking God for the torrent of joy she had felt. Piet loved her, they were going to be married, and all her most cherished dreams had come true. But on this glorious morning a year later she could not bring herself to pray, either for mercy or for peace. Her conversations with God had ended when he had taken away her love, allowed Piet to die without her. There was nothing she could say to such a cruel, implacable deity. She was relieved when Anthony appeared at her side and took hold of her hand as if to absorb some of her grief.

They exchanged simple gifts over breakfast and then set out for the day, driving through the thick forest to reach the Chania waterfall, admiring the soft green of distant, folded slopes and the sight of a world that was a place of apparent order and harmony. The hours passed in slow motion. Sarah took photographs, portraits of Hannah and Lars and the baby, a smiling family unit whose closeness tore at her lonely heart. Camilla accompanied her father and Anthony as they walked down the river with rods and fishing flies, returning with several fat trout. At noon the camp staff arrived with a picnic that included a turkey, roasted to miraculous perfection in an oven made from a converted kerosene drum. But in spite of Anthony's efforts and their determined cheer, they were left with a deepening sense of loss that they could not overcome.

'It's a milestone, and we've passed it,' Hannah said as they sat around the camp fire in the evening. 'We'll have to go slowly like this, one step at a time, and hope that time will do its work like they say. But when we get home, I'm going to phone Ma and Pa. Because they're down there in that awful place with no one to share their troubles, while we all have each other.'

'We must persuade them to come back,' Lars said. 'I know it will be hard for them and for us too. But it's time to set the ghosts to rest, and they'll never do that from a distance. Janni will find a role for himself at Langani and I'll make adjustments to help him. It won't be easy, but I know we can do it. In the meantime, we have another day in this great camp of Anthony's, and I'm planning to show my daughter her first leopard. And maybe a rhino or two.'

On the morning of their departure George said his farewells and set off with the local game warden to discuss the problem of relocating rhinos, and to rendezvous with friends in Nyeri. It was the anniversary of Piet's death, and they were in a sombre mood as they prepared to break camp. Anthony watched as Camilla packed her belongings into a canvas bag, taking in the way she moved, the glow of her skin, the silk of dark lashes on her cheeks when she closed her eyes, and the perfect curve of her mouth.

'I love you,' he said. 'I want you to be mine.'

She sat down and put her arms around him, drawing his head down between her breasts. 'Be patient,' she said. 'My little factory is doing well, and once I've finished the modelling contracts I promised to do in London, I'll be able to see my way better.'

'I want you with me now,' he said.

Camilla was smiling as she kissed him. 'Only for a few days, though,' she said. 'And then you'll be off into the *bundu* again, and you'll forget all about me.'

'No,' he said. 'I want you to come with me for part of my next safari. There are three men hunting, and only one of them has brought his wife. I thought you could spend some time with us. Take her out on game drives, or organise whatever she'd like to do on days when we're shooting. What do you think?'

'I'd love that,' she said, hugging him with delight. 'If Hannah is prepared to supervise while I'm away, then yes. I'll be there.'

*

They left the camp in the late morning and headed north to Langani, breaking the journey for a beer and a sandwich and making a brief stop for petrol and farm supplies. Sarah was silent, steeling herself for what was to come. She had formed a few words in her mind that she wanted to say at the cairn that was Piet's memorial, but she did not know whether she would be able to say them aloud. Her throat ached, and she was sick at heart as the ugly memories invaded her head. It was after three when they drove past the line of trees leading to the driveway and the garden. Lars pulled up first with Anthony only a minute behind him. They were lifting the baby and their bags out of the vehicles when Mwangi came down the steps. His face was grey and his gnarled hands were clasped together. There were tears in his rheumy old eyes.

'Mama Hannah,' he said. 'Mama Hannah . . .'

Chapter 6

Kenya, December 1966

They stood in the ruins of Camilla's workshop and surveyed the devastation. Trestle tables had been overturned and wood splintered. Machines were smashed beyond repair. Bolts of cloth had been unrolled, scored and ripped into shreds by the blade of a panga, or trampled and covered in mud and dirt. Boxes of trimmings were scattered across the floor, braids chopped into unusable pieces. Glass beads had been bludgeoned, reduced to tiny shards of light that crunched on the floor wherever they walked. It looked like the work of a madman. Camilla stared around her in disbelief. Every single piece of equipment and stock had been systematically destroyed.

Sarah stood beside her, speechless. She was reminded of the wanton destruction she had witnessed at Buffalo Springs when poachers had slaughtered herds of elephants for their ivory, leaving the wasted carcasses to rot where they had fallen. But that was something she could understand – a matter of poachers and money and corruption. Here, in Camilla's workshop, nothing had been taken as far as anyone could see. The raid seemed to have no purpose.

Hannah moved through the room, holding her daughter close and making small sounds of distress, picking up scraps of fabric from the floor, running her fingers over the remains of the table that had been demolished with hideous force. She caught Sarah's eye and looked away, frightened by the reflection of her own fear. Lars was swearing, lifting the fallen chairs and furniture that littered the room. Anthony put his arm around Camilla as she began to tremble with shock. She bent down, and gathered up fragments of an embroidered suede jacket that had been almost finished before she went away. It was sliced through, seams ripped, beadwork and feathers on the borders mangled.

'Who would have done this to me? And why?' She asked the questions knowing there would be no answers. 'I've only just started here. All the women seemed to be happy, and we had finally reached the point where they were turning out perfectly finished things. I can't understand it.' She turned to Anthony, dropping the soiled garment on the floor. 'I'm not even insured,' she said. 'It never occurred to me.'

Mwangi and Kamau stood in the doorway, discussing the presence of bad spirits in low voices. The police arrived and two *askaris* began to take statements. It must have happened during the night, Juma the headman said. The second night watchman they had recently taken on had disappeared. Perhaps he was responsible and had let the marauders in. Or maybe he had just run off.

'Come away, Camilla,' Anthony said, taking her hand and leading her away from the ruins of her enterprise. 'There's nothing we can do for the moment. Let's go back to the house. I think we all need to sit down and talk about this.'

In the sitting room Lars poured drinks. The news had spread through the labour lines, and a number of the farm workers gathered on the lawn in front of the house, muttering and shaking their heads. There was a *shitani* at work, they said. Or the ghost of Simon Githiri had come to haunt the farm. It was a bad omen for Langani. Lars went out to address them and to explain that they must answer the police questions with great care. Every observance would be valuable, no matter how unimportant it might seem. But as they dispersed he could see that they were more concerned with the work of the bad spirits, than with the ability of the *askaris* to find reasons for what had happened.

'We all know this is not a coincidence.' Lars sat down in the living room beside Hannah and placed his arm around her. 'Piet died a year ago today. This is a message of some kind, although God knows who could be responsible. I'm going to phone Jeremy Hardy. The local *askaris* can't sort this out, and we need fast results in order to stop a walk-out. These *watu* are full of superstition, quick to believe in the power of the dead to affect the living.'

'We are affected.' Hannah's expression was bleak. 'But I don't think this is anything to do with the power of the dead. Jeremy always said that Simon had other people helping him. On the night when the farm was raided last year, for example, there were five men here. They must all have been connected with Simon. And he couldn't have killed my cows without help.'

'Are you saying that someone else has taken up where Simon left off?' Camilla shivered. 'That's horrible.'

'Simon Githiri was a loner.' Lars was definite. 'He was an orphan with no family, and no visits from friends while he was at Langani. In fact, he seems to have existed in a vacuum, even before he came here. So who would want to carry on what he started?'

Sarah turned away. She could not get rid of the sickening certainty that had assailed her as soon as she saw the workshop. It bore all the markings of the earlier attacks – the same furious, wanton destruction that had characterised the first incident on the farm, when Hannah's cattle had been slaughtered and left disembowelled, with their throats cut and their hocks severed. This was the work of an evil mind. But she could not fathom the reasoning behind it, any more than she had ever understood why Simon had murdered Piet, the patron who had given him a chance of a good job and a secure life. Simon, whose presence she could still feel in the air although he too was dead and gone. Her thoughts churned in circles of despair, and her head began to ache. She left the sitting room and went out to the verandah, hoping the cool of the night would ease the pain. But she found the darkness menacing, and soon she began to see ominous shapes in the shadows of Lottie's garden. She wanted to run back inside, but she could not face the rest of the gathering or allow them to see the terrible thought that was in her mind. And she was afraid to go to her room alone. She gripped the rails of the verandah, frantic to get rid of the image of Piet that had risen up before her. After a few moments, Lars came out to join her, sympathetic and concerned.

'I'm sorry,' she said. 'It's hard to deal with the idea that someone is still trying to destroy us. That Simon's hatred is being kept alive.'

'We are grasping at straws,' he said. 'This has terrible implications. I don't think we can stay here, if these threats are starting again. Because there is no logic or motive behind them, no road to follow in order to find a reason or a solution, and no way to protect ourselves. We have been determined to stay on at Langani. To put all that happened last year behind us. But my priority is to create a secure life for Hannah and Suniva. I have no idea what we could do or where we could go, but—'

They were interrupted by the flicker of approaching headlights. A car pulled up in the driveway and Jeremy Hardy stepped out, his face tight.

'This is a bad *shauri*,' he said. 'The fact of its being the anniversary of Piet's death makes it very serious. I'm going to start by questioning the house staff, and then everyone in the labour lines. I will personally get through every single man and woman on this farm over the next forty-eight hours. Find out where each one of them has been over the last few days, and whether they saw anyone they didn't know or heard anything unusual. Even some snippet of gossip that might be a hint. Where did you find this night watchman who has disappeared?'

'He came from Nyeri. He'd worked at the Outspan Hotel for more than a year and he had a good reference,' Lars said.

'So why did he want to work on a farm, presumably for less pay?' Jeremy asked.

'He said he had a wife from around here, and a small *shamba* that he wanted to keep an eye on,' Lars said. 'I hope I haven't opened the door to some—'

'He's more likely to have run away because he's afraid of being blamed for what happened,' Jeremy said. 'He's the last man you took on, so some suspicion has to fall in his direction. But if he trashed the place himself or let someone else in, it won't be hard to find him. Everyone around here will remember him because he was a stranger, and he's bound to leave a trail. Let's get going with questions for your staff, and see what we can turn up.'

No one slept that night. The hours crawled past in a nightmarish replay of the scenes that had taken place only a year ago in the same room. Jeremy came and went, drinking coffee, talking to his *askaris*, interviewing frightened people from the labour lines. At dawn, Hannah collapsed into bed, still holding Suniva whom she had cradled in her arms since the moment of their homecoming. Later in the morning Camilla returned to her workshop and began the task of clearing up. Sarah and Anthony worked beside her, sifting through the debris, looking for anything that could be salvaged. It was a financial disaster. Makena, the seamstress, offered to help, but the other Kikuyu women were too terrified to set foot in the building. It could be bad luck to work in such a place. By late afternoon fatigue had overcome them, and Anthony insisted on closing up.

'After the horse has bolted,' Camilla said bitterly, her feet dragging, body aching with exhaustion as she walked back to the house.

In the sitting room Mwangi brought tea. Sarah's head was nodding, drooping with weariness, and when the telephone woke her it was almost dark outside. Lars answered and beckoned to her from the hallway.

'It's for you,' he said. 'Allie Briggs.'

'Sarah, my dear.' Allie's voice was cheerful. 'I hope you had a good Christmas. I tried to contact you on Christmas Day, but Mwangi told me you had all gone camping in the Aberdares with Anthony. Good plan.'

'Yes. But we got back to find something bad had happened here,' Sarah said, finding it hard to keep her voice under control. 'Camilla's workshop was broken into. Everything has been smashed to pieces. Jeremy Hardy and his *askaris* have been here since last night, questioning everyone.'

'Good God! I'm so sorry. The poor girl had only just got the whole thing up and running. Were the machines stolen? Is any of it salvageable? Do they know who did this, or why?'

'Nothing was taken at all,' Sarah said. 'It was pure vandalism. And it was on the anniversary of Piet's death. Jeremy doesn't like the implications. Allie, there's something really sinister happening here. It's frightening and I have this feeling . . .' Sarah trailed off, unwilling to articulate the fear that was mounting in her. 'Anyway, the police are here and now we can only wait.'

'You must be terribly upset. Hannah too.'

'Yes. And Lars is worried about their future here,' Sarah said. 'Anyway, for the moment we can only hope that Jeremy will turn up something in his investigation. Let's move on to something cheerful. How was your Christmas?'

'Good,' Allie said. 'I'm ringing you from Nairobi. You won't believe it, but I managed to drag Dan down here for a couple of days. He's really enjoying it, although he'd never admit it. And we have amazing news which may cheer you up a little.'

'Tell me.' Sarah tried to summon some enthusiasm.

'We had a call from Rabindrah,' Allie said. 'He has indeed persuaded his uncle, Indar Singh, to donate a brand new Land Rover to the project. We can hardly believe it. And the same Indar is willing to put a reconditioned engine into the old heap you're driving. What do you think of that?'

'It's astonishing,' Sarah said. 'I can't believe it.'

'Me neither,' Allie said. 'Of course Dan is full of dark suspicion.'

'Suspicion?'

'He says there must be conditions attached to such a big gift, particularly from a member of the Indian community. He's convinced there's a payback expected somewhere down the road, and Uncle Indar has an agenda of his own that will compromise us in some way. There are no free lunches, Dan says, and most Indians want something in return for anything they do.'

'I can understand his reservations,' Sarah said. 'It is a hugely extravagant gesture from someone you've never met, or even heard of until recently. Rabindrah must have remarkable powers of persuasion. I'd be more concerned about his agenda than his uncle's. He's very ambitious and he wants to get this book published with his name in big letters on the front, no matter what.'

'I still don't see what harm either one of them can do. So far we have everything to gain,' Allie said. 'They have no influence over our work, and they haven't asked for anything at all in return for this gift. Rabindrah has arranged for us to meet the uncle tomorrow morning. He has a big garage in Westlands, and that's one of the things I was phoning about. When he hands over the Land Rover he wants to put something about it in the paper. With a suitable photo.'

'Oh dear,' Sarah said. 'So there are conditions.'

'Those kinds of conditions are fine,' Allie said. 'A piece in the newspaper can only help us. As I pointed out to Dan. Anyway, you must come down for the handing-over ceremony.'

'When will that be?' Sarah realised that she could not refuse.

'I'm not entirely sure. It depends when Rabindrah can get the thing into the paper. I told him you'd phone, so here's the number. And Sarah?'

'Yes?'

'Try not to worry too much,' Allie said. 'I know this incident has come at a terrible time, but you have a good man in Jeremy Hardy, and friends around you. If this is a *rafiki* of Simon Githiri, I'm sure he'll be found. Now ring Rabindrah and see what he's been able to set up.'

Sarah dialled the number reluctantly, and he picked up on the second ring.

'I was hoping it would be you,' he said. 'Happy Christmas, if it isn't too late to say that. I take it you've already heard the news from Allie.'

'It's very generous. They're both delighted.' She tried to sound upbeat, but she was aware that her voice sounded flat.

'My uncle is suggesting a ceremony with a photo in the paper,' Rabindrah said, disappointed by her muted enthusiasm. 'It will be good for your elephants, and for Indar Uncle and his garage. Not that he needs any coverage. He has more work than he can handle. But he likes to be seen as a pillar of society, saving the world for future generations and all that.'

'I suspect he never thought of saving Kenyan elephants, even for his own generation, until you got to him.' Sarah could not help laughing. 'How did you pull it off?'

'He only has daughters, you see. Daughters are charming and beautiful, but they are also a liability until such time as they are safely married off, isn't it?' Rabindrah spoke the words with a strong Indian accent before switching back to his usual form of speech. 'I've always been his favourite nephew. He treats me like the son he doesn't have. But you will be meeting him soon, I hope. We're thinking of the day after tomorrow for the event?'

'I'll be there,' she said.

'We'll meet at the garage in Westlands, then. Allie knows where it is. Around three? The photographer would like to see you for a minute or two and discuss how to do the pictures.'

'Oh no.' Sarah realised that she too was expected to play a role in the ceremony. 'No. I don't want my picture in the newspapers. And it's not good that I have to leave the farm right now. I'm only coming down because Allie asked me to.'

He heard the change in her tone, and remembered that her fiancé had been killed around Christmas time. About a year ago.

'I understand this is not the best time for you,' he said. 'But it might be good to get away, even for a few hours and—'

'I've been away,' she said, her tone curt. 'Camping in the Aberdares over Christmas. But things were not so good when we got back here yesterday.'

Rabindrah listened with growing apprehension as she described the scene of havoc they had faced on their return.

'This can't be a random incident,' he said, grasping the situation immediately. 'The date makes it a definite statement.'

He questioned her about the extent of the damage and the initial conclusions of the police, and after a few minutes Sarah began to wonder if he was taking notes, preparing a sensational story that he could file as soon as she had hung up.

'I sincerely hope this won't become one of your headline pieces,' she said, cutting him off as he pressed her for further details.

'If it appears in the papers it won't be my doing,' he said, offended. 'But I think you need to keep at your friend Hardy. Make sure he follows up every detail, no matter how small. He should go over the old police report again, and look for any little point that wasn't followed up last time.'

A jolt of memory hit her. 'You said there was something lacking in the last investigation,' she said. 'What was that?'

'It was a minor thing, and—'

'Tell me.'

'There was nothing of importance,' he said. 'The police were very thorough.'

'Tell me, goddammit,' she said, her voice rising. 'You can't make insinuations like that, and then back off and leave me dangling. What was it?'

He was silent, taken aback by the flare of her anger.

'I'm sorry,' she said wearily. 'But you have no idea what this is like. How it feels to have the horror starting all over again, to be looking over your shoulder every moment. I was only beginning to get rid of the fear. We all were.'

'There was someone mentioned in the police files,' Rabindrah said. 'A priest who taught Simon Githiri at the mission in Nyeri. Looked after him when he was first brought there. Bidoli, his name was – Fr Bidoli. But no one ever interviewed him.'

'Why not?' Sarah was puzzled.

'He had retired from teaching and then he became ill. He was in hospital in Nairobi at the time of the murder He's old and rather forgetful, apparently. I suppose no one considered that he might have anything to add, and there was no point in troubling a sick man. But I thought someone should have gone to see him. He might have provided an insight into Githiri's character, or known his friends or someone connected with him. Even your inspector friend thought he wasn't working alone.'

'Did you follow up on the priest?' she asked.

'No. But I made enquiries, and he's still in Nairobi. In a retirement place for missionaries. Now that this has happened, maybe the police should talk to him. Or maybe you should go and see him yourself. You might be better able to jog an old man's memory than a policeman with a notebook and no tact. Because you are all vulnerable at Langani while there is someone around with a grudge connected to the farm . . .' He did not finish the sentence and the silence hung between them.

'No!' She tried to control her rising panic. She did not want to talk to anyone about Simon or even hear his name. It would be more than she could bear, to revive all the pain she had so carefully buried. And she was still not sure of Rabindrah's motives. 'No, I don't think I could talk to the priest.'

'Perhaps you could get a friend to go with you,' he said. 'Or I would, if you wish.'

'No. But thank you, all the same. By the way, how did you manage to read the police reports? I thought those things were confidential.'

'I'm a journalist. Every good reporter has ways to access such things.' He paused. 'I'd appreciate it if you didn't pass on this fact to Inspector Hardy. It could mean trouble for my source in the police department. He could lose his job.'

'I won't tell anyone.' Sarah was frowning. 'But it's hardly reassuring to know that confidential police reports are not secure. That people like you can read and interpret them whatever way they like. That's how things get twisted and put into the papers all wrong. It's not helpful at all, in my view.'

'There are responsible journalists,' he said defensively.

'Well, I hope you're one of them,' she said. 'I'll see you in Nairobi.'

After she had hung up Sarah sat for a long time, thinking about the retired priest and the faint possibility that he might throw some light into this new nightmare. At last she went back to the sitting room, knowing what she wanted to do.

'Rabindrah Singh's uncle is giving Dan and Allie a new Land Rover,' she said. 'And he's going to put a new engine in my old wreck too. Allie wants me to go to Nairobi for the handover. I'll have to stay the night, because it will take time to get the registration papers and so on. But I'll be back as soon as it's sorted out.'

'A new Land Rover?' Hannah stared at her, open-mouthed. 'That's a fortune. What do they want in return?'

'Nothing, it seems,' Sarah said. 'Although Dan asked the same question.'

'I wouldn't trust any of them an inch, those Hindis,' Hannah said. 'I'll bet you there's an expensive service agreement tied into it. There have to be strings attached.'

'Not that anyone can see,' Sarah said. 'And the Sikh community is known for charitable gifts. I often heard Dad talking about their generosity.'

'Take it and don't ask too many questions, is my advice,' Anthony said with a broad grin. 'Maybe the uncle wants to curry favour with the government, or with the wildlife organisations that are always in the market for cars. Whatever the reason, it's bloody marvellous. Although if Allie drives it regularly, Uncle Singh should be warned about including a service agreement.'

'That's true,' Sarah said, laughing. 'Can I use the phone and try to find a hotel room?'

'You can stay at my place,' Anthony said. 'There's no one there, and Joshua will look after you. It will give him something to do. I'll ring and fix it up if you like?'

'He can practise folding table napkins and lighting candles for you,' Camilla said, smiling for the first time. 'Otherwise he might forget everything I've taught him about the finer things in life.'

'Maybe you should go to Nairobi too, Camilla,' Hannah said. 'Stay at Anthony's place or with your father, until things get sorted out.'

'I'd prefer to stay here, with you and Lars,' Camilla said, and saw the unspoken gratitude in her friend's eyes. 'And Sarah will only be gone for a day or two.'

For Sarah, the thought of the house at Karen was suddenly daunting. In the year since Piet's death she had always been at Langani or Buffalo Springs, apart from one or two nights in a Nairobi hotel. Now she would have to face the prospect of a solitary stay in Anthony's cottage with its large garden, immediately after this new, inexplicable act of vengeance. But she could not think of any good reason to turn down the offer, and she did not want anyone to see her fear.

'Thanks, Anthony, that would be grand,' she said, with an attempt at a bright smile.

Sarah could see Camilla's influence everywhere in the house. She looked out of the window across the garden, telling herself that she had no need to be nervous. The neighbouring property was hidden from view by a band of shrubbery and a mass of bougainvillea, but it was close enough to be comforting. She would be fine, and it was time that she braved a night on her own. She gave herself a pep talk and then telephoned Dan and Allie who were staying with friends.

'Our chums are out for dinner tonight,' Allie said. 'So maybe you'd like to come and take pot luck with us? I can pick you up if you like.'

'I'd love to come. Thank you. But I'll make my own way over. What time?'

'About seven-thirty. See you later.'

Sarah replaced the receiver and turned her attention to the phone book. Her heart was hammering as she looked up the listings for Religious Orders, leafing through the pages until she found the number of the Consolata Mission House. Fr Bidoli, they told her, was in the retirement home in Mathari. She scribbled down the number and dialled again. Yes, it would be all right to visit, the receptionist said, but only for a short time. He had been in hospital again and he tired easily, but a brief visit would be good for him. Stimulating. Within minutes she was on her way.

The mission house was in an overcrowded area bordering a shanty town. The simple whitewashed building looked startlingly clean, its green-painted roof and small garden hemmed in on all sides by crumbling shacks with open drains and leaking roofs of rusted, corrugated iron. She pulled up outside, and sat for a few moments in the car, building up her courage. A variety of excuses slid into her mind. It was unfair to disturb the priest when he had recently come out of hospital, and he was unlikely to have anything helpful to tell her. She should go away and leave the poor man alone. But there was an outside chance that he might remember something about Simon's past, or about anyone that might have been close to him. She braced herself, and got out of the car.

'*Hodi!*' she called out as she went up on to the verandah. 'Anybody home?'

A young African in starched white shirt and trousers came out to meet her.

'Yes, madam, Fr Bidoli is here,' he said, in answer to her query. 'I will take you to him.'

He led her to a shady corner of the verandah where a figure reclined on a chair. The priest was old and fragile. His head was sunk on his chest, and folds of skin hung loose across his jaw. At one time he had evidently been plump, but now the sagging flesh was evidence of illness and decline. His face was deeply lined and he seemed to be sleeping. The white cassock he was wearing was slightly frayed at the sleeves and at the hem, and his hands were folded across his chest as though he had nodded off in the middle of prayer. Sarah was already regretting her intrusion. She stepped back, uncertain, and was about to turn away when the priest's eyes opened and she found herself the object of a shrewd appraisal. He studied her in silence for a few seconds, and then held out his hand in greeting. When Sarah took it in hers, she was surprised at the strength of his grip, and the warmth of the smile. She wondered how old he was.

'I'm sorry to have disturbed you, Fr Bidoli,' she said. 'My name is Sarah Mackay. I hope you don't mind me coming to see you. I know you've been ill, and I won't trouble you for long.'

'You are welcome, Sarah.' His English was heavily accented with the musical inflection of all Italians. 'What can I do for you?'

Now that the moment had come, Sarah felt the familiar constriction in her throat taking hold. She made a huge effort to keep her voice steady.

'It seems to me that you have some deep trouble?' Fr Bidoli sat forward a little, wincing as he shifted position. He took her hand again, and indicated a chair. 'Come, child. Sit down beside me. There is no hurry,' he said. He waited for her to seat herself as she struggled for composure. 'Tell me about yourself, first. Where do you come from?'

She found a certain calm in reciting the details of her childhood, taking time to describe her growing up at the coast, and her father's work. She told him about her years at the convent boarding school, and finally explained to him her connection with Langani Farm. At the mention of the place, Fr Bidoli nodded.

'Ah. I begin to see what has brought you to me.' He sighed and folded his hands. 'You have come about Simon Githiri.'

The mention of Simon's name opened the dam of her memories, and the whole story poured out of Sarah in a torrent of dislocated sentences. She talked about the lodge that Piet had built, and his pride in its completion. She described him then, laughing and golden as he had left the farm on that cloudless morning, wanting to check that everything was in place, ready for the opening and the first guests. He had promised to contact her in the afternoon and she remembered her growing unease when there was no call, and no response to her efforts to reach him on the radio. Anthony and Hannah had driven out to the lodge with her then, all of them thinking that Piet's vehicle might have broken down. But there had been no sign of him. They had searched the building, calling his name, looking for Simon who had accompanied him on the last, fatal day. There had been no trace of either one. Nor could they locate Kipchoge, the tracker and friend whom Piet had known and loved since childhood, and who had gone everywhere with him. Finally, Sarah had stepped out on to the viewing platform straining for a movement in the bright moonlight, or hint that might offer her some kind of lead.

She no longer saw or felt the hot Nairobi afternoon, as she sat beside the priest and allowed the forbidden images to crowd into her mind. She shuddered as she remembered the feeling of the hand clamped on to her shoulder, almost dragging her down in its strength and desperation as she turned to face Kipchoge, maimed and bloody, clinging to her, trying to tell her something, dying there at her feet. Moments later came the discovery of Ole Sunde, the night watchman, whose body had been slashed and torn to pieces along with Piet's dog. Then the frantic drive up to the ridge with Anthony and Hannah, listening to the hyenas cackling and calling through the night, praying that Piet had somehow escaped whoever had killed his companions, but filled with sickening dread. She had run ahead of the others towards the place he loved best, clambering up the last part of the hill in the darkness, fear lending her the strength to scramble over the rough scree. Close to the top she had encountered the male hyena, crouched low on the rocks above her, eyes glittering, mouth open and slavering, waiting to attack. In her head she could hear the whoosh of the spear through the air and the thump of the animal's body as it fell. The image that she constantly sought to suppress rose in her mind as she spoke. She saw the warrior, his feathered headdress and tribal ornaments gleaming in the moonlight, his face turned towards her. Simon Githiri. She pressed a clenched fist to her mouth, unable to find a way to tell the priest how she had, at last, stumbled on her love.

'I saw him, then. Piet. He was lying on the ground. Pegged out like an animal.' Sarah was gasping as she said the words for the first time. 'His body had been cut open, and his innards were spread out, his blood making a stain on the earth. I could smell his blood. And then I saw his face.' She stopped, her breath rasping, her arms wrapped around her in a hopeless attempt to stop the shaking.

'My poor girl, you do not have to—'

'Yes, I do. I have to say how it was. Because it lies in wait for me day and night, buried in my mind. Always there, no matter where I go or what I do.'

The priest nodded and took her hand, watching with compassion as she tried to stop the tears. It was several minutes before she was able to continue.

'He was so beautiful, you see, with his blue eyes and his smile that could melt the whole world. And his hair that was pure gold in the sun. But when I found him his head was dark and matted with blood. And his – his manhood had been cut off and stuffed into his mouth.' She was gagging now, as she tried to continue. 'And his eyes were gone, gouged out of his head with the sockets just gaping, bloody holes. Oh God.' She bent over and rocked to and fro, her sobs harsh and choking, tears pouring down her cheeks and falling on to the priest's frayed cassock. 'Oh God, I can never close my eyes and look for Piet without seeing that. Never.'

Fr Bidoli sat still, holding her hands, his lips moving in soundless prayer.

'I told Hannah that there was nothing we could have done, even if we had been there an hour before,' she said, her voice strained. 'But his blood had not congealed. It was still oozing, and the hyena had only just found him. They never take long to track fresh blood. And no matter how hard I try I cannot stop myself from imagining him, lying there in agony, blinded, crying out for us to help him. But we didn't get to him until it was too late. Who knows how long it took him to die, or what pain and fear he endured. Piet died alone. I'll never know how it was in those last moments, and that is unbearable in itself.'

'It is hard to think of it that way,' the priest said.

'I've never talked to his sister about it. I never wanted Hannah to wonder whether he might still be alive, if we had found him earlier.' She wiped away the tears. 'But maybe we could have saved him, if I'd insisted on going to look for him straightaway. Or I could have been with him, to comfort him in those last terrible moments.'

'My child, when we are faced with tragedy we always think of what might have been. But that cannot change what is. Suffering is the greatest of all mysteries. You must not scourge yourself with what you might have done. It was not ordained that you should be there.'

'I've tried to tell myself that. I've asked myself if he would have wanted to go on living, with his body mutilated, and his eyesight gone. With everything taken from him—' Sarah gripped the arm of her chair, her every nerve and muscle straining for control. 'Because he loved to look at the world, to be a part of everything in it. He loved to ride his horses and walk over his land. And he loved me. We loved each other so much. I don't believe he would have wanted the kind of life that would have been left to him, if we'd found him earlier.'

'May our merciful Lord help and comfort you in this terrible loss,' the priest said, placing his hand on her head. 'I hope that you are able to pray, to find comfort in that.'

'Pray? I cannot pray any more, Father. Because no merciful God could have allowed this to happen,' she said. 'No merciful God would have destroyed him at the peak of his life, when he was so beautiful. When our life together was about to begin and we were so happy. So blessed and grateful. The cruelty of it is beyond me.'

'You were going to marry?'

'He had asked me the day before. But we never had time to be together. Not even a week or a month to share.' The tears began again. She rested her head in the priest's cupped hands and sobbed out her misery as he stroked her hair and prayed. He held her as she railed against the pitiless power that had granted her a brief insight into love, and then snatched its promise away, leaving her cleft in two and wandering in a desert of loneliness and desolation.

'And Simon Githiri, the boy you knew.' She looked up at Fr Bidoli at last. 'Why would he do such a thing? Why?'

'You are absolutely certain he did this?'

'I'm certain.' She wiped her eyes and rubbed at her swollen cheeks and eyelids. 'Piet took him in, gave him the chance of a bright future. Simon had no grounds for what he did. I do not understand it.'

'There are never any simple answers, Sarah. When man chooses evil, terrible things occur. I understand that you are angry with God, for the act that has destroyed your future, your whole world. So you cannot pray, for the man you loved, or for yourself.'

'I was brought up to pray. But I cannot find a God of love or compassion in any of this, Father. No one should suffer what Piet suffered. I cannot communicate with a God who allowed one man to do that to another.' She shuddered, and her eyes stung and ached with the shedding of more tears.

'So what is it that you want of me?' the priest asked with great gentleness. 'It is not just for words of comfort that you have made this journey to find me.'

'You heard that Simon was killed by hyenas? When that happened we thought it was finished. That's what the police said. That it was over. But three days ago, on the anniversary of Piet's death, there was another act of destruction on the farm.' She told him in a few words abut Camilla's workshop. 'It cannot be a coincidence,' she said. 'It's all beginning again. So I thought perhaps you could tell me something about Simon that might give us a clue as to what made him kill Piet. And maybe you know who his friends were. Because that could also be linked to what is happening now. Perhaps there is someone you saw him with, someone who wants to continue what Simon started.' She slid to her knees beside him. 'I came because I believe you are the only one who might tell me something, any small thing you remember, that will show us what to do. Otherwise I do not think we can live our lives like normal human beings, ever again.'

The priest looked away from her into the distance. For a minute, Sarah feared he was going to refuse, out of some sort of principle. But then he began to speak.

'Simon was a small boy when he was brought to us. He looked about four years old, but I think he must have been seven or eight. His size was probably a result of bad nutrition. He did not speak for a long time. At first we thought he had an impediment. But when he had been with us a while, and he was no longer hungry or frightened, he began to make sounds. The man who left him with us did not give any name. He was clearly afraid, and he left the mission as quickly as he could. He told us the child's name was Githiri. His parents had been killed, he said, and there were no close relatives who could take care of him.'

'How were they killed?' Sarah asked.

'At the time we thought perhaps they had been the victims of a Mau Mau massacre. These took place often around Nyeri. Many Kikuyu compounds were burned, the people killed and their animals butchered, if they did not take the oath.' Fr Bidoli paused, collecting his thoughts. 'There were also women in the villages who were secretly feeding the men who had joined the gangs hiding in the forests of the Aberdares. The police and the army came regularly to question them, and some of the troops were as barbaric as the oath-takers they were hunting. People were imprisoned or shot in those days if they were captured up in the forests. Everyone was afraid. So perhaps the boy's parents were caught up in that. We baptised him Simon, because he had no name or papers. He was silent, but from his eyes I knew that he was intelligent. I liked the boy, and when he eventually began to talk I gave him extra tuition to bring him on. I provided him with books – encouraged him to read.'

'He told me about the books.' Sarah's voice was heavy with sadness. 'I gave him one of my own, you know. On the last morning, before he left with Piet, I gave him an anthology of English literature. A prize that I had won as a student.' She brushed her hand across her face to dry new tears. 'Oh, Father, why did I not see what he really was? Do you remember anything special that he might have told you? Or anyone he knew?'

Fr Bidoli shook his head. 'No one ever came to visit him. He worked hard and he was not troublesome. I believe he was happy as the years passed, and he grew strong and became more confident. He got on well enough with the other boys, but he was always a little apart. Not gregarious as most children are, but of a good disposition.' He paused. 'Until about three years ago.'

'What happened then?' Sarah felt the current of anticipation run through her body.

'A man came to see him. A relative who said he wanted to take Simon to visit his family. No one had come before because they would not have had the money to feed an orphan, or send him to school. That was why they had left him at the mission. But now that he was ready to work, to take his place in the world, his clan wanted to meet him. Simon was excited, but also nervous. He asked me not to tell anyone why he was going out, because he did not know if the visit would be a success. I could see that he would not want to lose face. I respected his wish and I was glad for him. Young men are not given holidays, or time off, from the mission. They must work to repay the food and schooling they have received. But I always tried to arrange a little freedom for my students, when it was possible.' The old man smiled, and shrugged. 'I gave Simon some money, so that he could bring a gift to his new family, and I told the other priests that he was going to Nanyuki to visit someone who might give him work. He was away for two weeks.'

'And then he came back?'

'Yes. But he was changed.'

'Changed in what way?' Sarah leaned forward, not wanting to miss a syllable of the reply.

'I could not say, exactly.' Fr Bidoli was frowning. 'Only that he had a different way of looking at me. At all of us. Withdrawn, you might say. Even sullen. He did not smile any more. He did not read. In his free time he chose to be alone.'

'Did you ask him what had happened when he met his family?'

'Of course. He said they were not his clan after all. That it had been a mistake. I thought he was trying to overcome the disappointment of not finding the relatives he had hoped for. It was also possible that the so-called cousin had tricked him, in the hopes of getting money from him. Or that his clan had rejected him for some reason. That has happened before. I asked him if there was anything else worrying him, but he said nothing. I said that perhaps he had found the meeting with his family harder than he had expected, and I told him he could always come and speak with me about whatever troubled him. But he told me nothing more.'

'But he stayed on at Kagumo?'

'For a short time, yes. Then, about a month later, he said he wanted to go and look for work in the towns. He did not want to stay at the mission any longer,' Fr Bidoli said. 'I felt that he was right. He was a young man, ready to live his own life. His childhood days had been confined, and now he wanted a taste of freedom. He had obtained his school certificate with good results. I thought, also, that after the disappointment of not finding his family he should be encouraged to make a life for himself. So I got our Father Bursar to write him a reference and to give him some money. He left right away. That was about two years ago. I never saw him again.'

'Two years ago?' Sarah thought back, calculating Simon's movements. 'But he only came to Langani in June of 1965. Where did he go during the interim?'

'He must have been working somewhere else.'

'I don't think so. His only reference was from the mission, and Hannah understood that he had come straight from there. He never said that he had worked for anyone else.' Sarah was puzzled, and a knot began to form in her stomach. This could be the first clue leading them to someone else Simon had possibly worked for, or lived with. 'Did you ever hear from him at all, after he left?' The priest shook his head, troubled by her question. 'Do you have any idea at all where he might have gone, looking for work?'

'I became very ill soon after he went away,' Fr Bidoli said. 'I was moved to Nairobi, because I had to spend a lot of time in the hospital.' He smiled with resignation. 'Well, if I have to say the truth, it is that I am still too often in the hospital. I am old now, and there is not so much time left for me.'

'I'm so sorry.' Sarah had only just met the priest, but she recognised in the gentleness of his voice a man who had seen the pain and confusion of humanity, and who understood. He took her hand again and she half closed her eyes, drawing comfort from his spirit.

'When I was in the hospital last year, one of our community came to visit me,' the priest said. 'He told me that Simon had come to the mission in Nyeri, asking for me. It must have been four or five months after he left. He was upset, apparently. And agitated when he found that I had gone. They gave him my address in Nairobi, but I never heard from him.' Fr Bidoli passed a hand wearily across his eyes. 'Maybe he could not get a job, and he fell in with people whom he recognised as bad. He may have come to ask for help, for some counsel. And perhaps I could have said something that would have changed his mind about what he was going to do. But he might not have listened to me, and for some reason God ordained it otherwise.'

'Do you think, as I do, that he had planned what he did? That he came to Langani to kill?'

'I do not know. Perhaps no one will ever know that, my child.' He sighed, and she saw that his hands were shaking a little and that he was very tired. 'I am sorry I cannot tell you more. But I will pray for you, and for your friend Hannah and her family, and for the young woman whose workplace was destroyed. I pray that you will receive protection, and comfort, and that there will be something to show you the way.'

'Thank you. I wish I still had your faith, Father. I think I could accept illness, or an accident, but not that unspeakable savagery. I cannot pray to that kind of God.'

'I understand this. But do not give up on prayer, even if you cannot accept what has happened now. In the end it will help you, more than anything else.'

'You've been very kind, Father, and very patient.' Sarah did not want to embark on any further discussion about faith. Or prayer. 'I've kept you from resting, for far too long.' She took a small notepad from her bag and wrote down her address in Buffalo Springs, and the radio phone link. 'In case you remember anything else.'

'I will tell you. And you must promise me something in return.'

'If I can, yes.'

'Do not blame yourself. You could not have guessed what was in Simon's heart, any more than I did. We all fail, because we cannot see the whole tapestry, only the little strands that are close around us. And do not give up on God.' His eyes were full of wisdom and kindness. 'You are angry now – that is part of your mourning and it will pass. But anger can consume you. You must let it go. Then you will have need of Him, more than ever.' He sank back into his chair. 'Come to visit me, whenever you need to talk to someone who cannot be hurt or frightened by what you say or feel. That can be important.'

She stood looking down at him for a few seconds, wondering if she would ever see him again. Then she spoke softly. 'Goodbye, Father.' As she walked down the verandah steps she thought that he said something, but when she looked back he seemed to be asleep.

At Anthony's house the fire had been lit in the sitting room. Joshua hovered, waiting to see if there was anything he could do for her, tactfully avoiding any direct look at her blotchy face and swollen eyes.

'I'm going out for dinner this evening,' she said. 'So you don't need to stay, Joshua. Thank you.'

She decided to pour herself a stiff drink and take it to the bath. The prospect of having dinner with Dan and Allie was no longer appealing, and she lay in the steaming water for a long time, utterly drained, sipping from her glass and wondering if she could back out. But it was too late, and she felt it would be rude to cry off at the last minute.

Dan greeted her at the door.

'Great to see you, kid. Come on in. Fortunately, our hosts have an excellent *mpishi*, so we're not going to be victims of Allie's cooking. She may be a brilliant scientist, but a chef she ain't!' He was laughing as he led her into the sitting room.

She stopped short in the doorway. Rabindrah Singh had risen from the sofa, smiling. It took Sarah a few seconds to recover from the surprise of seeing him there. She was less than pleased and Dan noticed her hesitation. He took her arm firmly.

'Rabindrah introduced us to his uncle, Indar Singh, this afternoon. A remarkable guy by any standards, and just as enthusiastic about his generous gift as we are. I hope he'll come and visit us up at the camp one of these days. You'll meet him yourself tomorrow.'

'I'm looking forward to that,' Sarah said, puzzled that Dan's reservations about Indar Singh had evaporated so quickly.

'We tried to get you at Anthony's place earlier, but the houseboy said you had gone out,' Dan said. 'Now, I've mixed a pitcher of ice-cold Martinis. Up to James Bond standards. Try this, kid. We saw the new Land Rover by the way, and it's one hell of a car. So the least we could do was to invite Rabindrah round this evening to thank him.'

'Come now, Dan. It is my uncle who is donating the car.'

'With a bit of arm twisting,' Dan said.

'Has anything developed at Langani that might help the investigation?' Rabindrah turned to Sarah.

'There's nothing new up there.' She had feared that he would mention the priest, but after his initial enquiry he confined himself to general pleasantries.

'I'm so sorry about what happened at the farm.' Allie joined them, embracing Sarah and accepting a Martini. 'I want to warn you that these are lethal concoctions. One of Dan's favourite tricks. You don't notice the effect until you stand up, and then – wham!'

Sarah had never tasted a Martini before, and she was enjoying the icy bite of the gin and its distinctive aroma. She wondered if it would cause any ill effects, after the whisky she had drunk in the bath. But after a short time she was surprised to find herself relaxed and extremely hungry. The sick feeling she had carried away from her meeting with Fr Bidoli gradually dissolved. During dinner she drank several glasses of red wine, her head buzzing slightly. The talk was mainly about Buffalo Springs, and Rabindrah was keen to return and to draft the remaining text for the book. As the night wore on, they all seemed to have drunk a prodigious amount. The men had an extraordinary capacity, and Allie appeared quite capable of keeping up with them. Sarah realised that she must be the only one who was very drunk. She could hear herself babbling, becoming increasingly incoherent, but nobody seemed to mind. Dinner came and went in a haze, and she had no recollection of anything she had eaten. Then they were back in the sitting room, and when the coffee had been served and the fire was burning low, she knew it was time to leave. But now that the moment had come, it was harder than she had anticipated. Anthony's cottage seemed remote and solitary, a place where she would be alone with her visions and nightmares. She was suddenly afraid. Dan leaned across and patted her head.

'Looks like it's time for your beauty sleep, young lady,' he said, looking at her with some amusement. 'Why don't you crash out here?'

'Good plan,' Allie said, coming to sit beside her.

Sarah was finding it difficult to focus and she was desperately sleepy. She thought hard, but it was like trying to wade through cotton wool.

'I think I should go,' she said at last.

She was not too sure how she would drive. Rabindrah was speaking. His outline was blurry, but she thought he was smiling. Always smiling, with those shiny white teeth in the dark face.

'If you want to go back to where you are staying, I will drive you,' he said. 'It's only ten minutes from here. Dan or Allie can collect you in the morning. Bring you back here to get your car.'

She concentrated hard. A bed down the corridor, not having to walk very far, that was an attractive proposition. But the people who owned the house would be back soon. She didn't fancy explaining to total strangers that she was too drunk to leave. And now that she was well and truly pickled, it would probably be easier to spend the night in a strange house on her own. She did not want Allie and Dan to know how cowardly she was. Her head was spinning and she blinked her eyes hard.

'Sarah?' Allie's voice was coming from a great distance. 'I think you conked out on us there! Maybe we should just cart you off to bed.'

'No, no.' Sarah sat up straight. 'I'd rather go back to Anthony's place – if you really wouldn't mind driving me, Rabindrah? I'll just go and freshen up first.'

She stood up carefully and made her way to the cloakroom where she splashed water on her face, in an attempt to clear her head. Her legs felt rubbery. Balance was tricky. But at least she was feeling no pain. Feeling nothing really. That was good. Feeling nothing was just fine. She was fine. All she had to do was to remain upright long enough to get to Rabindrah's car. She smiled at herself in the mirror.

'You are as drunk as a skunk,' she mumbled, stabbing a finger at her reflection. 'If the nuns could see you now!'

She opened the door, and began to make her way slowly towards the hall. Her head was reeling and she put out a hand to steady herself against the pulsating walls. She could see Allie talking earnestly to Rabindrah, her hand on his sleeve.

'This is a very hard time for her. Piet's anniversary, and now the trouble on the farm. She's very vulnerable, so look after her. We're extremely fond of her, Dan and I – she's a very special and extraordinary young woman.'

Sarah stopped in the shadows, holding her breath as Rabindrah took Allie's hands in his own. He was still smiling.

'I shall care for her like a baby,' he said, turning as he heard Sarah's unsteady steps.

'All ready, then.' Her bright words sounded slurred, even in her own ear. She wanted to protest that she was not a baby and had no wish to be treated like one. She wanted to let everyone know, in a dignified manner, that she could look after herself perfectly well, thank you. That was all. But the effort of getting the words together was too much, and she allowed Allie to shepherd her out to Rabindrah's car.

'I didn't say goodnight to Dan,' she said.

'I'm sure he'll understand. And we'll see you tomorrow. I'll come and get you, but I think you'll need your sunglasses.' Allie was grinning as she shut the car door. 'Best sleep on for an hour or two in the morning – I'd say you might need it!'

Sarah muttered her thanks and shut her eyes tight as they drove off, hoping to minimise the ominous lurching in her gut as the car gathered speed. She did not want Rabindrah to know that she was afraid to be alone, but she did not seem to have any control over her tongue. Her words and phrases seemed to melt into one another and disappear inside her head, so that she was not sure if she had actually said any of them, or just dreamt that she had. The noise and smell of the engine were making her dizzy and nauseous. She wished she had the energy to open the window.

'I don't think I'm very well,' she said solemnly. 'Actually, I think I might be sick. Yes, I might be very sick. Vomit is what I mean, actually. I've always suffered from car sickness, you know.'

When she opened her eyes again the car had stopped, and Rabindrah was half lifting her out into the driveway. She stumbled on the doorstep, holding on to him tightly, laughing because she could not keep her balance. Once inside, she leaned against the doorway, trying to take in her surroundings. But the walls were moving in a strange way and she had begun to feel very ill. Her knees gave way without warning and she started to slide to the floor. It was a shock when he picked her up unceremoniously and carried her down the corridor.

'What are you doing?' It was an effort to ask.

'I am taking you to the bathroom, because your host will not wish you to puke on his Persian rug. Point at the right door. Good. Here we are, then.' The noise had brought Joshua from the back of the house, and he was staring at the Indian with a mixture of astonishment and grave suspicion. Rabindrah issued instructions over his shoulder.

'The memsahib is not well. Please open the bathroom door for me, and then go to her bedroom and turn down the bed. Straight away.'

Joshua sprang into action and they made the bathroom just in time. Sarah sank to her knees over the toilet bowl and Rabindrah held her head as she retched and moaned, and felt every vestige of sophistication and dignity being flushed away with the shameful results of her excesses. When she slumped against the bath, empty and shivering, he cleaned her face, and sponged her neck and shoulders. Then he led her to the bedroom and helped her into bed. His face loomed over her as he held out a glass of water and two white tablets that she swallowed without protest. She thought he might be frowning, but she could not make out if he was angry, concerned, or plain disgusted. At least he was not smiling and she was grateful that his voice was so low and soft. Focus was proving difficult. One thing was very important. She had to get it across.

'I am not a baby, you know.' She frowned in annoyance. 'I don't need a nursemaid. I can look after myself. No problem. I just can't stand up at the moment, that's all. You don't have to baby me, no sirree . . . wheee!' She lay back on the pillow. 'Not a baby. I should make that quite clear. Virgin, yes. Baby, no.' She giggled, and then gave another small moan. 'Bloody hell, I'm making a right dog's dinner of this. I'm sorry. I'm so sorry.'

'Goodnight,' Rabindrah said, patting her on the head. 'I'm sure you will not have trouble with sleeping tonight, but I will stay here at any rate. In the circumstances, I'm sure your friend Mr Chapman won't mind. And tomorrow we can talk.'

A beam of sunlight pierced her eyelids and made her head thump. Sarah squinted at her watch, trying to let as little light into her brain as possible. God! It couldn't be half past eleven! She sat up quickly, then lay down again with a whimper of pain, feeling as though someone had unscrewed her neck and her head was about to fall off. What was this? Where the hell was she? As her memory returned, she turned her face into the pillow and groaned. What a show she had made of herself! Puking in the bathroom, babbling on about virgins and babies! Oh God! Oh God! She was a shameful, walking disaster. What must the wretched man have thought of her? All respect would be gone. How would she be able to work with him ever again on the book? On anything. And Joshua! She had an image of his impassive features swaying past her as she was carted along the corridor. What if he told Anthony? Of course he would tell Anthony. She would never live this down.

She sat up again, very cautiously this time, wondering if there was anywhere she could hide for at least a week. But as she swung her legs over the side of the bed the door opened and Rabindrah was standing there. She looked at him in horror. Had he spent the night here? He looked disgustingly fresh and healthy although he had drunk a great deal last night. But he could down gallons of it without any effect, like Dan and Allie. It wasn't right. Sikhs weren't supposed to drink alcohol. Even she knew that. He was a lapsed Sikh. Like she was a lapsed Catholic. Sarah turned her head, and the slight effort made her wince.

'Not feeling so good today?'

He was smiling again, his teeth gleaming white, so that they seemed to hurt her eyeballs. She was torn between shame and fury. Now he was going to patronise her. It was an effort to meet his gaze. She cleared her throat, and addressed him formally.

'I owe you an apology. I was absolutely out of order last night.'

'Yes. Completely out of order. Nothing working properly at all.' He laughed loudly, his head thrown back. 'Joshua is making breakfast.' He saw her grimace and advanced into the bedroom. 'I have a foolproof remedy for hangovers that I learned on dark mornings in the north of England. You will take these aspirins with water, and then a whole bottle of Coca-Cola. After that a hot shower, and then breakfast with bacon and eggs and sausages, and a Bloody Mary and strong coffee. Then, I guarantee you will feel much better. Ready to take delivery of a Land Rover, in fact!'

It sounded like torture but she followed his instructions meekly and tried to think of a way to explain her behaviour. When she had finished breakfast, she was surprised to discover that Rabindrah had been right. She felt almost human again. He too had put away a large plate of food, several cups of black coffee and one of the tomato and vodka drinks laced with Tabasco that made her cough. He had not spoken much during the meal, but now he looked at her directly.

'I really am sorry,' she said again. 'For last night. I'm not used to that much alcohol. I should have stopped sooner.'

'It was nothing,' Rabindrah said. 'You were very civilised, compared to some I have seen. But now we had better get a move on.' He glanced at his watch. 'Dan called earlier on and I told him I would drop you off there to pick up your car.'

Sarah stared at him in dismay, realising that her employers must know the whole story.

'I will meet you at Indar Uncle's garage, at three o'clock,' he said. 'Before that I have some interviews to write up, so we will have to leave soon.'

She nodded. He was being terribly polite, she thought, but distant. He had not mentioned Fr Bidoli at all. Either he was the soul of discretion, or he was trying to extricate himself from her problems without causing himself further embarrassment.

'Thank you. But you don't have to drop me. I can get a taxi. It's not far.' She did not want him to think she expected any further help or attention from him.

He put a hand to his forehead. 'Sorry. That reminds me. Your friend Anthony telephoned and I said you'd ring him back.'

Sarah's heart sank.

'I took the liberty of telling him I had come to collect you for the handing over of the Land Rover,' Rabindrah said.

His expression was unreadable, and she could not tell if he was laughing at her or not. Of course he was laughing at her. She went to the phone and dialled Langani.

'Sarah? Is everything all right?' Lars's voice was concerned.

'Yes. I had a stomach upset last night, so Rabindrah drove me back here after dinner. He was very kind.'

She knew it sounded lame but she did not wish to expand with Rabindrah sitting in the next room, probably listening with amusement to the conversation.

'Is Hannah there?' she asked, contrite.

'I'll put her on. See you tomorrow.'

'I know it was stupid,' Hannah said. 'But I was afraid you had gone out somewhere and been held up on the way back. There are robbers in Nairobi who do that at night. They block the road and wait for cars, and especially for women driving on their own.'

'I wasn't alone. Rabindrah gave me a lift, because it was so late.'

'What was he doing there?' Hannah sounded accusing. She still had not forgiven the journalist for his appearance at Langani.

Sarah sighed. 'Look, I was nervous and upset last night. I drank far too much at dinner, and when it came to the moment, I was scared of going back to Anthony's on my own so late at night. Can't you understand that, Han? I hadn't realised it would be so hard to be by myself.' She waited for Hannah to say something, but there was no response so she plunged on. 'I was really tipsy and when I finally got back here, I didn't think of phoning anybody. I should have left a number where you could reach me, but I never thought of that either. My brain just wasn't working properly.'

'Why didn't you stay with Dan and Allie if you didn't want to be alone?'

'Hannah, I was dead drunk, for God's sake! So Rabindrah offered to drive me back here. I nearly threw up in his car and when I got here I conked out till this morning. And that's the brutal truth of it. I behaved like an idiot altogether, so please don't make me feel any worse.' She knew she sounded sharp and defensive, but it really was nobody's business whom she spent her time with, or where.

'I'm sorry.' Hannah's voice changed key. 'For being a stupid cow, and for getting in a panic over nothing. Everything is so hard since the workshop was smashed up. And you're my lifeline, Sarah, 'specially now. Just keep in touch, heh? Please.'

'I promise.'

Sarah put down the phone. Rabindrah was standing on the steps that led to the garden, smoking a cigarette.

'Everything all right?' he asked.

'Wonderful. We're all one big happy family. Shall we go?'

She picked up her bag, ready to leave the house and take care of the everyday tasks demanded of her. But her body was aching and sluggish, and she wished there was somebody she could lean on. Someone who would lift all the burdens and the grief and the fear away, and let her sleep. She closed her eyes. Out on the veldt, Piet was standing in the sunlight, his back to her. She called out his name, and he turned. Stared at her from empty, leaking eye sockets. Her hands flew to her face, and she gasped and bent over. Rabindrah moved quickly to her side, and she let him take hold of her arm and turn her round to face him. She could hear the sound of birds in the treetops, smell the honeysuckle that covered the porch over the front door. The sky was a perfect blue and the day was sunny and warm in God's beautiful world, where the man she loved had died in unspeakable agony.

'Talk to me,' Rabindrah said.

'There's nothing to say.' She made an attempt at a bright smile, but he could see the tears brimming in her eyes.

'If you don't talk to someone, you will fall apart,' he said.

'But there's no one,' she said. 'No one who could know what it's like to be in my skin. To be this lonely and afraid. To wake up every morning and know that no matter what I do I'll never see him again. Never, as long as I live. And now it has all been brought back.'

'You went to see the priest.' It was an intuitive statement, and he was filled with compassion when he saw that he had guessed the cause of her distress.

'Yes.' It was a relief to tell someone. 'He's a good man, and we talked about Simon Githiri.'

'Do you want to tell me what he said?'

She did her best to repeat what Fr Bidoli had told her, and when she had finished she shrugged, resigned and helpless.

'I didn't tell anyone that I was going there,' she said. 'I wouldn't want Hannah to start galloping down a false trail, hoping to find someone who knows why Piet was killed, and why we are still being attacked at Langani. And I don't know if Fr Bidoli is just another dead end. So all I've really done is to bring back my most terrifying nightmares.'

'I can see how painful that must be.'

'But there is something else.' She hesitated and then the words came out in a spate of misery and distress. 'It's something that I cannot say. An idea that sounds insane, and it would hurt too many people to express it.'

'What is it?'

When she finally said the words her voice was so low that he had to lean forward to catch them.

'What if he's not dead?' she said.

'Who?' He was puzzled.

'Simon Githiri.'

'But he is dead. You were the one who saw him that night, standing on the ridge. So you were able to identify what he was wearing, after the police found the headdress and the ornaments close to the remains in the forest.'

'That's true,' she said in a low voice. 'But I have always felt that I would have known if he had died. If the hyenas had killed him in the forest. People have made fun of me since I was a child because I have these premonitions, but they're mostly true. And now the terror has begun again at Langani and I can feel the same menace in the air, hanging over the farm. And I am afraid that Simon is alive today.'

Chapter 7

Kenya, January 1967

'This is the busiest time of year for tourists, Mary, and I'm offering to supply you exclusively,' Camilla said. 'I have an exceptional selection of clothes and accessories, and you know you'll sell every item.'

'You promised me three times this amount of stock, my dear. And if your workshop has been put out of commission, how are you going to go on supplying me?' Mary Robbins ordered coffee. 'This is a far cry from our agreement, and my shop isn't dependent on a few tourists. Every well-dressed woman in Nairobi buys from me, and I'm not limited to any season. If I take on a new line, I spend time and money promoting it. Obviously, my main concern is continuity.'

'I'll be up and running again in a matter of—'

'So, in view of what's happened, I think we should make a new arrangement. Let's agree that you will start supplying me in, say, nine months from now.'

Mary did not want to discuss alternative proposals. In her view, there was something radically wrong at Langani Farm. She did not believe that Hannah and her husband would stay on after the incident that had taken place on the anniversary of the brother's death. If the Olsens left now, they would not be the only farmers to abandon the attempt to hold on to their land in the difficult circumstances of a newly independent African country.

Camilla would probably end up leaving too. It seemed extraordinary that the girl had set up a business in Kenya, when she was the toast of London and New York. Her affair with Anthony Chapman had brought her back, but Mary did not believe it would last. He was too much of the tomcat around town. Camilla was one of many glamorous women who had fallen for the charms of a white hunter, and the excitement and romance of being out in the bush. It was incredible how frequently it happened and how completely they were taken in. But the reality of everyday life in Africa was another matter, and the girl looked too fragile to stay the course. Mary remembered her mother who had been one of her best customers. Marina Broughton-Smith had been a beauty too, and it was sad to think that her life had been so brief. Rumour had it that George was queer, but his wife had turned a blind eye to it during their marriage. God only knew what sort of relationship Camilla had with her father. Precarious at best. All in all, it would be better if the girl went back to Europe and her glittering career. It was possible that the workshop at Langani would never reopen. There was too much uncertainty about the whole situation and there were plenty of other suppliers pounding on Mary's door with quality merchandise.

'I'd like to sell your clothes,' she said to Camilla, trying to inject a more friendly note into the discussion. 'They're beautifully designed and made. But I'm about to open shops in the three most expensive hotels in Kenya, and I need more volume than you can guarantee right now. Let's talk again in six months or so when your workshop has reopened. Then we'll see if something can be worked out.'

Camilla's heart sank, but she was determined to remain calm and to make a deal with Mary Robbins. She would have to leave for London in a few weeks to fulfil the commitments she had made to Tom, and to Saul Greenberg. The situation at Langani was borderline with cash flow very tight. Some of the labour had walked out, and Lars was struggling to keep the farm running efficiently.

'I put most of my available cash into setting up the workshop,' Camilla had told him before leaving for Nairobi. 'Once I've done these new contracts I'll have money I can use to start up again. And I'll soon receive my percentage on the first batch of Saul Greenberg's dresses. But it will take a few weeks for that to happen.'

'You don't have to go on, you know.' Lars was impressed by her willingness and determination. 'We would understand only too well if you didn't want to continue at Langani. Maybe you should look for a suitable place in Nairobi that you could work from.'

'No,' Camilla said. 'If you're staying on, then I'm staying too. I have to be in London towards the end of February, as you know. I'm booked for several big fashion campaigns. But Hannah can run the workshop while

I'm away. She's been with me nearly every day, training the *bibis*, and supervising the cutting and sewing. She can take care of things. It's a question of teaching some new women, if none of the old ones will come back.'

For several days after the destruction of the workshop, Hannah had been tight-lipped and morose, living in a closed-off place in her mind, unreachable.

'I don't know what she is thinking,' Lars had said to Camilla. 'At night she turns her back on me, won't talk to me at all, although I know she's not sleeping. All day she sits with the baby beside her, saying nothing. Maybe she wants to pack it in. Leave Langani.'

It was on New Year's Day that Hannah made her announcement.

'We don't know what is happening here or why,' she said, her expression haggard, her eyes shadowy with fatigue. 'But I am not giving up the farm because some bloody *kaffirs* are trying to frighten me.' She saw Lars wince at the word she had used and flicked her hand, paying no heed to his disapproval. 'My grandparents created this place, and my father fought the Mau Mau to keep our land. Pa went away so that his son could hold on to Langani, and Piet himself died believing that we have a right to be here as citizens of this country. So, I am going to do whatever it takes to keep the farm. Because of what they have already given to this country, and for Lars and Suniva and me.' She turned to her husband. 'We will open the lodge Piet built, and repair Camilla's workshop. We will stay on our own land, Lars, and in what is our own country. And no one will take it from us, by fear or by force.'

Camilla had listened, admiring the conviction and courage that inspired the words. Her own first instinct had been to turn away from the ruins of her business, and move to Nairobi where she could re-establish herself. But when she heard the catch in Hannah's voice, saw her glance at Lars and the baby and at the gun on the shelf beside her, Camilla had decided to stay.

But she needed money. Urgently. She had spent most of her available funds on the renovation and running of the workshop. It had needed a new roof, new plumbing and electricity, partitions and shelving. In addition she had purchased the machines and materials, paid out three months of salaries, and insisted on contributing to the household expenses at the farm. She needed cash to tide her over the next few weeks, and Mary Robbins was the best source.

The waitress brought more coffee and set it down, spilling a little in Camilla's saucer and splashing a tiny drop on her white linen shirt. She glanced up, faintly irritated, and found herself looking at one of the most beautiful girls she had ever seen. A Somali, she thought. Or an Ethiopian. The face was a perfect oval, set on a long, swan-like neck. Her eyes were almond-shaped and fringed by thick, curling lashes. The nose was fine, slightly tilted, the mouth round and full and sweet, like a ripening fruit. A possible solution flashed into her mind in that instant.

'I understand what you're telling me, Mary,' she said. 'I know you would prefer a larger inventory. But I have an alternative plan to put to you.'

'If it's risky or expensive, I don't want to hear about it,' Mary said.

'I think we should create a demand that can't be filled,' Camilla said. 'Sell a number of exquisitely made articles that only come into your shop two or three times a year, in very small amounts. True couture items. I propose that we organise a fashion gala and charity dinner sometime in the next two months, and show the clothes and accessories. On Valentine's Night, for example. Yes, that would be good. We'll pick a cause and donate some of the takings – limit the tickets and sell them at a huge price. I'll put on a Paris catwalk performance. Me, and two other girls, one Indian and one African. The new face of Kenya fashion. We'll show the inventory I have right now, and create a real scramble to buy items that will never be available again.'

'You couldn't arrange something like that in such a short time,' Mary said. 'And publicise it too.'

'I can get one or two famous names to fly out from London for the show. Party people who are always in the papers and the glossy magazines. There are several who owe me a favour or two.' Camilla was already wondering how she could possibly pull off such a thing, and whether there was a single glamorous personality in Europe who would be willing to support her. 'I'll train the two other girls myself, and I can promise you they'll look as though they've done the best collections in Paris or London.'

'Where would you find these girls?' Mary was sceptical. 'It sounds like an awful lot of work for no guaranteed result. This may be a small city, but people here are quite sophisticated and they do expect high standards.' She was silent for a moment. 'Who do you think would come out from London? It's very short notice.'

Camilla could see that she had struck a chord. They parted half an hour later with a date for delivery and payment of her available inventory. She sprang up from the table and looked around the café for the waitress, but there was no sign of the girl.

'Where's the manager?' she asked the waiter who came to clear the table.

'Is there something wrong?' he asked, a little surly.

'No. Everything is fine,' Camilla said, leaving him an excessive tip. 'I was just wondering – what is the name of the new waitress?'

He wrinkled his large nose, and pursed his lips disapprovingly. 'She is Zahra. A Somali. But she has gone now.'

'Could you give her a message?' Camilla asked.

He shook his head. '*Hapana*. We do not mix with that one,' he said. 'She is not doing good things when she is off duty. And she does not talk to us.'

'I can imagine,' Camilla said. 'Where does she live?'

'*Sijui*.' He shrugged, pocketed the tip before she changed her mind, and made a show of attending to another customer.

In the cramped office the secretary smirked as she explained that the manager had gone out and she had no idea when he would be back. And no one knew where Zahra lived. Except the manager himself. Camilla drove back to her father's house where she was staying while Anthony was out on safari. She should have been with him but there was no chance of that now, with the organisation of the fashion show. She lifted the telephone.

'I'd like to book an overseas call,' she said. 'To London.'

Tom Bartlett laughed out loud when he heard her plan. 'You must be bloody joking, darling,' he said. 'You can't set up something like this in the timeframe you are talking about. No one I know is going to jump on a plane and take pictures of an amateur fashion parade in darkest Africa. I'm still living in the real world, remember?'

'You're getting on the plane, for one,' she said. 'Come on, Tom, use your imagination. This can be an amazing thing. I'm sure Joe Blandford would come, too. There's a Somali girl here who is so beautiful you'll make a fortune if you sign her up. I promise you, the fashion editors and photographers will go mad when they see her. You need only be in Kenya for a few days.'

'You're suffering from delusions,' he said. 'The heat must be getting to you. Or your jungle man has put something in the water that's affected your wits, just as I predicted. What date were you thinking of for this crazy event?'

She spent the remainder of the day making the basic arrangements and by evening she had extracted a reluctant promise of support from both Tom and Joe Blandford.

'I'm going to arrange a fashion gala,' Camilla said to her father as they had dinner together that evening.

'That old witch Mary Robbins ropes everyone into her extravaganzas,' George said. 'How did you get involved?'

'It was my idea, not hers. This will be the most gorgeous spectacle Nairobi has ever seen.' She explained the reasoning behind her plan, and was disappointed to see that George was frowning when she had finished.

'I needed to placate the old witch, as you call her,' Camilla said. 'Fortunately, I have just enough stock to keep her happy. I've been bringing the finished things to Anthony's house and storing them there, otherwise I would have lost everything. I had to ship two thirds of them to Saul Greenberg yesterday. If I'd let him down completely it would have cost me a great deal more than the sale of a few dresses in a Nairobi boutique. Meantime, I need Mary's cheque in my local account, to set everything up again at Langani.'

'I think you should wait until the police get to the bottom of this incident,' George said. 'There's something sinister about that whole situation, my dear. It's not safe up there, and I'm sure Hannah would understand if you didn't reopen the workshop for the moment.'

'Why do you use the word "sinister"?' she asked, and was irritated when he looked away and did not reply. 'You always evade the issue of Langani. Hannah is trying to save her farm and you, of all people, should understand that. You seem to have forgotten how Jan and Lottie looked after me, when you sent me away to boarding school up there. They acted like parents for all those years, while you were busy in Nairobi, or you had flown off to London again with hordes of politicians. And the beautiful Marina was up to her neck in charity events and cocktail parties. I saw more of Sarah's parents, and of the van der Beers, than I ever did of you. Langani was more like home for me, until Mother ruined it all.'

'Camilla, there's no sense in going back over old wounds. Right now, Hannah has a good, sensible husband who is more than capable of looking after the farm, better than Jan van der Beer ever did. And there's no reason for you to feel you have to make up for an indiscretion of your mother's, or to take risks now.'

'She was responsible for Jan and Lottie leaving Langani,' she said. 'She was the one who said Janni was on a blacklist drawn up by the new government. That he would probably be thrown off his farm after Independence because of something he'd done years ago. You must know what that was.'

'I don't know anything for certain,' he said. 'Conjecture in such circumstances is foolish and dangerous, and doesn't help anyone. And it's all history now. If you're determined to reopen your workshop on the farm, let me advance you the money. And then you won't have to run around in circles just to please an old witch like Mary Robbins.'

'That's sweet of you.' Camilla flashed a smile, seeing that she had hit a sensitive spot in his memory, wondering if he sometimes felt guilty about Jan and Lottie's departure from Langani. 'I'm not going to accept your offer, though, because this is my business and I can get by on my own. It's a temporary problem. From March onwards I'll have plenty of cash. More money than you, probably. And in the meantime, Mary's payment should be just enough to see me through.'

'My dear, you're awfully loyal and brave,' he said. 'But I still don't think you have enough security at Langani. I know, I know,' he said, holding up his hand to prevent her from butting in. 'You don't want to abandon Hannah. But it's not safe up there, Camilla. We all thought that Piet's death was like a line drawn under the past. A settling of scores. And now there's this new incident.'

'What scores?' She stared at him, troubled. 'You said something like that when he died. You said it might be something to do with the Mau Mau years. But Janni wasn't the only farmer who fought during the Emergency. Bill Murray next door, and most of the other settlers around there, all joined up to fight the Mau Mau. No one is attacking them or their livestock, or wrecking their property. Besides which, Jan and Lottie aren't even there any more.'

'What's their situation?' George asked. 'Are they going to stay in Rhodesia?'

'I don't know,' Camilla said. 'Hannah spoke to them at New Year. We all did. She told Lottie what had happened to the workshop. She said that she and Lars were staying on, and that as her parents they should come back. Make a show of strength. Lottie cried, but Janni wouldn't talk to any of us. Hannah thought he'd probably been drinking.'

'She's a brave girl,' George said. 'They're a tough breed, those Afrikaners.'

'Oh, it's all so dreadful,' Camilla said. 'Whenever I think of the happy times at Langani, when I was a child, I want to cry. Janni was so wonderful then, letting us drive the tractor, teaching us how to ride and fish, making us laugh. I remember planting roses with Lottie in the garden, and standing beside her in the kitchen, learning how to make delicious Italian puddings with thick, yellow cream from her dairy. And Piet was full of plans for the way he would run the farm one day. We had such lofty dreams, and they've all turned into bloody nightmares.'

George saw that his daughter was on the brink of tears and changed tack. 'When do you have to go to London?'

'Soon after this gala thing,' she said. 'But I'll only be away for a matter of weeks.'

'Well, think about all this while you're in London,' he said. 'It's always good to step back and look at a problem from a distance. Gives one a much better perspective. There are plenty of places in Nairobi that would be suitable for a workshop.' He smiled suddenly, but his tone was pensive. 'You'd see more of Anthony, and it's lovely for me too, having you around.'

'Are you happy here, Daddy?' Camilla caught a hint of loneliness and reached for his hand. 'I know you have friends from the time when you were with the High Commission. But—' She stopped, unsure as to how much she wanted to ask or to know. 'Are you lonely? Do you miss London. Do you miss Giles?'

He was shocked at the bluntness of her question, and she saw the effort he made to recover his customary air of unruffled confidence. 'I'm very happy to be living here again,' he said, finally. 'And I'm enjoying the challenge of this job.'

'And what about Giles?' Now that she had brought up the subject of her father's lover, she wanted to pursue it to a conclusion.

'It was too complicated. I have friends here that your mother and I . . . well, it would have been inappropriate right now. So soon after she died. Besides, he didn't really want to come to Kenya,' George said, his face taut. 'There would have been difficulties with work permits and the restricted number of things he could do here, and so on. I'd prefer not to discuss it, actually.'

'I'm sorry,' Camilla said, surprised at his answer, remembering how Giles had begged her to accept their relationship and his love for her father. 'I wasn't being nosey. I only wanted to see if you were . . . well, to know that you're not lonely.'

'I'm not,' he said firmly.

'Do you think you could get your friend Johnson Kiberu to be one of the V.I.P.s at this gala?' It was her turn to change the subject swiftly.

'I'm sure he'd love it. I'll make up a table and include him, and his wife.'

'Thanks, Daddy.' Camilla kissed his cheek.

'Will Anthony be around for this?'

'It's hard to say. He's very busy, but he is supposed to be in town for four days from the twelfth of February. So I hope he'll be here.' Camilla crossed her fingers, smiling.

'He wants to marry you. I wouldn't keep him waiting too much longer if I were you,' George said.

'You're not me, Daddy. And I need to be sure.'

'My dear, he's madly in love with you. He's a young man with rare qualities who loves this country like you do, and wants to contribute to its future. He's on a new committee I've set up to study two interesting issues. One is the question of culling wildlife and subsidising the sale of the meat to feed the hordes of people suffering from protein deficiencies and malnutrition. And the other is the translocation of endangered animals from agricultural land into National Parks. He's had some very interesting and sensible things to say on both subjects.'

'He told me he'd spent an afternoon up a tree a few weeks ago. Running away from what he had taken to be an unconscious rhino that got up again and charged everyone in sight.' Camilla was laughing as she remembered Anthony's vivid description. 'He said you were no help at all, and that you were roaring with laughter as he ran for his life.'

'Yes.' George was chuckling. 'But he's always badgering me for more funds to pay for these operations. He's very persuasive, I might add. He convinced me to hand over a fat cheque last month for the relocation of some Rothschild's giraffe later this year. Anyway, my dear, I think he's sown his wild oats. I'd be happy to have Anthony as a husband for my beautiful, valiant daughter.'

'We'll see,' Camilla said, tilting her head at him and smiling. 'Maybe Valentine's Night will be significant for more than a fashion gala.'

She returned to the coffee shop on the following morning and watched as Zahra served the crowded tables. It was strange, Camilla thought, how the customers mainly did not notice her beauty, simply because she was black.

'I'd like a large coffee with cream,' Camilla said when her turn came. 'And I want to talk to you when you've finished work.'

'I have done nothing wrong.' The girl's eyes widened with alarm. 'I am not making any trouble here.'

'I know,' Camilla said. 'I want to offer you a job. I think you can do better than being a waitress. That's all.'

It did not take long to uncover Zahra's story. She had come over the Kenya border into the semi-desert of the Northern Frontier area, in an attempt to escape a life of drudgery and hunger in a Somali village. For the first few months the man she had travelled with had set her up in a brothel in Maralal where she was frequently beaten. Finally she had run away, begging a ride with two Italian tourists who were returning to Nairobi after a hunting trip. They rented an apartment in the city for two weeks, and used her as they wished. But they had bought her clothes and taken her to restaurants, and one of them had given her a gold bracelet and some money when he left. She had found a hovel in which she could live, and then looked for a job. To her surprise, her beauty had worked against her. She was constantly propositioned by the owner of the coffee shop and by several of his customers. Fearful of losing her position, she submitted to her employer whom she hated with a burning passion.

Camilla found a room for her in a flat shared by two young Nandi women training to be secretaries. They did not like or trust the Somali girl, but the money Camilla contributed to the rent made them accept her grudgingly. From then on, Zahra spent her days learning the art of modelling, walking miles up and down Anthony's living room and verandah, and then up and down again, and yet again, until Camilla had taught her the insolent, deliberately sexual sway and slide of the international catwalk. Her hair was frizzed out in a large Afro, but Camilla took her to the hairdresser and insisted that she have it cropped close to her head, so that nothing would take away from the smooth beauty of her features. The only problem was Zahra's feet. They were large and broad and rough, from her years of walking barefoot. After days of pumice stone and pedicures it was still impossible to find shoes that looked good on her, and she did not walk well in high heels. Camilla decided on open footwear. She bought beads and sequins and other ornaments in the Indian bazaar, and had them sewn on to plain leather sandals. The girl herself was clever but wary. Once or twice she did not turn up for a training session, and Camilla wondered if she had gone back to her old trade. The only thing that had been a certainty in her earlier, sordid life.

It was through Rabindrah that an Indian model was found.

'This is Rabindrah Singh,' George said to his daughter, as they took their places in the Taj Mahal restaurant one evening. 'He's working with—'

'I know,' Camilla said, shaking hands with him. 'You're doing the book with my best friend Sarah. I gather you'll soon be going back to Buffalo Springs.'

'I wish I could spend more time up there,' he said. 'I did start out focused on the financial success of the book, and the recognition it would bring me. But I'm now captivated by the elephants and the Briggses' project, and by Sarah herself.'

'I had planned to go back with her after the new year,' Camilla said. 'But it didn't work out.'

'I'm sorry about your workshop,' Rabindrah said. 'Is there any progress with the police investigation?'

'None,' Camilla said. 'But I'm determined to keep my business going. So I'm organising this fashion gala to raise money for the repairs at Langani. I suppose you wouldn't know an Indian girl who'd like to be one of the models for my show?'

'I have a cousin who might do it,' he said. 'I could arrange a meeting with her, if you like.'

Camilla hesitated. She did not want to be in the position of having to reject one of the journalist's relatives. He might be offended, and that could reflect on his work with Sarah.

'I'll send her on the pretext of delivering something to you,' he said, as though he had read her mind. 'That way you can take a look at her without being obliged to go any further, if she's not right. But I think she might suit you well. She walks beautifully, because she is a good dancer. Or you could try the lady in the corner over there.' He was grinning as he indicated a couple seated on the far side of the restaurant. 'Twinkle Kiberu. She has aspirations in that direction. In any direction that will bring attention, in point of fact.'

George made a small exclamation. 'Johnson and Twinkle. We'll stop at their table on the way out.'

'Nobody could be called Twinkle,' Camilla said, laughing. 'It's absurd.'

'She is both.' Rabindrah was grinning. 'Come, and we'll introduce you.'

Johnson rose to his feet and shook hands with Camilla, betraying no sign of recognition. She was relieved that he had apparently forgotten their ill-fated encounter in London when she had gone to his suite in the Savoy to ask for help in protecting the wildlife at Langani. He had listened to her concerns about poachers and security for a brief time, and then lunged out in a clumsy but rough attempt at seduction.

'Your father and I are allies and friends,' Johnson said. 'And Rabindrah sometimes gets coverage for us in the papers. George, I don't know if you have met Twinkle.'

The young woman stood up and leaned across the table, her ample breasts threatening to flow out from the low-cut bodice of her dress. Her waist was tiny, and she had wide hips and a large, perfectly rounded bottom that she displayed to full advantage as she turned to retrieve a fallen napkin. She had straightened her black hair and tied it back in a small knot. Her face was exceptionally pretty, with full cheeks and lips that were luscious and painted an iridescent pink. When she smiled her teeth were very white, and she giggled and fluttered her eyelashes as she took Rabindrah's hand.

'This is Camilla Broughton-Smith,' he said. 'You've seen her in all the newspapers and magazines. And maybe at the designer shows in Paris or London.'

He was well aware that she had never been to London or Paris, but she nodded her head with enthusiasm. 'I know them, yes,' she said. 'I would love to come to one of your shows there. In London.'

'You should get Johnson to take you with him, the next time he goes to England,' George said. 'In the meantime, Camilla is arranging a fashion show here in Nairobi, and I hope you will both join my table.'

'My goodness, she oozes sex appeal,' Camilla said as they left the restaurant. 'It's like an aura around her. What a woman. But she'd never fit into anything I've made, with that magnificently big bum. I need to design a whole new line of clothes for girls that shape to wear. Now that really would be fun.'

Rabindrah's cousin, Lila, had a cascade of raven-black hair, and a demure but sensuous way of moving. Her gestures had the stylised precision of a classical dancer, and her natural, effortless grace made her look as though she were floating across the ground. For three weeks Camilla practised every day with the two girls, making them model at least twenty outfits at each exhausting session, checking the speed at which they could change, experimenting with make-up and hairstyles and jewellery. Mary Robbins sent out cards and was bombarded with calls for more places. In London, Tom arranged airfares for himself and Joe Blandford. *Tatler* agreed to send someone to cover the event for their social pages. It was the height of the season and there were numerous European socialites and aristocrats on holiday in Kenya. Mary Robbins hastened to track them down and issue special invitations. The *Daily Telegraph* agreed to publish an article from Rabindrah, based on the new multiracial sophistication of the former colony. A generous donation had been pledged to a hospital for children with incurable diseases. The local press and radio stations were thoroughly excited about the entire event.

When Sarah arrived from Buffalo Springs she was greeted by a version of her friend that she had never seen before.

'I don't know how I could ever have thought of doing this.' Camilla was wan and distracted. 'We can't get the lighting right, and the sound system was truly dreadful this afternoon. Thin and brassy. And I don't think anyone at the back of the room will hear the introductions.'

'It hardly matters, as long as they can see the clothes,' Sarah said. 'They'll speak for themselves. Oh my, I never thought I would see you as anything but calm and organised. I rather like this new panic thing.'

'Oh, shut up, for God's sake. Look, I ordered white flowers for all the tables, and they've sent these multicoloured arrangements that make the place look like a bloody funfair. And the catwalk is about four feet shorter than they said it would be. I've got a potential disaster on my hands, and you're laughing at me. What's the news on your book?'

'Dan is doing a last check on Rabindrah's manuscript before it is sent to London. I think we will be offered a contract after that. I might even have to go there myself to look at the layout.'

'By the way, I didn't see the Briggses on the list of people coming tonight,' Camilla said. 'I'd so like to meet them.'

'I offered them tickets, but they said it was too much razzmatazz for their taste.' Sarah was smiling. 'Too much for Dan, anyway, although I think Allie was furious with him for not coming down. I tried to dodge that particular discussion.'

'Rabindrah's aunt and uncle are only coming under duress,' Camilla said. 'Well, the uncle is willing, but I gather that Kuldip Auntie is not entirely pleased.'

'She's doubtful about semi-naked girls, one of whom is her niece, displaying themselves in public. I met her at the Land Rover event. She reminded me of the nuns who tried to drum a sense of shame into us at the very thought of bare flesh. And failed – in your case, anyway.'

'Well, Lila's parents booked a table for their friends,' Camilla said. 'I hope they won't be too shocked.'

Anthony arrived three days before the gala, but Camilla saw little of him during the run-up to the show. She was working frantically, shuttling between his house and the hotel where the gala would be held, supervising the pressing of the clothes, setting up hanging racks and a long table of accessories which would be set out in the order of wearing. It was early afternoon when he appeared, and she was on her knees adjusting an embroidered hem on Zahra's dress. Lila was sprawled on his sofa, dressed only in her underwear, eyes closed, legs and arms spread out as she took full advantage of a few minutes' catnap before it was her turn to practise again. Anthony stood in the doorway, gaping for a moment at the scene in his living room before clearing his throat.

'Am I in the right house? I used to live here. A quiet bachelor's residence. But I could learn to prefer this.'

Camilla rose to kiss him. Lila, hearing a man's voice, leapt up in alarm and ran into the bedroom in search of clothing. Zahra stood very still, looking at him in silence from her tawny eyes, like a wild creature ready to spring to an attack, or to flee.

'I didn't think you'd be here until later this evening,' Camilla said. 'It's a long drive from Meru.'

'I flew in with the clients and left one of the drivers to bring my vehicle.' He looked around the room and whistled. 'Well, well. Joshua will never be the same again.'

'He's banned from the main part of the house while the girls are here,' Camilla said, laughing. 'This is Zahra, from Somalia. And here's Lila. You know her cousin, Rabindrah Singh. We were planning to work for another hour or so. This is the final selection of clothes for the big night, and we're trying to decide on the jewellery and all the other junk that goes with them.'

'You can do a private showing for me,' Anthony said.

'No, we can't,' Camilla said, sternly. 'Why don't you do the boring paperwork you always bring back? And by the time you've gone through all that we'll be finished too.'

'Can you have dinner with my clients tonight?' he said. 'They'd love to meet you.'

'That would be fine,' she said, although she had planned a quiet supper in the cottage for just the two of them. 'But from tomorrow on, I don't have a moment to spare. And I may not be all that much help tonight because I'm dead tired.'

Tom arrived from London on the following morning. He brought Joe Blandford with him and a make-up specialist called Gino who went to work on the two girls, muttering about the problems of dealing with dark skin and frizzy hair. Anthony made it clear that he was amused by the three men, and quite unimpressed by their so-called careers in the frivolous world of fashion.

'I can't believe two grown men can spend all day talking about the colour of a pair of shoes, and whether or not you should have false eyelashes,' he said to Camilla. 'I think the photographer has designs on you. And the other one definitely has designs on me. Can't you get rid of all these posers and stay at home tonight?'

'Are you out of your mind?' she said. She was half laughing, but disappointed at his disdain for the friends who had travelled so far to support her. 'They've come all the way from London for this. For me. Besides, we're all supposed to be having dinner at the Grill tonight with the old bat who reports on the British social scene for *Queen*. The people she's staying with are throwing the party. Do you have any idea at all what is happening here?'

'None,' Anthony said, grabbing her around the waist and slipping his hand up under her skirt to stroke the silky skin of her thighs so that her knees threatened to buckle. 'But I know it will be magnificent. A real blast. Come to bed with me. I want to make love to you. Now. Let's close the door and forget all this other stuff for an hour or two.'

Camilla extricated herself from his grasp, exasperated that he considered her work trivial. She threw him a withering look and left the cottage, her car spitting gravel on the driveway as she roared away for a last meeting with Mary Robbins.

In spite of his grumbles, Anthony joined the dinner party and made an effort to amuse the guests from London. The dinner table was long, and after the dessert had been served several people changed places. Tom came to sit beside Camilla.

'Brilliant, darling,' he said. 'Everyone is thrilled with the whole thing. They all think they're back in the Happy Valley days. I only hope your jungle boy isn't going to shoot me. I can see we're never going to be pals. But he's been handing out his business cards to some of the punters, so it can't be all bad for his business interests.'

Camilla smiled and looked around for Anthony. He was at the opposite end of the table and she saw that Zahra was on one side of him. She was staring at him with rapt attention as he told one of his safari tales, her eyes fixed on his face, her full mouth curving upwards in a smile, long arms resting on the table, almost touching him. Camilla felt a twisting sensation in her gut and looked away. But later, when they were at last alone in the quiet of the small hours, he held her and stroked her and made love to her with ardour.

'You're so beautiful,' he whispered, kissing her throat. 'And clever too. Maybe too clever and sophisticated for this bushbaby. I still don't know what you're doing here with me.'

'Don't be so silly,' she said, surprised by his remark. 'You were great company this evening. All those London people were riveted by your stories.'

'Not usually my kind of thing.' His voice was already slurred with sleep.

'I saw you telling Zahra tales of high adventure.' Camilla could not stop herself from raising the subject. 'She seemed spellbound.'

'Nothing like the tale she told me. What a frightful life. It's fortunate that she has such stunning good looks, otherwise she'd never have escaped. She's a brave girl.'

Camilla was about to respond, but changed her mind. The girl would never have risen above her sordid circumstances without her help, but she did not want to point that out now. Instead, she reached out to take Anthony's hand and turned to kiss him. But he had already fallen asleep, and for a long time she lay with her eyes wide open in the dark and tried to convince herself that she was, and always would be, the love of his life.

Lars and Hannah arrived on the morning of the gala. They had brought Esther, the ayah, to look after Suniva, so that their brief time in the city would be their own. The girl had never been to Nairobi before and she was overwhelmed by the traffic, by the numbers of people in the streets, by the tall buildings and broad, flower-lined avenues. It was all too large and frightening for her, and she was relieved when they installed her at George's house with the baby. Lars and Hannah spent the day together, dawdling over lunch in an Italian restaurant, and shopping for a few items that were a pleasurable extravagance in their uncertain circumstances. It was late in the afternoon when Sarah joined them, fresh from a meeting with the African Wildlife Foundation. George served drinks before leaving for the gala, and they raised their glasses to a successful evening. At the hotel, Hannah went backstage for a brief moment and hugged Camilla fiercely.

'I love you, and you're brave and wonderful and it will be a success,' she said. 'Lars and I, we know how much you've done for us, and tonight will be your reward. You know, I didn't think he'd come. With everything up in the air at Langani, he was worried about being away, even for one night. But then he said we had to be here to show you what a great thing you're doing for us all.' She peered over Camilla's shoulder through a chink in the curtains at the top of the catwalk. 'Oh no! Oh no, no!'

'What is it, Han? What's the matter?'

'It's bloody Viktor,' Hannah said. 'He's sitting about four tables back. Oh God, if Lars sees him—'

'Lars won't see him. Go down to our table right now, and change the place cards so that Lars is sitting on the same side as Daddy with his back to the room. Stay close to him all evening. Keep cooing over him and holding his hand so he doesn't notice anyone but you. And warn Sarah that you may need help. Where exactly is Viktor?'

Hannah pointed him out and disappeared to change the cards. Camilla took a deep breath and headed for the dressing room. Both girls were suffering from stage fright. They sat in front of the mirror like nocturnal creatures frozen in the headlights of a car, their make-up unable to mask the dread in their eyes.

'Get up,' Camilla said. 'We're putting on our first outfits now, and we're on in fifteen minutes. The moment you walk on to the stage the terror will go. I know, because I've been twice as frightened as you are now, but I've done it. The lights and the people and the music will carry you through. We're all beautiful. A trinity of goddesses, and this is our great night. *Harambee*. Let's go.'

It was a triumph from the first moment. They moved down the catwalk, swaying to the music. The dresses were provocatively short, with cap sleeves and collars and hems embroidered in bright silk thread, the shapes taken from swirling African designs that Camilla had found on Maasai and Kikuyu clothing, on pots and shields and water gourds. Longer skirts and jackets followed, beaded and tasselled and cut on the bias. Trousers had decorated pockets and seams. Shoes and boots and sandals came in exuberant colours, with matching handbags made of canvas and leather and velvet, the straps and clasps decorated in the same manner. Kaftans and evening dresses glittered with starbursts of semi-precious stones, feathers and seed pearls sewn into arm bands, seams, necklines and hems.

The finale produced a standing ovation as Zahra appeared at the top of the runway, her skin lightly oiled and gleaming in the subdued light. Her gold halterneck dress plunged at the front, revealing the curve of her breasts, the thin silk barely concealing her nipples. The skirt was slit up one side and her legs moved in slow, sinuous motion, exotic and feline. A tassel hung down her bare back, weighted by pieces of pink quartz, and around the crown of her head she wore a band of gold, fashioned into a serpent. Lila walked behind her, in an evening coat made from shot silk that reflected the light, and changed colour with every step. Her long hair had been braided, threaded through with sequins, and her earrings formed a glittering cascade. It was Camilla who brought the show to an end, drifting out on to the stage like a lost spirit, the one remaining spotlight trained on her. She moved, trance-like, down the runway into the heart of the audience, her arms spread out, chiffon sleeves beaded with silver and fluttering like diaphanous wings. The white dress was almost transparent, floating like a cloud around her body, worn over an embroidered slip that shone like a mirage. Her feet were shod in sandals made from white leather, bound with thin straps of glass beads and pearls. When she reached George's table she looked down at her father and her dearest friends, and blew them a kiss. And then the lights went out and she was gone, disappearing like the ghost of beauty into the sudden darkness.

There was an electric silence followed by wild applause before the lights came on strong and the music loud, and the three girls appeared to take their bows. Behind the stage they hugged one another again and again, adrenalin still coursing through them. Mary Robbins rushed into the makeshift dressing room, ecstatic. Guests crowded at the door and had to be dispersed. Tom elbowed his way through the crowd, shouting Camilla's name, grinning broadly as he reached her side. Behind him, Anthony pushed past a couple of journalists and a photographer and waved a hand over the crush of bodies.

'I can't believe what you did tonight,' Tom said, throwing his arms around Camilla. 'In the middle of bloody nowhere. In darkest bloody Africa, for God's sake. You'll help me sign up those girls tomorrow, especially that luscious black bombshell. Joe is panting for a chance to do some pictures of her in the jungle. Everyone out there is bowled over. What an amazing bird you are. A bloody fucking little genius! But you're wasted here, my darling. You've done your trial time, just like I suggested. Proved you could do something brilliant, all by yourself. And now you can stop playing games with the noble savages and the farmers, and good old Tarzan who obviously has no idea what you're worth. Not a bloody clue in his shell-shocked little head. It's time you came home, darling.'

'Of course I could do it,' she said, putting her arms around his neck and laughing up at him. 'You should have had more confidence in me. I told you exactly how it would be. I said I could make a life for myself in Kenya. That it wasn't about him. And I was right. On all counts.'

Standing in the doorway, Anthony's face reddened and he pushed forward again, seething with anger. But Camilla was surrounded by raucous, jostling admirers and she did not notice him as he tried to move into the circle of her success.

It was almost an hour before the press had finished with her and she made her way into the restaurant. Everyone else was already seated, and Zahra had chosen a chair on Anthony's left. Sarah frowned as the Somali girl set out to charm him, and she looked around for Camilla. But her attention was quickly diverted by the unwelcome presence of Viktor Szustak. He was sitting with a group of Nairobi artists who were known for their appetite for alcohol and orgies, and more recently for experimental drugs. For the moment he was engrossed in conversation with his immediate circle, and did not even glance in the direction of the main table. Lars had been placed between Twinkle Kiberu and Hannah, and it was clear that he was mesmerised by the sight of his wife in an evening dress he had never seen her wear before.

Camilla arrived and sat down on the other side of Anthony. She kissed him on the cheek, but he did not respond and she felt a twinge of unease for which she could find no explanation. The tide of her success swelled around her, and she allowed herself to revel in the pride she saw in her friends' faces, and the pressure of her father's hand when she stood to acknowledge the congratulations of guests. She drank the first glass of champagne very quickly and then sipped at the refill, watching with amusement as Tom dedicated himself to the business of seducing Lila.

Initially, Sarah had been dismayed to find herself between Rabindrah and Johnson Kiberu. She did not want to be reminded of her drunken experience with her cool, professional colleague whom she had not seen since the day of the handover, and she had no idea what she might say to the black politician. But she soon found that in Johnson Kiberu, she was talking to a man who understood all the advantages and problems of conservation.

'Education is the key,' he said to her. 'It's slow, but it is the only way to achieve balance in a country where the need for arable land and livestock is always going to be at odds with the necessity to protect our wildlife.'

'It won't be easily resolved,' Sarah said. 'It's political and tribal, and international too. A tricky set of ingredients.'

'It's a difficult mix in our halls of legislation,' he said. 'The fact that Kenya's wildlife has become an international issue is a double-edged sword. We are bombarded by recently arrived experts who are often academics, and not experts at all. Many are too idealistic. And there are people here who will take advantage of this and prevent large areas being set aside for conservation, in order to claim it for themselves. But I have met Dan and Allie Briggs several times, and I am impressed by their work and their attitude. In fact, I hope to visit you within the next few weeks. Perhaps I'll travel up with George who is a sensible man in all these matters. Have you known him for long?'

'Oh yes.' Sarah was smiling at the memory of those years. 'I went to school with Camilla. And with Hannah, too. We've all been friends since childhood.'

'In George we have a good friend in common, then,' Johnson said. 'I will look forward to visiting you in Buffalo Springs. And I hope you will give my *salaams* to the Briggses. We need balanced people like them, to help and to teach.'

Camilla ate her food in a daze, realising with surprise that she was hungry and that she had not sat down or relaxed during a meal for a long time. As they drank their coffee she heard Hannah make a small sound of dismay, and looked up to see Viktor leaving his group. But although he glanced at them for a brief moment, he made no attempt to approach their table.

'Another of your admirers?' Tom leaned towards her with raised eyebrows, his voice heavy with suggestion.

'God, no. He's an architect and a well-known stud,' she said.

'Unlike the terrific chap you have here tonight,' Tom said. 'He's exactly as I'd imagined him, your great lover. I can see you're not the only one who has the hots for him, darling.'

The runway had been rolled away and the band arrived to play dance music. Anthony and Zahra rose together and walked on to the small dance floor. Camilla looked down into the black depths of her coffee cup, trying to mask the jealousy and disappointment that had lodged like poisoned darts inside her.

'Dance with Camilla.' Sarah prodded Rabindrah urgently.

'What?' he said, with an expression of surprise that was comical. 'Why?'

'Just do it,' she said. 'Do it now.'

Hannah sat beside her husband, holding his hand, waiting for Viktor to burst in on the evening and ruin her pleasure. But when she finally summoned the courage to steal a glance in the direction of his table there was no sign of him, and she gave a silent prayer of thanks.

'He's gone,' she whispered to Camilla. 'I was terrified that he'd come over, and there would be a scene, or even a fight. We're leaving early in the morning, because Lars doesn't want to be away for another day. I only hope Viktor doesn't turn up at the farm again, because I don't know what would happen then.'

'If he didn't come near you this evening, then I don't think he'll bother you again,' Camilla said. But she could see that Hannah was not convinced.

'Will you come back to Langani before you leave for London?' Hannah asked.

'Probably not,' Camilla said. In the distance she could see Anthony, now sitting at another table, talking to a middle-aged woman with expensive jewellery. As she watched, Zahra appeared at his side and introductions were made. The Somali girl joined the group and accepted a glass of champagne.

'I think I might even fly back with Tom,' Camilla said.

Her voice was utterly forlorn and Hannah was filled with compassion. 'Men are such fools,' she said. 'Plain stupid when they get the scent of some conniving little bitch. But it doesn't mean anything, even though it's hard to stomach.'

'Come, Han. We must do some dancing.' Lars took his wife's hand and Hannah gave herself over to making the most of the glittering evening.

The floor throbbed with people and Zahra was making no secret of her attraction to Anthony, dancing close to him, spinning and twisting her long body, looking at him with liquid-brown eyes and a smile that was openly inviting. Camilla ordered more champagne and set out to dazzle her guests, stopping randomly at different tables to talk to people she had never met or seen before, dancing with Johnson Kiberu and Rabindrah, with Lars and her father, flirting outrageously with Tom. The distance between herself and Anthony grew and the room buzzed with excitement and gossip as the party blazed on through the night. It was George who finally decided it was time to leave and Sarah went with him, since she would be starting out for Buffalo Springs at dawn. Camilla was very tired now, and she searched the crowd for Anthony, anxious to repair the rift that had opened between them, and to prise him away from Zahra. But there was no sign of him and she sighed to herself and made her way to the dressing room to freshen her make-up.

They were standing together in the deserted corridor, Zahra leaning back against the wall, one arm draped snake-like around Anthony's neck, the other hand drawing him closer as she lifted her mouth to him. He was smiling as he bent towards her.

'Get out. Get out of here right now.' Camilla spoke to the girl, her voice clear and low and very cold. 'You can collect your things and leave this minute. After that, I never want to see you again.'

She did not look directly at Anthony, and he turned on his heel and left them without a word. In the dressing room Zahra gathered up her personal belongings in silence, making no attempt at explanation or apology, and within minutes the door closed behind her and she was gone. Camilla's icy rage dissolved into tears, and she swallowed the burning lump in her throat and clenched her teeth, determined not to succumb. She looked at herself in the mirror and saw only disillusionment as she brushed back her hair and put fresh lipstick on her trembling mouth. Then she straightened, pasted on her most professional smile and returned to the party.

'Ah! There you are,' Tom said. 'I thought you'd gone off with your boyfriend and abandoned me. Lila has left me high and dry in spite of my best efforts to get her into the sack. The watchful eye of her parents was too much for her. And the black beauty seems to have vanished into the night. Joe is half out of his mind over her.'

'I want champagne,' Camilla said. 'Let's get out of here and go to the bar. Now.'

'Champagne it is,' Tom said, recognising her distress and escorting her from the room. 'Better yet, why don't we go up to my suite where it's peaceful and there's no one to disturb us? You must be whacked now.'

'Whacked. Yes, that's exactly what I am,' she said. 'Completely whacked, in every bloody direction.'

Tom did not ask where Anthony was, but he watched as Camilla drank two glasses of champagne in quick succession.

'There are interviews set up for the morning, darling,' he said eventually. 'The old bag from *Tatler* is staying with Lady Carghill, and she wants to talk to you. Plus Rabindrah tells me he's doing something for the *Telegraph*.'

'And you're going on a lovely little trip,' she said, her voice brittle. 'You can't come here and not see a single wild animal. I've arranged for you to visit Treetops. It's an amazing platform built into the trees in the Aberdare Forest. That's where Princess Elizabeth was when her father died, and she became Queen.'

'Marvellous,' Tom said, without a trace of enthusiasm. 'I do love a bit of history. Did she pee down on the tigers when she felt the urge?'

'Coarse and ignorant is what you are,' Camilla said. 'There are no tigers in Africa. But you'll be able to sit up all night and freeze, and watch the rhinos and elephants and maybe even see a leopard. Commune with nature.'

'I don't much care for communing with wild animals, although I do value the fur collar on my winter coat,' Tom said. 'But I suppose I should be grateful that I'm not in a tent with lions tearing at the zippers, and your jungle boy beating them off. Are you sure you can't come with us?'

'Quite sure,' Camilla said, her head drooping. 'I'm rather drunk now, darling. So I think I'll stay here tonight, with you. If that's all right?'

She had fallen back on to the cushions on the sofa and was asleep before he could answer. He took a blanket from the bed and laid it over her. She would feel like shit in the morning, and he would be there to rescue her and to help her through the day. Good old Tom, reliable agent and friend. With any luck she would come back to London now, and leave her nice farming friends to look after her workshop. All in all, things were turning out very well and Tom was smiling as he turned out the light.

In the morning Tom was dispatched to the dressing room where he picked up Camilla's belongings and arranged for the place to be cleared and the clothes boxed up and sent to Mary Robbins's shop. As he made his way back to the lifts he came across Joe who was hovering in the lobby.

'Have you seen Camilla?' he asked. 'I was rather hoping to get hold of this Zahra. Do a few headshots to take back to London. Show them around.'

'I'll have to get back to you on that one,' Tom said.

'Yeah. I saw her make a play for Camilla's man. I'd say that wasn't a smart move,' Joe said. 'Still, she's a looker and you should sign her up, Tom. What I call hot and exotic.'

'Do you want to talk about last night?' Tom ventured the question as Camilla showered and dressed.

'That little bitch went for Anthony, and he fell for it,' she said, matter-of-factly, although her insides were churning with humiliation.

'I met Joe in the lobby. He was hoping to take some pictures of her.'

Camilla came out of the bathroom and planted herself directly in front of Tom. 'Let me make one thing clear to you,' she said. 'If you sign that girl up, I am off your books, and you will never see me again. Do you understand that, Tom Bartlett? Because if you don't, you can get on the plane for London and forget that we ever knew each other.'

'I wouldn't touch her with a bargepole,' he said hastily. 'If she gets herself into fashion, I swear it won't be anything to do with me. Now off you go for your interviews. *Tatler* first, then your Indian chum, isn't it?' He wagged his head from side to side and rolled his eyes, and was relieved to see that she was laughing as they left the room.

'Can we do this over lunch?' Camilla asked, as Rabindrah took out his notebook and pencils. 'I'm rather hungover, and I've already been grilled once today. I need serious food and a Bloody Mary, if I'm to go any further.'

By the time they reached the Equator Club she was weary and depressed. She was tempted to telephone Anthony, but she had no idea what she could say without breaking down and hurling accusations at him. Perhaps she should go back to his house in the afternoon and try to talk to him calmly and reasonably. But when she thought about it, Camilla found herself close to tears and she left Rabindrah and took refuge in the powder room, lingering at the mirror, summoning up the courage to get through the rest of the day. When she had regained a firm hold on her emotions, she pushed the door open and returned to the restaurant. The dining room at the Equator Club was dark and smoky and very crowded. And the smell of Chinese food made Camilla realise that she was a little queasy. Lunch had probably been a bad idea.

As she made her way back to the table she heard a woman giggle, and the sound was oddly familiar. She glanced around, curious. Seated in a small alcove, at a table for two, were Viktor Szustak and an African woman with an unmistakable hourglass figure and an aura of pure sexuality. Twinkle Kiberu. He was laughing as he showed her how to use her chopsticks, one of his hands covering her long, scarlet-tipped fingers, his other hand reaching up to touch a few grains of rice on the corner of her mouth. He murmured in her ear, and her tongue flickered out to touch his fingertips as she smiled at him with unmistakable lust. No wonder he had not come near their table last night. Camilla turned away quickly, a parallel vision of Anthony and Zahra forming in her mind. Perhaps they were together now, panting for each other like these two. She quickened her steps and sat down at the table.

'I see Viktor Szustak lurking over there,' Rabindrah said. 'With Mama Kiberu. I'm not surprised he didn't come over for a chat last night.'

'Is that an ongoing liaison?' Camilla asked. 'Part of the perennial "Are you married or do you live in Kenya?" question? Am I witnessing a local scandal?'

'The local gossips are lapping it up,' Rabindrah said. 'But I don't think there will be duelling or pistols. Now let's order, and talk about multi-cultural baubles and beads.'

It was mid-afternoon when Camilla finally arrived at Anthony's house. His Land Rover was in the driveway, and her heart was jumping and skittering as she walked into the sitting room.

'Where on earth have you been?' His face was tense, his speech clipped. 'I waited up for you until dawn. You look all in.'

He came towards her, putting his arms around her waist, trying to draw her close to him. But she shook her head and pushed him away.

'Come and sit down,' he said. 'I can see that you're really tired.'

'I'm not tired. I'm just sad,' she replied. 'It's my second name, I think.'

'You had a tremendous night,' he said. 'Spectacular.'

'So did you, it seems.' She could not conceal her jealousy.

'Now wait a minute,' he said, clearly on the defensive. 'You were too busy last night to even notice me, and you were flirting like crazy with that idiotic fellow, Bartlett. But I realised it was all a put-on. Just good fun. Everyone was flirting with Zahra, and it was unfortunate that she happened to make a beeline for me. It didn't mean anything. It was her big night.'

'It was my big night,' she said bitterly, turning away so that he would not see the angry tears in her eyes. 'And I don't want to talk about it, Anthony, so don't say anything more. Please.'

'I think you're being a bit harsh,' he said. 'She phoned here this morning, looking for you. Practically hysterical. She said she never drinks, and she knows how badly she behaved and she's terribly sorry. So maybe you should give her a chance to apologise to you in person.'

'How dare you tell me what I should do!' She turned on him, her fury blazing out across the room so that he felt it like a physical force. 'You have no idea what this whole thing meant to me. How important it was for Hannah who will share whatever we made in sales. Because when it comes down to it, you're totally self-centred and hollow, Anthony. You can't see past skin deep, and you can't resist any woman who sets her sights on you. Loyalty isn't a word you've ever stopped to analyse, much less put into practice. That's the reason I didn't want to talk about marrying you five months ago, and now I see how right I was.'

'You're overreacting because you've been under so much strain.' His tone was placating. 'Let's forget the whole silly episode, Camilla. Look how Joshua has arranged the flowers, and he has everything ready for dinner. I have to leave in the morning, and this is our only time alone. You've been so busy, and I've hardly seen you.'

'I'm going to a cocktail party with my father,' she said stiffly. 'I won't be back tonight.'

She threw a haphazard selection of clothes into a tote bag and left him standing with his back to her, looking out of the window at the soft afternoon that was now marked by anger and regret. As she started the car he stepped out on to the verandah, but he did not speak or make any sign and she was too proud to get out of the car and return to the house.

George greeted her affably, and made no comment as she put her bag into the guest bedroom. She longed to say something, to confide her hurt and her uncertainty. More than anything she wished that her friends had not left Nairobi, and for a crazy moment she thought of driving north to Langani or even Buffalo Springs. Instead she bathed and dressed with meticulous care.

'You look beautiful, darling,' George said fondly. 'And it will all turn out fine with your young man. These little storms are a part of every life and every love affair, and they don't count for much, or for long, in the greater scheme of things. There's no one else who really matters to him. You know that.'

'No, I don't know that at all.'

'Men often behave foolishly when they feel they're not the centre of attention,' George said. 'And I'm sure Anthony had no idea the girl would show up today, at his house. He rang here right away, looking for you, but I had no idea where you were. I don't think you should hold that against him.'

Camilla stood still, the air knocked out of her body by the realisation that Anthony had lied to her. She felt deathly ill, and small beads of sweat stood out on her forehead and she stared at her father, speechless and white-faced. He saw that he had unwittingly divulged a confidence and looked away. Camilla clenched her fists, feeling nothing but disgust for him and for Anthony whom he had sought to excuse.

'You're absolutely right,' she said. 'It doesn't matter at all. Let's go to the cocktail party, Daddy, and have fun.'

Half an hour later she drifted through the crowded room, accepting congratulations on the previous night's spectacle. She wished now that she had not agreed to come, and she was about to go upstairs to the quiet of the bar when George beckoned her to join him.

'That was a wonderful night,' Johnson Kiberu said to her, his eyes travelling very slowly over her body. 'I hope I will be able to obtain an invitation to one of your fashion exhibitions next time I'm in London. Meet some of your modelling friends, perhaps.'

'Oh yes,' Camilla said, shuddering inwardly. The man might be a good politician, but he was a lecher and a bore when it came to women. He put a hand on her bare arm and squeezed gently.

'We have some friends in common, actually,' she said, 'and we met briefly in London one evening last year. You probably don't remember, because you meet so many people.'

'Indeed.' Johnson's eyes narrowed slightly and she could detect alarm in the smooth face. He swallowed most of his drink in one gulp. 'It is hard to remember everyone. I'm delighted that your father has made his base in Nairobi. He's already done so much to advise us on our wildlife policy. Will you be staying on for a while?'

'I'm not sure,' Camilla said, smiling from beneath her lashes, flirting with him deliberately, leading him into her trap. 'It depends on what is on offer in Nairobi.'

'I hope we will see one another again,' he said, confident now that she was not going to present a problem. He tried an opening gambit. 'You don't always have a chaperone, do you?'

'No, I certainly don't.' She looked at him with studied innocence. 'How is your sister today?'

'You know my sister?' He was puzzled.

'Your gorgeous, sexy sister who was with us last night,' Camilla said. 'I've met her many times, with a friend of mine. Viktor Szustak. He's mad about her, and they've been having such a wild time together. We always converge on that place where I saw them the other night. I can't remember the name, but you must know it too. A dark little hideaway, ideal for steamy affairs and hot romances. They have jazz and dancing until the small hours. Perhaps we could meet there. Make up a foursome.'

She saw the politician's eyes alight with rage, and felt George's frantic grip on her arm.

'My dear, I want you to come and see an old chum of mine from the High Commission,' he said desperately. 'Johnson, I'll see you at the wildlife rescue meeting.'

'You didn't have to drag me away so abruptly,' she said. 'He'll think us very rude.'

'Jesus Christ, Camilla, you know damn well that's not his sister,' George spluttered. 'Twinkle Kiberu is his wife, for God's sake. I introduced you when we were with Rabindrah. Don't you remember? You can't possibly have thought she was his sister. And Szustak is a dreadful womaniser. Where on earth did you bump into them?'

'Oh dear. I seem to have got it all wrong,' Camilla said, her smile sly. 'Or maybe I'm mixing her up with someone else.' She could see Johnson Kiberu eyeing her from the other side of the room, his expression wary. 'Well, never mind,' she said. 'He's a real old groper anyway, your friend Mr Kiberu. Can we go home now? I'm near collapsing.'

As they left the reception she gave Johnson a small wave of her hand and a dazzling smile, and he turned on his heel and disappeared into the crowd.

The telephone was ringing as they walked into George's drawing room.

'Please come home now,' Anthony said. 'I'm leaving in the morning and I really want us to be together tonight.'

'You quite forgot to tell me that Zahra called on you today,' she said, shaking with rage.

'Camilla, I had meant to tell you. But I thought you would be even more upset. I got rid of her immediately because she was impossible. Hysterical, as I said earlier. And none of this means anything whatsoever to me. Nothing at all. Camilla?'

'It means something to me,' she said furiously.

'Come home, please. I want to see you. I want you, right now. I only ever want you. Please let's put all this nonsense behind us.'

'I'm having supper with Daddy,' she said, a red mist of rage descending on her. 'And I am leaving for London tomorrow night. With Tom.'

'What? But when will I see you? When are you coming back?'

'I don't know,' she said. 'I don't know at all.'

Chapter 8

London, April 1967

It was Rabindrah who had been responsible for Sarah's visit to London. He had returned to Buffalo Springs for several days before disappearing on assignment to Tanzania, and the time had passed quickly. When he was not following the herds, he would sit under the acacia tree with a small folding table in front of him, his fingers hammering the keyboard of an ancient portable typewriter in a clip-clap rhythm, sweat dripping, unheeded, from his forehead. The plain steel bangle that he always wore glinted on his wrist. He had a lock of black hair that flopped into his eyes when he bent over his work, and every so often he jerked his head back to flick it out of his eyes.

'I have a good, sharp pair of scissors I can use on that,' Sarah said to him. 'And Allie is a dab hand at haircuts. Save you a lot of energy, and lessen the danger of your head falling off.'

'Some Sikhs never cut their hair or their beards,' he said, grinning at her. 'Apart from my bracelet, this is my only nod to tradition, and it makes a good fly whisk.'

He had a black sense of humour, and a quick understanding that made him a stimulating companion. In the evening he read out sections of his text, accepting suggestions and criticisms with good grace, laughing at his occasional mistakes. He got on well with the Briggses, and stayed up late at night with Dan on several occasions, discussing the world at large and the frail hope of Kenya ever becoming a truly multiracial society. Even the African camp staff grudgingly came to accept the *mahindi* in their midst. Only Erope remained unimpressed by his woeful lack of knowledge in the field.

'Have you heard any more from the priest?' Rabindrah asked Sarah on the day of his return.

She shook her head. 'You know, I was far too emotional after I went to see him. It brought back all the bad memories, and I couldn't see straight for a while.'

'Are you telling me that your feeling about Simon Githiri was wrong? That you don't believe he could be alive after all?'

'I don't know,' she said. 'And I don't want to brood over it, because it's an instinctive thing. It's not based on anything scientific or sensible, so I'd like to try and forget about it for now. Not talk about it any more. Are you ready to go out in my fine, revamped jalopy, and look for some elephants?'

'Of course,' Rabindrah said. 'I told Indar Uncle I would be riding in his new vehicles. We will take photographs in the middle of the herd, so that he can see what benificence he has wrought in the wilderness.'

'Why doesn't he come up and see for himself? We'd love to show him around,' Sarah said.

Rabindrah did not answer and she looked at him curiously. 'I'll bet he's scared of wild animals,' she said, smiling. 'You'd be amazed how many big, strong men end up cowering in the back of the car when they see a bull elephant strolling towards them.'

He had no wish to tell Sarah that his aunt and uncle had become a little wary of his association with her, and had mentioned their reservations in a discreet but clear exchange.

'You must also be working on some good stories in Nairobi,' Kuldip Singh had said, when her nephew announced that he was returning to Buffalo Springs.

'There are always a few interesting issues,' he said. 'But being up there is something I'd never imagined. It's a place that gets under your skin. The whole experience takes hold of you. I want to take you up there, Kuldip Auntie. It is something mystical, to go out with Sarah in the morning and sit so quiet in the middle of those huge beasts, and watch them go about their business in such an orderly, dignified manner. She is full of courage, that girl. She knows each one of the elephants, can tell you what they are going to do before they even do it. Day after day she is out there alone or with a Samburu tracker, following the herds, not afraid of them or the buffalo or the Shifta poachers. Not afraid of anything. I've never come across a woman like that. This is like watching a legend in the making.'

'I'm sure she is a good girl,' Kuldip said. 'She did not say much to us, when she came to take the Land Rover.'

'You didn't meet her on a good day,' Rabindrah said. 'You know, she was engaged to the Afrikaans farmer who was murdered just over a year ago. Up near Nanyuki. And there was a break-in on the farm recently, just before you met her. So she was very nervous on that day, and full of bad memories.'

'Poor girl,' Kuldip said. 'She probably needs more time to grieve. For some people, these things are with them for the rest of their lives. They can never be normal again, you know. Will you be here tomorrow, Rabindrah? I have someone I want you to meet.'

'You never give up, Auntie,' he said, laughing. 'No doubt it's another of your possible bride choices, and you will only be disappointed. But I'll be here.'

'Best to stick with your own kind,' Kuldip said. 'Marriage is demanding enough, without adding anything extra to the problems a couple has to face together.'

'Your aunt is right.' Indar had come in on the tail end of the conversation.

But Rabindrah could not define his own kind, except as a small, alien tribe that did not truly belong on any continent. The British had brought them to Africa and would now abandon them, to survive as best they could. They were no longer Indian, these descendants of the Sikh policemen and soldiers and farmers, and the grandchildren of the Hindu coolies brought to lay railway lines in a far land. But they were not Africans either, although they had prospered in Kenya and their children had been born on African soil.

'And what is my own kind?' Rabindrah asked, although they had often discussed the subject before with no satisfactory conclusion.

'You are an Indian. That is your heritage. And you are a Sikh, even though you do not seem to be interested in the practice of religion,' Indar said.

'I'm a Kenyan,' Rabindrah said. 'I was born here and I've never set foot in India. Even you have only been there once, and you felt like a foreigner. "Indian" is just an idea we have of ourselves. A sentimental notion that exists only in our hearts. This is our home, for better or worse.'

'We are British citizens also,' Kuldip said.

'My dear, I think the boy is right.' Indar's tone was sombre. 'My brother is working and settled in his semi-detached house in the UK, but he will never be English. And they will not allow many more of us in there. The British have used us to further their colonial aims. But they do not like us, and they will soon find a way to stop us from coming. The Jews of Africa, they call us, and it is not a compliment.' He looked at his nephew. 'Your aunt is a wise woman,' he said. 'You have been talking a great deal about this Irish girl, over the past few weeks. Her name is cropping up regularly in all your conversations. It is good that you are making this book together, but you should take care not to look for more than that. True companionship and love is best found within your own community.'

Remembering his uncle's stern expression, Rabindrah smiled as he drove through the rose-coloured evening with Sarah. The sun was beginning to set. Birds scuttled along the sandy track and rose into the cool air ahead of the Land Rover. He could see the solitary beauty of the evening star and the pale shape of a crescent moon. He was dusty and tired, and completely in tune with the world around him. Sarah was looking straight ahead, her small, tanned hands gripping the steering wheel. She was humming under her breath, something she did when she was relaxed and content, and Rabindrah was absurdly pleased that she felt that way.

Two days earlier, he had received a message from John Sinclair, the London publisher. It caused Sarah excitement and considerable heart searching.

'We can finally afford to celebrate,' Rabindrah had said, as they sat under the stars enjoying a quiet moment before dinner. 'There's a publishing contract ready to be signed at last.'

'I presume they'll post it to you in Nairobi,' she said. 'If we have to sign it together, then maybe you can bring it up here?'

'I can,' Rabindrah said. 'But decisions have to be made about the layout of the book. John has suggested meeting in London. And you should be there.' He turned to Dan. 'A week would do it, if you could spare her.'

'I guess we can let her off the hook, since she's going to make us famous.' Dan was smiling at Sarah. 'Maybe you should take your dad up on his offer of a ticket to Ireland, kid. Visit your family, with a stop in London on the way. Isn't your brother getting married soon?'

Sarah had looked away. 'At the end of April.'

'Maybe Rabindrah can arrange things so you could combine the two events,' Dan said. 'What do you say, Allie?'

'If Sarah would like that, yes.' Allie had been careful not to force the issue, aware that Sarah might not feel ready to join a family celebration, particularly a wedding.

'We'll see.' Sarah's tone was abrupt and she knew she sounded ungracious. In the back of her mind was the probability that she could not avoid the journey. It was time to take her first steps out into the world at large, to visit her family who had begged her for so long to come to Sligo. To come home. It wasn't home and it wasn't her wedding, but she knew she would have to go.

It was late spring when she arrived in London. Camilla was at the airport to meet her, and they took a taxi to the Knightsbridge flat. She had forgotten how cutting the wind could be, and how the grey sky seemed to glower down on the scurrying crowds in the streets.

'Why don't you sleep for a couple of hours? I'll give you a key in case you want to go out and look at the shops,' Camilla said. 'I have a studio shoot at noon, so I won't be back until after five. I thought we could have the evening all to ourselves, if that sounds good to you.'

They had dinner in a crowded trattoria, too noisy for anything but superficial conversation. Sarah wondered if it had been chosen for that reason. It was late when they returned to the flat and she was able to penetrate the patter that Camilla had been using as a screen.

'Want to try some?' Camilla clicked a gold lighter and proffered a sweet-smelling cigarette. 'It's good quality stuff. If it makes you sleepy, you haven't far to go. And if you get hysterical with laughter or overtaken by hiccups, there's only the two of us here. You won't start hallucinating or jumping out of windows or anything.'

'I must say, since I moved to the Briggses' camp I've consumed more alcohol than I ever thought I would,' Sarah said. 'But I've never tried a joint. No. I don't think so, thanks.'

Camilla was lying back on the sofa, her eyes closed as though she had fallen asleep. Neither one of them spoke for a while.

'Do you still get nightmares?' she asked suddenly. 'After the raid, when my face was so badly damaged, I was afraid to go to sleep, afraid of being alone in a room, afraid of everything. For months. And when I arrived at Langani last year, I was even more scared. It took a while before I began to feel comfortable, and to sleep well. But since my workshop was destroyed, the old dreams have surfaced again and I see the panga rushing down towards my face, feel it slicing into my head, as though it was yesterday. Now I'm beginning to wonder if I can go back. If I have that kind of courage.'

'It's hard,' Sarah said. 'When you don't understand why you've been attacked.'

'How does one deal with faceless hatred?' Camilla's voice was angry. 'It affects the Africans even more than us. Look at the jobs lost, the local women whose work had become important to them, even in a short space of time. And it could happen again, because no one can work out the reasons behind it.' She dragged on her cigarette. 'I don't want to let Hannah down. I'm sure *she's* never thought of turning tail and fleeing Langani. But I'm not strong like her. I've developed a real fear of going back.'

'It's her home, and she still says she's staying on, no matter what,' Sarah said. 'But you could go back and set up in Nairobi.'

'That wasn't my idea. I had such a good plan for Langani, but it's been completely derailed. Ruined. And I don't know what to do. About any of it.'

Sarah realised that she was talking about Anthony now, as well as the disaster at the workshop. What a shallow, heartless fool he was. Protocad, she had called him once. She wondered how he would ever make things come right, and whether he deserved a chance to try.

'Is there anything left between you?' she said at last.

Camilla did not open her eyes. 'No more than between Anthony and every other female that crosses his path.'

'He behaved like an idiot,' Sarah said, knowing how lame it sounded.

'I'll never understand' – Camilla gestured with a languid movement of her wrist – 'about love. Why, in some circumstances, it's wasted, thrown away, while in other unlikely situations it survives, despite everything. Look at George and Marina.'

She had never mentioned her mother since her death. Sarah sat very quiet, saying nothing, not wishing to interrupt the flow of words. Camilla rarely confided.

'I cried, you know, when she died. I didn't expect to, but she made me cry. She said we were her life, Daddy and me. That she adored us, and he was the only man she had ever loved. She said if she were given a wish, she'd choose to live on until she was fifty, so she could try and make us really happy together, no matter what it took. She didn't want to go back and live her whole life over again. Her only wish was for everything to be right for a little while, so that we would remember that first whenever we thought of her. That's all she wanted. To stay, until she was fifty. And then she laughed, and said that fifty would be enough, because after that she'd have wrinkles and sagging skin which she'd always dreaded, and then she'd start behaving badly again.' Tears were brimming but Camilla did not allow them to fall. 'She was very brave,' she said. 'It made everything much harder.'

'They did love each other, then. In spite of everything?'

'I suppose so. A kind of love, at any rate. But how could anyone stay in a marriage like that? All those years spent with a man who was out chasing his boyfriends. He wasn't a real husband. But she settled for that. Secrecy and silence, at a terrible cost to herself. To all of us. Because he could never be free of his guilt, and she couldn't envisage life without him. And I was left to sink or swim in their misery.' She sat up and leaned forward, staring down at her feet. 'It's no wonder I don't understand love and relationships.'

'And Anthony?'

'He's probably out on safari. Surrounded by women ripping the canvas to get into his tent at night, while he charges them thousands of dollars for the privilege of making fools of themselves.' Camilla's laugh was thin and high. 'Just like I did.'

'No, you didn't,' Sarah said. 'He's a first-class twit. An adolescent disguised as a man, still on the rampage sowing wild oats. Not grown-up yet. But I do think he loves you, even though he doesn't know it. Or know how to really love anyone.'

'He's in love with his life exactly the way it is, and he doesn't see any reason to change it. I was beginning to think he was ready for a commitment, but I certainly read that wrong.'

'He proposed to you. That was a commitment, wasn't it?'

'That was a worthless romantic gesture, Sarah. You saw him with that little tart Zahra. And I did so much for her too.'

'He'll wake up one of these days and realise how stupid he was. Then he'll be over here and on his knees, begging your forgiveness.'

'Oh, for God's sake, Sarah, you're such a bloody optimist! A latter-day Pollyanna. No. No, he won't. And I'd never trust him again, anyway. Trust has been in short supply in my life, so it's become important to me. Trust and love and peace, and all that shit. That's what I'm after these days.' She waved the joint in the air. 'Come on, have some of this. It's good for you. You'll sleep well after it.'

'Oh, why not? Here goes.' Sarah pulled on the thin cigarette with its fine, crackling paper and untidy strings of tobacco, inhaling the smoke gingerly. It wasn't bad. She puffed again, lying back with her head against the thick cushions. Camilla had such fat, comfortable cushions and chairs.

'I don't sleep well any more,' she said. 'I'm like you. The bad dreams have come back since Piet's anniversary. I suppose they'll fade again, and in the meantime I have to take it day by day. That's all I can do. All anyone can do. As for trust – well, I trust you. And Hannah and Lars. And the Briggses. They've become true friends and we get along very well, even though we're on top of each other so much of the time. We work together, live together in that small compound, and mostly eat and drink together. Just the three of us. But it works, because we have a common aim.'

'It's so isolated up there,' Camilla said. 'Doesn't that make it harder?'

Sarah thought about Dan and Allie, and the deep bedrock of love and companionship that kept them together.

'Sometimes their partnership makes me feel lonely, because they have each other,' she said. 'But I can't imagine sharing my life with anyone. Piet's gone, and I have to accept that and learn to live without him. It's the only way to go on living. And I love my work. I've been lucky in that respect.' Her limbs were beginning to feel heavy and listless, a sinking sensation that was pleasant. 'We're not isolated in Buffalo Springs. We see plenty of outsiders.'

'Like who?'

'Like visiting scientists, people from the Game Department and from Samburu Lodge.' Sarah let her head fall back, although she was not quite sure whether it was still attached to her neck. It seemed to be floating inches above the rest of her body, but her mind was peaceful and she was content to be talking openly. 'We see George and Joy Adamson, and extraordinary game wardens like Peter Jenkins and Bill Woodley who keep the parks going against all odds. They're an inspiration, believe me.' Sarah became more expansive. 'And there's the occasional film star on a tented safari who drops in and sometimes gives Dan a fat cheque for our research work. The hunters and safari guides bring them along.' She stopped, realising that she was moving into tricky waters. 'I wish you'd been able to come up and stay with me. I really wanted you to see it all.'

'I had intended coming in January. So much for making plans.'

'And now I have the book to think about, which is good.'

'It's better than good,' Camilla said. 'When are you meeting up with your journalist?'

'I have to phone him in the morning,' Sarah said, frowning. 'I don't know why everyone keeps calling him "my journalist". It's a short-term, purely business partnership. He came looking for me because he liked my photographs. He writes well, he has useful contacts, and we're working together on a book. That's all.'

Even as she said the words, she could see Rabindrah hauling her along the corridor of Anthony's cottage. The joint was acting on her like a truth serum and she rambled on, describing the disastrous evening in Nairobi, joining in Camilla's peals of laughter as she recounted the drunken episode and the stunned expression on Joshua's face as she was carried into Anthony's bathroom.

'I have to admit that Rabindrah was gallant beyond the call of duty. And kind too. I went to pieces next day and ended up telling him the whole story, although I suppose he knew it already, being a journalist. His uncle must have thought me strange when I arrived at the garage for the presentation of the Land Rover. It makes me shudder to imagine it. My nose was red, my eyes were all puffy, and I had a nasty hangover to boot.' She began to giggle. 'Rabindrah even lent me a pair of sunglasses that would have cost me three months' pay. He's very conscious of how he looks. A bit vain, I think.'

She dragged on the joint again, more accustomed to inhaling it now, drawing it deep into her lungs. As she blew out the smoke in a slow stream, she felt as though she was being lifted out of herself. She could see things from up here that she had not noticed before.

'When he came back to the camp last month, I was actually glad to see him,' she said. 'He's not part of the turmoil of the past, you see. I've tried to hide all that, not allow anyone to see inside me. But now he knows my story, knows all about me. So there isn't any reason to skirt around things any more. I feel comfortable with him.'

'So that's really why you're in London. Because he's here.' Camilla gave her a sly smile.

'Oh no!' Sarah sat up in protest, then flopped back. She shook her head to clear the mist that seemed to be curling around her brain. Camilla was watching her from half-closed eyes. 'No, I came to meet the publisher. Discuss the layout of the book and how my pictures should be used. And I'm going to Tim's wedding, even though I don't really want to, and I can't honestly see why he's marrying her.'

'Dreary Deirdre. I can't understand it either. We should have made more of an effort to head her off in the beginning,' Camilla said. 'I should have fallen for him myself, darling sweet Timmy.'

'Would you do something for me, Camilla?' Sarah sat up straight. 'Would you come with me to Ireland? Because it's going to be hard, coping with all that sympathy, seeing the awkwardness in people who have heard what happened to me and don't know what to say. My parents will probably try and persuade me to stay, and that will be difficult, too. I could do with some moral support.'

'Yes, I'll come with you.' Camilla did not hesitate. 'Help you through. And maybe we'll save Timmy. Persuade him to run off with the local barmaid instead. Or maybe I'll seduce him myself. In a good cause.'

'I'm glad we've had this time to spend together,' Sarah said. 'You didn't answer our letters, and Hannah is upset about that. You shouldn't cut your friends off completely whenever things are bad. Run away and never let us know what you're feeling.'

'I haven't run away,' Camilla said. 'The workshop will open again, and I won't let anyone down. I just need a little time to get over what happened. What might have happened.'

Sarah wanted to say more, but her eyelids were drooping and her head had definitely been disconnected from the rest of her body.

'No more tonight,' said Camilla, her voice dreamy. 'You should see yourself. You're stoned and so am I. Let's go to bed.'

Sarah's meeting with the publisher was at two o'clock. She sat on the edge of her bed in the morning, a little dazed, casting around for something suitable to wear. She wanted to make a good impression. Camilla looked up from the morning paper and made an exclamation of dismay. Then she lifted the telephone and made several calls.

'Hairdresser, manicure, new trousers and a jacket over a silk shirt,' she said. 'I have the perfect shirt for you. I've never worn it. And I know where you can find the rest. I'll meet you in Fenwicks around twelve. And by the way, we've been invited to dinner with Edward this evening, if you're available. Would Mr Singh like to join us, do you think?'

'Edward? I thought Edward was history.'

'We meet from time to time.' Camilla's tone was casual. 'But we haven't . . . I'm not . . . Anyway, you can let me know later.'

Sarah emerged from the luxury of the hair salon to join Camilla for shopping that was decisive and mercifully quick. She had never met a publisher before, and she had no idea what was expected of her. A selection of new photographs, slides and notes made her portfolio awkward and too heavy to carry easily. The shoulder strap kept slipping, forcing her to stop frequently and put down her other packages, in order to readjust it. When she arrived at the offices she was hot and tired, her hair had frizzed up in the damp air, and her clothes were slightly crumpled. She did not feel at all like the composed professional she had intended to portray. Rabindrah was waiting in the reception area. He looked urbane and elegant. Within a few moments John Sinclair had emerged to greet them, and put her entirely at ease. He had published a number of books on Africa's wildlife and flora, and the quality of the printing was outstanding. He patiently explained the process and outlined the number of words and illustrations he planned to use, studying Sarah's pictures with grave attention. They left his office more than an hour later, each of them carrying copies of the publishing contract.

'You'll probably want to have a lawyer or an agent look it over,' John had said. 'Just to make sure everything is clear to you both. There'll be one advance to split between you as you see fit. It's not very large, because this is your first book, but it is against future royalties and I expect that in time you should earn in excess of double the advance. You need to instruct us as to how and where you want the money paid. It will take more than a year before this appears in the bookshops, you know. First there is the selection of pictures and editing of the text. Then we will make the photographic plates, finalise the layout and design, decide on the jacket, then have it copy-edited, proofread and printed. I'll be supervising the progress with you personally, and I believe we're going to have a great success on our hands. It's ideal timing, with all this fuss about the

Adamsons and the film about their lions and so on. My congratulations to you both.'

'I think we should succumb to the old English tradition of afternoon tea,' Rabindrah suggested as they left the publishing house. 'Brown's is just around the corner. It's not every day you sign a book contract.'

'I don't know any lawyers here,' Sarah said. 'But Camilla might.'

'My father is a lawyer,' Rabindrah said. 'We could ask him to look over the contract. If you have no objection.' He was pleased when she nodded assent. It had crossed his mind that she might not be happy with an Indian lawyer, and a member of his own family. 'You look very different. Is this your smart, London image?'

'I suppose you could call it that.' She was laughing. 'I'm staying with Camilla and she always tries to make me look more respectable. Properly groomed, as she puts it. She's been doing it since we were at school.'

'The results are lovely,' he said, and was amused at the instant red flush that crept up from her throat and into her cheeks. 'What is Camilla going to do now?'

'I don't think she's made up her mind yet.'

'She's brave but a little mad if she decides to start again in Kenya. Have you heard anything new from the police?' He saw her hands tense on the arm of the chair. 'Indian or China tea? I may eat two of these scones with the clotted cream and jam. Very civilised, the English, when they're at home having tea, instead of out suppressing dark-skinned savages in the colonies.'

'Are you doing anything this evening?' Sarah asked as they finished their tea. 'Camilla has invited us both to join her and a friend for dinner.'

'I'd like to see her. And tomorrow we could visit my father. I'll let him have the contract this evening and we could go to his office, or maybe see him at home. It's not far, and my parents would very much like to meet you.'

'Are you staying with them?'

'No, I prefer to visit. My mother is very orthodox, very religious. And I have not followed in the Sikh tradition. So when I am here I prefer to have the freedom of doing what I please without provoking family arguments.'

'Did your father practise law in Kenya?'

'Yes. He was a senior partner in a Nairobi law firm. But he was convinced that the Asian community would be dispossessed and thrown out after *Uhuru*. That he would lose his property and have his bank account frozen. So he left ahead of the exodus, and took the family to England. He works for a firm of solicitors in Southwark now.'

'What did you feel about the move?'

'I had already been sent to university here, and I was staying with relatives. When my parents first arrived they had my two sisters with them, and their first house was very cramped. So I never went back to live with them.'

'And your sisters?'

'They are both married now.'

'Do your parents not miss Kenya?'

'My father likes his job, although it's lowly compared to what he was doing in Nairobi. They have plenty of friends also settled here, and now they've managed to buy a house. I think they are satisfied with that, even though their lifestyle is modest and my mother has no servants here.' He shrugged. 'My sisters married good Sikh husbands who follow the rules and go regularly to the gurdwara. They're not rebellious and impertinent like me. I think for my family that is enough.'

'But it would not be enough for you?'

'The Indians who have settled here have lost something. Their roots, I suppose. Settling in Britain, living in their enclave, surrounded by other Asians who have all come from somewhere else. But perhaps they have no roots. They all talk about India as their homeland, and Kenya as some kind of stop on the way there. But my father was born in Nairobi and only visited India twice. He thought it was a dreadful, dirty place and he could not leave it fast enough. My grandfather came to Kenya in 1898 and soon brought his wife and his brothers, and their wives too.'

'Rather like Hannah's grandparents,' Sarah said.

'Yes, but I do not think she would like the comparison,' he said wryly.

'You'll get to know her one of these days,' Sarah said. 'And then you'll see that she is not as prejudiced as you think.'

'Perhaps. India was never my parents' homeland. And England? Here we are like refugees, second-class citizens grudgingly given the right to stay. I think my father made a mistake, but he will never admit it. And my mother goes where he goes. Makes the best of things whatever they are, like the good Sikh wife she wants me to find.'

*

It was just after seven when Sarah returned to the flat. Camilla was sitting on the sofa beside a tall man in his forties who stood up and held out his hand.

'You're the famous Sarah.' His smile lit his eyes. 'I read about you in the *Telegraph*. I'm Edward Carradine. Congratulations are in order, I hear. It's quite a feat to have a book published.'

Sarah liked him at once. He had a good face, she thought, although it was rather too long because of the high forehead. His hair was greying a little at the temples. He held himself well, as though he had a firm grasp on his life. When he smiled his hazel eyes were warm, although there was something hawklike about his features. His affection for Camilla was evident. He listened attentively when she spoke, and guided her into the taxi and the restaurant with his hand protectively in the small of her back. Interesting, Sarah thought. But would it ever be possible for him to oust Anthony, flawed as he was, from Camilla's heart?

The restaurant was smart and noisy and crammed with people. Sarah spotted Rabindrah, standing at the bar. Several people waved to Camilla, while others watched covertly as she negotiated her way gracefully between diners and scurrying waiters. Rabindrah saw that they had been given the best table in the house. Edward ordered the wine.

'Cheers,' he said. 'I always need this first drink when I've run the gauntlet through one of these fashionable venues where Camilla is in the spotlight.'

'And you're normally so modest and retiring.' Camilla's brows were raised, slightly mocking.

'Of course I am,' he said, smiling. 'I can't greet anyone in here unless they wave at me first. There are several women in this room who are pretending they don't know me at all, in case anyone guesses they've had their faces done. They behave as though we meet in some secret, underground cave, where I cut and stitch and no one ever finds out about it. And the men are even more coy.'

'Don't tell me men have facelifts?' Sarah was incredulous.

'Men are happy to have all kinds of lifts. Especially over-the-hill celebrities in show business. Now, Sarah, how do you like this lovely, light stuff we're drinking? It's from a small vineyard in the Bouche du Rhône. I'm trying to persuade Camilla that she should come with me to the south of France this summer, and see the whole enchanting area for herself. That there is life outside of the Paris couture houses and the frenzy of Manhattan.'

'The wine is delicious, but one glass is enough,' Sarah said, giving Rabindrah a sideways glance. 'I don't want to disgrace the company. Do you know Paris and Manhattan?'

'I know both of them well,' he said. 'In fact, I lived in New York for a time, honing my trade on the faces of Park Avenue ladies of a certain age. It's a great city.'

'New York was love at first sight,' Camilla said. 'I adored everything, from the minute I stepped off the plane. London is awfully slow in comparison. But for all his talk about knowing it well, Edward has never been to the top of the Empire State Building.' She smiled at him. 'That was a most spectacular view of the world! I wouldn't mind living there, if—'

'You could do that for part of every year,' Edward said. 'Your American enterprise is going well. I have a small apartment that I hang on to, overlooking Central Park. What better position could you have?'

'The position I'm in right now is just perfect, thank you,' Camilla said. 'And my calendar is very, very full.'

The talk turned to Rabindrah's visit to Tanzania where he had interviewed Jane Goodall in her research camp at Gombe.

'I was impressed by her. By the whole set-up, in fact. And the chimpanzees are extraordinary, although it's unsettling to watch creatures that are so close to ourselves. There was a polio outbreak recently, that spread from some of the villages near the reserve. Jane started a vaccination programme at the research centre straight away. It was a dangerous time for both scientists and animals.'

'They immunised the chimps too?' Camilla was astonished.

'Oh yes. But it wasn't a straightforward operation, because if the dominant animals had taken more than their share of the bananas spiked with the vaccine, they could actually have contracted polio, instead of being immunised.' Rabindrah's eyes darkened with regret. 'About nine contracted the virus. Four of them died and two of those had to be shot, which was traumatic for the team. They become very attached to their subjects, as Sarah will verify.'

'And the others?' Edward asked.

'Five were left with paralysed limbs and it was astonishing to see how quickly they learned new skills to compensate for their disability. Tragic though the outbreak was, it proved valuable for the scientists to see how the chimps coped with a health crisis.'

'Are you specialising in interviewing slightly mad women who live with wild animals?' Camilla's question was amused.

'I'd be delighted to interview all and any slightly mad women,' Rabindrah said. 'It strikes me that they have more obstacles to overcome, both physically and in other peoples' perceptions of them, particularly in Africa. I've interviewed Mary Leakey recently, and I hope to talk to others, yes.'

'I'm not mad,' Sarah said, laughing.

'Only a little,' Rabindrah said.

Camilla caught a slight inflection in his voice that she recognised. He's attracted to her, she thought. She is not aware of it, and maybe he isn't either. But the beginnings are there. They ordered dessert and the talk moved on to Edward's work and his visits to Third World countries where he treated children who were burned or disfigured in some way.

'I've been to Kenya a number of times,' he said. 'Camilla's mother used to raise money for a charity that paid hospital expenses and medicines for my patients. But I haven't been back for a while.'

'You should come out again,' Sarah said. 'Take care of your surgery and then go on safari. Drop in on us in Buffalo Springs and visit Samburu. It's a magnificent area, especially if you're camping somewhere on the Uaso Nyiro River.'

'There are people all over the world who need help,' Camilla interrupted, her voice sharp. 'I think you should spread your bounty around, Edward. You've been to Kenya six times.'

'She's right,' Edward said smoothly. 'I'm going to do some repair work in the Bahamas later this year. We'll spend a couple of weeks there.' He smiled at Sarah. 'We have mutual friends who own a wonderful house on the beach, and an old ketch on which we can sail from one island to another. We're going to stay with them.'

Camilla was looking fixedly at her plate. Sarah backed away from any further discussion about safaris and travel. What had possessed her to mention tents in Samburu, an early setting for Camilla's passionate affair with Anthony? The wine must have loosened her tongue. She wondered again what the situation was with Edward. Camilla had said that she saw him from time to time. But here he was, talking about taking her to France and New York and the Bahamas. He obviously believed that she was back to stay. He must be twenty years older than Camilla, but he was charming, full of energy and obviously successful. It might be a better partnership for her in the long run. One that offered the kind of trust and security she needed. Yet she had spoken so casually about him earlier. Had been almost dismissive.

'I'm delighted to have spent the evening with you, Sarah,' Edward said later. Rabindrah had gone to make a phone call, and Camilla was returning from the powder room, stopping here and there to talk to people she knew. 'You're an extremely courageous person, and I know how much you mean in Camilla's life. Friendships like yours are very rare.'

'I'm happy to have met you too,' Sarah said. 'I can see that you care about her a great deal.'

'I do, yes. And who knows, she may get used to me after a while and keep me on.'

'You mean you'd like to marry her?' Sarah immediately kicked herself for being so blunt. It was none of her business.

She was dismayed to see Edward's face change instantly. He turned away, signalling their waiter to bring the bill. When they walked out into the street it had started to rain and he ushered them back inside while he and Rabindrah organised taxis.

'What's your programme tomorrow?' Camilla asked as they huddled in the doorway.

'We have another session with the publishers. There's a meeting with the art director in the morning, and then Rabindrah wants me to meet his father.' She saw Camilla raise her eyebrows, and she hastened to explain. 'Mr Singh is a lawyer and he's going to read through our contract before we sign it. Look, Edward has found us a cab. Goodnight, Rabindrah. See you tomorrow.'

Back at the flat, Sarah put two cups of coffee down on the table. 'Is Edward turning himself into a permanent fixture?' she said.

'What's permanent?' Camilla threw her bag on to the sofa and sat down. 'I could get run over by a bus tomorrow. He could slip on a banana skin and break his neck. Permanent means nothing.'

'I'd say he is permanently in love with you,' Sarah said. 'So you can start by telling me what you feel about that. And don't try that bright chatter you hand out to the rest of the world. I want to know the real story.'

'I'm not going to let Anthony destroy my life.' Camilla's voice was strong, but she looked delicate, almost breakable. 'I've promised myself that I'll never let him hurt me again. I ran into Edward soon after I came back. It was inevitable – we have mutual friends. Now we see each other occasionally, for dinner or a concert or a film. I like him. I feel safe with him, and he makes me laugh. Makes fun of me, too. He seems to understand where I've been and what it felt like to be there. He's a workaholic, though. Often busy in the evenings and even at weekends, and he travels overseas too. We see each other when it's convenient, and I have plenty of time to myself. That's enough for me.'

'But is it enough for him?' Sarah pressed her. 'Doesn't he want to marry you?'

'He's not . . . well, the fact is that he's married. Oh come on, Sarah.' Camilla was exasperated by her friend's startled expression. 'It's 1967, for God's sake, and we're in London. His wife had a terrible brain haemorrhage some time ago. She's alive but little more than a vegetable.'

'How dreadful,' Sarah said. 'Did they have any children?'

'They were separated for some time before it happened, because she had an affair and a child with someone else. But Edward's never divorced her. Anyway, you don't have to get married these days, you know. Many of our friends are living together. Not everyone believes that they will burn in an eternal hell if they don't have a marriage certificate. Besides, I have no idea what my long-term plans are. It's only a few weeks since I came back here, and I've made my terms quite clear. He's a sophisticated man who knows the drill. It's bedtime.' She rose to her feet. 'I've got one really early session in the morning, so I'll be gone long before you get up. And I'm tied up for the day. I've managed to juggle my other commitments, though, and we can leave for Ireland the day after tomorrow. Just in time to rescue Timmy.'

'I can't thank you enough for doing this,' Sarah said. 'And I'm sorry – I'll shut up about Edward. It's none of my business.'

'There's nothing more to say on that subject. Your parents sent me a wedding invitation, by the way. I'm a legitimate guest, though not Deirdre's first choice, I imagine.' She paused at the door of her room. 'Why is he doing it, do you think? He's so fabulous, with his innocent expression, and the little round wire glasses, and that helpless, rumpled look. The nurses and patients must have been swarming all over him.'

'They were and I still can't figure it out,' Sarah said. 'Maybe he likes the fact that she needs him, and she's probably the kind of girl that will never look at another man. I asked him, when they got engaged, if he loved her. He kept telling me how kind and good she was, but he never mentioned the word love. He was quite defensive about it. To me they didn't seem like an engaged couple at all. I couldn't see any real excitement or passion between them. But I'm sure they'll be blissfully happy.' She could not disguise the undercurrent of envy and wretchedness in her voice, and Camilla put an arm around her shoulder.

'It won't be as bad as you think,' she said. 'We'll get through it together. Now, I have to get to sleep, or I'll look like shit in the morning.'

'I phoned my father,' Rabindrah said, when their introductory meeting with the art director ended. 'We're expected at the house for lunch.'

They crossed the river to Southwark, the largest Asian enclave in the city. Everywhere there were women with coats bundled over colourful saris. Many of the men wore turbans, or were dressed in the Pakistani *salwar kameez* tunics with astrakhan hats and long shawls. The taxi deposited them outside a neat, semi-detached house on a quiet side street. The door was opened by a woman in traditional Punjabi dress, a knee-length tunic with side slits worn over loose trousers, and an embroidered scarf draped across her shoulders. Rabindrah greeted her respectfully but with obvious love, and made the introductions.

Nand Kaur Singh was in her early fifties, slight in build, with deep, dark eyes in a narrow face. Her long hair was black with no traces, as yet, of any grey. She wore it in a plait down her back, with coloured threads woven through it. She looked exotic and elegant. Quite a beauty, Sarah thought. It was easy to see where Rabindrah's good looks and style had come from.

'Please come in. You are welcome in our home, Miss Mackay.'

Sarah was not sure whether she should ask to be called by her first name. As they stepped into the hall, she was assailed by the redolence of curry and spices that emanated from the kitchen. Nand Kaur brought them into the sitting room, and indicated two armchairs. Her voice was low, and had the lilting inflection that Sarah had always liked in the Indians she knew.

'Rabindrah, bring a drink for our guest, please,' she said. 'There is orange juice, or we have Coca-Cola.'

Sarah glanced around the room. The furniture was dark and heavy, and adorned with fringed cushions embroidered with gold thread. Deep velvet curtains were partly drawn across the windows, giving the room a gloomy quality. The floor was covered by a fine carpet, probably Persian. On the walls were a number of what Sarah took to be religious tracts, gilt-framed and surrounded by colourful landscapes. All the pictures were mounted very high, and the chairs in the room were arranged carefully around the walls. It reminded her of a waiting room.

'Please make yourselves comfortable. My husband will be home soon,' Nand Kaur said. She sat down opposite them, her feet together and hands folded neatly in her lap. It reminded Sarah of the way the nuns had taught her to sit when she was a child. 'I am sorry Rabindrah's sisters could not be here,' she said. 'Of course, he did not give us sufficient notice. But we are happy to have you visit us. Do you know London well, Miss Mackay?'

'Not really,' Sarah said. 'I was sent to university in Dublin, so I know that better. My parents are Irish, you see.'

There was an awkward silence and then they heard the front door opening. 'That will be my husband, now,' Nand Kaur said. She rose, excusing herself, and went out to the hall to greet him.

'Do you think your mother would mind calling me "Sarah"?' she asked, turning to Rabindrah, 'Because I'd feel more comfortable with that. Miss Mackay makes me feel slightly nervous.'

Rabindrah laughed. 'I don't think I've ever seen you even slightly over-awed by anything. Rhinos, charging buffalo and herds of elephants – you weave in and out among them without any signs of unease. But my little mother makes you nervous!'

Jasmer Singh was as tall as his son. Like Rabindrah, he was dressed in a charcoal-grey suit, but he wore the traditional turban and beard of his people. His greeting to Sarah was formal, and he kept their initial conversation to the clauses of the publishing contract, making several useful suggestions. But when Nand Kaur called them for lunch, the atmosphere relaxed over a richly flavoured vegetarian curry.

'We are very proud that you are doing this book with my son,' Jasmer said. 'It will be a great thing for both of you, in your professions. Good for Kenya too, I suppose, with all its current problems. But Rabindrah has not yet told us how he met you.'

'He does not tell us much, you know.' Nand Kaur's eyes flashed a smile. 'I only hear his news from my sister-in-law. This boy never writes home.'

Sarah laughed. 'I think my parents have the same complaint,' she said. 'But I'll explain how we met. The book idea was all his, by the way.'

She described their initial encounter, and went on to tell amusing anecdotes about Rabindrah's first days in the bush at Buffalo Springs.

'I don't think he was prepared for some of the things that happened up there. Like lying under the car to mend a tyre, and seeing a snake sliding towards him. He banged his head trying to escape, and we were laughing because it was a completely harmless *nyoka*. And he found a hyrax under his bed one night, shrieking and chattering with fright. He'd left his door open earlier in the day and it came in and got trapped inside.'

'I am glad he has taken up a cause, Miss Mackay,' Jasmer said. 'Nowadays there are many young men who are too fond of money and the pursuit of pleasure.' He looked sternly at his son. 'But you should be careful with the issues you choose to highlight.'

'We Indians have as much right to make our voices heard as any other citizens,' Rabindrah said, plainly annoyed. 'I'm not going to be cowed into writing any old rubbish, because of some corrupt African politician. I'm as much a Kenyan as any of them. I was born in the same country, and you were born in it too.'

'You are an optimist, my son,' Jasmer said. 'We will never be like them, or equal to them. We are Indian and they are black.'

'We're all Kenyans,' Rabindrah said stubbornly. 'We have an Indian heritage, but we are Kenyans, born and bred.'

Sarah's heart contracted as she thought back to her schooldays, and to Jan van der Beer presiding over the dinner table at Langani, warning Piet in exactly the same way. It sounded as though this was an old argument in the Singh household. She wondered if they clashed often in their opinions and aspirations. Jasmer Singh was charming and cultured but obviously conservative, while his son held more liberal views. Rabindrah turned the conversation quickly to Indar's gift of the Land Rover, and Sarah saw that he was quite expert in dodging uncomfortable topics. But it was not long before another issue caused a disagreement between them.

'When you have finished the writing of this book, you might think of coming back to London,' Jasmer said. 'You have had several pieces in the *Telegraph* now, and your uncle in Manchester also sent me your articles in the *Manchester Guardian*. Your time in Kenya has given you a chance to build a good reputation, Rabindrah, and you could use that to look for a permanent position here. Where it is secure.'

'I don't want to live in England, any more than I did a year ago,' Rabindrah said. 'And now I'm really interested in the subject of wildlife, and in what the Briggses and Sarah are doing up there in the north.'

'But you have written about Miss Mackay, and you are publishing a book together,' Nand Kaur said. 'So you must soon find a new subject, or you will become stuck again with only one thing to write about. That is what you disliked when you were working in Manchester, isn't it?'

'It's not the same at all,' Rabindrah said.

'I know our son is grateful to you,' Jasmer said, his eyes fixed directly on Sarah. 'But I am sure you understand the importance of moving on, of keeping a broad perspective in his profession.'

'I hope our book will give Rabindrah a chance to choose his direction,' she said, feeling an undercurrent in the conversation that she did not understand. 'He is a good writer, and in the end that is what counts.'

Nand Kaur smiled and kept her counsel for the remainder of the meal, plying everyone with ample food and soft drinks. After lunch there was sweet, milky tea and small pastries which were addictive. At Rabindrah's request Sarah had brought her portfolio and they spread the pictures out on a low coffee table. She was pleased at his parents' admiration, and the remainder of the time in their company was relaxed and pleasant. Finally, it was time for Jasmer to return to his office. He shook hands with Sarah briskly, but his eyes were full of pride as he embraced his son.

'I wish you good fortune, Miss Mackay,' Nand Kaur said. 'Perhaps one of these days we will see you again, although we do not plan to go back to Kenya for the moment. Our family base is here now, and we hope that all of us will be able to make a good life here together.' She reached up to touch her son's cheek in blessing. 'Do not stay away so long,' she told him. 'Your father worries and you should heed his advice. At least try and write more often.'

'What now?' Rabindrah asked when they were out on the street. He was visibly relieved to be free of the little threads of tension that had sewn themselves into the time spent with his parents. 'I'll take the contracts back to Sinclair and Lewis tomorrow, and see if they will accept the changes my father suggested. Then we'll sign, and you should receive a cheque before too long. Not very much, but worth having all the same.'

'I don't think I've ever taken this many taxis,' Sarah said as he hailed a cab. 'I feel totally decadent, squandering my money like this. But I'm glad I don't have to drag this big folder on to the tube. Do you want to come back to Camilla's flat with me? Maybe we can do something with her later on.' She was suddenly embarrassed by her presumption. 'Although you're probably busy already.'

'I'd like to come to the flat,' he said. But he did not respond to her second proposition.

'I have no plans for this evening,' Camilla said. 'I've escaped an awful party, and Edward is tied up with some professional thing. Why don't we go to a film?'

She made tea, and they argued cheerfully over what they wanted to see.

'It should be Sarah's choice,' Camilla said. 'She never gets to the cinema, so she should make the selection.'

'What about *Alfie*?' Sarah asked. 'I hear Michael Caine is a sensation.'

'No.' Camilla was definite. 'No cads.'

'I thought you said Sarah could choose.' Rabindrah was chuckling. 'What's wrong with Michael Caine?'

'I refuse to spend the evening learning more about feckless men,' Camilla said. 'I'm an expert already.'

They settled on *Blow Up* and afterwards had supper in a bistro, discussing the nature of reality and the genius of Antonioni.

'I think I should change my job,' Rabindrah said. 'I've come to the conclusion that I'd rather be a fashion photographer than a lowly journalist. I could spend all my time with beautiful half-naked, or even wholly naked, women. And be paid handsomely for it.'

'What rubbish,' said Sarah. 'You'd much rather be investigating some scandalous government conspiracy, or interviewing Shifta bandits to find out what it takes to be a poacher! You're far more likely to enjoy the *bundu*, now that you've got used to it. I think you'd be bored out of your mind in ten minutes, taking pictures of half-naked girls in silly clothes.'

'What's so bad about half-naked girls in silly clothes?' Camilla demanded. 'I've heard some people do that for a living.' She turned to Rabindrah and smiled knowingly at him from beneath long lashes. 'We need to watch my friend here, or she's going to turn into a feminist crusader, on top of her existing urge to do good. And that would be a bit much.'

'If it's half-naked girls you want to look at you should do a study of the Samburu tribe,' Sarah said. 'There are lots of them up there, and you could write something useful about their way of life and the hardship of it, and female circumcision and so on. Although your father might not think of that as an ideal subject.'

'Shifta bandits and Samburu virgins,' Rabindrah said thoughtfully. 'I could do that, yes.'

'Riveting,' Camilla said. 'And there's something you can do for me, Rabindrah.'

'What is that?' Rabindrah asked.

'I want you to talk to my father,' she said. 'About Langani Farm and Jan van der Beer.'

Rabindrah sat back, taken by surprise and distancing himself from her request, aware of the stiffening in Sarah's body and the distress that flashed across her face.

'What could your father have to say on that subject that we haven't heard already?' Sarah said wretchedly. She did not want to think about Langani and the past. It had been a good day and she wanted it to end happily. 'Jeremy Hardy is doing his best to find out why your workshop was trashed, and I don't see what George can contribute.'

'There are things you may not understand about all this.' Camilla spoke directly to Rabindrah. 'Things that Sarah and I have discussed in the past, but were never able to resolve. About a year before Independence, we were all at a party and my mother accused Janni of being a criminal. She said he wouldn't be allowed to keep his farm after Independence, because he had done something wrong in the past. She was always jealous of my love for the van der Beers, and she was very drunk that evening. But Janni fled the country soon afterwards, suddenly and without explanation. I think my father knows the reason, but he has always evaded my questions.

I'm convinced he has some piece of information that could throw some light on what happened to Jan van der Beer years ago, and whether it has any bearing on everything that has taken place at Langani since. And he might tell you what it is.'

'I don't think George would tell me anything. But I may have another source that—'

'I don't care who you talk to,' Camilla said. 'But you must do this for Sarah, who lost her fiancé and her future, and for Hannah, who is fighting to keep her home. And for me, because I love them both, and because Langani has always been the closest thing to home that I ever knew. Swear to me now, and to Sarah, that you will do it.'

'I will do it,' Rabindrah said, looking into Sarah's eyes. 'I promise you both that I will.'

Chapter 9

Ireland, April 1967

Their reservations were on the early flight to Dublin, and Sarah had chosen to take the train to Sligo so that they could enjoy the countryside.

'I can't look at the countryside,' Camilla protested as they sank on to opposite seats in their compartment. 'I need sleep. And darker glasses to protect me from all this loud greenery. Let's go to the dining car for some blotting paper. Tea you could trot a mouse on, eggs, bacon, sausages and fried bread. It's the perfect cure for everything, an Irish breakfast. And let no one ever try to tell me that Sikhs don't drink.'

'He's not a proper Sikh,' Sarah said. 'He doesn't wear a turban or go to the temple, and he eats everything in sight. He became detribalised while he was in England.'

'Being far from home often does the opposite,' Camilla said. 'Makes people long for their roots. Shores them up even if they didn't think about the issue before. He has that bangle, though, and I wouldn't be surprised if there's a traditional dagger tucked away on his person, since he can't hide it in his turban.'

'They don't hide daggers in their turbans,' Sarah said, laughing. 'They're worn in a holster.'

'Really? Maybe he even wears the warrior's knickers they're all supposed to have. You should ask him about that. Or take a look. Almost as intriguing as finding out if a Scot wears anything under his kilt.'

'You are outrageous.' Sarah's face had flushed scarlet. 'I don't know how I put up with it. But thanks for coming with me.' She hesitated. 'I have another favour to ask, though.'

'Out with it,' Camilla said. 'Get me while I'm weak and helpless.'

'I don't want them to know about the workshop,' Sarah said. 'My parents, I mean. They'll try to persuade me to come home permanently, and that would give them more ammunition.'

'I won't say a word. We're in this together. Like we promised, when we were naive and foolish schoolgirls, and very, very wise.'

Raphael was at the station to meet them and Sarah flung herself into his arms, clinging to him like a small child. At last he set her gently aside and welcomed Camilla. He helped them into his battered old car, and they drove through country lanes bordered by wide fields and budding trees, with the great flat shape of Ben Bulben sailing out of the horizon towards them. It was a crisp, cold day but the sun had decided to shine. Sarah's heart turned over each time she glanced at her father's lined face, saw his lopsided smile and the bristles on his cheek where he hadn't shaved too well. He was unchanged, and she loved him more than she could ever hope to tell him.

'Sarah! Oh, I'm so glad you're home. Thank God, thank God!'

Betty wept unashamedly as she held her daughter, thankful that she was back in the shelter of the family, and they would all be together for Tim's wedding. Then she turned to Camilla who was standing a little apart, watching the reunion with a pensive smile.

'My dear,' she said, opening her arms, 'it's been such a long time, and we're delighted you were able to come too. I hope you'll be as much at home as ever you were. I was sorry to hear about your mother.'

'Where's Tim?' Sarah asked, not wishing to dwell on the subject of Marina. 'Why isn't he here, rolling out the red carpet?'

'He'll be in soon.' Betty smiled fondly. 'He went into town with Deirdre to organise a few last things. They'll be back for their tea.'

'We have a surprise for Deirdre.' Raphael was looking pleased with himself. 'We found an old cottage on the road to Colloony. It's been empty for years, so we bought it for a song and had it renovated for the newly-weds.'

'Your father and I felt it would be better than living with the in-laws, 'specially since we all work together.' Betty's face was glowing with anticipation at their reaction. 'Tim is in on it, of course, and thrilled to bits. But Deirdre hasn't an inkling. We plan to give them the keys tomorrow.'

'What a fantastic wedding present,' Sarah said. 'A place of their own. They'll be over the moon.'

She looked around the hall where they were standing. The house had been little more than a building site during her last visit. Now it was a home that exuded welcome, with brasses shining and flowers in a large vase on the hall table. Raphael's favourite Persian rug was in place on the polished oak floor, and the furniture from Mombasa gave the rooms a familiarity that was warming. But it carried the nostalgia of times and places past, of happiness that could never be recovered and lives that would never be the same. In the sitting room she was surrounded by the trappings of her childhood and she reached out to touch a teak table, a carved Lamu sideboard, and brass-studded chests from Zanzibar, all part of their African history. The overgrown jungle that had surrounded the house when they had taken possession was now transformed. Hedges were neatly cut back, shrubs and beds of winter pansies burgeoning but orderly. Sarah was reminded of Lottie's garden at Langani, and she turned away from the window abruptly. Betty disappeared into the kitchen and returned with the tea tray. As she poured they began to talk, and Sarah realised that it had been a life-saving plan to bring Camilla. The awkward and painful topics were shelved as they listened to descriptions of swinging London and New York, and stories of the fashion world.

'It's a miracle we got here today,' Camilla said. 'We didn't part company with Rabindrah until after two, and we had to get up around six. Without Sarah's insistence I'd still be lying in bed in London. But it was fun, and he dances like a dervish.'

'Tell us about this man who is doing the book with you,' Raphael said, smiling proudly at his daughter. 'We're all thrilled that your wonderful photographs are going to be published. I hope his writing is good enough to set them off in the way they deserve. Has he been around for a long time? I don't remember his name on anything in the Nairobi papers in my day.'

'You wouldn't have read anything he wrote,' Sarah said, giving an outline of Rabindrah's background.

'I imagine him as one of those burly Sikhs with a big turban and whiskers, and fierce, hawklike eyes,' Betty said. 'A pillar of the temple and the Indian community in Nairobi.'

'Absolutely not. Rabindrah is hawkish. But he's also young and too smart by half,' Camilla said. 'He's clean-shaven with short hair and amazing eyes that are a green-gold colour. Sarah gave him a hard time at first, but now they have a good working relationship.'

'In the beginning I wasn't happy with the idea of having him in my vehicle and asking questions all the time,' Sarah said. 'I thought he was only interested in making a name for himself. But he has turned out to be as good as his word. I wrote to you about the Land Rover he persuaded his uncle to give Dan. That was impressive, to put it mildly. Uncle Indar. Now there's a traditional pillar of the Sikh community. He doesn't quite approve of his favourite nephew, although he's proud of him at the same time. I met Rabindrah's parents in London, too.'

'My goodness,' Betty said. 'You've been received into the bosom of the family. What do they want in return for all this generosity?'

'Dan wondered that at first. But I don't think they want anything,' Sarah said.

'It's rather unusual to have an Indian writing about wildlife and the countryside,' Raphael said. 'They do current affairs and politics very well, but for subject matter this is a little out of the ordinary, isn't it?'

'Yes, it is,' Sarah said. 'But Rabindrah is out of the ordinary, and he has become genuinely concerned with our study and the fate of the elephants. The word "Singh" means lion, but there certainly wasn't any resemblance between Rabindrah and the fearless king of beasts when we started out. He was scared stiff of all wildlife.'

She began to recount a series of amusing incidents that had left the journalist in a state of near terror, and everyone was laughing when Tim came into the room. There was a moment's silence as he looked at his sister and then she ran to greet him and he held her tight, hugging her until there was no breath left in her. Afterwards he turned to Camilla.

'Long time no see, Timmy.' She ruffled his hair with delicate fingers and dropped a light kiss on his cheek.

Deirdre was standing in the doorway. Sarah saw her blinking anxiously and crossed the room to embrace her and include her in the reunion.

'Come and tell us how the preparations are going.' Sarah took her arm. 'We want to hear everything.'

'Yes. I will, but I have a few things to finish up this afternoon. Patients' reports, and the dispensary list.' Deirdre sounded flustered, and she looked at Tim with a pleading expression. 'Maybe Raphael should take you to see the new surgery now, before it opens for the evening session. And we can chat about the other things later on.'

'We're doing pretty well on all fronts,' Raphael said with some pride, as they followed him down the path to the surgery. 'I think a few "ould fellas" were afraid I'd be a witchdoctor with a bone in my nose, after all those years away in Africa. But now we have more patients than we really want. Your mother has been grand, of course, doing more than her share, looking after reception half the time and keeping the house going. And Deirdre is a hard worker. The best nurse we could have hoped for and a great asset. Come on, Tim, let's show them around.'

The surgery had been set up in the old gate lodge at the entrance to the property. The place was bright, even on a blustery evening. There were pictures on the walls, and the waiting room had comfortable chairs, a table with magazines and a basket of toys to occupy fractious children. Evening surgery would start in twenty minutes, and Tim was taking it.

'I'll be off in a few days, swanning around Paris on my honeymoon,' he said, drumming his fingers on the desk, obviously keen to get rid of the visitors. 'So I'm doing double shifts this week. Very busy. You take the girls back to the house, Dad, now that they've seen the place. I'll be up as soon as I'm finished here.'

'Tim seems a little abrupt,' Sarah said, as they made their way up the drive in the dusk.

'Wedding nerves,' Raphael said cheerfully. 'I nearly ran away the night before I married your mother. But I got over it. And wasn't it just as well?'

He smiled at his daughter and Camilla and opened the front door. An appetising smell came from the kitchen and Raphael called out to his wife.

'We're back, love. Now, I think you girls should have a bit of a rest, and come down for drinks at seven. We've splurged on some champagne. It's not something we have very often around here, but this is a special night.' He went towards the study, then turned. 'Sarah,' he said softly. 'It's good to have you home.'

Dinner was a light-hearted affair as they discussed the wedding plans. It was not going to be a large gathering, and the reception would take place at the house.

'We all decided against a hotel. Much nicer to have it here,' Raphael said. 'Betty was going to do the food herself, but I've prevailed on her to get a caterer. That way she can enjoy the day, and not be trapped in the kitchen.'

Sarah was glad now that she had come. There would be plenty for her to do, and her contribution would be valuable to her mother. Extra tables and chairs had been ordered, and would be delivered the day before the reception, along with the flowers and linen, plates, glasses and cutlery. The church would have to be decorated on the eve of the wedding, and in the afternoon there would be a rehearsal with the priest and the organist. Deirdre said little at dinner and Sarah watched her covertly, noticing that she barely touched her food. Tim is not the only one with wedding nerves, she thought. Gifts had already arrived, and after dinner they went to Raphael's study where a table had been set out to display them all.

'What about the dress? We'd love to see it,' Camilla said. 'Or are you keeping it at your flat in town, in case Timmy is tempted to peep?'

'No,' Deirdre said. 'It's here. Betty set aside one of the bedrooms upstairs to use for the wedding. It has my dress and going-away suit, and all the other things in it. A place to change, and so on.'

'Can we go up?' Sarah said. 'You could put on the dress, and give a few sweeps around the floor.'

'That's a grand idea,' Betty said. 'Go ahead, Deirdre. Dad and Tim and I will clear away the supper things, and you get into your finery.'

'I'll go in first and put it on' Deirdre was clearly troubled when they reached the first-floor landing and the door to the bedroom. 'But it's not a dress that . . . well, you know, I just bought it out of a shop. So it wasn't made specially. It's not a designer dress or anything.' She was twisting her hands as she stared at them, pale and apprehensive.

'Go on,' Camilla said, giving her a little push. 'We can't wait to see it.'

It was a long time before the door opened. Camilla leaned against the wall outside, her brows raised. Sarah shrugged and held out her hands, palms up, in a gesture of helpless enquiry.

'I think she's scared,' she whispered.

Seconds later they heard the click of the door knob. Deirdre stood in front of them, lips pressed together tightly, body tense. Her expression was defensive as she looked at Camilla, and Sarah was suddenly sorry for her. Here she was, a country girl, wearing the most important gown she would ever own. But she was being inspected with the critical eye of a famous model she had seen in magazines, and even on television. Someone who wore the world's most beautiful and expensive clothes and jewels. It must be nerve-racking. The dress had a wide tulle skirt, with a high neck and long sleeves of lace. It should have looked like a birthday cake but, strangely, it was flattering on Deirdre. She had lost a considerable amount of weight, and her hair was tied back, smooth and sleek and away from her face, so that her perfect complexion was evident. Camilla made no comment and the silence stretched out uncomfortably. Deirdre gripped the door as though she was about to shut it in their faces.

'You look absolutely stunning,' Camilla said at last. 'I hadn't realised what lovely bones you have. And that tiny waist, and unblemished skin like a baby's. Perfectly lovely! Can we come in now? Is there a veil?'

There was relief on Deirdre's face, and she let out the breath she had been holding, in a soft sigh. Soon she was walking up and down, turning this way and that, as Camilla adjusted the skirt and fixed the headdress.

'I have a gold chain I'd like to give you,' she said. 'It's my present for you, personally. Something new. What about the old and the borrowed and the blue? My goodness, Deirdre, you are quite gorgeous. Timmy will be mesmerised.'

Deirdre's eyes filled with tears. 'Thanks. Thank you both.' Her voice was low. 'I wasn't sure, you know. I think I'll put it all away now. I have an early start in the morning because it's my last day at work.'

The next morning was bright but cold and the emerald grass shimmered in the sunshine. Tim had suggested an early morning ride. There was no sign of Deirdre as they saddled the three horses and took off along the beach at a gallop, the icy wind whipping colour into their cheeks and making their eyes water. It was pure exhilaration.

'Has Deirdre not got over her fear of the horses?' Sarah asked as they trotted back up the track to the stables. 'Or would the ride have made her late for the surgery?'

'I'm afraid she's never going to be a horsewoman,' Tim said. 'She has tried, but she's terrified all the time, and it's no fun for her really. The horses sense that she's not in control and behave accordingly, even old Ben. I thought she'd get over her fright in time, but now I've sort of given up on it. For the moment, anyway.'

Sarah thought it a pity that he would not be able to share one of his great pleasures with his wife. But they had other things to enjoy together, she was sure. Back in the stables, they put the tack away, and Sarah strode ahead, wanting to help her mother with the breakfast. She could hear Tim and Camilla behind her on the path, laughing and poking fun at one another as they had done since childhood. It struck her that she had never heard her brother tease Deirdre. She was far too sensitive to give as good as she got, and there was not that ease between them that would allow him to make even gentle fun of her. This was going to be a tough sinecure for Tim, she thought. She spent the morning with her mother and Camilla, tidying and moving furniture to accommodate the extra tables and chairs for the reception. Betty fussed and laughed, repositioning vases and ornaments and candlesticks a dozen times, until Raphael and Tim arrived for lunch. They were drinking their coffee when Raphael tapped his spoon on the side of the cup to gain their attention.

'Tim and Deirdre, we have a surprise for you,' he said. 'We're going for a little spin. It's not far, so I think we can all squeeze into my car.'

The old cottage was set back from the road and standing in its own garden. It was of red brick, with a high-pitched slate roof and sash windows. Rambling roses grew around the newly painted front door and window frames. Inside, everything looked fresh. Betty had found a selection of basic furniture at auctions and in second-hand shops, and the polished wooden floors were covered in bright rugs. The only extravagance was the four-poster bed in the main bedroom, an Irish antique that she had hung with curtains and decorated with a hand-stitched quilt. They waited in the sitting room as Tim took Deirdre slowly around the rooms. Betty stood beside her husband and daughter, her kindly face glowing with satisfaction. But when Deirdre reappeared her face was like a mask, and she turned to them with a tight smile.

'It's very nice, really it is. We're grateful. But I should get back now, because there's a lot to do in the surgery before I hand over to the temporary nurse.' She left the room quickly, heading for the car in what was almost a run. When they reached the main house she fled down the path to the surgery without a word.

'She doesn't like it, Raphael,' Betty said, collapsing into an armchair, her hand pressed over her eyes. 'I suppose she thought we were interfering, getting in furniture and all that. She probably would have liked to pick it out for herself. I should have realised. But with her own mother not being around to do things for her I thought—' She was almost in tears. 'I'm so sorry, Tim.'

'No, Mum. It's the most wonderful, generous present you could have given us.' His voice was grim. 'I don't understand her reaction, I really don't. She couldn't be anything but thrilled with the cottage. It's a dream and you've made it so perfect. Look, I'll go down now and speak to her.'

'Maybe I should go,' Sarah broke in. She could see that her brother was angry, and hurt on his parents' behalf. It would be a bad time for a confrontation. 'She might feel awkward talking to you right now. Let me see if I can get to the bottom of this.'

'She's right,' Camilla said. 'Why don't we go for a walk, Timmy, and let Sarah sort this out?'

But there was no sign of Deirdre in the surgery, and Sarah retraced her steps to the house, puzzled.

'She's upstairs,' Betty whispered to her daughter. 'She came in the back way, obviously trying to avoid seeing us. I'm sure she's feeling bad, poor girl. Embarrassed. I didn't realise she was so strung up.'

Sarah ran up the stairs two at a time and knocked on the door. There was no response, and she tried the handle. It was locked.

'Deirdre?' she called. 'Can we talk? I'm sure you're nervous about the wedding. About everything. It's a very common thing, and it might help to have a chat. Open the door. Please.'

'I'm fine.' Deirdre's voice was muffled. 'I just need some time to myself. Don't worry, I'll be down in a while.'

Sarah waited, unsure of what to do, feeling helpless and half angry, unable to figure out Deirdre's frame of mind. Finally, she turned and went back down the stairs, knowing that she could not force a confidence from this girl whom she hardly knew.

'Mum? She wants to be on her own for a bit.'

'She wouldn't talk to you at all?' Betty appeared from the kitchen. 'Oh dear. I suppose it would only make it worse to press her right now.'

'Yes. I think I'll go for a walk,' Sarah said. 'Do you want to come?'

'That sounds grand,' Betty said. 'But we'll need to wrap up.'

In the hallway they put on jackets and scarves before stepping out into the watery sunshine. Sarah saw her brother immediately. He was standing at the end of the garden with Camilla, talking earnestly, holding both her hands in his. She listened for a time until he put his arms around her waist and dropped his head on to her shoulder so that the fall of her long hair hid his expression. When he straightened, he took her face in his hands and looked at her without speaking. She kissed his forehead and slid her arms up around his neck and they stood together, swaying slightly. Finally he bent towards her, but she put a hand up to stroke his cheek and then distanced herself from him. The words she said were carried away by the wind but Tim nodded, smiling now as she moved off ahead of him, beckoning him to follow. When he caught up with her they took the path that led towards the sea, arms entwined as they vanished from sight.

Sarah looked after them, transfixed, the pulse in her throat jumping. She glanced sideways at her mother. Betty's face was set as she went back into the house. When Sarah turned to follow, a movement caught her eye and made her glance upwards. Above her she saw Deirdre at the bedroom window, her hands pressed against her face as she stared out across the lawn to the beach, straining forward, standing like a statue as though mesmerised. Then she disappeared. Sarah stood for a while on the terrace trying to figure out a way to talk to Deirdre. But the tossing waves and the whistle of the cold wind did little to inspire her, and after a while she made her way back into the house.

She was sure it could not be the way it seemed. Tim was upset, confiding in a childhood friend. But she remembered how he had looked at Camilla years ago, when they were in Mombasa. And later, when they had been students and had gone to spend Easter with her in London. There had been an obvious attraction there. Camilla had known it too. She was savvy in a way that Tim would never be. Only a few days ago she had joked about seducing Tim. They had both joked about it.

Sarah hung up her jacket, wondering if trying to talk to Deirdre again would make things even worse. But she might be able to persuade the girl that there was no significance in the scene they had witnessed, and to discover what had upset her earlier in the afternoon. She climbed the stairs and knocked on the bedroom door. There was no answer. When she tried the handle the door swung open, but there was no one inside. Downstairs she went in search of her mother and found her in the kitchen.

'Did you see Deirdre going out?' Sarah asked, with a sense of foreboding.

'I heard her come down the stairs and go out the back door,' Betty said. 'But I didn't like to confront her, or risk making things worse. She's probably at the surgery with Tim.'

'Tim is with Camilla.' Betty looked up, recognising the concern in her daughter's voice. Realisation came quickly. 'Oh Lord. She didn't see them, I hope. God in heaven!'

'There's nothing between them,' Sarah said. 'You know that.'

'Maybe not. But what would you have felt, if you'd been looking down on that? If you'd seen your man in her arms.'

Sarah shivered and turned away. Inside her head she could see Piet, all those years ago when she had still been at school. Even then she had known that she loved him, and her heart had cracked as she had stood at the window in Langani and seen him kissing Camilla in the cold, bright moonlight, before they had vanished into the darkness.

'I'm going to take my camera and go for a walk,' she said, hoping that she might find her brother and warn him that he needed to offer Deirdre an explanation.

But the garden was deserted, and Tim and Camilla were nowhere to be seen. Frustrated and angry, Sarah took the track that led to the beach but the afternoon light was fading and she had to be content with a solitary walk and a half-hearted attempt to photograph the empty strand and the sea, sullen and dull under the flat light of a dying day.

The house was silent when she returned, and she ran a hot bath and dressed for dinner slowly, delaying the tensions that would surely form part of the evening. When she joined her parents downstairs it was plain that something was terribly wrong. Betty was standing by the fire, clutching her handkerchief, her eyes red. Raphael stood beside her, puffing anxiously on his pipe. Sarah looked from one to the other.

'What's the matter?'

'It's Deirdre.' Betty took a deep breath. 'She's gone.'

'Gone where?' Sarah tried to make sense of the phrase.

'She's left for good. As far as we know,' said Raphael. 'Tim found a note from her on his desk in the surgery, about half an hour ago, saying that she was leaving.'

'Why would she leave?' Sarah asked.

'He hasn't told us,' Raphael said heavily.

'Well, what has he told you?' The news was bewildering.

'That it was all a terrible mistake. That he should have known. They both should have known. He says she won't ever come back. But he hasn't offered any reason for her decision. He told Dad that he doesn't want to discuss it right now.' Betty's hand shook a little as she patted at her hair. 'Do you think it's the long hours he was working, Raphael? Was that it?'

'My dear, I don't know what it was,' Raphael said. He slumped down into a chair and tapped out his pipe. 'I don't know what has happened at all.'

'Maybe it's a severe case of pre-wedding nerves,' Sarah said. But the vision of Tim and Camilla was fresh in her mind. The same image that Deirdre must be carrying with her now. She glanced at her mother, but Betty did not meet her eye. 'Could Deirdre be with her parents? Do you know their telephone number?'

'She doesn't get on too well with them,' Raphael said doubtfully. 'The father's a sour kind of a man, and the mother has a bad problem with drink. I think we've been more like parents to her than they ever were.'

'But it doesn't make sense to run away now, without even asking for an explanation,' Sarah said.

'An explanation for what? It's Deirdre who has to give an explanation.' Raphael looked at his daughter, hearing something unusual in her tone. Betty gave a small shake of her head.

'Asking . . . oh, asking Tim to sort out whatever it is that's bothering her.' Sarah tried to sound vague.

'Looking back on it, she's been a little peculiar in the last few months.' Betty was calm now, and more reflective. 'She put off the wedding several times. First she said there was too much going on here, what with setting up the practice and everything. Then it was because you couldn't be here, Sarah. And when Tim set the date for this month, she was doubtful that any of their friends from Dublin would be able to come down. Only last week she was worried about being away on the honeymoon, so we took on a temporary nurse for that period. At the time we were impressed with how thoughtful she was, but now I think it was odd.'

'Your mother is near demented, wondering if she made the girl feel we were trying to get rid of her out of the house, by giving them the cottage. Or that she felt left out, because everyone knew about the house except her.' He pushed his glasses up, and pressed the bridge of his nose with his thumb and finger. 'Even Tim knew, and didn't tell her. But I don't think either of those could be the reason.'

'Of course not,' Sarah said impatiently. 'That's ridiculous.'

'I'm going to get the dinner into the oven,' Betty said. 'I'll join you both in a few minutes.'

Raphael and Sarah sat staring into the fire, looking up when the door opened and Camilla appeared.

'Have you seen Tim?' Sarah knew her tone was sharp.

'No. We went for a walk earlier and then I left him at the surgery,' Camilla said. She showed no sign of unease and Sarah wondered what, if anything, she knew about Deirdre's extraordinary behaviour and disappearance.

'He probably needs some time to himself,' Raphael said. 'I don't think he's ready to deal with questions yet.'

They were prevented from saying more by the appearance of Tim himself.

'I'm sorry about all this,' he said awkwardly. 'You've done so much to make the wedding a great occasion, and I'm desperately sorry. I don't know what else to say.'

Sarah was filled with compassion for him as Betty reached out and patted his arm, as if comforting a child. Camilla did not express any curiosity or surprise, and she asked no questions. It was clear to Sarah that she already knew what had happened. They dined quickly and mostly in silence. When Tim rose from the table and went into the study, Sarah followed him.

'What happened, Tim?' She took his arm. 'What can I do that would help?'

'There's nothing anyone can do,' he said. 'I made a mistake, that's all. We both did.'

'I don't understand how she could have left like that,' Sarah said. 'Just before the wedding, when everything is ready. What was she—'

'Maybe you don't ever know anyone,' Tim said miserably. 'Anyway, she's gone, and that's all there is to it. I can't talk about it, and I don't want to. But I'll have to start making phone calls now to tell the guests it's all off. I can only thank God there weren't many of them. Please, Sarah, don't press me. Let me just do what is necessary so I can close off the whole subject. I'm truly sorry, and I love you all. Everything else is shit.'

Sarah stared at her brother, trying to analyse exactly how he looked. Stretched. Remote. But she could not see the overwhelming grief she would have expected after losing your true love on the eve of your wedding. She knew how that felt. Perhaps if she told him about it, he would be better able to confide in her. He opened the window a little to hear the sea and she went to join him, speaking softly, describing the time when Piet had asked her to marry him and everything had seemed perfect.

She talked about the plans they had made, sitting close together on the ridge, surveying the farm and the lodge, discussing their dreams and the glorious future they would have together. She wanted Tim to know that there was a way forward, no matter how hard it seemed. So she spoke about her own slow journey out of despair, realising that she had never really confronted the whole truth before. She had just wanted the pain to fade but it had not, and she thought it would never truly be gone.

Sarah shivered. Thousands of miles away, Piet's spirit still hovered above the cairn and the tortillis tree, waiting for justice, drifting over the same beautiful, cursed spot. For a while all she had wanted was to stay there with him. But she had forced herself to move on, to leave him there. In a sense she had turned her back on him, because otherwise she would have died too. And she knew now that despite all the agony of the past fifteen months, she did not want to die, and that she need not be ashamed of this. Tim listened without interruption until she came to the end of her narrative, and then he put his arm around her.

'It's getting cold,' he said.

But he did not move, and they stood there in silence, listening to the sound of the waves and the cries of seabirds as they wheeled over the rushing surf, staring out of the window into the ghostly moonlight.

'Piet's gone,' she said at last, looking up at him. 'I can never have him back. But if you love Deirdre and you want to sort this out, then go after her. Now. And whatever happens, I want you to promise that you'll come out and visit me. Meet the Briggses, see the elephants. Like Mum and Dad did after Piet was killed. I want you to see how I love my work and need to do it. And what it does for me.' An idea struck her and she took his arm. 'Then, if it's really over between you and Deirdre, maybe you should come back and work in Kenya for a while.'

His smile was wan as she left the room, not wanting to intrude on the painful explanations he would have to make to his friends. As she closed the door he was standing beside the old leather armchair, his fingers gripping the back of it, head bent and shoulders drooping.

The day that followed was thick with gloom. No one had been able to locate Deirdre. The caterers were cancelled, presents boxed and returned to their donors. Camilla said little as she wrapped gifts and addressed packages. But she was the only one who could raise a smile from Tim. Watching them, Sarah could hear the words echoing in her head. They should get him out of Deirdre's clutches, Camilla had said, laughing. Rescue poor Timmy. The atmosphere in the house became strained and uncomfortable, but Sarah could not bring herself to talk about what she had seen. What Deirdre had seen, before her unexplained disappearance. Raphael spent all day in the surgery, and there was a noticeable coolness in Betty's attitude to Camilla.

'Look out of the window.' Betty had just pushed the last piece of furniture back into its usual place. She straightened up and gestured to Sarah.

Outside, under the oak tree, Camilla's blonde hair caught the dappled sunlight. She was sitting on the swing seat with Tim, their heads close together. They rocked gently to and fro, as if to some music that they had created for themselves.

'Has he spoken to you at all?' Betty's face was pinched as she looked at her daughter.

'No. Only to Camilla.' Sarah was ashamed of the resentment and jealousy she felt.

'Sometimes it's easier to talk to somebody who is one step removed,' Betty said. 'But I'm not sure he chose the right confidante. He's very vulnerable now. On the rebound.' There was a pause and then she spoke again. 'You know, it's a terrible thing to say, but I'm relieved, in a way. About poor Deirdre.'

Sarah looked at her mother in surprise.

'She wasn't right for him,' Betty said. 'She was too . . . needy is the word, I think. Tim is generous and cheerful and well balanced, but he has to have love and support like any other man. I don't know if she would have been able to give him that.'

Raphael had come into the room, and Sarah stood between her parents, knowing she had to leave them soon, wondering how to break the news, ease the separation. They had been dropping hints, making references to the lack of security in Kenya, hoping that she would decide to stay in Ireland.

'I have to go back,' she said. 'On Monday.'

'You can't take a few more days?' Raphael could not hide his dismay.

'I'm only here because Dan gave me extra time off for the wedding,' Sarah said. 'The London trip was business, but this visit home was a favour.'

'Are you certain you should go back?' Betty's anxiety hovered around her like an aura. 'I know you love the work, but it's a dangerous place now. You could have been killed by the Shifta bandits last year, when you were out that night with the dead elephants.' She hesitated. 'According to news reports there's increasing tribal violence in Kenya. Maybe it would be better to live somewhere else for a while. Come back and get your master's degree. Make a fresh start, without the tragedy of the past being so close all the time. You could always go back to Africa after that.'

'It wouldn't be any better if I was somewhere else.' Sarah stood firm. 'I want to continue working with the Briggses. There are still details to be finalised on the book, too. I couldn't leave it all to Rabindrah. And there are other things . . .'

She stopped, not wanting to tell them about her meeting with the Italian priest, or her illogical fear that Simon might still be alive. Her mother would be frantic with worry if she knew about the latest attack at Langani and the police investigation that was now underway.

'It's the place I love,' she said. 'Kenya is where I want to live. It's my home. The place where my friends are and my work.'

Betty sighed and leaned into Raphael. They had been through this same discussion once before, in this very room, when Sarah had given up her chance to continue at the university and had insisted on taking up the research job with the Briggses. She had been so young and carefree and glowing with hope on that day. And three months later she had telephoned from Langani to say that she and Piet were going to be married. Raphael had smiled at his wife then, and told her that all her concerns had been unfounded.

'I see that I can't persuade you to change your mind,' Betty said. 'But I want you to promise me that you will come home if things become . . . well, any more dangerous.'

'I'll be fine, honestly I will,' Sarah said. 'The newspapers always make things sound worse than they are.'

She left them and made her way down to the stables. She had ridden with Tim every day on the wide strand, with the rolling surf on one side and the distant smudge of violet hills on the horizon. As she rounded the corner and entered the stable yard she came across her brother. He was resolutely casual. There was no sign of Camilla.

'I was coming to look for you,' he said. 'I thought you might need rescuing from parental concern. Dad said he'd take surgery. So I've saddled up for the two of us. The sea's far out, and the sand should be perfect for a good gallop.'

They set out in silence, the horses dancing through the swirl of the tide, snorting with impatience to be given their heads.

'Are you all right about going back?' he asked.

'Yes. And they've had to accept it. They know not to press their counter-arguments any further, and I'm grateful for that. I want to go on with the Briggses, and finish the book with Rabindrah.'

'I hear he's a good bloke,' Tim said. 'Camilla thinks he's attracted to you, by the way.'

'What rubbish,' Sarah said, flushing with annoyance. 'In Buffalo Springs you can't stop work at five and go home, or potter off down the road to the local pub or restaurant. So we've spent a great deal of time together. With Dan and Allie, of course.'

'All right, all right,' he said, amused. 'You don't have to get all riled up. But Camilla is pretty observant. If it's true, then I'd be a little careful if I were you. The cultural differences would certainly be a challenge.'

'There's nothing between us, I tell you.' Sarah was angry now, and cursing Camilla for her idle speculation and for sharing it with Tim. 'I don't know where she got such a stupid idea.'

'She told me about her father,' Tim said suddenly. 'That he's queer. I'd never have guessed. He's not the obvious type at all. And she talked about Anthony, and how he behaved like the brainless stud he is. She's very brave.'

'She hides things well. Like you do,' Sarah said, determined to break through the carapace. 'So tell me, now that I'm about to leave, how are you coping? I'm trying not to pry, but I'm desperately anxious about you.'

But Tim shook his head and spurred his horse so that she was obliged to follow him, splashing through sea foam and pebbles which seemed like jewels in the glittering rush of the water. The air was pure and cold and salt-laden and she gulped it in with pleasure, storing it in her lungs and in her memory for the days when she would sit in the blistering heat of Africa and long for her family. She was laughing with exhilaration when they came to a halt at the end of the beach.

'My little sister,' he said. 'You look grand, with your wild hair and bright eyes, and your face all pink from the wind. And so much courage.'

When the moment came it tore at her heart, and she had to swallow down the tears of separation. 'Come back with me, Tim,' she said, urgently. 'Come to Buffalo Springs now. Stay in our little guest hut for a while, and get away from all this. It would be so good for you.'

'Go on, son,' Raphael urged. 'It's a grand idea. Old Mallory was coming in to help me when you went on your honeymoon, so—' He stopped, as Tim's face twisted. 'What I meant was, we can easily handle things for a couple of weeks.'

But Tim shook his head. 'Not now,' he said. 'I'll come, later in the year, though. When things are . . . well, later. You know?'

Camilla put her arms around Tim, struggling to remain bright, but unable to summon one of her glib remarks or to make them all laugh.

'If you do decide to visit Sarah, you can drop in on me too,' she said. 'Come any time. You know where I am, and maybe big city noise and lights would be just the thing.'

Sarah found herself inconsolable as she boarded the train. Camilla sat beside her, offering handkerchiefs, making no attempt at small talk, pouring strong tea and ordering a brandy for each of them. After a while Sarah blew her nose and tried not to listen to the sound of the wheels on the track, taking her away from the people who loved her. She had not mentioned the scene she had witnessed between her brother and Camilla, or the fact that Deirdre had seen it too. She was ashamed of the suspicion that lurked in the back of her mind, and Tim's refusal to confide in her still rankled.

'I saw you with Tim,' she blurted out. 'You were hugging each other, and you kissed him. On the day that Deirdre left. And she saw it too.'

'Oh, for God's sake!' Camilla said angrily. 'Now I understand why you and Betty have been so cool with me. I suppose I can see how she might have jumped to the wrong conclusions. But you? Surely you didn't think for a moment that I would try to influence Tim in any way. Sarah?'

'No, of course not.' Sarah knew the denial did not sound convincing. 'But it looked so intimate from a distance, and you spent a lot of time with Tim after she left.' She paused and then flung restraint to the winds. 'He said you told him about George. And you hinted that Rabindrah . . . that he liked me. Which is nonsense. True confessions on all sides. I suppose Tim poured out all his troubles to you. Told you why Deirdre ran off.'

'Yes. As a matter of fact he did.' Camilla's eyes were cold.

'And?'

'And I promised not to discuss it. With anyone. So I have to respect that, and not talk about it.'

'Yes, of course you do,' Sarah said, resentment close to boiling point.

Camilla opened her bag and took out a book, but she could not read it. It seemed to her that she had been judged unfairly. She had tried to persuade Tim that he should attempt to overcome his humiliation and discuss the whole debacle with his family.

'It's the only thing to do,' she had said. 'Besides which, things often resolve themselves when they're brought out into the open. You must tell Raphael, at least.'

'I will talk to Dad, but I can't do it right now.' Tim had taken off his glasses and rubbed his eyes. 'Thanks for listening. For not preaching or being shocked, or going all sentimental on me.'

It was then that he had taken her face in his hands, but she had dodged his clumsy attempt to kiss her, walking away from him and calling him down to the beach. Camilla sighed with frustration. She had put aside all her appointments in London to provide support when it was needed, and she thought Sarah's assumptions were hasty and self-righteous.

The atmosphere between them remained cool for the remainder of the journey. They arrived at Camilla's flat in the late afternoon. Sarah found herself unable to relax, and she made an excuse and went out to do some last-minute shopping. But her emotions were ragged after the wrench of leaving her family and the quarrel with Camilla, and the rain and cold soon found their way into her tired bones. After an hour she returned to Knightsbridge, weary and depressed.

'I'm afraid you're stuck here,' Camilla said, as Sarah struggled out of a damp jacket and kicked off soggy shoes.

'Stuck?'

'Allie phoned from Nairobi. There's a function in London tomorrow night, organised by *National Geographic* who were at your presentation last year. Dan would like you to stay on for it. Also, the Briggses have been given an increase in their grant, and Dan wants you to collect the papers. So you should try and change your plane ticket, and let them know.'

'I should be thrilled,' Sarah said, when she had booked the flight for a day later. 'And I am, really. But I wish it had happened before we went to Ireland, because now I just want to go home. I've offended you and I'm really sorry. I'm sure you don't want me here for another day. And I've said enough painful goodbyes.'

'I've said a couple myself lately,' Camilla said. 'But I've realised that I can't spend time brooding over them. Edward wants to know if we'd like to have dinner at his flat this evening.'

'Three's a crowd,' Sarah said. She wanted to be alone, to distance herself from the mess she had made. 'I'll go to a film, or better still, stay here and go to bed early.'

'Martyrdom is out,' Camilla said. 'Besides, he has friends joining us. An American couple. So you'd better decide what you're going to wear.' She adopted a threatening pose, her eyes showing a first hint of laughter. 'Or go shopping.'

'I'm a penniless researcher from Africa.' Sarah started to smile. 'I don't think I need to look like someone who shops in Bond Street or Knightsbridge. Look, I'm terribly sorry for being such a fool. Please forgive me.' She was close to tears.

'You're hopeless,' Camilla said. 'You *and* your brother. Come and look in my wardrobe, and then do exactly as I say. You know the drill, and it always works.'

Dinner with Edward was casual. His friends were impressed by Sarah's tales of charging elephants and crocodile-infested rivers, and the roar of lions at night under huge, starlit skies. They had always wanted to go on safari, they said. But they felt that it would be better to travel with a professional guide who had been referred to them on a personal basis.

'I think you should contact a friend of ours,' Sarah said, as Camilla went to organise coffee and Edward poured brandy. 'If you give me your address, I'll pass on your name and make sure he gets in touch with you. He is one of the best there is in today's safari business. Do you have any idea what you would specially like to see or do?'

They discussed the merits of the various national parks and the different birds and animals to be found in each area. As she was leaving, Sarah was astonished when they pressed a cheque into her hand. Her work was so vital, so important for mankind as a whole, they said. And they would like to visit the Briggses' camp when they came to Africa later in the year. Her face was glowing with pleasure as they said goodnight and left the party.

'I can't believe this.' She looked at the amount of the cheque and gave a little hoot of surprise. 'I can't believe you can sit around at dinner, telling stories about the things you love, and at the end of it someone hands you a piece of paper that will cover half a year's salary. My God, it's just . . . well, I'm so grateful. Thank you, Edward. For introducing me to your friends, and for dinner and everything.'

'You're a born storyteller and fundraiser,' Camilla said. 'You can fire people's imaginations so easily. A useful talent.' She allowed Edward to kiss her lightly on the cheek and took Sarah's arm. 'Let's be off. I'm booked for an early morning session.'

'I'm going to do a little sightseeing tomorrow,' Sarah said. 'But I'll be back around five to get myself tarted up for the dinner.'

'Don't worry. I'll be around to help. Goodnight.'

Sarah managed to wheedle a hair appointment in the morning, using Camilla's name. Then she dropped into the Royal Academy. It would be shameful to go back to Kenya without having seen a single exhibition. In a camera shop she stocked up with film and splurged on two new lenses. Her luggage was already full and definitely overweight, and she had spent far too much money. She decided to avoid any further temptation and return to the flat early. At Knightsbridge she emerged from the underground into the sunshine, and glanced at her watch. It was only three. She would have time for a nap and a long bath before she had to go out again. Brompton Road was busy with afternoon shoppers, and it was a relief to turn into the side street that led to the flat. A cup of tea would be good.

Outside Camilla's building, she saw a taxi waiting at the kerb, the engine growling, light turned off. The street door opened and a man hurried out, probably conscious of the ticking meter. He had his back to her, but as he turned and bent towards the driver's window to give instructions Sarah halted in astonishment, wondering if her eyes had deceived her. Then she half raised her arm and began to run towards the taxi as it pulled out from the kerb, speeding away from the confines of the square. She stopped to draw breath and to take stock. It was Tim. She was sure of it. But what was he doing in London, and why had he not waited for her at Camilla's flat? They must have known she would be back shortly. Her head was spinning with possibilities. Maybe he had decided to come back to Kenya with her. Her spirits rose.

She was smiling as she climbed the stairs and put her key into the lock. In the sitting room Camilla was talking on the telephone. She signalled that she would be free shortly and pointed towards the kitchen. Sarah made her way to the counter to put on the kettle.

'I can't do tomorrow evening, Tom,' Camilla said irritably. 'It's too last-minute and I've got something else on. No, I can't bloody cancel it. If they really want me to come to dinner, then they'll have to try another date. I'm sure you can sort it out. Bye, darling.'

As Sarah warmed the teapot she noticed the two empty glasses in the sink. There was a click as Camilla hung up.

'You're back early. How was your day? That was dear old Tom on the telephone. There's a client who has chosen me for a new jewellery collection, and he's asked us to dinner. I'll never understand why these people can't sign deals in an office, over a cup of coffee. Why they all want to be seen in some swish restaurant or club, with the model in tow. Your hair looks good. Do you want to have a siesta? I've got something you might like to wear if you want to knock them dead.'

Camilla was speaking very quickly, gabbling, and Sarah could see that she was flustered. She did not mention Tim.

'Here's some tea,' Sarah said. 'Anything earth shattering happen today?'

'Not a thing.' Camilla's reply was airy. 'Totally uneventful. Edward's dinner guests phoned to say how marvellous you were. Having given you a cheque, they probably think they own you, along with Dan and Allie and all the elephants too. I'm sure they'll turn up in Kenya later in the year. Been to the place, talked to the scientists, stayed in their camp. All that.'

Sarah turned away. What was happening? Tim had just been here, that much was certain. But he had not waited for her or even left a message. And Camilla was hiding the fact that he was in London. Why was he in London at all, come to that? Each question that flashed across her mind led to another, and she felt the beginnings of a headache. Perhaps she should say something, admit that she had seen her brother outside in the square, watched him drive away in a taxi. Anger began to smoulder in her, making a sour, acrid taste in her throat.

'I'm going to sleep for an hour and then jump into the bath,' she said. 'And then I'll get myself all tarted up. I'll wear the same thing I wore last night.'

As she left the flat for the function, her mind was a whirlpool of doubt. Now that she was safely out of the way, she wondered if Tim would come back. Perhaps he and Camilla were planning to have dinner together, or to meet at his hotel. Where he would have a room of his own. No, that was impossible. But it looked very suspicious. She was concerned for her brother, confused by his actions. When she boarded the plane on the following morning she was angry. Very, very angry.

It was early afternoon when Camilla answered the door, to find Tim Mackay standing in the hall. He looked like a lost dog, and she was as irritated by his helplessness as by the fact that he had put her in an impossible position with his sister.

'I'm sorry about turning up unexpectedly yesterday,' he said. 'I thought Sarah had left for Nairobi.'

'She saw you in the square,' Camilla said.

'Are you sure?' he said, miserably.

'She was decidedly cool with me before she left, and I can't think of any other reason. You'd better come in.'

'What did you tell her?' Tim said.

'Nothing. As promised.'

'I looked around before I went out into the street,' Tim said.

'You didn't look hard enough. Why the hell didn't you stay and talk to her?'

'It's complicated.'

'*Life* is complicated. And now that you've blown a hole through my friendship with your sister, maybe you'd like to explain what you're doing here? I'm assuming you didn't just hop on a plane and come over for a cup of tea.'

'No. Good, solid, dependable Timmy doesn't do that sort of thing.' He looked sheepish.

'Where do Raphael and Betty think you are?'

'I suppose they think I went to look for Deirdre.'

'Well, she's certainly not here,' Camilla said.

'I'm sorry about all this,' he said, pushing his glasses up on to the bridge of his nose. 'I know I should have come back while Sarah was still here. But everything's so jammed up inside me. Besides, she's got problems of her own.'

'And I haven't?'

'It's no use being sarcastic. I need to talk to someone. Explain what happened.'

'So you've cast me in the role of agony aunt,' Camilla said, annoyed by his assumption. 'I'm supposed to drop everything because you turn up on my doorstep without a second's warning. And then disappear like the bloody white rabbit, because you're terrified you might bump into Sarah.'

'It doesn't sound too bright,' he admitted. 'I haven't made things clear.'

'You told me on the beach in Sligo that Deirdre ran away because she couldn't face the marriage. That her parents had been desperately unhappy, and her family was a mess, and she got cold feet. And you were angry because she hadn't told you any of this earlier, and then she left you in the lurch at the last minute. That's clear enough for me. What I don't understand is why you couldn't explain this to Sarah.'

He shook his head, not looking her in the eye, not answering.

'You're closed up tight as a buzzard's bum,' she said. 'We're not going to make any progress like this, and I have things to do.'

'What kind of bum does a buzzard have?' A smile crept across Tim's face and they both started to laugh, breaking the tension.

'I'll make some tea,' she said. 'And then you'd better start talking. Fast.'

'I wanted to find her,' Tim said, as he finished his second cup. 'Deirdre has a sister in London, so I thought she might have come over here. The address and phone number were on our wedding invitation list. When I rang from Sligo, it was Deirdre who answered the phone. I hung up without saying anything. But then I thought I should try and talk to her. I wasn't angry any more. I thought she might have calmed down, like I have. Changed her mind, you know, but felt too ashamed to tell me. And if that was the case, then we could get married here. Quietly and without any fuss.'

'You still love her enough to do that?' Camilla could not hide the surprise in her voice.

'I don't know. I thought she'd be an ideal wife,' Tim said. 'I went out with plenty of girls in my student days, and they were good fun. But I wouldn't have wanted any of them permanently. They'd been around, slept with half my friends. You know the score.'

'You were looking for a vestal virgin, in spite of your own efforts to make them an endangered species?' Camilla said, her eyebrows raised.

'When it came down to it, those birds would dump you in the blink of an eye for a successful consultant or a well-heeled lawyer. Or even a dentist. The truth is that I had my fingers burnt a couple of times. But she was different.'

He stood up and began to pace the room, coming to a halt at the window, telling his story with his back to her. They had met on night duty, he said. He had been impressed by Deirdre's efforts to soothe an old man whose family had abandoned him. He was a difficult patient, lonely and bitter, and most of the nurses tended to him quickly and moved on. But as he neared the end, Deirdre sat with him whenever there was a lull on the ward. He had been a schoolteacher and she made him smile by quoting passages from textbooks she had loved or hated. He died peacefully as dawn crept into the ward, and afterwards Tim had taken her to a local café for strong tea and bacon and eggs.

'When we started going out regularly she told me she had had a difficult childhood, with her mother being an alcoholic. She never spoke about her father, except to say that he was always hard on her. I was stretched to my limits as an intern, working long hours, not able to take a girl out two or three times a week. I liked the fact that Deirdre was steady and sensible. She wasn't someone who changed her boyfriends as regularly as her shoes.'

'Sounds reasonable,' Camilla said, wondering if Deirdre had ever had any other boyfriends. 'If a little dull.'

'I felt comfortable with her,' he said. 'Of course, after a while, I wanted to sleep with her, but she turned me down outright. Said she would never consider going to bed with anyone who wasn't her husband. And I had to respect that. It might seem old-fashioned and pointless to you, but I admired her for it.'

'Oh my,' Camilla said, with a sly smile. 'Poor Timmy – hooked by unconsummated lust.'

'I suppose. Anyway, when Dad decided to set up in Sligo, Deirdre said she'd come and work with us. She said she'd had enough of Dublin.' Tim sat down again. 'I'm making a bit of a spectacle of myself, aren't I? Sitting here, blathering away like this.'

'You're not alone when it comes to making a fool of yourself,' Camilla said. 'So far this story could have happened to anyone.' She lay back on the sofa.

'I was flattered,' Tim said. 'She'd been offered a promotion in Dublin, with more money. One of the senior consultants had invited her out a couple of times, but she'd turned him down. She was ready to chuck it all in and come with me, down to the back of beyond. I asked her to marry me at that point. And she said yes.'

'And you thought you were on the "happily ever after" track.'

'We agreed on a small wedding,' Tim said. 'When Sarah said she wouldn't come, Deirdre suggested we should put the whole thing off, but I wanted to press ahead. I went to meet Deirdre's parents. The mother was quite pleasant, and sober as far as I could tell. But there was a bad atmosphere between Deirdre and her father, and he made no attempt to disguise it. He was none too pleased at her choice of a humble country doctor, and he made a whole lot of disparaging remarks about my prospects. I felt uncomfortable, to say the least, and I was glad when the visit was over.'

Camilla waited for him to continue, but he sat staring into space until she prodded him gently. 'Come on, Timmy. Don't seize up on me now.'

'I couldn't talk to Sarah about any of this,' he said. 'She never warmed to Deirdre. When she decided to take the job in Buffalo Springs instead of continuing at university, we had a bit of a row. She left for Kenya, and next thing Piet had asked her to marry him. They were so madly in love, and perfect for one another. I don't know how she survived what happened next. And finally, I was the one getting married. I had the chance she wanted so badly. But I got it all wrong, and it seems so unfair, so cruel, whatever way you look at it. And not something I want to talk to her about. Do you understand what I'm saying?'

'I do.'

'Deirdre wanted to put off the honeymoon, because of Dad's workload. But I'd had enough postponements and I said no. And then she saw the house. Our own place where we could be together. I made a big thing of it that day, pulling her down on to the four-poster bed with me, kissing her and fooling around.' He stopped, his face reddening. 'Oh, you know. I'd told her we were going to Paris on our honeymoon. The city of love. But she was nervous because she didn't speak the language, and she found the French intimidating.'

'That's what the Parisians like everyone to feel,' Camilla said. 'They're very successful at it.'

'Well, I got annoyed with her. Told her I was fed up with all her fears and objections, and then she rushed out of the cottage, past you all, and back to the surgery. I shrugged it off, thinking she was finding the whole thing overwhelming, with no family of her own to talk to.'

'Bridal nerves. Old-fashioned and charming,' Camilla said. 'This sounds more and more like a Barbara Cartland romance, Timmy.'

'Well, it's not,' said Tim. 'It's a bloody horror story. Because when I got back to the surgery she was there, crying her eyes out. She'd written me a letter, she said. And she couldn't marry me. Ever. She said she'd been . . . well, she'd been hurt. Attacked when she was young. Ah shit, she was raped by her father, for Christ's sake! It was an ongoing thing for years. And she couldn't get it out of her head. She couldn't have sex with anyone, she said.'

'Oh God, how horrible! Poor girl. Poor Timmy.'

'I suggested she should go to a psychiatrist. Talk the whole thing out of her system. But she was furious. She wasn't crazy, she said, and she wasn't going to see any head shrink, because it would be all over the country the minute anyone saw her going into his office. And then she disappeared.'

'You haven't heard from her since?'

'No. In her note, she said she'd kill herself if I tried to find her or make her come back.' He paused. 'She knew all along that she wasn't ready to be a wife. But she still agreed to the engagement, and let Mum get on with all the plans for the wedding. I couldn't get over the fact that she hadn't told me the truth. That she had made a complete fool of me.'

'Have you seen her?'

'I tried,' he said. 'After I left here yesterday. But she won't see me. Ever again, she said. I feel bad for her, but I feel guilty, too. Because now that she's turned me away again, I'm actually relieved. Worse still, I'm selfish enough to be wondering how I'm going to handle the tittle-tattle in the surgery every day, and the whispering and clucking behind my back in such a small place. I've found out that I'm a coward at heart, and it's hard to take. So I'm well and truly screwed, whatever way you look at it.' He smiled suddenly. 'Well, *not* screwed, I suppose, is the problem And my sister is probably livid with both of us.'

'The situation is less than ideal.' Camilla looked at him with sympathy, her head tilted to one side. 'Raphael should know all this. You must talk to your father, Tim.'

Tim took off his glasses and rubbed his eyes. 'I suppose you're right,' he said wearily. 'But I couldn't have explained this to Sarah.'

'You have to write to her, though. Tell her in a letter.'

'I don't want to—'

'I don't give a damn what you want,' Camilla said, temper flaring. 'Your sister's friendship is the most important thing I have, and I'm not going to risk damaging it for any reason. You can stay here tonight and we can talk some more. But only on condition that you tell Sarah what has happened. You owe me that.'

'Yes, I do. And I will.'

The telephone jangled and Camilla picked it up. 'Edward. No, unfortunately I can't do anything this evening. You're sweet to ask, but there's a studio shoot with very bright lights tomorrow, so I'm having an early night. I'll phone you during the morning. Yes, I promise. 'Night.' She turned to Tim. 'Now look what you've done. I've had to turn down a dinner date for you. So you'd better buy me dinner at the nearest bistro and make up for it.'

In the morning Camilla rose early. Tim was still asleep in the guest room, his mouth slightly open, making small puffing sounds, snoring lightly. He looked defenceless without his thick, wire-rimmed glasses, and his hair was tousled like a character in a boy's comic book. Camilla bent down and kissed him on the forehead as she might have kissed a child. Then she made a pot of coffee and some toast, and the smell reached into his sleep and brought him into the small kitchen.

'Thanks,' he said awkwardly. 'For last night and for everything. And I'm sorry if I've caused a problem between you and Sarah.'

'Just sort it out soon,' she said. 'What's your plan today?'

'I have a plane to catch at noon, so I'll leave in the next hour or so.' He peered at her short-sightedly and smiled. 'I hadn't allowed myself to think it all out, to talk about it. It was just a big, black ball lodged in my brain. But now it will be easier to go on.'

'You're hopeless,' she said. 'If you want my advice, then you should think about taking Sarah up on her invitation. Get on a plane to Nairobi. Away from all this. She'd love to show you round her elephant kingdom. And Hannah would be thrilled to see you again.'

'Not yet,' Tim said. 'I need to sort things out at home first. I'll get my belongings together now, because I know you have a busy day ahead of you.'

He placed his arms around Camilla's waist and bent his head to kiss her, but she disengaged herself and patted his cheek with affection.

'I'd better be off,' he said, a little shy and red-faced. 'Another hour alone with the world's most beautiful girl and I couldn't promise to remain either chaste or chastened.'

'I'd be insulted if you could,' she said, laughing. 'Sounds like the beginning of recovery, I'd say. Talk to Raphael. Let me know how you're doing. No dark secrets.'

From the window, Camilla watched him walk away into Brompton Road. She sighed, thinking of the ache he must be carrying in his heart and the sting of humiliation in his mind. Feelings with which she was well acquainted. She was already running late for her shoot, and she showered and dressed quickly, jammed several books and a jumble of cosmetics into her tote bag and left the flat. It was a long day with a demanding photographer who had a hangover. The studio was too hot, the bright lights made her eyes feel gritty and gave her a headache. By the time she arrived back at the flat in the evening, it was after seven and she was shattered. The telephone was ringing as she unlocked the door.

'You were going to phone me this morning, remember?' Edward said.

'Sorry. I've had a frantic day.'

'So have I,' he said. 'I had a particularly complicated list this morning. But I could be revived. How about dinner?'

'You can come over here, if you like,' Camilla said. 'I'm too tired to move.'

He arrived with a bottle of chilled champagne and an armful of pink tulips. 'You look drained,' he said. 'I thought you were going to have an early night.'

'I did. I left here at nine this morning for a gruelling day. But I have four days off, now. I've told Tom I will not appear on or at anything, no matter what it is.'

'Sounds like something to celebrate,' he said. 'I'll open the champagne and put it on ice.'

In the kitchen sink there were two cups and saucers, and a couple of plates with the remains of breakfast on them. He looked at them, frowning. She must have had a guest, although the early morning was not Camilla's preferred time. If there had been someone here overnight it was strange that she had not mentioned it. He filled the ice bucket and returned to the sitting room, his heart beating a little too fast. It was ridiculous to be suspicious, to feel uneasy, but he could not banish the tentacles of jealousy that had wrapped themselves around his heart. What was she hiding, and why? He looked at Camilla, her hair shining pale gold in the lamplight, her face calm and innocent and utterly beautiful. His passion for her made him uncertain, took away his accustomed self-assurance. He only knew that he wanted her for his own. She came to stand beside him and he took her quickly into his arms and kissed her, feeling something close to panic.

Camilla remained very still, allowing him to caress her and murmur his words of love into her ear. She thought of Tim and his lost dream of happiness, and of Sarah who was so straightforward and loving and generous and who would never be able to smile up at her beloved Piet and be thankful for his presence. In her mind's eye she pictured Lars, with his big arms around Hannah, protecting her through thick and thin. And the loneliness and futility of celebrity struck her with force.

'Come,' she said, leading Edward by the hand into the bedroom, moving like a sleepwalker in an uneasy dream. 'Come and make love to me. It's been a long time, and I've missed you.'

When she lay beside him afterwards, looking at his lean body and fine features, she found that she was calm. And grateful for what she had.

'Do you love me at all?' he asked, his voice slightly hoarse.

She was surprised by the intensity of his expression and by something like fear in his voice. She kissed his mouth, but when he wanted to make love to her again Camilla pushed him aside with a smile and a whispered promise. She bathed and dressed, and went into the kitchen to find the makings of dinner. As she lit the candles on the dining table Edward came up behind her and put his arms around her waist.

'Marry me, Camilla. I love you very much, and I think I can make you happy. Will you marry me?'

'I'm not ready for that, Edward.'

'I'm ready,' he said. 'We're good together. I'm good for you, darling. You know that.'

'I seem to recall that you have a wife already.' It was cruel, but she did not want to be pressured.

'I never went through the motions of a divorce,' he said. 'It seemed disloyal, somehow, to divorce someone lying helpless in a coma. And in any case, I had no reason to do it. Until now. But it wouldn't be difficult to organise, after all this time. I'm very much in love with you, Camilla, and I want you to marry me. I can't imagine the rest of my life without you.'

'It would be all too easy to say yes,' she said, adopting a kinder tone. 'But I don't think it's a good idea. I'm not the nurturing kind of person that a wife should be. There's something in me that still needs to be separate. I don't want to disappoint you, or to spoil the happy times we have.'

'Perhaps you don't need to be the nurturing one. Maybe that's my role.'

'No, Edward. Marriage is not something I can consider now. Maybe it's a throwback in my mind, an inbuilt thing I have, from watching my parents in their daily strife. But it's not for me.'

He bowed his head, dejected and unable to hide his disappointment. 'Is there something I don't know?' he asked her. 'Is this about Anthony Chapman? Have you seen anything of him?'

'This has nothing to do with anyone but me,' she said. 'Let's not talk about it any more. You'll have to try and put up with me as I am for the moment, and hope I'll change for the better.'

'Yes,' he said. 'I'll hope for a change of mind, at any rate. In the meantime, here's to us and what we have shared already.'

He left early next morning and she watched him go with some regret. She loved him, in a way. It was not an all-consuming passion that made her feel desolate and incomplete when he was not with her. The hours did not drag when they were apart and she did not spend time waiting impatiently for him, or wondering when he was going to telephone. But she was comfortable when they were together, at ease in his home and with his friends who clearly envied him his beautiful prize. Edward offered a sense of security that she recognised as being important. He listened to her, encouraged her to open herself to his understanding, took an interest in her work. She would be safe with him. He would never cheat on her. Camilla thought that might be enough.

Chapter 10

Kenya, May 1967

'I don't think she will come back,' Hannah said. 'She's given us all the money from the gala to start up again. And we can keep everything we make from local sales, instead of the original percentage. In Camilla's eyes that's what is important – extra income for the farm. She knows we need it and that I'll be grateful. And flattered, too, that she is leaving the running of the workshop entirely to me. She has been true to her word.'

'Don't you think she would have told you if she'd decided to stay in London?' Lars said. 'Or told Sarah.'

'Not necessarily. She has a habit of disappearing without explanations when things go wrong.'

'I suppose from London things might not look so good in Kenya,' Lars said. 'She almost had her livelihood ruined here before. The scar is only beginning to fade. Then, for no reason we can fathom, her workshop was wrecked. And her man treated her very badly. Why would she come back?'

'I can't imagine,' Hannah said. 'She has everything in London – a flat in a posh area of the swinging city, money, fame and security. But we'll know soon enough.' She closed the door of the workshop and put the keys into her pocket. 'I'll have to write to her this evening, and tell her everything is ready now. Not that she ever replies. I still can't get over the fact that she sent the cheques through her accountant, without even a note attached to them.'

'Gone to ground, as you said.' Lars touched her cheek. 'But you know she's with you in her heart.'

'I suppose so. Anyway, we can start up again when the sewing machines arrive next week. Makena has agreed to come back to work, and one of the other girls. I'll have three raw recruits on my hands, but I can manage that.'

Lars took her hand. 'So strong, my little Hannah,' he said, smiling down at her. 'So strong and sweet, like my favourite tea with honey. Do you really want to drive up to the lodge now?'

'Yes,' she said. 'We must open in June, if we can. Anthony will bring the first guests, and several safari firms have promised us bookings. We must open the lodge and show them that we are going to stay. That they cannot frighten us away.'

He nodded and helped her into the Land Rover. But he wondered who she thought 'they' were, and what chance he had of keeping her safe from the faceless enemy that was trying to destroy the farm.

From the moment of her decision Hannah had initiated a routine that was punishing. But it allowed her no time to think back or to harbour doubts or reconsider. Mwangi brought tea at six each morning and she drank it in bed, drawing her strength from Lars's big, comforting frame beside her, and from the smiles and gurgles of the baby in her cot. The dairy was her first port of call, and then breakfast and household decisions made with Mwangi and Kamau. The cook was full of good humour these days. The young people were not going to abandon the farm, like Bwana Jan had done. The lodge would soon open, and then his son, David, would have a position of the highest importance at Langani. The *wazungu* would come from far away and praise the kitchens and he, Kamau, would be recognised for having taught his firstborn to make the best food in Kenya. He moved around his domain like a whirlwind, banging pots and pans and scolding David for the way he peeled carrots or folded egg whites into a cake mixture.

Hannah had never liked being in the office, but she kept her files and her accounts with a precision that would have passed a national audit, and she was always present at meetings with the bank, armed with facts and figures and plausible reasons why they should continue to extend their loan. She allowed herself several breaks during the day to feed and play with Suniva. Then she left the infant with the ayah and took off once more to ride or to drive around the fields with Lars, inspecting her cattle, judging the quality of the wheat, always mentally calculating their revenue and their outgoings. But she rarely talked to the *watu*. Lars was concerned at her refusal to acknowledge the older workers, many of whom had been on the farm since before she was born.

'You've barely spoken to Juma in a week,' Lars said to her, troubled by her dour manner when they came across the headman on their rounds. 'He was offended, Hannah. He's a loyal worker, and he's doing a good job. Look at him over there, breaking his back to get that fence mended.'

'No one knows who is loyal and who is not,' she said, her eyes narrowing. 'We cannot trust any of them.'

Lars did not answer her. It was a difference of opinion that he had never been able to resolve. Since her brother's murder, Hannah had been unable to separate herself from her mistrust of all the farm staff. Only Mwangi and Kamau were above suspicion, and since the ayah had worked for years with the Murray family she, too, was tolerated. But Lars could no longer leave her alone on the farm. While she tried to hide her fear he was acutely aware of it. An air of menace hung over them day and night, so that they were constantly alert and wary. It was exhausting, draining them both mentally and physically, and their mutual solace could not overcome their disquiet. Lars had even telephoned Jan in Rhodesia and talked to him at length about the incident at Camilla's workshop. But his father-in-law had been no help, and had made it clear that he could not return to Langani. Not that he would have been much use. In his present state of alcoholism and melancholy he would be more of a liability than anything else. But Hannah might benefit from having her mother close to her, even for a short time, and Lars wondered if he could persuade Lottie to take a holiday.

The Land Rover bounced along the rough track littered with sharp pebbles and memories, and soon they hit a pothole in the road. The vehicle lurched sideways and Lars gripped the steering wheel and turned his attention back to the road.

'It looks good up there,' he said, slowing for a moment to point up at the outline of the lodge. 'You can see the thatch of the buildings, but they look so natural with their curved walls. As though they've grown out of the rocks, all by themselves. Just as Piet said they would. His vision created something exceptional.'

Hannah gazed out of the window and Lars did not see her sudden smile. He had not mentioned Viktor who had designed the buildings with such genius, and she did not think either of them would ever say his name again. She knew that Lars must have seen him at the Nairobi gala, but he had said nothing. Three days after their return to the farm, Hannah had driven into Nanyuki to do some shopping. When her chores were completed she had sat down at the Silverbeck Hotel and glanced through the day's newspapers as she drank her coffee. There was nothing of interest on the front page, but when she opened the paper she saw Viktor Szustak's wolfish features grinning up at her, causing her to choke and spill some coffee from her raised cup into her lap. She dabbed at the stain on her skirt and tried to compose herself. After a minute or two she picked up the *Standard* again, telling herself that she had misread the brief article. There were only a few lines of type beneath Viktor's image. His work permit had been revoked, and he had been deported for irregularities in his business dealings. Mr Johnson Kiberu had made a statement to the effect that Mr Szustak was a talented architect who had done good work in designing the National Parks headquarters, and he had created several fine tourist hotels. But he was still not above the law, and his deportation should be taken as a warning to others who did not respect government regulations.

Hannah gave a loud hoot of laughter, her body rocking to and fro, and then covered her mouth with one hand as several people looked at her curiously. She gathered up her belongings and made her way to the car, humming to herself as she drove through the gates of the farm. In the office she put the paper down on the desk, still open at page two, and set about tidying away her accounts files. Lars took the *Standard* and read the article. Then he turned to look at his wife for several moments before slowly nodding his head. He was smiling broadly as he threw the newspaper into the rubbish bin and walked out into the sunshine. Hannah had stared after him in amazement. He did not seem at all surprised. Suddenly, she was sure that he had arranged this. Her wonderful, clever husband had saved her from distress and shame, and she loved him more than she had ever imagined possible.

Hannah was still smiling when they came to a halt in front of the lodge.

'Hannah?' Lars nudged her. 'You haven't answered the question.'

'What question?'

'That is so typical of a woman,' he said. 'I was asking you something really important, and you've been daydreaming, not paying any attention.'

'I was daydreaming about you,' she said, leaning over to kiss him. 'What did you ask me?'

'Whether you want to plant some flowering shrubs around this reception area,' he said. 'And if so, what colour should they be? I can get one of the *shamba* boys up here tomorrow to start digging the holes, if you tell me where you want them.'

They walked into the main reception area and through the lounge. Hannah stopped here and there to move a chair into a better position, to alter the lay of a rug or the combination of cushions on a sofa. All of the furniture had been made on the farm and she had sewn the cushion covers and bedspreads and curtains herself, proud to be a part of Piet's plan to create a game reserve and viewing lodge on the farm. It was more than fifteen months since she had stood in this same spot with her brother, surveying their handiwork with satisfaction and dreaming their impossible dreams. For a long time she had been unable to come here, had relied on Lars to take care of the place. But since the workshop had been destroyed Hannah had thought about the lodge in a different way, determined to suppress her deep-seated dread of going there.

When she opened the storeroom for the first time, her hands were trembling as she fumbled with the padlock and then threw open the doors, disturbing an owl that had taken up residence on one of the ceiling beams. He watched her solemnly as she lifted up the dust-sheets and looked at the beautiful things that had been put away after Piet's death. If only she had known that he would soon be gone. She had not told him often enough how she loved and admired him. So many of their hopes still lingered in the air of this place, and now they gave her the will to continue what he had started. In memoriam.

'It will be all right, won't it?' she said to Lars, and her voice was shaky.

'Yes. It will be fine, Han. And he will be proud of you.'

She pressed his hand and they went to stand together on the viewing platform, looking down over the ripple of golden wheat in the distance, and the curve of green that followed the river. The sky was a chalky, bleached-out colour and the glare hit her eyes and made them water, so that she lifted her hand up to shade her face. High above the plains several vultures made loops in the still air, waiting to settle on a kill. She did not see or hear the man hidden in the trees beyond the waterhole, squatting on the ground and rocking slowly to and fro on his hunkers, making circles in the earth with bony fingers, muttering his prayers and spells as the *wazungu* stood looking out at the land of his fathers. His hatred welled, festering like a wound, and Hannah felt a tremor in her body. Were the vultures waiting for her too? Circling over the death throes of the farm? She squared her shoulders and took her husband's hand.

'Anthony will be here later in the week,' Lars said. 'He's dropping off some clients in Nanyuki for the usual break at the Safari Club while his camp moves. We can talk about the lodge while he's here. See how he wants to handle things, as a shareholder.'

'He dropped in at the Briggses' camp recently,' Hannah said, her tone reproving. 'Allie asked him about Camilla, in her forthright way. But it was not a subject on his list at all. Ach, he's no better than an old goat, or a dog with the scent of a bitch on heat. What he did was bad. We all know where his brains were located that night. He has no real heart, no sense of loyalty. He may be clever and charming and knowledgeable about the bush, but there's some part of him that's missing. Unable to connect. He's a bad boy when it comes to women.'

But when Anthony arrived, Hannah was glad to see him. He was tanned and laughing and full of stories about the small party of clients who had travelled with him before. On this occasion he had taken them through the Mara and into Tanzania's fabled Serengeti Plains where they had witnessed lions mating, found leopard and cheetah and wild dogs, been charged by an elephant and recorded more than two hundred species of birds. They had booked again for the following year.

'You're going to open the lodge, then,' he said. 'That's good, Hannah, and I'm with you all the way. What's the plan?'

'I thought we would try for July,' Hannah said. 'That gives us almost two months to get ready. It's not a busy time of the year, so we can start slowly and get the staff used to their jobs. If the rains are good, the view will be green as a billiard table and bursting with wild flowers. The new grazing will bring in big herds of plains game, too.'

'Ideal, yes,' Anthony said. 'Let me know what my share of the money will be and I'll arrange to have it transferred into the lodge account. Fortunately, I'm feeling rather flush after a good season. And now that Sarah has her tame journalist in tow, we can get some good publicity for the lodge before it opens.'

'I don't like that man,' Hannah said. 'I don't want him around here.'

'Why not?' Lars said. 'He seems to have brought the Briggses some attention, and even rustled up a new Land Rover for them. Plus his uncle has repaired that dreadful old banger Sarah drives. To say nothing of the publishing contract he has landed. Rabindrah seems like a reasonable type to me.'

'I still don't like the fact that he went to see Jeremy and then came barging up here asking about Piet's death,' Hannah said. 'They're all the same those newspaper people. On the lookout for something sensational, and it doesn't matter whose life is ripped apart by what they write. I don't believe he's any different.'

'But he didn't publish anything about Piet,' Lars pointed out. 'There was a three-line mention of the wreckage in the workshop, but it wasn't written by him.'

'He probably passed it on to someone else so his name wasn't on it,' Hannah said stubbornly. 'Ach, I suppose it's just that I've never met an Indian who wasn't far too clever for his own good. They're always trying to figure out some angle that will give them a better deal, a bigger slice of the pie. They treat their African workers very badly, too. Money is all they think about. I'll bet there will be strings attached to this new vehicle at Buffalo Springs.'

'That's a bit harsh,' Anthony said. 'As a community they work hard, they have strong family units, and the Sikhs in particular have done a great deal for this country. I'm ready to believe that this was a purely philanthropic gesture.'

'We'll see,' Hannah said. 'They're smarmy. Especially this one. He's not a proper Sikh in any case. In my view he's not to be trusted. Sarah should be careful. She's so willing to see the good in everyone and be taken in.'

'I don't think you need worry about him, Han.' Lars touched her hand, stroking the inside of her wrist, trying to placate her. But she was clearly in no mood to mince her words this evening, and he knew it would be hard to talk her round to a more reasonable point of view.

'Are you going to Europe or America later this month?' Hannah switched her attention to Anthony. 'For your annual marketing trip.'

'I've no idea,' he said, evasive and uneasy. 'No firm plans as yet.'

'In that case, I think maybe you should make some,' Hannah said bluntly. 'Make plans and make amends.'

'Look, I was stupid to have flirted with the Somali girl,' Anthony said. 'But I think—'

'It's hard to believe you were thinking at all,' Hannah said. 'The way you were carrying on makes me think you're a couple of bananas short of a bunch. And you really hurt Camilla again. Ruined the evening that she'd worked so hard to create, largely for us here at Langani. In fact you're a bloody *domkop* fool, Anthony Chapman.'

'It didn't mean anything. It was—'

'I'm off to bed now.' She cut him off. 'I'll be going out early tomorrow so I may or may not see you in the morning. But I suggest you come back at the end of your safari, and then we'll finalise our plans and our accounts and so on. In the meantime, you should go back to thinking with your brains, heh?'

She was smiling a little as she kissed his cheek and rolled her eyes at Lars. 'Don't stay up all night,' she said, leaving them to bridge an uncomfortable silence.

It was Anthony who spoke first. 'She's pretty forthright, your wife,' he said sheepishly.

'She's brave,' Lars said. 'And very loyal and true to the people she loves. That's what she is, above all else. Would you like a nightcap?'

'I don't think so,' Anthony said stiffly. 'I'm going to turn in now, and be on my way early tomorrow. Before breakfast. I ought to be in camp before my next clients arrive on their charter plane. I'll see you soon, old man.'

During the week that followed Hannah was at the lodge every day. The two girls she had taken on before Piet's death were eager to start again and she spent long hours with them, making and remaking beds until they were perfect, folding towels in neat stacks, dusting and polishing so that every inch of stone and wood and glass was gleaming. In the kitchen she worked with David, adapting some of the recipes that Lottie had taught Kamau years ago, inventing simple dishes based on the fresh produce available on the farm and from local market stalls.

A postcard arrived from Sligo. The wedding would take place in three days' time. Everything was ready. They wished she could be there. It was signed by Sarah and Camilla.

'Can we go to Europe one day?' Hannah said to Lars. Her face was wistful as she studied the card with its picture of white cottages and soft fields, and the flat-topped mountain in the background. Camilla and Sarah were right there, in the heart of that green land, and she had been left out again. 'It's like a fairy tale,' she said.

They were sitting on the viewing platform, with the baby on her lap. Below them the waterhole was quiet, but they could hear rustling in the bush and they leaned forward as a family of warthogs appeared and trotted briskly to a patch of wet soil on one side of the clearing. Contented grunting sounds carried on the evening air, as they took turns to roll over and cover themselves in the red, oozing mud.

'There's nothing like this in Europe. Certainly not in Norway, that's for sure.' Lars was laughing at the antics of the pigs. 'On my parents' farm the cows are so clean and glossy that they might have been to one of those places they have in America for dogs. An animal beauty parlour. Not like our *ngombes* here, with their layers of dust and muddy feet. But we will go there, yes, and I will take you on the packet boat to see the Northern Lights.'

'And we must go to London,' Hannah said. 'When we were at school, Camilla and Sarah and I, we thought we would all go there together one day and see all the mods and rockers and the shops and museums, and the Horse Guards and the Tower.'

'We'll go next year,' Lars said, reaching out to take her hand. 'We will have had a good season at the lodge. And whether Camilla comes back or not, the workshop will be making her designs. So we should have enough money for a holiday, ja. We'll do a little marketing tour for the lodge, like Anthony, and see the sights.'

'Yes. And we'll come back and think how wonderful it was, and how glad we are to be home,' Hannah said, smiling. 'Because it is just about perfect right where we are now.'

'It is,' Lars said. 'And when Sarah comes back, she will be amazed at what you've done in the last two weeks.'

'Do you remember how spooked she was the first time she came here?' Hannah said. 'She wanted so much to tell Piet that his lodge was perfect, but she had this bad feeling in her and she tried to hide it. She never mentioned it to me until a couple of months ago. She's always been like that, you know – able to sense things. I don't know whether to wish I was like that, or to be glad I'm not.'

Lars said nothing, realising that the ever-present spectre of unease had raised itself in Hannah's mind.

'But I don't feel anything like that right now,' she said. 'Except that I miss Piet and I know he'd like to be here with us. He'd be so proud to see that his dream is alive after all, and that I'm working hard to make it so.'

'He would. Now I think we should go home and have a bath and some food. Then I want to hold you and love you, Han. Come on, we'll watch the sun go down as we drive. And we might come across a jackal, or even a leopard, on his way out to dinner.'

It was early when they retired, and they lay very close, kissing, tracing lines and messages on one another with their fingertips. Their lovemaking was gentle and profoundly tender, and afterwards sleep came swift and warm to claim them. It was Hannah who woke suddenly, in the dead of the night. She pressed her body into Lars's strong back and slid her arm around his waist. The curtains were half drawn, fluttering slightly at the half-open window, and she could feel the chill wind of the highland night on her face. A night that smelled faintly of the *kuni* that burned under the old water heater. She opened her eyes, puzzled, wondering what time it was. Perhaps the kitchen *toto* had lit the fire early. Hannah took a small torch that she kept on the bedside table and shone it on the face of her alarm clock. Two o'clock in the morning. It was very cold, but she slid out of bed, pulling on her dressing gown, inhaling the hint of smoke that she now realised had woken her. She saw it as soon as she looked out of the window. A thin orange line, creeping along the side of the ridge. Fire.

'Wake up! Wake up, Lars!' She shook him hard. 'There's a fire on the ridge.'

But she was not the only one who had seen it. As she pulled on trousers and a sweater there was hammering on the bedroom door.

'Bwana Lars.' Juma was out of breath, his scrawny chest heaving, spittle collecting in the corners of his mouth as he tried to speak. 'Bwana Lars, there is a fire on the hill. It is very dry up there and we need to go now. I have put buckets in the truck, and *debbies* of water. *Haraka, haraka!*'

Lars ran to the garage, Hannah following. 'You have to stay here,' he told her. 'You can't leave Suniva.'

'I'm coming with you. We'll call Esther.'

'No,' he said. 'You have to stay down here. That's an order. Keep your gun handy. Mwangi and Kamau will stay with you, and the night watchman. Ring Bill Murray now. We'll need all the help we can get.'

He left her standing in the black night, holding a kerosene lantern, her eyes fearful. His brain was racing, filled with doubts as he drove away and up the track towards the ridge. Maybe he should have taken them, Hannah and Suniva. It might not be safe to leave them at the house. But the watchmen were there. He hoped they were there. His heart was beating too quickly, he was driving too fast. Behind him, in the back of the vehicle, the *watu* were clinging on to the sides, calling out to each other. Ahead he could see the fire beginning to leap up in thin, red fingers, as the line spread quickly along the side of the hill. He knew with sick certainty where it was, that it was not an accident. Juma was sitting beside him in the front passenger seat, hanging on to the dashboard.

'When we get there, you start a chain of *watu* with the buckets,' Lars said. 'Eight of us will walk out along the ridge with the water. The rest will start cutting the *bundu* to make a firebreak.'

'They are burning the lodge,' Juma said, and his eyes were rolling with terror. 'They are taking Bwana Piet's lodge away from us, and burning it to the ground. There is a bad man doing this, or a *shitani*.'

Lars came to a skidding halt at the bottom of the driveway that led to the main building. The thatched roof was on fire now, blazing against the black night. All around him the bush was flickering as sparks flew through the air to ignite the dry brushwood. He ran to the storeroom and dragged out the fire hoses that he had not yet installed in the lodge itself.

'Here,' he said to Juma. 'Get this connected to the pump and the tap behind the kitchen. Go. And turn it on as quick as you can. Aim at the trees closest to the lodge.'

The heat was intense, searing his lungs with every acrid breath. He ran along the chain of men with their buckets, directing and cajoling and shouting encouragement, and then left them to help with the cutting of a firebreak. The flames rose in bright peaks, jumping the short distances between the bedroom cottages, flaring suddenly in some new direction. The sound of the fire smothered the frantic shouts of the men as they cut and hacked and threw water into the ravenous inferno. But its appetite was unquenchable, and its huge, all-powerful mouth devoured all that lay before it, roaring and crackling and snapping at every twig and broken shrub, its tongue probing every gap in the bush, consuming each twisted branch that fell in its path. In the distance Lars could hear screaming and trumpeting and barking, and there was the pounding of hooves as scores of terrified animals ran from the conflagration.

It was almost an hour before the police and the fire brigade and the neighbours arrived, alerted by Hannah. Bill Murray worked alongside Lars as they fought through the rest of the night, fleeing a safe distance when the lodge became a dazzling, scorching fireball that seemed to bound across the rocks and tumble down the side of the *kopje*, so that all attempts to extinguish it were futile. But the firebreak and the hoses slowly began to make their mark and at last, as dawn broke, Lars felt that they had gained control. He staggered back to his truck, his face and arms covered in soot, his eyes bloodshot, limbs torn and bleeding. All around him lay the ruins of Piet's dream. Drifts of smoke hid the pink glory of morning as the peaks of the mountain, remote and pristine home of the great god Kirinyaga, looked down on the smouldering air. There were men scattered all around the ridge, seated on the ground, leaning against tree stumps, slumped on the boulders and wiping their faces, coughing and spitting, murmuring and even weeping at the decimation that surrounded them.

At the farm Hannah was waiting, her face as grey as the ashes on the ridge. She ran out as Lars opened the door of the truck, flinging herself into his blackened arms, her body shaking with sobs.

'Thank God, thank God you're safe,' she said as he held her and smoothed her hair and kissed her forehead with his blistered lips.

'We'll need water and tea and food for everyone,' Lars said. 'We couldn't have got through without Bill here. We owe him for the fact that we haven't lost half of the forest behind the lodge.'

'Barbie is here too,' Hannah said. 'She came to keep me company, and I was glad of it.'

Jeremy Hardy arrived minutes later, and food was arranged for the exhausted men who had beaten down the flames. Out on the lawn the farm workers sat in silence, drinking tin mugs of hot sweet tea, eating bowls of *posho* and thick slices of bread and butter. In the dining room breakfast was a brooding affair with everyone lost in their thoughts, overcome by the enormity of the fire and its meaning. The Murrays left as soon as the meal was over.

'Phone me any time you need a break, or some help,' Barbie said to Hannah, deeply worried about the girl whose anxiety might soon bring her to breaking point.

As soon as they were gone Jeremy sat down in the sitting room and motioned for Hannah to close the door.

'My dear, this is now an emergency,' he said to her. 'I will put a police guard on the house, round the clock. But I think Lars should consider the possibility of you and Suniva taking a short holiday, getting away from here. Maybe you should go to the coast for a while, or visit some friends. And I think you should talk to your father. Let him know what has happened here. That could be important.'

Hannah looked down at her plate, mute with anxiety. There was something he was trying to tell her, but she could not fathom what it was. She wanted to leave right now, run away as far as she could go, flee with her husband and her child and keep them safe. Feel safe herself. She was close to screaming, to losing all control, and she pressed her knees together and clenched her fists to stop her body from shaking. Anger saved her, smothered her fear.

'And what do you think Pa could tell us?' she said. 'He left here four years ago, your old friend Jan van der Beer. You wouldn't even recognise him now, Jeremy, and that's the truth. So if you think someone should talk to him, then I'll give you his phone number and you can ring him yourself.'

Jeremy spread his hands out in a gesture of defeat, and glanced at Lars for direction. But there was no answering signal, and the policeman rose from the table and began to take his leave of them.

'I needn't tell you that—'

'That you'll do everything you can.' Hannah was openly bitter. 'I'm sure you'll be able to bring us news of a breakthrough soon. Just like you promised more than a year ago. You'll soon be able to tell us what is happening on our farm and why we have had our cattle slaughtered, and our house raided and someone in our family hacked to pieces. And why no one in the police force can find the *kaffirs* that trashed the workshop and burnt down the lodge.' She stood up to face him, her face scarlet with anger. 'Piet thought that no one really gave a damn what was happening on this farm because we are Afrikaners, and I am beginning to believe he was right.'

'I don't think that is a plausible explanation for what is happening here,' Jeremy said. 'For wrongs or imagined wrongs.'

'A plausible explanation?' She was shouting now. 'This is not about any wrong that we have done here. Piet always offered work and fair pay and the chance of a good life to our *watu*. Just like my friend Camilla tried to do. Our lodge would have employed more than twenty people, and our wildlife area is the only real protection for the game around here, otherwise it will all end up on somebody's cooking fire, or as horn and claw earrings or dagger handles, while the last rhino carcasses rot in the sun. So you'd better send your local *askaris* out into the towns and the reserves, Jeremy. You'd better put them out there right now, and find an explanation for what is happening on my farm.' She spun on her heel and left the room, slamming the door behind her.

'This is a bad business, Lars,' said Jeremy. 'I think you should try and persuade her to—'

'She won't leave Langani,' Lars said. 'You heard her. And she's bloody well right. We must be able to rely on the law to keep our daily lives in order, and we have to know that the police will do everything in their power to enforce that law. Otherwise there is no hope for anyone in this young country of ours. Black, white or brown.'

Jeremy sighed. 'There are so many old scores to settle around here,' he said. 'Kenyatta is an astonishing man, a statesman who is willing to let bygones be bygones, to wipe the slate clean and to start with a spirit of genuine goodwill for the benefit of the country. *Harambee*. But that's not true of other politicians and officials. Most of them are willing to ignore an incident that involves damage or injury to white people. Particularly old settlers.'

'We're not talking about "an incident", man,' Lars said furiously. 'We're looking at armed robbery, slaughter of livestock, assault and murder, vandalism, and now arson. All on one farm. There has to be something you've overlooked. You must have some clue as to what's behind all this.'

Jeremy picked up his hat and his baton. 'It's unusual, but we haven't had a whisper from any of our regular informants.' He hesitated. 'But there may be a connection with the bad old days of the Emergency, you know.'

'What connection?' Lars said. 'All the settlers round here opposed the

Mau Mau, and fought alongside the British Army and the police. I know Jan's brother was killed, and Janni himself was up in the forests tracking the gangs up there, along with hundreds of others. So, if your theory has any foundation, maybe you can explain why our neighbours aren't also being attacked?'

'I'll be back as soon as I can,' Jeremy said, making no attempt to answer the question. 'And we will get to the bottom of this. I give you my word. In the long run—'

'In the long run, we'll be dead,' Lars said. 'In the meantime, I want my wife and child to be numbered among the living for many years to come.'

Jeremy looked as though he was about to make a further comment, but then changed his mind and nodded briskly. 'You'll hear from me again before the end of the week,' he said. 'And I'll be working on this night and day, I can assure you.'

Lars found Hannah in the bedroom, gazing out of the window. The ridge rose up before her, stark and blackened and bare, the scars of the fire partly concealed by a pall of drifting smoke, burnt tree trunks and branches reaching out in grim supplication. He came to stand behind her, putting his arms around her waist so that she leaned back against him. For a time they surveyed the smoking ruins of the lodge in silence. Then he felt her body begin to shake and he turned her around so that she could weep in the circle of his arms. He held her for a long time, until she dried her eyes and stepped back from him.

'Do you think we should go now?' she said. 'Tell me, Lars, is it time to leave Langani?'

'I think we must talk it over,' he said. 'In the meantime there is a telegram from Sarah in London. She will be here tomorrow, on her way back north. She is collecting her Land Rover as soon as she gets off the plane, and driving straight up here.'

Sarah saw the ridge long before she reached the gates of the farm. She stopped the car and stared out at it, black and still smoking so that the pungent, bitter smell hung in the air and made her choke. She gunned the engine and raced for the house.

'What happened?' she said to Hannah as she jumped out of the vehicle. 'Was it a bush fire?' But as she asked the question she knew what the answer would be. 'Oh God. Was anyone hurt?'

Hannah shook her head. 'It happened two nights ago, and the lodge is gone. I'm so frightened, Sarah. I'm so terrified that someone will hurt Lars or the baby. Jeremy has *askaris* here, asking all the usual, endless questions just as before. I can't sleep or concentrate on anything.'

'Doesn't he have any clue at all?' Sarah said, putting her arms around her friend's shoulders.

'He says there's nothing coming out of the reserve or the townships. Not a scrap of information.' Hannah's mouth was turned down at the corners and her eyes were dull with anger. 'I feel beaten, Sarah. To the point where I don't know whether we can stay on any longer. Lars wants me to take Suniva and go to the coast for a while, but I don't want to leave him here. And I don't want them to think they have chased me off my land.'

'You could come to Buffalo Springs with me tomorrow,' Sarah said. 'You and the baby. And Lars could come for a day or two when he feels he can get away.'

'I don't know.' Hannah was doubtful. 'Here's Lars, in any case. I'm going to lie down for a while. I can't sleep so well at night, now. So I try to get a little rest during the day. I'll see you later.'

'Sarah.' Lars's normally ruddy face was grey and tired. 'We've some real trouble on our hands now, and this latest incident is ugly, in view of all that has gone before.'

'I gather Jeremy hasn't given you much encouragement,' she said.

'There are times when I wonder if there is something we don't know about all this,' he said. 'He's a good policeman and an old family friend, but I have this odd feeling that he is holding something back. Maybe it is even something to do with Janni. Although I can't imagine why he would do that.'

'That's what Camilla thinks. And Rabindrah too,' Sarah said. 'But I've never mentioned it to Hannah, because I knew she would be angry. And it's only a hunch.'

For a moment she was tempted to tell Lars about the priest and her irrational fear that Simon might still be alive, hiding in the thick, dark protection of the forest, waiting to strike again for reasons that were beyond their understanding. Then common sense took hold, told her that there was no evidence, that her feelings were not logical and could only lead to false alarms. And things were bad enough already.

'How was London? Tell me all about that and cheer me up for a while,' Lars said. 'Although you'd better save the description of your brother's wedding until Hannah is here.'

'Deirdre called it off at the last minute,' she said. 'So the whole situation is a bloody disaster. Tim is a bloody disaster.'

She sat down and told him the whole story of her visit to Europe, including Camilla's ongoing liaison with Edward, and finally she described the shock of seeing her brother leaving the Knightsbridge flat.

'I've racked my brains for an explanation,' she said, resentment still smouldering in her like the remains of the fire on the ridge. 'I can't imagine why they would want to keep his visit a secret from me. Right up to the last minute I thought she would mention it, or Tim would turn up and explain. But she said nothing at all, and we parted on pretty strained terms. So much for friendship. I don't think we should tell Hannah about this, though. She has enough on her plate already.'

'I agree,' Lars said. 'Camilla hasn't written since she left. She sent money for the workshop, as promised. But not a line or a phone call from her personally, and Hannah is upset by that.'

'Typical,' Sarah said bitterly. 'And we never learn.'

'Is that your old Land Rover you're still driving?' Lars asked, seeing that she was distressed, and seeking to focus her mind elsewhere.

'It is,' she said. 'But Rabindrah's uncle has taken it to pieces and put new parts into it – a reconditioned engine, in fact. The poor old thing is going like a bird. So we have a second, good-as-new vehicle and Dan is thrilled.'

'Ah yes, Dan,' Lars said. 'There is a message from Dan. He says there was a radio call for you yesterday. From a priest in Nyeri. A Fr Bidoli. He wants to talk to you.'

'Oh, no.' Sarah felt that her heart would burst out of her throat.

For a moment she longed to be back in Ireland with her family, away from the fear and violence that seemed to cling to this place which she had always loved. There had been too many shocks, too many reminders and omens and messages from the past. She could not deal with any more. Lars was looking at her curiously and she hoped that neither he nor Hannah would ask questions about the priest. Hopefully they would think that she had finally decided to return to the practice of her religion.

'Damn,' she said. 'I've just come from Nairobi and that's where this priest lives.'

'No,' Lars said. 'Dan said that he's in Nyeri. And he gave me the phone number.'

It took a long time to get through and to locate Fr Bidoli. But then she heard his voice, quavering and feeble on the line.

'Sarah, they have brought me back to the mission. To Kagumo,' he said. 'So, I hope to be here for some time. For the remainder of my time. I have contacted your camp and they told me that you would be at Langani. So I am wondering if you would come to see me. To visit me. Maybe tomorrow. Because there is something I remembered. Something that I want to show you, my child. It is about Simon Githiri.'

Chapter 11

Kenya, May 1967

Fr Bidoli was waiting for her at the mission in Nyeri, so frail that she could see the individual bones in his fingers as he took her hands. She sat down and tried to conceal her impatience as he settled himself.

'You are back in your original mission, Father,' she said. 'I hope that means you are feeling better?'

'The doctors in Nairobi have done what they can for me,' he said with calm resignation. 'And now I am better off here. This is my home, after all these years.' He looked at her, taking in her drawn face. 'Your friends in Buffalo Springs said you had been away?'

She told him about her visit to London and the time she had spent in Ireland, and then about the fire at the lodge. 'I should have gone back to the camp today,' she said. 'But they have given me extra time to be with Hannah. Because of the fire.' She sat back, her voice shearing off into silence.

'It will never stop, Father,' she said. 'Whoever they are, and whatever their reasons, it will go on and on until Hannah has been driven out of Langani. Or worse. And we are helpless to prevent it.'

'That is why I asked you to come,' Fr Bidoli said. 'When you first visited me, I was unprepared. There have been so many boys under my care over the years, and I needed time to think about Simon. To remember. And I have been doing that since I last talked to you. Thinking about him, trying to recreate the details of the time I spent with him.' He smiled at her. 'One advantage of my age is that I have time to think. And I remembered one thing which might be helpful to you.'

There was a tattered ledger on his knee, and she saw the date on the outside, in large print. Two years ago. He was leafing through the pages as he spoke.

'At Kagumo, they keep a record of where the boys go whenever they leave the mission compound,' he said. 'When a student leaves the mission to visit relatives or to attend a training course he has to sign a book before he goes out. He must write in the name of the person he is going to visit, and the place where he will be. I remembered how excited Simon was, on that day when he thought he had found his family at last. And it struck me that he would have no reason to hide the details. He would have felt proud to have people of his own to see, so what he wrote in the book might be a genuine address – unless the relative who took him away was, for some reason, not being truthful. So I asked for the registers when I came back to Nyeri last week, and I have been going through them.' He held out the book. 'Here it is.'

His finger was pointing to an entry near the end of the page and Sarah looked down at it, sick at heart when she recognised Simon's neat script. For a moment she had a clear memory of him, writing carefully into his notebook as Hannah or Piet gave him his instructions for the day. Her fingernails dug into her palms as she clenched her fists, feeling the pain he had caused them all. Fr Bidoli put a mottled hand over hers.

'I see that you know the handwriting. He was always methodical. It was what made me think that he would have written the name down in the book.'

'Simon Githiri. To Mwathe Reserve with Karanja Mungai.'

Sarah stared down at the page, absorbing the words, wondering if Simon had left them a first, vital clue.

'Do you think it's a genuine address, Father?'

'Someone will have to go to this place and ask,' the old priest said. 'It is not so far from Nyeri. But even if this is where he went, the people there may not admit such a thing. He is dead, and they will not want to take on his shame. Write down the name, Sarah, and the district. But do not hope for too much.' His words were full of weariness.

'I'm sorry, Father. I know he was dear to you, as a boy.'

'He was so small when he first came.' The priest rubbed his forehead. 'Young, but with an old face that was pinched with fear. I thought he was a child who had seen what children should not see, and was struck dumb by whatever it was. When he first responded it was because I was reading a book aloud to the younger ones, a simple Kikuyu folk story about a poor boy and a donkey. I was making the donkey noise and, suddenly, he smiled. He had a most beautiful smile. It changed his face and made him a little boy at last. I saw that I had found a way to give him back a childhood. Not what he should have had – I could not restore that to him. He had no father or mother, no family. But through the books, and the stories I told, his mind came to life. He learned to play and to laugh, although he remained shy. He tried very hard to please me. He was so serious about everything. I think he never felt truly safe, even in the mission.'

'So you believe he had some terrifying experience when he was very small.' Sarah thought about Simon's manner, his gestures and expressions. He had always struck her as being a modest young man, with a quiet confidence in his own abilities. 'But you never discovered what it might have been?'

'I tried to get him to tell me what had happened to him, before he came to us. But after a while I stopped asking, because whenever anyone questioned him he would become silent for days, sitting alone, unable to eat. He did not want to remember. In time he found a life. He was clever and he studied hard and made good progress. Many children here never find a way forward. We cannot help them all.'

'What changed him?'

Fr Bidoli shook his head. 'I only know it must have been something very terrible, to make him throw away all he had learned. To turn him into a murderer. If I had been at the mission when he came looking for me, perhaps . . . But I was gone when he needed me most. We cannot understand these things, my child.'

Sarah leaned back in her chair, tired of not understanding, jarred by the memory of Simon's face, at his evident pleasure as she handed him the gift of her book. Could he really have been this Jekyll and Hyde creature, one part of him full of hope for the future, the other so full of hate that he would mutilate and kill? She shut the thought away.

'I'm sure he admired you,' she said, wanting to offer the priest some comfort. 'He must have been grateful.'

'Not enough to stay true to what I taught him,' Fr Bidoli said. 'But perhaps this one line of handwriting will be of some help to you now. I will give you my blessing, child. You know that you are welcome to come and see me at any time, for any reason. May God grant you peace.'

All the way back to Langani, Sarah wrestled with the problem of what

266

to do about the information she had uncovered. Maybe the person who had come for Simon had given a false name and address. But he would hardly have known that his details would be recorded. So if Mwathe Reserve was where they had gone, somebody there would have to remember Simon's arrival. She decided to discuss the matter with Lars before raising it with Hannah. It was still vague and could prove to be a dead end, creating another crushing disappointment. There was more than enough of that already. She considered passing the information on to Jeremy Hardy. He had said that even the smallest snippets, when added to what was already known, could put them on the right trail. Sarah decided she would phone him after her conversation with Lars.

At Langani the dogs hurled themselves at the car, barking their welcome. Mwangi emerged to tell her that Memsahib Hannah was at the dairy, but that the bwana was in the office. She went along the verandah and knocked on the door.

'*Hodi!* I'm back. How is everything? Is Hannah all right?'

'So-so.' Lars rose to greet her.

'Have you heard anything from Jeremy?' She was eager to broach the subject of her visit to the mission.

'Nothing. It's so bloody frustrating.'

'Lars, I have something I want to tell you, although it may not turn out to be of any significance.' She looked at him directly, demanding a pledge from him. 'But I don't want you to tell Hannah. Not yet.'

'If you say so,' he said, with more curiosity than reluctance.

'I've been to see one of the Italian priests from Kagumo,' Sarah said. 'He's an old man, retired now and very sick. But he had a lot to do with Simon during his childhood. Actually, it was Rabindrah who noticed that no one had ever interviewed him after Piet's death—'

'Rabindrah? What is this to do with him? Why is he still poking about in the case?'

'Listen to me, Lars. Rabindrah may have given us the first useful piece of information we've had since the start of this investigation. Since Piet died. Now, do you want to hear about it or not?'

'I'm sorry. But you know how Hannah feels about that man.'

Sarah ignored his comment and ploughed straight into her narrative, not wanting to become embroiled in an argument about the Indian journalist.

267

'As I was saying, Rabindrah noticed that no one had ever interviewed this priest because he was ill and in hospital at the time. So I went to see him. Twice, in fact.'

'Twice? When was the first time?' Lars was taken aback.

'I visited him in Nairobi. Before I went to London. But I didn't mention it then, because I wasn't sure if he would tell me anything useful.'

'And has he?'

'Not the first time, no. But I saw him again today because he had remembered something.'

She produced the piece of paper with the name Simon had written in the ledger, and the location of the reserve, and told him what Fr Bidoli had said. Lars studied it in silence.

'I know where Mwathe Reserve is,' he said eventually. 'Just outside Nyeri, on the edge of the Aberdare Forest. It's one of the largest Kikuyu tribal districts.'

'It isn't much to go on, but we do have a name. Karanja Mungai. It might be a help. Do you think we should tell Jeremy about it?' Sarah asked. 'So that he can send someone in there to make inquiries.'

'That's exactly what he would do. Ja.' Lars nodded. 'He might even go himself. But that land belongs exclusively to the Kikuyu. It was the heart of the Mau Mau operations during the Emergency.'

'Meaning?'

'What do you think these people in the reserve will tell a white policeman who is looking for one of their tribe in connection with the killing of a white bwana, or the burning of his property?' Lars said. 'Nothing. They won't say a damn thing, and we won't learn a damn thing.'

'Then we should go ourselves,' Sarah said. 'You and I should go in there without any threat of the law, or prison, or any of that. Talk to them ourselves. You're always saying that's the best way to deal with the Kikuyu. And if we don't get anywhere, then we will ask Jeremy to go.'

'Definitely not.' Lars shook his head. 'It would be unwise for us to go in there unaccompanied.'

'We could take a Kikuyu with us, to smooth the way. Someone from here that you trust.'

'We can't do this, Sarah.'

'Then I'll go,' she said. 'And I'll take David with me. He is Kamau's son, and completely trustworthy. He doesn't have a job now, since the lodge was burnt down. I'm sure he would be only too glad to try and find out who was responsible for that.' She knew that Lars would try his best to dissuade her, so she rushed on. 'This is the only lead we've got and it could be important. So I'm going to Mwathe, with or without you.'

'You can't go into the reserve on your own, Sarah.' He wanted to tell her that she was headstrong, too impulsive, but he knew it would be no use. She had made up her mind. 'All right. I will go with you, and we will take David. That, at least, is a good idea.'

'And what should we say to Hannah?'

Lars did not answer for a moment, torn between his desire to keep Hannah away from any further danger and the knowledge that he would be lying to her if he kept the expedition a secret.

'I think it's best not to tell her anything yet,' he said, with reluctance. 'Not until we have some definite information. If she knew, then she would insist on coming with us. We will need slow, careful questioning that is indirect. Hannah is too wound up. She would not be able to stay calm and patient at a meeting like this. So, for now, we say nothing.'

'But we'll be gone for most of the day. What would we tell her?' Sarah sat down, her eyes filled with doubt. 'I don't know, Lars. Suddenly this doesn't feel right.'

'What doesn't feel right, Sarah?' Hannah opened the office door and came to stand beside her husband, her hand stroking the back of his neck.

Sarah looked at Lars, seeking direction, wondering how long Hannah had been there and what she might have heard. He shook his head very slightly, and the lie slid from Sarah's mouth, smooth and easy in spite of her moment of indecision.

'It's a problem with one of the photographs in the book. I think I need to change it.'

'You can still do that?' Hannah was surprised. 'Tell me which one you are not happy about. I can't imagine how you could improve on what you showed me. Come with me now, to fetch Suniva. We can take her for a little walk.'

They left the office together, Sarah throwing a distracted glance at Lars, Hannah smiling with the soft bloom of a mother about to rediscover the miracle of her child.

*

269

'I'm planning to drive into Nanyuki tomorrow,' Lars said at dinner.

'Maybe I could go with you.' Sarah stared down into the swirl of her soup, not wishing to make eye contact with Hannah.

'What on earth for?' Hannah was puzzled. 'I was hoping you would do the dispensary with me in the morning.'

'I'm sorry, Han. But I need to post some negatives and slides to London, and to send a note to Rabindrah explaining my change of mind. It's pretty important. Urgent.'

'Why can't Lars do that for you?'

'There are a few other things I need to buy before I go back to work. Personal things – you know. There wasn't enough time yesterday.' Sarah knew it sounded less than believable, but she could not think of any better excuse. She moved her glass around in circles.

'Well, it's up to you,' Hannah conceded, but with bad grace. 'What time will you be back?'

'Sometime in the afternoon.' Lars was vague. 'I might have to wait for a part for the harvester. I'll take David with me.'

Hannah looked at him. 'David? Why?'

'His morale is pretty low, now that his chance to be a cook at the lodge is gone. So I thought it would be good to give him something to do.' Lars tried to ignore her mounting irritation and dug himself a deeper hole. 'It's not as if you are actually using him for anything.'

'I put him back in the storeroom, where he was working before.' Hannah was red-faced with annoyance.

'Well, I'm sure he can be spared for one day,' Lars said. 'I wonder if you can't find something else for him, Han. David may not have much schooling, but he is bright, and he really needs something more challenging. Otherwise we may lose him.'

'I can't see that a shopping trip to Nanyuki would be much of a challenge,' she said, angrily. 'And I don't think you should be critical of the kind of job I've given him. He's lucky I've kept him on at all. If you start favouring him it will cause discontent and jealousy with the other *watu*, and then we'll have even more problems.'

'Possibly,' Lars said, 'but I'll take him anyway.'

'Do as you please,' she said, flinging her dinner napkin down on the table. 'But after tomorrow David should go back to working in the store.'

She left them immediately after dinner, irritated by Sarah's proposed outing. There had been an outbreak of dysentery on the farm, and it was difficult to take care of everyone who came to the dispensary. Some of the women brought *totos* suffering from dehydration and high fevers. It seemed to Hannah that the expedition to Nanyuki was unnecessary and ill-timed. She had also relied on Sarah's company to boost her morale for the few days that were left, before her friend's return to Buffalo Springs.

Lars sat staring at the table, his face like granite. Sarah felt a great deal of sympathy for him, but she did not know what she could say. At last she rose, and touched his shoulder.

'It's the strain of the last few days,' she said. 'No. It's the strain of more than a year, in fact. Be patient. I'll see you in the morning.'

They set off early, aware of Hannah's continuing displeasure. Lars had rolled his eyes when she stood up from the breakfast table, turned on her heel, and left to face the demands of the day alone. Sarah felt as though they were truant children, and she was tempted to run outside and tell Hannah the truth. But then Lars would be in hot water for not having confided in her the day before. Either way, there would be trouble. She sighed with frustration.

In Nanyuki they made a brief stop to place their order for farm supplies, arranging to pick up the goods on the way back. Sarah bought several lengths of *kitenge* cloth, and some brightly coloured wool.

'What's that for?' Lars said. 'It's amazing how women are always shopping, no matter what the circumstances.'

'It's for the women in Mwathe,' Sarah said, somewhat scathingly. 'Karanja must have a wife or two. It could be useful to offer a gift.'

'Good idea.' His expression was a little sheepish as he went back to the shop. 'I'll get some tobacco for the men.'

As they drove south towards Nyeri, they explained to David where they were going and what they hoped to discover. The young man was decidedly uneasy.

'You must be careful,' he said. 'These men at Mwathe – if they were helping Simon, or if they have done the things that have happened at Langani since Bwana Piet was killed, then they are very bad. They might kill you too. It would be better for Memsahib Sarah to wait in Nyeri.'

'He's right,' Lars said.

'I'm not going to be left behind.' Sarah was adamant. 'I can talk to the women while you concentrate on Karanja, if we find him. The *bibis* might be more likely to tell me something than to talk to you or David. This whole thing may be a wild goose chase, but I am going to Mwathe. And that is final.'

'David has a point about our safety,' Lars said. 'We'll have to tell them that there are people who know where we are. And if we don't get home by a certain time they'll be out looking for us.'

Sarah nodded agreement. But in the end, she thought, it won't matter what we say to try and protect ourselves. Because the moment they know we are from Langani, we will become sitting targets for anyone bent on further destruction.

At Nyeri they stopped to ask directions, and half an hour later they turned on to the road for Mwathe Reserve. The Aberdare Forest towered, green and dense, above the human habitations. Sarah sat in the front seat beside Lars, silent and tense as David made enquiries about Karanja Mungai's homestead. There were curious looks from people walking along the mud tracks, going about the business of their day. Some called out a greeting, others watched with suspicion, talking in undertones as the strangers passed. David sat up straight and stern in the back of the Land Rover, apprehensive but not prepared to vocalise his concern.

All around them the thatched mud and wattle dwellings of the Kikuyu were clustered in a series of compounds, surrounded by heavily cultivated smallholdings. Further up the hillside, *totos* tended goats and cattle, and in the space in front of each hut chickens clucked and scratched. Women carrying huge bundles of firewood toiled along the narrow paths, bent under the weight of their burdens. The men walked in front of their wives, or stood together, talking amicably and smoking their pipes, watching the domestic work in progress. It was a peaceful scene from another age. They came to a halt at a point where the road was too narrow to drive further, and got out of the car. David pointed up ahead of them, to a group of huts on the edge of the encroaching forest.

'This is the place,' he said.

Lars and Sarah followed the direction of his finger. Smoke was rising from the vents in the circular huts. As they drew closer they could see two women outside, and a number of small children playing in the dirt around them. A third, younger woman stood in the shade of a tree to one side of the compound, with a baby on her hip. She was watching them, motionless and wary.

'This Karanja is well off, judging by the number of huts in his compound,' Lars commented. 'Three wives at least, he seems to have. And that one is very young, even by their standards.' He indicated the girl standing alone.

'What are you going to say?' Sarah asked. Now that they were here, she felt unsure. 'We can't just walk up and ask them to tell us all they know about Simon Githiri.'

'David will introduce us in the acceptable tribal manner,' Lars said. 'Then we will have to feel our way. A number of serious crimes have been committed, and if anyone has information they will try to hide it, so we'll have to watch everyone for a sign.'

'What kind of sign?' Sarah said.

'I don't know exactly,' Lars said. 'But David can read his own people's reactions better than we can. He's more likely to know if they are lying. And my Kikuyu is poor. It's difficult for me to follow when they speak quickly, so I could miss something. In any case, it may be better to look like an ignorant white man.' He smiled encouragement. 'You're the one who is famous for picking up on bad spirits, Sarah. Just keep your antennae on full alert. Here we go.'

They stopped at the entrance to the compound. Sarah looked around, suddenly aware that they were being watched from all the surrounding huts, and that they were the only white people here. Several young men appeared and stood close to her, not speaking, their expressions guarded. Like her own. She felt a prickle of unease. David called out a respectful greeting in Kikuyu, and one of the older women nodded to him. He asked if the *Mʒee* Karanja was at home. The woman jerked her head towards the largest dwelling, and the young girl with the baby went to the entrance and called inside. Eventually, a man emerged from the narrow opening. He had been sleeping, Sarah thought, and he peered at them through eyes that were bloodshot and yellowed. His face was lined and dour, with a long scar that ran from his forehead down his left cheek, almost to his chin. He carried a tribal stick marked with coloured patterns picked out in beads down the haft, and although he was slight he gave the impression of wiry strength. It was hard to gauge how old he might be – perhaps in his sixties, or even seventies. He wore a pair of threadbare khaki trousers and an old shirt rather than tribal garments, but his ear lobes were long and decorated with copper wire, and he had an intricately beaded cap on his head. As they approached he stood outside his home, unsmiling and forbidding. David spoke again, asking permission for the *wazungu* to enter the compound to discuss an important matter. Karanja considered them for what seemed a long time. His womenfolk nudged one another and whispered behind their hands, and the children gazed at them, round-eyed and solemn. Two younger men crouched in the low entrance to a second hut, waiting to see what the *mzee* would do. Finally, he nodded, and beckoned them forward.

'Tell him we are grateful he has allowed us to speak with him,' Lars said to David. 'We have brought gifts for the *mzee* and his wives. We are seeking his advice on a very delicate *shauri*. Because he is a wise man, and we hope he may be able to help us.'

While David translated, Sarah opened her brown-paper package and offered the lengths of cloth and beads to the women, enjoying the delight on their faces as they fingered the material. Lars presented Karanja with a pouch of tobacco. The old man nodded again, then issued instructions to the women. They disappeared into his hut, and came out with three carved wooden stools, placing them on the packed earth outside the larger hut. Lars and David sat down opposite Karanja, but Sarah was left to stand to one side. It was something of a balancing act for Lars, with his long legs folded under him at an awkward angle. Sarah caught a malicious gleam in Karanja's eye as he watched the big white man trying to seat himself with dignity. The younger Kikuyu squatted on either side of their leader. Everyone waited as Lars produced a packet of cigarettes, and offered them to his host. Karanja accepted one, then the other two extended their hands, and after a few seconds of low-voiced discussion between the men and the women, the older wife also took one. Lars lit Karanja's cigarette with his Zippo lighter, and as it was passed around the embossed design on the panel was inspected by all the members of the gathering. When it came back to Karanja, he held it thoughtfully in his hand.

'Tell him it would do me great honour if he would accept the lighter as a gift,' Lars said to David.

The Zippo with the packet of cigarettes disappeared into the pocket of Karanja's trousers. He puffed on his cigarette, and regarded the *wazungu* with hostility through the smoke, murmuring something in an undertone to one of the other men. Sarah's Kikuyu was minimal and she was unable to understand what he was saying. Now Lars asked David to explain that they were looking for information about a young man whom he believed might be a relative, and who was known to the people he had worked with as Simon Githiri.

Sarah stood very still, observing them all carefully when Simon's name was mentioned. There was a perceptible stiffening among the men, and a surreptitious glance between the two younger ones. But it was the girl with the baby who betrayed the most obvious reaction. She had been standing at the edge of the circle out of any direct line of vision, and the men did not see her start and clutch at the bundle in her arms, digging her fingers into the child. There was a wail of distress and Karanja turned to glower at her. She slunk away to one side, explaining that the baby had just woken up and was hungry. Her face was troubled as she tried to calm the child, apologising to the old man for disturbing him. His expression as he looked at her was one of sour disdain. Sarah watched the girl carefully. She had seen the flash of panic in her expression, and she was now convinced that this young woman knew Simon, or knew of him at least. Sarah moved towards her, nodding with respect to Karanja, masking her interest in the mother by paying attention to her child. He must be over a year old, yet he was not playing with the other *totos* in the compound. One of the older women gave a cackle of mirth and then spat in the dust as Sarah reached out to touch the baby. He wriggled out of his knitted blanket, and she realised with a shock that he had a badly deformed foot. The girl saw the direction of her gaze, and pulled her own clothing around him in a protective gesture. Sarah smiled at her, trying to show reassurance, but there was no response.

Karanja spoke for several minutes in a rapid undertone to the other men. Then he turned to David, shaking his head, disclaiming all knowledge of Simon Githiri. His two henchmen had moved closer to him, shaking their heads in denial. Lars demonstrated his regret by holding out his hands, palms turned upward, as he shrugged his shoulders.

'We are sure there must be a mistake,' he said. 'But we have been to the mission school in Kagumo where this man, Simon Githiri, was brought as a child. There was an entry in their record book that said he was going with a relative, Karanja Mungai, to visit his family in Mwathe Reserve. The priests have told us that Simon Githiri definitely left the mission with Karanja Mungai. Perhaps there is another man with this name in Mwathe?'

Karanja stood up, indicating that his companions should do the same. David understood the signal, but Lars was slower. He was at a disadvantage now, as the only man sitting down. He rose with difficulty and faced the three Kikuyu. The atmosphere had become taut. The old man waved his stick in front of Lars's face and spoke angrily, the sides of his mouth flecked with spittle, and he thumped the *rungu* in the dirt to emphasise his rage. There was no longer any attempt at a polite exchange, and he leaned towards them aggressively. Through David, he said that he had indeed gone to Kagumo Mission once, but it had been a long time ago. He had heard that there was a boy there who had some connection with his tribe. But when he questioned the young man, he realised that it was a mistake. This boy had nothing to do with him, or with his tribe. This boy was dishonest. He had tried to make claims that were not true. If he had put Karanja's name down as a relative, it was false. He had lied, perhaps to go out of the mission, to go somewhere that the Fathers would not approve of.

Karanja spat in the dirt and spread his hands. There was nothing further he could say, except that the *wazungu* had wasted a journey. As Lars tried in vain to obtain more information, Sarah moved close to the young mother and reached out again to caress the baby, speaking in a mixture of rudimentary Kikuyu and Swahili that she hoped the young woman would understand.

'My father is a doctor of white medicine,' she said in a low voice. 'He has helped many children with the trouble that afflicts your baby. If you bring the child to me at Langani Farm, near Nanyuki, I can help you. I know doctors who can make your baby well. It will take time, but he will be able to walk like other children.'

The girl's eyes widened, and she turned away. David was explaining to Karanja that the police had wanted to come to the reserve and question him. But this Bwana Olsen had said it must be a mistake, and he would come himself to speak with the *mzee*. He agreed that Simon Githiri was a dishonest man. Indeed, he was a very bad man, wanted for murder. And now he was dead also. A judgement of the great god, Kirinyaga. But if they did remember anything about him, and who his friends or family might really be, they should inform Bwana Olsen or the police in Nyeri.

Karanja gazed back, his manner increasingly antagonistic, and repeated that he knew nothing of the man in question. And since he was dead that was the end of the matter. He spat again on the ground, barely missing David's feet. Lars nodded, and signalled that they should go.

The young woman had disappeared inside one of the huts. As Sarah left the compound she thought she caught a glimpse of her, standing in the shadows of the doorway, watching. But the sun was low in the sky, and in the blinding light she could not be sure.

They drove back to Nanyuki very fast, concerned that they might not be in time to collect the farm supplies. If they returned to Langani empty-handed, Hannah would be justifiably angry.

'They know something, that's for sure,' Sarah said as they hurtled along the road. 'The reaction when you mentioned Simon's name was a dead giveaway.'

'But it hasn't left us with anything firm to go on,' Lars said. 'I don't believe for one moment that Karanja travelled all the way to Kagumo, and then decided Simon wasn't a relative. I'm sure they came back to Mwathe together. Your old priest was right, though – he never realised that Simon had written his name in a book.'

'It's the first hint of someone who might be connected with him,' Sarah said. 'And as a result we may be able to track down whoever it is that still wants to harm us all.'

'No one at Mwathe is going to volunteer any more information,' Lars pointed out. 'Maybe we should get Jeremy and his boys to lean on them now.'

'But if the police start asking questions, this Karanja may move off somewhere else. Disappear into the forest. If he was involved in the last two incidents at Langani, then he could conduct his campaign from anywhere round here. It's better if they think we've accepted their story. Act like stupid *wazungu*. Maybe Jeremy could set up some sort of watch on the compound.'

'What about you, David?' Lars asked. 'What did you think of Karanja?'

'He is bad, bwana. And he takes *bhang*.'

'Yes. He was high on something. He had that feverish look they get, when they are addicted.'

277

'The thing that interested me was the girl with the baby,' Sarah said. 'She nearly jumped out of her skin when she heard Simon's name. I wish we could have talked to her on her own.'

'It would be dangerous for such a woman to be seen talking to *wazungu*,' David said. 'They would kill her. She is young, only a junior wife. And with a deformed child. That is a bad omen for her tribe. It brings evil on the whole clan. Some husbands would make their wife leave a *toto* like that one out in the bush. For the hyenas.'

'The poor child has a club foot,' Sarah said. 'Dad saw a number of children with that problem, and it can be treated very successfully. I told the girl, you know. That I would try and find medical help. But I'm not sure she understood. She disappeared before I could make it clear.'

She felt let down, discouraged by the lack of anything concrete they could use or follow up.

'I have a gut feeling she knows something about Simon,' she said.

'Perhaps David can think of some way of talking to her again,' Lars said. But he did not hold out much hope.

'We must tell Hannah now,' Sarah said. 'Even though there's not much to relate. But we can't hide it any more. I can't, at any rate. If we are going to talk to Jeremy about this, then we have to tell Hannah first. Please, Lars? I'm no good at this cloak and dagger stuff.'

Lars nodded agreement. 'We'll explain it to her this evening.' He glanced in the rear-view mirror. 'And you, David—'

'*Ndio*, bwana.'

'You cannot tell anyone where we have been today. No one at all. It is very important that the people at Mwathe think we are finished with them, understand?'

'*Ndio*, bwana. I will tell no one.'

They reached Nanyuki with seconds to spare before the store closed.

'How about a quick drink at the Silverbeck?' Lars asked when they had loaded the Land Rover. He was keen to release some of the day's tension before getting back to the farm.

'I think we should keep going,' Sarah said. 'It's almost dark, and Hannah isn't comfortable on her own.'

Lars smiled and put an affectionate hand on her arm. 'You're right. As ever. We'll press on.'

'Maybe we should phone her?'

Lars hesitated, then shook his head. 'I don't want to start explaining on the telephone and we'll be home in about forty minutes. Let's go.'

They headed out towards Langani, driving at top speed, each wrapped in private thought until they rounded a bend and almost ran into a young bull elephant. Sarah gave a cry of dismay as the great shape loomed in the windscreen. Lars braked hard. The car slewed wildly from one crumbling verge to the other as he fought to control it on the rutted surface. It seemed that a crash was inevitable, but in the last seconds before impact, the elephant lifted his trunk in alarm and cannoned off into the bush. The front wheel struck a boulder on the side of the road with a crunching sound and then the vehicle came to a halt, canted over to one side. For several minutes Sarah was stunned, looking into the thorn tree that had stopped their headlong rush. Then panic took over.

'Lars? Lars, are you all right? David?' She found that she was shouting their names.

Beside her, Lars began to cough, trying to clear his lungs of the dust that swirled round them in choking red clouds.

'I'm good! I'm good – I'm alive, anyway! Are you OK?'

'Yes.' She looked across at him, weak with shock and relief. 'David? Are you hurt?'

'No, memsahib. I am very fine.' His voice was shaky and he was half lying across the back seat, clinging to the window frame.

'We'd better take a look at the damage.' Lars climbed out of the vehicle and it rocked violently as he stepped on to the ground. 'Watch out,' he warned. 'This thing might turn over. It's sitting up on a bloody great rock. Get out very carefully, Sarah. Then you, David. Here, grab my arm. We'll have to see if we can get it back on the road, and whether we can still drive it.'

They crawled from the damaged vehicle, listening with trepidation to the groaning noise of metal as the change of weight altered the angle of the car. Now that they were out and apparently unhurt, Sarah felt sick and began to shake.

'Sit down,' Lars said. 'David, there's a thermos in the back.' He poured coffee into the cup, ladled in a large amount of sugar and handed it to her. 'It's shock. Drink this, and stay quiet while David and I try to pull this jalopy off the boulder. You're not bleeding, are you? You haven't broken anything?'

Sarah shook her head, not trusting her voice. She sat down on a stone nearby and sipped the syrupy coffee until the tremor in her hands had stilled, her breathing was easier, and the nausea had passed. The men were wrestling with the car, trying to lift or push it off its resting place, but the boulder was wide, and they could not get enough leverage. Lars was cursing in dismay.

'Bloody hell! I can't see any major damage to the wheels or the chassis, but we're stuck fast and I don't want to turn it over altogether. Get the rope, David.'

David searched the back of the vehicle. The car gave a sideways lurch when he leaned on the back board and Sarah sucked in her breath. Finally, after Lars had put his shoulder against the side panel to steady it, the young Kikuyu managed to pull out a length of rope. They attached it to the tow bar and Lars disappeared into the bush. He returned, dragging a heavy bough from a fallen acacia tree, laying it down on the ground.

'If I can get this under the front of the car, I might be able to lever it up, and then David can pull it off,' he said.

Sarah walked over to join them. Lars was about to refuse her assistance, but she silenced him.

'You have to let me help. It's dark now, and we don't want to be stuck out here all night. It's unlikely that anyone will come by for hours, and Hannah will be out of her mind with worry if we're gone much longer.'

'Right,' he said. 'Take the rope. When I give you the signal, you and David pull as hard as you can, and I'll push.'

He disappeared round to the front of the car and she heard him struggling and cursing as he tried to push the branch into place, underneath the axle.

'Now, on a count of three, pull like hell!' he shouted. 'One, two, three! *Harambee!*'

It took twenty minutes to haul the car off the rock. Twice, the improvised lever snapped and Lars had to forage for stronger wood.

'Be careful,' David said. 'The elephant may be waiting for us to move, or he might be thinking about chasing us away. I will come with you to get the wood.'

There was no sign of the elephant, or of any other wildlife, much to

Sarah's relief. But when the Land Rover eventually began to move there was a grinding noise, and she feared they would destroy the entire underside before they got it down. Finally, with one last shriek of metal, the vehicle landed on the road in a puff of dust and they collapsed, filthy and gasping for breath. David and Sarah had rope burns on their hands and Lars's arms were gashed and bleeding from wrestling with the thorny branches. They sat breathless and recovering in the gathering darkness, and then Lars made another inspection. A tell-tale streak of oil followed the track of the car over the boulder, and he lay down under the chassis to see where it was coming from.

'Hell! There's a leak from the sump,' he said. 'We'll have to try and patch it up with a rag, and limp home. But it's anyone's guess how long it will last.'

The car crawled along, and twice Lars had to stop and replace the rag he had stuffed into the sump. The oil was leaking fast. There was no one else on the road, and Sarah felt an increasing sense of dread that they would be stranded out in the bush all night, with no means of telling Hannah where they were. When the inevitable happened and the engine seized completely, they sat helpless, listening to the steam escaping from the overheated bonnet.

'This is bad news,' Lars said. 'Very, very bad news.'

Then David gave a shout. 'Someone coming, Bwana Lars. From Nanyuki direction.'

Lars jumped out, waving frantically into the headlights of the approaching car. A police vehicle pulled up beside them, and Jeremy Hardy wound down the window.

'Thank God I've found you,' he said. 'Hannah has been on the line, totally hysterical. Convinced you were lying dead in a ditch somewhere after an accident or an ambush. Are you all right?' He peered at Sarah's raw, bleeding hands. 'What happened?'

'We very nearly were dead in a ditch,' Lars said, grinning with relief. 'We came up to a jumbo rather fast, hit a rock, and the sump is gone. We need a tow.'

Lars attached the Land Rover to the police truck, while Jeremy sent a radio message to Langani. As they drove back to the farm Lars described where they had been, and what had led up to the crash.

'We'll discuss this in detail tomorrow,' Jeremy said, his expression stern and disapproving. 'But you were bloody stupid to go into the reserve like that, without letting me know. This is no time to play at amateur sleuths. What the hell were you thinking of?'

It was past eight o'clock when they reached Langani. Mwangi rushed out to greet them and David began to tell him about the accident, throwing his arms wide to describe the elephant, proudly showing his torn hands like a warrior displaying battle wounds. Sarah stood apart, stiff and drained. There was no sign of Hannah. Kamau appeared from the kitchen and his son repeated the story, with added dimensions of danger and drama in the retelling.

At last Hannah appeared with a first-aid box. She stood looking at them for a moment, then swallowed hard.

'Where the hell have you been?' Her voice was pitched high, driven by anxiety. 'Especially since sundown. Wherever you were, you could at least have phoned. Did it never bloody occur to you that I'd be worried sick? Mwangi tells me you turned the car over.'

Sarah moved forward, dismayed by the force of Hannah's anger, anxious to offer an explanation.

'Han, we're so, so sorry,' she said. 'We almost ran into an elephant and we're all a bit of a mess, I'm afraid. Rope burns, cut arms and legs, and stiff muscles. But at least no one was badly hurt.'

'When did that happen?' Hannah was looking at the marks on Lars's arms.

'About six,' he said. 'We were bowling along, trying to make up for lost time and—'

'Six o'clock?' Hannah cut in. 'What were you doing in Nanyuki until six o'clock? You were only going for supplies, and the post. I didn't realise you were going to lounge around there all afternoon.'

But they could not explain, not in front of the staff. Hannah opened the first-aid box in stony silence, took out disinfectant and poured some on to several wedges of cotton wool.

'Clean your hands,' she said to David, her tone short. 'And put some of this yellow ointment on them.'

He retired to a corner of the verandah, listening with interest to see how they would escape the anger of the young memsahib and whether they would tell her many lies. Sarah felt for him as he tended to his hands, alone in the dark. She was bone-tired, suffering from the after-effects of the crash, conscious of the searing sensation in the palms of her hands, and the aching muscles in her body.

'David was terrific today,' she said. 'We had a couple of anxious hours trying to get back here, so that you wouldn't be on your own all night.'

'Oh, really? Well, it's great that you made the effort.' Hannah turned on her, eyes blazing. 'I hope you've had a good time in Nanyuki, after telling me some cock and bull story. The shopping you mentioned this morning couldn't have taken more than half an hour. When you didn't come back I phoned the club and the hotels, but no one had seen you all day. I'm trying to run a bloody farm here, and look after a baby, and cope with raids and arson and—' She choked for a moment on her anger, then raced on. 'And with everything that's happened. Lars has work to do here, Sarah. He's not free to spend the day running around with you on shopping trips.'

'We weren't on a shopping trip, Han. We—'

'You took off for the day with my husband and one of my staff, both of whom were needed here.' Hannah's voice was shrill with anger. 'And between you, you've managed to crash my car, probably because you were driving too bloody fast.'

She knew she was saying all the wrong things, that she should be explaining how relieved she was to see them, how frightened she had been when they did not come home. She wanted to put her arms around Lars, to tell him that she was afraid he had come to some harm, that she could never live without him or get through a single day unless he was there to love her. She had tried for so long to be resolute and steady and brave, only to discover that her husband and her best friend were involved in some plan from which they had deliberately excluded her. Where had they been all day? What were they keeping from her? All her pent-up terror exploded in an angry release, and she could not stop the words. Sarah was staring at her, contrite and silent. Lars stood with his back to her, shoulders hunched, hands in his pockets.

'I suppose you think I should be full of sympathy, because you've come back here with a few scratches,' she said, rounding on Sarah. 'But you should have been back by three o'clock at the latest, and I couldn't think what had happened to you. So don't try and tell me about how my husband and my staff behaved in this mess that you've created, Sarah Mackay!

Because you are a guest here on my farm. You have no right to tell me anything.'

Sarah's face crumpled. She placed her torn hands on the back of a chair for support, and then quickly withdrew them as pain shot through her palms.

'I'll be getting along now.' Jeremy Hardy cleared his throat, plainly embarrassed. 'We'll talk about all this in the morning, when everyone has had time to recover. In the meantime, the less said the better. I don't think this visit should become common knowledge.' He patted Hannah on the arm. 'Goodnight, my dear,' he said kindly. 'I'm glad I was able to be of help. Sleep well, now, all of you.'

'Whom did you visit?' Hannah turned to Lars as the policeman drove away.

'Hannah, I think we should take this discussion inside,' he said quietly. 'Before you say anything else you might regret.'

She stepped away from him but he took her arm and steered her towards the office, leaving Sarah alone, rooted to the spot, her eyes blinded by the onset of tears and Hannah's words weighing like stones in her heart. After a few minutes she heard David move away down the steps, and she walked along the verandah, past the drawn blinds and closed door of the office, and shut herself into her room.

'I do not appreciate being told off in front of the servants,' Lars said. 'You should not have spoken to either of us like that, no matter what you were feeling. No, don't talk, Hannah. Listen.' He thumped the desk with his fist to silence her. 'Rabindrah Singh put Sarah in touch with a priest who had looked after Simon as a child.'

At the mention of the Sikh's name, Hannah gave a hiss of fury. 'That bloody raghead! I knew he was trouble. He rang here tonight. I wish he'd bugger off and leave us all alone!'

'Shut up, Hannah! Just shut up.' Lars gripped her hard, forcing her down into a chair 'Don't talk like that. He may have led us to the first break we've had. This priest gave Sarah the name of a man who claimed to be a relative of Simon's. So we went to Mwathe Reserve today, to try and find him. And I was the one who decided not to tell you, because it might have turned into a dead end.'

'But you felt more comfortable explaining it to David, rather than your wife?' Hannah's voice was cracking, and her knuckles were white as she clutched the dark wood of her father's old desk.

'I took David as an interpreter, because I trust him,' Lars said. 'And he has promised not to talk about where we went. This is not something that can be discussed in front of the other staff. And neither is my work on this farm.'

'So what did you find?' she asked.

'I'll tell you that in a minute,' Lars said. 'But in the meantime, you have no right to accuse me of behaving irresponsibly, or to assume that I would take a day off to amuse myself and Sarah, without including you. You'd better see to her hands, by the way, and make sure she takes something for muscle strain, after pulling up the car. You should have been out there thanking her, and David too, instead of—'

'Why are you taking her part, putting her first?' Hannah stood up, her arms folded and her back stiff. 'Can you imagine how it was when you didn't come home?'

Lars sighed and reached out to touch her, compassion taking over from resentment. But she jerked away.

'I'm sorry I didn't tell you where we were going,' he said. 'And I do understand how it must have been for you. But you are not the only one who is suffering. You seem to have forgotten that Sarah lost everything with Piet's death – the man she was going to marry, and the future they had planned together here on this farm. But she has always done her best to help you through the pain, to try and protect you, to stay here whenever she can. It must have been terrible to talk to that priest about Simon, to say nothing of making the journey today. Taking the risk of coming face to face with whoever is trying to destroy you and your farm. None of that is easy for her. You have a beautiful daughter, and you have a home at Langani despite its present difficulties. And you have a husband who loves you. But Sarah has lost all her dreams.'

She looked at him, all her anger fading, and tried to smile. But he did not respond.

'I deserve more respect than you have shown me,' he said. 'You should understand that, Hannah, the next time your temper takes hold of you. Sarah is the best and most loyal friend you have ever had, or are ever likely to have, and she should be treated as such. That kind of friendship is rare, and you may have put an axe through it for good tonight. Now, I am going

285

to clean up, and you should find some *dawa* for Sarah and then go to the kitchen and ask Kamau to organise something for us all to eat.' He left the room, closing the door firmly behind him.

In the office Hannah sat at the desk her father and grandfather had used for so many years before her. She bowed her head as a picture of Janni came into her mind, bloated and drunken, embittered by the knowledge that he had turned his back on Langani, and taken Lottie to live a life of drudgery and despair in a country they hated. He had lost his son in a brutal, senseless slaying. And all for the sake of holding on to the land their forebears had carved out of the bush at the turn of the century. Langani, the joyous place of her childhood and her fondest memories, had become an albatross. A burden with a cost which had already claimed the life of her beloved brother, and which was now destroying a vital friendship, even threatening her marriage and the security of her child. She wondered if it was time to go.

Chapter 12

Kenya, May 1967

Sarah was awake before dawn. The discord of the previous night had embedded itself in her mind, and her first thoughts made for a bitter start to the day. In the refuge of her bedroom, she had created a physical distance between herself and Hannah. But the harsh words had stayed with her, and she had been too distressed to make an appearance when Mwangi had come to call her for dinner. It had not been long before she heard another knock on the door.

There had been a strained silence, widening the chasm between them. Then Hannah had spoken. 'Sarah. Ach, Sarah, I'm so sorry. I've brought you some sandwiches, and a salve for your hands.'

Sarah had nodded, unable to find any words to say.

'I can't deal with anything any more.' Hannah had sat down on the bed, hiding her face in her hands. 'I was frantic when it got dark, terrified that something awful had happened to you and Lars. That you would never come back, and Suniva and I would have no one left. No one at all. Then Jeremy found you and I was sick with relief, but angry at the same time. And then Mwangi came to tell me there had been an accident, and I came out on to the verandah, and everyone was laughing at David's story about the crash, and no one seemed to have thought about me.' She'd stopped, waiting for Sarah to say something, to reach out a hand in reconciliation. But there had been no gesture.

'I always get angry when I'm scared. You know that. Maybe it's the Italian in me. Ma used to be the same way, if I disappeared without telling her where I was going. She'd be convinced I'd fallen into the river or been eaten by a leopard or something, and she'd be livid with me when I came home. It was her way of letting go of the fear. I'm sorry, Sarah, and I can understand why you don't want to talk to me.' Her eyes had been pleading. 'I have to go back to Lars now. He is angry with me too, and he's right. But I wanted you to know that I love you and I'm sorry. I'll see you in the morning.'

When she had gone Sarah had sat without moving for a while. Eventually she'd tried to eat something, but it was difficult. Her hands were still smarting in spite of the salve she had smeared on them, and she was aching all over. After a while she had given up on the food and lain down, but she had not been able to sleep. They should have told Hannah where they were going. She had a right to be angry. But the cruelty of her words were indelibly printed into Sarah's consciousness. She was a guest on the farm, someone who could not be trusted. Not part of the family, not a sister or a treasured friend, as she had always believed. And that was the truth of it. She did not belong here any more. Hannah had a husband and child to care for, and a home to run. She did not want her dead brother's fiancée disturbing her already troubled life, emphasising his absence, acting as a constant reminder of her loss. Sarah had tried to quell the rising grief. Piet was gone, and the place that should have been her home was no longer a real part of her life. She should have recognised it sooner.

The remainder of the night had passed in a series of uneasy dreams. Karanja Mungai's menacing presence had filled the darkness each time she'd closed her eyes. He had known Simon, she was sure of it. And so had the girl with the baby. But the visit to Mwathe had brought them no closer to identifying who or what was behind the threat to Langani. Sarah now felt that she had only succeeded in creating misunderstandings and recrimination between them all. She had lost Piet and now she had lost Hannah too. In London even Camilla had betrayed her. She would leave Langani in the morning.

As the first sliver of light stole across the sky, Sarah dressed quickly. She scribbled a note for Hannah and slipped out to the car, waving to the night watchman and moving off as quietly as she could in the hopes that the engine noise would not wake anyone. In the cold, hazy dawn she turned on to the main Nanyuki road, hoping for a sense of relief now that she had left the farm. But as she drove into the rising sun, the glory of the morning seemed only to underscore the isolation that had engulfed her. Passing the scene of the accident, she saw the rock where the car had landed, and the long black streak of sump oil that had stained the ground. She found herself shivering at the memory of the impact. What if Lars had been killed, or badly injured? They had been lucky to get away with a few scratches and a damaged engine.

The road stretched out in front of her, long and empty and red as the sun hit the rich clay. She had always enjoyed travelling alone, content to observe the wildlife that teemed in the bush on either side of the road, to identify wild flowers and plants and bird calls. But now she longed for someone to talk to. Another human being who could understand how lost she felt, wandering in the alien, hostile world that had become her life. She drove on, staring straight ahead, hardly aware of her route, until she reached Nanyuki. She had begun to feel sick and shaky, and remembered how little she had eaten over the last twenty-four hours. When she saw the sign for the Silverbeck Hotel she decided to pull in and order some breakfast. There was no one around except the night porter who told her that breakfast would not be served until seven. Sarah walked out to the car park, aware that she had not had enough sleep and that she was hungry, cold and dejected. The car keys had vanished into the bottom of her bag and as she rummaged for them her need for solace increased. She stopped searching and leaned against the door of the Land Rover, kicking at a stone and scuffing a pair of new shoes that had been an extravagance in London. Then she returned to the hotel.

'I'd like to make a phone call,' she said, scribbling down the number and handing it to the porter.

He gestured towards the phone kiosk and dialled the operator. Sarah installed herself in the small booth, gripping the receiver awkwardly in her blistered hands as she waited to be put through. When she heard the voice her heart sank. She had obviously woken him up. Another mistake.

'Indar Singh here. Who is speaking please?'

Sarah considered putting down the receiver. This was beyond embarrassing. She looked at her watch. What had she been thinking? A phone call at this hour would cause all kinds of speculation. This was a disaster. But she needed to talk to someone. Anyone.

'Hello? Hello! Who is this please?' Indar Singh's question carried alarm.

'Hello,' Sarah found her voice, 'I'm awfully sorry to disturb you, Mr Singh. This is Sarah Mackay. I wonder if I could speak to Rabindrah? If he's there?'

'My nephew is still in bed, Miss Mackay. It is only six o'clock in the morning and everybody is asleep.'

'I know. I'm dreadfully sorry. But I do need to speak to him. Urgently . . .'

Her face was scarlet. Why had she done this? In the background she could hear Kuldip, incredulous that she had telephoned at such an hour. There was a muffled conversation between Indar and his wife, and Sarah's discomfort grew. But it was too late now. She had made the call, and suddenly she did not care what they thought. She wanted to talk to Rabindrah.

'Please hold the line. I will call him.' Indar's irritation was evident. Then silence.

'Sarah? I've been on a story in Tanzania and I only heard about the fire yesterday. Did Hannah tell you I'd phoned?'

Sarah could hear surprise and concern in his voice, but it was difficult to get any words out in reply. She made a few strangled sounds as she tried to explain what had happened, before the dam of emotion overwhelmed her and took away her capability of speech.

'Stop,' Rabindrah said. 'Take a few deep breaths and tell me the details. About the fire. And the car accident. Was anyone hurt?'

Gradually she managed to describe everything, beginning with the burning of the lodge, and her sense that Piet's memory was being erased from the land. That even the last symbol of his dreams had now been eviscerated. He listened to her account of the visit to Fr Bidoli in Nyeri, and the journey to Mwathe Reserve.

'I'm sure they knew Simon,' she said. 'Even though they denied it. The old man, Karanja – I found him evil. Full of malice, although I can't exactly say why I felt that. But the girl – she really gave them away, because she was too scared to pretend. And I kept thinking, afterwards, that I could be right about Simon. What if they were hiding him there? What if he was watching us all that time? It was horrible. And then on the way back there was the accident. At that moment I thought Lars had been injured and that we might all die and it would be my fault, for making him come with me. But the worst thing was Hannah. How angry she was. I've made such a mess of it all. Not being honest with her.'

Her sentences were fractured, disconnected, and she kept apologising because she could hardly make sense of the broken narrative herself, let alone explain it to anyone else.

'Sarah, you're suffering from an accumulation of shock, after everything that has happened in the last twenty-four hours. Nobody could cope with all that and remain clear and calm. Where are you, exactly?'

'In Nanyuki. I ran away. This morning. I couldn't stay there any longer.'

She could feel herself starting to hiccup, and a new wave of humiliation rolled in across her misery. He would think she had been drinking. Again. 'I'm sorry. I shouldn't have disturbed you.' She tried to swallow the next hiccup, but it emerged like a squeak. 'Your uncle and aunt must be horrified.'

'Really? Why is that?' She could hear that he was smiling.

'Ringing you at the crack of dawn. Hysterical. Waking up the household. I know they weren't pleased.' She hiccupped again, and began searching for a handkerchief, but her hands were still greasy from the ointment she had put on that morning, to make driving possible. The phone slid from her grasp and fell on to the floor. 'Oh shit!'

'Sarah?' Rabindrah's disembodied voice was coming up at her from the tiles. 'Are you all right? Sarah?'

She sat down on the ground and lifted the receiver carefully to her ear. He would hear her sniffling now, and she thanked God he couldn't actually see her, dishevelled and red-eyed. The porter was watching her curiously from the reception area, but she was past caring.

'Sorry. I dropped the phone. Look, I don't want to run up a big bill and—'

'Give me the number there. I'll phone you back and then you can talk as long as you like.'

She was not sure how long the call lasted. At least a half an hour, she thought. He allowed the conversation to wander from topic to topic, and they discussed the publisher in London, the elephants, their book and her family, until her voice had stopped shaking and the hiccups had subsided.

'I feel better now,' she said. 'Thanks for calming me down. For listening.'

'Eat some breakfast before you start up that bumpy road,' he said. 'It's a long journey, especially when you're tired. By the way, I'm planning to come up soon, to discuss a few details in the text. And I may have another assignment in the area. Sarah?'

'Yes?'

'Don't forget how frightened Hannah must have been. She's living under siege, and people often say things they regret in those circumstances. Don't read too much into words that were spoken in panic.'

Sarah went into the dining room, hiding red-rimmed eyes behind the dark glasses Rabindrah had lent her on the day she had broken down in Nairobi. She had tried to return them to him, but he had insisted they would be useful in the glare of the semi-desert lands in which she worked. She put away a large cooked breakfast, and drank several cups of strong coffee. The sun was blazing in a bronzed sky by the time she left Nanyuki. She considered ringing Langani, to talk to Hannah, but she did not think she could face another emotional conversation. The note of apology and explanation would have to do. More than three hours of dusty, rutted road stretched out before her, and for the first time she found herself dreading the solitary journey. She gripped the steering wheel hard, and then winced with pain. It was going to be a long ride.

'She's gone, Lars.' Hannah's face was desolate as she held out the letter Sarah had left for her. 'I've driven her away.' She watched as Lars read the note. 'I should have stayed with her for longer last night. Explained better.'

'The circumstances weren't right last night,' he said. 'But you should write to her. That would be the best way to mend things. She needs some time and space to come around herself. But now we need to talk.'

'Yes. I'll take care of my chores, and see that Esther has everything right for Suniva, and I have a couple of things—'

'No, Hannah. We are going to talk now. And not only about what happened yesterday. We are going to talk about every other day too.'

Lars led the way into the sitting room and closed the door. He felt a rush of sympathy when he saw her dread. She sat on the sofa beside him with her hands clasped tightly in her lap, and he was tempted to take her into his arms and stroke her hair and kiss her sad, anxious face. But it was time for plain speaking.

'Since the workshop was destroyed, Han, you have become more and more angry,' he said. 'I know it's because you are frightened. But if this is how you are going to be, then we will have to leave Langani. For all our sakes. Because you are becoming more impossible with each day.'

'I don't know how to manage.' Hannah's shoulders drooped with defeat. 'Every time we deal with a crisis and start again, something else is destroyed. I've thought of giving up, but when it comes down to it, this farm is my home. Our home. It's my heritage, and it's all I have left. Everything good that I love and remember about my family and my childhood is here. We were married here. Suniva was born here, like Piet and me. And Pa. It's our home, Lars.'

'What heritage will we have if something happens to one of us, or to Suniva? You know we would never forgive ourselves.' He stared out of the window, choosing his next words carefully. 'Your fear and hatred are spreading like a poison on our farm. You can't go on like this, seeing everyone around you as a potential enemy. Even Sarah. Is that the kind of heritage you want?'

'I've lost my way.' Her words were pitiful. 'But I'm not ready to give up my home. And if Jeremy arrests this man you saw yesterday, then perhaps it will all be over and we will feel safe again.'

'Will that really finish it, Hannah?' He looked at her sadly. 'I'm not sure. And it could take a long time to prove that Karanja Mungai has any connection with what has happened at Langani. Maybe there will never be evidence that is strong enough to stand up in court. And we still do not know why Piet died. By the time we have laid all this to rest it could be too late for us. There might be nothing left of the Hannah I knew.'

'We can hold out a little longer. I love you, Lars. I couldn't live without you. That's what sent me out of my mind last night. And I'm so sorry.' She looked at him, imploring. 'I'm going to do better from now on. I really am.'

'If you want us to have a life together, Hannah, then you will have to accept that it might not be here,' Lars said. 'We may have to begin again, somewhere else. It won't be the same, I know. But we will have each other and that must be more important than anything else.'

'But not yet.' Her eyes were pleading. 'We must give Jeremy one last chance. We must discover whether Karanja Mungai is the key to what has happened here.' Her fingers ground into his arm as she tried to quell her anxiety. 'And from today I'll try harder for you and Suniva. If you'll help me.'

She was looking away towards the blackened ridge, beyond Piet's cairn to the burnt-out ruins of his dream. Lars reached out to touch her cheek and she turned to him, her face solemn and trusting and sweet. Breaking his heart.

'Come, Han,' he said. 'We'll finish the accounts for the week. And then we'll give ourselves a little holiday and take Suniva to the river for a swim. It's a beautiful day out there.'

It was early evening when Jeremy Hardy arrived. Hannah's look of enquiry made him shake his head.

'It's too soon for results,' he said. 'But I have a good undercover man in Mwathe. He went in late last night. An experienced fellow who was born there and goes back regularly. No one will be suspicious if he comes home for a while.'

'What about this old man that Lars met yesterday?' Hannah said.

'Karanja Mungai has no official criminal record. We've tried in the past to get him for a string of robberies and stock thefts, and for selling stolen goods. But he's crafty, and he uses several younger men in his clan to do his dirty work.'

'So he's known to the police?' She was frowning.

'That's right,' Jeremy said. 'He might have organised the first raid at Langani, you know, and the slaughter of your cattle. But it's difficult to see why he would choose to attack a farm so far from his reserve. In the past he has always operated in the Nyeri area. The link with Githiri can't be a coincidence, though, and we have to follow him up.' He turned to Lars. 'In my opinion your excursion yesterday was unwise. Taking a white memsahib into the reserve, and asking questions. And now this man, Karanja, is alerted to the fact that we know of his connection with Githiri, so we have lost the element of surprise if we want to question him ourselves. These things are best left to the police, Lars. When it comes to teamwork, I think we should stick to our tennis partnership.'

'If you had followed up on the priest at the start of this investigation, you might have caught this Karanja long ago.' Hannah turned on the policeman, in defence of her husband. Out of the corner of her eye she saw Lars's warning look, and ignored it. 'And then we might never have lost the workshop, or Piet's lodge which we will never be able to rebuild, because we cannot afford it. I think Lars and the Indian journalist have done a better job of investigation than you, Jeremy.'

The policeman took time to light his pipe, and chose not to answer her accusation directly. The poor girl was at the end of her tether, he thought, and there was no point in discussing what might have been. Since the previous night he had been cursing himself for not noticing that the priest had never been questioned. He wondered how and where Rabindrah Singh had been granted access to the police report. Hannah rose and pressed the bell for Mwangi. When she had ordered drinks she sat down again, making an effort to remain composed as Lars went over everything he had seen and heard in Mwathe.

'I think we should try and talk to the girl with the baby,' Hannah said when he had finished. 'Sarah had a strong feeling about her. Do you think your undercover man could arrange for her to meet us outside the reserve?'

'That's a possibility,' Hardy said. 'I told him to look for her, but he hasn't seen her at all since he went in there last night. Where is Sarah, by the way? I'd like to have a word with her.'

'She had to go back to work,' Hannah said. 'But you can get her on the radio.'

'Good. Well, I'll push off now.' Jeremy stood up to leave. 'We will nail that old bastard. And maybe that will finally give us an inkling as to why Piet was killed.'

'I'm scared, Lars,' Hannah said, when they were alone. 'If this man attacked us before, then he might try again. Especially now that his connection with Simon has been discovered. What if he comes back and tries to attack us and harm the baby?' She bit her lip, chewing at the inside of her mouth until she could taste blood. 'Am I asking too much, risking too much by playing for a little more time? Should we leave now, Lars? Tell me. Tell me what to do.'

Lars pounded on the table as he searched for an answer to this impossible question.

'There is no land worth the risk to either you or Suniva,' he said. 'I know you've been determined to stay on because of your family history. And for Piet. But he would not want to see any of us harmed in any way.' He saw her shudder. 'I love this farm but I am not willing to die for it, or to let you die for it. And that's how it is.'

'So. We must make a decision.' Hannah's voice was bleak. 'I say that we should give Jeremy a couple of weeks. After yesterday the old man may be frightened and the violence might stop. Or Jeremy will find a reason to arrest him. And I will try to be calmer. And kinder. Would you consider that?'

'Yes, Han,' he said. 'I would consider that.'

Three days went by, and they heard nothing. Hannah wrote to Sarah, begging for forgiveness, but she knew it would be some time before any answer came from Buffalo Springs. If there was one at all. Lars, too, seemed to have burrowed into himself and closed off any channel to his thoughts. Then Hardy telephoned with a progress report. During the Emergency years Karanja Mungai had been detained as a known Mau Mau sympathiser. But the police had never been able to prove his involvement in oath taking or specific killings.

'His *shamba* was on the edge of the forest,' Jeremy told Lars on the telephone. 'We were pretty sure he was supplying food and stolen ammunition to the gangs up there. And he was in a good position to pass on information about police and army patrols, and to hide wanted men.'

'He was never charged?' Lars asked.

'Insufficient evidence,' Hardy said. 'I understand he rules that compound and the younger people are frightened of him. He has three wives, but the young woman with the baby is not one of them. She is married to one of his clan. The husband works in Nairobi somewhere. The usual situation – he's gone off and left the *bibi* to till the soil and take care of the child. He'll come back on leave when he's ready, and make more children. How is Hannah?'

'Doing her best,' Lars said heavily. 'But I don't know how much more she can take.'

'She's a courageous girl,' Jeremy said. 'She's seen far too much tragedy for someone of her age. She and Sarah Mackay both. By the way, I'll be in Nanyuki all day tomorrow, so I'll drop in on you during the afternoon, if that's all right. *Salaams* to you both, and take heart. We will get this man, believe me.'

'It's news, but it's not progress,' Hannah said. 'Still, we must be patient for a little while longer.'

On the following morning Lars was working in the office, sorting the post and paying bills, when he saw David standing in the doorway, his face grave.

'Yes, David? Is there a problem?'

'It is the *bibi* from Mwathe, bwana. The young one with the child. She is outside and she wishes to speak with Memsahib Sarah.'

Lars got up quickly. 'Where is she? Does she have the child with her?'

'Yes. And she is very afraid.' David was afraid too.

'Has anyone else seen her?' Lars was relieved when the young man shook his head. 'Good. Bring her in here straight away.'

He looked out of the window, but he could not see anyone in the heavy shade of the flame tree. He hoped that their visitor had not attracted any attention. David disappeared into the dark foliage that had hidden her well and she emerged with reluctance, holding the child against her breast, wrapped tightly in the folds of her *kanga*. Her expression was a mixture of fear and defiance. Lars felt a deep compassion for her when he saw how thin and poorly she looked. Glancing down, he noticed that her feet were cracked and bleeding, and she was walking with difficulty. He asked her in Kikuyu what her name was, and she looked at him in silence, her eyes wide with fright.

'I think it would be better if she spoke with you,' he said to David. 'She'll be less nervous. Get her name first.'

'Wanjiru,' the girl replied.

'Tell her she is safe here. That no one will harm her. But it would be best to come into the office where it is more private.'

Wanjiru looked around, afraid to enter the building but even more fearful of remaining outside. Lars smiled reassurance as she sidled through the door and positioned herself against the wall, her eyes downcast. He stood for a moment, in a quandary as to what he should do about her. Then he made up his mind.

'Ask her to sit down. Then find Memsahib Hannah, and tell her there is something urgent I need to discuss with her.'

David looked at him in trepidation. What would Memsahib Hannah do about this *bibi*?

'Go.' Lars gave him a small push. '*Haraka!* Oh, and David . . .'

'Yes, bwana?'

'Bring a basin of water and the medicine box with some *dawa* for her feet. She has walked a long way.'

Wanjiru stared around her, watching the door with apprehension. When it opened, and she saw Hannah standing there with David, the young woman looked as if she might make a run for it. She burst into an urgent flurry of questions and it took some time before he could persuade her to sit down.

'She wants to know where the other memsahib is, the one who came to the reserve,' he said. 'She says that the memsahib told her she would help the child. This is why she has come.'

'Tell her she will receive help for the baby, as it was promised,' Lars said. 'But first, she needs some help herself.'

Hannah took the basin and put it down in front of the girl, encouraging her to lift each foot into the warm water and wash off the grime and blood. Wanjiru flinched, but made no sound, as Hannah took out the thorns and small pebbles that were lodged in her cracked soles, and then applied disinfectant. Wanjiru clutched the sleeping child tight against her.

'How long has she been walking?' Hannah asked, and listened as Wanjiru responded in a low voice.

'She has been on the journey for three days,' David replied. 'Since the time we went to the reserve, she was waiting for a chance to escape. It was very hard. Each time she asked the way she was frightened of being caught and brought back to Karanja. So she kept off the main roads most of the time and hid in the *bundu* at night.'

'She must be hungry,' Hannah said. 'Three days is a long time to walk through the bush, carrying a child. Could you find some food for her, please, and bring it here? Lars, maybe you should ring Jeremy – see how quickly he can get here from Nanyuki. But tell him not to come in uniform. If she sees that he is a policeman she may not tell us anything. She might even try to run away. David, explain to her that we need to ask some questions, and we have another friend who will also want to talk to her. But we will help her with the baby, and she need not be afraid.'

Lars lifted the telephone in an attempt to track down Jeremy Hardy. Wanjiru was plainly agitated that another *wazungu* was coming, but gradually she accepted that the memsahib could be trusted, and she was heartened at the prospect of a meal. She sat meekly, waiting for the food to come. Hannah rubbed antiseptic ointment into her feet, and put a clean towel under them. Then she touched the baby, talking in the calm, soft tone that she used with a frightened horse.

'David will bring your food, and when you have eaten, we will talk about what we can do to help your son.'

'I have a couple of urgent things to see to with Juma,' Lars said. 'I'll leave you with the girl until Jeremy arrives. He should be here in about half an hour.'

Hannah sat patiently with the young woman, talking to her in a mixture of Swahili and Kikuyu, as Sarah had done, to make her meaning clear. After a few minutes, Wanjiru loosened her *kanga* and let Hannah examine the child's foot. It was turned in at a bad angle, and would certainly make walking very difficult in the future. The child was young, however, around fifteen months at the most. Hannah had seen this condition before, and she knew that surgery followed by physiotherapy was generally successful in dealing with a club foot.

There was a knock on the office door and Mwangi peered into the room, his rheumy old eyes coming to rest with curiosity on the young woman.

'Bwana Hardy is here,' he said. 'He is in the sitting room and I have given him a Tusker. Bwana Lars asks if he should bring him now?'

'Yes, Mwangi,' Hannah said. 'Tell them they can come right away.'

She held the baby's spindly little leg in her hand, and tried to demonstrate how a doctor could straighten the ankle, and put it in a cast for a while. Wanjiru would have to go to Nairobi, she explained, and stay with her baby at the hospital for the operation. But afterwards he would be able to walk like other children.

The girl burst into a tumble of words, most of which Hannah could not follow. She wished David would come back, to translate accurately. But she could make out that Wanjiru had no money and nowhere to live. She was afraid she would be found by her husband's clan, and taken back to the reserve. They would kill her, she said. That part Hannah understood perfectly. It would be simple enough to get Dr Markham to refer the child to a specialist in Nairobi. But finding a safe place for the young woman to live for the duration of the baby's recovery was another matter. If Karanja Mungai discovered that she had come to Langani, her life could be in danger. All their lives might be in danger. But perhaps Wanjiru's husband could be contacted, and she could stay with him while the child was being treated.

'Wanjiru, where is your husband?' Hannah's tone was gentle. 'I am sure he will be glad to know that someone is going to help his son. Is he working in Nairobi? Could you stay with him while the baby is in the hospital?'

The girl stared at her in misery, shaking her head over and over again. And as Hannah tried to follow what she was saying, the realisation dawned. She felt a tide of nausea and revulsion rising in her, sweeping her away, so that she found it hard to think or even to breathe.

'Wanjiru,' she said at last, unable to keep her voice steady, steeling herself for the answer. 'Was Simon Githiri your husband? Is that why you are alone with your child?'

The young woman began to wail. In a state of panic she launched into a tangle of sobs and explanations. Hannah barely heard the broken sentences as she stared, dumbstruck with horror, at the girl and then the infant. Simon Githiri's baby. She was helping the son of Piet's murderer. Bile rose in her throat as the first beads of sweat broke out on her forehead. She swallowed hard and sat back in her chair, unable to utter a word. Oh God! This was too cruel, too much for any human being to accept. The child was innocent of any crime. But his mother? How much had she known about her husband's actions? Wanjiru's pleas died away and she placed her arms around her son and began to rock him. Her agitation had disturbed the child, and he was squirming and fretful. She sat down on the floor, drew his mouth to her breast and began to feed him.

Hannah stood up on shaking legs and went to stare out of the window. She thought of Sarah who had promised the young woman treatment for her child if she came to Langani for help. What would she do, faced with this awful truth? If Piet had lived, they would have been married now, maybe with a child of their own. But Simon Githiri had taken his life away, and there would never be a son for Piet and Sarah to love and care for.

An eye for an eye, a tooth for a tooth. That was what the Old Testament said. Simon's son would not die as Piet had died, pegged out like a sacrificial animal on a mountainside. But he would be maimed. A cripple in a society that saw physical deformity as the judgement of the great god Kirinyaga on his clan. He would be an object of scorn, his days difficult and barren, punished for the sins of his father. Let the police take the girl away – question her and hold her in custody until she provided evidence that would incriminate Karanja. Then she would be sent back to Mwathe where the clan could deal with mother and son in whatever way they saw fit. There was no reason to offer healing and security to this infant, who might grow up to be a murderous savage like his father.

300

Hannah leaned her head against the cool glass of the window pane, and looked out into the harmony of Lottie's garden. Then she turned back to watch the sucking child, his fingers opening and closing on his mother's ebony skin as he fed. His eyes were closed, his world was bounded by Wanjiru's protection and bounty, her scent in his nostrils, her nipple between his lips. These were his securities. Hannah was moved by his dependency, by that same trust that she saw in Suniva when she lay on her lap. And she could not ignore the desperate appeal in the mother's eyes.

'There has to be an end to it,' she said aloud. 'An end to the hatred, and the killing and the pain. It should finish now. And I can make it stop, if I have the courage and the strength to do it. For myself and Lars and Suniva. And for Sarah.'

Wanjiru was staring at her, uncomprehending and frightened. Hannah squatted down and placed a hand on the girl's shoulder.

'Don't be afraid,' she said. 'I will take you and the baby to a good doctor, and he will help you. You have my solemn word.'

When Lars arrived with Jeremy, the girl jumped to her feet, and Hannah put a restraining hand on her arm.

'Wanjiru, you need to tell this bwana about your husband and Karanja. Because they have done something very bad. You know that, don't you? And here is David with some food for you to eat. Take it, and then Bwana Hardy will ask you some questions. Do you understand?'

Wanjiru ducked her head several times. She took the bowl of *posho* and stew and ate very fast, glancing around occasionally, her eyes darting between the three white people who were standing over her, preventing escape. Hannah moved close to Lars and placed her hand in his, making a silent prayer for strength to see the nightmare through. He saw that she was overwrought and wondered what had transpired since he had left the room.

'I have something very difficult to tell you,' she said at last. 'This is Simon Githiri's child.'

She saw the shock in Lars's eyes and on the policeman's face. David let out a hiss of breath from between his teeth. She tore on, not wanting to lose her resolve. 'I'm convinced Wanjiru knows what happened, and how Karanja fits into the story. But she's petrified with fear. If we want to learn anything from her, we will have to go carefully. And she will need a safe place to stay, while the child gets the treatment we promised.'

'Hannah.' Lars put his arms around her, and he could feel her quivering. 'This is too much for you. It is too hard. Why don't we let Jeremy take her away now, and question her. And later we can think about the child's foot and what can be done.'

'I've considered that.' Hannah shook her head and forced out the words, hearing them as if from a long way off. 'It was the first thing I thought of doing. But I doubt that a girl this young and simple would have had anything to do with Simon's actions. She certainly wouldn't have had any influence over him, in any case. Look at her. She's little more than a child herself. You know how it is – she was probably given to him. There wouldn't have been a choice. In the end, she's just a mother with a disabled child, and she is already suffering because of that.' She put her arms around Lars and held him very tight as she made her decision. 'There has been enough suffering.'

And so the questions began. David squatted down beside Wanjiru and asked the questions. Jeremy sat at the desk, taking notes. After a few words of encouragement and reassurance, Hannah and Lars moved away and stood by the window, listening with horrified absorption as the story unfolded into the stunned silence of the room.

Simon had come to Mwathe Reserve about two years ago, as the nephew of Karanja Mungai. The girls of the compound had thought him a fine-looking young man, smartly dressed, well educated and directly related to the most powerful member of the clan. He had excited a great deal of attention. Wanjiru had looked at him with interest and he had noticed her too, smiling at her fleetingly when she was allowed to carry the beer to the men's hut and serve him. That was during the lengthy meetings that had taken place during his first visit. The women did not know what these meetings were about, but Karanja's senior wife revealed that Simon was the old man's nephew. Wanjiru asked why he was only coming to the family homestead now, and why they had never heard of him before. But the woman frowned and cuffed her on the head, warning her not to ask so many questions.

Initially, Simon had seemed happy to be reunited with his family. But soon he became troubled and distant, and after a few days he left. After his departure no one mentioned him and Wanjiru's life continued as before. Her people were of Karanja's clan but they were poor and had no land of their own, so she had been sent to help his third wife during her pregnancy. The woman was capricious and hard to please, and when Wanjiru did not carry out her wishes adequately she was beaten. Most of all, she tried to keep out of Karanja's way. He had a reputation for cruelty, and when he looked at her he made her feel afraid.

A month passed before Simon reappeared. This time he stayed longer, but his mood was dark and he often argued with his uncle. One day, when Wanjiru had gone into the forest to collect wood for the fire, she saw the young man on the path ahead of her. He was muttering to himself and she was curious, so she put down her kindling and crept after him, careful to keep out of sight. When he reached a small clearing some yards off the track he stopped suddenly, cried out, and then fell to the ground, weeping and beating his head with his hands. She was worried that he might be having a fit, and she had no idea what she should do. If she revealed her presence he might be angry. If he told Karanja she had followed him, she would be beaten. But she felt a great pity for him, alone and in such distress. Eventually, she went to his side and touched his shoulder tentatively. He whirled around and grabbed her by the throat, shouting, and she was sure he was going to throttle her. But after a few seconds he seemed to come to himself. He let go of her and sat with his hand over his eyes, explaining that he had some bad memories, that he thought he was somewhere else. At last she found the courage to ask what was troubling him, but he would not say.

He begged her not to disclose what she had seen, and she understood immediately that he did not want his uncle to know about his weakness. She promised to keep his secret, and she left him there alone and went to retrieve her bundle of sticks. It was unwise to be away from the compound for too long. An unexplained absence would incur the wrath of Karanja's wives and perhaps result in another punishment. In the days that followed she often saw Simon and was brave enough to smile at him, but they did not speak. He spent many hours sitting in Karanja's hut, and then he disappeared again. Wanjiru tried to find out where he had gone, but she could not ask direct questions. It was not her place.

Some time later she was on her way back to the compound with a load of kindling strapped to her back, when she saw Karanja emerging from a narrow track which she had not noticed before. She stood silently under her heavy load, eyes downcast, hoping he would ignore her and pass her by. But he stopped and asked her what she was doing in that place. His tone was belligerent, and she knew he had been taking bhang. It always made him aggressive. She answered in a respectful tone, keeping her gaze on the stony path but, suddenly, he knocked the firewood off her head and struck her across the face. She looked up, her eyes watering, her cheek stinging from the force of the blow, and he threw her to the ground, shouting that she was a spy, and he would teach her what happened to a woman who went about spying. He knelt over her, hitting her repeatedly and ripping the *kanga* cloth from her body. She began to cry and to plead with him, assuring him she had only been collecting wood, that she had seen nothing and heard nothing. But he continued to beat her until she knew she was going to die. He would have his pleasure with her, and then he would kill her. She was too terrified to struggle.

Then she heard Simon's voice. He was remonstrating with his uncle, and after some minutes, the old man stood up. Wanjiru gathered her torn clothing around her and struggled to her feet. Karanja looked at her with disgust. His nephew wanted her for a wife, he said. She was worthless, but he would give her to Simon. She fled back to her hut, fearful that the evil old man would change his mind. For the rest of the day she worked in the compound, in spite of her cuts and bruises.

On the same evening one of Karanja's sons appeared and told her to follow him. She obeyed with dread, sure that she was going to be tortured and punished, perhaps killed. They turned down the track from which she had seen Karanja emerge earlier, and went deeper into the forest. In a dank clearing far up the mountain she found Simon waiting for her, with Karanja and some of the elders of the clan. A goat was tethered by a fire in the centre of the glade, and she was stripped naked and made to kneel down beside it. Karanja took a panga and slit the animal's throat. As it bled into a gourd, he turned to her and made a slice across her back with the blade. Now she was convinced that her life was at an end. She kept her head down and her eyes closed, waiting for the final stroke. Then Karanja spoke. Her blood would mingle with the goat's blood in the gourd, and she must now take an oath of silence and walk around the sacrificial animal seven times. If she broke her promise she would die, as this goat was going to die. She swore the oath as the goat was dismembered, still living, and its testicles burnt on the fire. A brand from the flames was laid across the wound on her back, and she screamed as her flesh sizzled.

Afterwards Simon came forward and lifted her up. She belonged to him now, he said. He was dressed in traditional Kikuyu warrior's garb, naked except for his feathered headdress, a leather loin-cloth, a cloak made from colobus monkey skin and beaded armlets. His eyes were bright from bhang, his body was oiled, and his breath smelt of raw alcohol. He took her into a cave at the edge of the clearing and pushed her down on to a bed of wattle. There he took possession of her, as she lay beneath him in a fog of pain and fear. That was her marriage night. There was no courting, no tenderness, no gifts or days of celebration with the members of the tribe as other young women might have enjoyed. For two nights she lay in a fever from the agonising wound on her back. Close by she could hear the men, chanting as her new husband went through some kind of ritual. He brought her a piece of the roasted goat which he made her eat, although she gagged on it. Then he forced her to swallow a bitter herbal drink that gave her terrifying hallucinations, and finally she lost consciousness.

She did not know how long she lay there, but when she awoke daylight was filtering into the cave. Simon came in and squatted beside her, looking at her sternly, but the rest of the men were gone. She must get up, he said, and tend to her domestic duties. The cave would be their dwelling place and she could not go back to the village. If she heard anyone coming she must hide until they were gone. She must not speak to anyone. He would bring food for her to prepare, and she could gather kindling for the fire from around the edge of the clearing. He had saved her from the wrath of Karanja and made her his wife, and she had taken an oath. She knew what would happen to her if she tried to run away.

Stiff and sore and numb with despair, Wanjiru rose to make a fire and to cook her first meal for her husband. Simon ate in silence, and when he had finished she took a portion of the food for herself. She was too frightened to ask any questions. During daylight hours she collected wood, tended the fire, cleaned the pots with water from a nearby stream, and wondered what would become of her and how long she would be imprisoned in the forest. The wound on her back healed eventually, but left a jagged scar. She had no clean clothing, so she washed her one *kanga* in the icy river and rewrapped it around herself, still wet. There was no pride or pleasure in displaying her young, firm body to her man. Simon barely noticed her, except when he wanted sex. Then she was just a vessel for his seed, and when he was finished he always turned away from her with a grunt and slept with his back to her. Later he would rise and go to sit alone at the entrance to the cave. He drank a great deal of alcohol and his expression was dark and brooding, but he was not violent with her. She knew that she was better off with him than if she had been left to the mercy of Karanja.

Her life in the forest was a time of unrelenting hardship. She suffered from the cold of the high altitude, from the mists and the rain, and the isolation. But she made what she could of her circumstances, and over the months, a relationship began to develop between herself and her husband. He was gone for many hours during the day, and she could not ask what he was doing. Men came to the clearing to take him away, and when they approached she hid in the cave until they left. Karanja came from time to time but there was no communication between them, and she was grateful for that. She felt both dread and resentment at the way he had treated her, and she believed it was because of him that her husband was so changed from the young man who had first come to the reserve. Whenever Simon had been away with Karanja he returned surly and drunk, and often high on drugs. At night he would toss in his sleep and cry out, but she did not dare to waken him from his troubled dreams because he might react as he had that first time in the forest. She still remembered his hands squeezing her neck, and the madness in his eyes. She did not want to give him any excuse to hurt her again.

Early one evening he came back carrying a package and when she walked out to greet him, he handed it to her. Inside were three *kangas*, and a small necklet of beads. Her eyes filled with tears as she held up the first gifts she had ever received. She looked at him tentatively, unsure if these riches could be for her. He nodded, and for the first time since the travesty of their wedding, he smiled at her. Emboldened by his reaction, she shed her tattered cloth and stood before him in the soft light of the forest so that he might look at her. He took one of the *kangas* and wrapped it around her, touching her breasts and her flanks with appreciation as he did so. Then he led her in to the cave, caressed her, and made love to her as though he was seeing her for the first time. They lay entwined afterwards, and as he slept she began to hope. Her husband was not a bad man. She had won his approval. In time, perhaps, he would bring her out of this dark, gloomy place, and they would go far away from Mwathe and build a life together.

But the weeks wore on, and she remained a captive. They spoke more often now, shared their meals together, and when he lay with her at night he held her in his arms. But he slept badly, waking in a lather of sweat with his eyes bulging in his head, and then she would stroke his head and cradle him against her breast to quiet him. Finally, after a particularly bad night, she begged him to tell her what it was that made him suffer from these terrible dreams. Timidly, she pointed out that she had taken an oath of silence, so whatever he said to her could do him no harm. And at last he told her what had brought him to Karanja, and to the reserve.

During the Mau Mau uprising, he said, his father had joined the oath takers in the forest. He had been part of a group that carried out raids on white farms and African villages. Simon was about five, the only son of his father's favourite wife, and he and his mother had been brought up into the forest to hide in a Mau Mau enclave. His father's older brother, Karanja, was the man who organised supplies to the camp, and passed on information about the movements of the police and the army. The arrangement worked successfully and they avoided capture for some time, until one of the special patrols discovered their camp. The Mau Mau had been on a raid, and had brought back a bullock from the farm they had attacked. Elated by their success, and close to starving, they built a fire in the clearing and roasted the animal on a spit. It had been a long time since they had tasted meat and they became careless. Soon the sentries were drunk and the tell-tale smoke rose above the trees. The police set up an ambush, waiting in the dark for the fugitives to finish eating and go to sleep. Then they descended on the encampment. A vicious confrontation took place and many of the gang were killed.

Simon's mother hid with him in the dense undergrowth until the fighting was over. She watched as his father and others were captured, and then she decided to escape into the forest. But her movements were noticed by one of the *askaris,* who raised the alarm. She pushed the child into thick cover and ran down the track, intending to draw the police away from her son's hiding place. Shots rang out, and the child saw her fall to the ground, then rise and try to crawl away. A white man who was with the patrol raised his rifle and shot her again. After that, she did not move any more. The child sat in the thicket, too frightened to stir, watching everything that was happening in the clearing. The police began to interrogate their captives. He saw his father brought before two white men. When they questioned him he spat at them, and shouted that all the *wazungu* would be driven from the land, and their womenfolk killed as they had killed his woman. He refused to give them any information. They beat him, and his companions too, but they all refused to talk. One of the white men issued an order, and the *askaris* laughed and dragged his father over to the fire. They tied him to the spit where the bullock had been roasted, and one of them taunted him, asking if he would be so full of fire when he felt it under him. Then they brought brushwood and stoked up the flames. The two white men looked on in silence as the *askaris* continued their questioning. A third white man, the one who had shot Simon's mother, appeared from the forest and ordered them to stop. But the others taunted him, saying he was only a farmer, not a real soldier, and after some argument he shrugged and walked away. Simon saw him sitting on the edge of the clearing, looking into the forest as his father began to scream.

It was a long time before the screaming stopped, but he never told them anything. Others of the group, when they were dragged before the police, began to weep and to say whatever they knew. They did not want to be tortured like Simon's father. Eventually, the white man who had shot his mother ordered the *askaris* to take his father down off the spit. But it was too late. When they lifted him to the ground, his skin was burned to charcoal, and he died on the floor of the forest. One of the Kikuyu policemen asked what they should do with the bodies of the Mau Mau, and a white man told him to leave them there, as a warning to other terrorists. Then the police set fire to the remains of the camp and left with their prisoners. Simon remained hidden in the bushes, frozen with fear and shivering, for a long time. When he was sure that the police had all gone, he crept down to sit whimpering beside his mother. He was afraid to go near the other charred, smoking thing beside the fire. He did not remember how long he sat there, or who found him and brought him to Karanja. There were questions about what had happened, but the little boy was unable to form any answer. He could not speak at all. They kept him at the reserve for some weeks, and then someone said that he was useless so they took him away and left him at Kagumo Mission.

The Fathers were kind to him. He himself knew that something very bad had happened to him. But when they asked him what it was, a cloud came into his mind and he could not remember anything, not even his name. They called him Simon Githiri. It took him a long time to learn how to speak again. He could not recall any of his early childhood until Karanja came to take him back to Mwathe. At first he was glad to find that he had a family. For many years, he had wondered who he was and where he had come from, and why no one ever came to visit him. But the events of the past had been buried deep in his mind and he only began to fear the truth when Karanja took him to the place where his father had died. He had gone back to Kagumo after that, but had told no one about the terrible incident. It must be a lie. Or they had mistaken him for someone else. He had heard all about the Emergency from the priests, and from Kikuyu teachers who had been loyal to the British. He did not want his father to be one of the evil terrorists. The priests of the mission had given him a home and an education. They might throw him out if they thought his father had been in the Mau Mau. He would lose the little he had.

Plagued by doubt, and no longer able to find satisfaction in his work at Kagumo, he decided to go and look for work outside the mission. The Fathers gave him a little money, and a good reference. He left, intending to go to Nairobi. But on the bus he had felt an ungovernable urge to return to Mwathe. To find out for himself, once and for all, if what Karanja had said was true. The day that Wanjiru had found him in the clearing was the day that he finally knew. He had gone for a walk and something about the place had triggered his memory. Suddenly he was sitting once again by the body of his mother, remembering the stench of his father's blackened corpse lying by the fire. It was all as Karanja had said. Now he would have to do as his uncle had told him.

Horrified by his story, Wanjiru tried to find out what Karanja wanted his nephew to do, but Simon would not say. He had spent the whole of that day with her, worn out by the retelling of his childhood tragedy. She did not question him any further. He was already nervous, afraid that he had said too much. For the next week, he spoke little. When he wanted to have sex she gave him her body willingly and generously, and at night when the nightmares came, she comforted him as she would a child. He did not leave the clearing. Some time later, Karanja appeared. There was a heated discussion. Wanjiru, sitting in the cave, could not make out what was said. Soon afterwards, Simon left with him, and this time he was gone for many days. Wanjiru was alone in the forest.

The food ran out, and she tried to subsist on berries and anything else she could find. She began to wonder what she would do if he did not return. No one would know, or care, if she died here of starvation. And she was sick. She had begun to suspect that she might be pregnant, and the prospect filled her in equal measure with fear and elation. If she bore her husband a healthy baby, he might take her away from this place. It was no home in which to bring up their child. He would see that. A child of his own, a son – she hoped it would be a son – might lead him away from the awful memory of his past. He would not want the boy to spend any part of his childhood hiding in the forest, as he himself had done. Three more days went by, and the last scraps of *posho* were gone. Wanjiru knew that if she did not act soon she would be too weak to save either herself or her baby. In the end, she resolved to walk back to the reserve. Simon would not have left her alone to die. Something bad must have happened to him.

Terrified of the consequences, now that she was breaking her oath, she started down the track. But in a short time she realised that she was lost. There were trails in all directions, made by elephants and buffalo, and she had only come up the path once, at dusk and led by Karanja's son. She had been too fearful then to pay proper attention to the route. As night fell, she found herself in dense forest. All familiar landmarks had disappeared and she could hear the rustle of feeding elephants and the snort of a buffalo close by. There was no water. Her stomach was empty. She had vomited up the last meagre meal she had eaten, and she was overcome by exhaustion. In despair, she lay down and tried to cover herself with leaves, convinced that the curse of the oath was now being visited on her.

It was Karanja who found her, and his rage was so terrible that she wished she had died in the cave, or been torn apart by some wild beast during her wanderings. She awoke, dazed, to find him standing over her, his eyes glittering with fury. She did not dwell on the beating he gave her. It was impossible to say how she had survived the journey back to the cave where Simon was waiting for her. He gave her no consolation or support when she staggered into the clearing and when she looked into his eyes there was only emptiness there.

Karanja told her that she must pay the price now for her disobedience. He had a panga in his hand. In a last desperate attempt to save herself and the child in her belly, she threw herself at her husband's feet and begged him for mercy. She had not been trying to escape, she lied. She was hungry. She had wandered beyond the boundary of the clearing searching for food, and then she had got lost. It was because of her pregnancy that she was confused. She was sick. She had only tried to sustain herself for the sake of their child. If he killed her now, the baby would die as well. He would be killing his own son. Karanja was grinding his teeth, warning his nephew that the woman was worthless, and not to be trusted. But her words struck home with Simon. He stared at her with a new intensity and then told his uncle that he would allow her to live, until he was sure she was carrying a child. If she was lying, then he would kill her himself.

When Karanja left, muttering angrily, Simon went to the stream, filled a gourd with water and brought it back to her, telling her to drink and clean herself, and then to go into the cave. She lay down in the half darkness, her face swollen, her eyes almost closed from the force of Karanja's blows. Her limbs were bruised and bleeding and she wept with pain and desolation. Her husband, this man whom she had served and cared for, had offered no explanation of where he had been, or why he had been away so long. He was her husband and he should have provided for her. Instead, he had left her alone and without food, and when he came back he had allowed his uncle to beat her. The only reason she was alive was the prospect that she was going to bear him a son. Whatever bond had grown out of their time together, it was gone for ever. The child was her only hope. She put her hands on her belly, and curled into sleep.

As the months passed and the baby grew inside her she spent most of her hours alone, talking to the child and singing to it. As far as she could be, she was happy. Simon left her to herself, but he made sure that there was always food at the cave. She thought that he kept Karanja away, because the old man did not come up to the clearing any more. Then one evening, Simon walked into the cave, smartly dressed in a clean shirt and trousers, and told her she was going back to Mwathe. He had found work, he said, and he would be away for a long time. She could not stay up here any more. She begged him to take her with him, but he was adamant in his refusal. In spite of all her tears and pleading he insisted that she return to Karanja's household, and give birth to her baby there. He led her down the mountain and left her alone at the edge of the forest.

The last part of her journey was the hardest. She was filled with the terror of what would happen to her when she reached the compound. It was Karanja's senior wife who took her in. The old woman was a formidable matriarch but she was not unkind, and Wanjiru was surprised to find that she had gained a powerful ally who offered her protection. There was no sign of Simon, and no one mentioned him. She was told that as long as she worked hard and kept quiet, no harm would come to her.

The last months of her pregnancy were almost joyful, as she waited in eager anticipation for the arrival of her son. Somehow, she thought, when Simon returned and saw his child, he would become the man he had once been, and things would be resolved.

Her labour was long and painful. The midwife who had come to assist made increasingly anxious incantations as the hours passed. And then it was over. She heard her child give his first cry, and a great flood of happiness poured through her weary body. All pain and effort were forgotten. She sat forward to see her baby, but as he was lifted up to cut the cord the midwife gave a cry of alarm and looked around at the rest of the womenfolk. It was then that Wanjiru saw the child's deformity, his right foot turned in on itself at an unnatural angle. The women were muttering among themselves, about a sign, a bad omen. The child should be taken away. It would bring ill fortune on the clan, on the tribe. Wanjiru was trouble, and her child was trouble. They should both be driven out of the reserve. She snatched the baby from the arms of the midwife, and severed the cord herself. Then she clutched the wailing infant to her breast, defying them to take it away.

In the tense moments that followed, Karanja's senior wife was the only one who spoke up for her. And it was she who had saved the baby and the mother as well. No one should take any action now, she said. There would be a meeting of the elders, and a decision would be made. Until then, the mother and child would remain with her, and be cared for like any others. She had pushed all the women from the hut and squatted down beside Wanjiru, telling her she must nurse her baby and trust that all would turn out well. It was important to keep the child covered. He looked quite healthy if people did not see his foot. Then she too left the hut, and Wanjiru was alone with her son. He seemed to look at her with all the knowledge of his turbulent beginnings, and she vowed to protect him with her life. But as she lay back, exhausted, the tears flowed down her cheeks and on to his tiny head. She knew the hardships he would face if he was allowed to stay on the reserve. And the worst of these would be at the hands of Karanja.

She did not know what was said at the meeting of the elders, but Karanja's wife must have put up a powerful defence on her behalf because she was allowed to stay, and to keep her child. Perhaps the old man thought that she would not give up her baby without a fight, and he did not want to draw attention to her or her missing husband. Whatever his reasons, he put out the word that the baby was illegitimate, and it was only through his benefaction that Wanjiru was allowed to remain in his compound. But whenever he saw her his gaze was malevolent, and she felt that when Simon returned she would somehow have to persuade him to find another place to live, although she had no idea where they could go. Her greatest fear was that her husband might disown the child, if he ever did come back. Then she would have to find someplace to bring him up alone. But, for the time being, she remained with Karanja's senior wife, and was grateful for her protection.

It was about six months later that Simon had returned. He came late at night, his body streaked with sweat and grime, and his eyes full of the madness she had seen the day he had attacked her in the forest. Karanja's smile was malicious when she brought the baby for her husband's inspection. But Simon barely looked at the child. He seemed to be in the grip of a fever, and his breathing was fast and laboured. His hands kept clenching and unclenching, and there was dried blood on them and spattered all over his body. He said he was going into the forest, and would remain there for some time. In another month or two he would return to see his son, and in the meantime she must remember her oath. If she said anything about seeing him, he would have her and the baby killed.

Wanjiru dropped her gaze, and murmured that she understood what he was saying, that she would keep her silence. All the pity she had felt for him shrivelled inside her and she went back to her quarters, resolved that as soon as the opportunity arose she would try to escape. She was no longer safe with her husband. But she knew in her heart that she was trapped. With a crippled child, she would be recognised wherever she tried to hide, and no one would give her shelter because they would say that she was cursed. And in the end, she had come to believe that maybe she was. Until Sarah and Lars had appeared at Mwathe with David, and she realised that these *wazungu* could be her last and only chance. So she had left the reserve in the darkest hours of the night when everyone was asleep, and walked through the bush to Langani.

When she had finished speaking, Jeremy's expression was grim. If the girl was telling the truth, and there seemed no reason for her to have made up the story, they could bring in Karanja for questioning. But they would have to move fast.

Hannah stood like a statue at the door. She was staring into a void, the way she had stared on the night of Piet's death. Looking at her, Lars wondered for a moment if this would break her, destroy her increasingly tenuous hold on reality. The silence crawled about the room as they waited for her to speak, or to give some indication that she had taken in Wanjiru's story. Lars put his arms around her and she stood stiffly against him, her face was ashen, her stillness unnerving. When she spoke at last, her voice was low and hoarse.

'Janni,' she said.

'What is it, Han?' Lars stroked her hair, not understanding. 'What about Janni?'

'It was Pa,' she said. 'It was my father, up there in the forest on that day. Piet was killed because of what the farmer did. Because of Pa.'

Then she stirred, and looked at her husband.

'I have to speak to Sarah,' she said, her words barely above a whisper. 'I have to tell her myself. And say that I am sorry. That I will do anything to make things right between us. But Lars, oh God, Lars. If Wanjiru's story is true and Simon went back to Mwathe after he killed Piet . . . Do you understand what that means, Lars? It means that Simon Githiri is alive.'

Chapter 13

Kenya, May 1967

The radio call, punctuated by static and sudden breaks in the conversation, made it more difficult to tell Sarah what had happened. And the effort had swallowed up the last vestiges of Hannah's resilience and courage.

'Simon is alive.' Sarah's flat repetition of the words did not express horror or even surprise. 'It's what I believed, but I couldn't say it. It would have been too hard to explain how I felt, and you would have scoffed at me.'

'You shouldn't have kept it to yourself.' Hannah was ashamed.

'I told Rabindrah,' Sarah said. 'But then I buried the idea, because it was just a feeling and there was no point in brooding over it. Have you spoken to Jan or Lottie?'

'I can't do that yet. I can't.'

'What will happen to Wanjiru now?' Sarah thought of the girl and the deformed child that was Simon's baby, and she felt ill.

'Dr Markham will arrange for the child to see a specialist. But we cannot keep Wanjiru at the farm,' Hannah said. 'Karanja might come looking for her. She is a terrible risk for all of us here. Jeremy is trying to organise a safe place, without putting her into the jail. He can't afford for anything to happen to her, or for her to run away. Otherwise he will lose a star witness.'

'She could go to the mission. To Kagumo,' Sarah said. 'I'm sure they would be willing to keep her there, safe and out of sight. I'll contact Fr Bidoli. I have to drive into Isiolo tomorrow, and I'll phone him from there.'

'Sarah? I'm so sorry. I miss you.'

'It's all right, Han. Over and out.'

'She has not forgiven me,' Hannah said. 'Wherever I turn it is as if I had

315

committed some heinous crime myself, and I am paying for it over and over again, in everything I do. And the worst is still to come.'

'No, Han. We have seen the worst. Today is the beginning of—'

'Can't you see the court in Nyeri?' she said, leaning over Lars in his chair. 'Can't you hear Simon's evidence? And the girl, too. Jan van der Beer shot a defenceless woman dead. And then he took her man and trussed him up and roasted him over the flames and listened to him screaming and screaming, and—'

Her own voice had risen to the brink of hysteria and Lars took her wrists and shook her.

'Stop, Hannah. Stop right now. Simon may still be hiding in the forests, but he could also be dead. We don't know. And if he is alive, Karanja may find him first and kill him, to prevent himself from being implicated. But whatever happens, we must stay strong. You cannot give up now. We will get through this together, because we have each other and Suniva. So do not lose heart now, or Simon will have destroyed us all. I will go and take care of Wanjiru, and then I will come to bed.'

Lars organised a mattress and blankets in the storeroom where the girl spent the night. But he was troubled by her presence. He had explained to Mwangi and Kamau what she was doing there, and had seen them shake their heads, frightened that she and the crippled child would bring some new misfortune to the farm. The son of Simon Githiri should not be given a place to stay at Langani. He carried a sign. They refused to go near the storeroom. When Wanjiru and the child were settled for the night, Lars locked the door from the outside and put David on guard, afraid that they might have disappeared by the time he returned in the morning.

It was almost noon when Fr Bidoli telephoned to say that the young woman and her baby could be brought to Kagumo. The nuns would keep them safe.

'Will you come to Nyeri with me, Han? I'm going to drive them down there myself, just to be sure.' Lars thought that the priest might be of some comfort to her. 'You might like to meet Fr Bidoli. Sarah says he is very kind.'

'The child of a murderer,' Hannah said in a hard voice. She had not risen at her usual time to go to the dairy, nor had she come to breakfast, and Lars had found her still lying in bed. 'He is the child of a murderer. Like me.'

'Don't say that, or think it.' Lars tried to draw her close but she pushed him away, blinded by the awful realisation.

'My father was a murderer,' she repeated. 'A man who tortured and killed other human beings. And we are paying for it. First Piet, with his life. And now you and me and Suniva.'

'In times of war many men become crazy for a while,' Lars said soothingly. 'You and I, we have known only peace during our lives. We cannot understand how a war affects those who are trapped in the heart of it.'

'I am trapped in the aftermath,' she said. 'I have not hurt or killed anyone, but I cannot escape my father's war.'

'Han, it's no use driving yourself mad over what has already passed. We have seen too much violence and sadness here, and we can never forget it. But we must find a way to rise above it.'

'I've tried to think of it like that. Tried to imagine how Piet would have acted, if he had known. But I can't reach the place where you want me to go. And everywhere I turn he is there.'

'Piet will always be with us, Hannah. His memory will—'

'I'm not talking about Piet,' she said harshly. 'It is Pa that I see. He is there at his desk, or standing out in the wheat, or waiting by the fire in the evening. Pa, who destroyed what his parents and grandparents built here, who took away his children's future. I see him everywhere I look, and I cannot forgive him. Because he is to blame for all this. For the fact that Piet is gone.' She spoke the words as though she had been endlessly repeating them to herself, drumming them into her heart.

'But we did not die with Piet,' Lars said quietly. 'You've tried to continue what he planned to do, and I have supported you in that. And now we will find a way to make our own lives bearable.'

'Don't lecture me,' she said. 'I cannot listen to you if you talk to me as though one of my cows was sick. I am lying in the bed that was once my parents' bed and is now ours. The place where they must have talked about what he did. About how he roasted a man alive. Like the Nazi criminals you read about in books. And she must have lain here and comforted him. So do not talk to me like a child that has fallen and scraped her knee.'

'Will you come with me to Nyeri?' Lars tried again.

'No. You take them. We've kept Sarah's promise, and we should get rid

317

of the girl and that child as quickly as possible. After today I don't want to ever see them or hear about them again.'

She had turned her back on him then, and for three days she shut herself away in the bedroom, lying with her eyes wide open, stirring only to feed her daughter and hand her over to Lars or Esther. Trays of food prepared by Kamau were left untouched, and she refused to see Dr Markham. Lars thought it unwise to raise the question of contacting Jan and Lottie. But he knew that sooner or later they would have to be told the dreadful truth about Simon, and it weighed heavily on his conscience day and night.

'Hannah, I need you,' Lars said. He was determined to bring her back, to rouse her from her misery. 'I cannot work the farm alone. You have to start your life again, and there will be good things in it. I want you to get dressed now, and come to breakfast. I will tell Mwangi and Kamau that you will be there.'

'Leave me alone, please.' She hid her face in the pillows.

Lars stood up. 'You will get dressed now, Han,' he said firmly. 'And we will start the day together.'

In the dining room Mwangi appeared, downcast and solemn.

'Memsahib Hannah will be here for breakfast,' Lars said.

He had no idea whether she would come, and if she did not he would look like a fool. But the change in Mwangi was instantaneous and carried its own particular reward. When Hannah appeared and took her place at the table he fussed over her like an old nurse, bringing fresh coffee and extra helpings of bacon, hovering at her elbow so that finally she turned and pressed his hand. They ate in silence, but for Lars it was enough that she was there. She was fighting back at last.

'Will you come to the dairy with me?' he asked her. 'There is a new calf that you have not seen yet. He's doing well, and you must find a name for him.'

She shook her head. 'No.'

But he saw the flash of interest in her eyes and he pushed his advantage further.

'I know you want to see that calf,' he said. 'He's your favourite colour, and already as stubborn as you are and full of character.'

She looked down, her fingers pulling at the tablecloth. When she answered him he could barely hear her.

'There's something I want you to do for me first,' she said. 'And then I will come out on the farm. I want you to do it this morning. Because I cannot.'

'I'll do anything for you.'

'I want you to telephone Pa.'

'I don't think I'm the one to—'

'You will phone and tell them what has happened, and why. But I will not speak to him. For now, it is not possible, Lars. Maybe it will never be possible again.'

His heart plummeted. The dining room was flooded with sunlight, but he felt cold. She had not mentioned Jan or Lottie since the afternoon when Wanjiru had told her story. And he himself had chosen to ignore the problem of informing them, because of the pain it would inflict. Now he felt a constriction in his chest as he imagined Lottie's reaction.

'Maybe we should wait until Simon is caught,' he said, clutching at a possible reason for delay. 'Until we are sure that the girl was telling the truth.'

'You know it's the truth,' she said. 'You know that is what happened. That's why Piet is dead, and why we may all be dead soon. You're still Pa's manager and his son-in-law, and you must tell him the truth.'

'I don't think that is the right way to do it,' he said. 'I cannot phone the man, out of the blue, and tell him that his actions have been responsible for the murder of his own son. Not in a telephone call. And the effect on Lottie would be unimaginable.'

'I cannot do it,' Hannah repeated. 'You will have to be the one.'

'Then I must go there,' Lars said. 'Tell them in person. Offer them some comfort by being there with them. I will try to find someone to look after the farm for a few days. And we will go to Rhodesia.'

'You do what you want,' Hannah said. 'I will not go there to see him.'

'Your mother will need you,' Lars said.

'She was not here when I needed her. She chose to be with Pa. Just as I choose to remain at Langani, even though he has caused our land to be soaked in blood. I will go to the office now, and do the letters and accounts. And later, when you have talked to them, I will come with you to the dairy. That is all I can manage.'

He went out on to the farm, making his usual rounds and stopping to talk to the herdsman and the *watu* whom he met in the fields. But his spirits were low and he wondered how they would all react when they discovered the reason behind Piet's murder, and realised that Simon was still alive. He thought of Jan and Lottie and was even more convinced that they should not hear the grim story on the telephone. It was clear that he would have to leave soon. News travelled regularly between the expatriates in Kenya and their beleaguered counterparts in Rhodesia. He knew that Lottie kept in touch with old friends, and he had no idea how long the true reason for Piet's death could remain a secret. When he returned to the office later in the day it was to find Hannah at her desk, typing with furious concentration. Suniva lay in her crib, sleeping peacefully, an innocent in the war of attrition that tore at her mother's soul. Lars's blood ran cold. There was no knowing if or when there might be another attack on the farm, on his wife and child. Clearly Simon was determined to wipe out everything the van der Beers had created, in his thirst for revenge. If only Hannah would come with him to Rhodesia.

'Did you hear anything more from Sarah?' he asked.

'Nothing,' Hannah said, without looking up. 'But I spoke to Anthony. He doesn't have any more safaris until June. He was planning to drive up and talk to us about the fire, so I asked him if he would come now. Stay with me for a few days. So that you can go south.'

'Hannah—'

'You can leave as soon as you like,' she said in a flat, matter-of-fact tone. 'Anthony can stay with me for a week. Maybe a little longer. He will drive up tomorrow. Now I will come and see the calf.'

It was after dark when the sweep and flicker of headlights beamed around the sitting-room walls and woke Hannah. She froze, all her fear and torment rising to the surface as the dogs raced outside, barking hysterically. Lars placed a reassuring hand on her arm.

'It's bound to be Anthony. I'll go out and see.'

The two men returned together, and Hannah made an effort to be cheerful as she greeted their friend. But her face was strained as Lars filled in the details of the fire and results of the visit to Mwathe.

'I'm sorry to hear all this,' Anthony said. 'But it looks as though justice will finally be done for Piet's murder. I only hope they have the girl somewhere secure in that mission.'

'Jeremy had reservations about that,' Hannah said. 'He opposed the idea of taking Wanjiru to Nyeri, and so did I. But we couldn't keep her here, and he couldn't think of a better alternative.'

'I'm confident that they understand the position at Kagumo,' Lars said. 'I drove her down there myself, and I spoke to the old priest and to the nuns who will be looking after the girl. There isn't anywhere she can go, with no money and a child to take care of. And she's terrified that someone from Mwathe will find her and bring her back to Karanja. I think she is relieved to be somewhere safe where no one wants to ask her any more questions.'

Wanjiru had become increasingly withdrawn as Jeremy Hardy pressed her for information, making her repeat her story several times. Finally, after a renewed promise of a safe haven and treatment for her son, the girl gave him a detailed description of the path to the clearing, and to the cave where she had lived for so long. *Askaris* were sent out but when they found the place it was deserted, although there was evidence that someone had been there recently. Trackers agreed that the fugitive had gone further up into the forest, and then doubled back on one of the many buffalo trails that criss-crossed its dense growth. Despite an exhaustive search, they found no trace of their quarry.

On the same afternoon two police officers went directly to Karanja's compound at Mwathe, but no member of the Mungai clan admitted to having known or seen Simon. And Karanja himself had disappeared, slipping out under cover of darkness, in spite of the surveillance that Jeremy had organised. When he came to break the news, Hannah reacted with cold resignation.

'I knew it would be like this,' she said. 'He and Simon can stay up in the forests or on the slopes of the mountain for the rest of their lives, and we may never find them. Until they choose to attack us again.'

'My dear, I don't think either of them will come back,' Jeremy said. 'You have *askaris* here round the clock, and there are more of them combing the area. This is a full-blown man hunt, with every available officer engaged in it. We will catch them.' But the words sounded hollow, even in his own ears, and inwardly he was cursing the inept surveillance of his juniors.

Hannah had turned on her heel without a word, leaving the policeman with his hand held out in a gesture of farewell never acknowledged. And another day had now passed with no news.

'I have no faith in the police,' she said to Anthony. 'I don't know whether they are simply inefficient, or whether this is a case where a white farm is under attack and they don't care.'

'That's a little unfair on Jeremy,' Lars said. 'I think he is doing his best, but his back-up isn't up to much these days.'

'I've had enough of this subject,' Hannah said. 'I'm going to put the baby to bed while you have a drink. And then we'll have dinner.'

'She looks stretched to the limit,' Anthony said as Lars handed him a whisky. 'I could hear that she was in bad shape when we spoke on the phone yesterday.'

'We're under siege here,' Lars said. 'And I'm not at all happy about going down south. It's going to take me another day to organise everything, and to go over a few odds and ends with Bill Murray in case there are any problems while I'm away. But I am convinced that I must tell Jan and Lottie this news face to face. It's very good of you, to hold the fort in these circumstances.'

'We'll be fine,' Anthony said. 'The place is bristling with policemen, as well as your own watchman and the game rangers. And I'm a pretty good shot. So go and do your duty, and don't worry.'

During dinner there was no mention of Wanjiru and her child, or Lars's departure for Rhodesia. The evening was punctuated by tense silences, followed by a barrage of conversation. Anthony brought the only bright news. After several days of haggling with the insurance company in Nairobi, he had forced them to agree that they would pay the cost of reconstructing the lodge.

'At first they offered a pitiful sum,' he said. 'We argued for a while, until I mentioned that I would be happy to take all my safari and vehicle insurance elsewhere. Then we got down to some serious talking. So they have agreed to pay up, and we can start again. When and if you're willing to do it.'

'We haven't discussed the lodge,' Lars said. 'But I think it's too soon to—'

'No. It's not too soon at all.' Hannah addressed her remark to Anthony. 'We know the whole story now, the truth about Pa and Simon, and the risk of trying to start something new on the farm.'

'It will be hard to make decisions,' Anthony said. 'But don't judge your father too harshly, Hannah, because—'

'Because good old Jan van der Beer was only protecting his family and his farm, and men do crazy things during wartime.' Hannah could no longer contain herself. 'Isn't that what you were going to tell me? What everyone wants to tell me? Well, I'll save you the trouble. Instead, I want you to consider that as a result of Pa's little brush with madness, Piet is dead and our home is under threat day and night from this murderer who is out to destroy everything that was ever built here. And where is Pa now? Is he here to protect us from the wages of his sins? Oh, no. Not at all. He ran away before Independence, knowing that Langani might be taken from us because of his past. And he even forgot to mention that the farm was nearly bankrupt. It was Lars who saved us from going under.'

'I'm not defending Jan, but he must have thought his leaving would give you a clear—'

'Unfortunately he omitted to tell us his little secret, to warn us or prepare us in any way.' Hannah did not give him a chance to finish his sentence. 'He just walked out and left Piet and Lars and me to live with the consequences of what he did. It seems strange to me that you can't grasp that.'

'What he did was terrible beyond belief,' Anthony said. 'If it's true. But you have to remember that the Mau Mau raids and oaths and killings were utterly barbaric, too.'

'So it was all right for us to sink to the same depths?' Hannah's fury made her thump the table.

'No, of course it wasn't,' Anthony said. 'But you must take into account that Jan found his own brother up in those forests, hacked to pieces and—'

'And left to die, like his son died later,' Hannah said. 'So that makes it excusable.'

'It's a reason, not an excuse,' Anthony said. 'The British Government and the army and the police were all committed to putting down the Mau Mau movement, whatever it took. Fighting those savages saved the lives of far more Kikuyu than white farmers. But now I think we have come to a point where forgiveness is the only way forward. Otherwise this will go on for another generation, and then another, and everyone involved will die from the bitterness and the hatred and the repercussions.'

'I can't listen to another sermon,' Hannah said, throwing down her napkin. 'We have to promise each other that we will not talk about this while Lars is away, Anthony. Otherwise we will not remain friends. I'm grateful that you're staying here. But I can't look at any of this from where you're standing, and you can't feel the rage and the shame and the grief in my head. So let's agree not to talk about it again. Not for a very long time. Maybe never.'

'You're right,' Anthony said. 'I cannot imagine what you feel like at all. We'll talk about other things from now on.'

Hannah rose to her feet. 'I'm dead tired,' she said. 'And I don't sleep well any more. What with Suniva still waking up to be fed, and everything else that comes to haunt me in the dark, I need to get an hour or so when I can. I'll see you all in the morning.'

'At least she is up and talking again,' Lars said, as Hannah's footsteps died away. 'Although she's frightened and still angry. I think this may be the beginning of acceptance. A turning point. And right now, that is the best I can hope for.'

When Sarah had returned to Buffalo Springs, Dan was sitting on a canvas chair in the main building, editing his daily observation report. He was bending forward over the typewritten pages with intense concentration, muttering to himself. His bush jacket was frayed and peppered with occasional burrs, and his glasses were sliding down his nose, crooked and taped together on the bridge with a piece of Elastoplast. Sarah's heart contracted at the sight of him. How fortunate she had been to meet these people, to work alongside them and count them among her closest friends. He looked up as she came into the *boma*, her face lit with the delight of being home. She would have time to sort her thoughts, to find harmony and order again, to rid herself of the heartache that was always with her at Langani. And now rejection and a renewed fear. These would all retreat as she resumed the work that she loved.

'I hope you like Irish whiskey, as well as your usual mash,' she said as she went to embrace him.

'Good that you're back, kid,' he said with affection. 'How was the wedding? How are they coping at Langani?'

'The wedding was cancelled,' she said, and was forced to smile at his astonishment. 'And the fire at the lodge has been a terrible blow. But I'll save the details until Allie is here. Then you won't have to listen to the whole story twice.'

She spent an hour helping him to update his charts, moving the coloured pins as he squinted at his notes recording routes taken by the elephants in recent days. In her own hut she put away her luggage, sat down at the rough table that passed for a desk, and began to sort through a sheaf of memos and letters. After a time she felt calm, surrounded by the whirr of crickets in the still afternoon, and the chatter of hyrax as they watched her from their vantage point on a small outcrop of rocks outside the fence. The heat was intense and she felt as though all the trappings of the world outside were melting away, leaving her with an inner softness, a sense of being cleansed and new. When her papers were in order and she had checked her cameras, she called for water in the shower tent.

Sarah was towelling her hair dry when Allie appeared, standing just outside the door in the shade of the thatch. The sun was sliding down behind the tracery of thorn trees and the first sounds of evening drifted in through the opening, along with a hint of cool, silky air.

'You've cleared most of the desk already?' Allie was smiling. 'That's impressive.'

'I certainly needed a shower this evening,' Sarah said. 'Standing under that bucket of streaming cold water was heaven.' She crossed the room to hug Allie and held out a package. 'It's Irish linen,' she said. 'Trousers and a shirt. They always feel comfortable, no matter what the temperature. And I brought some odds and ends, like marmalade my mother made, and . . . well, I'm really sorry I was away for a couple of extra days. I know it must have been difficult to follow up on everything with one person short. I'm sorry, Allie.'

'Don't be. Things have been less than idyllic here, by the way. There was a Shifta raid a couple of days ago. They brought down four elephants, and as usual no one has been able to say how they came in unnoticed, with a huge, noisy lorry and a barrage of guns. Right through an area that is supposed to be patrolled every day. Someone was paid off and turned a blind eye. Dan is so mad he can't trust himself to talk about it.' Allie sat down on the edge of the bed. 'But I hear you've had troubles of your own. I came to say that he is opening your bottle of Irish whiskey, and he wants to know if you'd like to share it.'

'I can't drink that stuff,' Sarah said. 'But I can definitely be lured by a cold Tusker. I'll be there in five minutes.'

The lamps hissed, geckos scuttled in the thatch, and outside in the

African night she could see the glimmer of stars in the night's black bowl, and hear the sounds of nightjars and frogs and hyrax. Nursing her glass of beer she described her days in London, the disaster of Tim's wedding and the fire at Langani. When she talked about the disturbing visit to Mwathe Reserve, Allie could not disguise her alarm.

'I hope there's some extra security in place on that farm,' she said. 'It's not safe for Hannah. In her shoes, I think I would leave before some other terrible thing destroys all she has left.'

'I think she is close to that point,' Sarah said.

She was relieved to have talked about her brother and the problems at Langani. But she could not bring herself to include Hannah's tirade of the previous evening, or the garbled call she had made to Rabindrah. They were painful and embarrassing moments, and she wanted to bury them, to escape the sting of their memory.

In the morning she left the camp as dawn spread ribs of scarlet cloud across the wide sky and birds called out their songs. The Land Rover slid along the sandy tracks, new tyres crackling over fallen sticks, the air fresh and laced with the scent of wild flowers. Erope sat beside her, grinning when she asked him about the postcard she had sent from London. He had taken it to his *manyatta*, he said, and shown it to the elders as an example of the madness of the *wazungu* in their own land. But all in all, he felt that the white men and women in the picture, with their bright clothes and beads and feathers, were more akin to his own people than the stiff British officials he had come across in Kenya, with their starched shirts and trousers, and shoes that had to be polished three times a day because of the dust.

It did not take long to find her group of elephants. They were standing beside a baobab tree, its huge trunk and delicate fingers pointing towards the blinding disc of the sun. There was no hint of rain, and the threat of drought could not be ignored.

'There is not much for the cattle and the goats to eat now,' Erope said. 'Everything is drying up quickly. We are already forced to go very far for water, and the Shifta and the government are chasing us. One or the other, they are always here, in our land, stopping us from living the way we have always lived in the history of the world.'

'What do the elders feel about having less children and fewer cattle?' Sarah saw his eyes widen. 'I mean, the government thinks that the women and children would be healthier, and it would be easier to find enough food for everyone.'

'The government sees that if we had less people, they could take away our land more easily,' Erope said. 'We have only our children and our animals. These are our lives and our riches, and we cannot lose them. I know you are surprised, Sarah, when I say this. But we have nothing else and we ask for nothing else, and no one has a right to take these things from us. Not the British, nor the neighbouring tribes like the Rendille or the Boran who steal our cattle and our water. And not the Somalis who have nowhere of their own, now that some official bwana in a faraway land has drawn a line through their country and ours, without thinking about who lives on either side. This war between the Somalis and Kenya has been caused by someone who has probably never been here, has never met a Somali or a Boran or a Rendille in his life.' He glanced at her. 'Is that the truth, do you think? You are my friend, Sarah, and we can talk about these things.'

'It's certainly true that the people in the far north wanted to be part of Somalia,' she said. 'And they are different in the way they look and in their beliefs. But at least the government is trying to find a solution now. There are talks going on to stop this war.'

'It will never be over,' Erope said. 'It is like your land.'

She stared at him in surprise. 'My land?'

'One of the teachers told me that. When I was at school. He came from Ireland like you, and he said they had drawn the wrong line across your land. That is why you understand this country so well. Because your people are suffering too. Fighting over where the line was drawn.'

'You're right,' she said. 'I hadn't thought of it in that way, but it's true. Like most other things you point out to me. I wish we could just stop fighting and figure out a way to share what we have. But when I say that everyone laughs at me and tells me how foolish I am.'

'In this you are foolish, yes,' Erope said, with quiet amusement. 'Because you have forgotten that every creature is born to fight over their territory. Look now, at this herd of buffalo coming down to the river. There are plenty of places for them to drink, and still they will try to take the same spot that the elephants have chosen. And they are also pushing away the zebras, but they will not win because the *ndovus* are stronger. And that is what happens to us all.'

When she had been back in camp for a few days Sarah wrote to her parents. But she could not bring herself to send anything beyond a stiff thank-you note to Camilla, and she did not write to Tim at all. She was sealing the envelope for Raphael and Betty when the radio call came through. As she strained to hear Hannah above the static and the full significance of the news struck her, she sat down in a canvas chair, grasping the receiver in hands that were shaking. It seemed as though the world was careering away from her, shattering the veneer of calm she had so recently and gratefully put in place. When the invasive buzz and crackle of conversation was over, Allie led her away from the radio.

'What . . . ?' Dan's question was silenced by the look in Allie's eyes.

'He is alive,' Sarah said after a few minutes. 'Simon Githiri is alive. I always felt that I would have known the moment when he died, although it seemed irrational. Fey, Camilla always says, when I have those feelings. But I was right.'

She was filled with foreboding and she sat in her camp chair as though paralysed, until Allie reached out and patted her briskly on the arm.

'Tell us,' she said. 'It will help.'

'An act of revenge.' Sarah's explanation came out bald and hard. 'Janni was part of a patrol that killed Simon's mother. During the Emergency. She was shot, running away from a Mau Mau camp. The father was killed too, although Jan could have given an order to prevent it. So Simon killed Janni's son. Killed my Piet. It was an act of revenge, and God only knows where it will all end.'

She could not bring herself to admit, even to her friends, the exact circumstances of that day in the forest that had changed all their lives, setting in motion a cycle that might never be complete until Langani had returned to the wilderness from which it had been created. And she was unable to deny the revulsion that had already begun to eat into the loving memories of Jan van der Beer that she had carried with her since childhood.

'At least Hardy is a family friend,' Dan said. 'And now that he has a lead, he will surely find these two men. But I'm glad Hannah is trying to help the girl and her child, too. That's the kind of thinking that shows balance and compassion. It's what we need in these difficult years of transition.'

'Yes,' Sarah said in the loud silence that followed his pronouncement. But in her heart she saw that his words were those of an academic, a gentle, privileged man whose personal life had never been touched by murder and revenge. 'I don't think I can talk about it any more. Not tonight, at any rate.'

'Let's fill you in on some of Dan's new ideas on four-legged creatures,' Allie said, seeking to bring Sarah back to the one part of her life that could still give her a solid base. 'And we can mull over the things they teach us that we have long forgotten.'

Sarah spent the next week following the herd, photographing and making notes. She and Erope drove and walked in the dry, hot wind that scuffed up dust devils and turned the land into a hovering, shifting mirage that swirled away into a formless distance. Only the tracks along the river offered any relief from the searing heat, and on a breathless, bleached-out afternoon she was tempted to walk down the bank and splash the brown water over her face and arms. But Erope shook his head when she suggested it, pointing to what appeared to be a log embedded on the opposite bank. On closer inspection the two small eyes of the crocodile could be seen above the waterline. Within an hour a herd of zebra came down to drink, and the long, scaly predator vanished without a ripple, only to erupt with terrifying speed in their midst, thrashing wildly as the zebra scattered and the muddy water turned red with the blood of an unwary victim. The bush rang with the high-pitched barking of the survivors and alarm calls spread through the canopy of trees, carried by monkeys and birds.

She was shocked to see how thin and lethargic the animals had become, in their relentless hunt for food and water. The carcasses of those that could not withstand the harsh conditions littered the trails. Elephants dug their pits deeper and deeper around the dried-up watercourses, but without much success. The dust rose in fiery circles and the grass crackled dry underfoot, until it was like walking on spears. There was a terrible frustration in watching the hopeless foraging of dying animals, their bones showing through their skin long before they sank down for the last time on the unforgiving ground. Only the carrion eaters flourished. Hyenas and jackals, foxes, vultures and huge crocodiles lurked in the sluggish rivers, waiting for their thirst-driven prey to descend into their gaping jaws.

Erope's clan had a *manyatta* less than an hour from the Briggses' camp, and many of their animals had fallen victim to the drought. For the Samburu, their livestock represented life. The cattle were more than just animals, they represented riches and status in the community, and loss on this scale was catastrophic. Erope owned a small herd himself, and two of his prized cows had already died. Sarah had visited the *manyatta* on several occasions, photographing his family and friends as they went about their daily tasks and later presenting them with framed prints of her pictures. She felt they were some of the best portraits she had ever done. Now she racked her brains to think of some way to help the children whose hungry faces and distended bellies signalled malnutrition. The clan normally lived off their animals, taking the milk from the cows and supplementing their diet with roots and herbs. They only ate their cattle when there was a ceremonial ritual, or when prolonged drought made it necessary to kill in order to survive. The Samburu did not plant crops, looking with disdain on the Kikuyu and other farming tribes. Grain and other dry goods came from a *duka* in the nearest township, and Sarah took Erope into Isiolo to bargain with the Indian shopkeeper for better prices. When she had beaten him down, she drove back to the *manyatta* with a carload of *posho* meal, sugar and salt.

'He is different from those ones, your *mahindi*,' Erope said. 'But I do not know how he treats his servants in Nairobi. These Indians look down on us, and one day they will pay for this.'

It was a conversation Sarah did not want to pursue. She had never seen Rabindrah dealing with African staff, but she had not liked the way that Indar shouted at some of the workers in his garage. On the other hand, he was training three African mechanics whom he treated fairly, and they obviously liked and respected him. It was a difficult subject about which she knew very little, and she did not wish to generalise.

'We are better off discussing elephants and dik dik spoor,' she said to Erope, and he was smiling as he nodded agreement.

The earth was still parched and baking when Rabindrah appeared in a rolling cloud of dust. Sarah left him to stow his bags in the guest quarters and to shower off the thick layer of grime from his journey. When he reappeared she was elated to see that he had brought a copy of the proposed layout from the publisher. After dinner they sat out under the glitter of stars, but even at night the air remained hot and dry.

'Good stuff, you guys,' Dan said. 'When will it be on the shelves?'

'They're hoping to have it out in the spring,' Rabindrah said in the low voice that Sarah had come to like. 'Sooner than expected.'

'I agree with Dan,' Allie said, smiling at Rabindrah. 'You've done a great job between you. And we're grateful for your uncle's generous gifts. I hope he'll come up here and see us, one of these days.'

'He keeps promising,' Rabindrah said. 'But he's very busy. Always building.'

'Building what?' Allie asked.

'Building safari vehicles, temples, shops and houses,' Rabindrah said. 'And fences to sit on.'

'Do I detect a tone of disapproval?' Dan was intrigued.

'You know how we Asians are, these days,' Rabindrah said. 'Always trying to keep a low profile, to gain favour with African politicians, and worm our way into the new system. Avoid any controversial issues. Most of the community doesn't even want to sit on the fence. It's too high up, and they might be noticed with their heads above ground.'

'I know that only a small percentage of the Indian community took out Kenya citizenship, and they must be questioning that decision now,' Allie said. 'But surely those who can't stay on, or don't want to, are entitled to live in England.'

Sarah leaned back in her chair, mentally distancing herself from yet another discussion on the problems of race and background, thinking of Jasmer Singh and his semi-detatched refuge in the grey, uninspiring streets of Southwark.

'I don't want to keep writing about this question,' Rabindrah said to Allie. 'But in England, Enoch Powell has stirred up a fine old kettle of fish. Technically, those of us who decided against Kenya citizenship still have the right to go and live in the UK. Or return to India. But "return to India" is an absurd phrase in this context, because many of us younger Asians were born here and have never set foot in India. We could never build a life in all that chaos and squalor.'

'Surely most of you have British passports?' Dan said.

'We have the passports, yes,' Rabindrah said. 'But there's a difference between those issued in a former colony and the ones issued in the UK. Right now there is real fear in Britain that the country will be swamped by Asians. More than ten thousand have arrived from East Africa over the last two years. And that's a trickle that will only grow into a flood. Soon Africanisation will really take hold. It will turn many of the old *duka wallahs* into penniless refugees, and they will find themselves stateless, too.'

'You chose to come back here, though,' Allie said. 'To become part of a community in danger of being disenfranchised by both Britain and Kenya.'

'Ah yes. And is that not a true folly?' Rabindrah's smile was crooked, his voice conspiratorial. 'But in England I could find no sense of belonging, no loyalties, no vision of myself that I could accept. I sat in my room with its small electric fire and linoleum floor, with the kitchen hidden behind a limp curtain and the streets outside flat and grey. And I wanted to be here. In a place that looks and sounds and smells familiar to me. But I am neither British nor Indian, and I have not yet found out what it is to be Kenyan. Or whether I will be allowed to stay in the country of my birth. It is a tightrope I am walking, and it appeals to me.'

'You have conviction, man,' Dan said. 'And that's all I have, when I think about it. It's enough, though.'

'What's next, now that this book is almost put to bed?' Allie said.

'I'm interested in the talks aimed at ending the war with the Shifta,' Rabindrah said. 'The government sounds far too optimistic on the issue. The people north of here are a different race. In Wajir or Garissa you only have to see their physical features and their way of life, or hear them speak or pray. The flat-roofed buildings and the mosques could be on the Arabian peninsula. There may be a temporary halt to the violence, but these Somali nomads and bandits will not change. They are like medieval warlords and that is how they will stay.'

'That's right,' Dan said. 'Only they no longer rely on swords and camels and poisoned arrows these days, when they go out on cattle raids or poaching expeditions. Now they have guns and trucks with which to defend their way of life.'

'They're afraid that if they give up their arms, the government will take their land and their wells and give them to farmers from the south. Kikuyu mainly, because they have the most influence. If that happens, the northern territories will be fenced in and the nomads will lose their way of life. So I'm going to spend a few days around Wajir, talk to the Somalis and to the Rendille and the Boran up there. Listen to their versions of what's going on.'

'That's pretty wild territory,' Sarah said, a knot of disquiet forming in her mind.

'I'll only be there for a short time,' Rabindrah said. 'And then I have another project in mind that we could all discuss.'

'And that is?' Allie was curious.

'It's an idea I've managed to sell to John Sinclair. I'd like to do a book on the nomadic tribes of northern Kenya. The people who still follow the old way of life, in spite of education and Independence, and all the other changes here. I'd like to live and travel with them for a year, get to understand their customs, their diet, their rituals, sexual and family relationships within the tribal structure. All that sort of thing. They're exotic, handsome, photogenic, and the area they inhabit is magnificent and wild. No one has done anything serious about them yet. There are the odd scientific papers, but no illustrated books that would appeal to a wide readership.'

'Sounds great,' said Dan, raising his glass. 'Here's to it.'

'A year with the nomads.' Allie was thoughtful. 'I'll take your deposit money now, for the use of our shower facilities. And it'll cost you. I can see you staggering in here, reeking of camel hide, covered in those hungry lice and smelling of cow dung. Wait till you've had a week or two on urine and curdled milk – oh my! No knife-edge line down your trousers and starched shirts.' She took his expensive shirtsleeve between her finger and thumb and rubbed, her eyes laughing. 'You'll be Dan's slave when he asks you if you'd like a Scotch or a cold beer. Or even a glass of clean water. This is going to be fun, my boy.'

'The thing is, I need your help,' Rabindrah said. 'I'm not an anthropologist, as you well know. This will be a true portrait of the area, but the text will be written for a popular audience. Like our elephant book. And it can't live without illustrations. Photographs.'

'Ah,' Allie said. 'I see it all now.'

'I'd like Sarah to do the pictures,' Rabindrah said. 'But she'd have to be away from here now and again, for several days at a time. If there was a big celebration like a circumcision or a wedding, for example. I'm not sure whether that could fit in with her commitments here. The same deal would apply, though – some of the sales revenue would be donated to your research fund. Would that be feasible?'

'I think Sarah should tell us whether she wants to take these pictures,'

Allie said. 'If you're going to be here for a year, then it might work.' But she could see from Dan's expression that he was less than certain. She tried to head off an immediate discussion, knowing that the subject needed reflection on all their parts. 'Have you considered that you might not be able to afford her fees? Once this first book is published she might be bombarded with offers. Have your publishers thought of that?'

'They are mad about your pictures.' Rabindrah turned to Sarah. 'You know that. John Sinclair has seen your Dublin portraits and the pictures of Erope's *manyatta*. This is the kind of book that will show both the beauty and the plight of such people. What do you think, Sarah?'

'It's too late in the evening to discuss it, and far too early to make a decision,' she said, rising to her feet. 'Besides which I need to talk about it in detail with Dan and Allie. Are you coming out with Erope and me in the morning?'

'No, I don't think so.' Rabindrah was disappointed at her reaction. 'I'd like to leave these last corrections of text with Dan, for his approval. And while he's looking them over I'll drive up to Wajir tomorrow. I'll leave early. Do some of the journey before the heat turns my brain and the rest of my body into a puddle.'

'Don't you need a permit to go roaming around up there?' Dan asked.

'I've arranged to spend a couple of days in a guest house with government security, whatever that means,' Rabindrah said. 'And I have a guide who comes from the area. Although I suspect I may have to get rid of him if I want to hear any real opinions.'

'Watch your back, is my advice.' Dan shook his head. 'I assume you'll drop in here again on your way back to Nairobi?'

'If that's convenient, yes. It will give you time to note down anything you don't like in the text. And for Sarah to comment on the layout. After this, we won't be able to make changes.' Rabindrah hesitated, a little self-conscious. 'Was there anything that struck you at a first glance, Sarah?'

'We'll leave you to it,' Allie said, rising from her camp chair and beckoning to Dan. 'Be careful, Rabindrah. Writing about the problems of Somali bandits isn't worth your life.'

'I don't want to discuss this new idea,' Sarah said, when they were alone. 'I've been away too much recently, and I need to concentrate on my work. Make up for lost time and be grateful for all the consideration they've shown me over the past eighteen months.'

'I'm sorry I brought it up like that, without thinking about all the implications. But it would be an extraordinary project for us to do together.'

'I am grateful to you, you know,' Sarah said awkwardly. 'You've been awfully kind, and I owe you a lot for listening and—'

'You don't owe me anything,' Rabindrah said. 'But one of the most handsome and colourful tribes is on the doorstep, and I wondered if Erope would make arrangements for me to talk to the Samburu round here. Perhaps we could start – I could start, I mean – by talking to the people in his *manyatta*.'

'I'll ask him in the morning,' Sarah said, glad that she could contribute something. 'If he's happy with the idea, then maybe you could visit his elders and family.'

She did not hear Rabindrah drive away before dawn, but he had left a note of thanks and set out for the north. Erope was waiting for her when she stepped out of her hut, ready for the day's work.

'I thought the *mahindi* would be with us,' he said, looking at her sideways as she started the car. 'I thought he had come to see you and stay for a while.'

'He's gone to Wajir,' she said, a little cross at his suggestive tone. 'To talk to camels instead of elephants.'

'That is a bad plan.' Erope spat into the dust to illustrate his disapproval. 'He must have good luck up there, or he will soon be lying in the desert with all the other skeletons. And there are many.'

Sarah revved the engine to erase the chilling image from her mind. She had been taken unawares by the disappointment she felt at Rabindrah's brief stay.

'He wants to write a book about the tribes in this northern area,' she said. 'Including the Samburu. It could be useful, Erope. It will help people to understand your way of life and to respect it. And he has asked me if I will take pictures for it. I was wondering if you might bring him to meet your family. Your clan.'

'I will ask the elders.' Erope did not sound enthusiastic. 'They will not refuse if you are with him, because they are grateful for the food you brought.'

But three days later there was no sign of Rabindrah. By the end of the week Sarah had become increasingly anxious, and at last she raised her fears with Allie.

'Don't you think we might have heard from him?' she said. 'A radio message or something?'

'No news is good news,' Allie said cheerfully. 'If he was in trouble we would certainly have heard about it. What are you going to do about this new book proposal?'

'I don't know,' Sarah said. 'I'm not ready to think about it.'

'Well, Dan and I have been thinking about it,' Allie said. 'Because you have an outstanding talent with your photography, my girl. And we don't want to hold you back. So if you feel you'd like to move on, do something purely creative, then God bless you, is what we would say.'

'Oh no!' Sarah's stare was filled with dismay. 'No, Allie. I want to go on with the elephant study. Stay here with you and Dan. This is my work and my home, and I can't imagine being anywhere else. If it's possible to spend some time taking pictures for Rabindrah over the next year, then I'd like to do it. But my real life is in our camp.'

'You'd better think about that,' Allie said, poking fun at her. 'Staying on here with two grizzled old scientists, sleeping alone in your rondavel and driving your Land Rover can't hold a candle to sharing a flea-infested shelter and riding a camel with the dashing Rabindrah.' She was laughing out loud as she drove off in search of her elephant group, leaving Sarah no chance to respond.

All through the day temperatures soared, and the only relief came when Sarah took her shower. But it was brief. Dan had begun to ration the water and the sensation of being cool did not last long. Even the night's dark breath felt unrelentingly hot and dry. She was still awake in the small hours, lying naked on her bed, mosquito net and sheet pushed aside as she tried to find a cool place and a hint of fresh air. Outside she could hear a chorus of frogs, and in the distance a lion calling to his mate. The unaccustomed noise on the thatch made her sit up in bed, a prickling sensation on the back of her neck as she tried to analyse the sound and the smell around her. The smell of dust rising, the noise of great fat drops of water hitting the dry soil, smacking the grass roof, running down the tin gutter and splashing into the water drum at the side of her hut. Rain! The rains had come.

Sarah scrambled out of bed and flung open the door. Outside, a cascade of water obscured her view, and after half an hour the first, small puddle had turned into a lake that was edging closer to her threshold. She peered into the driving rain and saw the flicker of a lamp. Dan was shouting, and she pulled on shorts and a shirt, and ran out into the downpour as the first rumble of thunder shook the compound. In the office Allie was already moving boxes and files, pushing the furniture into the middle of the room, lowering canvas blinds and fastening them to the window frames. The camp staff appeared, soaked to the skin and grinning broadly, their dark faces glistening wet in the lamplight. Tarpaulins were found and thrown over the chairs with their already damp cushions, and across the ancient typewriter and the radio telephone and the jumble of papers still remaining on the desk. Finally, when everything seemed to have been covered, they all went to stand in the deluge, holding out their arms and allowing the sweet water to pour into their mouths and eyes and over their hair and their skin, laughing and clapping their hands in celebration, jumping up and down in the puddles like children.

It was Allie who came to her senses first. 'I'm cold,' she said, wrapping her arms around her compact frame. 'This is all very well for *totos* down at the coast, but I'm for a whisky and a dry towel and back to bed.'

They made their way back into the upheaval of the main building and Dan poured measures of whisky into tin cups.

'Here's to the rainy season,' he said 'Let's hope—'

But the rest of his words were obliterated by a sound that started as a low rumble and then turned into a roar as the swollen river burst across its banks, covering the sand flats, rising up on to the land, hurling logs into the black night, snatching low-hanging branches, scattering small creatures, tearing apart the delicate construction of weavers' nests and the tree-trunk homes of cerval cats, filling the round depressions of pig holes, knocking down the spires of anthills. Everything crumbled and fell before the foaming water, defenceless in the face of its unstoppable force. Beyond the fence there was a groaning sound as part of the bank collapsed into the torrent and was carried away, changing the shape and character of the land for all time. Lightning tore through the curtain of rain, followed by an ominous lull in the storm and then a new roll of thunder. Standing ankle deep in water, Sarah suddenly felt something attacking her feet and she leapt into the air, shrieking in alarm. Laughter followed as Dan shone his torch downwards and discovered the contents of the kitchen hut, adrift in the muddy water. Pots and pans, kettles and sieves and bowls were all afloat, and an occasional potato or carrot sailed past until, at last, the noise abated and the water ceased to rise.

'Better take a look at the vehicles,' Dan said, disappearing into the night.

Allie and Sarah stayed put, waiting for an exclamation of dismay or a sound of relief, alarmed when Dan stopped in his tracks and gestured with the torch that they should join him.

Standing on the other side of the fence, looking into the compound with small, wise eyes, were two of Sarah's elephants. She walked towards them very slowly, hoping they would recognise her scent, trying not to cause alarm. It was Lily who put out her trunk first, curling it over the wooden poles, the curve of her mouth suggesting a smile as she reached out and blew softly on to Sarah's outstretched hand. And then the calf reached up and touched her arm. For an eternal moment they stood together in the patter of rain, and then the mother rumbled a message and backed away, fading silently into the darkness.

When dawn broke the sky was massed with clouds, ponderous and grey, and the air felt muggy. Sarah worked beside Allie in silence, wiping down surfaces, drying out books and ledgers, placing the furniture in positions well clear of windows and doors in case of another deluge. Dan's precious charts had been blown off the wall and several of the coloured pins had fallen on the floor, a painful reminder of the storm for the unwary with bare feet. Sarah picked up the torn papers and taped them together carefully. Then she put the coloured pins into a small tin and left them for Dan to put back in place. It would take him a long time. The camp staff whistled and sang as they swept mud out of the kitchen hut and the stores, puzzling over the ragged remains of paper labels once fastened to tins and bottles. Dan checked the vehicles and pronounced them sound, but the radio link was not working at all.

They set out in his Land Rover after breakfast, hoping to ascertain the amount of damage caused by the storm and to locate some of their elephants. But the tracks were littered with debris and the roads were treacherously wet and slippery. When they had pushed the vehicle out of two holes and the first raindrops splattered on to the windscreen, they gave up on their excursion and returned to camp.

'That was quite a visitation you had last night,' Dan said, as they skidded along the muddy track. 'I think they came to see if you were safe, kid.'

'It's not like you to be so fanciful,' Sarah said lightly, but her heart swelled with delight as he confirmed her own feelings about the elephants.

'He's getting soft,' Allie said, winking at Sarah. 'The rain has made his brain soggy. Let's hope it continues – I could learn to live with this kind of romanticising.'

The rain fell for three days and soon everything was damp and mouldy. Insects that Sarah had never seen before came crawling out of the thatch and in from the compound, lodging themselves in her shelves and cupboards and her shoes. Dan became increasingly cranky as he tried without success to repair the radio and to dry out his notes, cursing as the soggy pages peeled away into layers.

'What about trying to get to Isiolo this afternoon?' Allie suggested. 'That road can't be too bad, and there are things that the staff claim we can't do without.'

'Sarah and I could try it,' Dan said. 'Give me the list and we'll see how far we get.'

The drive was largely uneventful and they managed to reach the town with only one stop to put brush under the wheels and manoeuvre the Land Rover out of a ditch.

'I've been trying to contact you on the radio,' said the local police commissioner. 'There's an Indian fellow here who says he's a friend of yours. A journalist who is lucky to be alive.'

'What happened to him?' Dan was frowning.

'A couple of my *askaris* found him, stranded way north of Wajir with a few bullet holes in his car. No food or water and a smashed-up *gari*. Apparently he was following a lorry-load of Shiftas. He managed to talk to them for a while before one of them got annoyed and took a pot shot at him. I don't know how he got away without a bullet hole through his head.'

'But he's not hurt?' Sarah tried to sound calm.

'A few cuts.' The commissioner turned to Dan. 'We're not terribly pleased to have journalists around here, stirring things up like this. If he'd been killed or blown up we would have had a serious incident, and there's enough trouble already, with these Somalis. I hope we're getting close to some kind of peace agreement, and I think it would be better if your team stuck to tracking elephants and left the bandits to us.'

'He's not part of my team,' Dan said angrily. 'And we had no idea where he was or what he was doing. I'm not responsible for the antics of the Nairobi press. And I don't like the idea of my research facility being used for anything other than studying elephants.' He turned to Sarah. 'You'd better find your friend Mr Singh, while I organise the things on Allie's list.'

'I'll have to leave my car here,' Rabindrah said when Sarah tracked him down. 'It has openings in vital places, and Indar Uncle is sending up a mechanic.'

'Fine. But I warn you, Dan is not too pleased with you.'

Rabindrah's face had been cut by flying glass, and the car itself was riddled with bullet holes. Sarah's stomach lurched as she realised how close he had come to death. Nothing was said until they reached the camp in the late afternoon and unloaded the provisions. Then Dan addressed Rabindrah.

'We have a special position here,' he said. 'There are no restrictions on our movements as we follow the herds and go about our research. I don't want my work compromised by some smart arse using this base to write political stories. We're fully accepted by the District Commissioner and the police and the Game Department, because we're scientists and we steer clear of politics. I won't have any visitor using this compound for anything other than elephant research. And if you wish to start writing about the political situation around here, then you'd better do it from somewhere else. Because this is not a jumping-off point for chats with the Shiftas. Is that clear?'

'I had no intention of implicating you in anything I was doing,' Rabindrah said. 'And I certainly didn't suggest that I was part of your set-up. I simply told one of the *askaris* that I had to get back to Buffalo Springs and pick up my belongings, and I'm afraid they assumed I was one of your researchers.'

'Well, you should have made it clearer that you had no connection with my camp,' Dan said. 'Those Somalis have caused nothing but chaos here, killing and shooting and maiming people and wildlife. Even if there is a political agreement, I don't believe these skirmishes will end any time soon. The Shifta are cattle rustlers and raiders by nature and tradition, and they'll continue in the same way no matter how many pieces of paper are signed.'

'They have a story that deserves to be told, though,' Rabindrah said. 'True, some of them are violent bandits who kill at the drop of a hat for ivory and rhino horn. But there are ordinary herders and traders with wives and children, and old people too whose needs are modest. And they will soon starve, because they have become a dispossessed people since the British drew their arbitrary border line across the map. The Kenya Government has taken some of the grazing land they've been using for centuries and given it to farmers from other tribes. And they will take more as time goes on. The Somalis are not allowed to integrate here in Kenya, and they're no longer part of Somalia either. No one wants them. No one has really tried to figure out who they are, or where they belong. Ordinary Kenyans are paying the price for this, and I think they will be paying the price for a long time, unless something is done about this question.'

'Hell, man, the Somalis have fought for grazing and water, with the Boran and the Rendille and other nomads, long before the British ever got here,' Dan said impatiently. 'Don't try to tell me that their elders ever sat down over a cup of tea, or a gin and tonic, and worked out how they felt about where they belonged?'

'No, sir. But they never pretended that they were taking a superior moral stance. They just went out and fought with spears and shields for what they thought was their territory, and the strongest men won the day. We, however, have set ourselves up as a moral authority on social order. We've tried to change their way of life beyond recognition or reason, and now we're surprised at the outcome.'

'I guess you have a point there,' Dan said wearily. 'But it's not my role to be a part of it. I'm just a boring old scientist trying to figure out a way to protect some of what's left of this fragile environment.'

'I'm sorry I caused you a problem,' Rabindrah said stiffly. 'I've contacted my uncle and he's sending someone up from the garage tomorrow, to repair my car. In the meantime, I'll take my belongings and stay in the nearest rest house or *banda*, if Sarah doesn't mind driving me there.'

'That won't be necessary,' Dan said. 'You're welcome here until your

341

transport arrives. Just as long as you keep to the house rules. See you for a drink before dinner.'

He strode away towards the sleeping and shower quarters, leaving Rabindrah and Sarah mired in an awkward silence. It was Sarah who spoke first.

'You were shot at?'

'Yes. I'd been with them for two days, in this makeshift camp beyond Wajir. I slept in one of their huts, if you could call it that. Some woven mats fastened to a few sticks. They had their goats and a few scrawny cattle, and some camels. But there were a couple of lorries parked in the bushes a few yards away, and they were stuffed with automatic weapons. All Russian. That's where they get their arms from – from the Soviets, coming in through Somalia.'

'There's no way this government can police that border,' Sarah said. 'It's hopeless, the whole situation.'

'Anyway, I seemed to be getting along with them, although they were pretty jumpy. Until a dispute broke out between two of the men over a question I asked about the guns. And then there was a fight and it was clearly time to leave. In a hurry. So I ran for it and they shot at the car. Punctured one of the tyres and smashed the back windows and the radiator. Narrowly missed the back of my head. But they didn't follow me, and a few miles down the road I patched things up and drove for a while longer, until the car died and a patrol came by. So here I am. I'm sorry about Dan and his reaction.'

'So am I,' Sarah said. 'He's right, too. You're staying with us to write about elephants. That should be enough.'

'And what does enough mean?' he asked, his voice low but intense. 'They have a story, these people, and their situation is desperate. Things are not as simple as you imagine.'

'I don't care whether they're simple or not,' Sarah said. 'I've seen the results of Shifta poaching raids. I've seen elephants speared or shot down and left to rot, once their ivory had been hacked out of their skulls. The Shifta kill men and castrate them, and they steal and rape the women from other tribes, and take the livestock too. They're a bunch of bloodthirsty killers and I don't want to know about extenuating circumstances.'

'What do you think a journalist should be, then? A writer of fairy tales?

Someone who trudges through scenes of starvation and unfair practices and prejudice, and makes it all look good on paper because the powers of the day say it should be so?' He leaned over and took her arm, the pressure painful on her skin. 'I saw you as someone different. When I first met you in Nairobi, there was something about you that struck me as exceptional. I saw the courage in you, the determination to see that corruption and greed do not win over justice. And now you are telling me that I should not search for those same factors in every situation, and bring them into the light.'

'I'm not suggesting that at all.' She stood up, confused and defensive. 'It's none of my business how you think or what you write, and I have no reason to comment on your judgement one way or the other. Excuse me. I'm going to have a shower. I'll see you later.'

She left him cursing himself, sitting in angry silence and suddenly aware that he was very tired. And cold. He shivered and rubbed his arms briskly with the palms of his hands, trying to warm himself. Then he went in search of hot water for his shower.

The atmosphere before dinner was strained. The air buzzed with mosquitos and flying insects that had emerged in droves after the rain. Rabindrah was withdrawn. His eyes, usually alight with interest in everything around him, seemed dull and flat. He was wearing a long-sleeved shirt and a safari jacket, and he had wound a scarf around his neck.

'You're dressed for the mountain slopes,' Sarah said. 'It's awfully hot and muggy for all those layers.'

'Maybe it's because I didn't have many square meals up there,' Rabindrah said. 'And my limbs are aching from sleeping on the floor.'

'This should help.' Dan handed him a large whisky, smiling broadly in an attempt to get past their earlier exchange. 'You didn't have any good Scotch up there either, I'd say.'

But Rabindrah did not finish his Scotch, nor did he eat much of his dinner. Immediately after the meal he left them, saying that his days and nights in the north had left him more than tired.

'I guess I was a little hasty earlier on,' Dan said. 'When it comes down to it, we all have our methods of trying to make a balance between man and his environment. Between the demands of progress and ancient nomadic ways.'

'And maybe we'll fail,' Allie said. 'Because we seem to be hell bent on setting up a rigid system that forces people to change their ways without a backward glance, and embrace a very uncertain future charted mainly by politicians. And Rabindrah sees the necessity for pointing that out.' She turned to Sarah. 'What do you think?'

'When he first started asking questions about this project, I was impressed. But then it all became personal and I didn't like that at all. I thought he was digging for scandal and sensation. But now I believe he has integrity.' Sarah thought for a moment, wanting to get the words right for her own sake. 'He's not someone who will take the easy option or toe the official line, just to please his bosses or readers. I think he's genuinely trying to get to the heart of what is happening in the country. And he's not afraid of doing it.'

They all retired early. Sarah turned out her lamp as soon as she was ready for bed, in an attempt to minimise the insects that burrowed through the thatch and squeezed in through the window and door frames, drawn by the light. She fell asleep quickly and at first she did not hear the tapping on her door. But after a few minutes it fractured her sleep and she sat up, tense and anxious.

'Sarah?'

She lifted the mosquito net and pushed her feet into her sandals. Rabindrah was at the door, wearing several layers of clothing with a towel wrapped round his shoulders like a cloak. She stared at him in surprise.

'I think I'm sick,' he said, his teeth chattering. 'Yes. I am sick. And very cold.'

'There's a blanket here, in the cupboard,' she said. 'You'll find another one in a box on top of the wardrobe in your rondavel. There are more in the storeroom, but I'm afraid they may smell rather mouldy.'

She took her lantern and found the store keys. Soon she was in the guest hut, armed with three more blankets. Rabindrah was buried under the bedclothes, his body shaking, teeth still chattering.

'Malaria,' Sarah said. 'I saw my father with it several times. That's why he left Kenya – the doctors told him he couldn't afford to get it again.'

In spite of his feeble protests she sat down beside him, folding the blankets in two, watching him burrow deep into the mound she had created. But the shivering did not stop.

'I'm going to call Allie,' she said after an hour. 'I'm sure she has some *dawa*.'

'No, please don't wake her,' Rabindrah said. 'I've caused enough trouble as it is.'

But Sarah had already gone. She came back with more blankets and a mug of hot tea that she urged him to try and drink. His hands were shaking and she was obliged to hold it up to his lips and wipe his face when some of the hot liquid spilled from his mouth. Moments later he vomited it all on to the floor and lay back, gasping his apologies.

Allie arrived with a thermometer. 'Oh my,' she said. 'One hundred and two. And it may climb some more. The radio isn't working, so we can't call anyone. But I do have some medicine, although I'd rather not give it to you until we have a doctor's approval. We may have to drive you to the nearest hospital in the morning. Meantime, we need to try and keep you warm. And soon we'll be trying to cool you.'

It was an impossible task, and on several occasions he was shivering so violently that Sarah had to hold him down. Three hours had passed by the time the rigors stopped and Rabindrah lay limp and exhausted, his breathing shallow. Then the fever rose and he began to sweat, tossing and turning on the narrow canvas cot, throwing off the blankets, calling out in a language that Sarah did not recognise. They changed his sheets several times until there were no more dry sets available. Dan appeared as the rigors began again and helped to swaddle him in towels. Once he tried to get up and make his way out to the tent with the long drop, but he was too weak to walk, even with Dan's support. Allie appeared with a chamber pot and Rabindrah turned his face away in shame, so the women withdrew outside. When dawn came he was drifting in and out of a restless sleep. Dan recorded his temperature and said it was time to move him to hospital. But Allie disagreed.

'He's too sick to be moved,' she said. 'I vote that we give him high doses of chloroquine. But we may have to start with a jab, because he probably won't be able to keep down any tablets. Sarah, we need to bathe him again. It may help to bring his temperature down.'

They washed him down with cool water and sprinkled his back with talcum powder, although his skin was so sensitive and feverish that even the lightest touch made him groan. Allie tried to feed him small amounts of water, but for the most part he was unable to keep it down. As the day grew hotter he began to shiver again, and Sarah ran outside to collect the blankets and sheets that were drying in the sun. Dan left the camp in search of a retired mission doctor who lived near Isiolo, and returned with a supply of quinine.

'If he doesn't respond to the chloroquine within the next three or four hours, we have to fill him up with this,' he said. 'Otherwise he may have breathing problems.'

The cycle began again in the late afternoon, and sheets were drenched and changed and drenched again. By nightfall Rabindrah lay shattered on the canvas bed, his limbs aching, his head throbbing with the fever. But Allie insisted on turning him and keeping him sponged down and dry. The old mission doctor arrived, his thick Scottish burr and gentle manner soothing them all.

'If the fever hasn't broken in the morning you'll have to get him to Nanyuki,' he said. 'Or arrange for him to be flown out of Isiolo or Samburu. Ye're in for a rough ride tonight, I'd say. I've set him up with the quinine now, and we'll have tae wait and see. But he's young and strong, and I have an idea he'll have turned the corner by tomorrow. Another six or eight hours should make the difference.'

Rabindrah continued to shiver and sweat in turns, and Sarah fed him water through a small dropper and kept his lips moist by smoothing them with Vaseline. She was finding it difficult to stay awake as the night wore on, and her own joints ached with fatigue as she and Allie took turns to pile blankets on top of him and then remove them as the fever rose again. They filled bowls of water, wrung out the soft cloths and sponges used to cool him, put his sheets out to dry, and searched for more bed linen. All through the day and night they took turns to stay in his hut, waiting for the shivering to begin again.

Just before dawn Sarah had fallen asleep in a chair, her head lolling, her body slumped sideways, when Allie shook her gently.

'The fever has broken,' she whispered. 'He's like an old rag, but the worst is over. I'm going to lie down for a couple of hours and I think you can safely do the same.'

Sarah nodded, a strange feeling of exhilaration coursing through her cramped limbs, flooding her thoughts as she stretched her arms and legs. Her neck was hurting and it was impossible to understand why she felt like crying and laughing at the same time. She stood looking down at

Rabindrah, at his closed eyes and black lashes. His hair was standing out in black spikes against the pillow and his face seemed deathly pale beneath several days of dark stubble. There was a line of sweat beads along his upper lip, and she thought that his mouth looked carved and perfect like a classical statue. When she placed her hand on his forehead, his skin was cool and slightly damp. She bent down, leaning closer to him until she could feel his breath, faint but regular on her cheek. His eyes were shut and she did not think he was aware of her as she kissed him, slowly and gently, on his beautiful lips.

Unnoticed in the open doorway, Allie nodded to herself, tucked her hands into her pockets, and went to find Dan.

Chapter 14

Rhodesia, May 1967

The road shimmered with dust that cut visibility to a few hundred yards and veiled the glassy blue canopy of sky. There had been no other traffic for more than an hour, and Lars was glad to be undisturbed, alone with his thoughts. He had spent the previous night in Salisbury, where the hotel bar and dining room had been full of people drinking gin slings and whiskies and tankards of beer, ready for the round of weekend parties at the club and at one another's houses. They were hospitable and friendly, interested in making the acquaintance of a stranger in town, and a shade too loud in their optimistic view of their country's future. A girl with long, dark hair and an inviting mouth installed herself on an adjacent bar stool, and set out to seduce Lars with an undisguised enthusiasm that made him smile. The fact that he was from Kenya became a talking point, and there was heated discussion about the way in which the country and the white community had been betrayed by the British Government.

'You're right to come south.' A jovial, red-faced man with eyes like chips of granite placed a gin and tonic in front of Lars. 'This is where things will last, where we won't lie down like yellow-bellies and give everything over to the *kaffirs*. Look around you over the next few days, man. You'll see this is a booming country where things are still in the right hands. I'm sure you can find something to do, if you're inclined to stay. There are plenty of people here who've left Kenya and found a new future in Rhodesia. We've got everything in this country – copper and gold, tobacco, tea and cotton, coffee and sugar and good cattle. Ian Smith will see us through. He'll work something out with the blacks. And in the end the British Government won't kick up too much fuss, because they don't want the Commies in here, taking over everything.'

But Lars found their political vision of Africa alarmingly isolationist, and soon after dinner he retired to his room. He had tried earlier in the evening to contact Jan van der Beer, but there was no reply from his telephone. When he spoke to the operator she confirmed that he had the right number. The line was down, she said, but she could not give him a reason or a time when it might be in working order again. He telephoned Hannah at Langani.

'I'm setting out for Kobus's place first thing in the morning,' he said. 'I haven't been able to rouse your parents on the phone — the line is out of order, which is quite a common thing, apparently. I'm sure Lottie will be around, even if Jan is out on the farm. It just means I may not be able to ring you from the house when I get there. Are you all right? And Suniva?'

'We're fine. Anthony is here and everything is quiet.'

He could hear the slight tremor in her voice. 'Goodnight, Han. I love you,' he said.

He slept fitfully. In the morning he checked out of the hotel, rented a car and bought a small thermos bag with some water and beer and sandwiches. By ten o'clock he was driving fast through the city suburbs and out into the countryside, his mind focused on his destination. He still had no clear idea what he was going to say to Jan and Lottie when he arrived. What would Jan's reaction be when he was confronted with the truth about his son's death? And as for Lottie, he could not imagine how she would be able to bear this new revelation and still struggle on.

Lars now wished he had not insisted on coming down here to see Jan. The man he had known and admired was responsible for an appalling crime. Revenge for the murder and mutilation of his brother at the hands of the Mau Mau could not excuse the savagery of roasting another human being alive on a spit. Even if, as Wanjiru had said, he had made a protest of sorts at the start. The shooting of Simon's mother could barely be considered an acceptable casualty of war. But the other. The thought of it filled Lars with revulsion. And then Jan had left Kenya and the farm without any warning, thereby allowing his son to be killed in his place, and leaving his daughter to face a future poisoned by terror and hatred. What kind of man would do that to his family? He must have known, or at least suspected, what was behind the attacks at Langani. Yet he had chosen to say nothing, even after Piet's death. If he had spoken out then, they might have tracked down Karanja earlier. Now he would have to face up to the consequences of that horrendous act in the forest years ago. The time for running away was over.

Lottie would take the news hard. Lars was at a loss to know what comfort he could offer in such circumstances, and he wondered if she had any close friends who would be able to support her. From all that he had heard, the cousin, Kobus van der Beer, was a rough brute of a man who would be of little help. Perhaps Lottie, too, had always known the truth, although Lars did not think so. He wished that he did not have to be the messenger, but he was still sure that the news could not have been broken to them over the telephone.

His thoughts turned to Hannah. He imagined her, sitting in the office with her glowing skin and her thick blonde hair tied back, bending over the accounts ledger or the order books, frowning a little, her tongue touching her upper lip as she trailed her finger down the line of entries. Or lifting little Suniva, laughing, into her arms. Hannah with her lovely wide mouth and her strong, curved body, and her up-and-down, sing-song way of speaking. She would have completed her tasks in the dairy, and be back at the house, most likely finishing off the day's paperwork so that she could spend part of the afternoon playing with their daughter. Pray God they would be safe in his absence. If anything happened to her, or to the baby . . . He thumped the dashboard, raging at the evil that had turned his home into a place of seige.

He was catapulted back into reality when, without warning, a shape loomed up in front of him. He swerved, barely missing the man on the bicycle. The car spun as he wrenched at the steering wheel, swearing at his own carelessness. He skidded across the surface and came to a halt in the choking dust, with the vehicle tilting into the shallow ditch on the edge of the road. The lone cyclist picked himself up off the stony ground, remounted and wobbled towards him.

'Sorry,' Lars said, climbing out of the car. 'I didn't see you in time. It's the dust.' He was at a loss as to what else he might say. The man probably didn't speak English in any case.

'It is all right, *nkosi*. Maybe you have had some beer and you must sleep now, and not drive until it is cool again.'

'No. It was the dust. But there is beer in the back of the car, and I will give you some bottles, because I caused you to fall from your bicycle.'

'Maybe you will give me a lift, *nkosi*.' There was a flash of white teeth in the dark face.

'But you were going in the opposite direction from me,' Lars pointed out, smiling.

'It is true, *nkosi*. But now I am thinking that by the time I have helped you to take your car out of the ditch, it will be too late for me to reach the place where I was going. We are not allowed to be on the roads at curfew time. So my bicycle can be tied on to the roof rack, and I will return to my house.'

'Where is your house?' Lars asked, realising the futility of the question. He would not recognise the name of any local village. But the fellow seemed co-operative and was not demanding money or threatening any trouble. It was the least he could do to make pleasant conversation. He opened the boot and looked for a rope with which to secure the bicycle.

'It is not far.' The cyclist gestured over his shoulder. 'I will tell you when we get there. Do you have a farm where there is work, *nkosi*? I am looking for a job. I am strong and I can do anything. I can work hard for a good boss.' The eyes regarded him hopefully and then recognised a further opportunity. 'Do you also have cigarettes in your car? As well as the beer?'

'I'm not from round here,' Lars said, proffering a cigarette and bending his head to light his own. 'I'm visiting a friend. Do you know where Kobus van der Beer's farm is? I'm going to stay there, so maybe you can ask him if he has work.'

There was no response and Lars looked up, puzzled. His potential travelling companion had remounted his bicycle and was pedalling away with remarkable speed. After a hundred yards or so, he turned sharply into the bush and disappeared from sight. Lars shrugged, and reached into the cold bag for his sandwiches and a beer. The bread and cheese and ham tasted fresh, and he drank from the bottle, savouring the chill in his throat. When he had put the rope away he got back into the driver's seat and turned on the ignition, relieved that he was able to back away from the edge of the ditch without a problem. He pulled out into the road and set off once more. Less than five minutes had passed when the first rock hit the passenger window, smashing the glass and showering his lap and legs with splinters. He pressed down hard on the accelerator and raced through the hail of stones that came at the car, cursing the group of men on the roadside. They were shouting abuse as he drove past them, increasing his speed until he reached a curve in the road where his attackers were lost from sight. The windscreen had cracked and the car was filled with dust. Lars could feel small pieces of glass sliding down between his legs and on to the floor of the car. There was no one in sight, but he drove on until he was well clear of the place where he had been ambushed. Then he stopped and climbed out of the car, leaving the door open and the engine running as a precaution. It took some time to clear the remains of the windscreen from the front seats, and he found himself looking over his shoulder frequently, peering into the bush on either side of the road as he worked. When he set off again it was with considerable relief. The next hour passed without incident and he finally turned off the main road and bounced down a rough track that led to a gatepost, and a barrier pole. There was a watchman on duty, sitting in the shade of the thatched mud hut beside the barricade.

'I've come to see Mr van der Beer,' Lars said.

The man did not answer, but looked at him out of sullen eyes for a long moment before lifting the wooden barrier. Lars raised a hand in salute and drove on, surrounded on both sides by a tangle of bush for the first mile or two and then by lines of tobacco plants, clattering and whispering in the white, pitiless glare of the sun. When he reached a fork in the road, he made a guess and took the narrower track to the left. Within moments he saw a painted name board nailed to a tree trunk. Jan van der Beer. The driveway was short. In front of him there was a small bungalow with a sagging verandah that looked as though it might soon collapse. The roof was made from corrugated iron and he could hear it cracking and shifting in the blinding heat. The steps up to the verandah were framed by dust-laden shrubbery, the branches hanging listless and heavy. In front of the house was a flowerbed, bordered by a strip of grass that had been coaxed into reluctant life. Lottie's unmistakable signature. He was smiling as he stepped out of the car, only to be swallowed by an eerie silence. Birds and insects seemed to be holding their breath in mid-song as he called out a greeting.

'Jan? Lottie? It's Lars. I tried to phone, but there's something wrong with your line.'

Now that he was closer to the building he became aware of a strange, thick odour that hung in the air. The front windows were broken, and the outer walls were black in several places as though they had been scorched. He called again into the echoing silence, and then turned the door handle and entered the house. Inside he could smell smoke and the all-too-familiar scent of singed cloth and burnt wood. A pile of furniture lay haphazard and broken in the centre of the room. Books and magazines floated in a stagnant pool of water. Shelves and chairs had been overturned. Shards of glass and a few ornaments and framed photographs littered the floor of what had been a sitting room. In one corner Lottie's sewing machine lay on its side, the cover splintered into small pieces, the handle ripped from the wheel, tumbled spools of thread shining like a web in the dim ruins of the room.

Visions of the workshop in Langani and the charred shell of the lodge rose up in Lars's mind as he walked slowly through the house, his skin crawling with a terrible sense of foreboding. With dread, he opened each door, looking into the poky bedrooms and the bathroom that led off the main corridor, expecting at any minute to come upon a blackened corpse. But the rooms were empty. There was nothing of value left anywhere, and it was plain that the fire had not reached the heart of the building. In the kitchen two aluminium pots stood on the gas cooker, but the place had been ransacked. Drawers hung open, their contents scattered on to the floor, and there were broken dishes on every surface.

The back door of the house was open, creaking a little in a breeze that heralded an end to the stifling afternoon. Lars stood still for a moment, listening for any sound of life, alert to the slightest of movements in the tangled bush that surrounded the back yard. But there was only silence and the stench of the extinguished fire. The remains of a wire chicken coop lay scorched and twisted on the ground. Above the shrivelled, blackened bodies of the birds, a flurry of grey ash and feathers drifted across the hedge that framed a vegetable patch.

The light was softening with the advent of evening, and Lars realised that there was nothing he could do here, apart from putting his own life in danger. He strode around the outside of the dilapidated bungalow and started the car, revving the engine and reversing down the driveway to the fork in the road where he followed a second track that meandered through the tobacco fields. After several miles he thought that he would have to return to the barrier on the main road to ask for directions. He slowed down and was looking for a suitable place to turn the car when he caught a glimmer of light in the distance. Minutes later he parked the car in front of a solid, stone house and walked up the steps to the verandah. A small woman emerged, closing the front door on a horde of dogs that barked and scrabbled at the windows behind her. She looked at Lars with faded eyes, a cigarette hanging from the corner of her mouth, her face sagging with years of hardship and disappointment.

'I'm looking for Jan van der Beer,' he said. 'I'm his son-in-law. From Kenya.'

'Their place was burnt. Petrol bomb a couple of nights ago. They're in my son's house. In Faanie's place.'

'Were they hurt? Is Lottie—'

'Who's out there? What are you standing around for, Ellie? Don't you bloody know it's not safe to go outside this time of the day?'

The door swung open to reveal a burly man whom Lars took to be Kobus van der Beer. He was similar in appearance to Jan, but his face was grim and unforgiving and his eyes held no hint of interest or sympathy, or even curiosity as to the identity of his visitor.

'I'm Lars Olsen from Langani. I've come to see Jan.'

'Over there.' Kobus flung an arm towards the gathering darkness. 'Take your car round the side of this house and you'll see another driveway to the right. He's staying in my son's house until we can fix up something else for him.' His eyes shifted to Lars's car. 'Did you have an accident?'

'Someone threw a rock at me.' Lars shrugged. 'Probably because I almost ran him over. He found a few friends and they attacked me further along the road, but I'm not hurt.'

'How far? When did this happen?'

Lars described the incident. He was unprepared for the immediate reaction.

'I'm not having a bunch of bloody *munts* throwing stones at anyone on my road,' Kobus said. 'I'll bet I know who's responsible for it. Lazy bastard who used to sit around scratching himself, until I fired him a week ago. You can tell Jan that we're going out to get the whole frigging lot of them. Tonight I'll be over to fetch him later. We'll catch these buggers when they don't expect it.'

'Tell Lottie she can keep me company tomorrow, if she doesn't feel like being on her own.' Ellie's voice was hesitant and she looked away as Kobus turned on her.

'Lottie can stay where she is,' he said, taking his wife's arm and pushing her back inside the house. 'They should be grateful we've put them over there, in our son's place.' His eyes flickered over Lars again. 'He's dead, you know. Killed by those bloody *kaffir* savages. Tell Jan I'll be round in a few hours, and he'll need to have his wits about him. So he should go easy on the bottle, heh?'

'I think what happened was partly my fault.' Lars tried to diffuse the tension. He did not want to precipitate any more violence. 'I was ambushed well before I passed through the barrier on to your land.'

'This whole area is full of *kaffirs* who need to be taught a lesson. I'll collect Jan after dinner.'

Kobus disappeared into his house and Lars returned to his car and drove around the side of the cheerless building to the adjacent property. The second house was smaller, but it had the same gloomy appearance, with thick bars on the windows and a large sign warning of ferocious dogs. When he knocked there was no immediate response, but he could see the glow of a lamp behind the drawn curtains and he raised his hand to knock again. Before his hand touched the door it was flung open and he found himself looking down the barrel of a gun.

'Lars! Jesus Christ, man! What the hell are you doing here?' Jan lowered his rifle and stepped aside, shaking his head in astonishment. 'Is everything all right at Langani? Hannah? Why are you here?'

Before Lars could answer he heard footsteps and then Lottie had flung her arms around him, exclaiming in surprise and drawing him into the house. He stood looking at them both in the lamplight, dismayed by Jan's bloated face and red-rimmed eyes and by the apprehension in Lottie's face.

'Everything is fine at Langani,' he said quickly, wanting to reassure them. 'Hannah is fine, and Suniva is growing more beautiful every day.' He held out his hand to Jan. 'I haven't seen you since . . . well, it's been a long time. I hope you got my letters. And all the monthly reports. Piet was my best friend and I miss his company and everything that he was. Every day of my life I miss him.'

'So you've taken some holiday time at last?' Lottie asked. She looked anxiously at Jan's darkening face. 'We're so happy to see you,' she said. 'But it's a shock. We weren't expecting you at all. Hannah didn't say—'

She stopped, instinctively aware that there must be a significant reason for his being there. Lars was not a man to do things on the spur of the moment. He would certainly not leave the farm, and his wife and child, at short notice. She wondered whether he had come to mend the breach that still existed between Hannah and her father, and maybe try and persuade Jan to go home. For a few moments her heart lifted.

'Here – this is what you need after your journey. Wherever you've come from.' Jan held out a glass of neat whisky and a jug of water. His hand was shaking as he poured. 'Say when.'

'That's a little strong for me. I'll take it filled up to the top with the water, please,' said Lars. 'I've driven from Salisbury today.'

Lars watched as Jan poured an even larger measure of neat Scotch for himself and sat down heavily in an armchair, his rifle propped against his knee. Lottie positioned herself on the edge of the sofa and leaned forward with impatience. She looked pale, and lines of tension had traced their story across her face. Neither of them had mentioned their burnt-out home, and Lars was about to ask what had happened when Lottie broke the silence.

'Tell us all about Langani, and Hannah, and Suniva. And what is happening on the farm? How are dear old Mwangi and Kamau and Juma, and everything at home. We're so anxious to hear your news, Lars.' She was smiling encouragement but her eyes were apprehensive.

There is no easy way to do this, Lars thought. Best to get it over with, all the horror of it, straight away. He began with the destruction of the workshop, then the fire at the lodge. But before he could move on to Karanja, and Wanjiru's subsequent arrival at Langani, Jan had drained his glass, and was staring at him belligerently.

'So what are you doing down here, man?' he asked.

He attempted to rise from the chair, causing the gun to clatter on to the floor at his feet. He bent unsteadily to pick it up and lean it against the sideboard. Lars looked away, conscious of Lottie's eyes on him, making some kind of silent appeal. Jan poured himself another whisky, ignoring his wife's murmur of protest.

'What has happened to my daughter? It can't be safe for Hannah, to be left on the farm like that. You should not have left her alone.'

'It was Hannah who asked me to come. There is something I have to talk to you about.'

Lars caught the question in Lottie's glance, but she said nothing.

'Hannah is fine, and the baby is fine,' he said. 'Anthony Chapman is staying at Langani while I am here, and the Murrays will call in regularly.'

'So tell me if this is right,' Jan said, the alcohol fuelling the anger that lived in him. 'After two vicious attacks, you walk off the farm and abandon your wife with a new baby. Leave her to run Langani with someone who knows nothing about farming?' The question was filled with contempt.

'Of course he didn't leave like that,' Lottie protested. 'I'm sure Lars has very good reasons for coming all this way. You know he would never leave Hannah and the baby unprotected. And he has always run his farm in the best way.'

'It's my bloody farm. Even if I have not been able to go back there for some time.' Jan glared at his son-in-law.

'I'm fully aware of that.' Lars was having difficulty remaining polite. 'Although one day you will have to address Hannah's position, and whether you are going to hand Langani over to her. Since you do not seem to have any plans to return to Kenya. But that's not what I—'

Jan came to stand beside Lars, his gait unsteady, his face red and angry. 'She wants me out, is that it? Or is it you that wants to own the place, now that you've got her to marry you? Is that what was in your mind all along?'

Lars could feel anger boiling inside him.

'Jan, stop it!' Lottie pleaded. 'How can you say such a thing? Lars loves Hannah, and you know that's the only reason he married her. So now we need to hear whatever he has come to tell us. But not for a few moments.' She stood up. 'I think you should calm down now. I'm going to make up a room for him, and then we'll have supper and he can tell us everything. About the farm, and our daughter, and our granddaughter. And you will listen, Jan. Without flying into any more of your pointless rages.'

Jan gave a snort and sat down again, clutching the whisky bottle in his hand.

'What happened to your house?' Lars asked, putting off the moment of truth. 'I went there first. Saw the mess.'

'Bloody *munts* came and threw a petrol bomb in the window. Lucky we weren't there, or you wouldn't be talking to us now.' Jan's words were bitter. 'I was out with Kobus on a night patrol, and Lottie had gone to spend the evening with a friend who lives about ten miles away. When she drove home she saw the smoke and flames. The house was on fire, and the bloody chickens were on fire, and the store and the shed were burning. And of course the servants had run away. They were probably responsible.'

'I don't think so.' Lottie stopped at the door leading to the corridor, and spoke directly to Lars. 'I think this is one of the local gangs that have been going around damaging white property. There are so many of them now, all riled up by the terrorists who sneak in over the border from Zambia. They've tried to get Kobus and Ellie a couple of times recently, and their son Faanie was killed in an ambush a while back. Janni almost lost his life that day too.'

'It seems to be hard going down here,' Lars said. 'In spite of the determination of Ian Smith and the white population. I myself think it's too late to try and rule an African country without a vote for everyone. That time has passed.'

'Things are going from bad to worse,' Lottie agreed. 'What with sanctions and shortages, and the increasing political rift between black and white, I don't see any reason for optimism. I think the whites are fooling themselves, and local Africans are being pressganged and beaten, almost like it was during the Mau Mau. Only it's more sophisticated here. Young people are being forced to join the black political parties who promise them everything, and then send them away to be turned into thugs and killing machines. We hear some of them are even shipped off to Russia and China. The violence is increasing every day. I keep telling Jan we should leave.'

'Don't start on that subject.' Jan glowered at her, and his voice rose as he topped up his glass once more. 'Anyway, things aren't so great in Kenya either. People are being killed there too. Our own son was hacked to pieces. And the killers aren't being caught. I think we know that all too well. Too bloody well.' His voice quavered, and he wiped his face with the back of his hand,

'Come with me,' Lottie said, beckoning to Lars. Her movement did not quite hide the fleeting expression of despair that he saw in her face as she listened to her husband's mutterings. 'I'll show you the bathroom and a bedroom you can use, and then you can bring in your things and freshen up. We'll talk over supper.'

'I almost forgot.' Lars turned back to Jan. 'I met your cousin. He's coming to collect you later in the evening. A group of people threw stones at my car on the way here, and he says he knows who they were. He wants to go out and look for them.'

'Oh God.' Lottie's shoulders drooped. 'This is just an excuse for another patrol, for another beating or killing. Or both. Kobus is a brute, no better than a common thug, and he's obsessed by revenge.' She put her hand on Lars's arm, and he could feel urgency in the pressure of her fingers. 'Since his son was killed, he'll use any pretext to hunt down and shoot any black man he sees.'

'He's defending his property and his family, like thousands of other white Rhodesians,' Jan said angrily. 'But you've taken a dislike to him, and no matter what he does it won't be right in your eyes. You could have been killed by that petrol bomb, or on the road coming back here the other night. We need patrols and we have to defend ourselves, Lottie, because no one from the outside is going to help. Here in Rhodesia we're up against a crowd of ignorant *kaffirs* who are being brainwashed into thinking they'll own every scrap of land, and every building, and every bloody car and bicycle, if they keep attacking us for long enough. If they murder a few more farmers and throw more petrol bombs, they believe the whites will turn tail and run, and leave them everything we've built.'

'*We* haven't built anything here,' Lottie said icily. 'This isn't our land or our war, and we shouldn't be involved in it at all. We shouldn't be sleeping with guns under our pillows and the windows closed and barred at night, jumping up at every little noise in the darkness. It's months since I had a decent night's sleep. When you're out with your cousin for days and nights at a time I never sleep at all. I never feel safe for even a moment. And I don't want to be shot or burned or raped, for Kobus and his farm.'

'It must be tough for both of you,' Lars interjected, but he was gazing at Jan, and wondering at the man's talent for self-deception. What had he done at Langani but turned tail and run away? And worse still, he had left his children to deal with the consequences. 'It seems to me that things are not going to improve in Rhodesia. Unless all sides can come to a compromise here, and that doesn't appear to be imminent. Maybe it's time to leave, Jan. This is no place for you or Lottie. Surely you can see that?'

'Yes,' Lottie agreed desperately. 'For God's sake, Lars, help me to persuade him. We have to get away from here, before it's too late and what's left of us is shipped back to Kenya in coffins.'

'Back to Kenya where my son was butchered and my daughter hates me

359

and someone else has taken over the running of my farm? Is that where you want to go? Is that the safer choice you're always bleating about?' Jan's words were slurred and he staggered a little as he moved towards Lottie, shaking his fist at her. She stepped aside with a swift movement born of practice.

'You can't run away from the past for ever.' Lars grabbed Jan's coat and stood between them, appalled that the man would raise a hand against his wife. The angry words broke from him before he could stop himself. 'You bloody fool! You can't bury yourself permanently in this godforsaken place, and leave the rest of your family to bear the punishment for your guilt!'

'What do you mean? What the hell do you mean by that?' Jan was roaring at the top of his voice. 'Who are you to talk to me in those terms? A farm boy who married the boss's daughter, and now wants to take everything for himself. You're the one who has left your wife and child to the mercy of some *kaffir* thugs, so that you could come and persuade me to give you my farm. What else are you doing here, when you should be at home protecting them, not haranguing me?'

'I'm here because of what you did in the forest that day,' Lars said, speaking the words very quietly, his large frame absolutely still, arms hanging down by his side in a stance that was filled with sadness and futility. 'The day that you shot Simon Githiri's mother, and his father was roasted alive on the fire. As a small child he saw it all. And that is why your son is dead, and your farm is under attack, and your daughter lives in terror every day of her life. That is why she is afraid for herself, for Suniva and for me. Hannah is living with the consequences of your actions, while you hide down here and take out your guilt on your wife. While you go out hunting Africans with your cousin Kobus.'

Lottie made a high-pitched sound like an animal in pain, and then she put her hands over her ears and sank down to crouch on the floor. Jan stared into his son-in-law's eyes, seeing the accusation and the revulsion in them. Then his body sagged, and he leaned against the wall and covered his face. Lars turned away, unable to look at the ruin of the man whose strength and integrity he had once believed in. Wearily, he finished his narrative, describing the visit to Mwathe and the meeting with Karanja, and ending with Wanjiru's story and the discovery that Simon was still alive. When he had told them everything he could hear only the rasp of

Jan's breathing in the silence. Lottie was still sitting on the floor, her arms crossed in protection over her head, and the sight of her filled Lars with remorse. This was not the way he had intended to tell them the truth. And now, as he looked again at Jan, his anger dissipated and he found himself pitying the morose, drunken wreck who stood before him. Jan turned to Lottie and held out a hand to help her up. But she shook her head and rose without his assistance, standing aloof from him, her arms folded tightly across her chest. Seeing her like this, in the harsh overhead light that hung from the ceiling, Lars was saddened by the way that she had aged, by the lines of disillusion that had eaten into her luminous goodness.

'I'm sorry, Lottie. More sorry than I can say.' He tried to make his voice gentle, to let her know that he loved her. 'I'm sorry for all that has happened, and for the way I told you. I didn't mean to be so brutal. I'm terribly sorry.'

'I'll go and get the sheets and towels for Lars,' Lottie said, her voice dull, her face white as chalk. She did not look at her husband. 'And then I'll make something for us to eat.'

'No. I'll get the things for him,' Jan said. His eyes were downcast, and he moved slowly, unsteadily. 'You go into the kitchen and make the dinner, Lottie. The bloody cookboy hasn't come back because he's scared and useless. Lars will get his luggage. Here, take my rifle with you. You never know if there are going to be a couple of *terrs* out there, waiting to finish you off.'

He handed the gun to Lars and then made his way down the corridor to the storage cupboard outside the bathroom. His hands were shaking as he opened the door and reached inside, searching for the whisky he had hidden there earlier in the evening. Lottie was always on the lookout for liquor, but he had reasoned that she would not open the linen press for a day or two. His fingers trembled as he tried to find the place where he had pushed the flask deep into a stack of towels. He must have something now. Quickly. Before what Lars had said penetrated the fog of his brain, and the pain became unbearable. He tried twice without success and he was cursing softly when he slid his hand in again and touched something. Not the whisky. It felt like paper. He grasped the small bundle and brought it out into the light. Letters. Letters addressed to Lottie. Envelopes with an Italian postage stamp. He could not think who might be writing to her from Italy, and he took a letter and put it into the pocket of his bush shirt.

Reaching into the cupboard once more he replaced the package, and was relieved when his fingers touched the cool exterior of his flask in the layer of towels below. He withdrew it and swallowed a draught before slipping it inside his jacket. Then he took the bed linen and brought it to the guest room. Lars appeared in the doorway. The two men stood frozen in the small room, unable to look at one another.

'There's plenty of hot water,' Jan said. 'You can get yourself cleaned up, then we'll have a drink and some dinner. Lottie is still the best cook you're ever likely to come across.'

It was a meal where anything of true importance was left unsaid, an hour of long silences and strained observances.

'I'm afraid we don't have any wine,' Lottie apologised. 'I haven't had a chance to replace what was taken or destroyed in the other house, after the bomb and the fire and so. In any case, we don't know how long we're going to be here in Faanie's place, so I don't want to buy much for the moment. Until we know—'

'Kobus says he has another house for us. Near the water pump and the stores. It needs fixing up and that will take a week or two. But I looked at it today and it's not bad. Not bad at all.' Jan could not meet his wife's eye and he addressed his remarks to Lars. 'There's plenty of water over there, and Lottie can start on a new garden that will be much better than what she's been able to do so far.'

'I don't want to start another garden.' Lottie's eyes were glittering, and her face crumpled with despair. 'I want to go home. I want to see Hannah and my granddaughter. I want to get away from here.'

Lars put down his knife and fork and cleared his throat. 'You could come back to Langani, Lottie. Hannah needs you.'

Jan stared at Lars across the table, perhaps waiting to be included. But when nothing more was said he pushed back his chair, stood up and walked over to the sideboard to pour himself another drink.

'Don't take any more, Janni. Please. Especially if Kobus is coming for you and you're going to be driving around all night. Please?' Lottie had also risen from the table and was moving towards him, but he pushed her aside.

'Sit down and finish your dinner,' he said. 'You and Lars. I'll drink what I bloody well want, whenever I want. Because I don't get any support around here. Only complaints. When I've left the house, you and

Lars can discuss your daughter, and going back to Langani. You can tell him how you long to return to the place where your husband fought to preserve his farm and his family, where my brother and several of our friends died for their land. Where I paid the price with nightmares and misery for weeks and months afterwards. Langani is the place where Lars has left our daughter alone and defenceless, to live under the threat of being murdered herself. Langani took our son. To me it is now a place of death, whether I am to blame or not. Because this kind of hatred doesn't need reason. The desire to kill is enough. And it will go on and on. So when I get back in the morning, you can let me know what conclusions you've come to. Yes.'

He drained the liquor in one long swallow and staggered from the room. Lars sat in silence, listening through the flimsy walls as Jan crashed around in the bedroom next door, pulling open cupboards and drawers and swearing as he hunted for warm clothes and ammunition.

'I'm sorry.' Lottie's head was bowed in misery. 'He is not the same man. I know you have left Hannah well protected. Only, I wish she had not stayed—'

'I wanted her to come,' he said. 'But she could not face Janni. I thought I might prevail on her to take Suniva and to go and stay with Sarah until I get home. But she refused to leave the farm. Luckily, Anthony has been a true friend, and I believe that she is safe with him. As safe as we can be, just now. But I can't stay long.'

'She is so strong-willed, Hannah,' Lottie said. 'Since Piet was . . . since he died, there has been a barrier between us that I have not been able to break. And now, to learn this! Oh, my poor little girl. Poor Hannah.'

Before Lars had time to respond Jan reappeared, weaving his way across the room and coming to a halt at the dining-room table where he stood over them.

'I'm leaving now,' he said. 'I'm going to drive over to Kobus's, so that we can get going right away. In the morning, Lars, we will talk. You and I, man to man. When my wife has gone out to do her shopping and deliver her sewing, and so.'

The door slammed, and outside in the darkness they heard the sound of the truck backing out into the driveway. Headlights pierced a chink in the curtains and then all was quiet. Lottie remained at the table, her head lifted in defiance and resentment.

'This is very hard for you,' Lars said. 'And maybe Jan is right. I shouldn't have allowed Hannah to stay at the farm. We have even talked about leaving for good, if these attacks continue. But she cannot bring herself to think of it as something definite. Everything we have is tied up in Langani, and there was so much destroyed in the fire. Not just the building, but all the equipment and furniture. We would have big problems trying to find somewhere else. Still, I cannot take much more of this, Lottie. I always thought I was strong enough for every eventuality, but the risk of something happening to her, or to Suniva—'

His voice was so sad that Lottie left her seat at the table and took him by the hand. 'Come,' she said, with a faint smile. 'You are the best of men. I admire your love for Hannah, how constant you have been, the way you have taken the baby and loved her as your own. Come, Lars, let's have a little brandy. I keep it hidden so that poor Janni can't get at it. Because sometimes I need a drink myself – when I'm alone at night. I'm frightened that I'll be attacked and no one will know or care, and I'm afraid that he won't ever return, or that he will come back maimed and totally broken. Fear is always pumping through my blood these days, Lars, and I can't find a way to get rid of it.'

They sat in silence for a while. Then Lars looked at her and spoke out the question that had been plaguing him since he had first heard Wanjiru's story.

'Did he know?' he asked. 'Did Janni realise that Piet's murder and the trouble at Langani had something to do with the burning of that man?'

'I think in the recesses of his memory he knew, yes. After he came back from fighting the Mau Mau, he had nightmares for a long time. He was afraid to close his eyes and sleep. I knew that something bad had happened up there. That he had killed somebody. But it was a war, and he was not the only one. I tried to help him through the aftermath. Many of us wives had to do that, for our men.' She pressed her fist against her mouth, trying to compose herself, but Lars could see her body shaking. 'I heard what you said tonight. About the way that Simon's father died. But I don't want to ever hear it again. Because I would spend the rest of my days wondering how I could have lived with a man who was responsible for such a barbarous act.'

'What will happen now?' Lars asked her.

'Now he will have to confront the reason that Piet was killed. In as far as he is able to face the fact of death at all. Most of the time, he drives out all feeling with a bottle.' Her mouth twisted. 'Already, he tortures himself over the fact that he didn't go back last year. That he passed up his last chance to see his son alive. He blames himself for Hannah's leaving here. She stuck it out for a long time, tried her best with her business course, gave me as much love and support as she could. But finally it was all too much. I was almost relieved when she ran away. When she went back to Langani to be with Piet. She had to escape from this hopeless place, from her drunken father. And Janni also believes he was responsible for the death of his nephew, Faanie. But he has never explained why.' Lottie made a gesture of dismissal. 'Faanie would probably be dead by now anyway. He was just like his father – short-sighted, ignorant and intolerant. And Kobus will one day be responsible for Jan's dying, if we stay here much longer.'

'Lottie, you must leave,' Lars said. 'I know that the choice must be yours, and I don't want to interfere. But if you stay in this place you too will be destroyed. If you came back to Langani, or went to stay in Johannesburg with your brother for a while, then maybe Jan would follow you, and even return to being the man he was.'

She shook her head, her mouth forming a hard line as she refused to give way to tears. Lars watched with compassion as she searched in her pocket for a handkerchief.

'Janni is right about Langani,' she said finally. 'It has become a place of death, and I cannot see him ever returning there. And he would never go to Johannesburg. We have argued about that in the past.'

'Not Johannesburg, then,' Lars said. 'There is good farming country in Natal, and—'

Lottie stood up. 'I don't know if I want him to follow me,' she said. 'After tonight, I don't know anything.'

'I can understand why you feel that. You've supported him, stuck by him all these years, put up with his drinking. You are so good, Lottie. So—'

'No!' She saw Lars's startled expression and realised that she had shouted. 'Don't make me out to be some kind of saint, Lars. I'm not that type of person at all. I'm not the perfect wife, suffering in silence and without hope. I'm not a martyr.'

She was crying now, sobbing without restraint, and he put his arms around her and tried to quiet her. But she could not stop herself from pouring out her wretchedness. It had been so long since she had talked to anyone, allowed herself to think beyond the grim necessity of surviving another day in this hateful place.

'I've made terrible mistakes,' she said. 'I'm here because I'm a coward. I should have left him long ago and gone back to help you and Hannah. I should have stayed on at Langani after Piet died, and been there when Suniva was born. But I couldn't face the ghost of my son. So I abandoned my daughter, even though she needed me so badly. Because I didn't have enough courage.'

'Don't berate yourself, Lottie. Hannah was angry for a while, it's true. But she understands now, she really does. We both know that you have given everything you could, that you have been alone and without help for too long. You are the bravest person I know. You've had no one to love you or care for you for a long time, and there isn't a human being alive that can survive without love.'

'But I even threw that away,' she said. 'I threw it all away.'

'Of course you didn't,' Lars said. 'We love you so much, Hannah and I, and there is nothing we would not do to—'

'I had an affair,' she said.

Lars stared at her in silence, his mouth slightly open. The baldness of her statement left him without any words.

'I don't want you to think of me as a saint,' she repeated. 'And I'm not a hypocrite. I want you to know the truth, because otherwise you will pity me, and your love for me will be based on a myth. Another lie. We have had enough of those.'

'I can only hope it brought you some happiness,' Lars said.

'I was happy, yes. For a short time. It happened when I went to visit my brother in South Africa last year. I met a good man, and I fell in love with him. He's a widower, and he wants me to leave Jan and go to him in Italy. But I came back because Janni was injured on one of Kobus's patrols. I could not abandon him. Leave him with his demons and nightmares. I would have felt too guilty. I was afraid to turn my back on him and go away with Mario. Scared that Hannah would never forgive me, that I would be vilified for leaving my husband when he was critically ill in hospital. I was afraid that God would not forgive me.' Her expression was immeasurably sad. 'We had good years, Lars, when Janni worked hard and was a real husband and father.'

'But they weren't all good years, Lottie.'

'You are thinking of him as a murderer,' she said. 'But he was not like that before the Emergency. The British Government treated the Mau Mau situation as a just war, and called up all the able-bodied men. They brought in extra police and sent an army to back us up. Then Janni's brother was killed by the Mau Mau. Hacked and cut and sliced through, just like Piet was. With his belly ripped open and his entrails spread on the ground, and his testicles in his mouth. We knew that some of the *watu* on our farm had taken the oath. Most of them were forced into it, afraid they would lose their lives if they refused, but we could never be sure which of them was loyal. Our lives and our farms were under threat. And yes, there were terrible incidents and abuses on all sides, especially between Africans. They were the ones who suffered the most.'

'I know about those years,' Lars said. 'My uncle was already living in Kenya. There were troubles on his coffee farm near Kiambu.'

'Of course there were,' Lottie said. 'Times were different then, and some of the methods used by the British would be questioned now. After it was all over Jan suffered for a long time, with remorse and nightmares. He was like many men who fought in trenches and on the battlefield, in dark places and brightly lit prison cells, where they had to beat or kill other human beings with their bare hands in order to survive. He knew what he had done was wrong. And when the Emergency was over he did try hard to be a loving husband and father, and a fair employer.'

'When I first came to Langani it was like that,' Lars said. 'Everyone in the area spoke well of him. They still do.'

'But it's no good, is it?' she said with despair. 'It doesn't count now, and he will never stop paying for what he did on that one day. He feels that I will never forgive him for the death of our son, for the rift with Hannah, for the loss of our home. He knows that the people he loves no longer respect him. So he allows himself to go out there with Kobus, soaked in whisky, with a heart that carries no hope. He does whatever his cousin tells him to do, because he can see no way out.'

'But you cannot achieve anything by remaining here,' Lars said. 'I believe you should come back to Langani and bring Jan with you. Even in his present state.'

'Back to Langani.' Lottie's laugh was a hard, rasping sound. 'Oh, I dream about it. I say it out loud sometimes, just to torture myself. But what would be the reality? He would know that Hannah did not want him there, on the farm. He would live with Piet's ghost stalking him day and night in every familiar place. He would drink. And if they find Simon Githiri, there will be a court case, and what Janni did will become public. You are so kind, so brave and loyal, to consider having us there. But we can never come back, Lars, and that is the truth.'

'I'm so sorry, Lottie.' Lars could not think of any other words.

'You are a compassionate man, and Hannah is very fortunate,' she said. 'But I cannot talk any more, for now. I think I must go to bed, Lars dear. It is several nights since I had any sleep, and tonight you are here with me so I can close my eyes and not be alone and frightened in this horrible world. I will take that gift and be glad of it.'

She leaned against him with her eyes shut and he put his big arms around her, hoping she would feel the deep affection he had for her, and the sympathy he felt for her predicament.

When the doors and windows had been double bolted and locked, and the lights had been turned out, Lars lay awake in his bed, alert for any sound that might indicate the presence of an attacker waiting outside. He wondered where Jan was, and thought back to the bluff, kindly farmer he had known when he first came to Langani. He had been impressed by the school Janni had started on the farm, and the number of children he had sent to be educated in Nanyuki. In his mind's eye he could see Lottie's clinic, and the women queuing up outside the stores for their monthly portions of rice and sugar and meat that they received in addition to their husbands' wages. Jan van der Beer had been a firm but fair employer. A decent man, well respected in the community. A man who had tortured and killed.

Lars turned out the light, and thought of his own parents' farm in Norway, and the neighbours who could never understand his love for the chaotic beauty and the fierce, relentless dangers of Africa. He tried to imagine himself back in the orderly farmlands of Europe, in his father's brightly tiled dairy with its gleaming machinery, mixing with prosperous farm hands who owned radios and washing machines and cars, who sent their children to free schools with new textbooks and polished desks, who expected to live in stability and security all their lives long. But he could never go back to living in Norway. He had to stay and watch over Hannah and their daughter, the two people who meant everything to him. He must find a way to save the farm, and all it represented. And to help Jan and Lottie, too. Somehow it must be possible to create a life that would be bearable for them all.

Twenty miles down the road, Jan lay flat on his stomach on top of an overhanging rock, his body concealed by the protection of the surrounding scrub. He was confident that he had rendered himself invisible in the murky night, where even the glimmer of stars was intermittent beneath the thick canopy of cloud and trees. Kobus had parked some distance from the place where Lars had been ambushed earlier in the day, pulling a tarpaulin over the vehicle and covering it with branches that he had brought with him in the back of the lorry. The eight members of the patrol set out from the truck with blackened faces and dark clothes, creeping forward at a snail's pace, moving with stealth and caution, stopping regularly to crouch down and identify every sound. It took them almost two hours to reach the high ground where they could look down on the circle of huts. A cooking fire blazed and crackled outside the largest dwelling, and several men in tattered army fatigues sat around the burning logs, holding automatic rifles. They were haranguing the villagers with passionate speeches, holding out handfuls of banknotes, urging them to join the revolution, assuring them of wealth and freedom from toil, promising ownership of vast tracts of land that now belonged to the white man.

'Bloody geeks – trained over the border and sent back here by Nkomo and his friends,' Kobus muttered. 'And the one to the right of the fire is the brainless *munt* I fired. We'll get them all. Shoot the bastards and hang them up in the trees where they came from.'

'There are women and children down there.' Jan was weary of his cousin's obsessive desire to kill without discrimination or reason. 'We should wait a while, until they leave the fire to the men. It won't be long, because they've finished eating and the women have no reason to stay.'

'You're not going bloody soft on me, are you? Kill them all, what's the difference?' Kobus whispered. 'Man, the more we get rid of, the better. Look at that pregnant one, about to give birth to another troublemaker. Shoot the lot, for Chrissakes. What's the bloody difference?'

'I think we should wait.' Jan was insistent. 'If we hang on for a while we'll have a better chance of getting the leaders. When there are less people around. We should hold our fire until they send the women and children into the huts. If we start shooting now there'll be confusion, and too many people all over the place, and the *terrs* will use that to get away.'

'They'll run for cover on the other side, even if we wait,' Kobus said.

'Then we should split up,' Jan said. 'You stay here with three of the boys, and I'll take the other three through the trees and round the other side of the compound. When we're in place, I'll signal you with my torch and you can start shooting at the *terrs*. When they start to run, we'll get them from both sides.'

Kobus stared at him, smelling the whisky on Jan's breath, searching for a sign of weakness. Then he nodded. 'Right. I'll wait for your signal. But I hope it won't be too bloody long.'

An hour passed before Jan had positioned himself in a strategic place, facing the group around the fire. The light was brighter here, and the clouds had parted to reveal a pale moon. He retreated into the cover of the bush and a rumble of fear crept through his belly. He closed his eyes and thought of Lottie, seeing again her closed expression and the unmistakable look of pity in Lars's eyes. His hands began to tremble and when he reached for the flask of whisky his fingers touched the letter he had pulled out of the linen cupboard. He drew it out slowly and opened the envelope, squinting at the pages in the feeble light.

Darling Carlotta,

Every day I feel your despair and your loneliness and your pain. And every day I love you more and I am more certain that you must come to me. I have known from that first evening in Johannesburg that we should be together, that we were made to share our lives. There is no reason for you to throw away your beauty and your love, and all the remaining days of your life for this pitiful man.

You have done enough, my darling, my love, and I am waiting for you here in Italy. I want to show you my home. Our home. I want to see your pleasure and your delight when you look at what has already been done to this old place, and I want to feel my own joy when you make your first suggestions as to how we will continue. I am longing for your touch, to kiss you, to possess you again and to keep you safe.

There were three pages in all, but Jan could not read them. He put the letter back into his pocket and lay still, trying to prevent the shaking that had taken over his sweating body. Was Lottie preparing to leave him for some unknown man in Italy? He thought of her as she had once been, saw her glowing face as she cut the roses in her garden at Langani, as she held out their tiny son in the hospital on the proud day of Piet's birth. He remembered her as she braided Hannah's thick, golden hair, and kissed them both before he drove his daughter to school. Lottie, who had lain beside him in the night, loved him through all that had taken place in their lives. She was in Faanie's house now, talking to Lars, confiding her unhappiness, describing her husband's drunken, useless existence in this hell-hole he had chosen as a cowardly escape. Admitting to what he had done.

He owed her so much. He owed her everything. Once he had been able to defend her. He had done his best to protect their home, crawling, hungry and cold, through the dark, high forests of the Aberdares, fighting alongside the British officers who had never considered the Afrikaans farmer as one of their own, although he had been born a citizen of their country. But he had only led his family to the brink of destruction. He had lost his son and alienated his daughter, and his wife was going to leave him. The capture of Simon Githiri would reopen the case that had been closed as part of an amnesty at the end of the Emergency. He could see the loathing and revulsion on Hannah's face, feel her shame as the details of his actions were read out in the public courtroom. And Lottie would suffer most of all. Lottie, whom he loved. Lottie who deserved the happiness and security that he could no longer give her. Lottie, whom he must set free.

Jan stood up abruptly. His companions looked up in surprise, but he did not even see them as he strode down towards the clearing, shooting straight ahead, aiming for the figures in combat fatigues, watching two of them fall. He had a sense of triumphant savagery, a certainty that these were the men who had tried to burn down his house and kill his wife. A strange, growling sound rose from his throat and passed his lips, stretched back into a terrible grimace of bared teeth and deadened eyes as he went forward. He felt only relief as the first bullets entered his chest and his shoulder and then hit his legs, so that he stopped and looked down in surprise as his knees buckled and he fell on to the ground. His eyes closed and he drifted away, although for a time he could hear the sound of shooting and screaming, and the cries of the women and children. Then everything was quiet and he let go of his rifle as Lottie came towards him, and then Hannah with her hands held out and her long braided hair swinging over her shoulder. And as he was carried towards the light, he could see his beautiful son, young and vital and alive and waiting for him. Waiting to help him begin again.

Lottie was awake the instant she heard the lorry in the driveway, but it was Lars who opened the door, holding her gun in his hand, motioning her to stay back inside the house. Kobus stood outside, gesturing over his shoulder for the three remaining men to bring in the body. They laid it inside on the dining table, wrapped in a grey, bloodstained blanket. Jan's eyes were closed, and his expression was soft. Almost childlike. Lottie stared at her husband's body from a distance and then ran from the room without a word.

'We got the bastards. All of them. Sorry about Jan, but he went in without giving the signal. No back-up. I don't know what got into him.' Kobus shrugged. 'Tell Lottie I'm sorry. I'll talk to her in the morning. Just as well you're here, man. You'd better start cleaning him up, and we'll arrange the funeral as soon as we can get hold of the undertaker. Can't delay in this heat.'

He left the house, slamming the door behind him. Lars stood beside the body, listening to the sound of Lottie's weeping behind the closed door of the bedroom, thinking of Hannah and Suniva, whom he loved and must protect always and at all costs. He found a large bowl in the kitchen and filled it with warm water, took several clean dish-cloths out of a drawer, and searched for a pair of scissors. When he had set them down on the sideboard, he made his way to the linen cupboard and pulled out a clean sheet. He bathed the spatters of blood from Jan's face and then began to cut open his shirt. There was a letter in the breast pocket and Lars removed it, thinking that it might be a last message for Lottie. He began to read, his face blanching with sorrow.

When he had scanned the first paragraph he took the cigarette lighter from his pocket and watched as the flame consumed the last tragedy of Jan van der Beer's troubled life.

Chapter 15

Kenya, May 1967

It was late in the evening when the dogs began to bark and Hannah heard the sound of a car.

'It's Lars!' she called out to Anthony as she ran down the verandah steps. 'Lars! Thank God you're here. When I got the telegram I didn't know what—' She stopped in mid-sentence, as a second figure emerged into the dusk. 'Ma? Ma? Is it really you? Ma! Ach, I'm so happy!'

She rushed to embrace Lottie who stood, unmoving, in the driveway with her daughter's arms wound tight around her. Hannah was laughing with delight. Lars had achieved the impossible. He had brought her mother back to the farm to see her grandchild. Dear, wonderful Lars.

'You are so amazing,' she said to him, still clinging to Lottie's hand. 'How did you talk her into coming, into leaving—'

Her words died as she noticed her mother's unnatural stillness. 'What's wrong? What has happened?' Then her hands flew to her mouth. 'Has something happened to Pa?'

'My darling.' Lars gathered her into his arms. 'He's gone, Hannah. He was killed in an ambush. Shot down. It was very fast, and he wouldn't have felt any pain. The lines at the house were down, and I couldn't reach you. I was going to use a neighbour's phone, but then your mother and I thought it would be better if I was here when you heard the news. That's why the telegram only said that I was coming back. I've brought Lottie home so that we can all help each other through.'

'Pa is dead? He can't be. I never . . . Ma? Oh, Ma, I can't believe this.'

'It's true.' Lottie put her arms around Hannah. 'I thought it would be too hard for you to bear the news alone, with Lars so far away.'

'God, oh dear God. Ma, you didn't leave him in that horrible place? He wouldn't want to be left there alone.' She stepped away from Lottie, her voice rising.

Lars held her face in his hands and spoke with his lips close to her ear. 'He was cremated the day before yesterday,' he said. 'It was the only thing to do, in the circumstances.'

'We had no choice,' Lottie said. 'With the heat, and the time that had passed, there was no other way. I have brought his ashes home.'

'Let's go inside now, Han,' Lars said gently. 'Look, here are Mwangi and Kamau to greet your mother.'

They stood aside as the two men came forward and took Lottie's hands, murmuring their sorrow, tears running down the furrows of their old cheeks as they heard her news. Bwana Jan had been a good man. They were so sorry that he was gone. *Pole sana*. After a few moments they retreated to the kitchen, Kamau shaking his grizzled head. When would this curse be finished? Was there no stronger magic, no spell that would counteract the power of Simon Githiri's evil? Now Bwana Lars was the only one left to take care of the women. Would he be the next victim?

'Lottie? My dear Lottie.' Anthony came out on to the verandah and embraced her.

'Anthony, man.' Lars shook his friend by the hand. 'It was good of you to take care of everything. And you see who has come home. But I'm afraid we have some bad news.'

When Lottie had settled in an armchair, close to the crackle and blaze of the log fire, Lars took Hannah aside, kissing her face, putting his arm around her and keeping her close beside him.

'Your mother is at breaking point,' he said. 'Exhausted. But we will sit down now, so that I can explain what happened. And then you will bring Suniva. Because that will surely help to bring Lottie a little light and happiness. She has been through too much.'

Lars told the story in plain terms, but it was a kindly version, from which he omitted details that he felt were unnecessarily painful. There was no mention of Jan's drinking or violent behaviour. Nor did he repeat Kobus's assertion that Jan had walked out into the line of fire, uncaring and unprotected. And the letter he had found and destroyed would never come to light. There had been too much suffering already. Instead, he concentrated on the good things he remembered about his father-in-law, and tried to make it appear that Jan had died bravely in an unexpected ambush.

Lottie sat and stared into the fire, thinking of her last sight of the wooden box sliding away into the crematorium. When they had closed Janni's coffin she had felt her own spirit shut in there with him. Suffocating in a dark place, feeling as though the flames were searing her too. She had hoped for an ending, a sense of peace. But it had not yet come to her. In those last months, she had grown almost to hate the man her husband had become. Sometimes, when he left the house after an episode of drunken abuse, she had found herself hoping that he would not come back. Then she would be racked with guilt, for wishing that any harm should come to the father of her beloved children, no matter how he might have changed. But as the dreary weeks and months dragged on, broken only by the rages of a hopeless man, she was assailed by weariness and a longing to escape. She had turned away her chance of love, of a new beginning, and she felt trapped in the grim, termite-ridden house and by the cruelty and squalor in which she lived. She longed to be somewhere clean and quiet, to be alone.

Now it was over but she did not know if there could be any freedom from suffering, even in the finality of Janni's passing. When she thought of him, she saw his red, sweating face, his raised fist, and heard his voice loud with fury and recrimination.

On that night, after Lars had cleaned the body and laid it out on the makeshift bier, Lottie had crept into the room to look at her husband. A bloated corpse, riddled with gunshot wounds, lying on a table in this miserable house, under the glare of a naked light bulb. This was what he had come to. Gazing down at the ruin of the man to whom she had given her best years, she had seen only the waste of life that had brought him to this last indignity. She found that she could not touch him, and she was ashamed of her inability to give him a last benediction of love and compassion. On the bright, joyous morning of their wedding day she had sworn she would never abandon him, no matter what happened. But now she wondered if the cost of that promise had been too high. Because there was nothing left of her to give to anyone. Back in her old home, with her one surviving child, she felt paralysed. Unable to break free from the constraints of despair that had overtaken her since Janni's death. So she sat, huddled and alone in the company, unable to speak or to touch the food that was brought for her.

It was the sight of her grandchild that began the transformation in

Lottie. For the first time in many weeks she smiled out of pure delight. The little girl, with her wide, happy smile, reminded her of Hannah at the same age and brought back memories of a family life that had been taken from her. She wanted to say something about the joy of holding the baby for the first time, but she could not speak. Instead she sat and rocked the child, holding tight to this one symbol of hope in a world of chaos.

Anthony guided them gently through the evening, describing an expedition he had undertaken with Piet in the Mountains of the Moon, recalling fishing and hunting expeditions that he had shared with Jan, coaxing Lottie into eating a few morsels and insisting that she sip a little brandy, turning on the radio to listen to the familiar tones of the BBC World Service. At last Lottie rose and embraced each one of them.

'I must go to bed,' she said. 'It's been a long, long day. Lars, I don't know what I would have done without you. And Hannah must feel the same about you, Anthony. You are exceptional young men, and the best friends that anyone could wish for.'

'Lars will put Suniva in her cot,' Hannah said. 'And I'll help you to get ready for bed, and see that you have everything you need.'

'Goodnight, Lottie, my dear,' Lars said. 'Anthony, thanks again for holding the fort. I'll see you in the morning.'

'Glad I could help. I'm heading out on my sales trip next week, so I'll leave after breakfast tomorrow. There are things I have to do in the office before I take off.'

'I'll talk to you on the phone before you leave,' Lars said, taking the baby. 'And now I'll put my daughter to bed. A pleasure I've missed out on these last few days.'

It was not long before Hannah opened the door and slipped into their bedroom.

'Lottie has gone to bed?' Lars asked, looking at his wife's tired face. She nodded and he held out his hand to her. 'Han,' he said. 'Come and let me hold you. I missed you being close to me. Every moment of every long day and night.'

She lay down beside him, with her head on his chest.

'Did you tell him?' she asked, after a long silence. 'Did he know why Simon killed Piet? Did Pa know that, before he went out on the patrol?'

'Yes, he knew. They both knew. It was a dreadful business, breaking that news. I don't think I handled it well, but . . . I tried my best. That was all I could do.'

'I never spoke to him. Never made it up,' she whispered. 'And now it's too late. He died thinking I hated him. And I did. I blamed him for what happened to Piet. But I should have tried to understand, because he was my pa.'

'He struggled for years with what he did. I don't think he ever forgave himself.' Lars stroked her hair. 'Given time, you would have found a way back to him.'

'It's Ma who is the worst off. Four long years in that place with no one to love her or take care of her.' Hannah's voice was breaking. 'In the bedroom she put her arms around me and I could feel her shaking underneath. And when I tried to talk about it, she just shook her head and didn't speak. I helped her into bed, and then she just turned her face to the wall. I stayed for a while, and then I came away. I don't know what to do.'

'Be patient, Han. What is important is that she is here. She will need time to grieve, and then she will begin to find the memories of the good years. They are here too.'

'But they are buried deep. You will have to help us to find them.' She was grateful for this extraordinary man who was her life, and her refuge and her joy.

'Patience,' he repeated. 'That is what we need. Tomorrow, we will sit down together and plan a farewell for your father. Arrange for a service with the dominee, here on the farm. Jan's old friends and neighbours can come and pay their respects. Remember the good in him. Because the other – that was only a part of him for a short time. We must think of the good, Han.'

In the morning Anthony left early for Nairobi, and his sales trip. No one raised the subject of Camilla, reluctant to bring more discord and sadness into their already fraught circumstances. But Hannah embraced him with affection, grateful for his unquestioning loyalty and support.

Lottie slept until noon. When she woke, it took her some seconds to realise where she was. Beyond her door, she could hear the familiar sounds of her old home – Mwangi whistling as he polished the floor, the dogs barking, Kamau instructing the kitchen *toto* on what he should bring from the vegetable garden. And birdsong. She got up and went slowly to the window, to draw back the curtains. Outside, the garden was luminous with flowers and the lawn was velvet-green, stretching away to the boundary of shrubs she had planted so long ago. She breathed in the scent of jasmine under her windowsill, and turned to look back into the room of Hannah's childhood, glad that she was not in the bedroom that she and Jan had shared. No painful recollections here, only the echoes of her daughter's growing up. It was going to be hard, facing her old life, dealing with the darkest memories. But the past could not be undone, and she had to find a way to move on. For the moment she would help Hannah and Lars to build a future for themselves and the child, and in doing so her own path might become clear. She showered and dressed with care, and went to look for her daughter.

In the afternoon they discussed the arrangements for the memorial service. Lars had telephoned the dominee and fixed a date for the weekend, allowing time for newspaper announcements and for old friends to make travel arrangements where necessary. Hannah was amazed at her mother's extraordinary transformation from the previous night. Lottie made decisions about the service and the guests and the catering, delving into some hidden reserve that Hannah envied.

'There is one important thing I want to settle now,' Lottie said. 'I would prefer it if only the three of us scatter his ashes. I don't think I could—' Her voice wavered, and she put a hand up to her eyes. 'No people watching this last journey, except his family. I'd like to do it tomorrow. Is that all right?'

'Where do you want to scatter them?' Hannah asked. 'On the ridge? Beside Piet's cairn?'

'No!' Lottie cried out. She covered her face for a moment before she could continue. 'No. I couldn't bear that. I think the river. Where the deep pool is, and the big trout he was always after.'

Lars nodded. 'And the river will carry him on, through his land. Ja. That is a good choice.' He stood up. 'I am going out to look at the wheat now, and to drive round the fences with Juma. Hannah, you and Lottie might like to take the baby for a walk. But take David with you. I do not want you going anywhere alone.'

In the end, the rain kept them in the house, where they watched over the baby as she rolled and crawled on the rug and played with the dogs. Lottie looked at Hannah, noting the signs of tension she was trying to hide.

'Do you want to tell me about it?' Lottie asked, after a while. 'About what you felt when the Kikuyu girl walked in with that child, about what she said? When Lars came, I didn't have a chance to talk to him. Our house had been burned just before he arrived. A firebomb through the window. It happens often now, on the white farms. And your pa didn't want to think about what Lars was telling us.'

'He was drunk, wasn't he?' Hannah said. 'Making sure he didn't feel anything. No, Ma, don't deny it. You can't protect him any more. What is the point? He's gone. I lived with it too, remember? I'm sorry I left you to face that on your own, but I had to find a life for myself. I wanted so much to be here on the farm, part of what Piet wanted to do.'

'You were right to leave,' Lottie said. 'I never thought otherwise.'

'I believe Pa was drunk on that last night,' Hannah said. 'He didn't want to understand what Lars told him. So he drank himself senseless, and then he walked out and got himself killed.' She saw from Lottie's eyes that she had hit on the truth. 'That is what we have to live with. What else can we do?'

'We have to hope that Simon and Karanja Mungai will be arrested. And then we will pick up what's left of our lives. And this farm.'

'It's your farm now, Ma. So you will have to decide what you want to do with it, and whether you want to stay.'

'My dear, Langani is not mine.' Lottie took her daughter's hand. 'Your father made a will. I insisted he should, if he was going to keep going out on those patrols. We could not know from day to day what might happen. So I went with him to a lawyer and he made his will. I put it in an envelope and posted it to your Uncle Sergio in Johannesburg, for safe keeping. Langani is yours, Hannah.'

Hannah sat in silence, taking in what her mother had said. In spite of their estrangement Pa had trusted her enough, loved her enough, to leave her the farm. She had been born on this land, had always worked to preserve it, although it had never truly belonged to her. But the giving of it was a poisoned chalice, because now she was tied to it more than ever before. She was also aware that Jan had made no provision for Lottie. And they had not yet discussed the implications of a court case in which Simon Githiri's defence would bring disgrace to Jan van der Beer, and the possibility of further retribution. Hannah leaned her head into her mother's lap, like a small child.

'This place is yours as well, Ma. It's your home to live in too. You know Lars and I would be happy to—'

'I know I can always come here, and spend time with you and your wonderful Lars,' Lottie said. 'But I don't think I could live here again. I will stay for a while, to help you. I should have done that long ago, Hannah. I shouldn't have—'

'He needed you more. I don't know how you stuck by him. But we're together now. And that's good, isn't it?'

Lottie looked away into the distance, thinking of the glowing Italian countryside, and the man who wanted her to join him there. Mario. Their affair in Johannesburg had been so brief, but they had known immediately that they could share a future. He had written to her regularly since then, love letters that she treasured and read, again and again, to keep her soul alive. But it was too soon to think about him. Or too late. She must see to Hannah now. Make up for what they had lost.

'Yes,' she said. 'We are together again, and that is good.' She stood up, smoothing her hair back, bracing herself. 'I'm going to ring Sergio now. I told him I would let him know when I had decided what to do. I'd like him to come for the memorial service if he can get away. You should contact Sarah, too. She would want to know about Janni, because she always loved him. And Camilla. Lars told me all that she tried to do here. He said she went back to England, because Anthony hurt her.'

'I'll write to Camilla,' Hannah said. 'I bet she's over Anthony by now. She's so beautiful and famous and successful, and it can't be long before someone comes along and blows the last of him out of her mind. I met her manager, Tom, when he came for her fashion gala. I think he's in love with her, although she hasn't noticed it. And Sarah said the doctor who operated on her face is mad about her too.'

'She has a brittle surface,' Lottie said. 'She always was a fragile, lonely girl who was easily hurt. I'm sorry it didn't work out with Anthony. He's a good man, until it comes to his dealings with the opposite sex. Tell me about Sarah.'

'She's going to be famous too. With her book. It will be coming out in the spring.' Hannah hesitated, then decided on the truth. 'We had an argument. I said some bad things to her and I don't know if she has forgiven me. I've spoken to her on the radio, but that's all.'

'She's not one to hold a grudge,' Lottie said. 'Too generous in spirit. If

380

she comes down for the service, maybe you should take a few days off and go back with her to Buffalo Springs. It would be good for you.' She kissed her daughter's forehead.

The idea of going to Buffalo Springs was appealing. But Hannah thought she might not be wanted there. She went in search of Lars.

'Would you mind if I went to stay with Sarah for a few days? I mean, if she comes down for Pa's service, maybe I could go back with her.'

Lars made the radio call at once and Sarah's reaction carried its own static in the air. She would be at the memorial service. And take Hannah back with her.

'Maybe you should leave the baby here with me,' Lars said. 'It might be good to have the time to yourself, and Lottie would love to look after her.'

But Hannah would not consider leaving Suniva behind. Not at Langani. Not while Simon Githiri was still at large. The thought of being separated from the child was terrifying. Impossible. When Lars saw the panic in her eyes, he did not press the issue.

The clouds cleared briefly on the following morning. They made their way down the riverbank in silence. The ground was moist from the rain, and a rich, loamy smell rose from the print of their footsteps. Sun-stars glinted on the rushing water, bouncing off the ripples as the wind stirred the surface. All around them was the music of the bush, the whistle and whirr of bird calls, the rasp of insects, and the distant bark of zebra on the plains. A kingfisher dived for minnows, feathers flashing cobalt and orange and turquoise, and the stones along the bank shone like marble. A rocky island broke the flow of the current, creating small eddies and channels, dappled green from the reflected leaves of overhanging branches. The sound of water filled the bright air, and a trout rose suddenly in a silver arc, to capture a fly and sink from sight again. Lottie stood on the shingle, her hands holding the urn that she had carried to Janni's final destination.

'Do you want to say anything, Lottie?' Lars asked, with his arm around Hannah's shoulders.

'Only this,' she said. 'You are home now, Janni. This land that took so much from you must now give you rest. I pray that your presence here will end all the vengeance and hatred. Your debt has been paid. And if you are watching us from some better place, then I beg you to ask for protection for your family. And peace. I wish you peace.'

She opened the lid and tipped the ashes into the swirl of the river. Grey particles hung for a second in the sunlight, then drifted down into the water and faded away like a sigh. Hannah leaned against her husband.

'Goodbye, Pa,' she said softly. 'I loved you. Goodbye.'

She turned, her eyes filled with tears, and strode up the path from the bank. Lottie stood for a while with her head bowed. Then she handed the urn to Lars.

'Throw it as far as you can,' she said. 'Into the deepest part of the river. It is empty. I do not want to bring it home.'

She walked away from him and did not look back. Lars took the small, metal chalice that was all that remained of a life. Only the inside was still smudged with the evidence of Janni's passing.

'I am sorry, old friend, that it ended this way,' he said. 'May God grant us all peace.'

With a last murmured farewell, he gripped the vessel in his palm. His arm swung wide and high, and he watched as it sailed into the air and splashed down in a foam of bubbles a great distance downstream.

In the arid surroundings of Buffalo Springs the countryside was spattered with a mass of wild flowers and the stubble of new grass. Sarah had been out, following the elephants in this newly watery paradise, observing and photographing their behaviour now that the grazing was plentiful again. Rabindrah was still in camp. His car had been towed into Isiolo and Uncle Indar had sent a mechanic from Nairobi. But more spares were needed and there was a delay. The extra days allowed him to regain some of the strength that had been sucked out of him by his illness. The day after the fever broke, Sarah had argued with him about leaving for Nairobi.

'I should go tomorrow,' he had said, when he woke from his first fever-free sleep. 'Dan and Allie have put up with me for long enough. And if you are sitting around looking after me, then I am hampering your work.'

'Not at all,' she said. 'I can't drive far at the moment. Most of the tracks were washed away in the storm, or reduced to quagmires, and all the *luggas* are full of water. Erope and I are tired of digging the Land Rover out of holes and ditches. I've been doing short excursions near to the camp, and catching up on paperwork. Most of Dan's charts were blown away or soaked through, and we've been trying to reconstruct them from the blotchy remains. Allie's notebooks are damp, too. I've been drying them in the sun and typing up what's still legible inside.'

'The storm took you by surprise, then,' Rabindrah said.

'Yes. We weren't paying enough attention to the clouds. They'd been threatening for so long that we'd stopped watching the sky.'

She perched on the edge of his bed and handed him some barley water. His hand trembled with weakness as he held the glass to his lips and she wanted to reach out and steady it for him, but she sat still. It was a relief that he had not been conscious of the foolish thing she had done. It had been a spur of the moment reaction, she told herself, born out of the relief that he had come safely through the night. Dealing with severe illness did that to you – broke down your natural reserve.

'You've been very kind.' He was looking at her directly, and his voice sounded croaky. Probably from the aftermath of the fever and the vomiting, she thought. 'Every time I woke up, you were there. You must have been up day and night.'

'It was no trouble.' She smiled. 'My dad used to get malaria often, so I know the drill. And Allie did her share too, keeping you warm or cooling you down. I'm glad you're over the worst of it. We were worried about you.'

'It's not an experience I would like to repeat,' he said. 'But I've recovered now, and I shouldn't impose on you any longer.'

Sarah looked at him, at the drawn, thin face, the whites of his eyes still yellowed from the malaria and the medicine. All her protective instincts rose. She knew that she wanted him to stay, so that she could look after him. But she did not think she could say that. It was ridiculous and it would certainly embarrass him. She was embarrassed by the idea herself.

'You're not ready for that journey,' she said. 'The roads are treacherous – miles of slippery mud that require concentration and physical strength. You have to keep going at a steady pace and not stop at all, or you'll get stuck.'

'I'm a good driver,' he said. 'I've driven with Indar Uncle in the East African Safari Rally. You can't get into worse conditions than that.'

'Right now you don't have enough *nguvu* to dig yourself out,' she said firmly. 'Anyway, your uncle's mechanic has gone back to Nairobi for more parts. He left on the bus from Isiolo this morning. That was a wild ride you had up there. So you're stranded until the spares arrive, and then the mechanic can drive you down.'

'But I could get a lift on a plane, or in a safari car from Samburu, or—'

'No buts.' She leaned forward and took the glass from him, putting her finger across his lips to silence his protests. 'You've been seriously ill, and you need rest.'

'Your employers can't be happy that I'm still here,' he said.

'Dan was angry about the Shifta story being connected with his camp,' Sarah said. 'But that's all past, and they think well of you. Now, relax and get some sleep.'

His hand stretched out and covered hers, and then he raised it and put his lips against her wrist. She felt a jolt like electricity pass through her as he touched her skin. His eyes were closed.

'And you, Sarah,' he said. 'What do you think of me?'

She gazed at him in silence, tingling from the pressure of his mouth, shocked by the desire she had to lean across and slide her arms underneath him, and kiss him again. She had not felt this way for a long time. Not since Piet. With a shiver of guilt, she drew her hand away and busied herself, fussing with the bed covers around him.

'I think you're remarkable,' she said. 'You have integrity and courage and vision, and you're a little crazy. A good mix. But most of all you're a sick man in need of rest. And food. I'm going to organise something for you to eat.'

She stood up and left the room quickly, rushing away from him before she could make a fool of herself. Before she was forced to analyse what she had felt.

Rabindrah lay with his eyes closed, drawing in the scent of her and the memory of the kiss she had bestowed on him. He had been in the grip of the fever, but he did not think he had imagined it. It was good karma that he could not travel for the time being. It would give him a chance to be sure. The rain began again, spattering down on to the soggy ground, dripping from the thatch outside his window. He hoped that Indar Uncle was short of spares.

'How's the patient?' Dan looked up from his papers as Sarah ducked in from the downpour. Allie gave her a knowing smile and she flushed. Nothing ever escaped Allie's sharp eyes.

'The fever is gone,' Sarah said. 'If his temperature goes up tonight it won't be all that high. He's been sleeping, but now I'm going to get him something to eat. Then he can sit up for a while. He'll be very weak for the next few days. I don't think he could drive himself to Nairobi.'

Dan leaned back in his chair and took off his glasses. 'There's no rush about Rabindrah leaving,' he said. 'Unless he's desperate to file his article about almost getting murdered by the Shifta?'

Sarah laughed. 'He's in a bit of a tizzy about being here. He feels guilty about taking up time and space.'

'Hmm. I guess he took his dressing-down to heart.' Dan grinned at her. 'Well, you go and tell him he's welcome to stay as long as he likes. Provided he steers clear of bandits and government officials. I don't want any of those dropping in on us.'

Sarah collected a bowl of soup and some bread from the kitchen, and carried it back to the guest quarters. Rabindrah was out of bed and leaning heavily on the back of the chair, his face grey and covered in sweat. Sarah crossed the room in a few strides and helped him back into bed.

'What on earth are you doing up?' she said, alarmed at his pallor.

'I thought I'd ask for hot water and have a shower. But my legs are not working too well.'

'No, you idiot, of course they're not. You can't go anywhere right now, except between that chamber pot and your bed.' She saw him flush, and realised she had been too outspoken. Young Indian ladies would probably not discuss such delicate matters with unrelated menfolk. 'Sorry if I sounded crude. But I'm a doctor's daughter, and you're my patient. Now, here's some soup and bread to put inside you. You haven't eaten anything for days. It's no wonder you're weak.'

She saw how his hand still shook so she sat down on the edge of the bed, took the spoon and fed him.

'Dan is coming in to see you later,' she said. 'He won't let you leave until he thinks you're fit.'

He nodded and finished the meal in silence. When she wiped his hands and face with a cool cloth he thanked her and closed his eyes again, and made a small sound of frustration. She wondered if he was uncomfortable at being so dependent, unable to do the simplest things for himself. And he did look a mess, clammy and unshaven and in need of a wash. During the worst of the fever, she and Allie had bathed him frequently. But it might be as well not to mention that. She fetched a basin of hot water, and set it down on the chair beside his bed. Then she left him to his ablutions and went back to her work.

He joined them in the main building on the following evening, a little unsteady on his feet but clearly glad to be up and about.

'I wonder if I could try the radio,' he said. 'I should find out from my uncle how long it will take to get the spare parts for the car.'

'We don't have a radio right now,' Dan said. 'I haven't been able to get the damn thing going since the storm.'

'I used to be one of those radio hams,' Rabindrah said. 'Maybe I can have a look at its innards. I'm not an expert, but I had a pile of receivers and equipment in England. A collection of old junk, in fact. But I was keen on it then.'

Late in the evening, when Sarah drove into camp with Erope, the radio was crackling and hissing and Dan wore a delighted smile.

'Will you look at this, kid?' he said. 'We're part of the wide world again. Great work from Rabindrah here. Join us for a drink?'

'A cold beer would be great,' Sarah said, and she felt a small fire in her veins as Rabindrah pressed the glass into her hands.

They spent the evening listening to Dan's and Allie's stories about their early years of research when they had lived in a tent in Tsavo National Park. The flimsy shelter was frequently knocked down by hyena trying to steal their meagre supplies of fresh food, and was trampled once by an elephant taking a short cut. There was much laughter at Dan's wildly dramatic recollections and Allie's dry modifications to her husband's anecdotes. Occasionally Rabindrah leaned closer to Sarah to share a reaction, and then he would touch her arm lightly with his long fingers. But she gave no sign that she had noticed his advances and he was puzzled and frustrated. Allie watched them, saw the way Sarah sometimes glanced at him. There was a special connection between them, she thought, and a vulnerability that was touching. But each covert look was followed by a stiffening of Sarah's shoulders, as she resolutely distanced herself from closer contact.

The rain came down intermittently, but there was no further flooding. On his second day out of bed Rabindrah insisted that he was fit to go out in the Land Rover, and Sarah decided they would pay a visit to Erope's *manyatta*. The Samburu had taken two days off to help repair storm damage in his home compound. It was a rough ride over waterlogged terrain, and she soon began to regret taking Rabindrah so far. His colour was poor and she feared he was over-taxing himself, but he assured her that he was strong enough for the outing.

The *manyatta* was a sea of mud. The arrival of the rains had been welcomed, and grazing for the livestock had improved. But two of the huts had partially collapsed, and in the wet conditions rebuilding was slow. Water had seeped through cracks and fissures in the low structures, and all the kindling for the cooking fires was wet. Inside, the rooms reeked of smoke swirling up from the damp wood. Sarah and Rabindrah found themselves spluttering, and their eyes were streaming from the acrid air. Several of the children were sickly and coughing, and the smell of wet dung pervaded everything. It was an eye-opener for Rabindrah, and Sarah saw that he was shaken by the primitive conditions and the hardship he was witnessing. She moved through the enclosure, taking photographs of the desolation, searching in her pockets for sweets and crayons and paper that she had brought for the children. Seeing the place as it was now, she wondered if Rabindrah would change his mind about living with the northern nomads for a year. He might opt for another project, and then she would not see him any more. The possibility made her feel bereft, and she moved away from him to work with her camera on the other side of the *manyatta*.

'I'm going to write a piece for the paper,' Rabindrah said to her as they left the *manyatta*. 'If I can use a couple of your photographs. Erope thinks that would be acceptable to the elders and it could bring some relief into the area. There must be more *bomas* like this, or even worse off. And I think I could arrange for some food and medicine for the children. One of my cousins is a doctor in Nairobi. I'd like to be of some help.'

Erope was surprised. He was not accustomed to being offered anything by an Indian. The *duka wallahs* in the townships were not known for their generosity. They had no respect for the Samburu, and in times of hardship they were more likely to charge exorbitant prices for their goods, knowing that the tribesmen had nowhere else to go for essential supplies. But this one was offering assistance. He was different. Sarah had explained the purpose of the book, and pointed out that they were travelling in the Land Rover that the *wahindi* uncle had sent from Nairobi. Erope leaned forward and held out his hand to Rabindrah.

'*Asante*,' he said, and in that moment a mutual respect and friendship were born.

Sarah was delighted that these two men, both so important in her life, had finally accepted one another. Her smile was warm as she touched Rabindrah fleetingly on his arm, and he grasped her hand for a brief moment.

But he was shaking with fatigue by the time they reached the camp. He insisted that he would be fine after a short rest and a shower before dinner, and Sarah walked with him to his hut. As they stepped inside he closed the door and drew her against him, swaying a little with weakness, but holding her very close. She could feel his body under the material of the cotton shirt. The malaria had taken the thin layer of padding from his bones, but she seemed to fit snugly against his shape. He felt her quiver and for a moment he believed that she would let him kiss her. He drew in his breath, realising with astonishment that he had fallen totally in love with this small, determined and beautiful girl.

'Sarah,' he said, his voice soft. His arms tightened around her. 'Little Sarah . . .'

In that instant, as he spoke the endearment that Piet had always used, her body went rigid and she pulled away from him. Then she was gone from the room, leaving him stunned, the pain of her rejection like a stab wound. There was a powerful attraction between them. Rabindrah was sure that she could feel it as well as he did. He could not understand what had destroyed that wonderful, fragile moment. At the dinner table Sarah said little, letting him describe the conditions at the *manyatta*. She retired immediately after the meal had been served, and Dan took a lamp and returned to his charts. Allie was left with Rabindrah.

'A little drop of brandy might kick-start your system again,' she said.

'I want to thank you for your kindness.' He accepted the generous measure she had poured. 'I'll be on my way as soon as it's possible, but I hope to be back in a couple of months with the final proofs of our book now that Sarah has approved the layout.'

'That will be a grand day,' Allie said. 'Here's to it.'

'This idea about nomadic tribes in the north will need at least a year of research,' Rabindrah said, encouraged by her enthusiasm. 'I'm still hoping that Sarah might provide the pictures, without it taking her away from here too often. It's something that can be done a few days at a time, over a long period.'

'It's been good for her, putting this first book together. After all that happened. And it was clever of you to interest your publisher in northern nomads. Fortuitous.' She gave him a searching glance, and in the lamp-light she thought she saw him flush. But he looked her straight in the eye.

'You're right,' he said. 'John Sinclair is keen to publish more of Sarah's work. She would be ideal for portraits of nomadic life, because she sees and understands more than any photographer I know.'

'Come on, Rabindrah. You're not fooling me for a moment,' Allie said. 'It's not just her talent as a photographer that interests you.'

'You're a smart woman, Allie.' He swirled the brandy gently.

'They were madly, passionately and ideally in love, Sarah and Piet,' she said, and saw him flinch. 'She waited a long time for him and then, when everything had turned into a fairy tale, he was taken from her in the most savage way. It's hard for her to put that behind her. It may take a long, long while, because that's the kind of person she is. You'll need patience, my boy, otherwise she'll close up on you. Run like hell. And then you will have ruined your chances.'

'I can wait,' Rabindrah said. But he feared that he might have already made a fatal error. 'In the meantime, we can build on our friendship.'

'Well, I wish you luck,' Allie said. 'We're very, very fond of Sarah, and she can't go on living with the idea of what might have been. But you'll have to tread carefully.'

He was casually friendly for the next two days, going out with Erope and Sarah, making notes, steering clear of any intimacy. But he felt the strain of not expressing what was uppermost in his heart. His standing increased further in Dan's eyes, however, when he was able to cobble together a spare part for the old kerosene fridge that cooled the beer.

'Nice work,' Dan said, opening two cold Tuskers.

'We're all supposed to be good mechanics, us Sikhs,' Rabindrah said. 'Although my father wouldn't be able to put a washer on a tap. But I learned a few tricks from Indar Uncle that have proved very useful.'

They were interrupted by a burst of static from the radio. Sarah listened in horror to the news from Lars.

'It's Jan van der Beer,' she said afterwards. 'He was killed in an ambush in Rhodesia. Lars went down there and brought Lottie home to Langani. There's a memorial service the day after tomorrow.' She looked at Allie, then at Dan. 'I'll need to go down, just for a night. I'm really sorry, but I must be there.'

'Yes, you must,' Allie said as Dan nodded agreement. 'That poor girl — what a chapter of disasters. You go and help her out. Really. It's OK.'

'Lars was wondering . . .' Sarah hesitated. Rabindrah was already here, and now she was asking whether she could have another guest. 'I think he would like Hannah to come up here for a few days after the service,' she said. 'She could stay in my rondavel. But she would probably bring Suniva as well, and you might not want to have a baby here.'

'Nonsense. A baby will be marvellous, eh, Dan?' She ignored the alarm in his eyes and looked directly at Sarah. 'Bring them back with you. We'll be glad to have Hannah as long as she wants to stay.'

'Will you be all right, driving down on your own in this weather?' Rabindrah asked her the next day.

'I'll leave very early and hope it won't rain all the way,' she said.

'I'd be glad to come with you, but I don't think my presence would be appropriate,' he said. 'But I could stay in a hotel in Nanyuki. In fact, now that I think of it, I could continue to Nairobi and let the mechanic bring my car down once it's repaired.'

'No, don't do that.' Sarah was aware that her words were too emphatic. 'You're not well enough. Honestly.'

'I'll wait until you get back, then,' he said.

He had seen a flash in her eyes, and he thought that she wanted him to stay. He put his arm around her lightly, and she turned her face in to his shoulder and closed her eyes.

'If only it would all end,' she said. 'If only life could begin again without the pain and the bad memories and the guilt.'

'It will,' Rabindrah said, touching her hair, his heart jumping. 'Soon that is how it will be.'

Sarah left at dawn on the day of the service, driving the long miles on a slippery surface, stopping several times as heavy showers reduced her visibility to zero. But mostly she crawled along, trying to keep a steady momentum, afraid that she would get stuck and be stranded alone for hours. The drive felt endless. These days she always seemed to be travelling towards or away from another tragedy. When she climbed down stiffly from the car, Hannah was waiting for her. Her hair was tied back in a half-plait, but her shirt was creased, her eyes dull.

'Han, I'm so sorry.' Sarah hugged her. 'So sorry. When did it happen?'

'Six or seven days ago. Ach, I don't really remember, it's a kind of blur. Lars was there. He went down to tell them about Wanjiru. That was bad enough. And Pa went out with Kobus that night and he was shot. Thank God Ma wasn't alone.'

She lapsed into silence, unable to say any more about her father. Then she took a long breath and exhaled slowly before she spoke.

'He was killed on a terrorist patrol. He died for that thug Kobus, who never gave a damn about him. Lost his life for a tobacco farm that he didn't own and never cared about. What an end, heh?'

'Poor, poor Janni. He was such a wonderful part of my childhood.'

'I don't even remember what childhood felt like,' Hannah said. 'I'm so tired, and I've hardly slept in weeks. Years maybe. Let's go inside and find Ma. She's looking forward to seeing you.'

'Sarah, my dear. I am glad you could be with us,' Lottie said. 'Come and have some lunch after making that awful journey, all by yourself. And then you can rest a little. The service is not until four. My brother Sergio is arriving this afternoon. He flew from Johannesburg yesterday, and is driving up now.'

At lunchtime, Lottie ate very little. She sat crumbling a piece of bread on to her plate, staring at the place where Jan had once presided over his table. She was still beautiful, Sarah thought, and always would be. There was something regal about her now, and her courage shone through, illuminating the large, dark eyes and the generous smile that had not changed. Her face was pale with the effort of sitting at the dining table, trying not to think of the service ahead and the image of Janni that she would have to portray to their old friends. His empty chair spoke to her of apparitions. Like Banquo brooding at Macbeth's feast, she thought. Piet, and now Janni, bloodied and present, just beyond her vision. *Stand not upon the order of your going, but go at once* . . . She had tried so hard to persuade Hannah to leave the farm after Piet's death. Maybe they should all have left the madness that had overtaken them. Perhaps that was what Hannah and Lars should do now, before the last remnants of Langani Farm crumbled into the African dust.

Later, from her bedroom window, Sarah saw Lottie in the garden. She had a basket over her arm and secateurs in her hand, and she was cutting flowers for the service, moving as if in a trance. We are all like automatons, Sarah thought. Going through the motions. The past was not something you could put away from you in this place. Memories crowded in at every turn, in every room, the happier ones as difficult to bear as the tragedies, because they offered, for a fleeting, tantalising instant, the joy that had been snatched away. No matter where Sarah looked, indoors or out, the ghosts rose up to meet her. She put her hands up to her eyes in weariness, longing to escape. The rain had held off, but the sky was overcast and the mountain looked menacing, a smudge of dark blue covered in sullen clouds, hunched and brooding over the land.

They were all oppressed by the thought of the memorial service, and the strain of preserving Janni's good name among those coming to bid him farewell. And if Simon Githiri was found and brought to trial, what of Janni's legacy then, or the future of the farm? The thought of the young Kikuyu filled Sarah with revulsion. If the police captured him he would probably be executed, and who could disagree with such a verdict? But the white officers who had killed his father had never been judged culpable. Granted, there had been an amnesty at the end of the Emergency. Thousands of Mau Mau fighters had come out of the forests and walked free, after years of indiscriminate killing. But still, to roast a man over a fire? To sit by and hear him screaming as his flesh seared and bubbled on a spit? These were the casualties of war, the law decreed, like Jan's murdered brother. Jan must always have feared that one day there would be a reckoning. But he had not dreamed that the vengeance would be visited on his son. Her beloved Piet. Sarah's thoughts became a maelstrom, and she went outside in order to distance herself from her solitary musings. A robin chat was singing, and the sun had begun to emerge from the clouds so that the wide plains were transformed into a place of dappled beauty, like an Impressionist painting. Perhaps the most costly painting ever coveted or owned.

Sergio arrived while they were still in the garden, and Lottie's relief and gratitude were palpable when she greeted her brother. But Sarah wondered if he knew the whole truth behind the tragedy.

People began to arrive around four o'clock, when the sun had vanished and rain threatened once more. Jeremy Hardy came with his wife, and old Dr Markham was a comforting presence. Many of the local farming community appeared, including the Murrays who were the closest neighbours. Old friends offered awkward words of condolence and stood talking among themselves. Hannah was relieved that the weather was too inclement to think of holding the service out on the lawn. The last ceremony there had been her wedding, and when she thought of that day, with all its joy and promise, she could not bear the shadow of her father's life and death casting its gloom over such a treasured memory.

The service was held in the sitting room. Lottie had arranged a table laden with flowers and a framed photograph of Jan. He was standing down by the river, looking straight into the camera. A genial giant of a man, with his wife clasped in the shelter of his arm, and his son and daughter at his side. It was Lottie's favourite image of him, the one she had struggled to preserve against later, bitter memories. Beside the photograph, the old Afrikaans family bible lay open at the page recording his birth. Two candles flickered from silver candlesticks, making the image in the photograph shift in the light, almost as though the man was moving, smiling, raising an arm in salute to his assembled friends.

It was a simple ceremony. The dominee invited them to remember their friend and neighbour, and to pray for him and his bereaved family in the circumstances of his tragic death. When the funeral prayers had been said, a blessing was given and the congregation sang the hymn that Hannah had chosen. Bill Murray spoke on behalf of the assembly.

'I had the privilege of knowing Jan van der Beer and his family since the day I came here, many years ago. We worked side by side, Jan and I, on our respective farms, sharing the rough and the smooth years, and helping one another out where needed. He was a good man – in all senses of the word. A man with a big heart, a loyal friend. A man of purpose who worked hard to provide for his family, and to offer a fair living to the workers on his property. That he should have died so far away from the land he loved is terribly sad. For Lottie, for Hannah and Lars, and for all of us. Coming so soon after Piet's death makes it doubly so. We, your neighbours, cannot begin to know the sorrow you are going through, but we want you to understand that we are with you as true friends. That we will do anything we can to ease your burden of grief. We stand here to support you today and every day, and to help you to defend your home and your family. We hope you will find consolation in the fact that you are not alone. May Jan rest easy now. We will always remember him with kindness and respect. God be with Lottie, and with you, Hannah and Lars and your beautiful daughter. And let us all pray that from now on, Langani will see only peace and prosperity. Amen.'

Lottie closed her eyes, wishing that it would soon be over, dreading the hours when she would have to recount the agreed version of her husband's death, listening to words of sympathy. Everything that had been said was both truth and lie, and she no longer cared to make a difference between them. Hannah felt her mother's desperation and reached out to take her hand. But later, as old friends crowded around them, anxious to offer whatever assistance they could, Lottie began to feel the benefit of the gathering. Many stayed late into the night, sharing memories and telling stories that brought affectionate laughter, and its own sense of peace.

The drive north brought a sense of release for Hannah, although for the first hour she had felt guilty at abandoning Lars and her mother.

'I have Sergio here for another week,' Lottie had said, in response to Sarah's invitation to join them. 'He has come all this way, and I want to spend time with him,' she said. 'Also, it is a pleasure to have a garden again, and I will enjoy being in the dairy and helping Lars. My darling Hannah, make the most of the break. And don't worry about anything. We will be fine, and you can talk to us from the camp.'

Hannah had leaned out of the window to wave at Lars and her mother, until distance blurred their outline. For a time she did not speak, worn down by the emotional roller coaster that she had been riding over the past weeks. Now that the memorial service was over, it was as if she had hit a wall.

'I'm not much of a companion,' she said at last. 'It's all I can do to breathe. Even that is an effort.'

'Then concentrate on breathing, Hannah. And relax. You haven't been able to do that for God knows how long. Look at Suniva – she's got the technique just right!'

The baby was fast asleep in her carrycot on the back seat, oblivious to heat, dust, joy or pain. Hannah reached back to touch her soft cheek, then smiled and allowed the countryside to slide past in a half-dream. The realisation that Simon Githiri was alive, followed so closely by the news of her father's death, had exploded like a meteor into the fragile defences that she had struggled to erect around her family. In the background of her consciousness she kept seeing images of her childhood. Pictures of her father, smiling, laughing, lifting her, teaching her to ride, to swim and fish and shoot, comforting her when she fell and grazed her knee. Part of her wanted to shut them down, never to dwell on them again. But she was frightened of what would rush in to replace them. Afraid of the other, secret part of Janni's life, and its deadly aftermath.

There was a tacit agreement not to talk about Langani. It was Hannah who brought up the subject of Tim.

'I don't know what he's up to,' Sarah said. 'Dad says he's back at work but very down. And Deirdre has never showed up again. But there's something you don't know.'

She told Hannah the whole story, describing her own anger and confusion at the discovery that Tim was in London, and the secret between himself and Camilla from which she had been excluded.

'He's hopeless, Tim, but sort of wily at the same time,' Hannah said.

'What on earth do you mean?'

'Well, he looks so rumpled and sweet. Whenever he gets into a mess he takes on that helpless, confused look. And soon everyone has dropped what they're doing and they're all caught up in solving his problems.'

'Yes, I suppose that's true,' Sarah said, with the beginnings of a smile. 'I'd never considered him in that light. But I have rescued him from many a scrape myself. And maybe Camilla has been cast in that role. But she should have made some effort to explain. They both should.'

'Camilla never tells anyone anything,' Hannah said. 'She reverts to radio silence, or disappears altogether. So don't hold your breath waiting for an explanation from her.'

There was no rain during the journey, and Sarah was thankful not to have to haul the car out of mud with a baby on board. They stopped twice for a cold drink and to eat the sandwiches that Kamau had prepared. Dan and Allie were still out in the bush when they reached the camp in the afternoon. Sarah took the carrycot with the sleeping child from the Land Rover and brought it into the thatched hut. A second bed had been put into her room, and she looked at her surroundings with a fresh eye, hoping that Hannah would see them in the same light and find comfort in their simplicity.

'I think I'll just stay here till Suniva wakes up.' Hannah collapsed on to the camp bed.

'Of course. Shall I rustle up something to eat, or some tea?'

'Not for me, thanks. I can't believe how tired I am. I might sleep for a while. I can't seem to keep my eyes open.'

Sarah took some notes from her desk, and settled herself under the acacia tree with a cold drink.

'How did it all work out?'

At the sight of Rabindrah she felt a small rush of gladness. She had wondered if he would still be here on her return.

'Hannah's on her last legs, I'd say. Each time she starts to rebuild, to draw in some happiness, her hopes are shattered again. God, how our lives have changed.' She leaned back in her chair. 'I wake up sometimes, feeling that I've been beaten over the head, punished for I don't know what. We've all been overtaken by such dark forces, ended up so far from the way we thought things would be. It seems utterly senseless.'

'God's grand designs. They're often hard to follow,' he said.

'I almost hate going back there now,' Sarah said, half to herself. 'We were so happy at Langani when we were at school, Hannah, Camilla and me. But the foundations have been pulled away, along with generations of love and dedication and hard work. First Piet, and then Janni. I can't imagine what Lottie will do now, or what will become of Hannah and Lars.'

The arrival of Dan and Allie from their afternoon sortie roused Hannah, and she came over to join them, holding a wakeful Suniva.

'It's so kind of you to let me come and stay,' she said. 'Hello, Rabindrah. You look as though you've recovered. Sarah wasn't sure if you'd still be here.'

'Malaria, bandits and rain have made him our prisoner,' Allie said. 'Although not in that order. You're welcome here, Hannah. I'm sorry about your father.'

Hannah nodded. It was still too difficult to speak about him. 'Have you finished with the book now?' She spoke to Rabindrah. 'When will we see a proof, or whatever you call it?'

'In about two months, when Sarah's beautiful plates are ready,' he said. 'I'm so sorry also, about your father's death. The situation down there can only get worse. I believe it will turn into a full-scale war. Was he with one of the Rhodesian regiments?'

'He wasn't fighting any war,' she said coldly. 'He was just a farmer trying to grow a few acres of tobacco. Not anyone of special importance. Caught in the crossfire, I think you'd call it. Certainly not worth following up for a newspaper article, anyway.'

'Well, I'm sorry he lost his life,' Rabindrah said, conscious of her animosity. She was a prickly one, this friend of Sarah's. He would have to be careful.

'Drinks for everyone?' Dan was in an expansive mood. 'I have a special mix for young mothers. Have one now, before you shower. Never known to fail.'

'To fail what?' Sarah asked, laughing. 'Come on, then, Dan. We'll try it.'

They sat in canvas chairs, nursing a potent mix of rum and lime and Cointreau whisked up for the occasion. Hannah felt the tension melt away as she sipped her drink and questioned Allie about her work. Later, Sarah heard her humming in the shower and smiled to herself as she gave Suniva her bottle. Hannah never could sing in tune. After dinner they sat outside under the trees, leaning back to look up at the glitter of the sky, their feet stretched out and warmed by the embers of the camp fire. In the distance they heard a lion roar, and then the heavy grunting sound before he roared again.

'There's a guy on the lookout for dinner,' Dan said. 'I hope he doesn't carry on like that all night.'

'I don't think he'll keep me awake,' Sarah said. 'I'll barely make it to my bed.'

Later, as they lay in the dark listening to the scuttle of geckos in the roof, Hannah propped herself up on her elbow.

'Sarah? Do you remember the last time we were here together? It was the summer of our twenty-first birthdays and we had promised we would spend it together. You came from Ireland, and Camilla from London. And I'd run away from Rhodesia and come home to the farm, to work with Piet. Do you remember how happy we were, and all the dreams we had then?'

'I remember.'

'Don't you think we should write to Camilla? Tell her what has happened?'

'I suppose so, yes.'

'There's no point in being angry with her over Tim,' Hannah said.

'You shouldn't make the same mistake I made, when I thought you and Lars had a secret.'

'No. It's not as though Tim is a master of deception,' Sarah said. 'And Camilla's the sort of person that would probably tell me if she was sleeping with my brother. Whether I wanted to hear it or not.'

'So?'

'We'll write to her tomorrow. Go to sleep, for God's sake, or you'll be sorry when I haul you out of bed at five-thirty in the morning.'

'I'm asleep already,' Hannah said. She lay with her eyes open, accustomed to the dark now and able to make out the shapes and shadows of the objects that surrounded her. She was bone-tired, but she had come to the moment when, closing her eyes, the images came flooding in.

'Sarah?' The response was no more than a murmur, a half-acknowledgement. 'Does Piet know we're here? Is he looking at us from somewhere?'

'I think so. I know he watches over me. Over us all.'

'But what about Pa?' Hannah asked. 'If what we learned at school is true, if what the nuns and the dominee believe is correct, then he's burning in some eternal terrible hell and he'll never escape.'

'I don't believe that at all,' Sarah said. 'I think Janni paid for everything he did long before he died. He paid his debt while he was still here. And now he is at peace.'

'I hope you're right.' Hannah lay back in the darkness, thinking of her father as she had once known him, before her innocent, orderly world had been blown apart. He hovered on the edge of her consciousness for a while and she was still struggling to see his face when she fell asleep.

The air was cool when Sarah woke at daybreak. She shook Hannah lightly and watched as she fed and changed the baby, and placed her in the carrycot. Then they carried her to the Land Rover, gurgling and waving her small arms and legs. There was no sign of Rabindrah.

'Will you come with us?' Sarah had asked him the night before.

'I think I'll stay here tomorrow,' he'd said, aware that Hannah might not be too pleased to have him on the drive, and he did not want to intrude on her grief. 'I'm sure you have things to talk about that don't require a third party.'

They drove out into the hiss and warble and chatter of birds and insects.

Sarah pointed out a handsome oryx camouflaged in the long feathery grass, and spotted both gerenuk and giraffe long before Hannah could see them. When they came to the river there was a small herd of elephants drinking and splashing themselves with trunks full of water. Above them, in the line of trees, a troupe of baboons screeched and chased one another, competing for berries and leaves, leaping and chasing through the branches, or sitting in tight groups and grooming each other's coats. A fish eagle patrolled the river and came to rest on a piece of bleached driftwood on the bank, its haunting call drifting on the soft air.

'How long is Rabindrah staying?' Hannah asked. 'I hope he doesn't raise the subject of Pa again. Start digging into the details of his death.'

'He's only here until his car is fixed. And I don't think he would dream of doing that. It's unfair to assume he writes up everything he hears about people's private grief. He's not like that at all.'

'I'm sorry,' Hannah said. 'I can see you've become very friendly with him, and he's impressed Dan and Allie too. I suppose we got off on the wrong foot, when he came to Langani that day.'

'I wasn't happy when he first appeared up here, either,' Sarah said. 'But I've enjoyed working with him.'

'Are you going to do another book together?'

'I don't know,' Sarah said. 'I'd like to, if it's possible to fit it in with what I'm doing here. It would be interesting to photograph the nomads and pastoral tribes between here and Somalia.'

'It's hard to see things straight, isn't it? God, Sarah, I hope we'll all be able to live like normal people again, one of these days. Including poor Ma.'

'Lottie is very strong. Janni was lucky that she stood by him through all those years.'

'But she didn't love him any more. How could she, when he had become such a soak?' Hannah was speaking with brutal honesty. 'It must have been desperately lonely, and he sometimes turned violent. I never understood why she wouldn't leave him. I don't think I could make that kind of sacrifice for someone who hurt me. I'm not that good a person. I still can't believe what he did, Sarah. My own father.'

'He paid a terrible price, Han.'

'It was Piet who paid the price,' Hannah said. 'With his life. And I can't forgive Pa for that. He should have stayed on, or warned us at least. That might have saved Piet from Simon Githiri. You know, I hated them equally, Pa and Simon, when I first understood what it was all about. I was barely able to tell which one I hated more.' Her voice was wretched. 'I should have sent Pa a message with Lars. Anything. But I didn't, and now it's too late.'

'He knows, Hannah. He knows everything now.'

Two days passed and Hannah's face softened as she fell into the routine of the camp life. Her smiles were wide and more frequent, and she began to look like the strong, optimistic girl that she had been before Piet's death.

'Aren't you coming with us this morning?' she said to Rabindrah on the second day. 'Or have you lost interest in Sarah and her elephants, now that you've finished your book?'

'Of course not,' he said, rising to the bait.

'Ach, if looks could kill,' Hannah said, laughing loudly. 'I hope you don't have one of those daggers hidden on you?'

'That's what Camilla wanted to know, too.' Sarah was grinning, adding to his discomfort.

'You're in a good position to know that,' Hannah said. 'You and Allie had him at your mercy for days, looking after him like a baby.'

'Now I'm sure I don't want to come out with you,' Rabindrah said, beginning to laugh as well. 'In any case, I've been promoted to camp mechanic. There's something Dan wants me to do this morning. A surprise. And talking of mechanics, my car should be fixed by tomorrow evening.'

Sarah felt her spirits plummeting. Now that he was going, there were things she wanted to say to him. But she was not entirely sure what they were, and she was afraid to analyse them or to try and find the words. He was watching her face, his own expression unreadable. She looked away, confused, wishing she could explain. More than that, she wanted to put her arms around him, ask him to be patient, not to give up on her. But she did not see how she would get an opportunity, with Hannah here.

When they returned in the evening, Allie was sitting under the acacia tree, writing. She glanced up and rolled her eyes.

'They almost burnt down the stores this afternoon,' she said. 'Hope you like the results.'

It was a vital piece of equipment, Dan explained as they gathered before

400

dinner. He and Rabindrah had designed and made it together, using some old pipes and a welding torch. The square structure looked like a small cage, but it had a wooden platform with a series of screws and wing bolts attached.

'It's for your cameras,' Dan said. 'This part can be bolted on to the top of your Land Rover and you can screw your cameras into the top to keep them steady. What do you think, kid? Come on, let's go and fit it right away.'

Sarah found herself on the verge of tears as she gazed at him, so conscious of her welfare, so anxious to see her happy. Rabindrah was looking at her with the same intensity that had unnerved her when they had first met, but there was a smile in the gold-flecked eyes. She hugged Dan and then Rabindrah too, and Allie squeezed her arm with deep affection as they watched the menfolk fastening the strange contraption on to her vehicle.

'This calls for a celebration,' Dan announced. 'And it's a farewell party tonight. Rabindrah's leaving tomorrow.'

'Would you mind taking me as far as Nanyuki?' Hannah asked him at dinner. 'It would save me having to take the bus from Isiolo. It's time I got back to work.'

'You're welcome to come with me,' Rabindrah said, but inwardly he was not best pleased at the thought of three or four hours alone in a car with Hannah.

They dispersed soon after dinner, in spite of Dan's protestations. Hannah declined a third nightcap on the grounds that she had to pack for the morning. She lifted up the baby and headed off to Sarah's hut while Allie took her husband firmly by the arm and led him away to their quarters. When Rabindrah stood up, Sarah rose from her chair. He hesitated for a moment before taking her hand.

Inside the rondavel she stood frozen and shy, not sure what to do or say next. The door swung closed with a small, groaning sound and he pulled her close and kissed her. She put her arms around him as his fingers trailed over her skin. He led her over to the narrow bed and they lay down together, face to face, looking at one another, kissing again and again. Her sandals clattered to the floor as he put his hand into the thick mass of her hair. She pressed herself into his body, feeling his hands move along her back and slide up under her cotton shirt, setting fire to her skin.

'I don't know,' she whispered. 'I don't know if—'

'It's all right,' he said as he drew away from her. His expression was already distant as she sat up and put her feet on to the floor.

'I'm sorry,' she said miserably.

'You're going to tell me you need time to think. And you do. You need to decide what you want, whether you will ever allow someone new into your heart. And whether it could be me, an Indian journalist, a man with a different colour skin, from a different culture.'

'It's not about who you are,' she said, hurt by his insinuation.

'It's about who I'm not.' Rabindrah lay back and stared at the ceiling. 'Because I am not Piet van der Beer, and I will never be anything like him. So you must decide if you can let him go. Otherwise any man who loves you will forever be competing with a ghost.' He sat up. 'When you have figured that out, you know where to find me.'

'I'm sorry,' she said again, reluctant to leave things between them in this way. But she did not know what she could say or do that would make a difference. She stood up. 'Goodnight, Rabindrah,' she said.

'Goodnight, Sarah.'

She sat outside under the stars for a time, thinking of the way he had touched her, and of her fierce desire for him. But how could she put aside her memory of Piet whom she had loved since childhood? He was gone, but her love for him had to live on somewhere, and she did not know where or how this could be. There was something real and thrillingly alive in what she felt for Rabindrah and she desperately wanted him to kiss her, to make love to her. Guilt rose in her as she thought of Hannah. Hannah, who was her childhood friend, who was Piet's sister, who still mistrusted Rabindrah. Hannah, who would be shocked at the thought that anyone might take her brother's place. Sarah sighed and stood up. If she stayed outside any longer, Hannah might think she was with Rabindrah. When she opened the door there was no sound. Hannah seemed to be asleep, or did not wish to talk. It was a relief, and Sarah made her preparations and slipped gratefully under the cloud of the mosquito net where only her dreams could reach her.

Rabindrah left after breakfast, with Hannah beside him in the passenger seat of his Peugeot, and Suniva in her cot on the back seat. He seemed pleased with the prospect of returning to Nairobi and was in high spirits.

There was no sign that he had been ill, except that he had lost weight. Farewells were quick and then they were gone, the car rounding a bend on the sandy track and heading for Isiolo and the main road south.

'I understand why Sarah always found comfort in this place,' Hannah said. 'I should have come up before. But we were all on safari here a few months before Piet died, and I thought it would be too hard to see it without him.'

'You look different,' Rabindrah said, surprised at the confidence. 'The strain has left your face over the last three days, and you look rested.'

'You look much better yourself,' she said, smiling at him. 'Where do you live in Nairobi? Do you have a flat somewhere? Or a house?'

'No. I'm living with my uncle. But if this book does well, then I'd like to buy a place of my own.'

'So you plan to stay in Kenya permanently?'

'I'm a Kenyan,' he said simply. 'Born and bred here. Like you.'

'Yes,' she said. But she did not feel entirely comfortable with the comparison. 'My family has been here since the turn of the century. My great-grandfather trekked up to Langani in 1906, when it was bush land. Most of the Afrikaners went further north and west. But my grandmother was very sick when they got as far as Thika, and the old man thought his favourite daughter was going to die. So three of the wagons stopped there for a month. And some Britisher they met offered them the land that is now Langani. For a while, I think they felt they'd made a mistake in not sticking with the rest of the Boers who had come from Cape Town on the same boat. But they stuck it out, and I'm the third generation on the farm.'

'My mother's family came from farming stock,' he said. 'In the Punjab.'

'I thought Sikhs were all soldiers,' Hannah said. 'A kind of warrior class in India who came here in the British Army.'

'That's a myth that has grown up around us,' Rabindrah said. 'Many Sikhs are farmers. The militant part of Sikhism only started at the end of the seventeenth century, and those who joined its ranks were called "Singhs" or Lions. When the British arrived in India, these Sikhs became an important part of the British Army, and were then brought here as soldiers and police, and guards on the railway. My grandfather arrived here in 1898. And later he sent for his wife, and two of his brothers. He only died last year, aged ninety-three.'

'So your family was different from the humble coolies who laid the tracks, then?'

'The Sikhs working on the railway line were mainly skilled workmen. Blacksmiths and masons and carpenters. Apparently the man-eating lions in Tsavo were especially partial to Sikhs and ate quite a few. But there are many Sikh sawmill owners, and sorghum farmers, and people with big garages like my uncle.'

'Is it true that anyone of any denomination is welcome to visit your temples, and to eat in the community centres?' Hannah had heard this but had never put it to the test.

'Absolutely true,' Rabindrah replied. 'I'll take you to one of the temples next time you're in Nairobi, if you like. You met my cousin Lila, at the fashion gala. She'd be happy to show you round the temples and to take you to the bazaar and the spice shops.'

'I'd like that,' Hannah said, fascinated by the idea. She had never been in an Indian home or place of worship. 'I can't imagine the dominee welcoming Hindus or Muslims, or even Catholics, into his church and feeding them.'

'We are not so bad, you see,' Rabindrah said, his smile twisted. 'Not all of us are *duka wallahs* who mistreat our African staff and force our children into arranged marriages.'

'I'm not ignorant enough to believe that,' Hannah said, flushing. 'And I'm sorry we got off to a bad start last year. After all the newspaper articles about my brother's death, I became very wary of journalists. I was scared when you suddenly turned up at the farm, because I thought you were going to rake it all up again. But I know you were responsible for our finding this man Karanja. And that you've become a good friend to Sarah.'

'It's an honour,' he said, 'to be counted among her friends.'

'Yes. And there is something else I'd like to say, even though it's hard.' Hannah hesitated, then took the plunge. 'I'm grateful that you haven't brought up the subject of my father again, or treated me as if I was a part of the terrible thing that he did. I know that if Simon is caught, and all this comes out in court, you will still be a friend to Sarah. And I hope to me.'

Rabindrah nodded, his face calm and his mind racing. What was it that Jan van der Beer had done? Hannah assumed that he knew. But Sarah obviously had not trusted him enough to confide this apparently painful knowledge. His spirits were low as he drove south, away from the girl he loved. He had no chance with her, he realised. The idea that she might fall in love with him had been a crazy dream born of his fever. It was just as well that they would not see one another again for some time.

Even the arrival of a new calf did not entirely capture Sarah's attention as she followed the herd through the terrain that she loved. Today the shape of the hills and the harsh beauty of the countryside made little impression on her. The hours dragged, and she wondered whether Rabindrah had reached Nairobi, and when he might return. If ever. She could think of no reason that would bring him back, and she certainly could not go running after him to Nairobi. She drove back to the camp early on the pretext of writing up her notes for the day. Allie was sitting at the desk, swearing as the typewriter carriage jammed for the fifth consecutive time.

'You look out of sorts,' she said. 'We'll have a cup of tea.'

They sat together under the trees, Sarah silent and withdrawn.

'You miss him,' Allie said.

'I don't know.'

'My dear, of course you do.' Allie leaned forward. 'Now I'm only going to say this once. Because it's no business of mine, except that you're very special to Dan and me. We know how much you loved Piet, and love him still. How you have grieved for him. But instead of dwelling only on his loss, you might want to consider that he was given to you for a short time, as a perfect, beautiful gift. A shining vision of how a young man should be. And he can never change, or become damaged or tarnished or old in your memory. He was a wonderful part of your life, a treasure to be thankful for. I believe he would want you to remember what you were to each other at that moment. But I think he would also want you to go on being the vital, loving girl he knew. To live your life in the way he so admired, and to recognise and celebrate the other gifts that come your way.'

'Thank you, Allie.' Sarah's response was barely audible. 'Thank you so very, very much.'

It was an hour later when the radio crackled into life and Dan pressed the receiver button.

'We've just had a call from Jeremy Hardy,' Lars said. 'Simon Githiri walked into the police station in Nyeri an hour ago and gave himself up.'

Chapter 16

London, June 1967

'Do you have any plans for tomorrow?' Edward sounded tense on the telephone.

'No. I have a few days off and I'm determined to keep my calendar free of work,' Camilla said. 'Do you need to change our dinner date?'

'I have to fly to Barbados tomorrow,' he said. 'It's only for three or four days. I have a burn patient. And I wonder if you'd like to come with me?'

He was surprised when she agreed. On the long flight she felt carefree and relaxed, full of anticipaton for the simple pleasures ahead. It would be a true holiday, and she dreamed about the hours they would spend walking on the beach and lying in the blue sea.

'They're sending a car to take me to the hospital,' Edward said, as they checked into the hotel. 'I need to spend some time with the anaesthetist as well as the operating team and, of course, the patient. I'll be back as soon as I can, darling. In time for a late evening swim. We gained an afternoon with the time change. That's the best thing about flying west. And look at that white, white sand and the colour of the water.'

Camilla walked the beach and lay in the sea, and then returned to their room where she fell asleep for an hour. She was dining alone in the restaurant when Edward telephoned to apologise for being so late. It was almost midnight when he returned, and he threw himself down on the sofa in their suite and ordered a large whisky.

'This is going to be a tough one,' he said. 'It's a black girl of sixteen with appalling damage to the left side of her face, and third-degree burns down her neck and one arm. It will be a miracle if she doesn't lose the sight in her left eye. She's sedated, of course, but the parents are demented with grief and fear. And rage.'

'An accident?'

'Her boyfriend threw a saucepan of boiling fat over her. Apparently she had made a rendezvous with another fellow that she met when she took her goats out to graze in the mornings. So this jealous young hothead decided to teach her a lesson.'

'God, how barbaric. When will you operate?'

'First thing tomorrow. I'm afraid I'll be at the hospital for several hours. There are a couple of local doctors attending, and I hope to teach them a new procedure. I'm going straight to bed now, because I need to leave around six.'

Camilla sat out on the balcony, listening to the surf and the clatter of palm fronds in the soft air. Starlight flickered on the sea and she watched the movement of light and was filled with wonder at its mysterious beauty. Images came unbidden into her head as she walked down the steps and on to the beach, visions of the dip and swish of the Indian Ocean, the long shapes of the *ngalawas* with their delicate outriggers and pointed prows, and the roundness of mooring buoys dancing in the waves. She was assailed by a longing for Africa as she paddled at the edge of the tide, placing her feet in the tickle of water, allowing it to run over her toes.

She knew that her sense of isolation was temporary. Tomorrow, she would spend the morning in the sea, and when the surgery was over she would take Edward to the market, lead him into the clash of tropical colour and noise and smells that always made her glad to be alive. In the distance she saw a couple, their arms wound around each other, heads close, soft laughter drifting towards her on the night wind. The sight of them tore at her heart and she returned to the suite, walking swiftly, and closed the glass doors and the curtains to separate herself from their world of shared pleasure.

The long hours Edward spent with his patients and colleagues did not usually bother her. He often stayed late at one of the hospitals, and in the past she had occasionally found herself alone at a table for two when he could not, or would not, leave a critical case. Her own work was demanding and often in the public eye, and she did not mind days or evenings she spent by herself. But here in the moonlight she wanted to share. She wished that he had been able to take her by the hand, to smell the salt wind and the air off the sea and to see the dancing lights of tropical boats and cottages and fishing huts reflected in the water, following the curve of the beach, echoing her memories of the African coast that was now so far away.

When she had spent another whole day alone, she rang the hospital with a suggestion that surprised Edward and delighted the entire ward. On the way from the hotel she stopped and bought several bunches of flowers from a market stall. Inside the whitewashed building she talked to staff and patients and their relatives and friends, arranged her flowers, fed the youngest inmates in the children's ward, and signed hastily produced cards that would later be pasted with pride into autograph books and on to the walls of the island houses. It was not long before a photographer arrived from the local newspaper, and Edward's burn victim and her parents found themselves on the front page. Gifts and money began to arrive, and on the second day an insurance company sent a secretary to sort out the cards and donations. The girl became a celebrated cause, and by the time the limousine arrived to take them back to the airport, Camilla was glad to escape.

'That was a wonderful thing you did,' Edward said, as the plane took off, and she craned her neck for a last glimpse of the turquoise sea. 'Absolutely inspired. That girl now has enough money for the next skin graft, and an eye specialist in New York has offered to take her case on.'

'I was tired of solitary walks on the beach,' she said. 'No, you don't have to apologise. You came out here to save someone from being terribly disfigured, and that's fine with me. But I wouldn't want to make a habit of travelling like this.'

In London, she threw herself back into her work. Her hospital visits had been picked up by the *Daily Mail*. Tom Bartlett telephoned to congratulate her on the publicity she had generated and did not even hear her protests. A new contract was waiting to be signed with *Harper's Bazaar*. Saul had produced new designs for the winter season and urged her to put her stamp of approval on them. There was a shoot in Morocco and the offer of a lucrative assignment in Paris. With papers to be studied and signed, she decided it would be best if Tom Bartlett came with her to France. He arranged a series of pictures for one of the couture houses to be taken over the same period and guided her through the business negotiations, but neither one of them enjoyed the trip.

'That was the worst bloody three days of my life, hanging around with those arrogant frogs,' Tom said, bringing her bags into her Knightsbridge flat. 'And by the way, I wish you'd live somewhere with a lift. Or get rid of that doddering old porter in favour of someone who can carry your luggage upstairs.'

'It's good exercise,' she said. 'After all those cigars and cognac.'

'When the plane was late, I was afraid we would be trapped in France for ever.'

'It was only two hours.'

'Seemed like for ever,' Tom said. 'How about a drink, darling? I fancy a glass of champagne. Even if it is French.'

'The French are always tricky,' Camilla said. 'And the photographer hated me, which didn't make things any easier. Open the fridge and take the glasses out of the sideboard, while I plough through this pile of mail.'

She saw the Kenya stamps immediately. The envelope had been addressed by Lars, and Camilla felt immediately uneasy. It was always Hannah who wrote. She put the letter aside to read later – when she had had a drink, and would not feel so guilty about the fact that she had not written. She had sent the cheques through Tom's office, and arranged for new sewing machines and fabric to be delivered. But she could not pick up a pen and put her feelings down on paper, or explain why she had not made plans for her return. Admit that she was a coward. Each day that passed made the situation worse.

'Tom? Did you send another cheque to Langani, before we left for Paris?'

'Yeah. Although God knows what it was for. The workshop isn't open and you're having the clothes made here, at ten times the price. Your friend Hannah isn't contributing anything to the process, and I don't know why you're still sending her money. Bloody ridiculous, if you ask me.'

'I didn't ask you.' Camilla accepted a glass of champagne. 'Stop pacing and sit down, for heaven's sake. You're making me nervous. I'm tired too, you know. It was no fun out there, dancing along the edge of a parapet in a dress that wouldn't keep me warm in the Sahara. And no one bothered to enquire whether I suffered from vertigo.'

'Do you suffer from vertigo?' Tom sat down on the other end of the sofa.

'No. But what's the use of asking me now?' She looked at him through half-closed eyes. 'Why don't you massage my feet before you go home? It always makes me feel better.'

'I don't want to go home,' he said. 'It's cold and dull and lonely at home. I'd rather stay here and get drunk with you. Or stoned.'

'I have no intention of being either,' she said. 'Isn't your blonde dolly bird waiting for you, with a steak and kidney pie in the oven and her best nightie on?'

'It's all over,' he said, looking forlorn. 'Didn't work out well, for some reason.'

Camilla burst out laughing. 'Of course it didn't work out,' she said. 'You always pick up these brainless little groupies that are only good for one thing. And then you're surprised that they don't last.'

He took one of her feet and began to apply expert pressure to the sole. 'Did Tarzan massage you like this when you were tired?' he asked, trying to hurt her.

'Don't, Tom.' Her tone was cold, and she pulled away from him. In spite of Anthony's duplicity, she could never put him out of her mind, and she resented his power to inflict pain in spite of the distance she had put between them.

'I'm sorry darling,' Tom said, backing away from a confrontation. 'Relax, and I'll make us some scrambled eggs.'

'Don't think you're going to worm your way into staying here, just by making supper,' she said. But she was depressed, and glad that he was there.

She sipped her drink and listened to him banging around in the kitchen. He was a good cook, but he seemed unable to produce a bowl of cornflakes without making a noise like an express train, and leaving the kitchen looking as though it had been struck by a hurricane. When he brought a tray into the sitting room she blew him a kiss on her fingertips.

'You're very sweet, really,' she said. 'Not bad looking, with your brown, bedroom eyes and your funny smile. I like your hair these days, with the fringe thing, and all the wheels turning inside that sharp mind underneath.'

'You don't fancy me, though,' he said, half hopeful.

'No, I don't. And I never will. Now eat your supper and afterwards we'll see if there's something on television.'

'How's Edward?'

'He's away,' she said.

'What's the news from Sarah? And what happened to Dr Tim? Did he ever track down his bride?' Tom was curious. 'Jilted at the altar and all. What really happened there, anyway?'

'I haven't heard from Tim,' Camilla said. 'Sarah hasn't written either, except for a terse little thank-you note. I'm sure she saw him leaving here. And I was stupid enough to promise I wouldn't tell her he was in London.'

Camilla turned on the television to avoid any more discussion. But she could not concentrate on the programme, and Lars's handwriting stared at her from the envelope on the coffee table. She reached out and opened it, and everything else faded into the background.

'What's the matter?' Tom leaned forward.

'The Kikuyu who killed Piet is probably still alive,' Camilla said. 'And Hannah's father died in Rhodesia.' She dialled the international operator to book a call to Langani and then cancelled it, realising that the time difference made it too late.

'Bloody hell,' Tom said. 'It's as if that family has some kind of curse on them.'

'Perhaps that's true,' she said thoughtfully. 'Although no one seems able to find out what it is, or the reason behind it.'

There was still no clue as to Simon's whereabouts, Lars had written. He had flown down to Rhodesia where Jan had been killed in an ambush, and had brought Lottie back to Langani. Hannah was taking it hard. The new sewing machines had arrived but the workshop was not up and running because of the sad events that had taken place over the last two weeks. There was a note from Hannah on the last page:

You are better off away from here. If I were you, I'd never come back, because there's nothing left here, except things that we would have been better off not knowing. I spent a few days with Sarah and she is fine. Ma is with us but I do not know how long she will stay. We haven't decided what to do, or whether we can continue here. I always wanted to fight for our farm, for Piet's hopes and in honour of his life. But I just don't know any more.

'I should go back,' Camilla said, handing Tom the letter. 'I could do something to help. Open the workshop, get some feeling of hope going for Hannah. And I could repair the situation with Sarah.'

'Are you fucking crazy?' Tom glared at her in angry disbelief. 'Or plain stupid, for Chrissakes? There's a bloody murderer at large over there, and everybody on that farm is a sitting target. And if you're not slashed to pieces, you'll run into that no-brained bushman. It won't take more than half an hour before he makes you feel like shit, instead of the beautiful, intelligent, desirable woman you really are. When you're not with him, that is.'

'I could go for a short time, and—'

'You're not bloody going anywhere, Camilla.' Tom was shouting at her, cords of anger standing out on his forehead and pumping through his neck. 'You made me promise that I wouldn't take on that Somali hooker in Nairobi, or you'd leave my agency. Well, I'm telling you now that if you go back there I'm cancelling our contract, and you can forget about your career. Because I don't work for people who play games with me, darling. And that's final.'

'I don't know why you're so angry,' she said, tugging at his hand as he stood up.

'I'm going home,' he said, ignoring her. 'Let me know when you've come to your senses. But don't take too long, Camilla, or I might have taken your number out of my fucking book.'

For two days she wrestled with the idea of flying to Nairobi. A letter came from Sarah, briefly describing the memorial service on the farm. The telephone rang, cutting through Camilla's thoughts about booking an airline ticket to Nairobi.

'I have a surprise for you.' Tom could not contain the excitement in his voice. 'There's a production of *The Seagull* going into rehearsal. I've persuaded them you should audition for the part of Masha.'

'Me? On a stage?' It seemed so long since she had failed at her audition for drama school. But Camilla had put the rejection behind her, made a success of an alternative career. Now her childhood dream had been revived once more. She stared in disbelief at the receiver in her hand, saw her radiant reflection in the mirror. 'Oh my God! When is the audition? Tom, I don't think I could do a play. Go to an audition. I'm so nervous. I've no idea how to—'

'This is what you've always wanted, isn't it?' he said. 'So here's your chance. I've set it all up for next Tuesday, and I'll come and hold your hand. You'd better not fluff your lines, darling.'

When she was given the part, Camilla's spirits soared. She cancelled all but the most essential photo shoots and settled down to study the part. Her sitting room was piled high with everything she could read about Chekhov and the history and literature of the period. Night after night she sat up late, steeping herself in the twilight world of the fading Russian aristocracy and their crumbling estates. Two weeks later she came in from a day's rehearsal that had not gone well. There had been frayed tempers and arguments between the director and two of the actors, and afterwards she had been unable to find a taxi in weather that was cold and wet. The invitation was on the top of her pile of mail. She opened the envelope and looked at the names of her would-be hosts on the engraved stationery. Chad and Ruthie Parker. They meant nothing to her, and she put the envelope on a pile that required a polite refusal note. Every day she received dozens of cards like this, usually from celebrity hunters who had talked to her at a cocktail party or a charity event. When she had bathed and changed, she took a taxi to Edward's flat where the housekeeper had lit the fire, and he had Mozart on the stereo.

'Did you get an invitation from the Parkers?' he asked.

'Yes, I did. Who are they? Do you know them?' Camilla was surprised.

'You're amazingly vague sometimes, Camilla,' he said. 'Don't you remember? They came here for dinner when Sarah was here. Gave her a donation for her elephants.'

'So they did,' she said. 'Oh dear, I suppose that means I'll have to make the effort. They were sweet, but frightfully earnest. She gushes.'

'They have a rather grand house in Mayfair,' he said. 'Stuffed with Impressionist paintings and a couple of Picassos, and all the expensive Chinese junk that decorators in New York are so fond of. I think we ought to look in on the party for a while, at least. We can have dinner afterwards, on our own, if we feel like it.'

The Parker house was imposing. A uniformed maid whisked away their coats and a waiter offered champagne.

'So lovely that you could join us.' Ruthie greeted them effusively in the hall. 'We have a surprise guest. I thought of telling you, but then I decided this would be more fun.'

She led the way to the sitting room and Camilla prepared herself for an hour of mindless chatter. And then stiffened with shock. Anthony Chapman was standing with his back to the fireplace, long and sinewy, a little aloof from the rest of the party. He had a drink in his hand, and he smiled at her across the room. Chad Parker stepped forward to greet her and then Anthony was kissing her cheek as Ruthie burbled on about the romance of white hunters and safari plans, and nights under canvas in the African bush.

'We sure are grateful to your friend for putting us in touch with Anthony,' Chad said. 'We've made up a great party of friends for September, thanks to Sarah.'

'Anthony. How unexpected. Have you been here long?' Camilla recovered herself.

'Since this morning. I'm on my usual sales trip, and the Parkers asked me to stop over in London.'

Camilla wondered whether he would have bothered to contact her if she had not been a guest tonight. She could see Edward watching her from the other side of the room where he had been captured by one of the guests. She flashed him a dazzling smile.

'Are you going to introduce us, darling?' Edward had moved across the room and was holding her lightly by the elbow.

'Of course I am,' she said. 'This is—'

'I'm Edward Carradine,' Edward said to Anthony, without waiting for the formalities. 'I've heard a great deal about you. Are you in London for long?'

'I flew in this morning. It's London for two days, then New York and Chicago and the west coast before heading back to Nairobi,' Anthony said, shaking Edward's hand and then turning back to Camilla. 'Everywhere I look, you're staring at me from shop windows and billboards and magazine covers. And now I hear you're going to be on the stage as well. That must feel pretty good.'

'Better than good,' she said. 'Although I'm nervous of the critics. They can close a play with a couple of ferocious reviews, and I might be the one responsible if I'm not up to scratch.' Her words were coming out too fast and she could not slow her pulse or prevent the dry feeling that threatened to close up her throat.

'I'm sure that won't happen,' Edward said.

'Of course it won't.' Anthony was staring at her, his eyes boring into her composure.

'I heard about Janni,' Camilla said. 'And about Simon being alive.'

'It's rough on Hannah,' he said. 'And Sarah, too, after what they've been through already. I don't know how or when it will all end, this series of tragedies.'

But Camilla did not want to dwell on the subject of Langani and her failure to offer any real support to her friends. She was relieved when another couple edged towards them and the conversation moved on smoothly to talk of the bush and life in an independent African country. It was easy to charm the large man with a Southern drawl who would be part of the Parkers' safari entourage, by telling him stories of her Kenyan childhood. Champagne flowed, and the room grew increasingly hot. She felt hemmed in, and when Anthony was lured away by his hostess, Camilla put down her glass and asked for directions to the powder room. She stood there for ten minutes, breathing in the cooler air, distancing herself from the rising hum of the party and from the fluttering in the pit of her stomach. She was returning to the drawing room when Anthony appeared in the hall, blocking her way.

'I have to see you,' he said in a low voice.

'You *are* seeing me.'

'I want to see you alone,' he said, taking hold of her arm.

'I'm very busy,' she said. 'Not available. Excuse me please, I'm leaving now.'

She spent the night at Edward's flat and made her way home after breakfast, glad that she had no appointments for the day. In the hall she found an envelope that had been pushed under the door. She opened it and read the note enclosed:

> *Camilla,*
> *I have to see you. Please.*
> *Ring me at the Chesterfield Hotel. My room number is 14.*
> *Anthony.*

She threw the note into the wastepaper basket and made herself a cup of coffee. When the telephone rang she knew it would be Anthony.

'I'd like to come over,' he said. 'There are things I have to say to you. Please give me a chance.'

'You can say them on the telephone,' she replied.

'For God's sake, Camilla, I want to see you. And if you're not there when I arrive I'll bloody camp outside the door until you get back.'

'It's too cold for camping around here,' she said, trying to make light of his threat. But she knew she would have to see him. That she desperately wanted to see him. She tried to think of somewhere neutral and safe where they could talk for an hour. Just an hour. 'Let's meet at the Royal Academy. There's an exhibition I've been meaning to see for weeks. Twelve o'clock.'

'I'm glad you came,' he said when she pushed through the revolving door. 'Although I would have preferred somewhere more private. I want you to know that I behaved like an idiot. Like a cad. I've regretted it every day since then. I want to know how you're faring.'

'I'm fine. I told you that last night. Shall we talk about something else?'

'I've seen a great deal of your father in Nairobi,' he said, afraid that she would walk away from him. 'We're working together on several projects. He's doing big things for the parks and reserves. George is one of the few people who gets results, because he knows how to handle the local politicians and officials. Employs huge charm but takes no nonsense from anyone. He has Johnson Kiberu totally on his side. A good bloke.'

'Very good bloke.' Camilla pressed her lips together to keep from laughing.

'Between the three of us, we've invented all kinds of checks and balances to prevent funds disappearing into the wrong pockets. And last month George managed to deliver five spanking new Land Rovers straight into the hands of the park wardens, for anti-poaching patrols. I think he's planning a quick visit to London soon.'

'That will be lovely,' Camilla said. 'Look at this wonderful landscape with its mauve glow. It's French, but it's just like the evening light in up-country Kenya. Isn't that amazing?' She saw that he was not concentrating on the pictures at all. 'How are things in the safari business? Are you booked up for next season?'

He ignored her question. 'Camilla, I don't know how to convince you that I'm truly sorry. I was utterly selfish. Childish, I think you'd call it. I was just flirting with the girl, and it didn't mean a thing to me beyond that. I never intended to upset you. Please listen to me.'

'It's not important now,' she answered, afraid to reopen an issue that would bring pain and recriminations. In any case it was too late. 'It all seems like a long time ago, and everything has changed so much.'

'Has it?'

'Yes. Our lives have returned to their accustomed tracks, just as you always thought they would.' The brittle smile did not reach her eyes, and she knew she should not have agreed to meet him.

'Are you in love with him?' he asked. 'Are you sleeping with him?'

'That's none of your business.' She was losing control. 'I'm leaving now. There are things on my list for today that I haven't even thought about, and I have to be at the theatre by two.'

'Look at me and tell me you're in love with him.'

'Leave me alone, Anthony. My life is well organised now. I'm good at what I do and satisfied with that. Just leave me in peace. Please.'

'I made a terrible mistake,' he said.

'No, you didn't. Tell me about Hannah. And Lottie.'

'It's been a bad time for them all. The shock of discovering Simon's motive. Of knowing what Jan had done. And of course Simon and his uncle are still on the loose and a serious threat to everyone on the farm.'

Camilla's mind was in turmoil. No one had told her about the motive for Piet's killing. And what had Janni done? She felt ill. Hannah had excluded her from the core of what was happening at Langani. She did not belong, was no longer part of the cherished circle of her childhood, in spite of the effort she had made with the workshop and the cheques she had been sending. She looked at Anthony, sick at heart but too proud to admit that she did not know the full story. In a flash of clarity she understood that this must be what her father had known all along. This was the reason that Jan had left the farm before Independence.

'I don't want to talk about Hannah,' Anthony said. 'I want to talk about us.' He was facing her, standing in front of a huge canvas but not seeing it, not seeing anything except Camilla with her beautiful face turned towards him and her blue eyes glittering. Several people were staring at them, and he saw that she had been recognised. 'Let's get out of here,' he said, taking her hand. 'Come on. We'll go across the road and have a coffee somewhere. Or we could walk a little in the park. It's a beautiful day out there, and you still have plenty of time.'

She followed him in silence, determined to regain a hold on her emotions. By the time they had walked along the park and found a café she was calm.

'Hannah's letter didn't fill in all the details about Simon and Janni,' she said. 'There's only so much you can put down on paper in those circumstances. Can you tell me the whole story?'

She heard the truth then, as she drank her coffee and tried to hide the shock she felt when Anthony told her about what Jan had done, and its tragic consequences.

'Poor Hannah,' she said. 'But at least she has Lars and the baby, while Sarah has no one to help her through all this.'

'She has gone back to her work. The only thing that keeps her going,' he said, reaching across the table and taking Camilla's hand. 'But now we must talk about us.'

'There is no "us". We had fun. We had a fling and it was great, but it's history.'

'I hurt you, and I've never stopped regretting it.'

'You hurt me twice. And I want you to stay away from me, because I've got over all that and I don't want to think about it ever again.'

'I was jealous. Of all the people from London and the razzmatazz around you, and my not being part of it. Hannah showed me how selfish I'd been, in plain words. How immature. And Lars, too. They didn't spare me, and they were right.'

'We all grow up at different rates. My life has changed now, Anthony. I have a chance to do the one thing I set out to accomplish when I was still a child, and I'm very excited about it. And that's what is important to me.'

'Are you happy?' he grasped her hands. 'With this doctor of yours?'

'Happy? What sort of question is that? Everything is going well for me. And he takes good care of me.'

'He's old enough to be your father,' Anthony said.

'He's twenty years older than me,' Camilla said coldly. 'And he's nothing like my father. It's none of your business anyway.'

'Look, after you left I felt like a shit. I was devastated. Destroyed.'

'I'm sure you were able to console yourself.'

'You're talking about that American woman,' he said, assuming that she had heard about it. Nairobi gossip was fast and cruel, and George had surely known about the affair. 'She was nothing to me and I didn't mean anything to her either.' He did not see her shocked face as she looked away.

'Poor girl,' she said bitterly. 'Another sex toy whose advances you couldn't resist. Just like me.'

'She'd come out of a broken engagement, and we were both licking our wounds. It's not worth talking about.'

'And the same applies to the other girls who've managed to comfort you or break down your defences since then.' Camilla was filled with an icy rage, more angry with herself than with him. Her stomach had begun to churn, and she found that she was twisting her cup round and round in clumsy, trembling fingers.

'Camilla.'

'I'm going now, Anthony. I think we should call it a day.' She stood up, looking at him with sad eyes.

'Come back to the hotel with me, Camilla. Let's begin again.'

She shook her head, unable to trust her voice. Then she walked away, her steps brisk, her mind focused on finding a taxi, on finding a bus, on crossing the street, on anything and everything except Anthony Chapman. In the refuge of her flat she stepped into the shower and stood under the stream of water, scrubbing the thought of him out of her system. Washing the man right out of her hair, she thought. But she felt the pain inside, as though he had knifed her in the chest.

When she got back from the theatre he was standing in the hallway, a whole shrubbery of roses on the floor beside him. He bent to pick them up.

'Please,' she said, turning away from him, putting the key into the lock with shaking hands. 'Please go away.'

'Tell me you're in love with this Edward. Tell me you don't have any feelings for me at all. Swear to me that you don't want me to kiss you. Because I want you so desperately I can scarcely breathe.'

She stepped backwards into the sitting room, her hands thrust out in protest. He followed her swiftly, throwing the flowers on to the coffee table and pulling her into his arms. When she pushed him away his grip tightened and he unfastened her shirt and covered her with kisses. She beat her hands against him but he only held her closer, groaning softly and mumbling into her ear, and his breath made her shiver. They fell on to the sofa, her arms and legs wrapped around his body, and made love like animals.

Later, when the telephone shrilled, she took it off the hook. The intrusion awakened a new urgency in them both and Anthony reached for her and made love to her again. They ate supper slowly and in near silence, looking at each other, smiling, touching fingers. When they had cleared the dishes away they lay on the rug in front of the fire, exploring the familiar and the new in one another, talking in sentences and phrases interspersed with long kisses. Then they went into the bedroom and fell asleep, hands clasped, faces close together so that they could feel each other's breathing. When she opened her eyes in the morning he was already awake. He placed his hand lightly on the silky skin of her stomach and desire spread through her.

'I'm leaving tonight,' he said quietly. 'I know you want to do the play. But then you'll come to Nairobi and we'll be together. Unless you decide to make some understudy's dream come true and fly back with me tomorrow.'

She studied him in silence, wondering if he could hear her heart cracking. 'I'm not coming to Nairobi,' she said. 'It's too late. I don't belong there any more. I'm not brave enough to live that life, to give up everything here and spend most of my time alone in a dusty house and garden in Karen or Langata, waiting for you to come back off safari every few weeks for a day or two. I can't do that.'

'Camilla,' he said. 'I've been in love with you for years, but I suppose I was scared of the commitment and the changes it would make in my life.'

'Your life won't ever change,' she said. 'Your work and your life are one and the same thing. And I don't want a life where my main role is to check stores and supplies, order booze and fresh vegetables, make hotel bookings for your next safari, and chat up your clients while you have a harmless flirtation or fuck the wives and daughters. You were right the first time. We don't belong.'

'I'd never do that if you were mine,' he said desperately. 'We can work this out. You know we can. We could set up a different kind of camp where you would be the hostess, with your own stamp on everything. We could make a huge success of that, and we'd be together most of the time, sharing the places you love as much as I do.'

'No.' She did not trust herself to say more than one word.

'We'd be in Europe and the United States at least twice each year. Besides which, there are all kinds of things you could do in Nairobi, with the beautiful things you were making at Langani. We're privileged people, Camilla, brought up between two cultures and able to keep a foot in each. We can work out a wonderful life that would fulfil us both.'

She turned her head away, steeling herself up to withstand whatever form his persuasion might take.

'I'm staying here,' she said. 'I don't have the guts to do what you are asking. I couldn't take the uncertainty of it.'

'Of course you have the guts,' he said with impatience. 'You're scared I'll let you down. But I won't, Camilla. I'll never let you down again, darling, for the rest of our lives. I'll care for you and keep you safe with me. We'll live together in a world full of the most wondrous things that only I can show you. I've seen you there, and I know you love it as much as I do. It's the only place for us both.'

Camilla shook her head. 'No.'

'You can't spend your life with this man because you think he's a safe bet,' he said urgently. 'You don't love him, Camilla. You're demeaning yourself, and it's not fair on him either.'

'I love him in some ways,' she said. 'I can rely on him and I know he'll always be around when I need him. I've seen the consequences when people hurl themselves into situations driven only by passion. I'm not going to do that any more.'

She reached for her robe and wrapped it around her. 'I'm going into the bathroom now,' she said. 'When I come out you'll be gone. You'll find a good girl, and in no time at all you'll have several blonde, tanned little Kenya children running around your garden. And one day, when enough time has passed, we'll see each other again and we'll be good friends.'

He said nothing, his jaw clenched tight with the shock of her rejection. She went into the bathroom, locked the door and turned on the taps at full blast so that she would not hear his movements outside. In the bath she allowed herself to cry, soundlessly and with so much sadness that she had to draw her knees up to her chest, in an attempt to dull the pain. At last she wrapped herself in a towel and opened the door into the empty bedroom.

It was seven in the evening when Edward arrived at the flat. Camilla smiled at him, but turned her face away so that he could not kiss her mouth that was still swollen and tender. Her eyes were slightly red, but she hoped that her expert attempts at camouflage were sufficient. He accepted her offer of a drink and sat down on the sofa while she poured it.

'You've been with Anthony Chapman,' he said without preamble. 'Don't deny it, because it will only make it worse. I rang and you didn't answer, and then the phone was off the hook. I know he was here with you. I know it in my heart. And now I can see it in your face, in your eyes. It's not over, the thing between you.'

She was silent, her pulse jumping into her throat, choking any response that came to mind. When she was able, she made her reply in a measured voice.

'He was here, but he's gone. There's nothing between us any more, Edward. We had a fling in Kenya when I went back last year. But he didn't want it to be anything else. He came here to say he was sorry for hurting me, that's all. So we've put the past aside, and I hope that we will be good friends in times to come. There's nothing else to it, I can promise you.'

Edward put his drink on the table and leaned towards her so that his eyes were on the same level as hers.

'I don't think you can say that with any assurance,' he said. 'If you do, then you're not being truthful, either to me or to yourself. And I know that he was here before. On his way to the United States. Because I saw the remains of breakfast for two in your kitchen. Ironically enough, it was the evening when I asked you to marry me. I wondered at the time who had been here the night before. And why you hadn't mentioned a guest.'

'Oh, no. It wasn't—'

'I think we shouldn't see each other for a while, Camilla. In fact, I've arranged to go away tomorrow, to do some surgery in Morocco, followed by a conference in San Francisco. I'll telephone you sometime after I get back, and then perhaps we'll talk. If you're still here, and if that bank of roses has faded from your mind.'

'Of course I'll be here,' she said, forcing a laugh. 'Can you really see me trailing around Nairobi in a beat-up truck, waiting for a Kenya cowboy to show up every few weeks and take me out for a leg of eland and a beer?'

'So he asked you to go back to Kenya? To live with him?'

'It doesn't matter what he asked me,' she said. A trickle of fear crept into her veins and she heard herself pleading with him. 'I'm here to stay, and you're going to have to resign yourself to the fact. Please, Edward, let's go out and get some dinner and see a film. And then I need to go to bed early because I'm supposed to be at a rehearsal tomorrow morning, and there's a fashion shoot in the afternoon that promises to be cold and wet, and very dull.'

Edward stood up. 'I'm not willing to play the role of the safer option,' he said. 'I need much more than that, and it's clear to me that you aren't able to give it. So let's take a break for a while.' He stared at her for a long moment before she heard the click of the opening door.

'Goodbye, Camilla,' he said.

And then she was alone.

Chapter 17

London, June 1967

'You could have stayed with me,' Camilla said to her father. 'I have a perfectly civilised guest room.'

'It's sweet of you to offer,' George said. 'But the club is nearer to my appointments. Besides, I'm going to be around for a couple of weeks and I don't want to be linked to the guests and fish theory.'

She was a little guilty that she had not invited him before, but her long hours at the theatre and on photo shoots made it difficult to look after a guest, even if it was her own father. And in the back of her mind was the certainty that she did not want to know too much about his private life. She wondered if he would see his former lover, who had unexpectedly remained in London when George had gone to live in Kenya. In Nairobi there had been no sign of anyone in George's life while Camilla was staying with him, no man who appeared regularly at dinner parties or weekend lunches. Perhaps he was afraid of gossip, of destroying his reputation as a successful, widowed diplomat-turned-aid-executive. He was probably surrounded by people like herself who accepted his homosexuality, as long as they did not have to come face to face with it. She was ashamed to admit that she was as hypocritical as they were.

He looked well, she thought. Life in Kenya obviously suited him, and he was tanned and fit from frequent field excursions. George was known for his insistence on familiarising himself with each project funded by his organisation. Unlike many aid officials he did not confine himself to his plush Nairobi office, making rare and fleeting visits into the bush. He preferred to spend several days at a time in any region that had asked for his help. Nor did he set up a temporary office under local government auspices. Instead, he would spend his time talking to park wardens and rangers, to local farmers and businessmen of all races, and to elders of the tribes that lived on the land or grazed their livestock there. He was happy to walk in the bush, to climb steep, rocky outcrops in order to look over game corridors used by migrating wildlife, or to take cramped and bumpy flights over areas that could no longer sustain the demands of a fast-growing human population and its resident wildlife.

'It's been a long time since I was in your club,' Camilla said. 'It's so comforting to be able to order shepherd's pie or a boiled egg, and to be in a place that never changes. Where no one gawps at me, or even recognises me.'

'They're much too discreet,' George said. 'But they know you. Old Alfred, at the porter's desk, asked me this morning how my famous daughter was. He'd read that you're an actress now, as well as a model.'

'I'm only an actress for another ten days. Small theatre and short run. Although there is talk of a West End transfer in the autumn.'

'I thought your performance last night was terrific,' he said. 'My beautiful, talented daughter – I was so proud.'

'Pride goes with prejudice.' She was as absurdly happy with his praise as she had been at six years old.

'Did you bring the notices? I saw the one in *The Times*, but you said you had more.'

'I do.' Camilla took a sheaf out of her tote bag. 'They're mainly about the production itself, and the other leads. All of whom were so kind and patient that even my most awful blunders came right in the end. But I did get an honourable mention.'

'Better than that,' he said. 'Best newcomer. Luminous and vulnerable presence. Intelligent performance.'

'I don't know why the public assumes that models have no brains,' she said, half indignant. 'The press seemed astonished that I could actually speak, never mind act. It's tiring, though. All those performances – two on Wednesdays and Saturdays. And several photo assignments I couldn't get out of. I'll need a break when it's finished.'

'Do you remember the day you were turned down for drama school?' He smiled fondly at her. 'You were so shattered. Said you didn't want to try again. We were here, in this very room. And now you've done a play with good notices and no training at all. That's quite a feat.'

'The reviews weren't all good,' she said. 'One critic wrote that I was beautiful but transparent, and another one hated my voice. Said I was like the stars that were ravishing on the silent screen, but should never be cast in talkies. What are we drinking with this nursery food?'

'There's an exceptional St Julien you might like,' George said. 'So, how are you, darling?'

'Busy,' she said. 'Like everyone else I know in this town.'

'Are you seeing anything of Edward these days?'

'No. He did come to the play one night, but I don't have time for socialising, and neither does he.' She dabbed at her mouth with a napkin and tried to look bored.

'What does that mean?' George knew her too well.

'We've decided not to see each other regularly.'

'Is this anything to do with Anthony's visit? No, don't clam up on me, Camilla.'

'Daddy, I can't imagine a life hanging around in Nairobi, while Anthony is out hunting lions and buffalo, and other women. Or they're all stalking him. It's not for me. Now let's talk about something else.'

'No, let's talk about this,' he said firmly. 'He behaved very badly on your gala night. But until then, it seemed to me that you were very much in love. Both of you. Then you rushed off and—'

'He was true to form,' she said. 'And I know he immediately fell into bed with some American girl. Besides, I had commitments here. I would have left anyway.'

'For a short time, yes.' He paused. 'You mentioned Edward in your letters.'

'I see him, occasionally,' she said.

'Darling, I do read the English papers. Even in Nairobi. They may be a day or two late, but I saw the thing about the girl in Barbados who was burnt and the money you raised for her.'

'I didn't raise money for her. I only—'

'You were there with Edward, is the point I'm making,' George said. 'I also know that Anthony was hoping to see you in London. And now you're not involved with Edward any more. So I'm asking you if you are still in love with Anthony Chapman?'

'I was infatuated with him for a while. I fell for the whole thing – the glamorous white hunter, lions roaring, flaming sunsets, tents under the stars. But it won't work, because I can never trust him again. He hurt me badly. Not just once. And I don't want to be that vulnerable ever again.'

'I don't want to excuse him in any way, but—'

'Then don't, Daddy. It's over, and I've moved on.'

'You can't protect yourself from all the risks of life, Camilla. Some of them are what make it worth living.'

'You seem to do well at that.' She wanted to hurt him, to prevent any further criticism.

'I've made terrible mistakes.' To her surprise he responded to the barb without hesitation. 'I hurt your mother and you, and myself, by pretending to be something I wasn't. I don't want to see you doing the same thing. I think you should be honest with yourself, Camilla.'

'I'm trying to be honest. I should have thought that was clear.'

'So tell me truthfully, then, what happened between you and Edward?'

'He thought it wasn't over between Anthony and me. So he broke off our – our thing.'

'And how do you feel about that?'

'Can we have pudding, Daddy? I do like the treacle pudding,' she said, infuriated by his persistent probing. 'I'd like you to stop giving me the third degree. And I'll have some more wine. Please.'

'Life never proceeds in straight lines, my dear,' George said. 'There are many paths waiting to confuse us, and wrong turnings we all take. Sometimes we have to recognise that. To go back and retrace our steps.' He swirled the wine in his glass. 'Sometimes backtracking is the only way to find happiness.'

'I don't think I want to put my life in reverse. And you sound pompous. Preachy, actually, which is worse.'

'Maybe you should come back to Nairobi for a short time,' he said, realising he would have to change the subject. 'Get away for a week or two. See how you really feel.'

'What I really feel is that Anthony Chapman humiliated and betrayed me, and right now it would be impossible for me to get away for more than half an hour,' Camilla said. 'And Tom Bartlett has my diary filled up day and night.'

'Don't let Tom take over your entire life,' George warned her. 'He's an ambitious young man who will try and squeeze every ounce of energy out of you.'

'He's a good agent, and a loyal friend,' Camilla said. 'Have you seen Hannah?'

Her heart was thumping as she asked the question she had been avoiding.

'No. I haven't had time to visit Langani lately. Lars seems to have their conservation patrols organised, so I—'

'Do you know about Janni and what he did?' Her voice was low but fierce. 'Do you know why Piet was murdered?'

George shook his head, his face sombre. 'I do know that it goes back to the Mau Mau years.'

'Jan killed Simon's parents. The mother was shot in the back, running away, trying to protect her child. To hide Simon.'

'Hannah told you this?' He was shocked by what she had said, and did not notice when she did not confirm his assumption. 'Well, those things happened, I'm afraid. The women often fed the gangs in the forest, and occasionally got caught in the crossfire.'

'And then Janni and his men tied up Simon's father and roasted him over a fire. To get information out of him. Roasted him on a spit until he died. And I think you always knew this.'

'No. My God, I've never heard anything so frightful. I knew Jan had killed a man, and that there had been some irregularity. But it wasn't unusual in those days. His brother had been brutally murdered, in much the same way as Piet was killed last year. There would have been an inquiry, but the Emergency came to an end soon afterwards and there was an amnesty. The files were destroyed – thousands of them, detailing crimes on both sides. Things were brushed aside, hidden. But just before Independence, Jan's name came up on a list. I saw it when you asked me to look into the situation at Langani, and see whether the farm was marked for government purchase and redistribution. Someone had obviously remembered. Jan knew he would have been refused any application for citizenship or permission to stay on. So he left.'

'You knew that Piet's death was an act of revenge.'

'I did suspect it, yes,' he said heavily. 'But I thought that would be the end of it. Particularly since Simon was also dead. Until I saw your workroom, I was sure it was all over.'

'It's far from all over,' she said, telling him Wanjiru's story. 'Simon is alive, and Hannah is living in fear of her life. She's also frightened that when Jan's story comes out, all her workers will leave Langani and there will be more attacks. More retribution.'

'My dear, I am horrified by what you've told me today. I'm sure they will find Simon, but as you say, the evidence in a court case may cause even more damage. In the long run, it might be better for Lars and Hannah to pack up. Maybe go to Norway where his parents have a farm. Start up again there.'

'Half of her wants to stay. And why shouldn't she? Her grandfather and Janni were born on that land and so was Hannah, and even Suniva. She's a Kenyan. Why should she have to hand over her farm just because the law can't protect her from being terrorised?'

'She shouldn't, in theory. It's tragic. But I don't believe any land is worth what she has been through. And in view of what you've told me, I think it would be better if you didn't go back to Kenya for the time being. And certainly not to Langani.'

'You're wrong,' she said. 'Langani is where I should be right now. To stand up with Hannah and fight for what is hers, and for all the happy years I had there. And when this play is over, I think that is what I am going to do.'

They parted on uneasy terms, and Camilla made her way to the theatre. When she reached the quiet and security of her flat after the performance, it was past midnight, but she could not sleep. She tried to read a book but it proved difficult to concentrate and she was filled with a sense of futility. She felt threadbare, starved of love and true understanding. She thought of Anthony and her heart began to beat at a different tempo. Where was he now, she wondered? Probably consoling himself with some new girl he had met in New York or Chicago. And she herself had set him on that path by rejecting him. She wanted him to come back and whisk her away to Kenya, without asking her whether she wanted to go. He should have known that, ignored her protests, realised that she wanted the decision made for her. It was not a realistic notion, but she clung to it in her loneliness and regret. Outside the window a weak moon cast its light across the square, and the rain speckled the window panes.

He had been cruel to come back and tempt her, to make her feel that her life was trivial, each day filled with the flash of camera bulbs and the endless wardrobes of clothes and jewellery worn for a brief moment, before being discarded and forgotten. She was an integral part of swinging London's glamour, a familiar image, an icon. But she had no commitment to this way of life. Her small workshop at Langani had given her far more satisfaction. Only she had not been courageous enough to go back, and as usual she had drifted into something else. She had not fought for what she really valued, any more than she had fought for Anthony.

During her childhood she had often heard her parents quarrelling, listened as Marina wept behind the closed door of her bedroom while George started his car and left the cold, sad house. Camilla had tiptoed away to her room, shaking with dread, afraid that her father might not come back, that her wraith-like, lovely mother would leave her in the care of another nanny or housekeeper, or simply vanish out of her life. She had promised herself during those lonely years that she would not fight with anyone, that she would let life take its course and make the best of whatever came her way. But on that childhood day, when she had first set foot on the van der Beer farm, Camilla had found the home she had longed for in Jan and Lottie, at Langani. The place where she should be now.

The telephone woke her, and she struggled up from the sofa, realising that she had spent the night in the sitting room. She was shivering in the cool morning air as she picked up the receiver.

'I thought I'd ring and see how you feel about the news,' Tom Bartlett said.

'What news?' Camilla rubbed her eyes and pulled a rug around her.

'The man who killed Hannah's brother. He's given himself up,' Tom said. 'There's a paragraph in the *Telegraph*. Anyhow, they've got him. That must be a relief.'

'Does it say anything about a trial? I need to be there with Hannah and Sarah, if there's going to be a trial.'

'No, you don't, Camilla. Let's not start along those lines.' Tom's tone was instantly hostile.

'I'm going, Tom. I have to. This isn't a straightforward court case. There is evidence that will change everything for Hannah. Ironically, it may be Simon's trial that finally causes her to lose the farm.'

'And you can change all that by skipping off to hold her hand in the dock?' he said. 'And I suppose you plan to kiss and make up with your Jungle Johnny while you're there. Has it slipped your mind, by the way, that you're in a play right now?'

'Only for another week. I can make the understudy's dream come true.'

'You're not seriously thinking of leaving now.'

'Yes, I am. I'm going to phone Hannah as soon as you get off the line.'

'Camilla, I want you to listen to this very carefully,' Tom said. 'If you leave for Nairobi, I will have to find a replacement for at least three shoots you've agreed to do.'

'It happens all the time,' she said. 'Models get sick, take on film or stage roles, get too stoned or too drunk, or they go off on last-minute holidays with their musician or film star boyfriends. I rarely back out of a booking. I'm known in this business for being reliable and non-temperamental.'

'Camilla, if you leave town now, I'm taking you off my books,' Tom said. 'Our association is over.'

She was surprised and angry. 'So, it's bloody over,' she said. 'Goodbye, Tom.'

She dressed and went out to buy the newspaper. The column was on page four and took up very little space, but the headline leapt out at her:

KENYA POLICE CHARGE KIKUYU MAN WITH MURDER OF
BRITISH FARMER

The article stated that Simon Githiri was in custody, and described the horrific and barbarous details of Piet's murder. Memories bombarded her brain and with them came the old, suppressed fear, flooding her body as she relived the night of the raid, the appearance of the five men with their knives, the sensation of blood trickling down her forehead. She thought of Sarah and Hannah, face to face with Simon, giving evidence against him in a courtroom, knowing that nothing they said would ever bring Piet back to life or lessen the horror of his death. There was no doubt in her mind that she must be there.

It was several hours before she managed to negotiate her way out of the play, and make her travel arrangements. She had just spoken to Hannah, said that she was on her way, when the doorbell rang.

'I've been trying to ring you,' George said. 'But the line has been busy since before eight this morning, and I had to go to a couple of meetings in between. Did you see the *Telegraph*?'

'I'm going to Nairobi,' she said. 'Tonight.'

'You're a valiant, loyal friend,' he said soberly. 'I'll be back in about ten days. You can use my house for as long as you like, and the keys of the car

431

are in my desk. I'll telephone the houseboy now, if you like, and set everything up for you.'

'Thank you, Daddy. I'll take a taxi there from the airport, and have a rest before driving up to Langani.'

She hugged him gratefully, and after a telephone call to Nairobi he left her, already running late for his next appointment. Camilla poured herself a drink and took it into the bedroom. She had just lifted down her suitcase from the top of the cupboard when the phone rang. For a moment she ignored it, almost sure that it would be Tom. But then she answered, thinking that by now he would have calmed down. There was no point in leaving without patching things up.

'Camilla?'

'Who is this?' The voice was familiar, but she could not place it.

'It's Giles. Giles Hannington.'

'Good heavens,' she said, less than pleased. 'What a surprise.'

'I know George is in town,' he said, and she could hear the strain in his voice. 'I've left messages at his club, but he hasn't contacted me. So I wondered if you would—'

'If he hasn't contacted you, it's nothing to do with me,' she said. 'You made your choice, and he went to Nairobi alone, and that was it.'

'What choice? I never had a choice.'

'Everyone has a choice, Giles,' she said. 'And you decided it would all be too difficult, living there.'

'No. That's not what happened,' he said. 'George didn't want me to come to Nairobi. He told me it was all over. That I mustn't try to change his mind. It was only a couple of days before he left. I was utterly wrecked and I haven't heard from him since, but I wanted to—'

'This isn't any of my business,' she said. 'And I don't like you phoning me. If my father wants to contact you then he will, in his own time. In any case, I'm going away tonight. Leaving the country. So I couldn't help you, even if I wanted to. I'm sorry, Giles.'

'Of course.' His voice was flat with defeat. 'I'm sorry too. I shouldn't have bothered you. Goodbye, Camilla.'

She hung up and tried to concentrate on her packing, but his words kept buzzing round in her head as she chose and folded her clothes. This was a different story from the one that George had told her. She had been under the impression that Giles had not wanted to move to Nairobi, to continue their affair or whatever it should be called. But it really was not any of her concern and she did not want to become involved in it. She shrugged mentally and closed the lid of her suitcase. There were still three hours left before she needed to go to the airport and she sat down and lit a cigarette, nervous and impatient. When the telephone jangled once more she lifted it quickly, wanting to dispel the ominous atmosphere that the day had taken on.

'I've just seen the article about your friends in the *Telegraph*.' Edward's voice was smooth. His comforting, consulting-room voice. 'I thought you might be feeling a little low, even though you must be relieved that justice will finally be done. Perhaps you'd like to have dinner. I could try to take your mind off all this, distract you for a few hours.'

'I'm flying out tonight,' she said.

'Will you be away for long?' he asked.

'I've no idea,' she said.

'I see. Well, I wish you luck.'

She heard the disapproval in his words. And the disappointment. 'Thank you for the phone call, Edward. For thinking about me. Goodbye.'

'Goodbye, Camilla.'

The click as he hung up made her feel as if she was letting go of the last line that bound her to the life she had made in London. An hour later she was on her way to the airport.

Chapter 18

Kenya, June 1967

Jeremy Hardy leaned back in his chair and stretched. In front of him a mountain of letters and reports still sat in a reproachful pile on his desk. He glanced at his watch. Six o'clock. He might drop into the Outspan Hotel and have a drink before going home. Unwind a little. He wondered whether he was too old for this job. Or whether the job was now too much for him. The Langani case was a bugger, made worse by the fact that the van der Beers had been personal friends for almost a decade. Jan's memorial service had been a wretchedly melancholy affair, with his old friends gathering to remember the man, without knowing the real tragedy of his life and death. Jeremy was still haunted by the look on Lottie's face, when she had asked if he had made any progress. He needed results for her, and for her family. And he wanted to prove that he was a good police officer. He took out his pipe and cleaned it, filled it, tamped down the tobacco and lit it, the ritual giving him time to think.

It was a few minutes before he became aware of the noise from the front office. The duty officer was talking loudly, summoning a second *askari*. Well, let them deal with it. He reached for his jacket and shrugged it on, hoping to leave before he was asked for advice. There was a knock on the door.

'*Karibu*,' he called, with resignation.

'Sir, there is a man in the front office who is asking for you.' His newly appointed assistant, Sergeant Adongo, stood in the doorway. 'He says he will only speak to the Chief Inspector. I have told him to come back tomorrow, but he says that he knows you are here.'

'Who is he?' Hardy asked, with some annoyance. He did not want to spend an hour listening to some *shauri* about stolen cattle, or a family feud that could easily wait until the morning. In any case, this was exactly the type of problem he wanted the African policeman to handle.

'He would not give his name,' Sergeant Adongo said. 'He says he will speak only to you.'

The inspector grunted with frustration as he walked down the corridor to the front office and emerged from behind the duty desk. The room was painted in government-issue green, illuminated by strip lighting down the centre of the ceiling. There was a man sitting on one of the benches that lined the walls. He was dressed in a long, threadbare greatcoat, and he wore no shoes. The harsh light showed that he was in bad physical shape, his hair long and matted, and the planes of his face hollowed, almost skeletal. His skin had an unhealthy, greyish pallor. He was hunched forwards, head hanging down, hands holding on to the bench, as if he might topple over.

'I am Chief Inspector Hardy. You wanted to see me.'

The man did not look up. When he answered, his voice was hoarse, as if he was having difficulty speaking.

'My name is Simon Githiri,' he said in careful English. 'I have come to give myself up. For the killing of my employer, Piet van der Beer.'

Hardy studied him, astonished, not believing him. Simon Githiri. He had seen the young man on a number of occasions at Langani. But the figure before him was shivering, his face and body wasted. His eyes were glazed and filmy and he looked as though he was starving. He had been on the run for a long time, hiding in the cold and damp of the Aberdare Forest. But yes, it was Simon Githiri.

'Bring him to the interview room,' Hardy ordered. 'Find him something to eat and get ready to take down his statement.'

He went to his office and telephoned Langani, glad that it was Lars who answered the telephone.

'He walked in here of his own accord. I've no idea why, or where he has come from,' Hardy said. 'I'll ring you back when I know more.'

In the interview room, a bowl of *posho* with a little meat had been placed on the table in front of the prisoner, and a mug of sweet milky tea. But Simon refused the food, turning his gaunt face away from any nourishment.

'Water,' he said.

He took the cup that was offered to him, and his hand shook as he lifted it to his lips and drained it in silence. The duty sergeant came in and sat down, ready to take notes. Hardy cleared his throat.

'For the record, we are in the interview room at Nyeri Police Station, where Simon Githiri has given himself up of his own free will, and has confessed to the murder of Piet van der Beer of Langani Farm.'

The sergeant read Githiri his rights in English and Kikuyu, and told him he would be required to make a formal statement and sign his confession. Simon nodded his assent.

'I have come to give myself up for the killing of Piet van der Beer,' he repeated in a low voice.

'And do you also admit that you were involved in the slaughter of livestock at Langani, and in an armed raid during September of the same year? As well as the destruction of the workshop in December of last year, and the burning of the property known as Langani Lodge? Would you tell us, now, the names of the other people also involved in those incidents?'

But the prisoner's response was an impenetrable silence. His face was devoid of expression, and it was almost as though he had removed himself from the room. Finally, after repeating the questions several times, the inspector lost patience with him.

'Simon, do you understand that you may now face the death penalty because of the confession you have made?' There was no reaction, and Hardy paused before changing tack. 'We already know that you were aided in these crimes by your uncle, Karanja Mungai,' he said. Then he leaned very close to the young man, his next words spoken in a soft, confiding tone. 'We know about your wife, Wanjiru. And the child who is your son.'

Simon's head jerked up, and he looked at the policeman directly for the first time. But he still did not say a word.

'The old man, Karanja, cannot harm you now,' Hardy said. 'He will be arrested and charged, because I believe that he persuaded you to carry out these terrible crimes. But your wife and son are innocent. If you want to protect them, then you must tell the truth.'

'The man's death was a tribal matter. A matter of honour.' Simon had broken his silence. 'My son was marked because I did not act sooner, to pay the debt. Now I have fulfilled my oath. Piet van der Beer is dead, and I have learned that Jan van der Beer is also dead. It is over. That is why I have come to give myself up.'

Simon's head sank back down on to his chest and he seemed to have entered a kind of trance. The policeman tried again and again to obtain more answers, but no other sound came from the prisoner's lips. He was clearly in a state of exhaustion, or perhaps a form of hysteria. Hardy had seen men like this before, people who thought they had been sentenced to death by a witchdoctor, or who had their minds altered by the use of powerful drugs. He beckoned the sergeant outside.

'Take him to the cells,' he said. 'Stay with him and talk to him in Kikuyu for a while. Quietly, and sympathetically. Keep on bringing up the subject of his son. And see if you can get him to eat. That might shake him out of his trance, and then we'll be able to question him in the morning with better results.'

Sarah was sitting, ashen-faced, staring at the radio receiver. She looked up at Dan. 'He gave himself up. Walked into the police station and confessed. It's beyond belief.'

'Do you want to go down there?' Dan asked.

'No!' The word came out as an explosion. 'No,' she said again, more quietly. 'There's nothing I can do. Nothing at all. But thank you.'

She sat silently through dinner, swallowing her food with difficulty. Allie watched her and gave Dan a warning look when he raised the subject again.

'Sarah's right,' Allie said. 'There's no sense in her going anywhere for the time being. Now, let's decide what route we're taking in the morning. Because one section of my "pachyies" has embarked on a detour, and I'm not sure which group to follow.'

In the sanctuary of her hut, Sarah lay down on the bed. She should be relieved that Simon was in custody at last, but instead she felt ill. There would be a trial, and she would have to give evidence, because she was the only one who had seen him on the ridge. She would have to face Simon Githiri across a courtroom, have to look into the face of Piet's murderer and tell a room full of strangers what he had done to the man she loved, and how she had found him there on the ground. When she closed her eyes, the nightmare played itself out in front of her and she imagined herself sitting in the witness box, with Simon's eyes glittering as he turned to look at her from the dock. As he had looked at her on the ridge that night. Her mind shied away from the memory, but it hovered on the edge of her consciousness like a ghost on a turret stair. Eventually, she got up and went to sit at her desk, tidying her notes and files, trying to bury the future in the welter of ordinary, everyday things. She started a letter to her family but she could not tell them, with any coherence, what was happening, so she tore up the pages and threw them into the waste-paper basket.

At first light she drank her tea, washed in the canvas basin outside her hut, and threw on her clothes. Her eyes were gritty and her head ached from lack of sleep. She went to the kitchen, filled a thermos with coffee and packed a small basket of fruit and bread. The thought of a breakfast discussion and bright conversation was too much, and she was relieved to see that Erope was ready and waiting beside the Land Rover. They set out in search of their elephants, but she could not rid herself of the idea that it was only a matter of time before she would have to face Simon, and she could not immerse herself in the world of the great creatures she studied. The glare of the sun's yellow eye was relentless, and after a couple of hours Sarah found an area of shade and stopped the vehicle on the brow of a small, tufted rise. Below her the herd made its way through a patch of riverine forest, their huge bodies creating a series of sounds like the crack of rifles as they pushed their way through trees and thick bush.

She climbed out of the Land Rover and took out her cameras to photograph the shimmering horizon to the north, with its border of jagged, volcanic hills rising like pointed teeth out of the tawny land. Erope stood close by, balanced easily on one leg, leaning on the spear he always carried. All around them the sounds of Africa rose into the white-hot air. In the centre of the river Sarah could see a submerged crocodile, its scaly form making a small island that was surrounded by a cloud of hovering butterflies. Hornbills hopped and spluttered in the trees, and they could hear the raucous shriek of baboons close by. Sarah sat down and poured coffee, putting three heaped spoons of sugar into Erope's mug.

A movement caught her eye. In a thicket just a few feet away, she saw a pair of dik dik, eyes moist, noses and ears twitching, on guard. She scrambled to her feet, reaching for her camera, but her sudden action put the tiny animals to flight and they bounded away on spindly legs, scattering a group of Thomson's gazelle grazing close to them. Erope clicked his tongue at her lack of caution.

'Sorry. I wasn't thinking,' she muttered.

'It is a heavy burden you are carrying,' he said.

'Too heavy,' she answered. Then, all at once, she was desperately tired of keeping it locked inside herself. 'Erope, I am in trouble,' she said.

'When you share your troubles they are not so bad.'

'Simon Githiri gave himself up last night.'

'The man who killed Piet.' Erope spat on the ground in contempt. 'He will pay for his crime now. The government will hang him?'

'I don't know. Yes, perhaps.' She shuddered. 'But first there will be a trial.'

Erope spat once more, this time in satisfaction. 'And after, he will die. Then it will be finished, Sarah.'

'No. Because Simon's uncle helped him with what he did at Langani. It was a matter of revenge. And I will have to give evidence in the court, but I am afraid to face him.' She closed her eyes against the pounding heat. 'They may execute him, Erope, but he will not die in my head. He will always be there, in my thoughts.'

'It was a blood feud, then?' Erope said.

'You could call it that, yes. During the Mau Mau times, Piet's father killed Simon's father. So maybe he did see it that way.'

The Samburu gazed into the distance, weighing the matter. 'Sarah, if a *fisi* waits in the dark for you, it is better to go out and hunt it with your spear than to hide from it,' he said at last.

Sarah felt her skin crawl at the memory of the hyena on the ridge. She could almost smell the fetid rankness of it in her nostrils, see the creature's heavy jowl and sense its thirst for blood. It had come for Piet whose ruined body lay dead on the ground. The scent of his blood was in the air and she had prevented it from tearing apart what remained of him. And then Simon had thrown the spear and the beast had fallen, knocking her over the side of the ridge.

'It is only a cowardly beast,' Erope said, lifting his spear. 'It can be hunted and killed, as a man can be killed. Then the smell and the fear are gone.' He swung his arm back, and the spear soared away in a swish of hot air, the blade landing with a dull thwack in the trunk of an acacia tree. It hung there, quivering. Sarah stared at it, mesmerised, remembering the spear that Simon had thrown to save her life, even though he had murdered her love, on that same moonlit night.

As the afternoon heat intensified, her head continued to throb and she was too tired to concentrate on the movements of the herd.

439

'I'm going back to the camp,' she said. 'I'll work on my notes for the rest of the day, and we'll go out again in the morning.'

They set off down the track, emerging from dense bush on to one of the wider trails that led to the Springs. Half an hour later, they saw a minibus filled with tourists from one of the game lodges. It had stopped on the dirt road ahead of them. Alongside was a Game Department vehicle. A heated argument had broken out between a uniformed ranger and the driver of the bus. As Sarah drew nearer she saw the official reach out and accept a wad of banknotes, stuff them into his pocket and drive away. She pulled up beside the bus, and greeted the passengers who were all Italians.

'Were you having some trouble there?' she asked the driver.

He scowled. 'We paid our park entrance fee at Samburu,' he said. 'But today we decided to drive out of the reserve, because one of the guides saw a leopard around here yesterday. Now this man has told me I must pay him another twenty shillings for each passenger and fifty shillings for the bus, to be in this area. He says this is a special fee, to cover security patrols. Because of the Shifta bandits. I have never heard of such a charge, but he said we could not pass through here unless we pay. And he would know my bus the next time.'

'Did he give you a receipt?' Sarah asked, already knowing the answer.

'He was very angry, shouting about the money.' One of the tourists leaned out of the window, talking to Sarah in halting English. 'It was a little . . . frightening for us. We are wondering, for a moment, if he was a bandit himself. If he would hurt us. He was telling that we might be attacked if we do not pay.'

'This is a question of local corruption,' Sarah said. 'Please don't be concerned for your safety. You are in a pretty secure area, and no one is going to attack you. I'm afraid you've come across a crooked official, and I'm going straight to the Game Department headquarters to report him.' She turned to the bus driver. 'You must report this man, too. He had no right to charge you anything extra, and he has pocketed that money for himself.'

The driver shrugged. 'Who can stop it?' he asked. 'I must come back here every few days, with different parties. I cannot argue with such a man. And it is better to pay him, than to be ambushed by his bandit friends, and have our throats cut, or get shot. If he pays the Shifta to keep away, that is better. And his boss will probably get a share of the money. I must go on now. We have to be back at the Samburu gate by sundown.'

Sarah drove away, seething with anger. She would go right now to the warden's office in Isiolo, and complain. The bus driver was obviously too lily-livered to do anything about it. Someone must put a stop to it. Erope made no comment. He clung to his seat, bracing himself as Sarah rattled along the rough track at breakneck speed. When she marched into the Game Department headquarters, he remained in the car. The official on duty recognised her at once. He was unprepared for her attack, and completely unmoved by it.

'What is the name of this man whom you saw?' he said, slowly taking out a notebook and a sheet of carbon paper, and licking the tip of his pencil. 'You will have to fill in this report, Mama, and we need his name and the number of his car.'

'I didn't take down his name,' she said furiously. 'And I didn't get the vehicle number. He drove off in a hurry when he saw me. You can't have many cars out on patrol. You must know perfectly well who he is.'

'We do not know what man you are talking about,' the ranger said. He leaned back in his chair and regarded her with insolent eyes. 'You must give his name and his vehicle number. And the number of the safari bus, with the name of the driver so that he can be questioned.'

A small group of Samburu who had been standing outside now peered into the office, curious about the *shauri* with the white memsahib, interested to see who would have the upper hand.

'You know very well who this ranger is.' Sarah was close to exploding with rage. 'And the safari driver is at Samburu Lodge. You can find him by asking around there. I want to see the warden. Right now.'

'He is out. He will not be back today. We have no one who can go to Samburu Lodge. We are busy here in the office.' The duty officer was not going to be ordered about by a *mzungu*, least of all in front of an audience. These white people should understand that they were no longer in charge. He put away his notebook and pencil, and Sarah heard a snigger in the little group behind her.

'Dammit, you're all the same!' She was almost shouting. 'God knows how many of you are in on this racket! People who abuse their positions don't deserve to work here. That ranger should be sacked, and so should any of you who are taking illegal money from tourists or Shiftas. And I will tell the warden when I see him, that you did nothing to help me. Nothing at all.'

She stormed out of the office and returned to the car. Erope glanced at her flushed face and grim expression, and retreated into his private thoughts. She could sense disapproval.

'What? What's the matter?' Her tone was belligerent, and Erope had no intention of being drawn into the conflict. He spread his hands, in a gesture of dismissal.

'Since we are here, maybe you will get the post for Dan,' was all he said.

Sarah collected the bundle of mail from the post office. There was a letter for her with an Irish stamp and Tim's near indecipherable scrawl. She put it into her camera bag and set off for the camp. Dan was in the office, bent over his old typewriter, sweating in the afternoon heat and muttering to himself. He waved a hand absent-mindedly, but did not look up.

'I brought the mail from Isiolo,' Sarah said. But she did not explain what she had been doing there and he did not seem to notice.

'Thanks, kid,' he said. 'It sure is too hot around here today. Take a break. We'll catch up later, when Allie comes in.'

Her hut was breathlessly hot, and she took Tim's letter outside to read under a tree. He had written, at last, to explain the circumstances of Deirdre's departure, and his visit to Camilla in London.

It's hard to put into words what a complete panic I was in, how ashamed I felt, and how humiliated by what had happened. I couldn't talk about it within the family. Misplaced pride, I suppose. I felt such a fool, that Deirdre had never been able to tell me the most important thing about herself. A doctor who couldn't recognise that serious a condition in the girl he claimed to love.

I am very sorry, Sarah. I know you would have understood, and you tried to tell me that, before you left. But I wasn't thinking straight then. I'm writing now to make things right, especially between you and Camilla. She was pretty angry that I had put her in such an awkward position, and I hope you can forgive the mess I've made of everything.

You did say I should come out there to Kenya and visit you. And one of these days, maybe I will. I might even come back there to work, if Dad

can find someone to replace me here. Try to forgive me for being such a
crass idiot, and give me a chance to make it up to you.

In the meantime, please patch up things with Camilla. She's one hell
of a friend. Don't lose her on my account. On any account.

Love,

Tim

Sarah read and reread the letter, feeling as foolish and guilty as her
brother. She had fences to mend. It was difficult to admit how judgemental
and stupid she had been, and she was wrestling with her conscience when
she heard the sound of Allie's vehicle drawing up outside the compound.

'Hello,' Sarah said, smiling at her. 'It's brutal out there.'

'The warden from Isiolo is right behind me,' Allie said. 'He'd like a
word with you. About some incident with one of his rangers, he says.'

The warden shook hands with her, but he was openly hostile and angry.
Dan appeared and brought them into his office where he sat without
saying anything. But Sarah could see that he was displeased.

'I have heard that you came to the office, to accuse my staff of taking
bribes,' the warden said. 'That is a serious complaint.'

'I saw it happen,' Sarah said, her chin coming up in defiance. 'One of
your rangers took money from a group of Italian tourists. The driver said
he had to pay a large sum, otherwise there would be trouble for him next
time, and maybe his bus would be attacked. The tourists were scared too.
That's bad for this reserve, and for tourism generally.'

'Did you speak to this ranger? What was his name?'

'No. He drove off before I had a chance. But I saw what was going on.
He took money from tourists, claiming it was for security. You can easily
find out who he was.'

'But if this ranger drove off before you stopped, then you would not be
able to identify him. Perhaps he was not a ranger at all.'

'He was in uniform. He was in an official vehicle. I saw that quite clearly.'

'So what was the number of this vehicle? Or the number of the safari
bus?'

'I explained all this to your staff.' Sarah could feel her anger rising
again.

'My staff.' The warden's smile was not pleasant. 'They told me a *mzungu* woman came into the office, shouting before members of the public that the rangers were all corrupt, and should lose their jobs.'

'Look,' Sarah glared at him. 'You have a corrupt official working for you, and maybe more. And if you're not inclined to do anything about it, then—'

Dan rose to his feet.

'It seems we have a misunderstanding here,' he said, gripping Sarah's arm to silence any protest. 'We recognise that complaints have to be made through the proper channels, and of course my assistant did not mean to suggest that all of your staff are corrupt. I'm sure you will now investigate the incident right away. And Miss Mackay will write a full report of what she saw, and leave the matter in your capable hands.'

Sarah stood open-mouthed as Dan and Allie walked out to see the warden off. When they returned, she could no longer contain her fury.

'How could you let him off like that? If we turn a blind eye to park rangers on the take, what hope is there for this place? Some of these parks people are in cahoots with the poachers. They even allow the Shifta in here with their guns and trucks. This kind of thing will ruin everything we are working for. I know what I saw! That ranger was guilty of extortion, and I could have done with your support back there—'

'Sarah!' Dan's voice cut into her diatribe, and brought her up short. 'There is a right way and a wrong way to deal with this kind of thing. Going into the warden's office with all guns blazing, firing accusations at all and sundry – that's not going to do it, kid. I'm sure this guy is taking money, but we're not going to nail these crooks that way. You should have got the number of the park vehicle, the names of the safari company and the driver, and the number of the minibus. And you should have told me, when you came in this afternoon, that you had been to Isiolo.'

'But I—'

'We know how committed you are to your work here. There's no question that the corruption issue is bad and getting worse. But that was poor judgement on your part, charging into the warden's office without first thinking things out. That alienates the people we have to work with, and doesn't achieve anything.'

'Yes. Yes, I suppose you're right.'

'Look, kid, you're under a lot of strain,' Dan said. 'The news about

Simon giving himself up and the prospect of a court case must be pretty hard to take. Allie and I have talked about the pressure on you, and we have a suggestion. We think you should go down to Langani for a while. Or take a holiday somewhere. At the coast, maybe. You're too wound up, young lady, and we don't want you making any mistakes that can't be undone.'

Sarah looked at them both in horror. They were sending her away. This was their way of saying she had lost her job.

'Is this . . . are you telling me you don't want me to work here any more?' She put her hands up to her face. 'Are you giving me the sack?'

Allie put an arm around her shoulder. 'Of course we're not giving you the sack. You've done a great job here from the beginning, Sarah. But right now your mind isn't focused on your work. We both understand that, and we think you should take some time off. And when this whole tragic business is sorted out, then we would love to have you back.'

'Now don't get all upset.' Dan's face was sympathetic. 'We've been worried about you for a while, with all that's happening between here and Langani. Your visit to the warden's office today was for the right reason, but it was the wrong tactic. So I figure you need a little cooling-off period. We'll hold your job for you because you're the best researcher we've ever had. Allie and I can manage with Erope for the immediate future. We've all taught him a lot, and the notes he takes are good. So you can take some time for yourself. I warned you before that this was a hard place to survive in.'

'Why don't you take your Land Rover and head for Langani tomorrow?' Allie suggested. 'If we need the car, or if you decide to go to the coast or somewhere, then I'll come down with Dan and drive it back. And don't worry, Sarah. You'll be fine in a little while, and then we'll all be back to normal again. Let's get Hannah or Lars on the radio and tell them you're coming. I'm sure they'll be glad of your support just now.'

Dinner was a strained affair, and Sarah went to bed immediately afterwards. The next morning, she packed her bag, gathered up her cameras and her notebooks, and closed the door of the hut that had been her home and her refuge.

'Safe journey,' Dan said. 'It's just as well that you will be at Langani. The police will surely be interrogating Githiri now, and you'll want to hear first hand what your inspector friend has to report. We'll be anxious to know what's happening.'

'Dan, I—'

'It's OK, kid. Really it is. Off you go. You have your notes and so on. Plenty of paperwork. We'll be in touch.'

She drove at speed, tears distorting the already dust-blurred windscreen. She had been evicted, sent on her way without being offered a choice. She had made a mess of her job. And Dan was right, she wasn't thinking straight. Recently she had quarrelled with both Hannah and Camilla, and she had lost contact with Rabindrah by refusing to face up to what she felt about him. She needed to calm down, before she made any more mistakes.

When she reached Langani, Lars took her arm and brought her into the sitting room where Jeremy was already ensconced, flanked by Lottie and Sergio. Hannah rose to welcome her, and they resettled themselves to hear what the policeman had to say.

'Simon looks very much the worse for wear,' Jeremy said. 'Close to starving, I'd say. He knew exactly what he was doing when he admitted to Piet's murder. Since then I've spent hours questioning him, but he won't say another word, apart from repeating his original statement.'

'Couldn't you get anything else out of him at all?' Hannah demanded.

'I've been at it all day yesterday, and most of this morning,' Jeremy said. 'And I've had one of my best Kikuyu blokes in the cell with him, talking around the issue, speaking to him in Kikuyu, asking him about his clan and his family. So far there is no response.'

'But he has definitely admitted to killing my son?' Lottie's eyes were huge with sorrow.

'Yes. Unequivocally. The problem is that he will not implicate Karanja, or anyone else. Nor will he say anything about the initial raid on the house, or the cattle or the incidents at the workshop and the lodge.'

'You are sure the uncle was behind all this?' Sergio asked.

'Wanjiru's evidence confirms that. Simon seems to have been a normal young man, until that evil old bastard got hold of him. I believe that Karanja brought him to the reserve specifically to plan Piet's death. He counted on the shock Simon would experience when he learned what had happened to his father, deliberately played on the young man's emotions, and then plied him with drugs and made him take the oath.'

446

'At least Karanja has been forced into hiding,' Lars said. 'That should prevent him from thinking about Langani for the time being. Particularly if he knows that Simon has given himself up.'

'It's clear that Simon thought his son's deformity was a punishment for not acting sooner,' Jeremy said. 'He could have murdered Piet much earlier. They were often out together, just the two of them. There was no reason for him to wait so long, unless there was a struggle of conscience going on in his head. I think Karanja arranged the killing of Hannah's cattle and the raid on the house in order to remind his nephew that he was there, waiting for the act of revenge to be carried out. But as long as Simon remains silent, we can rely only on Wanjiru's testimony. I'm not sure she will have the courage to hold up in the witness box, and in any case some of what she says will be regarded as hearsay.'

'So Simon will be convicted of murder because he's made a confession. But Karanja, and anyone else who was involved, will get off. Is that what you're saying?' Hannah's eyes were fixed on Hardy.

'Simon will hang. I've no doubt about that. He has admitted killing your brother, and there's no other possible sentence. But we cannot touch Karanja unless Simon talks.'

'You must find something that will force the truth out of him.' There was a savage note in Hannah's voice.

'He has nothing left to lose,' Lottie said with resignation. 'That is why he gave himself up. He knows that he is already a dead man.'

'Then this will go on. And on,' Hannah said. 'Because Karanja will not stop until he has taken everything. You have to break Simon's silence, Jeremy. Whatever it takes!' Her voice had risen, and Lars reached out to take her hand.

'Hannah, I will do everything in my power, but—'

'But you expect us to sit here patiently, and wait for you to ask Simon a few more polite questions. While Karanja is still out there, threatening us all.' Hannah's face was dark. 'Are we supposed to wait until we are all dead? Is that it?'

'Hannah,' Lottie said, gently, 'it does no good, this. Jeremy is doing his best for us.'

'What has he done for us, exactly?' Hannah asked. 'How come he never discovered the reason for Piet's death?' She turned to look at the policeman. 'Or were you protecting Pa's good name? Was that it?'

'Hannah, you know that's not the case,' Lars said.

'There is no record of the incident in the forest,' Jeremy said stiffly. 'I can only assume that any mention of it in official files was destroyed at the time of the amnesty. In any event, I can assure you that I was not aware of what Jan had done. Or that Piet's death could be a crime of revenge.'

'Simon has said that the debt is paid,' Hannah said. 'But I am still fighting for my family and my land.' She turned to Lottie. 'After Piet died, I was the one who stayed. You left and went south, for Pa's sake. And now he's dead too, and all that is left of our family history is this farm. I've thought of leaving it, of course I have. Because I'm so terrified of what might happen to Lars and Suniva and myself. But why should we leave? We're creating jobs and revenue and taxes and food, and contributing all that we can. What will happen to this country if thugs like Karanja can frighten people off their land? Where is the law, if Karanja can walk free?'

'That's right.' Sarah spoke for the first time. 'Simon must sign a statement, showing his uncle's role in what happened.'

'The police have ways of getting information from even the worst criminals.' Hannah addressed her remark to the policeman. 'Special methods of interrogation. We all know that. So, go and use them.'

'Hannah, I have to act within the law,' Jeremy said. 'Otherwise I am no better than Karanja and others like him. If Simon's confession is exacted under duress, he could retract it in court. Then the rest of our evidence would be tainted, and we could end up with nothing.'

'It is this family who will end up with nothing.' Hannah stood up, shaking her fist at him. 'While the law shields a murderer and a criminal. We know you have ways of making a prisoner confess, Jeremy. And Simon is barbaric. He deserves no mercy.'

Lottie rose and positioned herself in front of her daughter, staring into her angry face. They were like two lionesses, squaring up for a fight, Sarah thought. She was afraid for both of them, and for the damage they might do each other in their anger.

'You know who you sound like?' Lottie asked. 'Like your father. This place is making you just like him. What do you want Jeremy to do? Beat Simon up? Threaten and terrorise him? Put him on a spit and light a fire under him?'

'Lottie—' Lars leaned towards her but she ignored his outstretched hand.

'Is that what you want, Hannah?' she asked. 'To start this whole cycle of revenge all over again, until you too have to run away and hide from what you have done?' She stood back a little, shaking her head. 'Will you stay here until there is a sea of blood at your feet too, just to hold your claim to this farm? It's not worth it. It was never worth it. I want you to be strong, but not made of stone. I want you to have vision, not blindness. You are a wife and a mother now, like me. We have to know when to say "enough". And if you think I have failed you because I want to walk away from this, then so be it.'

'Walk away, then.' The words were out before Hannah could stop herself. 'Forget about us – your daughter and your granddaughter. Run away and hide, like Pa did. Go back to Johannesburg with Uncle Sergio.'

There was a shocked silence and Hannah froze, appalled by what she had said. But it was too late to retract. Lars sat forward and put his head in his hands.

'I said I would stay while you needed me,' Lottie said. 'But when this case is over, I will leave. Not to run away and hide, but to live. I can't take any more hatred. I will go because I have no desire to watch my only surviving child destroy herself and everyone around her for a piece of earth.'

She turned and walked out of the room. After a moment, Sergio went out after her.

Hannah slumped into a chair, her face twisted with remorse. 'Ach, don't look at me like that,' she said to Sarah. 'We lost Piet, you and I. And now I stand to lose the place he loved. The place where we were born. Where you would have built your lives together. Do you think he would have hung his head and walked away from his land?'

She turned to Jeremy. 'You must use the child,' she said coldly. 'Simon's son. Tell him the baby can have an operation that will take away the mark of deformity. The curse, or whatever he thinks it is. But if there's no statement about Karanja, there will be no treatment and the child will never be normal. He will spend his life as a cripple. An outcast from the clan, like Simon was. He will have no future.'

There was a long silence. The policeman sat in his chair, turning his baton round and round in his hands, not meeting Hannah's eyes.

'Why not tell him the truth, Jeremy?' Sarah said. 'Tell him that his child is deformed because Karanja beat up the mother when she was pregnant. Simon was there when the old man brought Wanjiru back, on the day that she ran away. He saw what had happened to her. Not that he cared much – she was only a chattel in his eyes. But a male child has some value. If Simon understands that his son was injured by Karanja he may speak out.'

Hardy regarded her thoughtfully, then stood up. 'It's a possibility,' he said. 'It might work if Simon has any real feeling for the child. But I'm thinking that the person who should tell him this, who might best influence him, is his old mentor. Fr Bidoli.'

'I could ask him to do that,' Sarah said. 'I could drive down to Nyeri tomorrow and talk to him. And perhaps see Wanjiru, too. I'll ring Dr Markham before I go, and see if he has been able to set up a date with the specialist.' She paused. 'Do you think she should still be at the mission? With Simon locked up in the same town?'

'It's not ideal, but I prefer to have her where we can keep an eye on her,' Jeremy said. 'Let me know what the priest has to say. I'll be in touch tomorrow.'

It was Lars who saw the policeman to his car, and he did not come back inside.

'He's furious with me.' Hannah was hunched miserably in a chair, and Sarah came to sit on the arm. 'Ach, Sarah, why can't I ever keep my big mouth shut? Ma was right, you know. I've turned into a stone-hearted bitch. It's not what I want to be, truly it's not. Simon may be in jail, but he is still a threat to us, and I'm so frightened that I want to scream with rage. Because of what I see and hear in my head all the time.'

'I know. I hear and see those same things. And when it comes to rages, you're not the only one. I've been sort of suspended from my job, because I had a run-in with one of the local officials in Isiolo and handled it all wrong. I'm even scared that Dan will start looking for a new researcher – someone who won't go off the rails, is totally focused on the job. I haven't been able to concentrate on anything recently. It's hard to know where we can go from here.' She stood up, and pulled Hannah to her feet. 'But we can find Lottie at least, and make peace with her. You don't want to let this push you apart again.'

They heard Lottie before they saw her, sitting with her brother under the flame tree. The sky was a mass of pewter-coloured clouds, and the wind that had come up carried the sound of their voices towards the verandah. Hannah stopped at the edge of the steps, wondering if she should disturb them. Sergio's words stopped her in her tracks.

'Have you written to Mario?' he asked.

'No.' Lottie shook her head. 'It's too soon. I don't know what I could say to him.'

'He loves you, Carlotta. You must at least tell him what has happened.'

'I know. I know.'

'I'm sure he would fly out to Johannesburg. You could come down and stay with us. Get to know him again, maybe go to Italy for a while and see his place.'

'Sergio, Janni has only been dead—'

'Jan was a brute during those last years in Rhodesia. I saw how you were when you came to visit us. Elena and I – we were very concerned. And we were happy about what had happened between you and Mario. If you had had more time together, I don't think you would ever have gone back. God knows, Carlotta, Jan didn't deserve you these last few years, and he very nearly destroyed you. But you are free of him now. Free to go where you want.'

Sarah signalled that they should move away, but Hannah was riveted. She stood, straining to hear Lottie's every word.

'I'm staying at Langani for the time being,' Lottie said. 'I will write to Mario soon, but for now I must be here for Hannah, because she is afraid. If they do not find Karanja, then I will try and prevail on her to leave. But it will be difficult. And that is my fault in a way, because of Janni's will. I made him give her the farm, you see. I told him it was the only thing to do. But now that it really belongs to her, she may find it even harder to abandon it. I am afraid I have created a millstone for her neck.'

'She is a stubborn girl, your Hannah. But she has a good husband who loves her, and a beautiful child. She is not alone like you. You have earned the right to live the best life you can, *cara*. You cannot exist only for your daughter and your grandchild.'

'I have to make up for the time when I wasn't here. How can I tell Hannah that I want to go away, to be with a man with whom I had an affair while her father was still alive? You heard what she said earlier, what she thinks of me. But I will write to Mario, and if he loves me, then he will be prepared to wait. At least until after this trial.'

Hannah walked away, hurrying towards the house and beckoning Sarah to follow.

'She had an affair.' Hannah was astounded by what she had heard.

'But she stayed with Janni to the end,' Sarah said. 'No matter how hard that was.'

'But what if this man turns up here? Asks her to go away with him, maybe even marry him?' Hannah paced the verandah.

'If he's a good man, and he loves her, then she should marry him. And if you love her, you will be glad for her. Sergio is right. She deserves to be happy, after all she's been through.'

'But she'll go away. He lives in Italy!'

'Hannah, she will go away in any case. Not because she doesn't love you all, but because Langani and its associations are too terrible for her. I can't see her living here as your dependant. Besides, it would be wonderful to think of Lottie in love. Like you and Lars. Wouldn't it?'

'Always the romantic! The strong, patient people like you and Ma make me feel so bad. I blunder around, kicking out in every direction, finding it hard to explain anything to anyone. Although I did talk to Anthony while he was here. Somehow it was easier to say things to him. I was surprised how much it helped.'

'The people nearest to you are often the hardest to confide in. It's too painful,' Sarah said. 'I suppose that's why Tim couldn't talk to me. I'll show you what he finally wrote to me. And then maybe we can compose a joint letter for Camilla. Because we also need to tell her about Simon.'

They stood at the window, arm in arm, and looked out at the silhouette of Piet's ridge, deep blue in the cloudy landscape, still scarred by the fire that had destroyed his last dream.

'Let's see the explanation from the helpless brother, then,' Hannah said. 'And afterwards we'll find Lars and Suniva, and go for a walk before the dark comes in and closes us into our night-time siege.'

It was close to noon the next day when Sarah sat down with Fr Bidoli. Although he looked frail, she did not think his failing health would prevent him from going to the prison. But would he agree to press Simon for a statement implicating Karanja? If he went to see Simon, he would be going as a pastor. And he would certainly not countenance Hannah's suggestion to use the child as a bargaining tool. Dr Markham had confirmed on the telephone that an orthopaedic specialist in Nairobi would see the child within a week. That would be good news for Wanjiru, at least.

The priest looked ghostlike as he took her hand and smiled his kindly smile.

'How are you, Father?'

'I am living each day as God gives it to me,' he said. 'But you have not come only to enquire about my health, I think.'

'I have come about Simon,' she said. 'He has surrendered and he is in jail. Here in Nyeri.'

The priest was visibly shocked by her news. But he listened patiently and without comment as she described all that had happened since she had last seen him. She finished with the meeting at Langani the day before, dwelling on the suffering of both Hannah and Lottie and on their fears about the man in prison across the street.

'You want me to go and see him?' he said.

'I think he might listen to you. He trusts you.'

'And what is it you think I can persuade him to say?'

'His uncle drove him to much of what he did. I think we all accept that. But if Karanja goes free, the vendetta will continue until he forces Hannah from her farm. Or kills her, too. She is already near to collapsing under that threat. But Simon has refused to talk about his uncle.'

'My dear child, if I go to the prison, it is not certain that he will see me, or that he will say anything that will be useful to the police. And if he speaks to me as his confessor, you know I can never tell you, or anybody, what he says.' He paused, looking at Sarah's bowed head. 'But I will go,' he said. 'I will try to save the goodness that was in him once. And I will appeal to him, for you and for Hannah and her family.'

'I realise it is a lot to ask,' Sarah said.

'No. It is my mission. Once a child is given into my care, he is always in my care. I will tell you when I have seen him. Give me the name of your friend the policeman, and I will make the arrangement with him. But do not expect too much, Sarah. This man in the prison is not the boy I knew at Kagumo. He has moved far away from any beliefs he held then, so we can only trust in God's goodness and redemption. Still, Simon must have had a reason to give himself up. Perhaps he is ready to make the reparation.'

'I think he turned himself in when he heard that the man who killed his father was dead. But I don't believe that will satisfy Karanja. I am afraid he will not stop until Hannah has left the farm.'

'Perhaps not. So you will go back to Langani now?'

'I am going to visit Wanjiru first. To tell her that the surgeon will see the baby, and do the operation in a few days.'

'You are a truly good and generous Christian. I met your friend's husband when he brought her here.'

'Lars?'

'Yes. A fine man. A good man. Hannah is fortunate, yes?'

'Very fortunate, Father.' Sarah's voice was wistful.

'And you, my little one?'

Sarah looked into his wise, rheumy old eyes, and began to tell him how Rabindrah Singh had stepped into her life and overturned all her certainties.

'It's crazy, Father. I never thought . . . The thing is, I never loved anyone but Piet from the first moment that I saw him. I was a child then, and he was Hannah's big brother. But I loved him on that first day when he jumped into the river beside me, laughing and splashing me.' Her eyes were shining as she saw him again on that glorious morning, with his blonde hair and the mountain water running off his golden skin. 'My love for him grew, even though he didn't pay any attention to me for so long. And when he eventually came to love me, and asked me to marry him, it was the culmination of all my dreams. I was completely, deliriously happy.'

She was silent for a time, and the priest closed his eyes and waited.

'The day before Simon killed him, Piet and I lay side by side up on the ridge that was his favourite place on the farm. We were looking at the sky, making marvellous plans for the future. There was so much passion between us, but we wanted to wait. For our wedding night. We were going to spend it up there, camping on the top of our world. It was all so perfect. And then he was gone. Ripped away from me, torn out of my heart and out of my life. I never wanted or expected to feel like that again. It was too beautiful, and too agonising.'

'But now you are beginning to come alive for someone else. And you feel you are betraying the memory of the one you loved?'

'It's frightening. And I'm afraid that it's wrong, that everything about it is wrong!'

'Tell me about this man who has woken your heart again. Why do you think he is wrong?'

Sarah ran her fingers through her hair, searching for a way to describe Rabindrah and his effect on her.

'He is an Indian. A Sikh. He is the journalist who first noticed that the police had never interviewed you about Simon. When we started working together on this book about the elephants I did not like him much. I felt he was only out to make money and a name for himself. But when I was in real distress he was kind, and I found I could trust him. And then, after a while, I wanted to share more with him. To tell him about myself, about . . . I don't know, really. Something changed. Maybe I realised it when he was ill with malaria. Then I was suddenly afraid I would lose him. I realised that I wanted more from him than friendship.'

'And he wants this too?' The old priest was smiling at her.

'I think so. No, I know he does. Well, he did. We kissed. And it was the first time I had felt that deep thing that you feel for—' She stopped suddenly. 'Anyway, I panicked and ran away. I thought I was turning my back on Piet, forgetting the promises we had made to one another. I felt so guilty. And so terrible. Because I wanted Rabindrah to want me. I still do. But where does that put the love and the years that belonged to Piet? I can't just forget them and move on. I can't.'

'Sarah, because you loved one person who is lost to you, it does not mean you can never find room in your heart for another. We are human, my dear child, and God has blessed us with an infinite capacity for love. It is his gift to us. Look at a mother and father with their children.'

'That's a different kind of love,' she said, still troubled.

'And what you have begun to feel for this new man is different from what you felt for Piet. Because you are another person now. Ready to love again. You have a faithful nature, Sarah, and that is good. But Piet is gone from his earthly existence. One day you will meet again, in another life. But for now, you must take this new gift of love that God has given you, and live with it and in it. You have grieved for long enough, and Piet himself would not want you to live in sadness for the rest of your days. If you have loved once, so strong and true, you can love again. Indeed you must.'

'There will be problems, though. Religious, racial, family——'

'You will have to think about these things carefully as you come to know one another, it is true. Marriage with someone from another race and creed can cause unhappiness, unless you work hard together to overcome the differences. It is often the families that make problems, if they do not approve.'

'I don't think his family liked me much. And Hannah doesn't get along with Rabindrah. That's difficult, because she is my closest friend, and Piet's sister. So being attracted to Rabindrah is almost like a double betrayal.'

'Sarah, Sarah.' Fr Bidoli reached out and patted her cheek. 'You cannot choose to love a man because he suits your friends, no matter how close they are. And if they are truly your friends, then they will want your happiness more than anything else.'

'But what if this is just an infatuation? For both of us.'

The priest laughed, his kindly face crinkling in amusement. 'If it is only an infatuation, it will pass. And you will have taken another step towards your new life. Try it. That is how you will know. Because if you do not try it, then you may find that the engine of your life is stalled!'

She leaned over and hugged him carefully, afraid she might crack one of his brittle old bones.

'Thank you. Thank you for switching on the lights for me. Now, I'd better go and find Wanjiru, and tell her about the baby's operation.'

Wanjiru was working in the kitchen with one of the sisters, the baby wrapped in her *kanga* and asleep on her back. She was nervous as she sat down at the kitchen table with Sarah. One of the Italian nuns joined them, to explain in Kikuyu what would happen to the child during and after his surgery. Wanjiru was grateful, but filled with dread when she learned that her husband was in jail.

'He will come for me now,' she said. 'Karanja will kill me and the baby.'

'The police will protect you, and neither Simon nor Karanja knows where you are,' Sarah said.

'Karanja said if I ran away, if I spoke to any of the *wazungu*, he would kill me, and throw my baby to the hyenas.' The girl was wringing her hands and wailing.

'Look, you can see the police station from this window here,' Sarah said. 'If Karanja is seen the *askaris* will arrest him immediately. He will not come here, because he does not want to be caught.'

Wanjiru shivered as she looked across the open square at the police compound. And Sarah felt the same, sick feeling. Simon was too close. She stood up quickly.

'Don't be afraid,' she said. 'Chief Inspector Hardy will catch Karanja. I will come back and see you when the baby has had his operation. It will all be well, from now on.'

When she reached Langani her idea was to slink away to her room and to try to sort out the chaos in her mind. But Hannah was waiting, her face alight.

'I've just spoken to Camilla,' she said. 'There was a paragraph in the English papers today, about Simon giving himself up. She's flying out tonight. She wants to be here with us, until this is over. We should get through it together, she said. George is in London, but she's going straight to his place to freshen up and nap, and then she'll drive up here.'

'That's a long drive after spending hours on a plane,' Sarah said, as the news percolated through her clogged brain. 'Why don't I ask Rabindrah to fetch her from the airport, and drive her up?'

'Rabindrah?' Hannah was surprised. 'Why him?'

'We have some last-minute editing to discuss. He could bring Camilla up and do that at the same time.' Sarah hoped that Fr Bidoli's blessing would cover a small, white lie. 'I'll tell you all about Fr Bidoli in a minute. But first I'll ring Rabindrah, if that's all right.'

She made her way to the telephone and was relieved to find Rabindrah at the newspaper office. She had not wanted to make a call to Indar Singh's residence.

'Sarah. What a surprise. Is there something I can do for you?' His voice was cool. Almost cold.

She was on the defensive immediately. Why was he assuming she had only rung him because she wanted something from him?

'Simon Githiri has given himself in,' she said.

'Yes. I'm aware of that,' he said.

Sarah was taken aback. He had known, but he hadn't contacted her. She was silent, disconcerted.

'I spoke to Dan when I heard the news,' he said. 'He said you had gone to Langani. That you were planning to spend some time with Hannah.'

'Look, Rabindrah, there was something I didn't explain to you before.

About the attacks on Langani, and the reason for Piet's murder. Not because I didn't want to tell you, but—'

'Sarah, I have to go out in a minute. Perhaps I should give you a ring at Langani later?'

His tone was neutral, and suddenly she knew that she must make him see why she had kept silent. She could not lose him now, just when she had accepted that he might be an important part of her life. She plunged into the narrative before he had a chance to cut her off.

'I couldn't tell you what Jan had done,' she said, when she had reached the end of the story. 'For Hannah's sake. No one except the immediate family knew, and they were trying to come to terms with what they had learned. So I didn't feel I could explain the facts to anyone else.'

'But you are telling me now.'

'Because there will be a trial. And the whole story will come out in court soon.' She suddenly realised how awful that sounded. She was informing him because it would soon be common knowledge anyway. 'No. That's not why I'm telling you,' she added quickly. 'It's because I've been thinking about you. About what you said before you left Buffalo Springs. And I want you to know that I would trust you with my life, and with all the revelations that could ever be made about me or my friends, or anyone I know. The thing is, I need to see you, Rabindrah.' Silence. 'Rabindrah?'

'I'm listening.'

'Camilla is flying out from London,' she said, feeling foolish now. 'And I wondered if you would mind meeting her. Maybe even bring her up to Langani, if you have the time. Because I'd like to talk to you, and . . . well, would you please do that? Please?'

'What time? What's the flight number?'

She gave him the flight number and time of arrival and waited, breathless.

'I have to rush out now,' he said, his tone clipped. 'I'm due at a family gathering and they are all waiting for me. I'll bring her. Goodbye.'

She was left holding the receiver, hearing the click of the disconnected call and the burr of an empty line, feeling a surge of pleasure and anticipation.

The following day seemed endless, and Sarah could hardly contain herself. She was afraid that Hannah would sense her restlessness, and demand to know the reason. She passed the time working with Lottie in the dispensary, and helping to prepare Camilla's room. No one asked if Rabindrah might need a bed, and Sarah was reluctant to suggest it. Finally she disappeared to her room to work on her research notes. She did not want Dan and Allie to think she had forgotten her elephants. If Allie came for the car, Sarah wanted to show that her reports were up to date and her contribution still valuable.

By noon she was on tenterhooks. Rabindrah had not commented directly on her desire to see him, but at least he had agreed to come. That was the main thing. The rest she would have to figure out when he arrived. Every time the dogs barked, or she heard what might be the sound of a car approaching, she jumped up and went out to the front steps.

'What on earth is the matter with you this morning?' Hannah asked. 'You're skittering around like a hyrax on a hot rock! Sit down, for God's sake, or have a walk. You're making me feel really nervous.'

'Sorry.' Sarah reopened the book she had been trying to read and stared abstractedly at the page she had been struggling with for the past hour. Lars arrived for a cold beer before lunch.

'Not here yet?' he asked. 'I hope they haven't broken down.'

He had barely finished speaking when Sarah heard the crunch of tyres on gravel. Now that the moment had arrived, she sat glued to her seat. It was Hannah who went outside, and then there was the sound of Camilla's breathless greetings and high, light laughter.

'Where's Sarah?' Rabindrah's first words were echoed by Camilla.

'Yes. Where is she?'

Camilla was standing by the car, surrounded by dogs with tails waving. She had an arm around Lottie and she was holding Hannah's hand as Lars opened the boot of the car to take out her luggage. Rabindrah stood a little apart, his hand still on the driver's door. Sarah walked out on to the verandah, aware only of his eyes fixed on her. She gazed back at him, taking in the suggestion of a smile on his sculpted lips, seeing the gleam of his black hair in the sunlight. There was a moment of total silence and then she flew down the steps and launched herself into his arms, holding on to him tightly, burying her face in his jacket, feeling his hand on her neck, lifting her head back so that she was whispering into his kiss.

'I missed you. I missed you. I'm so glad you're here.'

They stood clasped together, oblivious to the astonishment on the faces of the gathering that surrounded them. It was Mwangi who broke the spell.

'*Iko simu*, Memsahib Sarah,' he said. 'Telephone. It is a priest from Nyeri.'

Sarah looked at him, dazed, and then stepped away from Rabindrah and the incredulous onlookers.

'Phone,' she said foolishly. 'Someone wants me on the phone.'

She made her way to the small alcove outside the sitting room, and picked up the receiver.

'Hello? Fr Bidoli?'

Her heart was hammering as she waited for the priest to respond. His breath wheezed on the line, and it was a strain to hear the words.

'I have seen him,' he said simply. 'He drinks only a little water and has eaten nothing since he gave himself up. He wants to die. At first he refused to talk to me. But I told him that I, too, was dying. That we would be facing our last days together. He looked at me then, and he knew I spoke the truth.'

'Did he say anything about Karanja?'

'Not at first, no. I told him his child would be able to walk normally because he was having an operation. That the boy's condition was an injury and not a curse.'

'Does he know where Wanjiru is?'

'I did not say, and he did not ask me. But when he heard that you had arranged the operation, even though he had killed your Piet, he began to weep.'

'But is he willing to name Karanja?'

'He is caught between the two worlds. Between his tribal heritage, where his father's death must be avenged, and his mission upbringing, where we preach Christ's forgiveness. He understands that it was wrong to have turned to evil magic.' Fr Bidoli paused and Sarah could sense his exhaustion, but he pushed himself on. 'He said that Karanja forced him to take the oath.'

'Oh, thank God he's admitted it. Thank God,' Sarah said.

'He was very frightened when the ceremony took place,' the priest said. 'Karanja gave him a drink made from herbs and made him eat the raw heart of a goat and say the words. Afterwards Simon was afraid of what would happen to him if he did not carry out his promise. The power of

460

superstition is still strong in these people, despite what we have tried to teach them. It is a sad irony, my child, but I believe Simon came to like and respect Piet. He did not want to carry out his promise.'

'But he killed Piet anyway,' Sarah said.

'Karanja threatened to kill Piet and Hannah, and all the old-time workers on the farm, if Simon did not honour his oath. And when Simon still did not act, his uncle sent men to slaughter the cattle and the game, and to raid the house. Finally, Simon took a potent drug Karanja gave him, and that gave him the determination to carry out what he had sworn to do. Afterwards, he was very sick.'

'He is not sick, Father. He is inhuman.'

'He knows that what he did was terrible. Afterwards he did not feel less angry over his father's death. He did not find any peace. I told him Karanja's evil had brought dishonour to his clan. I said that if the old man remained free, he would find Wanjiru and kill her, because she could make a statement against him.'

'Has he agreed to make a statement to the police? About Karanja?' Sarah asked.

'It is not so simple. After the killing Simon returned to his hiding place in the forest. He thought that was the end. But Karanja had other scores he wanted settled. He threatened to kill Simon and have his child murdered, if he did not obey. According to the old tribal ways, the debt was paid — your Piet's life for Simon's father. But Simon saw that there would never be an end, that he would never escape Karanja's power, that the old man now owned his soul.'

'So he gave himself up,' Sarah said.

'He felt that Karanja had ordained that he should die, so he lay down in the forest and waited for death to come. And then someone brought food to his hiding place and told him that Jan van der Beer was dead. That it was in the paper. So Simon gave himself up. To finish it all.'

'But it will not be finished unless he signs the statement,' Sarah said despairingly. 'What he has told you is not enough for a court of law.'

'Perhaps he will find the courage. He is ready for death, but he fears for his son if Karanja finds him. That is what he said.' Fr Bidoli was seized by a bout of coughing. When he was able to talk again his voice was thin and weary. 'He has asked me to be with him when he dies, and I told him that

461

if God spares me, I will be there. Or I will be waiting for him on the other side.'

'No. You are still needed here, Father,' Sarah said. The old priest had become her friend, her guide, a tenuous link between her and the inexplicable God in whom she had once had unswerving faith.

Fr Bidoli chuckled. 'I am a sick old man. My time is limited. It would be foolish not to recognise that.' His next words were spoken just above a whisper. 'Sarah?'

'Yes, Father?'

'He has asked if you would see him. Just once, before he goes to execution.'

'No! Oh no, Father. I couldn't do that. I could not do it.' A wash of fear and revulsion made Sarah shudder and she turned to look for a chair to sit on, or something to support her shaking legs.

'I know it is hard to think about such a thing. But the most painful things can also be the most precious, because they cure us of fear. So I ask you to consider it. That is all that I have to tell you for the moment, my dear child. God bless you. You are very brave – more so than you realise. I pray for you every day.'

Sarah replaced the receiver with clammy hands, and went to her room to sit down. To arrange treatment for an innocent child, that was one thing. To go to the prison and visit the monster who had mutilated and killed the man she loved – no one could ask or expect her to do that. She took a handkerchief from her pocket and wiped away the sweat that had broken out all over her face. It made her feel ill. It was unthinkable. She would not do it under any circumstances.

Chapter 19

Kenya, June 1967

Camilla looked around the sitting room at Langani, soothed by the warmth of the place and her love for it. She ran her fingers over the faded slip-covers on the sofa and chairs, the colobus monkey pelt that still lay over the back of the large armchair that had been Janni's special place. Oil paintings of African landscapes and wildlife, watercolours of local flowers, sepia photographs of stern ancestors in formal poses, a selection of glassy-eyed hunting trophies, and a ceremonial Maasai shield and spears decorated the walls. Hannah's great-grandparents had brought several pieces of heavy Cape Dutch furniture on the ox-wagon that had carried their most prized possessions into the wilderness that was to become their home. The polished tables and dresser and bookshelves held lamps with faded shades, books and gramophone records, bowls of flowers and mementos that Hannah had put in place to make the house her own. There were silver-framed photos of her wedding and the baby's christening, of Jan and Lottie in happier days. A photo of Sarah, her unruly hair framing a laughing face, was on the sideboard. Beside her was a portrait of Piet that she had taken a few months before his death. He had been caught unawares by the camera and looked surprised, quizzical, his keen face and blonde hair gilded by the evening sun. The face of a vital young man who would never grow old. He would always be remembered as he was at that moment, full of dreams and plans and optimism and the expectation of a long life in which to fulfil them. On the bookshelf Camilla came face to face with a photo of herself with Anthony in his Samburu camp. She was leaning towards him, her expression filled with unmistakable love. Her heart constricted and she turned away, unable to look at it.

Lunch had been abandoned after the awkward moment in the

driveway, when Sarah had detached herself from Rabindrah and gone to the telephone. Lars had been the first to speak.

'Why don't we go inside, Han, and have sandwiches and a beer or coffee, instead of lunch?' he'd said. 'Rabindrah, give me a hand with Camilla's bags. She seems to be carrying a selection of rocks. I don't know what it is with women and suitcases.'

'Don't be too critical,' Camilla had said. 'I've brought all kinds of things from London for you and Hannah. Along with toys for Suniva, and new face creams and lotions for all of us girls. You'll eat your words when you see what's in there.'

They were all conscious of Sarah's voice in the background as she spoke to the priest, and then listened to whatever he had to say. Hannah sighed.

'I hope he has persuaded Simon to sign a statement,' she said when she had explained the situation to Camilla. She pressed the bell for Mwangi and then smiled. 'Ma is here, as you know. She went to have lunch with Barbie Murray, but she'll be back soon.'

'Rabindrah could use a cold beer after that dusty drive.' Lars had returned to the sitting room with Rabindrah following on his heels.

'Of course,' Hannah said. 'I'm going to take Camilla to freshen up. There's a cloakroom off the hall there, Rabindrah, if you want to use it. Lars will organise your beer.'

In the guest room she closed the door and clapped her hands to her head.

'My God! What do you make of that! I can't take it in, the way she literally flung herself at him. It's unbelievable! I don't know what to think. It's very strange. Hard to . . .' She sat down on the bed and looked at Camilla, waiting for a reaction.

'I noticed a little fizz between them in London,' Camilla said. 'But I don't think they were aware of it themselves, at that time.'

'It's very hard,' Hannah repeated the words. 'You know, I always thought of Sarah and Piet as inseparable, even though he took a long time to see how right they were for each other. And when he asked her to marry him, I assumed we'd all be here for years to come, running the farm and the lodge, bringing up our children together. Since his death we've been through so much, and I somehow never thought she would—'

'Would ever look at anyone else.' Camilla finished the sentence.

'It's a shock. Although it's not fair on her to be so surprised,' Hannah said. 'But he's an Indian. I have to admit I'm not too happy about that. It's difficult to come to terms with a Sikh journalist replacing my brother in her life.'

'But he's not some *duka wallah*. He's a well-educated and intelligent man, and he comes from a family that is as cultured as yours or mine or hers.'

'It's a different kind of culture,' Hannah said. 'They don't treat women in the same way.'

'Sikhs have a reputation for being tolerant of other races and religions. They're also supposed to consider men and women as equals, which is an idea most white males still seem unable to cope with. I rather like what I've seen of him, I must say.'

'I suppose,' Hannah said, but she did not sound convinced. 'I drove down from Buffalo Springs with him a while ago, and he made me see something about myself that I was ashamed of.'

'What was that?'

'He pointed out to me, politely but firmly, that our families were very similar. He saw that I thought of most Indians in Kenya as the descendants of illiterate coolie labourers who came to lay the railway lines and wound up as betel nut-chewing shopkeepers. But Rabindrah's family arrived here before mine, and they were educated soldiers and policemen and farmers. Probably better read and more worldly than old Grandpa van der Beer, who never read anything except his bible, and didn't think about anything outside his farm.'

'Did your family get on well with the other white farmers round here?' Camilla asked.

'The Afrikaners were not known for mixing socially with any other people, whatever their colour, unless they needed something on the farm that they couldn't supply themselves. Or, later, unless there were rugby matches. They were very clannish. When Pa married an Italian girl he'd met on a holiday down south it was frowned on at first. But it didn't take the grandparents long to fall in love with Lottie. Our family saw more of the Britishers than most Afrikaans families because of Ma, and because there aren't many of us *yaapies* in this area. We weren't part of a tight little clique, like the Dutch Reform communities in the Trans Nzoia area. But we weren't in the thick of the European social scene either. Piet played rugby in Nanyuki, and we joined the club for the tennis. But I was the only Afrikaans girl in the senior school, if you remember.'

'I thought that was because the Dutch Reformers didn't approve of frivolous Catholics and their craven images,' Camilla said.

'The Dutch Reformers don't approve of anything that looks too joyful,' Hannah said. 'In fact, the Kenya Asians understood British culture much better than we did. And they took full advantage of the British education and any jobs they were offered. Even though the English looked down on them, for the most part.'

'Indians were already accustomed to having us in their home country,' Camilla said. 'And their maharajahs were every bit as grand as the grandest British elite.'

'True,' Hannah said. 'It's odd, though, how the British and the Africans dislike Indians and us Afrikaners equally. That should have created a bond of some kind between us, except that we couldn't get past the fact that our skins were different colours. It will be interesting to see how the next generation turns out, now that we have passports saying we are all Kenyans first and foremost, regardless of colour.' She thumped her fist into the palm of her other hand, frustrated by her inborn prejudice. 'I understand all that, you know, and I want good racial relations. But the idea of Sarah and Rabindrah – that is still tough for me to accept.'

'I've met several mixed-race couples in Nairobi, at dinner parties I've been to with Daddy,' Camilla said. 'Not that this situation is necessarily going to get to that point.'

'My God! Do you think she would actually marry him?'

'Who knows?' Camilla threw her pale hands up in the air.

'There are European men with Indian and African girlfriends, or even wives, these days,' Hannah said. 'But the other way round is still rare. And I don't know about children. How would they be accepted? I want her to be happy. But I feel uneasy about all this.' She looked at Camilla, a plea for understanding in her eyes.

'Of course you do,' Camilla said. 'It's difficult to think of anyone stepping into Piet's shoes, as you say. He was her first and only love, from the days of our childhood. After he died, I was afraid that her life would shrivel and die too. Or she would become one of those eccentric female scientists that grow grey and isolated, stomping around in the bush. A crusty old maid with baggy clothes and wrinkles and hairy legs, unable to talk to anyone except wild animals and other boffins. We wouldn't want that for her, would we?'

'No, we wouldn't.' Hannah had begun to smile. 'I admit that he can be charming. But still, an Indian. Betty and Raphael won't be too happy with this. Betty won't, anyway.'

'I'm not sure Rabindrah's family will be thrilled either,' Camilla said. 'In spite of Sikh tolerance.'

'Why can't people stick with their own kind?' Hannah asked. 'It's so much better all around, not to mix too many ingredients into a love affair or a marriage.'

'Which is why you had a torrid romance with a mad Pole, and wound up married to a Norwegian,' Camilla said smugly. 'Good advice, Han.'

'Ach, you're always too smart,' Hannah said, laughing out loud. 'And while we're on this subject, I've found out that Ma has been carrying on with an Italian she met in Johannesburg. I don't know anything about him, though. He could be a gigolo, for all I know. They had an affair, and then she went back and stayed with Pa until he was killed.'

'Our parents are often a little too surprising for our tender expectations,' Camilla said, with a touch of bitterness. 'I'm so looking forward to seeing Lottie. Is this a love affair that looks as though it might continue?'

'Sounds like it,' Hannah said doubtfully. 'Sarah and I overheard her talking to Uncle Sergio about it. He left yesterday so I didn't get a chance to ask him about this man, and I haven't been brave enough to tackle Ma directly.'

'I wouldn't tackle her at all, if I were you,' Camilla said. She picked up a sweater and draped it round her shoulders. 'There are some things that parents shouldn't know about their children, and vice versa. Let's go and have something to eat with Lars and Rabindrah, while we wait for your mother to come home. Maybe she isn't having lunch with Barbie Murray at all,' she said wickedly. 'Maybe the Italian boyfriend is twenty-five years old, and she has him stashed away in a suite at the Mount Kenya Safari Club, where they're spending a wild afternoon together.' They were laughing as she opened the bedroom door and then shut it again immediately.

'What's the matter?' Hannah asked.

'It's Sarah. She's just come out on to the lawn with Rabindrah. I think we should give them a few moments to themselves, maybe.'

'I need a few moments to myself as well. So I can think of the right thing to say to her.' Hannah winced as she watched them, crossing the garden hand in hand. 'Tell me about you and Anthony, while we're waiting.'

'I saw him in London.' Camilla shrugged. 'But it can't work. I'm going to be here with you and Sarah for the trial and whatever problems that may cause. And we can start on some new designs in the workshop, if you want to carry on with it. But then I'll go back to London. I may get another acting role. It's what I always wanted, and I love the design side of the fashion business. The things we made here sold right away, and I have plenty of new ideas. But I can't live here. I can't take another chance on Anthony.'

'He is in love with you,' Hannah said.

'So everyone keeps telling me. Except that I don't quite understand the way he shows it.'

'He was ashamed of the way he behaved that night.' Hannah tried again. 'It was stupid to flirt with her like that, but I think he felt left out of everything. Eclipsed by your success and the people from London and so.'

'He wasn't just flirting with her. I caught them kissing outside the dressing room. Besides, I can't bury the best of myself, hide my light, so that he won't feel insecure,' Camilla said. 'I need a man who can love me and be proud of what I do, without feeling diminished himself. I don't want to live with someone who needs to seduce another woman every time he isn't top dog for a day or two. Above all, I need a man I can trust. Now lead me to some food and strong drink, otherwise I'll never make it through the rest of the day.'

'What did he say?' Rabindrah took in Sarah's pallor, the slight twitch around her mouth and the tightly balled fists. 'Tell me.'

But the words stuck in her throat. She licked dry lips, unable to form any words.

'Come and get some fresh air,' he said, taking her hand.

They stood close together, leaning on the gate that led out to the open plain, breathing in the thin, cool air of the high veldt.

'He wants me to go and see him,' Sarah said. 'At the prison in Nyeri.'

'Fr Bidoli has asked you to—'

'No. It's Simon. Simon wants me to visit him. He's the one who—'

'Sarah!' He held her tightly and put his lips against her forehead.

'I can't go into that prison. Look into his face, speak to him, hear his voice. I can't. No one should expect me to do that.'

Rabindrah said nothing, allowing her time to explain what the priest had said, to find her way through the terrible thing that had been asked of her.

'This is all my waking nightmares,' she said. 'Because he is alive and whole and seeing and talking, while Piet— No. No, I can't do it. I'll go and ring Fr Bidoli now. Tell him, once and for all, that I won't go.'

'You don't have to do anything right now,' Rabindrah said. 'I'm sure the priest understands better than anyone that you need time to think. Do you want to talk to Hannah and Lars about this? Or to Camilla?'

'No. It's my problem and I have to deal with it,' she said. 'It will be excruciating enough to face him in the court, but I can't avoid that. In the meantime, I will not be made to feel that I should go to the prison. That God expects me to be that merciful.' She turned away from him. 'We should go back in now. I haven't even said hello to Camilla properly.'

'I don't think she will mind,' he said, lifting his hand to smooth a strand of hair away from her face. 'I think she won't mind at all.'

'Did she tell you that she was angry with me?' Sarah asked.

'No. She only said that she wanted more than anything to be here with you and Hannah.'

'Well, she is. Angry, I mean. Because I thought she had persuaded my brother to back out of his wedding. Anyhow, I was totally wrong and she was justifiably upset by my assumption. It was a hypocritical way for me to behave, because I never liked his fiancée anyway. In fact, I made a right mess of everything. Maybe ruined our friendship.'

'I don't think that is the case,' he said. 'After all, she's here, isn't she? She came all this way to be with you and Hannah, so it doesn't seem likely. How many other people would drop out of a London play that still had a week to run, and travel thousands of miles to support their friends? She must have had other commitments too.'

'I didn't know she'd left the play early,' Sarah said. 'But I do know that the bond between the three of us is a rare and precious thing.' She was silent for a moment, not looking at him directly. 'I want to thank you for dropping everything at such short notice yourself. For collecting Camilla and bringing her here.'

'It was nothing.' He wanted to kiss her anxious face, smooth away her little frown, touch her ears and her throat and the freckles on her cheeks. Kiss her endlessly. But he did not move, remembering Allie's cautionary words and Sarah's own reaction when he had pressed her too far at Buffalo Springs. 'I wanted to see you,' he said simply.

She looked up at him. 'When do you have to go back?' she asked. 'I'd like us to have some time together.'

'I would like that too,' he said, his heart soaring. 'I'm going to be in Nanyuki for tonight, and I've booked myself into the Sportman's Arms. A good Indian-owned establishment with dreary rooms and strange plumbing and good curry, isn't it?' He said the words in a thick Indian accent, rolling his eyes and waggling his head and making Sarah laugh. 'So perhaps we can spend part of tomorrow together.'

'Yes,' she said, her face lit with pleasure. 'I'm sure we could. But right now, I'd like you to kiss me. I really want you to kiss me, Rabindrah.'

He put his arms around her waist and she leaned against him and opened her mouth a little so that she could learn the taste of him. She was smiling as they drew apart for a moment and looked at one another before he kissed her again.

'I'm in love with you,' he said. 'I hope this isn't the wrong time to tell you.'

'No. It's the best moment to tell me,' she said. 'Because I need you to help me through all this. I was too scared to admit it. To get past the crippling fear I've lived with since the night I found Piet hacked to death. But now I can see myself moving on, if you will help me to do it.'

'I can't know how it was or is,' he said, kissing her, thrilled by the sweetness of her trust in him. 'But I will be with you wherever you go. If you want me.'

'I want you,' she said. 'I think I'll always want you from now on.'

Her smile was more beautiful than anything he had ever seen, and he wished that they could stand in this beautiful garden for ever, under the eye of the mountain, alone and oblivious to the demands of the outside world.

'Come on,' she said at last, tugging at his hand. 'They're all waiting for an explanation up there and it's time to face the music.'

They were granted a reprieve by the arrival of Lottie. Camilla reached her first and was immediately folded into her arms, embraced with love and then held at arm's length for affectionate scrutiny.

'My dear,' Lottie said. 'This is a wonderful thing, that you have come back to Langani. A mark of love and loyalty that none of us will ever forget.'

'Lottie.' Camilla said her name several times as a deluge of memories rushed through her mind, and tears filled her eyes. 'We're together again, and that's the most important thing. I'm so glad you're home. So happy to see you.'

Lottie nodded. 'I have my my daughters with me again,' she said. 'The three little girls who were a part of life at Langani for so long. And while we cannot know what is going to happen tomorrow or next week, I would like us to celebrate tonight. I think we should put our troubles aside for one evening, and be glad that we are reunited.' She embraced Sarah and held out her hand to Rabindrah. 'You're Sarah's friend. I am very happy to meet you,' she said. 'I've heard about the book and I am so proud of her, and glad that she has found someone that can put her extraordinary work into words. Will you spend the evening with us? Stay on for dinner?'

'I'd like that very much,' he said, warming to the vibrant woman with her olive skin and the smooth black hair that was wound into a chignon on the nape of her neck. Her large, dark eyes were set above a straight nose and generous mouth, and there was no mistaking her southern European origins. Hannah's larger bones and fair hair and complexion had obviously come from her father's side.

'Good.' Lottie flashed a smile at him. 'I was out when you came here the last time, dropping Hannah off after her visit to Buffalo Springs. Old friends have been so kind since I came back, taking me here and there, inviting me for lunch and dinner. But we will make up for that last occasion when we did not have a chance to talk. I'm going to see Kamau in the kitchen, and we will prepare for a very special evening. Tonight we will not think of the bad things or the sad things. Not at all.'

Sarah felt a swell of gratitude. She had been wondering if she could slip away for an hour or two with Rabindrah, without alienating Hannah and seeming to abandon Camilla who had come so far. But Lottie had solved the problem in an instant, although Sarah knew that she would eventually have to answer some questions.

'I'm going to find Suniva and take her to the dairy,' Hannah said. 'If she does any more crawling today she'll wear the skin off her fat little knees. And she loves to see my cows. Does anybody want to come with me?'

'I'll walk down with you,' Camilla said. 'I've been sitting in planes and cars for too many hours and I need some exercise.'

'I think I'll go to Nanyuki and drop my bag off at the Sportsman's Arms,' Rabindrah said, unsure if he would be welcome in Hannah's dairy. 'What time should I come back for dinner?'

'You don't need to go all the way into town now.' Lars had emerged from the office. 'I'm sorry we have no spare room for you tonight, with Lottie and Camilla and Sarah all here. I'm going out to look at a field of wheat, and you're welcome to join me if you like. Everything all right, Sarah, after the phone call?'

'Yes. Nothing new,' she said in a clipped tone, not wanting to disclose what Fr Bidoli had asked her to do.

'Good.' Lars was aware that there was something she was not telling him. The priest must have said something to unsettle her, he thought. Or maybe it was the whole idea of Simon Githiri and the trial. He gave her a comforting squeeze. 'Are you joining Rabindrah and me, or do you prefer to go and talk to those spoiled heifers of Hannah's?'

'She's coming with us,' Camilla said firmly, taking her friend by the elbow, laughing inwardly as she saw the look that passed between Sarah and Rabindrah. 'We'll see you all later.'

They collected the baby and set out along the driveway, branching left after a few yards and following the path to the dairy. Juma, who had worked at Langani for thirty years, was shooing the milkers into the shed, and Suniva began to smile and gurgle as soon as she saw the cattle with their soft eyes and moist noses.

'So, tell us about this thing going on between you and Rabindrah,' Camilla said.

Sarah's colour rose at once as she tried to think of a glib answer. She could see laughter and sympathy in Camilla's eyes, but Hannah's expression was unclear. This was going to be difficult, but she felt that she had to be honest now. No point in hiding anything.

'It's something that grew out of our working together,' she said. 'It sort of . . . happened. First we were colleagues, then friends. And just recently, it all changed. Without my noticing. I didn't want to acknowledge that there could be anything else between us, but when I saw him today I had to admit that we have something more than friendship.' She looked at Hannah, appealing. 'And I think he feels the same. Well, he does. Yes.'

'You're right about that,' Camilla said. 'And I think it's great.'

'You can't help who you fall in love with.' Hannah had summoned a smile. She realised that this wasn't an ideal comment and she made another effort. 'What I mean is, you have to go on with your life, and I'm glad for you. Really I am. Whatever choices you make, you'll always be my sister and my friend. You and Camilla.'

'True to our promise, through thick and thin, across oceans and continents,' Camilla said, flinging her arms wide, making a grand gesture. 'Above and beyond black and brown and white, always and for ever. What happens next?'

'I've no idea,' Sarah said. 'We'll just find our way as best we can. See what happens.'

They stood looking into the milking stalls, watching as Juma took Suniva and held her so that her small hands could touch the soft flanks of the cows and their curled fringes, seeing her eyes widen with delight when the animals turned their heads and blew softly on to her skin.

'Ach, it's only important that we are grateful for the gifts we have, whatever guise they may come in,' Hannah said, hugging her daughter. 'I ought to remember that more often. What did Fr Bidoli say to you? Has he thought about visiting Simon?'

'He's going to talk to me again tomorrow,' Sarah said. 'In the meantime, we'll have a happy evening and celebrate the fact that we're all together again. As Lottie said.' She turned to Camilla. 'I owe you a big apology. I wrote you a letter when I finally heard from Tim, but it was the day before I came down here so I never got around to posting it. I'm going to give it to you later, though, because the written words make more sense than anything I can say to you.'

'Tim had a lucky escape.' Camilla's expression was wry. 'And I'm not as bad as you think.'

'Rabindrah told me you gave up the last days of your play to come here. That was beyond anything—'

'One has to prove to oneself that it's possible to escape the prison of success,' Camilla interrupted her airily.

'What rubbish you always talk!' Hannah put her hand over her mouth and they were reminded of the way she had made that same gesture at school, covering her laughter when Sarah had let a grass snake loose in the classroom.

'I'll push Suniva's pram back to the house,' Camilla said. 'She can watch us getting ready for Lottie's special evening. Just like we used to, long ago.'

It was an evening of rebirth, as they emerged from the long shadow of tragedy into the simple pleasure of a meal shared with family and friends. Lottie's face glowed in the candlelight as she looked around the table. The lines of strain and hardship had begun to fade from her face, and she was happy to be working in the garden and in the kitchen where she had presided for so many years. When Lars stood up to pour the wine he touched his wife on the nape of her neck and Hannah looked at him, her skin rising in small bumps of pleasure. Rabindrah pressed Sarah's hand beneath the table, aware of the monstrous request lurking in the back of her mind, moved by the fact that he was the only one she had confided in. For Camilla, the place that had almost been destroyed by heartache and anguish, was filled once more with love. And she felt that somehow they would all survive, and that the strength of the people around this table would conquer all pain, because they cared for each other so deeply. Only Anthony was missing, creating a void in her that she resolutely ignored during this one, lovely evening.

It was late when they drifted off to bed, leaving Sarah and Rabindrah alone beside the fire.

'Will you be able to sleep?' he said, stroking her hair, kissing her on the lips.

'I hope so. I'm sharing with Camilla, just like we did as children.'

She lay back against him, her eyes closed, feeling his fingers on her cheek, along the ridge of her shoulder, sliding down to caress her neck and her breasts. She made a small murmuring sound of desire and then sat up abruptly, her eyes wide open, looking directly into his face. He drew back at once. Now that he knew for sure that she wanted him, he could be patient. And she was right, in any case. They were only beginning to explore their feelings for one another.

'I should head off now,' he said. 'I'll be in Nanyuki for the morning, but I have to get back to my desk in Nairobi later in the day. Why don't you ring me after breakfast and let me know what you want to do?'

She followed him out on to the verandah, tendrils of disappointment curling around her happiness. He pulled her close and kissed her again and she wound her arms around him, not wanting to let him go. Now that he was leaving her, the dilemma of Simon's request crashed into her consciousness once more, and she did not know how she would get through the dark hours. She steeled herself to step away from him, and reached up to kiss him one last time.

'Until tomorrow,' she said, trying to glean some comfort from the words.

'Goodnight.'

She watched him drive away and then stood for a moment, looking at the hollow cavern of the midnight sky and the shimmer of stars. It was a long time since she had looked up at the beauty of the African night without sadness, and she wanted to share the moment.

'Piet,' she said softly. 'I believe you are watching over me, and I think you do want me to find the courage to love again. Because you know that I'll still love you, right to my very last breath. But I'd so like to know that what I'm doing is all right with you.' She saw the star at that instant, shooting through the inky sky, trailing its long, dazzling tail in a glorious arc before disappearing into infinity.

She was smiling as she crept into the dark bedroom, careful not to make any noise that would wake Camilla. When she lay down and closed her eyes she was immediately asleep, and the hovering uncertainty of Simon and his dreadful request did not haunt her dreams.

'We're taking a picnic to the river,' Hannah said at breakfast. 'Lars will join us at lunchtime. In the meantime, we can dunk ourselves and Suniva. And maybe do some fishing. Would Rabindrah like to join us? We'll set out around ten.'

They approached the riverbank through a stand of African olive trees, their trunks twisted with age, leaves gleaming grey-green in the sunlight. In their shade there was a smell of damp moss and aromatic ferns. Butterflies dipped and fluttered across the surface of the water, and the morning was full of bird calls. They spread rugs on the grassy bank and set the baby down. For a while they chatted about the farm, discussed local politics and conservation, and heard about Camilla's first experience on the London stage. But Sarah could not concentrate. The priest's words were now lodged in the forefront of her mind, and she was unable to banish them. Even the presence of Rabindrah, the occasional touch of his fingers, the curve of his lips when he smiled, failed to alleviate her growing sense of anxiety.

'We could take a walk,' he said, seeing her restlessness. 'Unless you think I might be eaten by something once we're out of sight.'

'That depends on your company,' Camilla said, enjoying Sarah's immediate and obvious embarrassment as they walked away.

'I'm going back to Nairobi this afternoon,' Rabindrah said, lifting Sarah's face to kiss her. 'Is there any chance you might come down there soon? Even for a couple of days. It might help you to come to a decision about Simon. Do you know how sweet and beautiful you are?'

'I don't know if I should leave Langani right now,' she said. 'But I'm tempted.'

'I'd like to bring you home, for Sunday curry lunch with Indar Uncle and Kuldip. My aunt is a marvellous cook. And my cousins and many more of the extended tribe gather for lunch at the weekends. It's sometimes better to jump in at the deep end.'

'They may not be all that pleased when they realise I'm not just the photographer who illustrates your books,' she said. 'We're bound to come across people who are not happy about us being together.' She looked out across the swirling current of the river. 'I did mention you to Fr Bidoli. I told him that we – that I . . . Well, anyway, he was encouraging. But we do come from different cultures, and I think we will face some disapproval.'

'I'm ready for that, if it happens,' he said. 'I love you, you see. And that makes me ready for anything I may have to overcome, in order to keep you with me.'

She hesitated, wanting to tell him that she loved him too, a little shy about saying the words for the first time. But the sound of Lars and Lottie arriving with the picnic broke into their private world and they felt obliged to rejoin the rest of the party. Lars took Sarah aside immediately.

'Fr Bidoli telephoned,' he said. 'I told him you'd be back after lunch. I didn't like to press you yesterday, what with Rabindrah and Camilla arriving, and Lottie's lovely celebration. But is there anything you want to talk over with me?'

'Not right now,' she said, grateful for his concern. 'I'll phone as soon as I get back to the house, and then I may have to ask you for some very serious advice.'

'I'm always here to help you,' he said. 'Now, look at this daughter of mine who has turned from a cherub into a plump little fish, in that icy water.'

It was mid-afternoon when they packed up and drove back to the house. Mwangi was waiting with a message.

'It is the bwana inspector who called about half an hour ago,' he said. 'He would like to talk to Memsahib Sarah. *Sasa hivi.* Urgent.'

She was filled with dread as she dialled the operator and asked for Nyeri Police Station.

'My dear, I'm sorry to break into your day, but I want you to know that Simon Githiri is very ill. The prison doctor has been to see him twice in the last twenty-four hours. He thinks Simon may not survive to stand trial. Fr Bidoli is with him, because he will not speak to anyone else.'

'What kind of illness does he have?' Sarah asked.

'He's in a catatonic state,' Jeremy said. 'Wasting away, eating nothing. The man has given up. I wouldn't be surprised if he died very soon. And if he rolls over and pegs out now, we are well and truly buggered. Sorry, but you know what I mean. Whatever he has told the priest will be worthless. Hearsay, and not admissible in court.'

'I know that,' Sarah said. 'But Fr Bidoli is trying to get something signed. I'm sure he will.'

'In the meantime, I've put an *askari* on duty at Kagumo Mission. Just in case Karanja has discovered that Wanjiru and the child are there. I'm going to move her somewhere else tomorrow, because the bush telegraph is pretty fast around here, no matter how we try to keep things hush-hush. The old devil must be concerned that Simon may sign a statement which allows us to arrest him. And that Wanjiru would be a fatal witness.'

'Oh God!' Sarah said. 'When is this nightmare ever going to stop?'

'Look.' Hardy hesitated. 'Fr Bidoli told me that Simon has asked to see you.'

'I don't want to talk about that. Please.'

'Sarah, I think you are the only one who might get Simon to sign the statement now. You are our last chance.'

There was a silence as Sarah braced herself for what she knew was coming.

'It's a terrible thing to ask, I know,' Hardy said at last. 'But if you would consider coming to the jail. Not necessarily into his cell, but—'

'I don't think—' Sarah wanted to protest, but the words died. She thought of what Erope had said. No use hiding away. Better to go out and face the worst of her fears. Fr Bidoli had told her she was braver than she knew. But could she summon up that kind of courage? The policeman spoke again, his sympathy almost crumbling her resolve.

'It's all right,' he said. 'It's too much to expect of you. Or anyone. I quite understand.'

Sarah found her voice. 'I'll come,' she said. 'I could be in Nyeri first thing in the morning.'

'Tonight would be better.' She could hear the relief in Jeremy's tone. 'Less *watu* to notice your arrival. The fact is, Simon may not last until tomorrow. Every moment counts.'

'This evening, then.' Panic and nausea rose in her as she said the words.

'When you get to Nyeri bring your car round to the back of the police compound. I'll have an *askari* waiting to open the gates for you.'

Sarah put the phone down carefully on its cradle. The walls around her seemed to be moving, and she sank down on to a chair, afraid that she was going to faint.

'Sarah?' Through the roaring in her ears she could hear Camilla's voice. 'Who was that? What has upset you?'

She became aware that Hannah and Lars were standing beside her, and that she had to tell them now. Then she must go to Nyeri, while her resolve held. If she could get her legs to work. She looked at the friends who needed her, to ensure the safety of their home and family. She stood up.

'Yesterday, Fr Bidoli told me Simon had asked to see me.' She heard Hannah suck in her breath, and she hurried on. 'And while we were out today, Jeremy phoned and left a message. So I rang him back.' She was finding it hard to breathe. 'Simon is going to die very soon. Maybe even tonight. And Jeremy feels that I might be able to persuade him to sign a statement.' The nausea hit her again. 'So I've agreed to try.'

'You don't have to do this.' Hannah's eyes were full of tears. 'You shouldn't go, Sarah. There must be some other way.'

'No. So the sooner I start out, the better.'

'You can't go alone,' Lars said. 'I'll drive you.'

'No.' Camilla was firm. 'You stay with Hannah and Lottie, and I'll go down with Sarah. I'm sure Rabindrah will come with us.'

She ran out into the driveway where Rabindrah was standing beside his car talking to Lottie, waiting to say goodbye before departing for Nairobi. Her explanation was brief.

'Of course I will come with you,' he said, as Sarah appeared on the steps. 'There is no one in the world as brave as you. No one else who would even think of doing this. No greater love. But you will come through it very strong, and it will be all right.'

'My dear, I want you to drink some of this strong, very sweet tea before you go,' Lottie said, taking in Sarah's trembling hands and pale face. 'And we'll put a thermos in the car. You're shocked, and it will help you to get through the journey.'

Sarah nodded, wanting only to leave, to be on her way, to reach her destination and finish what she had promised to do. Hannah was making an effort to remain calm, but her mind was in turmoil as she struggled against anger and disbelief.

'He has no right to summon you to his deathbed,' she said. 'To cause you more pain and grief.'

'But don't you see, Han?' Sarah said. 'It's something I have to do. For you and Lars and Suniva. For Lottie and Jan. For Camilla who loves this place and is trying to build up her workshop here. And for me. This is for all of us.'

Hannah covered her face with her hands. 'I know. And I should go with you, but I can't. I just can't. I'm not brave enough, and I wouldn't be able to control myself. If I saw him, face to face, I'd want to scream at him and beat him. Kill him myself. I can't be like you. I don't have the—'

'Ssshhh.' Sarah smiled at her. 'It's all right. It will all be all right.'

'You drive with Camilla,' Rabindrah said to Sarah. 'I'll follow right behind you. All the way.'

'You won't be alone,' Camilla said, handing Sarah a wool scarf and jacket. 'Here, wrap this around you because it's getting chilly now, and it will be cold by the time we arrive in Nyeri. Hannah, we'll phone you later, from the police station.'

'Yes. Don't worry about me. I'll ring Jeremy and tell him you're on your way.'

They hugged one another, murmuring words of comfort and encouragement before moving apart, fingers still entwined, reluctant to break the connection between them.

Mwangi and Kamau appeared from the kitchen and reached out to touch Sarah, talking to her as though she was a child in need of consolation.

'Mama Lottie has told us where you are going,' Kamau said, placing his hand on her head in an age-old gesture of blessing. 'May God be with you tonight, and we will be waiting for your safe return.'

Camilla offered to drive, but Sarah needed to be behind the wheel herself. It was a relief to be concentrating on the noise of the engine and the twists and corrugations in the road. She was thankful that she was not alone, although they drove without saying much. The Land Rover was sturdy and functional, but not designed for comfort. Camilla's body was soon aching and stiff from the hard seats and the cold air creeping in through the canvas that covered the back section.

As the moment of confrontation drew closer, Sarah was dreadfully afraid that she would not make it through the ordeal. The reality of going into the cell made her feel sick with tension, and for the first time since Piet's death she began to pray. It was a frantic reaching out into the unknown, a search for the strength to do what she had promised. She thought of the wild beauty of Buffalo Springs and her days in the bush, tracking her elephants with Erope. She dwelt again on what he had said about the *fisi*. Since the trauma of Piet's death, the images of Simon and the hyena had become inextricably merged in one monstrous visitation of evil, hurling her down into the horror of the sacrifice. It was the place where her nightmares always began. The top of the ridge, the odour of the beast mingled with its sloping shoulders and heavy jowls. She could see the gleam of the man's oiled body, the slavering muzzle and the stripped teeth of the animal as it sprang at her. The eyes of the warrior were turned towards her as she toppled, and then all became one with Piet's ruined face, staring sightless into the sky. The scent of his blood was in her nostrils, and on her body, when she was thrown down into the pit beside him. Hunched over the wheel of the Land Rover, she heard the swoosh of the spear, the dull, wet crunch it made as it struck the hyena, seconds before she fell. Simon had saved her life. She gritted her teeth, allowing herself to remember.

In the immediate aftermath, she had not wanted to be a survivor. She had hated Simon for making her live to see what he had done. But despite the long agony of her grief, she had come to a time when she was glad to be alive, to have something worthwhile to do with the rest of the life she had been given, to have found a new love so unexpectedly. She had to look at Simon Githiri one last time, and survive that too. Her muscles tensed when she leaned into another sharp corner, and her lips moved in prayer as she sped down the road to Nyeri.

When she drew up at the gates of the police compound, the night air seemed sinister and grasping. The town square was bounded by cedar trees and cape chestnuts, and by the low buildings of the market and the local bus station. Kagumo Mission, where Wanjiru had been given shelter, was situated nearby. Sarah shivered with apprehension. It was dangerous for the girl to be so close, even with a police guard at the convent. But Jeremy believed that the very fact of its proximity to the police station made it the last place that Karanja would look for her. Everywhere was in darkness, but under the trees she could make out the shapes of a dozen or more sleeping forms. A huddle of people, wearing cast-off army great-coats and sweaters and felt hats, lay wrapped in heavy blankets against the chill, surrounded by sacks of belongings, waiting for early buses or for the opening of the market in the morning.

She drove round to the back of the police station where Jeremy was waiting, his face registering surprise at the presence of the Indian journalist, although he made no comment. In his office he took a typed statement from the drawer of his desk, and handed it to Sarah.

'This is a record of everything Simon has told Fr Bidoli,' he said. 'If you can persuade him to sign it, then we'll have Karanja, even if Simon dies before the trial. Without this piece of paper, there's no evidence to hold the old man. I'm sorry you have been asked to do this, Sarah, but you're the only chance we have now. The last resort. I admire your courage.' He turned to her two companions. 'I'll organise some coffee, if you'd like to wait here in the office.'

Camilla had noticed Sarah's hesitation and her shaking fingers as she took the document from the policeman.

'Rabindrah and I will come with you, as far as we're allowed to go,' she said. 'We love you, brave, wonderful Sarah, and whether you go into that cell or not we will always love you.'

Hardy called the duty sergeant, and they made their way to the cell block at the back of the compound. It was a grim concrete building ringed by a chain-link fence and topped with rolls of barbed wire. A single high-voltage bulb burned white outside the main door. Circles of buzzing insects struck against the wire mesh, like meteorites penetrating the energy rings of a distant planet. All the windows were heavily barred. An armed *askari* stood outside and another guard patrolled the boundary, with an Alsatian dog on a leash at his side. They were taking no chances with Simon being sprung by his uncle, or finished off before he could give evidence. At the entrance, the *askari* sprang to attention as the duty sergeant unlocked the door.

Inside, a prison orderly sat at a small desk in front of the cells. He stood up as the inspector entered. A stale smell of latrines and unwashed bodies pervaded the air, mixed with the strong odour of disinfectant. Now that she was here, fear overwhelmed her and Sarah felt the sweat breaking out all over her body. The room began to lurch, like the car on the journey down from Langani. She stumbled. She was going to be sick. Then she felt Rabindrah's hand on her arm, helping her down on to a chair, aware that the statement was sliding from her fingers to the floor. But she could not lift it.

'Put your head down.' She could hear Rabindrah's low voice coming from somewhere above her, remote and disembodied. 'Close your eyes and take some deep breaths. That will take away the nausea. You're doing fine.'

When Sarah raised her head again, she was looking into the kindly eyes of Fr Bidoli. His face was grey, his breathing laboured, and his cassock hung off his frame like a shroud. She shivered. There was too much death around her. Always too much death. She wanted to run outside, to get away from the suffocating sense of decay and desolation that filled the place. She got to her feet shakily, glancing over her shoulder to locate Rabindrah and Camilla, wanting to be sure they were still there. They had promised to stay with her. In her panic, she could not see anybody except the priest.

'It's no good, Father. I can't go in there. I just can't.' Her throat was dry, and she heard the words rasp across it like sandpaper.

'Sarah.'

He said her name, and when he took her hands she felt an amazing strength begin to pour into her. She stared at him, seeing the myriad lines of pain and experience that etched his face. But his eyes were alight with life and kindness and compassion, and a shining courage that made her ashamed of her own weakness. She knew that he too might die soon, and that he too was suffering. But his concerns were not for himself. They were for her, and for the prisoner over whom he had been keeping watch.

'Help me,' she said. 'Help me to do this. Because I don't know why I'm here.'

'He needs your forgiveness,' Fr Bidoli said, and she gave a sharp cry of dismay. 'Simon is going to a judgement that he fears far more than anything the courts of this world can bring on him. He is going to die and he needs to know that God can forgive him. He needs to know that *you* can. And it is for yourself as well as for him, Sarah. Trust me, my child. This is the only way to be set free.'

Someone handed her the unsigned statement. She clutched it in her hand and clamped her mouth shut to prevent her teeth from chattering as she allowed Fr Bidoli to lead her to the door of the cell. One dangling light hung from the ceiling of the room, and a high, barred window looked out on the malignant, black night outside in the compound. There was an iron frame bed in one corner.

The prisoner lay on his side on a flock mattress, partially covered by a thin blanket. A chair stood beside the bed, a latrine bucket in the other corner. There was nothing else in the small space. Sarah stood looking down at the man who had destroyed her life, taken away her love, her happiness. He looked utterly pathetic. His body was emaciated, his skin dull and dry, his eyes milky. Unseeing. She could not equate this wretched creature in front of her with the eager young man who had started out at Langani, or the oiled, gleaming savage who had eviscerated Piet in his thirst for vengeance. What had happened to the evil being that inhabited her dreams? This was a shrunken husk of a man, flickering on the brink of eternity.

For a timeless moment she was engulfed by cold rage. Why should she forgive this vile animal for what he had done? Let him pay for it, pay for the pain and the despair that he had heaped on her, and on the people she loved. This would be her revenge. Why should he receive, in his dying, the consolation and compassion that he had denied to Piet? As the room see-sawed around her, she thought of the words of Hamlet, watching the murderous Claudius at prayer. Should she send this villain to heaven already purged, seasoned for his passage by her forgiveness? Or should she walk away so that his soul might be as damned and black as the hell where he was headed? Sarah wanted to take up some implement and strike him, bludgeon and disfigure him as he had destroyed Piet. The nausea rose again in her gullet, and she reached out blindly for something to hold on to. She found the hand of the priest.

She was not sure how she came to be sitting in the chair beside the bed. Fr Bidoli stood behind her, the pressure of his fingers light on her shoulder, and all at once everything became still. When she looked again at Simon Githiri, she saw a little boy, crouched in the forest, waiting for his mother to get up from the dirt, watching his father die an agonising death. And now he was Simon Githiri the prisoner, curled up like a child on his bed of fear and darkness and despair. She felt only pity. How could she judge him for what he had done in the madness of his grief? Let God be the judge. She must let him go, or be devoured herself by the same rage that had destroyed him.

'Simon.' She heard her own voice, hoarse, coming from somewhere far away. She held the statement in front of her. 'Your son will soon be healed. Able to walk and run like other children. Do you understand?' He made no sign. 'Simon, I need you to sign this paper. It is what you told Fr Bidoli. You need to sign it so that your son will be safe. Otherwise Karanja will—'

She realised then, with a shock, that he could not see her. His eyes were covered in some sort of film, or whitened membrane. They stared out of his dull, vacant face into an abyss of nothingness. She reached out, with a last silent prayer for strength, and touched his hand. His lips moved, and she leaned forward and bent her head to hear what he was trying to say.

'*Samahani.*' It was only a faint whisper. '*Samahani*, Sarah. *Samahani.*'

Sorry. Over and over he said the word, until he could not say it any more. Then he turned his head so that she could only see one side of his face.

'"Whose sins you shall forgive, they are forgiven."' It was all she could think of to say.

A single tear formed in his open, unseeing eye, and slid down his cheek. She fumbled in her pocket for a handkerchief and wiped it away, pressed his hand. The eyes closed, and she heard him sigh. Then he was silent. After a time, Fr Bidoli helped her up from the chair and brought her out into the corridor. She felt her knees begin to give way, but the sickness, the dreadful, surging fear was gone. The priest touched her cheek.

'You will be all right now, my little one. You have done something great-hearted and magnificent.'

'What is wrong with his eyes, Father?'

'Cataracts. Sometimes they come from a great trauma, sometimes from lack of food. He has had both of these. He is no longer able to eat.'

'What will happen to him now?'

'He is going to a better life. And you have made that possible for him.'

She caught a movement at the end of the corridor, and saw that Jeremy Hardy was waiting for her.

'The statement!' she said. 'Oh God, he hasn't signed it. He couldn't see to sign it.' She realised that she had failed, that they would never be free. She did not know how she would face Hannah. Or Jeremy, who was walking towards her.

'I have let you all down. I'm sorry.' She began to sob, her shoulders shaking.

'You did what you could. It was a great act of courage to go in there at all,' Jeremy said, placing his hand on her shoulder. The words were kind, but she could sense his disappointment.

'You will see that God is never outdone in generosity.' The priest's words were meant to reassure her, but Sarah could feel only desolation. 'Here are your friends, now, to take you home.'

As the priest turned to greet Camilla and Rabindrah, the harsh light revealed the ravages that the last days had wreaked on his failing health, and Sarah saw how grey his colour was.

'Father, you look ill,' she said. 'You need to get some rest now.'

'Do not concern yourself.' His smile was a mixture of humour and resignation. 'There will be eternity to rest. Will you walk over to the mission with me? The good sisters have prepared something for you to eat, and Wanjiru would like to see you.'

'She knows I'm here?' Sarah was surprised.

'I told her you were coming to visit Simon. She asked if she could see him herself, but the inspector thought it would be too dangerous.' Fr Bidoli turned to the policeman. 'Will you join us?'

Jeremy shook his head. 'That's very kind, but I have paperwork to finish off. You can leave your car in the compound, my dear. If you drop into the office before you leave I'll still be around.'

They left the cell block and walked across the floodlit compound. The *askari* unlocked the gates and they stepped into the open square. Sarah was still holding the unsigned statement in one hand, her other hand supporting Fr Bidoli as he walked slowly, looking as though he was close to collapse. Rabindrah moved towards them but Camilla held him back, thinking that Sarah might need a few moments to talk to the priest about what had happened in the cell. As they approached the mission house, a figure rose suddenly from the huddle of sleeping men and came after them. Almost too late, Camilla saw the flash of the raised panga and screamed out a warning. Sarah whirled, pushing the priest to one side, fighting off their assailant with flailing arms as he grappled with her. She felt his rank breath, saw the glittering hatred in his eyes as he threw her to the ground and tore the police statement from her hands. She was aware of shouts and the sound of pounding feet coming from the police station. A shot rang out, and when her attacker lifted the panga to deliver the death-blow she found herself looking into the malevolent gaze of Karanja Mungai. Sarah raised her arms as Fr Bidoli threw himself between them. There was a crunch of metal on bone, and she felt his frail old body sagging against her.

As if from nowhere she heard a high-pitched shriek of rage as the doors of the mission were flung open and another figure raced towards them. Wanjiru was screaming in Kikuyu as she hurled herself at Karanja. He turned to face her and raised the panga once more, bringing it down in an arc that sliced across her neck and shoulders, and into her chest. But she leaned into him, making a blood-curdling, shrieking sound as she plunged the blade of a kitchen knife into his abdomen. With a grunt of surprise, he looked into the face of his nemesis and crumpled on to the ground, the knife handle still protruding from his body.

Wanjiru sank to her knees, holding her neck, blood pumping from between her fingers as she leaned over the old man and spat into his dead, staring eyes. Then she collapsed on to the ground beside him. Rabindrah was at Sarah's side, lifting the priest away, calling out to her, asking if she was hurt as Camilla knelt in the dust beside the Kikuyu girl.

'I'm not hurt,' Sarah gasped. 'Look after Fr Bidoli – he's badly injured, I think.'

She crawled over to Wanjiru and lifted her head, trying to staunch the blood that flowed from the open wound on to the ground, spraying her clothes and shoes. But it was hopeless. The slash of the panga was too deep and too wide, and there was nothing she could do to stop the gush of arterial bleeding. Wanjiru's voice was a gurgle as she tried to speak.

'Karanja?'

'He is dead, Wanjiru. He will do no more harm.'

'My baby.' Her eyes were glazing over, but the appeal was still there.

'I will see that he is well,' Sarah said. 'I promise you that, Wanjiru. I promise with all my heart.'

There was a last, bubbling sigh, and then the girl was limp. Sarah sat holding her, watching the blood pool around her in the dust, thinking of the child that was now waiting in the mission for his mother who would never return. Waiting as Simon had waited. She looked up to see that an ambulance had arrived. Fr Bidoli was lifted on to a stretcher, and two nuns came from the mission to wrap Wanjiru's small body in a white sheet and carry her away.

Through the rest of what seemed like an endless night, Sarah waited at the hospital, dozing with Camilla on uncomfortable chairs as Rabindrah came and went with cups of coffee. Dawn was breaking when Jeremy Hardy joined them.

'Karanja is dead,' he said. 'I believe it's safe to say that without him there will be no more trouble. It's all over, my dear.'

'Wanjiru,' Sarah said. 'She should have a proper burial. I suppose the nuns will take care of that.'

'That poor little girl saved your life. And the priest's life, too.' He passed his hand over gritty eyes and the stubble on his chin. 'God knows how long Karanja had been watching the jail, or why he picked that moment to attack.'

'He must have seen me come out of the prison with the paper in my hand,' Sarah said. 'Maybe he thought that it was the signed statement we needed.'

She shuddered and closed her eyes. The numbness was wearing off, and she was beginning to feel very cold. Her body started to shake and Rabindrah took off his jacket and put it around her shoulders.

'I promised Wanjiru I would make sure that the baby was cared for,' she said. 'He can't be sent back to the reserve. Not with his history, and his disability.'

'I'm sure they'll look after him at the mission,' Jeremy said. 'He'll certainly be fine there for the time being. You should head home, you and Camilla. Or get a room and spend a few hours at the Outspan Hotel. There's nothing more you can do here.'

Sarah was about to protest, to say that she would not leave until she had seen Fr Bidoli, when the surgeon came into the small waiting room. His face was grave.

'He has lost a lot of blood,' he said. 'But his condition is stable. As you know, he is already a sick man and the next few days will be critical. He is conscious now, and he asked whether you were still here. You may see him if you wish, but only for a few minutes.'

He was in intensive care, heavily bandaged, wires and tubes everywhere. Sarah sat down at his bedside and wept, holding his hand, begging him not to die now, telling him that he had given her back her life, her faith, and hope for the future.

'Sarah.' It was little more than a whisper but his eyes opened and he squeezed her hand faintly. 'I always tell my parishioners: "*Kama Mungu na mwita wewe, hawezi kusema ngoja mpaka keshu.*" You understand? If God calls you today, it is no use saying "wait till tomorrow". If this is the time, I will go in peace.'

'No, please no. Don't die now.'

'Do not cry, little one. You have had enough grief. Your young man loves you, Sarah. I have seen it in his eyes. So now you must go out and find joy.'

He could not say any more, and Sarah sat listening to his laboured, uneven breathing until the nurse came in and gently told her it was time to leave. She would be informed if there was any change. Outside in the passageway Sarah stumbled into Rabindrah's arms, and he led her out to the car where Camilla was waiting. Then he kissed her and drove away. He would telephone later in the day, he said. For a long time Sarah and Camilla stood, wrapped together and holding one another steady, before climbing into the old Land Rover. It was time to go home to Langani.

Simon Githiri died two days later, at dawn on a Sunday morning as the sun rose and sent its summoning beam through the barred window of his cell.

When the call came through, Hannah and Sarah and Camilla drove out to the ridge. At Piet's cairn they laid flowers from the garden on the white stones, and then sat down on the wide natural seat of the rock where he had loved to look out over the tawny splendour of his land.

'I have something to tell you while we are here with Piet,' Hannah said after a while. Her voice was low, her face soft. 'I'm pregnant. Lars and I are going to have a baby. I was afraid to say it before. Afraid of bringing another child into a future where we seemed to be always fighting the odds. But now I can hope for him. Plan for him. And there is something else I have decided to do, although it may not be easy.'

'What?' Sarah took her hand. 'What is it, Hannah? Can we help you?'

'I have been thinking about the other child,' Hannah said. 'About Simon's son.' Her face was pale and set. 'I have a wonderful husband and a beautiful daughter, and another child on the way. But that little boy has lost everything. So I was thinking that perhaps he could live with us. Share our home and all that we have. It's only right, heh? It will make amends, at last. Finish all the hatred and the suffering that has gone before.'

Sarah and Camilla stared at her and then they hugged her, promising love and support, crying together, making plans for the future. After a while they stopped talking and stood together, each in their own private world of memory, looking out on the fresh world in front of them, and listening to the call of the African plains.

Chapter 20

Kenya, July 1967

'I've been invited to lunch in Nairobi this Sunday,' Sarah said. 'But I don't know. It's a regular family event. I'm nervous about it.'

They were lying on the bank of the river, their horses nibbling at the tender grass that had appeared with last week's rain. Slivers of sunlight pierced the leafy shade, offering glimpses of a sky bleached by the midday heat.

'This isn't the first time you've met the relatives,' Camilla said. 'You've known the aunt and uncle since the handover of the new vehicle. Some of the cousins came to see Lila in the fashion gala — there must have been ten of them at least. All charming and friendly.'

'Yes, but it's different now,' Sarah said, and saw Hannah's involuntary change of expression. She hesitated, realising it was still a touchy subject. They had not reopened the question of Rabindrah's new role in her life, but now she needed support. 'I've had a letter from Mum and Dad,' she said. 'I wrote to tell them about Simon, and everything that happened in Nyeri. And about Rabindrah.'

The reply had shocked Sarah. There were a few barely decipherable lines from Raphael, kind but cautious. It was good that she had feelings for someone new, he said. But there was no need to rush things. They hoped she might come home later in the year, maybe for Christmas, and then she could tell them everything. In the meantime, she should be careful. It was marvellous news that Langani could now return to being the peaceful place she had always loved and thought of as a second home. Betty's letter was longer and very different. Sarah fished in the pocket of her bush jacket and took out the pages, holding them out for Hannah and Camilla:

You are still so vulnerable, so defenceless. Especially after the most recent happenings. You've been working in close proximity to this young man for almost a year, and at Buffalo Springs there are precious few people you can talk to. None of your own generation. The encounter with Simon required an extraordinary frame of mind and great courage on your part, and Dad and I admire you beyond words. And then the terrifying attack on your friend Fr Bidoli, and the death of the poor little Kikuyu girl. I cannot think about the danger, and the possibility that you might have been seriously hurt yourself, without wanting to weep. It must still be extremely difficult to put these things into any reasonable context, along with the earlier memories of Piet's death.

I can see how you might feel grateful to Rabindrah Singh for being there with you, for seeing you through it all. And because you have suffered so bravely, it would be easy to mistake that gratitude for something else, my dearest Sarah. Especially in the emotional state you must still be in. It's right to feel that one particular part of your life is over, now that Simon is dead and the threat to Langani is over. A blessed relief to know that you can and should begin again. You have literally come out of the valley of the shadow of death, and your friend Rabindrah must look as though he could be the person to travel on with you, into a lighter, better place and time.

But, my dear, there would be many problems. Your father and I brought you up to be open-minded, to mix without prejudice with other races and religions. We always welcomed people with different backgrounds into our home, regardless of their colour or origin. And we had many friends within the Asian community in Kenya — Catholics from Goa, Ismailis, Hindus and Muslims — they were all part of our life out there. But our customs are so different when it comes to the everyday issues that arise between a man and a woman. I would not be a good mother if I did not tell you how concerned I am about your feelings for this young Sikh. No doubt he is cultured and clever. A sincere and good man, as you say. And I can see how you have come to depend on him over time, especially during a period when you were grieving and lonely. But there are other issues in this kind of situation.

I wonder if you remember Angela Patel who was one of my closest friends in Mombasa? She was a nurse from Monaghan, who met and married an Indian doctor from Kenya while he was studying medicine in Dublin. We always thought him a pleasant, intelligent man, and I know she worked hard to make a success of their marriage. But she has ended up back in Ireland, after having had a nervous breakdown. Her husband's family simply would not accept her. They made her life impossible in a hundred cruel ways, while he shrugged off the humiliation doled out to her by his mother and sisters in particular. Poor Angela stuck it out for years, because of the children. But she has no real rights as the wife of a Hindu. She only sees her son and daughter twice a year, and it's breaking her heart. He will not allow them to come to Ireland, and she is forced to go back to Kericho, where he is practising now, and stay in a hotel or with friends, when she wants to visit them. He has a new woman in his life, and Angela doesn't belong there any more. But she has no real home in Ireland either. People think her strange for having married an Indian, and disgraceful for having apparently abandoned her children. Her life here is bleak. She is not in a position to remarry in this Catholic country, and the amount of money she gets from her husband is pitiful. Yet they began their married life so much in love.

She is not the only girl I know with a story like this. Unfortunately, there are many who started out brave and confident, in the knowledge that their love would transcend all obstacles, only to find that centuries of differing customs and beliefs were beyond their most heroic efforts. In the end it is these apparently unimportant differences that chip away at the bedrock of marriage and erode the foundations to a point where they cannot hold.

So I think you should be very careful with this young man. He may seem ideal on the surface, but his religion and culture are as ingrained in him as your own. A close partnership between you may not bring either of you real happiness, after the first heady bloom of romance has been overtaken by the demands of everyday routine, and another kind of partnership is needed to take its place. You say he is not a traditional Sikh, that he does not go to the temple or wear a turban. In the same way, he and his family probably do not think of you as a traditional Catholic because you cannot attend Sunday mass or take the sacraments, living where you are in Buffalo Springs. But that does not mean your different religions are not a strong, vital part of you. And if you were to marry and have children, what then? How would you bring them up? In which society and culture? At what kind of school? You would both have to promise that they would be brought up in the Catholic faith, in order to be allowed to marry in the Church. And later you might find that this initial undertaking causes strife within your home.

Maybe there is no thought of marriage in either of your minds, for the present. But I know you so well. Your father and I have always been proud of your loyalty and your sense of what is right, even when it has made things difficult for you. From the tone of your letter I realise you have intense feelings for Rabindrah, and you are not the kind of person who would settle for a brief affair. So it is important for you to take all these issues into account, even if you have not yet discussed them between you. And what of his family? The Sikh community in Kenya is tight-knit, and generally does not take to marriages between themselves and Hindus or people of different castes, or unions with Muslim Indians, let alone with Christians and Europeans. I know that Sikhs are supposed to be tolerant, and Dad and I have been welcomed into Sikh homes and have been to a Sikh wedding. I also know that they expect anyone marrying into their society to do so in their temple and within the framework of their beliefs. My dear, this is an extremely serious situation that needs careful thought.

As your loving mother, I would suggest that you go back to Buffalo Springs now, and think this over for a while. Perhaps it would be a good idea not to see Rabindrah for a few months. That would allow you to test your feelings for each other. Your father and I love you very much, and we want you to find someone with whom you can share your life in a way that you, of all people, truly deserve. You have surmounted so many difficulties already, darling, and seen so much sadness. We don't want you to be hurt by anything else, ever again.

In the meantime you have Camilla and Hannah with you. The bond you have is a most admirable thing that will help to keep you going. And I'm sure your wonderful friends, the Briggses, will be waiting eagerly for you to get back to camp. We think of our time there with such pleasure, and we know that you are safe in their friendship and protection.

Dad and I love you more than we can say, and will pray that this will turn out for the best. If you could see your way to coming home for a while, we would love it. And so would Tim. He is doing his best to move on with his own life, but it is still difficult in this small community. We will send you an air ticket, if you'd like to be here for Christmas. We all

long to see you and to welcome you home again. Please write soon and let
us know how you are faring.

Mum

'Oh dear,' Camilla said, handing the last page to Hannah, who was reading more slowly, a frown of concentration on her face.

'I suppose his family will feel the same,' Sarah said. 'I mean, we've only just started to . . . well, we haven't had much chance to talk about our feelings for each other, and already the troops are lined up with full ammunition.'

'I think you should go to the lunch in Nairobi,' Camilla said. 'You'll never know what his family feels, or how Rabindrah might deal with opposition, if you don't push ahead.'

'Just don't go too fast.' Hannah's face was shaded by the brim of her hat and she turned her head so that Sarah could not see her troubled expression. 'There may turn out to be big differences that don't show up at the beginning, and you don't want to get into a situation where you—'

'So you agree with Mum, then?' Sarah's eyes flashed. 'You think I should beware of the dark-skinned stranger with the weird religion who might abandon me, or lock me up and treat me like a chattel.'

'Hey! Don't jump on me like that,' Hannah said. 'I'm doing the best I can to accept this. Of course I want to see you go on with your life. Fall in love again, like everyone our age. You know I want you to be happy. But this may turn out to be harder than you think.'

'When was the last time we were all happy?' Camilla asked, sitting up straight and directing a warning glance at Hannah. 'Do you realise not one of us has felt truly light-hearted and carefree and happy since that summer when we were twenty-one, before Piet died? Isn't there something wrong with that? Shouldn't we try to be happy now, above all else? Enjoy our lives, the people we love, whoever they are? And why are we all focusing on the subject of marriage? Why shouldn't Sarah start out with an affair and see where it goes?'

'You're right,' Hannah said. 'We're reading too much into this. Love should be full of excitement and the feeling of discovery.'

'It should make you beautiful and sexy and impatient and hungry,' Camilla said. 'It should be fun. Love shouldn't be overshadowed by responsibility and religion and guilt, for God's sake. I thought you'd got past Catholic fear and disapproval of all bodily pleasures, Sarah. You should abandon yourself to Rabindrah's advances, and time will tell whether you belong together.'

Sarah rolled over on to her stomach and lay face down, her head hidden by her arms, so that they could not see her disappointment. Surely they knew her better than this, understood that a casual affair was not her way. Even her mother had realised that. She pressed her lips together, feeling foolish and humiliated, biting off a heated defence of her ideals. There was no doubt that she was old-fashioned, but she could not find it in herself to excuse or abandon her most cherished principles.

'Let's all go to Nairobi.' Camilla leaned over and shook Sarah lightly. 'Drive down for a long weekend, share a cottage at the Norfolk, see a play or a film or both. Go shopping for the new baby. My father should be back from London today, so he can take us all out to dinner at the very least.' She turned to Hannah, laughing. 'Or he can take the two of us to Muthaiga for Sunday curry lunch, while Sarah has the real thing with Indar Uncle and the rest of the inspection committee. And we'll be waiting to prop her up when she gets back. What do you think?'

'Maybe Lars would come too,' Hannah said. 'We haven't been to Nairobi for months. If Anthony is around, between safaris, we could talk to him about the lodge. About starting to build again.'

Camilla's smile gave way to a pinched look around her mouth. 'I don't want to see Anthony,' she said. 'If you want to get together with him, then you and Lars have to do it when I'm not around.'

'He's phoned several times in the past couple of weeks,' Hannah said. 'Including the night that you and Sarah went to see Simon. Lars spoke to him two days ago. He was in Tsavo with some clients, but I think the safari is nearly over.'

'You didn't tell me any of this,' Camilla said.

'I didn't think you'd want to know.' Hannah shrugged. 'But you'll run into him one of these days. It can't be avoided.'

'I don't have to run into him at all.' Camilla's voice was tight. 'I'm very happy about staying up here, getting the new designs up and running in the workshop. I'll be fine at Langani where there's no chance of bumping into him. And if he plans to drop in for a discussion with you and Lars, I'll go and spend a day or two with Daddy in the big city. But I don't want to see Anthony again. Ever.'

'I'd call that hypocrisy,' Hannah said. 'You're pushing Sarah along, telling her to hurl herself into an affair, but you won't even consider giving Anthony another chance, heh? Maybe you'd better think about that – while you're dispensing so much worldly advice.'

'I'm not happy with any of this,' Sarah said. 'Besides, I've been thinking that it's time I contacted Dan and Allie. I should go back to work now, before they decide they don't need me or find someone else to do my job. Rabindrah could come up to Buffalo Springs in a week or so.'

'No.' Camilla rose to her feet and walked over to take up the reins of her horse. 'He obviously wants you to meet the family officially, and you may as well get on with it. Let's ride back, and try the Nairobi idea on Lars. See what the big man says. He's far more sensible and far-sighted than any of us.' She put her foot in the stirrup and sprang lightly into the saddle. 'I love the slower pace Hannah has adopted, now that she's pregnant again. I was always terrified of galloping across this plain, trying to keep up with the two of you, clinging on to the saddle or even the horse's mane, scared that my pony would fall into a pig hole, and even more scared that you'd see how pathetic I was!'

They set out across a wide area of feathered grass, the horses snorting and pulling on the reins, impatient to be given their heads on the ride home. An omnipotent sun beat down on them, and the sounds of the bush crackled and whispered in the shimmer of breathless air. After a while they broke into a gentle canter, and at the stables they handed over the sweating horses and headed for the house to slake their thirst. Lottie had prepared fresh lemonade and filled a bucket with ice and they sat with her in the garden, looking at the blue shoulders of the mountain and the approaching bank of afternoon cloud.

'Sarah has to go to Nairobi this weekend,' Hannah said. 'And we were thinking it might be good if we all went down for a couple of nights. Lars too. And you, Ma, of course.'

'I'll stay here.' Lottie's response was so quick that Hannah glanced at her in surprise. 'I have a few women and *totos* I need to keep an eye on, at the dispensary. And I want to finish sewing the new covers for the sofa and chairs. I love using Camilla's machines, while there's no one in the workshop.'

She bent her head as she spoke and looked down at her hands, resting in her lap. Hannah could see that she had smoothed them with some kind of cream, and shaped her nails into polished ovals. With a shock she noticed the band of white skin on one of Lottie's fingers, and realised that her mother was no longer wearing her wedding ring. The last symbol of her marriage was gone, and Hannah wondered what she had done with the gold band that Janni had given her so long ago, and why she had chosen to remove it now.

'Any chance of lunch?' Lars's measured step made them all turn around.

He bent down to kiss Hannah, placing his hand for a brief moment on her stomach in a gesture of tenderness that made her heart contract. She sighed, acutely aware of her good fortune, knowing at the same time that she had not been sensitive or generous enough with Sarah.

'There's an important event in Nairobi this weekend,' she said, looking up at Lars. 'Sarah's been invited to lunch by the Singh family, and she needs some back-up. Could we all go down for a night or two, do you think?'

'I'll stay,' Lottie said again. There was a softness in her face which Hannah noticed but could not analyse. 'Go on, Lars. You're brave enough to take these three girls on their outing. They need a chaperone. And I have something to tell you all.' She paused, aware that they were all staring at her, that they had picked up something in the tone of her voice. 'I'm leaving here at the end of this month,' she said. 'I want to spend some time with Sergio, in Johannesburg. He's going to phone tomorrow, when he has arranged the air travel for me. I need to consider my long-term plans. It's wonderful being here, and I'd love to come back and help when the baby is due. But I need a little time to myself. Time to think. So this is a good time for you to take a break in Nairobi, while I'm around to look after things here. And I'd love to keep Suniva with me, if you would consider leaving her behind with an adoring grandmother.'

Her announcement was greeted with silence, and Lars saw that Hannah's expression had darkened.

'I think Nairobi is a good idea,' he said. 'Thanks for your offer, Lottie. We'll leave Suniva with you and I'll take Hannah on a little honeymoon. It seems a long time since the last one.'

He was rewarded by the sensation of his wife's beautiful breasts pressed

497

briefly against him, as she reached out to put her arms around his waist and whisper a message into his ear. Her promise made him smile and adjust his schedule for the afternoon.

'Do you mind sharing with me?' Camilla looked at Sarah as they checked in to the Norfolk. 'We can take a cottage, and the lovebirds will have their own quarters just across the courtyard.'

'Sounds great,' Sarah said.

'Daddy will be here at around seven to take us to the theatre, and then on for dinner,' Camilla said. 'Did you ask Rabindrah?'

'He can't have dinner with us,' Sarah said. 'He's covering some conference. But he might join us for a drink later on, depending on how things go.'

'I'll toss you for first in the bathroom,' Camilla said. 'What are you wearing? Does any of this sound familiar?'

She was glad to hear Sarah singing to herself as they bathed and dressed and speculated on Lottie's announcement.

'Do you think she'll go and visit her Italian admirer?' Camilla drew expert lines along her eyelids with a dark pencil, making her blue eyes more startling. 'Or will he be waiting for her in Johannesburg, kneeling at the bottom of the steps as she gets off the plane, singing an aria? Do you think he looks like Mario Lanza? Or is he more Dean Martin?'

'I hope Hannah will deal with this calmly,' Sarah said, chuckling at the image. 'We're not brilliant at understanding our parents, are we?'

'No, we're not,' Camilla said, thinking of her father's apparent rejection of Giles Hannington, and the false assumptions she had made about that relationship. 'I suppose we've reached a time when each generation has to try and accept what the other one is doing. But it's not easy. Here's to parents and tolerance all round.'

'I've got the car parked outside. With an old friend who is looking forward to seeing you, Camilla.' George's words were not well received by his daughter.

'Oh, no.' She was both dismayed and angry. He knew she did not want to see Anthony again. She did not believe he had forgotten their discussion in London. 'That's not fair, Daddy. You shouldn't have done—'

'It's Saidi,' he said quickly. 'Our old driver. Do you remember how well he looked after you when you were a schoolgirl? How wonderful he was with your mother? He saw my name in the newspaper and came looking for me, so I've taken him on again.'

Camilla was weak with relief as she shook Saidi's hand, enquired after his family, and reminded him that he had also met Sarah before. George was silent, more than a little offended that she had not trusted him enough to know her heart. It was an inauspicious start to the evening, and things did not improve when the play at the Donovan Maule Theatre turned out to be mediocre. Camilla's heart sank when she had to pose for photographs at the New Stanley Hotel.

'I'm sorry,' George said. 'I should have warned Oscar that you would be here, when I booked the table for dinner. Like all the best hotel men, he knows how to head off the press and other unwelcome intrusions. But once we get to the Grill we'll be left in peace.'

'It can't be helped.' Camilla offered a dazzling smile to the photographer from the *Standard* and then leaned forward and whispered in his ear. His face registered surprise as he nodded and thanked her before hurrying away, cameras and light meters rattling on his skinny frame. 'He's gone to look for James Stewart,' she said in answer to her father's questioning look. 'I told him he'd just arrived at the Norfolk.'

'How on earth did you find out?' Hannah was wide-eyed. 'If I'd known that I would have stayed there myself, in the hopes of hearing his voice, just once.'

'Well, I think he's arriving this evening,' Camilla said. 'But it might be next week. Or maybe it's next month. But definitely sometime soon.'

They were still laughing when they reached their table. George arranged the seating and ordered drinks, and soon the talk was carefree and animated. He looked at his daughter and her friends and was touched by their happiness.

It was Lars who saw Anthony first. He was seated opposite a dark-haired woman whose dress was a little too tight and barely contained her overflowing bosom. His hands gestured as he leaned forward to emphasise a point he was making, and the candlelight caught the beaded and copper bracelets he always wore on his wrist, the curl of his mouth and the laughter lines that etched his face.

'Anthony is here.' Lars decided on the straightforward approach. 'I'll go over and say *jambo*.'

George cursed under his breath as he caught the immediate tension in Camilla's body. She picked up her champagne glass as she saw Anthony rise and move towards their table.

'Does anybody else have this amazing sense of déjà vu?' she said with a high-pitched laugh.

'I'm delighted to see these three sirens together again,' Anthony said as he greeted Hannah and Sarah with unreserved affection, and kissed Camilla lightly on the cheek. 'I'll be on a new safari next week. I'll stop off at Langani on my way, if that's good with you, and we'll talk about the lodge. Meantime, I'm in Nairobi for the next few days. How long will you be here, Camilla?'

'I haven't decided,' she said coolly. 'There are so many things pending.'

'I'll telephone you,' Anthony said. 'Are you staying with George?'

'No. We're all at the Norfolk tonight, but I'll probably move tomorrow.' Camilla looked away, deliberately cutting him off.

'I'm glad to see you down here.' Anthony turned to Sarah. 'So relieved that the bad times are over. I was camping in Amboseli when I heard what had happened. I couldn't get away, but I phoned from the hotel at Namanga. I'm sure Hannah told you. My next safari will take me north again, so I'll drop in on the Briggses. I hope you'll be there.'

'I'm sure they'll be glad to see you,' Sarah said.

'We're almost finished dinner.' Anthony nodded towards his table for two. 'George, would you mind if we joined you for a drink later? Is the chopper expedition still on for Tuesday?'

'It is.' George was increasingly uncomfortable, aware of Camilla's barely concealed agitation, and anxious to avoid further contact. 'I'll fill you in on the details on Monday.'

'Unfortunately, I'm not going to be able to join you for the flight. I was going to phone in the morning and let you know. And that's the end of any wildlife discussions this evening, I can assure you.' Anthony smiled, his brown eyes focused on Camilla. 'I'll see you a little later for a drink, though.'

He strolled back to his table, and moments later his companion was nodding with obvious enthusiasm. She leaned over to place her hand on his arm, allowing him a better view of her cleavage. Sarah gritted her teeth.

Camilla gave an impression of serenity, belying an inner sense of having been trampled. She was deathly afraid she was going to cry, but determined that she would not be affected by his presence, or make a fool of herself. It was not as though there had been any duplicity on Anthony's part. She had told him in London that she could not share his life, and it seemed now that she had made the right decision. In the space of a few weeks he had already moved on, found easy solace in another woman. Perhaps more than one. Clearly he had not been much affected by her decision. She swallowed hard, her stomach cramping with pain and humiliation.

'I rest my case,' she said looking round the table, her voice arch, brows raised, mouth forming a perfect smile that did not light her eyes. 'Now let's have ourselves a happy evening and we'll all be charming when they join us later. In the meantime, Daddy, what's this about a helicopter? I always hated them until Saul arranged for one to meet us in New York.'

'I'd love you to see this project,' he said. 'It's a rescue operation to move rhinos out of places that have become settlement areas, and to relocate them in one of the National Parks. Something I'm helping to finance.'

'They're so dangerous and bad tempered.' Camilla was intrigued, glad to be distracted. 'You can't just invite a rhino to come for a stroll to the nearest game park, or put a rope around one and lead it away.'

'This is a scheme where they're located from the air. Initially we follow the animal by helicopter, and the pilot radios its position to a Game Department lorry. The whole programme has been put together by a remarkable vet. He has perfected a tranquillising drug called M99. He shoots this knock-out dart at the rhino from the chopper, although it always amazes me that he can hit the target. Then we try to keep flying over the beast until it collapses. When it's down, the truck moves in and the rhino is winched on to the back, while it's still asleep. It's extremely tricky, though, because those huge, lumbering creatures have a habit of running for the thickest bush or into the heart of the forest, and it's sometimes difficult to locate the spot where they finally fall. And even harder to get to it.'

'I'd love to see that,' Camilla said. 'Could I really come with you?'

'I'd love you to join us.' George was beaming.

'That would be marvellous,' she said. 'If it's just the two of us, and the vet?'

'That's exactly how it will be,' he said, covering her hand with his own.

It was impossible to ignore the sight of Anthony, now dancing with the voluptuous young woman. Camilla brushed a napkin over her lips and left for the powder room. George watched her cross the small, crowded room and sighed.

'I don't understand it,' he said heavily. 'They were made for each other. I'd bet my life on the fact that Anthony truly loves my daughter.'

'I think you are right,' Lars said. 'But he is afraid. Not so much of the commitment, but of having something so beautiful that it might shatter at any moment. And she is so famous. He is not the kind of man to walk in her shadow.'

'Maybe there's an explanation for the girl,' Hannah said, watching the dance floor. 'He's not holding her close or anything.'

'She's certainly clutching at him, though,' Sarah said. 'But Lars is right. Camilla's and Anthony's beauty and their recognition in two different worlds is working against them both, I think. She sees him as one of those Greek images of physical perfection. Graceful when he moves. Like an animal, lean and powerful and effortless. And look at his profile – the aquiline nose, the mouth that is quite perfect in its shape. And his cheekbones make him look chiselled. I've taken many photographs of him, and always been amazed by those features. But I don't think he's all that sure of himself.'

'That's right,' Lars said. 'And she is like porcelain – so delicate and pale and fair. But she is very strong. Stronger than he is.'

'I hope that's true,' George said. 'I wouldn't want to see her hurt again.'

'Happily she has you as her rock,' Sarah said, smiling at him as Camilla threaded her way back to the table. 'And that is the thing that will see her through. Oh God, here he comes.'

The band had taken a break and Anthony arrived to join them.

'This is Charlene Moore,' he said by way of introduction. 'She's a travel agent from San Antonio. Her company specialises in horse riding holidays. I think we'll be working together a great deal from now on.'

'Bloody sensational,' Hannah said under her breath.

The girl was obviously captivated by Anthony. She spoke with a Texan drawl and was plainly happy to be in such glamorous company.

'Why, I never thought I would have a chance to visit with someone like you,' she said to Camilla. 'I've seen you in all the magazines, of course, but you are just so much more precious than your pictures.' She flashed a vivid smile at George. 'I can see from your daddy where you get your great looks from.'

'I'm a carbon copy of my mother,' Camilla said, her smile glassy.

'My sister was a beauty queen. She won all the pageants and she always wanted to go to New York and make it big. But she has a husband and six kids now, and she runs the best beauty salon. So I guess her chance at fame has passed.'

She spent the next half-hour regaling them with descriptions of her recent safari experiences. Anthony sat beside her, mute and unsmiling, his gaze fixed on Camilla.

'I decided not to say I was a travel agent when I booked my tour,' Charlene said. 'Even though this fine man would have given me a discount and all. But I wanted to be incognito. So I put my name down and came with a small party of friends. To see how he did things. And I can tell you that he does them well. There isn't a thing in his camp that could be better, and my customers are just going to love him. Especially the women! Oh my, when I show them my pictures they will be mad to come here and ride with Mr Chapman! And so jealous of me! You bet.'

'I think it's time to call it a night.' George rose from the table. 'Anthony, I'll talk to you next week if you're around. Goodnight, Miss Moore. I hope you enjoy the rest of your stay in Nairobi.'

'Oh, I surely will,' she said, glowing with pleasure. 'But it was so good to meet y'all and talk to such interesting people.'

'Maybe we can get together next week?' There was an edge to Anthony's voice as he spoke to Lars.

'Hannah and I are going back on Monday morning,' Lars said.

'I'm driving up with them,' Sarah said. 'Hopefully en route to Buffalo Springs. Time to go back to work.'

'I'll keep in touch, then,' Anthony said to George. He turned to speak to Camilla, but she was already walking out of the restaurant. 'Goodnight.'

At the Norfolk they collected their room keys and arranged to meet for breakfast.

'Not me,' Hannah said. 'Breakfast in bed is an essential part of this expedition. Not something I've done for a very long time.'

'Oh my,' Sarah said, as they climbed into their beds. 'There's certainly a crackle in the air when you and Anthony are in the same room. I know he's counting the hours until he catches up with you one way or the other.'

'Can you imagine the highlights of our lives together?' Camilla tried to sound flippant and failed. 'Can you see me in Nairobi, hanging around on my own for weeks on end, wondering if he'd surrendered helplessly to some female who'd pounced on him during a moonlit night in the bush?'

'Maybe he's not like that any more,' Sarah said. 'He might be ready for the one great passion of his life. Which is definitely you. The rest is almost certainly a question of marking time. Meaningless.'

'You should try writing Hollywood screenplays,' Camilla said witheringly.

'I think you're still in love with him,' Sarah said. 'Otherwise you wouldn't be so frightened of seeing him.'

But there was no reply. She looked around and saw that Camilla had shut her eyes and was feigning sleep.

'I can't cope with this.'

Sunday morning had dawned, bright and blue and filled with birdsong, and Sarah had panicked. She sat trembling on the side of her bed, still in her underwear. Her face was pinched and there were dark shadows under her eyes.

'Did you get any sleep at all?' Camilla asked. 'Here, put some of this stuff on the craters under your eyes and get your clothes on. Things are bound to go better with the relatives if you're fully dressed. And have some breakfast. It will calm you.'

It was midday when the hotel reception rang through to say that a Mr Singh was in the lobby.

'Oh God,' Sarah said. 'I should never have agreed to this.'

Rabindrah was dressed in a striped shirt with the sleeves rolled up, freshly pressed slacks and a bush jacket. He looked discouragingly normal and relaxed.

'I'm sorry I didn't make it last night,' he said, his lips warm against her cheek. 'The speeches dragged on and I couldn't escape. Did you know that your eyes are the colour of a forest in the spring? Are you all right?'

'No,' she said. 'Actually, I'm not. I'm very nervous. In fact, I think I'm going to be sick.'

'That's more or less how you felt when we went to see my parents,' he said. 'If my family continues to have this strange effect on you, I may have to curtail any further visits. In the meantime, we have time to make a detour.' He closed the door of the car for her. 'There's a place I like to go when I need to be calm. We'll stop there for a few minutes, even though it may be more crowded on a Sunday. Mostly with big Indian families, by the way.'

Ten minutes later he had parked outside the gates of the Nairobi Arboretum. He took her by the hand and they walked into the depths of its green tranquillity. All around them the trees and shrubs rose in a protective screen that hid them from the heat of the day and the noise and rattle of traffic on the main avenues that led out of the city. It was not long before they were alone, and Rabindrah stopped, putting a finger on her lips so that she could not say a word. He murmured in her ear, stroked her hair, kissed her neck and throat and her soft, round mouth.

'Stop,' she said at last, pushing him away, smiling and breathless. 'This is not calming. And my hair and lipstick and clothes are all mussed up.'

'I love you,' he said, putting his hands into her thick hair again. 'I love you, Sarah Mackay, small Irish girl with big heart. I love you because you are beautiful and brave, and true to everything that is good. This is all that you have to remember when we are with my family. Now we will sit here on this bench for five minutes, and think about that. And then we will go to Kuldip Auntie and enjoy her best cooking.'

The Singh residence was a large concrete structure with a curved balcony on the first floor, and a flat roof. There was a metal fence around the house, and the windows were barred on the outside. The entire façade looked in need of a coat of paint.

'Here we are,' Rabindrah said, and was surprised to see that Sarah was blushing. 'What? What is it?'

But she could not tell him that she was remembering her mother years ago, remarking with mild disapproval that Indians never bothered to look after the outside of their houses. She did not have time to dwell on the issue. Indar Singh had appeared in the driveway, his hand outstretched, his face smiling under a bright pink turban.

'Come, come,' he said. 'You are very welcome in our house, Sarah. We are most happy to see you. How is the Land Rover? And the old one we fixed up is still going, I hope?'

Sarah was swept into the cool, dark interior of the house, propelled across the polished floors by Indar's guiding hand, into a sea of colour, sound and smell. The contrast with Rabindrah's parental home in London came as a shock as she thought of the stiff, empty sitting room in Southwark, the silences punctuated by the ticking clock and the sound of Jasmir Singh's key turning in the front door. Here there was a swirl of chattering people in bright clothes and turbans and jewellery. Lila was the first to greet her.

'So good to see you, Sarah,' she said. 'You have met my aunt, Kuldip. This is my mother and her sister. And here are my younger brothers, who are silly boys.'

A glass of orange squash was pressed into Sarah's hand as she shook hands with a confusing assortment of people whose names she knew she would not remember. Senior members of the family sat on velvet-covered chairs and sofas, set back against the walls of the large room. A ceiling fan pushed warm air, redolent with a variety of perfumes, round the room. Watchful mothers eyed their sons and daughters, looking for connections that might or might not prove suitable. The older men had mostly congregated on one side of the room and were discussing cricket, business and politics. Some wore traditional Punjabi dress, but others were attired in suits, or slacks and jackets. All of them wore turbans in a variety of colours and styles.

'Miss Mackay is the one who has done the wonderful photographs for Rabindrah's book,' Kuldip said, introducing Sarah to an old lady seated a little apart on a red velour armchair that resembled a throne. 'This is my mother, Lakhbir Kaur Singh.'

The old lady offered a limp hand in greeting. Her plump arms were heavy with gold bangles, and she inspected Sarah with hawklike eyes.

'So you are the one living in the bush, no?'

'That's right,' Sarah said. 'Near Isiolo. I'm studying elephants around there, for a scientific organisation.'

'But you are not married?'

'No. I'm not married.'

'All alone in the bush, a single girl.' Grandmother Singh shook her head. 'Times have changed here, my dear.'

There was a long silence as Sarah searched for a reply. She glanced around the room, but there was no sign of Rabindrah.

'Come, we are ready for lunch now.' Lila came to her rescue. 'I hope you are hungry. Tell me about Camilla and how she is getting on. I'm sorry she did not come with you today.'

'Me too,' Sarah said, and immediately regretted the words, afraid that they might be considered rude.

'I saw in the newspaper that she has come back to Nairobi. I'm hoping she will do another fashion show. It was so much fun. Rabindrah has told me all about what happened in Nyeri. Look, here he is coming now with Kuldip Auntie, to take care of you.'

In the dining room a buffet-style lunch had been laid out. African servants scurried in and out of the kitchen with dishes made from spinach and soft cheese, carrots, peas, yoghurt and dal and lentils, served with flat chapattis, and a salad made from onions and the sweetest tomatoes Sarah had ever tasted. Most of the food was vegetarian, although she noticed that several of the men helped themselves to a chicken curry that looked and smelled delicious. But she did not see any of the women eating it, and she decided to stick to the vegetable dishes rather than make some kind of faux pas. A dish of yellow rice that she thought was an accompaniment to the curry turned out to be flavoured with almonds and raisins and very sweet. There were desserts that had been made from a kind of dough dipped in syrup and deep fried, but she found them cloying and a little heavy. Within an hour she was desperately casting around for a way in which to pass up any further dishes, without seeming to be impolite.

Rabindrah came and went, introducing her to more people whose names she could not catch. The hospitality was overpowering and her constant smile was making her jaw ache. She found herself either answering a stream of friendly questions about her work and her family history in Kenya, or searching for something with which she could fill a long, awkward silence. After two hours she wanted to curl up in a dark space and never see anyone again. Her head ached and she thought of the open spaces and the quiet of the bush, and wondered when it would be possible to leave. But Rabindrah was talking to a small group of older men on the opposite side of the room, and she could not catch his eye.

'It's a little hot in here; no?' Kuldip was smiling as she took Sarah's plate. 'Why don't you come outside and let me show you my rose garden. I'm not a real expert, but I've won quite a few prizes and I'm very keen.'

The large garden was at the back of the house, and Sarah was astonished at the profusion of roses in neat beds, and the range of colours and perfumes that made up Kuldip's great passion.

'This is extraordinary,' she said. 'My mother loves to garden. She was proud of the garden she had in Mombasa, and what she has now achieved in Ireland. But she has never dreamed of creating anything like this.'

'This is where I spend a good part of my day,' Kuldip said. 'Being a Sikh wife, I am obliged to be at home a great deal. You know how it is with husbands – they like to have their routine well established, and their meals at the same hour, and everything in order in the house. They are all the same, these men, no matter how old or young they are.'

'I think my mother would probably say the same thing.' Sarah knew instantly that there was a purpose to this conversation. She pressed clammy palms against her skirt and prayed for guidance.

'He is such a good boy, Rabindrah.' Kuldip's smile was as sweet as her milk puddings. 'He has been a little wild, like all his generation. Looking around all over the place, trying everything out, flirting with all the foreign girls. Of course, he spent so much time in England where things are different, and that brought other influences into his life. But now he has stopped running around with the Swedish air hostess, and the Italian and French girls. He has settled down at last, and he is ready to come back to the tradition of the family. We are all so happy about this.'

'I'm sure you are,' Sarah said.

'I suppose your parents are hoping that you will join them back in Ireland, one of these days? They must be worried that you are so far from home.'

'I don't really think of Ireland as home,' Sarah said. 'I grew up here and this is where I see myself staying.'

'But your family must be hoping you will soon want to settle down with a good husband, and give them some beautiful grandchildren, no? I'm sure you don't want to live alone, in all these wild, dangerous places, for too much longer.'

Sarah opened her mouth to answer, but Kuldip had turned away with a small exclamation of surprise.

'Oh, here is Anoop,' she said. 'She must be needing a breath of fresh air also. I will leave you in her hands, and you can come back inside together.'

She swept away, turning her head to leave them with a last, gracious smile. Just like Ava Gardner, Sarah thought, with the long black hair and the full, pouting lips.

'I am an old friend of Rabindrah,' Anoop said, holding out her hand. 'We have known each other since we were children. Our families have always been close friends, and done many things together. Rabindrah has shown me the outline of his book, and some of your pictures. It looks very fine indeed.'

'Thank you,' Sarah said. 'I've enjoyed working with him.'

'Yes. He is very clever and he deserves to be successful. We are all very happy that he came back here, instead of remaining in England.'

'Yes. It was a good choice, I think.'

'We spent some time together in England, you know. I studied in London for a while, when he was there, and I stayed with his parents for part of the time.'

'Is your family still in Kenya?' Sarah was curious about the girl. She looked like she was in her early twenties. Although she was a little plump, her face was pale in colour, and she was appealing if not pretty. Her almond-shaped eyes were striking and very dark with long lashes, and she had delicate hands and feet and a good figure. She was wearing the traditional *salwaar kameez*, and discreet but beautiful jewellery.

'Oh, you must have met them earlier,' Anoop said. 'But when you are introduced to twenty people all at once you cannot possibly remember who they are. My mother is best friends with Kuldip. They do everything together. Decide on what happens in their households, go to the temple, shop and exchange recipes, arrange their children's marriages. You know how it is.'

'Not really,' Sarah said. A prickle of unease lodged itself in her consciousness. 'Are you married?'

'Me?' The girl's smile was coy. 'Not yet. I only came back a few months ago.'

'What did you study in England?' Sarah asked. 'Are you going to work here in Nairobi, now that you have come back?'

'I studied economics,' Anoop said. 'But I don't know whether I want to find a job. That will depend, you know.' She lowered her voice for a confidence. 'Kuldip Auntie is optimistic, you see. And my mother too. Especially now that Rabindrah is going to make money with this book. It will give him a good base, and we are all so grateful to you for helping him with that. It is no wonder Indar and Kuldip are glad to welcome you today. I myself have not decided about working in Nairobi, although I'm sure a modern husband would not mind me having a job, but we will see.'

'Well, I hope things work out for you.' Sarah's head was spinning. 'I'm glad I had a chance to talk to you, but I think I'll go back inside now.'

In the sitting room Rabindrah was talking to his uncle and she headed straight for them, no longer caring whether she would be considered ill-mannered for breaking in on their conversation.

'I'm sorry to interrupt,' she said. 'But I'm afraid I have to leave now. I have an appointment this evening with someone from one of the wildlife organisations. So it's time to go.'

She saw Rabindrah frown for an instant before nodding, and placing his hand beneath her elbow.

'Come along, then,' he said. 'Let us say goodbye to my aunt, and I will drive you back to the Norfolk. I had forgotten all about your appointment.'

In the car she did not trust herself to speak, and he did not ask any questions. It was a few moments before she realised that they were not heading for the city centre.

'Where are we going?' Her voice sounded small.

'Up to Limuru, for a cup of tea at the hotel. It's beautiful in the garden, and we can look out over the tea plantations and be very peaceful. No one will interrupt us there.'

The air was considerably cooler when they walked across the lush grass and chose a table and chairs hidden behind a tumble of fuschias.

'What has upset you?' Rabindrah asked. When she did not answer he took her hand and kissed the inside of her wrist and her fingers. 'Did you not remember, among all those people, that I love you?'

'They'll never accept me.' She blurted out the words, snatching her hand from his to brush away the first tears. 'Your aunt made sure I met the girl she has chosen for you. And I got the message, loud and clear.'

He threw his head back and laughed out loud. 'She never gives up,' he said. 'But it is only a joke between us, and she knows that in her heart.'

'Don't bloody well laugh at me,' she said, standing up so suddenly that her chair fell over on to the lawn. 'You must have known it would be like this. That they had guessed there was more between us than our work. And you left me to fend for myself, while you played the charming nephew, the smart journalist, the returned conquering hero of your bloody clan. And now you're laughing at my humiliation, and calling it love. How dare you! How dare you treat me like that!'

'Sarah! I'm sorry. I'm really sorry. Please. I didn't realise—'

'No. You didn't,' she said. 'Because our cultures are too different. You brought me there and set me up as a target. You couldn't possibly have thought I would be accepted by your aunt and uncle. I'm not a traditional Sikh girlfriend from the Dark Ages. I'm a white Irish scientist and a bloody good photographer, with a life of my own and a career that I love and intend to pursue.'

She stopped and looked down at him, before continuing more calmly. 'It's no good. They're right. Your aunt, my mother, everyone around us. This could never work out. I've had enough pain and hardship in my life, and I can't cope with more.' She sat down again and stared out across the green of the tea plantations and the golden beauty of approaching evening. 'I want real peace,' she said at last. 'I can't deal with any more suspicion and unhappiness. I want a normal life now.'

They sat in silence as a waiter brought the tea, and then Rabindrah turned to her.

'Do you love me?' he asked. 'You've never actually said that you love me.' She bowed her head, unwilling to answer, but he was determined to force the words out of her. 'Do you love me, Sarah Mackay?' His voice was very low.

'Yes.'

'Then I will give you all the peace you need. I will create it for you and around you, and I will protect you and never leave your side when you need me. Ever again. I promise you this.'

She shook her head, not trusting herself to speak. The afternoon had grown chilly and the first tendrils of mist had begun to drift over the perfect ranks of the tea plantations. They finished their tea in silence and then Rabindrah stood up.

'I'll drive you back to the Norfolk,' he said.

'I don't want to go to the Norfolk.' Sarah was not ready to face any questions about her day. 'I can't take another set of questions, even from my best friends.'

'Would you stay with me?' Rabindrah took her hand.

'Stay with you? What do you mean? Where?'

'Would you stay here with me for the night? If they have a room.' His heart was beating fast and his mouth was dry. He was desperately afraid that he would lose her. 'We could talk quietly, have dinner together, time to ourselves. We've never had any real time to ourselves, and we need that.'

'But what would they say at the reception desk? I mean—' She was confused, frightened by the step she would be taking if they stayed here together.

'I know the owner, Mrs Lloyd, very well. Her husband is a journalist and we work together. And I've come up here regularly.'

'You've brought other girls here.' Sarah felt sick. 'Spent the night up here with other women.'

'No.' Rabindrah took her by the arm and shook her. 'No. I promise you I would never embarrass you in that way. I swear I've never done that. My God, Sarah, you can't believe I would put you in that position.' He was angry now.

There was a long, tense silence between them and then Sarah took a deep breath. 'You'd better see if they have a room,' she said. 'Although I don't know what I'll do for a toothbrush.'

'I have a small overnight bag I always keep in the boot of the car,' Rabindrah said. 'In case I'm suddenly sent off somewhere to cover a story. You can have my toothbrush. It's new and it's yours.'

Their room had a fireplace and chintz curtains and beams in the ceiling, and it looked out across the lawn and spread of the tea plantations on the steep hillside below the hotel. When the fire had been lit they sat down in two armchairs on either side of the fireplace. Sarah fixed her gaze on the orange and purple flames. She was already regretting her decision, wondering how she could explain her actions to Hannah and Camilla. It was Rabindrah who stood up first.

'Do you want to phone Hannah or Camilla? Tell them where you are?'

'No,' Sarah said. 'I'm my own keeper. I don't need to make excuses or explain anything to either of them.'

'I can see that you are uncomfortable,' Rabindrah said. 'But I didn't want you to go back to your friends and put today aside. Or put me aside. I am in love with you, Sarah. I can't lose you, and there is nothing I will not do to make you happy.'

He reached out his hand to her and she stood up and moved into his arms, caught in a tidal wave of conflict but unable to resist him. When he kissed her mouth with great tenderness she felt a surge of emotion and desire that led her like a sleepwalker to the bed. They lay down side by side, stroking one another, kissing, whispering endearments. After a while she began to describe her fears, as the memories of the day's events percolated in her mind and turned into words.

'I didn't know what to do with all the pain I carried around with me,' she said. 'When Piet was killed I wanted to die too, because my life was such agony. A continuous stream of nightmares whether I was awake or asleep. And then I found you and I was so frightened of that. Scared of leaving Piet behind. But there's a limit to how much anguish and pity you can take, and I know that he would want me to be happy again.'

'I will do my utmost to make you happy,' Rabindrah said. 'And our love will overcome everything that stands in our way.'

'But I don't want us to become a battleground between our families and our friends,' she said. 'I love my parents, and we are a close-knit family. They are trying to protect me from being hurt, from making a mistake or taking on something that seems like a great risk.' She left him for a moment, walked over to the chair where she had left her handbag, and pulled out her parents' letter. 'Read this,' she said. 'Because they feel the same way that your family does. And they are right about what lies ahead. I can see that now.'

Rabindrah read the pages without comment and then put them aside.

'I love you,' he said finally. 'Let me show you and tell you how much I have come to love you. This is something between the two of us, and only we can decide what we must do.'

She looked at him and was silenced by the message in his eyes. His hands unfastened her shirt and he kissed her breasts, making her gasp with pleasure. But when he began to unzip her skirt she drew back, her face troubled.

'Is this still about Piet?' he asked, rolling on to his back, looking away from her and up at the ceiling, trying to calm his desire.

'No. It's another stupid obstacle that is in our way. In my way. And I can't explain it logically, except to say that I was brought up as a Catholic, and—'

'And you don't want me to make love to you unless we are man and wife,' he said, smiling, touching her breasts, kissing her mouth again. 'That's not peculiar to Catholics, you know. Can you imagine what my parents would have said if one of my sisters had allowed their husbands to make love to them before they had been married in the temple? What I would have said, hypocrite that I am.'

She was forced to laugh as he drew her head on to his chest and lay quietly, holding her and making no further movement.

'Sarah?'

'Yes?'

'Will you marry me?'

'Marry you?'

'Will you marry me, for better or for worse, despite all our differences? Will you marry me, Sarah?'

'Yes,' she said. 'I will.'

Chapter 21

Nairobi, July 1967

'Where the hell did she get to?' Hannah's eyes were wide with alarm. 'What do you think we should do? Should we call the police, or the hospitals, or what?'

'I think that would be a mistake.' Lars stirred his coffee. 'If she had an accident, we would know.'

'She might be in a coma,' Hannah said.

'I'm sure she's somewhere with Rabindrah,' Camilla said. 'Otherwise he would be in his office. But they told me he hasn't come in this morning.'

'You mean she spent the night with him? Where? He has a room in his uncle's house, as far as I know.' Hannah was horrified. 'She'd never do that. Never.'

'They're madly in love,' Camilla said. 'We have to accept that. Only two days ago you agreed that she should have an affair with him. Abandon caution and religion and guilt, we said, and opt for passionate sex.'

Lars grunted, clearly disapproving. 'She could get hurt in all this,' he said. 'It's not an easy situation, and she's not the kind to have a fling.'

'Well, she knows we are going back to Langani this morning,' Hannah said angrily. 'We can't wait around for her all day. It's after eleven, and we told Ma we'd be back for lunch.'

'You go ahead, then,' Camilla said. 'I'll drive her up. It won't be until Wednesday, though, because I'm going with Daddy on the helicopter flight tomorrow. But I'll bring her back.'

'I'd be happier if I knew she was safe,' Hannah said. 'If I knew where she was.'

'Camilla has a good idea,' Lars said, rising to his feet. 'Come on, Han. Let's get started. And don't worry. I have a feeling that Sarah is not in any danger.'

'I'll see you in a couple of days.' Camilla hugged her friend. 'We'll get started on cutting the new patterns. In the meantime, I'm going to trawl the bazaar later today, and see if there are any new trimmings to be found. I can't wait to begin.'

She made her way back to the cottage and decided to spend the morning beside the swimming pool. The telephone rang as she was pulling a bikini out of her suitcase.

'I'm in the lobby,' Anthony said.

'I don't want to see you.'

'You could have a cup of coffee with me. In the Lord Delamere,' he said.

'I've had my coffee this morning. I don't need or want any more.'

'I'll come over to the cottage, then.'

'I'll meet you in the Lord Delamere,' she said quickly.

They sat without speaking. He lit her cigarette and ordered fresh lemonade for her and coffee for himself. The little pulse in the hollow of her throat was jumping as he said her name.

'Camilla.' He reached for her hand

She felt as though she was soaring. Excitement was making her skin exquisitely sensitive to the touch of his fingers. She felt light-headed and weightless. Her limbs seemed to be melting, and she was caught between fluttering anticipation and fear. She had made a mistake twice before and she must not make another one. In London her life would be under control, her career dazzlingly successful. And in spite of the fact that they had seen very little of each other, she was sure that Edward still loved and wanted her. Soon she would stop modelling, except for special assignments, and build on her first, modest success in the theatre and her reputation for good design. It would be insane to trade in her growing sense of security, to take another chance on Anthony. Except that she knew she loved him.

'Camilla.' Anthony leaned closer, his breath like a flame licking at her consciousness. 'Stay with me. We have to be together. Don't leave, Camilla. You'll be living the wrong life if you leave me.'

'We've been through all this before,' she said. 'Besides, I could see last night that you are more than fully occupied.'

'Don't be ridiculous,' he said. 'That girl is a travel agent. Our relationship is exclusively about safari bookings.'

He hesitated. Charlene was staying in his house at Karen. She had stayed on in Nairobi for an extra three days, to work out itineraries for a new brochure featuring Anthony's horse safaris, and a series of magazine advertisements for the programme. He was pleased with the deal they had made. It would boost the company income, and bring him into a lucrative market in the United States. But the Pan Afric Hotel could not extend her stay. There was an international conference in Nairobi, and they were full. On the spur of the moment, Anthony had told her she could use his guest room for the remainder of her stay. She was his best agent and it was easier than ringing around to find her another hotel. He thought about explaining this and immediately decided against it. The wretched girl had made it plain last night that she had a thing for him, and Camilla would certainly jump to the wrong conclusions if he said Charlene was staying in his house. In any case, she would be gone in two days, and there was no point in making an issue of the situation.

'We love each other,' he said. 'You know it, and so do I. Neither one of us will ever love anyone else like this. We are meant to be together. You can't deny it.'

She stood up, leaving her drink untouched. 'It hurts too much,' she said, aware that her resolve was draining away. She could feel the inescapable force of their need for each other, and she knew that it would be her undoing if she did not walk away now.

'You're afraid,' he said. 'I let you down before, but I'll never do that again. I love you, Camilla.'

She looked down at him, her eyes large with uncertainty.

'Camilla.' Another voice broke into her moment of indecision.

Sarah was standing a few feet away, her eyes shining soft and green, her mouth curved in a smile that was full of wonder.

'Where were you? We were a little worried last night,' Camilla said. 'Lars and Hannah left for Langani, but I can drive you up on Wednesday.'

'Rabindrah is going to take me up this afternoon,' Sarah said, as he appeared at her side and put his arm around her shoulders. 'We have something to tell you.' She glanced up at him and drew a breath. 'We're getting married.'

Camilla stared at her, speechless, her mind whirling. Her initial reaction was astonishment, but it was followed by a tingle of alarm. In her mind she could anticipate what Hannah would say, and the Mackay parents' dismay. A small worm of envy turned in the pit of her stomach as Anthony sprang up, holding out his hand to Rabindrah before sweeping Sarah into an enthusiastic embrace.

'Terrific news,' he said. 'What do you think, Camilla?'

'It's a complete surprise,' she said. 'Amazing. Congratulations to both of you.'

'I need to get my things from our room,' Sarah said, kissing Rabindrah lightly on the cheek. 'You stay with Anthony. I won't be long.'

'I'll come with you,' Camilla said, and they walked through the lobby and into the courtyard together.

'You're shocked,' Sarah said as they entered the cottage. Her heart was overflowing with happiness, but she was disappointed in Camilla's reaction.

'It's so fast,' Camilla said. 'It's wonderful that you've fallen in love again, and I'm so happy about that. I really am. But getting married is a huge step. Wouldn't it be wiser to give yourself a little more time? And I can't help thinking of Raphael and Betty, and Hannah too. They'll need time to adjust to this.'

'How about thinking of me?' Sarah's eyes were blazing. 'After everything we've been through, all the deaths and the sadness, why can't we all be grateful for love and happiness? Isn't that the most important thing? Why can't you be happy for me?'

'I am happy for you,' Camilla said, putting her arms around Sarah. 'But I'm a little scared too.'

'Because you don't have the guts to reach out and grab some unconditional happiness for yourself,' Sarah said, pushing her clothes into her canvas grip and tugging furiously at the zipper. 'So you're projecting your own doubts on to me, instead of seeing how lucky I am to have found Rabindrah. Instead of being glad for us.'

'That's not fair,' Camilla said. 'I only want you to be careful. To be sure. Not to be hurt.'

'He'll never hurt me,' Sarah said. 'Because I believe in him. We love each other and we're going to spend the rest of our lives together. I'm only sorry that you don't have enough faith in yourself or any other human being to make your life as rich as mine is going to be. But that's your loss, not mine.'

'Sarah—'

'I'll see you around,' Sarah said, picking up her bag and heading for the door. 'If you have the sense and the courage to stay on here, where you belong. You need to stop passing through other people's lives, Camilla. It's time you gave love a chance, and tried believing in something other than self-preservation.'

Camilla sat down on the edge of her bed, her hands gripping the frame, her shoulders shaking as she wept over her own stupidity. After a time she got to her feet and went into the bathroom to splash her face with cold water, and to repair her make-up. Putting a pair of sunglasses over her reddened eyes she went in search of Anthony, but he had gone. There was a message for her at the desk, but it was from her father. He was fully committed at the office, but wanted to know if she would like to move in with him while she was in Nairobi. If she telephoned, he would send Saidi to collect her.

'I'm checking out now,' she told the receptionist. 'You can send someone to collect my bag in about half an hour.'

In the cottage she rang George. 'I'd like to do the rounds of the market and the Indian bazaar before coming to you,' she said.

'Good. Saidi can take you wherever you'd like to go,' George said. 'And I'll see you at home, around five.'

She spent the afternoon browsing and buying beads, sequins and ribbon, and a selection of semi-precious stones and silver that she could use for her new creations. When she finally reached her father's house she was glad to be out of the swell and crush of people and afternoon heat of the city streets. When she had showered, she sat on the verandah with the newspaper, but she could not concentrate. She wondered what had happened to Sarah, and how Hannah would feel about the news of her engagement. Finally she lifted the telephone and rang Langani.

'She hasn't been here,' Hannah said. 'What time did she leave Nairobi? Why isn't she coming up with you? What is she using for transport?'

'Rabindrah is driving her up. Hannah, they're engaged. They're getting married.'

'Engaged?' Hannah's shock surged down the line. 'Oh, my God! I wasn't expecting that.'

'Listen, Han, I didn't handle the news well either,' Camilla said. 'She was upset with me when she left here. We have to be more tactful. Sensitive. Show that we're happy for her, above all else.'

'But are we?'

'They love each other,' Camilla said. 'She is certain that their love will carry them through, and I suppose he feels the same. I don't think we should try to erode that conviction.'

'Well, thanks for warning me,' Hannah said. 'When are you coming up?'

'I'm going on the rhino flight tomorrow, so I'll drive up on Wednesday. I'll phone you before I leave. And you'll be amazed by what I found in the bazaar this afternoon.'

Camilla hung up and stood staring at the telephone for a time. Then she picked up the receiver and dialled again. There was no reply from Anthony's cottage and she rang his office.

His voice on the line made her feel weak and she sat down on a stool.

'I came back to look for you this morning, but you were gone,' she said.

'I only have three days in Nairobi before my next safari.' Anthony's tone was guarded. 'One of my lorries is giving me trouble and I'm pushing to have the repairs finished today. And there's a pile of paperwork on my desk.'

'Yes,' she said. 'I know you must be busy. But I thought we could . . . well, spend some time together.'

He did not reply at once, and the silence lengthened on the line, making her anxious. She pulled at a choker of beads around her neck and the thread broke, spilling them all over the floor and rolling away under the furniture.

'Damn,' she said. 'The necklace I'm wearing has just fallen apart. Look, I'm staying with Daddy for the next couple of nights. So you know where to find me.'

'Yes,' he said, cursing the fact that he had not told her about his house guest, and the fact that he would have to spend the evening with Charlene. But she would be leaving in two days, and now there was something in Camilla's voice that sent a thrill of hope through his body. She had phoned him. She wanted to see him. He must be careful not to rush her now. 'I'll ring you tomorrow evening,' he said. 'See how the rhino rescue went. *Salaams* to George.'

She replaced the receiver and got down on her hands and knees to look for the beads. But her heart had plummeted and she sat back on folded legs, feeling wretched and close to tears. It was not the response she had expected. If only she had had the courage to tell him that she loved him, to make the leap of faith that would bring them back together. She was restless for the remainder of the evening, and after a quiet supper with George she went straight to bed, using their early departure as an excuse for not lingering. When she fell asleep she saw Anthony in her dreams.

Rabindrah had driven fast on the road north, aiming to be at Langani in the early afternoon so that they would have a shot at reaching Buffalo Springs before dark.

'Don't be upset,' he said to Sarah. 'They all have to get used to this. It will take a little time. You have been the cornerstone of your friendship with each other, and now you have done something out of character. Surprised everyone. They need time to adjust.'

'I don't see why they should need time to adjust,' Sarah said. 'Camilla doesn't usually display the kind of prejudice and fear that Hannah inherited from the Afrikaans side of the family. And if that was Camilla's reaction, can you imagine how it will be at Langani?'

'We'll weather it,' he said.

'No,' Sarah said. 'I don't see why we should even try. Look, we're coming into Nyeri now. Let's stop and visit Fr Bidoli at the mission. He came out of the hospital yesterday, because there are nurses at the mission so he's better off at Kagumo. We can say hello, and then go straight on to Buffalo Springs. I can collect my gear from Langani some other time.'

'I think you should see Hannah,' he said. 'Tell her the news. It's nothing to be frightened or ashamed of.'

'There you are!' she exclaimed. 'You're using the words "fright" and "shame" about the most beautiful things that will ever happen to us. It's not right, and we're not going to be pushed into that frame of mind by other people.'

'That may be the price you have to pay, for marrying a dark-skinned heathen,' he said, smiling at her. 'For taking on the handle of "Mrs Singh", isn't it?'

'We're stopping at Kagumo,' she said. 'And if it's too late to go on to Isiolo and Buffalo Springs, then we'll stay here, at the Outspan.'

'Oh my goodness gracious,' he intoned, in his exaggerated Hindi accent. 'You are leaving a trail of scandalous hotel bookings all over the country now, and you will soon have to admit to it, I'm telling you.'

'And I'm telling you that I have a reason for going to Kagumo right now. I have a plan that will make everything right,' she said, leaning towards him to kiss his cheek. 'Just turn off here and trust me.'

Fr Bidoli was installed in an airy room with a view of the vegetable garden framed by a line of flame trees whose blossoms flared scarlet in the afternoon sunlight. He was still weak and he spoke with an effort, but his smile was beatific as he nodded a welcome to Rabindrah and took Sarah's hands.

'You look happy, my children,' he said to her. 'What are you doing here, in Nyeri?'

'We've come to visit you,' she said, sitting down beside him. 'I was anxious to know for sure that you were making progress. And because there's something I want you to do for me.'

She pulled out her parents' letter from her pocket and handed him his glasses which were sitting on a prayer book beside him.

He looked at her through his faded, watery eyes and smiled again. Then he began to read, perusing the pages slowly without looking up or making any comment until he had finished.

'Rabindrah's family has the same fears and objections,' she said. 'And so do my closest friends. Just as you said. But yesterday he asked me to marry him, and I accepted.'

'You are strong young people,' he said. 'And if you love one another in the sight of God, then your lives together and your union will be blessed. I am sure of that, and you are obviously sure of it too. And in time your families and friends will see that you are right for one another, and there will be a marriage of mind and spirit in which you will all participate.'

'No,' Sarah said. 'We don't want to try and talk anybody into accepting our love for each other. Making them believe in us. And we can't go through a ceremony tainted by other people's suspicions and doubts. Our wedding day is for us. It will be the most memorable day of our lives, the day we start out together to build on our love and to make a family. There must not be any shadows falling on that day. And so . . .' she paused.

'And so?' Fr Bidoli had pressed his fingertips together in a steeple.

'And so we would like you to marry us,' Rabindrah said, his expression one of delighted surprise as he grasped Sarah's intention.

'My dear children, it would make me very happy to marry you. If you are sure that it is what you want.' He turned to Sarah, his expression grave. 'If you believe that this is the right thing.'

'It is the right thing,' she said. 'We are both sure of that.'

'In that case we will start today with the posting of the bans, and fulfilling the other regulations. And I will need to talk to this young man about allowing you to live within your faith, and to bring your children up as Catholics.'

'Then talk to him now,' Sarah said, leaning forward and taking the priest's hand.

Fr Bidoli turned to Rabindrah. 'I can see that you love each other. But before we talk about the sacrament of marriage, I must ask you to make a solemn promise.'

'Yes,' Rabindrah said. 'Sarah has told me that would be necessary.'

'Will you promise that you will allow her to practise her faith, and to bring up your children in that same faith, despite whatever pressures you may receive from your own people?'

'I promise that I will do whatever will make her happy, Fr Bidoli,' Rabindrah said. 'You have my word that I will never stand in the way of her faith, and that our children can be brought up in the beliefs of her Church.'

The priest gazed at the young man in silence for several minutes and Rabindrah looked back at him, composed and quiet.

'Let me be clear now what it is you are asking of me,' he said, his smile encompassing the two young people before him. 'Because the bishop is here, you know. In his office. What shall I tell him?'

'We would like to be married without delay,' Rabindrah said. 'Without families, without invitations, formal banquets and guests and gifts. Because we are the gifts we will give to one another, and that is all we need. So we would like you to marry us, Fr Bidoli, with only ourselves and the necessary witnesses.'

'Then I will do my best to arrange it. But it will take time to go through the processes of—'

'Fr Bidoli, there are ways of getting a special dispensation, especially in a small place like this,' Sarah said. 'You have brought me through anger and sadness, led me back into my faith. And you have worked with the bishop in Nyeri for more than twenty years. He trusts your judgement. So what we are asking is that you marry us quietly – in secret, if you like to put it that way. Tomorrow.'

Camilla and George left the house as the city woke to the pink light of dawn, and drove north to the rendezvous point where the helicopter was waiting. George introduced her to the pilot and to John King, the veterinary expert on immobilising game animals. To her surprise Johnson Kiberu was also at the rendezvous point. But he had chosen to ride in the lorry that would search for the rhino, once it had been darted and drugged. She did not enjoy the sawing, tilting motion of the chopper as they barely cleared the hump of hills, skimming the tops of trees as they reached the forest, ruffling the leaves and making the branches part and wave beneath them. They flew over the truck, parked on the edge of a clearing, waiting for their signal. George sat beside her, and in front of them the pilot bent forward, peering through the morning mist at the dense canopy of forest. John King held his dart gun lightly in his lap and leaned out of the door that had been left open, so that Camilla wanted to take hold of his bush jacket and pull him back. He cradled the rifle and gazed down, hoping that the sound of the helicopter would flush one of the great, armoured beasts out of the forest and into an open glade, where it would present a reasonable target. The clatter of the blades drummed in her brain.

She was beginning to wish that she had not come when the pilot gave a shout of excitement, and they dipped crazily downwards, hovering above the huge, prehistoric animal. It stood beneath them in a clearing, confused and angry, tossing its long, curved horn upwards towards the intruder. The helicopter slowed, and for a moment Camilla thought it had stalled as they lurched downwards, the skids almost touching the tops of the trees. She saw the small dart fly towards its target and admired the marksmanship as it hit the rhino in the chest. The animal hesitated, peered up at the sky and shook its heavy head, and then trotted away into the thick protection of the surrounding bush. To Camilla's surprise the vet hurled a roll of white lavatory paper out of the helicopter, and then made a thumbs-up sign.

'Acts as a marker for the trackers,' he shouted over his shoulder, grinning at her surprise. 'Now let's get down there, and join the troops on terra firma.'

When she stepped on to firm ground Camilla's knees were wobbly, and she was trembling. George took her hand to steady her and began to say something, but they were interrupted by the thrashing of the rhino as it staggered in their direction, thundering through the thick vegetation.

'It must be about five hundred yards away,' King said. 'Stay well behind me, and do as I say. I hope you can climb a tree.'

She waited, breathless with excitement, frightened by the snorting of the colossal animal as it approached, pursued by the Game Department truck. Then there was a crashing sound followed by a brief silence. Moments later Johnson Kiberu and two of the game rangers appeared on foot.

'It's down,' he said. 'It's a huge bull. It must weigh about two and a half thousand pounds, and the horn is more than two feet long.'

They pushed their way through the trees to the spot where the rhino was lying on its side, its small eyes closed. The park warden directed his staff as they jumped down from the lorry. The vet examined the animal, removed the dart and fastened a tag into its ear. A wooden ramp was hauled into place, and a block and tackle set up, enabling the platoon of men to winch the huge beast into the bed of the truck. It took more than an hour of heaving and shouting and grunting with exertion, before the rhino was safely on the vehicle. Then they set off again in the helicopter, to see their captive being transferred into a holding pen at the park headquarters.

'How long will it stay here?' Camilla asked, awed by the bulk and the strange vulnerability of the sleeping rhino.

'This one looks pretty strong and healthy,' George said. 'Unless there are complications, he should be safely on his way to Nairobi National Park in a week to ten days.'

'We could not manage without the funding from your father,' Kiberu said. 'And if we cannot continue to do this, I don't believe there will be any rhinos in Kenya for the next generation to see.'

'Why is that? Don't they breed well?'

'They're being killed off because of the press of people, and the need for more land on which to grow food,' George said.

'And poachers saw off the horns and sell them as dagger handles, or grind them into powder which is supposed to be an aphrodisiac,' Johnson said. 'I saw one of these poor creatures in Tsavo only last week. A rotting carcass, untouched except for its head with the severed horn. It was a nursing mother and we have no idea what happened to the calf. I cannot hope to pay my rangers more than the poachers offer them to turn a blind eye. Or even to lead them to the animals. And the areas are so large — Tsavo alone is eight thousand square miles. It is impossible to patrol such a vast area effectively. Too costly.'

'I can see why you're here,' Camilla said to George, when the rhino had been securely boarded into the pen. 'Much more satisfying to be in the thick of it, rather than writing the cheques and pushing paper around in London.'

'It's a privilege to be working with people like John King,' he said. 'He's an extraordinary man, and so are the remaining park wardens, like Bill Woodley whom you met today. But I fear they will soon be extinct, like the rhinos we're trying to save. It's good to have Johnson around. He's one of the few people genuinely interested in protecting this country's wildlife heritage, but he's up against a dreadful combination of inertia and greed and corruption. And plain ignorance.'

They were sitting in the shade beside the rhino pen, listening to the first sounds of its awakening, an irascible snorting and shuffling, and the push of the rhino's armour against the constraining walls. Camilla unpacked a picnic of hard-boiled eggs and sandwiches and cold beer that they had brought from Nairobi. She rose to her feet.

'I'm going to disappear into the bushes,' she said, smiling down at George. 'Don't try to steal any of my sandwiches while my back is turned. I'm starving after all that excitement.'

She was on her way back to the holding pen when she overheard the pilot laughing. He was sharing an anecdote with a young man from the Game Department in Nairobi.

'Bloody hell, I don't know how Chapman does it,' the pilot said with undisguised envy. 'This one's a famous model in London, you know. Her picture is in every magazine you open, but I hear she's crazy about him. I've seen him squiring all kinds of birds round town. One from every safari. He's even got some woman shacked up in his house right now. An American girl with the most spectacular tits, someone said yesterday in the Long Bar. Wish I knew his secret.'

Camilla froze, her stomach cramping with shock. For a moment she thought she was going to vomit. She wiped her hand across her face where beads of sweat had broken out. Then she took a slow breath, inhaling deeply, holding the air inside her to calm herself, counting as she let it go. She had heard gossip and comments like these before, most of them wishful thinking on the part of the hungry bachelors in town. All hunters and safari guides had to entertain their clients in Nairobi, and he had always said it was the part of his work that he liked the least. But he had not mentioned that the American girl was staying in his house, and she had to believe that it was not so. Camilla covered her face with both hands. It was surely true, what Sarah had said. She had to believe in him now. She took hold of her fear and pushed it down into the pit of her subconscious, and then returned to the shade of the tree beside the holding pen. But she could not eat.

It was just after four in the afternoon when they arrived back in Nairobi.

'I'm going to drop you at the house and go to the office for an hour or so,' George said. 'There are a few urgent things to sign. But I won't be too long, I hope.'

'That's fine,' she agreed, taking the keys from him. 'You can look forward to a home-cooked dinner later. Be it ever so humble.'

Back at George's house she showered and changed, making a determined effort not to think about Anthony. Anthony who had not phoned her, as he had promised on the previous evening. She went into the kitchen in search of ingredients for dinner. It was after six, but there was still no sign of her father. She sat down, composed herself, and dialled Anthony's home number.

'Hello there.' It was a woman's voice. An American with a Texan drawl.

'I'm wondering if Anthony Chapman eez zere,' Camilla put on a heavy French accent.

'He's out right now.' It was definitely Charlene. 'Can I take a message?'

'*Mais oui*, if eet ees not too much problem,' Camilla said. 'Will you be there when he comes back?'

'I surely will,' Charlene said. 'I'm staying here. He just called to say he'd be home for dinner real soon, so I'm busy fixing something for him. What message can I give him?'

'I'm a reporter from *Le Figaro* in Paris,' Camilla said. 'But I will contact him tomorrow. *Merci beaucoup*. Goodnight.' She hung up and poured herself half a tumbler of vodka over ice, dropped a quarter of lime into it and drank it quickly. Then she poured another.

'Are you feeling all right?' George asked Camilla over dinner.

'Yes. That was a wonderful day. But a little tiring.'

'I'm glad you enjoyed it,' he said. 'By the way, Saidi will take me into town in the morning, and you can use the car you left here earlier in the year.'

'Thanks. I might drive into the Nairobi Park and see if I can find some of your translocated rhinos.'

'I should think Anthony would take you, if you rang him. He was champing at the bit the other night, in the hopes of getting you to himself for a moment or three. You know, my dear, I think he is genuinely very . . . well, fond of you.'

'Bedtime,' she said, cutting him off. 'If I'm not up when you leave in the morning, I'll ring you at the office.'

She woke up feeling utterly wretched. The American girl's voice echoed in her head, and she wished that she had told George about the phone call. Since childhood she had always kept her insecurities to herself and tried to resolve her own problems or refused to confront them at all, and waited for them to disappear. Anything had seemed preferable to confiding in her mother, and George was rarely at home. Now she decided that she would try to have lunch with her father. She would open her heart to him, ask his advice. And talk to him more openly about his own life. She was pleased when his secretary could see no note of a midday appointment in his diary.

'Tell him I'll see him at one o'clock,' Camilla said, giving the name of an Indian restaurant that they had always liked.

She decided to leave the house at once and spend the morning in town, afraid that Anthony might telephone her and that she would make a fool of herself. He had deceived her again, and she realised that she could not deal with the experience by herself. If the American girl was strictly a business associate, why had he not told her that she was staying in his house? Camilla made a small sound of distress and opened the front door to be confronted by a young man. He was a Somali, with an exceptionally beautiful face and a tall, slender body, neat clothes, and delicate wrists decorated with bracelets made from copper and silver and beads.

'I am looking for Mister George,' he said. His expression was sullen.

'He isn't here,' Camilla said. 'Can I help you?'

'I want my money,' he said, his smile sly. 'He has not paid me.'

'Do you work in the house? Or the garden?' Camilla asked.

He shook his head at once. 'No work here,' he said.

'Tell me your name,' she said. 'And I'll let him know you were here.'

'Mister George knows my name.' The boy's expression was almost a sneer. 'I want only my money.'

There was something about him that made her feel uncomfortable, even threatened. She turned away from him, walked to the garage, and was about to open the door of the car when he spat. Straight down towards the floor tiles, hitting her right foot.

'Get out of here at once,' she said furiously. 'Or I'll call the police.'

'Mister George would not like that,' he said, openly insolent now. 'You tell him I come back tomorrow. I come only for my money tomorrow. Nothing else. He get nothing else.'

It was only when Camilla put the car key into the ignition that she allowed herself to recognise the full implication of the encounter. She opened the door of the car and rushed out of the garage, vomiting into the flower bed, sobbing uncontrollably. Then she returned to the house and packed her suitcase. She left her father a note, propping it up on the small table where the telephone squatted on a polished surface, next to a photograph of Marina and herself in a silver frame. His secretary had not yet seen him to pass on the details of their lunch date, and Camilla cancelled it. She rang for a taxi, and checked into a mediocre hotel where no one would think of looking for her. In her vanity case she found the tranquillisers she carried for use on long flights. After an hour, she was calm enough to contact the airline. There was a seat on the plane, and she reserved it and spelled out her name. Minutes later, the hotel operator connected her with London. When Edward answered the phone, relief flooded through her.

'I'm in Nairobi,' she said. 'But there won't be a trial, because Simon Githiri died and it's all over. I'm flying back to London tonight. Would you meet my flight tomorrow?'

'Are you coming back to stay?'

'Yes, Edward,' she said. 'I'm coming home. I'm coming home to stay. I'll hope to see you in the morning.'

There was a long pause before he spoke again. 'I'll come and meet you,' he said. 'On one condition.'

'What condition?'

'I want you to swear to me that you will never go back there, and you will never see or even speak to Anthony Chapman again.'

Tears were pouring down her face as she said the words.

'I promise.'

As night descended on the city, swallowing up the heat and swirl of colour and the noise and dust of the day, she made her way to the airport and checked in for the flight to London.

Epilogue

Nairobi, September 1970

She had never overcome her dread of hospitals. They reminded her of early childhood, when she had been taken by her father to visit Marina who always looked especially beautiful in the flower-filled rooms she had inhabited, lying back against large, white pillows, wan and delicate and frail. Her parents spoke in soft voices and never seemed angry on those occasions. But Camilla had always been afraid that her mother would never come home again, that she would die and then there would only be the big house, silent and waiting. The light tapping of Marina's high-heeled sandals, the breathless laugh and the scent of her perfume drifting in the air, these things would all be gone. Her father would be left behind, sitting alone with a distant look in his eyes, smiling a sad smile as the nanny took Camilla away, telling her not to bother her daddy, that he would come to see her at bedtime. She was almost a teenager when she finally understood that Marina would always come home. The antiseptic corridors, the squeak of the nurses' rubber shoes, the doctors who ruffled her hair and smiled down at her and told her she was a pretty child – these sights and sounds were familiar but temporary. A refuge for her mother, that usually followed a spell of muted sobbing behind closed bedroom doors.

Camilla had barely survived her own days in the clinic, following the operation that removed the scar on her forehead. Waking after the anaesthetic had brought a dry, suffocating feeling, but she had struggled not to fall asleep again, frightened of wandering through a dark world where she saw cruel faces, and the blade of the raised panga glinting in lamplight. Edward had sat beside her for several hours, and once she had opened her eyes to see that he had fallen asleep, a book in his lap, his reading glasses on the bedcover. She had been grateful for his constant presence, found it comforting. But she had left the hushed cocoon of the clinic earlier than he had recommended. She hated hospitals.

'Mr Chapman is in here.' The staff nurse broke into her memories, smiling brightly as they stopped in front of room 34.

Sarah and Hannah squeezed her hands and melted away to some bland waiting room. Camilla paused outside the door and opened her handbag, retrieving a lipstick that she applied indiscriminately. It was a way of delaying things, of searching for adequate words. Nothing came to mind. Her hand felt like a dead weight and she lifted it with effort, knocked gently and pushed open the heavy door.

He was lying on the white bed with his eyes closed. A cage-like structure was holding up the sheets so that he would not feel their weight on his body. They had told her that he was heavily sedated, that he needed to sleep through the early days of pain and shock. There was something almost church-like about the stillness of the room, and the banks of flowers in strangely assorted vases. A clutter of cards had been placed on the table beside him. She stood beside the bed, looking down at the motionless figure. His face was turned away from her and she was not sure whether she should touch him, but she put out her hand tentatively and laid it on his shoulder.

'Anthony.'

It had been a long time since Camilla had said his name. She had promised to forget him, had buried him in the deepest recesses of her mind, because she could not bear to shine the light of memory on his image. He did not appear to have heard her, and she pulled up a chair and sat down quietly, prepared to wait. There were tubes attached to him, and she could see the drip of some pain-relieving substance flowing into his body from a bottle hanging above the bed. He opened his eyes suddenly and looked at her. His face was startlingly tanned and healthy, hardly scarred. Only his eyes reflected the truth.

'I'm so sorry,' he said in a cracked whisper. 'I'm sorry.' Then his face tightened and he clamped his mouth shut, to prevent himself from making any sound that would betray pain.

She was frightened by the weakness of his voice, and the way that the silent room distorted the words he was trying to form. She leaned forward so that he would not have to make too much effort.

'I couldn't save him.' His lips moved with difficulty. 'There were flames everywhere. Fuel leaking on to the ground. People were yelling. Running in every direction and telling me to get away. That it would blow.' His mouth was dry, with a speck of something white at the corner. But his eyes were glittering as he struggled to explain.

'Hush,' she said. 'Don't try to say anything. I've just come to sit with you for a while. Hush now. We can talk later.'

She lifted a beaker of water and helped him to sip. There were dressings covering his neck and part of his chest and shoulders, and the only visible skin was blistered and marked by livid bruises. His arms were swathed in white bandages.

'We'll talk later,' she said again, putting her hand on to his forehead to soothe him. 'When you're stronger. I know how you tried.'

'He wasn't conscious. He couldn't feel anything.' He was determined to continue, in the same hoarse, despairing whisper. 'I tried to open the seat belt, but it wouldn't give. I had a knife and I cut it and pulled at him again, but he was very heavy. His legs were trapped in the twisted metal. I could smell the smoke and everyone was shouting, but I thought there was still time although it was so hot. The flames hit me when I reached across him, to get a better hold, to try and drag him out. But I couldn't move him.' Tears had formed in Anthony's eyes.

'I know. I know you did everything you could,' Camilla said. 'They told me he wasn't conscious, because of the impact, and the fire, and the glass and metal that cut through him everywhere.' She shuddered, trying not to picture it. 'There was nothing more you could have done. You would have been burnt. You would have died.'

'Part of me has died,' he said, shutting his eyes. 'I don't know the person who is left. I don't know who I am now, or what I can be.'

He had tried to save her father and failed. He did not know if she really understood and it was difficult to summon up the strength to explain. When the helicopter had spun out of control and hit the ground, he had run towards it and wrenched open the door, heaving and shouting and cursing as he tried to drag George from the front seat, beside the dead pilot. But George was strapped in, his head lolling forward on to his chest, his legs jammed under the weight of the damaged fuselage. The smell of the fuel and the thick smoke had made Anthony choke and had blurred his vision. He could hear sirens and people screaming at him, trying to pull him away from the aircraft. His clothes were torn and charred and bloody.

The fire leapt closer, turned into a wall of flame. He heard the explosion and made a dive to safety. There was a grinding, screeching sound of torn metal as part of the tail structure buckled and fell on to his legs, pinning him down so that he was unable to move. Sickening pain flashed through his entire body. He saw that his right leg had become a scarlet river of blood, pumping steadily through his trousers, making a puddle around him on the ground. After that he did not remember anything at all.

'I'm so sorry,' he repeated. His eyes were closed with exhaustion. When she did not answer he thought she was not there. Perhaps he had imagined her, along with the many visions that came and went in the haze of his mind. He licked his lips and spoke again, although his mouth was dry and he was desperately tired. 'Camilla? Camilla, are you here?'

'I'm here,' she whispered.

She laid her head down on his pillow and he lifted a clumsy, bandaged arm and put it around her as they wept together. After a time he fell asleep. Her body was twisted and cramped where she lay, but she did not move for fear of disturbing him. She had no idea how long she had been there when the nurse came into the room, her bright, professional smile in place.

'He won't wake up again for a while. You can stay with him, if you like, but I think he'll be asleep for a couple of hours at least.'

Camilla disengaged herself carefully so as not to wake him, and stood up, pushing her hair back from her face.

'I'll come back later,' she said. 'I'm at the Norfolk. Cottage number two. I'd like you to phone if he needs anything. Or if he wakes up and asks for me.'

'I'll do that.' The nurse was gentle as she lifted Anthony's hands and put them back under the covers. 'You can phone the floor whenever you like,' she said. 'I'll be on duty for another six hours. My name's Mary Thorpe.'

'Thank you,' Camilla said wearily. 'Thank you so much.'

'Your friends are outside,' the nurse said. 'They're bringing the car round the back. I'm afraid there are newspaper people downstairs at the main entrance, and I imagine you'll want to avoid them.'

She found Sarah and Hannah in a waiting room. Not trusting herself to speak, she stood in the doorway, her face taut. They embraced soundlessly, and she sat down for a moment and tried to repair her face, which was swollen with the tears she had shed and now wanted to suppress.

'The surgeon said he's very strong, both physically and mentally,' Sarah said. 'He can get through this. Come out of it and be even stronger. He just needs help.'

'Is there anyone . . . ?' Camilla did not want to complete the question.

Sarah shook her head. 'His mother's flying out in the next couple of days. I've never met her. She left here years ago, when his father was killed on a hunting safari, and she never wanted to come back. They haven't seen much of each other in the last few years, but she might be a help. There's no one else. What do you want to do now? We can stay here, or take you back to the hotel for a while.'

'He's sleeping. The nurse on duty will phone me if he wakes, or if he asks for anything. Asks for me,' Camilla said. 'In the meantime, I have to get through the awful paperwork and the formalities, whatever they are. I think it's best to deal with that while I can, and come back here later.' Her next words were hesitant, almost a plea. 'Do you think we can spend this evening together? Just the three of us? I know that might be unpopular and awfully selfish, but—'

'That's how we've planned it,' Hannah said. 'Lars isn't bringing the children down until the morning.'

'And Rabindrah is in Uganda,' Sarah said. 'He's covering a wildlife conference up there but he'll fly back early tomorrow, so he can be here for the funeral.'

'You should have been at the conference too,' Camilla said. 'Thanks, Sarah. For staying here instead.'

'I was only giving a brief talk,' Sarah said. 'What about Edward?'

'He's having dinner with a doctor he knows here. Someone who wants to talk to him about children with facial deformities,' Camilla said. 'He understood that we would want some time to ourselves.'

They left by the service entrance at the back of the hospital, successfully avoiding the two reporters in the main lobby, and drove through the broad avenues of bougainvillea and hibiscus and jacaradah trees, into the centre of the city. Camilla was tired and edgy when she arrived back at the cottage.

'I think an hour's rest might help,' Edward said. 'You look drained. If you want to keep going you should take advantage of this quiet moment.'

But she knew that she would not be able to relax, with all of tomorrow's arrangements hanging over her. There were papers to be signed and telephone calls to be made. A representative from the British High Commission arrived to offer assistance and official condolences. The undertaker came and went, discreet and obsequious. She refused to take any incoming calls, and decided on room service for a late lunch. Edward brought her tea, poured drinks, helped her to fill in forms. Initially he did not ask any direct questions about Anthony, but she could see apprehension in his eyes.

'Will he be all right?' he said finally.

'All right? What's all right?' she asked, her sorrow welling up again. 'He's thirty-two years old and he lives most of his life out in the bush, looking for animals, putting up tents and walking and climbing, driving trucks and safari cars and riding horses. And now half of his body is burnt, and he's lost a leg, and I don't know what other injuries he has. But if you discount all that, then he's doing really well.'

She put her head down on her arms and gave way to anguished sobbing, her tears making blots on the forms she had filled out so neatly. He was trying to help her, but there was no consolation possible in the dark whirling of her brain.

'I'm sorry,' she said. 'It was a terrible thing to see, and I don't know if the real significance of it has got to him yet.'

Edward did not try to reassure her, or to tell her that Anthony would survive. There were many definitions of survival, not all of them easy or welcome. He had not wanted her to go to the hospital today, and he was not yet sure what effect it might have on her. When she had learned the extent of Anthony's injuries her face had turned chalk-white and she had begun to shake, and to wail and wring her hands, and he thought that her accustomed and steely self-control had given way. She was already wrestling with the impact of her father's death, searching for a resolution that would allow her to live in peace with his memory. Now she had to consider the horror and despair that amputation and scarring would leave on the man she had once loved. Perhaps she still loved him. Edward's mind closed off the issue, his training allowing him to put it aside until the right moment came to deal with it.

'I've arranged a car and driver for this afternoon,' he said, watching her with grave concern. 'For the appointment with the undertaker, and so on.'

'I can't do that,' she cried out in protest. 'I don't want to see him, all patched up and sewn together as a corpse. I have to remember him as he was.'

'I understand that,' he said, sitting down beside her, taking her hand. 'I'll go there myself. There's no necessity for you to be there in person. All you have to do is sign the rest of these papers, and I'll finalise anything that's outstanding.'

In the end she went with him, and was grateful for his steadying presence as she looked down into the coffin at the man who had been her father. His silver hair was combed the way he had always worn it, and the cuts on his face had been cleverly concealed. He lay between padded, silk walls in an oak box, with his eyes closed and his hands folded across his chest. Someone had collected one of his linen suits and a pale blue shirt, with a tie that Marina had bought for him in Rome. Camilla wondered who had chosen the clothes and when. It was clear that his face had been made up, so that there was a faintly polished, waxen look about it. When she gazed down at him she felt a lead weight where her heart should have been. She had judged and abandoned him, shut away the image of him with her ugly recollections of his secret life. This man had given her life, and she had not recognised that his unconditional love for her was the only important part of their affiliation. Over the past three years she had avoided seeing him alone. During his infrequent visits to London she had not asked, or wanted to know, about his life in Nairobi or whether he was happy. In turn, he had never referred to the incident that had driven her away from him, and she had seen less and less of him. And now it was too late.

'Everything I've done has been wrong,' she said to Edward, as she bathed and dressed for the evening. 'My view of things, my conclusions – they've been so wrong.'

'That's not true at all. Look at your career. There isn't a better-known face in Europe or America, even though you don't do many photo shoots any more. Your design label has been hugely successful, and the clothes and other things just get better and better. Your stage appearances have been well thought of, and now there's the possibility of a film role. You've achieved everything you hoped for. You're an icon, Camilla, a fantastic example of determination and success.'

'No, I'm not,' she said, her voice as sad as the darkness swiftly descending outside. 'I've drifted into everything I've done. I've been lucky. I never had to make my own way, and I never fought for anything or anyone I really cared about. This is the only place I truly love, and I turned my back on it. Without thinking about my father or my dearest friends.'

'You've seen Sarah in London several times,' he said, talking patiently as if she was a child. 'And Hannah has done very well with the workshop you set up together.'

'I never had the guts to stay on,' she said. 'To see things through, like them.'

'You left here in a terrible state of shock,' he reminded her.

'I shouldn't have run away. I was never brave enough to try and understand who he was.' She did not notice Edward's increasing disquiet. 'You know, I've been afraid ever since I was small. Frightened of what was happening between my parents, scared of any kind of rejection or refusal, or anything that involved a major confrontation. I'm a coward. Every decision I've made has been about my own security, about being safe, about protecting myself. I don't want to be that way any more. I don't think I should live the rest of my life like that.'

'Camilla, I was the one who insisted that you should not come back here,' he said. 'I made you swear to me that you would never see Anthony again, never return to Kenya, because I didn't want him to hurt you any more. And I believe I was right. You couldn't have been safe or happy here. When these sad days have passed, darling, and we're back at home, you'll see that the life we've made together is the best place to be.'

'I didn't realise how much I missed my friends.'

'You have so many close friends in London.'

'No. Not like Sarah and Hannah. Not friendships like that. They're my only family, my sisters. And I've been lonely in London. So often.'

'Everyone has periods of loneliness, darling. If it's any consolation, I'm going to try harder not to let that happen again. George's sudden death has been a lesson for me. It's brought home to me that one never knows how much time there is left.' He took her hand and pressed his lips against her fingers. 'I do love you, Camilla, and our life together is mostly good. I promise you that I'll devote more of it to being with you, from this day on.'

'I know you mean that,' she said. 'But your work will always come first, and I truly admire that. You need the time you dedicate to all those ruined people whose lives, and faces and arms or legs, you've put back together.

But I don't know what I'm doing any more, or where I'm going. I only know that my life feels hollow and empty.'

'You're dreadfully upset by George's death, and the thought of the problems Anthony will face. It's turned everything upside down, made you anxious and unsure. But we'll help him in every possible way. I can arrange for the best medical specialists to see him, and for follow-up treatment overseas if he needs or wants it. When we go home in a day or two, we'll know that we've done everything possible.'

'You can't tick off the things he will need to live his life, like you might cross things off a shopping list,' she said, aggrieved by his pragmatic statement. 'I don't know what to do. I've never felt so hopeless in my life. So utterly useless.'

'It's the shock. Not just one terrible thing, but two. No one could absorb all this tragedy without the kind of reaction you're having now. But tonight you'll be able to talk about it with Sarah and Hannah, and that will help.' He touched her cheek. 'I'm going to join Dr Channing now. They telephoned from reception while you were dressing. He's waiting for me in the bar. You look lovely, darling, in spite of all this. I'm always so proud of you, and you know I'll give you every support.' His kissed her lightly on the forehead and left the cottage.

Camilla sat at the dressing table, looking into the mirror, mulling over his words and his promise to try and spend more time with her. She had tried to get used to his long hours, to fill in the solitary evenings when he was called out for emergency surgery, or when he was sitting with someone who was in a critical condition, almost willing life and hope into their broken bodies. There were times when she had asked him why he could not scale down his practice, see fewer patients, take more time for himself. Spend more time with her. It certainly wasn't a question of money. He often took on cases from one of the big public hospitals and did not charge a fee at all. But he was motivated by an all-consuming desire to be the best, and he had become a legend in his field.

At first his absences did not bother her. She had her own life, and a variety of places where she would go if she wanted company or entertainment. But after she had moved into his flat, she did not feel she could make the rounds of nightclubs and parties alone, and so she stayed at home, waiting. And waiting. And knowing that the people she cared about most were thousands of miles away, lost to her through time and distance and her own inertia and lack of honesty. She had never summoned the courage to tell them why she had left so suddenly, and never returned. Her sense of loneliness became more acute as time passed, and her memories of Kenya made her sad.

When Sarah and Rabindrah had come to stay in London she had thrown herself into their days together with near-manic delight, and sunk into a profound and silent depression after their departure. For more than a year she had hoped that Hannah and Lars would visit her too, and she had made plans in her head to take them everywhere, and introduce her friend to the boutique owners who sold the clothes made at Langani. But Hannah had not been able to make the journey. Her pregnancy and the birth of her son, the demands of the workshop, the decision to rebuild the lodge in partnership with Anthony, the pressures of running the farm in an increasingly hostile and corrupt political situation combined to prevent her travelling. Lars had flown to Norway to visit his parents, but Hannah had not accompanied him even then. She could not understand why Camilla did not come to Kenya. A distance unrelated to geography had gradually lengthened between them, and during the past year there had been no letters or phone calls at all.

'She's upset that your accountant forwards impersonal cheques and company statements, and there's never even a note from you,' Sarah had said. 'Not even when you send new designs, or cutting and beading instructions for the season.'

'I had to return a few of the handbags and belts,' Camilla had said. 'They weren't properly finished. Hannah feels that I should fly out and show the women how to do the new styles, but I haven't been able to go. And that has created a rift between us.'

'So why don't you come out for a week or two?' Sarah had asked.

'I'm too busy here.' Camilla's voice had been curt, cutting off any possibility of further discussion.

She had seen Sarah sigh with frustration, but she still could not bring herself to reveal the reasons for her abrupt departure from Nairobi. Anthony's deceit, and the horror she had felt at the boy prostitute outside her father's residence, were too much to drag out of the dark pit of memory to which she had consigned them. She had put it all behind her, closed it away, when she had made her promise to Edward, and she could not bear the thought of bringing any of it out into the light. But she was not overstretched in terms of her work. She had given up all but the most prestigious modelling assignments, and was concentrating on designing clothes and accessories that were now being made in India and Hong Kong and the Philippines. And she had played to good reviews in two West End productions, although her stage appearances had not given her the satisfaction she had expected. But they filled the time that she might otherwise have spent alone, the hours when she might have been tempted to look inside herself and reassess her choices.

All in all, she had nothing to complain about. She could accept that Edward would never change. His addiction to work was as vital to him as breathing. Sometimes he stepped into the noise and colour of the world outside, but they were brief sorties, exhilarating for a short time only. Then he would return to his medical journals and research notes and his patients, and they were back where they started. Still, he loved her. He was right in his assumption that she felt secure in his care, despite her occasional feeling of isolation. And he had not, even for a moment, thought of holding her to her promise when the dreadful news of the crash had come. Camilla looked at her reflection in the mirror and lifted her shoulders in a gesture of helplessness and resignation. It was impossible to have everything.

As soon as Edward had gone to meet his medical colleague, she telephoned the hospital for the fourth time. Mr Chapman was asleep. He had spent a reasonably comfortable afternoon. No, he had not asked for her. He had not asked for anything.

'I'll be there tomorrow,' she said. 'After the funeral. Perhaps you could leave him a little note with that information. For when he wakes up the next time.'

Hannah and Sarah were waiting for her in the hotel lobby.

'We're going to have dinner at Anthony's cottage,' Sarah said. 'No, don't object. It's quiet, and we can sit and talk for as long as we like. Hannah and I are actually staying there tonight.'

Camilla was silent and tense in the car, looking out of the window as the bright lights of downtown gave way to areas where large gardens and clipped hedges lined the sides of the road, and the glow of lamplight and log fires could be seen behind drawn curtains. She pressed her lips together, swallowing regret. At the house she walked up the steps and into the sitting room where Joshua was waiting to greet her. A wide, toothy smile lit his face as he greeted her, proudly pointing out his handiwork. Her heart turned over as she looked around the familiar room. He had lit the candles on the mantelpiece and the sideboard, plumped the cushions, set the table with the glass and silver she had chosen and folded the dinner napkins into flower shapes, just as she had taught him. There was an enormous lump lodged in her throat when she tried to thank him, to show her appreciation. He disappeared into the kitchen to prepare the dinner, and they sat down in front of the fire and smiled at one another, a little awkward now that they were alone together after so long.

'I wish something else had brought you back.' Hannah broke the stiff silence. 'I wish you'd come when Piet was born. I wanted you to be here for the christening.'

'I couldn't do it,' Camilla said, her eyes downcast.

'I can't imagine how it feels to be so famous,' Hannah said. 'Sarah has had a taste of it too, with her books and lectures. I'm the only one who has stayed the way I always was – a *yaapie* farm girl whose idea of city lights is downtown Nairobi. It must be hard, though, to have every hour accounted for, not to have the freedom to go where you want, and to have reporters following your every move —'

'Listen,' Camilla interrupted. 'Because I want everything to be clear between the three of us. I couldn't come back. I made a promise.'

'What promise?' Sarah was frowning.

'When I left Kenya the last time, Edward made me swear that I would never return here.' Camilla looked down, ashamed that she had not told them before. 'He couldn't live with the possibility that Anthony might suddenly reappear, turn my life upside down like before. Turn his life upside down. And then vanish.'

'But why did you leave without telling us?' Hannah's tone was brusque. 'I know Sarah has asked you the same thing, but you've never given her a straight answer. If you want everything to be clear between us, then I think it's time you explained. Because one moment you were going to stay, you wanted to help me with the workshop, you were coming back to Langani to cut new patterns and make samples, and you were still in love with Anthony – we could all see that – and the next, you'd left. Not a note, not a word of explanation. Nothing.'

Camilla was silent, looking for the words and the bravery to deliver them.

'He told me he'd asked you to stay,' Hannah said. 'We had a long discussion about it, when he came for the opening of the lodge. He said the same thing to Sarah.'

'I had decided to stay,' Camilla said, holding her glass tightly, turning it round in her hands. Remembering was an ordeal. 'I hoped he'd ask me to marry him again, especially when Sarah and Rabindrah said they were going to get married. But then I heard that the American girl was staying with him. The Texan we all met. And he hadn't said a word about her being at his house.' She laughed and the sound was harsh. 'The guest he had stashed away and somehow forgotten to mention.'

'He had that girl here in the house? Are you sure?' Hannah was incredulous.

'Yes. I'm quite sure, because I phoned and she answered. I said I was a French journalist and she said she was staying with him. Making dinner for the two of them, in fact.'

'But why on earth didn't you ask Anthony about this?' Hannah was incredulous. 'I can't believe there was anything going on between them. He only had eyes for you, that night at the Grill. I'd have asked him outright. That's what she should have done, isn't it, Sarah?'

'I'd been burnt before, remember?' Camilla felt resentment at their lack of understanding. 'We had different ideas on loyalty. On fidelity. I thought there was no point in going on because he would never change. So I left. And then I promised Edward that I would never, ever come back.'

'I agree with Hannah. You should have asked Anthony for an explanation,' Sarah said.

'And what about all the promises you made to me?' Hannah asked. 'You said you were coming back to Langani, and then you just vanished without saying a word because a girl answered Anthony's phone. The next time I heard from you it was a note attached to a set of instructions and cutting patterns and colour schemes. And not a line about why you'd run off, without even a telephone call to say goodbye.'

'It wasn't only Anthony.' Camilla's voice was barely above a whisper.

'This had better be a good explanation,' Hannah said. She was about to make a further comment but Sarah gave her a warning glance.

'It was George.' Camilla knew that she had to tell the whole truth now. 'I came out of his house the next morning. There was a Somali boy there. He couldn't have been more than fourteen or fifteen and he was hanging around, outside the door. A prostitute, waiting to be paid. Standing there in front of me, demanding money from my father.'

Hannah stared into the fire, white-faced and speechless.

'Oh God.' Sarah put her face in her hands. 'I never guessed he was referring to some specific thing that had happened.'

'What do you mean?' Hannah demanded.

'George came up to join Rabindrah and me, when we were working around Wajir,' Sarah said. 'He wanted to see the wells up there, and the way the Somalis and their camels shared the water with the giraffes and the local wildlife. We'd been out in the bush all day, and Rabindrah turned in early after dinner. George and I sat up talking. He got very drunk. I'd never seen him like that. He said he wanted to mend things with you, Camilla. That he had disappointed you, hurt you badly. That he was the reason you left.' She took Camilla's hand. 'He was weeping, sobbing like a child, telling me he couldn't change what he was, but it didn't alter the way he loved you.'

'You wrote and told me that,' Camilla said. 'But you couldn't have known what he was really talking about, and I couldn't bring myself to tell you. I've never told anyone. We all knew he was homosexual. But when I came face to face with that boy, little more than a child, I couldn't deal with it. It made me ill, every time I thought about it. I never really talked to my father again.'

'You shouldn't have carried that all by yourself,' Hannah said.

'I couldn't bring myself to say the words,' Camilla said. 'And now he's dead. Gone for ever. When I saw him in the coffin this afternoon, I realised that I've never tried to understand the people I really love. I've been afraid to see the flaws in them, and I've tried to hide my own shortcomings by keeping everyone at a distance. Or running away. I'm a coward. And for Daddy and me it's too late.' She stood up and gave a high-pitched giggle bordering on hysteria. 'So here I am, a sad little orphan. I have no family left. Except you.'

'You'll always have us,' Sarah said, taking her by the hand again and drawing her back down to the sofa. 'But there's no reason why you shouldn't create a family of your own. Are you going to marry Edward? Have children one day?'

'He doesn't want children,' Camilla said, her tone defensive. 'And I'm not sure I'd make a good mother, in any case. So marrying Edward isn't really an issue.' She turned to Hannah. 'I'm looking forward to seeing the children. I've brought clothes that I had made for my one and only godchild. I don't even have to ask if you and Lars are happy. I can see it all over your face, and in your eyes.'

'You can see it in the fact that I'm becoming more and more like one of my cows,' Hannah said, laughing. 'Ja, I have a good man and I love him like crazy. Little Piet is the image of him.' She swallowed some of her wine and looked up, with a sly smile. 'And Suniva still looks exactly like me. Luckily.' They were all laughing. 'And then there's James.' Her voice changed. 'I never thought I could come to love that little boy. It seemed impossible. I took him because I felt my family was responsible for what had happened to him, and he should not be abandoned like his father. But before you canonise me, I have to say that I also felt scared. I thought if he was left in the mission, or with strangers, then one day the whole cycle of hatred and revenge might start again. So it wasn't pure love that brought him to Langani. In fact, I was afraid that, deep down, I would hate him because of the past.'

'You did an extraordinary thing,' Camilla said.

'He was a brave little boy,' Hannah said. 'After the operation, he was so determined to get up on his feet and walk. Run, actually. He never complained about anything, and he would look at me with those big, trusting eyes, and smile. In the end, he completely won my heart. And he's so bright and ready to learn. He and Suniva are inseparable.'

'He's a great child,' Sarah said.

'You know, I see pictures of you and Sarah in magazines, and I read about your acting and designs and her books and lecture tours all over the world,' Hannah said. 'And sometimes I feel envious, it's true. But then I look at our farm and the lodge and my wonderful family, and I know how lucky I am.'

Sarah got up and went to the sideboard where the wine stood in an ice bucket. She poured each of them a glass, taking her time, thinking about Camilla and her aptitude for backing away from the feelings she aroused, unable to stretch out her hand and connect, always fearful of being hurt or betrayed.

'How is Lottie?' Camilla turned to Hannah.

'She's in Italy. They work hard, Ma and Mario, but his hotel is only open for six months of the year, and in the winter they travel. Last year they went to America. New York and Chicago and San Francisco and God knows where else. She was here in February, because she loves spending time with the children.'

'What's Mario like? Is she going to marry him?' Camilla asked.

'He's twenty-five. Looks like Mario Lanza,' Sarah said, her face grim.

Camilla stared at her, shocked, until Hannah began to laugh and then they were holding one another up, tears of laughter streaming down their faces, washing away distance and separation and sadness and bringing them back to the years of their childhood, to the day that they had become blood sisters and promised to remain true to their friendship.

'It's hard to believe we were once three girls at a convent boarding school who thought we'd never be parted,' Camilla said at last.

'We haven't parted,' Sarah said. 'We're sitting here together, talking about our lives just like we used to years ago. Our bond has been stretched to the limit, but it has never been broken. I think we can still say that our friendship is the best there is.'

'What about Rabindrah? And the two families?'

'It's been a bumpy ride, but they've come around. For the most part,' Sarah said. 'Mum and Dad are still upset that they weren't at our wedding. That they weren't even told.'

'Betty longed for a traditional ceremony with a long white dress and a reception on the lawn in Sligo,' Camilla said.

'She was hoping we wouldn't marry at all,' Sarah said. 'Especially after the shambles over Tim's aborted wedding. She wrote me a terrible letter after we were married. A real stinker. I suppose I deserved it. She was so hurt. And Dad was too, although he didn't say too much about it.'

'I admit I wasn't much help to you at the time,' Hannah said. 'Looking back on it, I know I was stupid and selfish. It's no wonder you didn't tell me beforehand.'

'You were less than enthusiastic, that's for sure,' Sarah said. 'And Camilla had completely disappeared. So we made our wedding an intensely private thing of our own.'

'When you turned up at Langani and announced that you had been married the day before, I was livid,' Hannah said. 'But I deserved to be left out. I should have been with you all the way.'

'We didn't want to spend our wedding day mired in other people's bad feelings, or being the subject of doubt and disapproval,' Sarah said. 'In the end, it was about Rabindrah and me, and making it the happiest, most important day of our lives. For just the two of us.'

'What's the family situation now?' Camilla was glad to be discussing someone else's life.

'In a way, I think the Singhs have accepted it better than my parents,' Sarah said. 'It helped that we didn't start off living on top of them, like most young married couples in their community. We spent our first year in the back of beyond, with no one looking over our shoulders. I'm not sure I would have done too well with an Indian matriarch clucking disapprovingly at my housekeeping methods, and trying to slot me into her way of things.'

'Betty has come round a little, though,' Camilla said.

'Mum and Dad still don't know Rabindrah very well,' Sarah said. 'We spent ten days in Sligo a few months after we got married. It was lovely, and Tim made a huge effort to smooth over the rough spots. But there wasn't enough time for them to make any real connection, and Rabindrah was surprisingly nervous. I'd never seen him like that, and it made me love him much more.'

'So, where are the babies?' Camilla asked. 'Are you deliberately holding off? Worrying about weaning them on to camel milk and goat stew?'

'It's not for lack of trying.' Sarah's smile held a twist of sadness. 'Every month I keep hoping, and then there's this terrible let-down when I realise it hasn't happened. And of course, Rabindrah's family shake their heads about it and look at us reproachfully, because I haven't produced the son and heir, or even a daughter. I'm sure they feel he'd have been better off with a good Sikh girl who stayed at home and concentrated only on making babies for him.'

'You do spend quite a bit of time apart, though,' Hannah said. 'I don't think I could do that. I hate being away from Lars for more than a few days, but sometimes Rabindrah can be gone for months. Or you go off for weeks on one of your lecture tours. How can you bear it?'

'We juggle the workload as best we can. Our first year was wonderful. We hardly saw anyone from either his background or mine. We had our Land Rover and our little tent, and we wandered around the country between Garissa and Wajir, and travelled on the Tana River with a canoe. Then we moved west, following the nomads and their livestock. Boran and Rendille herders, and Gabbra too. We walked across the Chalbi Desert, and we lived and fished with the El Molo at Lake Rudolph. We rode camels and climbed the mountain in Marsabit and camped on the edge of the crater above Paradise Lake. It was like a year-long honeymoon, and I never wanted it to end.'

Sarah's eyes took on a faraway look as she thought back to the perfect days and nights when she and Rabindrah had lived in a world that seemed entirely their own. There had been time to talk about their lives and their work, to get to know each other, to plan their future and to wonder at the miracle of their marriage. She thought of the days when they had swum in the Jade Sea, splashing each other like children, and the desert nights when they had made love under the eye of a stalking moon, glowing with the joy of being alive and together. Their tent had blown away in a storm, and they had fled from cattle raiders. Rabindrah had been bitten by a scorpion and Sarah had fallen into the Tana River within a few yards of a basking crocodile. They had learned from the tribesmen how to fish and hunt and light a fire from two sticks, how to smell an oncoming rainstorm, and where to seek shade and hide from the devouring heat of noon. The book describing their travels had been an instant success.

'Coming back to Nairobi was terrible,' Sarah said. 'Living in a rented flat and working on top of each other, with Rabindrah's manuscript and my photos spread out everywhere. Members of his family were always dropping in, trying to persuade us to come and live with Indar Uncle so that Kuldip could teach me how to run my household. I tried to adjust, to be polite, but they were invasive and they were always making pointed remarks about my getting pregnant. I thought Rabindrah didn't do enough to discourage them, because he started travelling, working on other stories, and left me to deal with the relatives. So there were a few months when things weren't quite so good.'

'Divorce is a word that comes to mind,' Camilla said smiling. 'Lucky for Rabindrah that he married a fervent Catholic.'

'And then Fr Bidoli finally died from his cancer, so I felt completely isolated,' Sarah said. 'It was Dan and Allie who rescued us. Gave us the use of my old hut, because they've built another one in the compound for their two new researchers. We'd go there for a few days whenever Rabindrah came back from a trip, or after I'd finished one of those awful tours. We still do. It's a busy life. And rich.' She stopped, and looked into the distance.

'But?' Camilla prompted her gently.

'I'd so love to have a baby. More than anything else. Seeing yours, Hannah, makes me really broody.' Her laugh did not sound quite genuine. 'Anyway, we have a fantastic marriage, even if it's not what either of our families would have chosen for us.'

'You must have to juggle your work and your private life too,' Hannah said, looking at Camilla with curiosity. 'Don't you find it hard, with all your public appearances, to sit down and remember that love is the most important thing?'

Camilla's eyes were sad. 'I'm the last one to talk about love, or what you should or shouldn't do about it.'

'It's different for everyone.' Sarah was still on the same track. 'Maybe I'll suddenly get pregnant when I'm not even thinking about it. Just like the way I suddenly felt right about Rabindrah. In the beginning, when I was first attracted to him, I couldn't see past losing Piet. I felt so guilty about the possibility of loving someone else. But a moment came when I was able to make the decision, and know it was the right one. What we have, Rabindrah and I, is so wonderful. I don't see him as a separate individual any more. We have each become a vital part of the other, and sometimes I'm afraid of how happy we are. After all that I have lost.'

'You had the brains and the courage to recognise that Rabindrah was the one,' Hannah said. 'Unlike the fool I was, when I had that steamy affair with Viktor and pushed Lars out of my life. Imagine if he hadn't come back, hadn't been big enough to marry me and take care of Suniva?'

'Each one of us has lost more in the last five years than most people lose in a lifetime,' Camilla said. 'We've seen illness and death, been almost destroyed by violence, had all our dreams blown apart. But we can at least say that we still have each other. And I can also say that Sarah Singh is pretty heavy-handed with that wine. I'm already quite drunk.'

It was late when they finished their meal, and Camilla could not disguise her exhaustion.

'Back to the Norfolk with you, before you fall down,' Hannah said. 'You need to be strong tomorrow, and you haven't had any rest since you stepped off the plane this morning.'

'I'm going to ring the hospital,' Camilla said. 'If there's any change maybe we can stop on the way.'

But the duty nurse informed her that Mr Chapman was sleeping. There was no change in his condition and little point dropping in now. Camilla glanced around Anthony's sitting room and thought of the evenings they had spent together when he had come back from a safari, hungry for her, happy to close off the outside world, to talk to her and to make love beside the fire.

'Could I ask you both a favour?' she said.

'Anything.' Sarah did not hesitate.

'I'd like to ring Edward and tell him I'm going to stay here with you for the night, rather than have you drive me all the way into town at this late hour. Would that be all right?'

'It would be fine,' Hannah said. 'Here's the phone.'

Later, Camilla lay in Anthony's bed, listening to the night wind as it skittered over the roof. A hyena whupped and giggled in the distance and she heard a sound like a leopard's rasping noise at the end of the garden. It had been a long time since they had shared his tent on safari and slept with their limbs entangled, the soft stir of his breath on her cheek as they lay in the narrow camp bed. Had he really loved her all along? She turned over and fumbled for the light switch, her eyes blurred with sudden tears. There were no handkerchiefs on the bedside table and she slid open the drawer in search of tissues, only to find her own face staring up at her. It was a photograph that Sarah had taken of them. Anthony was standing behind her, his head bent towards her as he whispered something into her ear that made her smile. Camilla lifted the photograph out of the drawer and looked at it for a long time. Then she slipped it under her pillow and put out the bedside light. In spite of the whine of a single, persistent mosquito she fell into a dreamless sleep.

It was after ten when she arrived back at the Norfolk Hotel. Edward was pacing the sitting room.

'Do you realise how late it is?' he asked irritably. 'We're due to leave here in less than an hour. I was beginning to wonder if you were going to turn up at all. I don't think it was a good idea to have stayed out at Karen overnight.'

'I don't see what difference it made,' she said. 'I arranged for my clothes to be pressed yesterday, and I've already had a bath. I only have to dress. I'll be ready in plenty of time.'

'Have you been back to the hospital?' He was drumming his fingers on the sideboard.

'Yes. We looked in on the way into town. There's no change. He was asleep. Do you think you could order some coffee?'

The funeral car collected them just before eleven, and Sarah joined them for the silent journey to the cathedral. Edward stared out of the window and Camilla closed her eyes and distanced herself from any conversation. The sleek, black limousine turned in at the gates of All Saints, drawing up in the shadow of the towers that flanked the great doors. The bishop and provost moved down the steps to greet them. Reporters and photographers surrounded Camilla with flashing camera bulbs and she realised, with a shock, that a large number of people had gathered for the service. The British High Commissioner greeted her and Edward took her arm. As he steered her into the cathedral she heard the wail of sirens, and looked back to see a Mercedes draw up, flanked by two police motorcycles. The Minister of Tourism, Johnson Kiberu, had arrived. He stepped from his car, accompanied by his wife and surrounded by assistants and bodyguards. At the top of the steps he bowed over Camilla's hand, and the cameras exploded around them once more.

Then they were walking into the cathedral, under vaulted arches of chiselled grey stone, to take their places in the pews. She stopped beside Lars and Hannah who were waiting just inside the door with their two blonde children. And a small African boy. James Githiri. Camilla gestured to them to join her in the empty pew at the top of the long aisle. Places reserved for the family she did not have.

The morning sunlight streamed through the rose window, washing them all in a cruciform pattern of stained glass. The congregation filed in to take their places, and the organ pealed out the tumbling cadences of Bach's *Toccata and Fugue* as the bishop and attendant clergy walked in solemn procession to the high altar. Incense rose to fill the air with aromatic smoke. The choir stood up in the choir stalls and deep voices rang out in an anthem of resurrection. Rabindrah slipped into the place beside his wife and reached for Camilla's hand, pressing her fingers.

She stared at the coffin, draped in its white pall, with her wreath of red roses on the top. Candles flickered in the tall brass holders that stood sentinel at its head and foot. The cathedral was full. She had not realised that her father was so well known and respected. More importantly, she had never known his friends. There were people here who had worked with him, laughed with him, perhaps even listened to his confidences, knew some of his hopes and fears. Except for occasional mentions that had caught her attention in the London newspapers, she knew little of his recent achievements. Now she felt a deep sadness at her scant knowledge of his last years. She could see Johnson Kiberu and his entourage, seated in the front pew on the other side of the aisle. There were officials from the Game Department and the National Parks, and from the numerous administrative bodies with which he had worked. She recognised Erope, from the photographs Sarah had sent her. He was now a chief game warden in one of the northern game reserves, and he had known her father well. There must be others here too, she thought, who had been an important part of his life. Men and women who had come to say farewell to their friend. But to her they were strangers.

As the ceremony progressed, she drifted through the readings from scripture, the responses of the congregation, the hymns, the bishop's homily. She rose and sat and knelt automatically on Edward's cue, vaguely aware of his hand on her arm, guiding her through the liturgy. George's coffin was there in front of her, but her eyes stared through it and into another place.

Anthony's face filled her mind, and she saw again the despair and grief in his eyes. He had almost lost his own life in his attempt to save her father. She thought of him striding ahead of her across the bleached grasses of Samburu, climbing a *kopje* to sit on top of the rocks with his arms around her, jumping into the saddle of his favourite mare with his long legs searching for the stirrups. She heard his laugh, remembered him leading her on to the dance floor in Nairobi, whirling her around until she was dizzy. Now he was a scarred man; he had lost a limb. Broken and crippled, he would find it almost impossible to envisage a future that held out true fulfilment. Camilla wondered if there was another woman in his life who would help him now, who would try to make him whole and laughing and confident again. She sank to her knees, her hands covering her face, and Sarah leaned over to ask if she needed any help. She shook her head and stood up again. There was another hymn and then they were seated as Johnson Kiberu climbed to the pulpit to deliver his funeral oration. Camilla raised her head to listen.

'My friends,' the Minister began, 'we have gathered today to honour the passing of our good friend and colleague, George Broughton-Smith. A man who loved our country and its people, and who served Kenya in several different capacities. He came here in the years before *Uhuru*, to assist in the transition of our great nation to freedom. And he returned after Independence to serve in the area of conservation and development, raising money and working with our government, supporting the game parks and my own Tourism Ministry, in our efforts to protect our greatest asset. He was always aware of the necessity to establish a balance between the protection of Kenya's wildlife and the provision of land and food for our people. We shared fruitful discussions and spent many hours working to devise a strategy that would achieve these vital aims. He was a man who worked well in politics and in administration. But he was also a man who loved to be out in the bush, actively involved in the projects for which he was responsible. And that is where he lost his life. In a tragic helicopter crash, while on a conservation mission in the Masai Mara Game Reserve.

'He told me, on the last occasion I was with him, that contributing to the future of our great country was his passion and his vocation. That all his energies would continue to be channelled into helping Kenyans build a prosperous future, into making this the finest sanctuary for wildlife in all of Africa. And he gave his life for that ideal. Now we must grieve with his daughter, Camilla, and with all his friends and co-workers, over the loss of a great man. And we must make a promise that his love for Kenya, and his sacrifice, will be remembered by the continuation of the valuable work in which he was engaged. So I call on you all today to join me in a symbol of unity that the people of Kenya will work together to bring harmony and prosperity to every citizen.' He raised his arm with a clenched fist, and shouted his last word in a loud voice. '*Harambee!*'

For a second there was silence, and then each man and woman in the congregation rose to their feet, and the roar went up through the soaring arches of the cathedral: '*Harambee! Harambee!*'

When the voices stopped the organ swelled again, and the choir began to sing the recessional anthem. The pall-bearers stepped forward and raised the coffin to their shoulders, and the procession moved slowly down the aisle. Edward escorted Camilla out into the hard, tropical sunshine, and she stood on the steps of the cathedral, receiving condolences from those who had attended, and thanking all who had participated in the ceremony. The cameras flashed again as Johnson Kiberu made his farewells. Then she was in the secluded peace of the cemetery, looking at the array of floral tributes which were being lifted from the hearse. She saw a huge wreath of white roses, with a message attached in a big, bold hand: 'Deepest sympathy. You know where I am, when you need me. Your friend for always, Tom Bartlett.'

She reached down and touched the scented blooms with gratitude. When the final prayers and blessings had been said, and the coffin lowered into the ground, a terrible weight of futility descended on Camilla. She closed her eyes and leaned against Edward.

'I need to go back to the hotel,' she said. 'I have to lie down. I need to be on my own for a while.'

In the cottage she tried to calm herself, but she was on the verge of tears, crumbling within her self-imposed emotional straightjacket. In one of the private dining rooms her friends were waiting for her, and she could not let them down. She took a great, shuddering breath and, for the first time in many years, she prayed for strength, ending with an appeal to her father.

'Help me, Daddy,' she whispered. 'Bring me through this and help me, please.'

When she finally walked into the room it was Dan and Allie who greeted her first.

'He was a great guy with a big vision,' Dan said. 'We'll miss him sorely, both for his contribution to Kenya's wildlife and as a personal friend.'

'We had good times together,' Allie said. 'He loved you very much, and I wish you could have shared some of them with us.'

'I wish it too.' Camilla's words were filled with remorse.

'Well, maybe you'll make your way up to our camp someday,' Dan said. 'With Rabindrah and Sarah on one of their visits, perhaps. We'd love to have you there.'

The reception was a strained affair and it was difficult to keep the conversation light and normal for the sake of the children. Lars introduced them with pride.

'You remember Suniva, your god-daughter,' he said to Camilla. 'She's a young lady now, going on four. This tiger here is Piet. And this is James Githiri.'

Camilla looked at Simon's son. He was of slight build, standing back and very shy, his small fingers clutching the sleeve of Lars's jacket. She glanced at Hannah and saw the soft encouragement in her face as she pushed the little boy forward. He stared back at her, his huge eyes round with awe.

'Why are you wearing a big black hat?' Suniva asked. 'Why are you so sad? Can I try on your hat?'

'You certainly can,' Camilla said. 'We'll do that right after lunch, and if it nearly fits you, then you may have it.'

All through the meal the children watched Camilla with questioning eyes, openly fascinated by the beautiful lady with the black dress and the pale gold hair. She noticed that Lars was withdrawn at first, and put it down to disapproval of her unexplained disappearance. He was probably angry that she had upset Hannah. But after a time he warmed to Camilla again, and she was moved by the small courtesies and kindnesses he pressed on her. There was talk about Langani and the lodge, and the book about the Rift Valley that Sarah and Rabindrah were working on. Time and again the conversation returned to the subject of wildlife and the extraordinary contribution that George Broughton-Smith had made to so many aspects of conservation. When coffee was finally served, Camilla stood up and drew Edward aside.

'I'm going back to the hospital for a while,' she said. 'Sarah will take me, and Hannah is coming too. Lars is going to stay here with the children, and they can go to the swimming pool. You could probably do with an hour or two at the pool yourself. Or a siesta in the cottage.'

'How long will you be?' he asked. 'Shall I book somewhere for dinner, for us all?'

'I don't know,' she said. 'I can't think about dinner reservations now.'

'We should also do something about air reservations. I need to be back in London over the weekend, because I have appointments on Monday.'

'It's too soon to decide on travel dates,' she said. 'I just have to make my way through today. I can't plan beyond that.'

'Camilla, we will do all we can for him,' Edward said. 'But it can be better organised from London. Whatever he needs in the way of help, we can arrange it from there. We must go home, darling. I was even thinking about the possibility of flying out tonight. There are first-class seats available on BOAC. I checked earlier.'

'I don't know.'

'My dear, I know this is the most difficult situation. But it won't help you to stay here for any length of time. It won't bring you any peace or—'

'How do you know what it will bring?' she said. 'Or where I will find peace?'

His expression changed and his tone was cold and reproving when he spoke again. 'It's time to go home, Camilla.'

'I don't know,' she said again. 'You shouldn't ask me to decide now.'

'I am asking you,' Edward said, his hands gripping her shoulders. 'I want you to tell me that you will be on the plane with me. If not tonight, then tomorrow. I do know what is best for you, my dear. I'm sure you realise that.'

She saw that doubt had begun to cloud his eyes, and she turned away quickly before he could press her further.

'I'm going to the hospital now,' she said. 'I have no idea when I'll be back, and there's nothing else I can say. I'll telephone when it's possible.'

When they crept into Anthony's room he was awake, his eyes slightly unfocused.

'All of you.' His voice was a rasp. 'Together. What an amazing sight!'

They embraced him, each one touching his face with tenderness, smiling down at him, composing small phrases of affection and support. Within a short time he was tired, drifting away from them.

'If you want to stay for a while, we'll wait downstairs,' Hannah said.

Camilla sat down and placed her hand on Anthony's bandaged arm. 'It's over,' she said. 'The funeral and so on. He's at peace now, and I think I can learn from that.'

'When will you be leaving?' he whispered, his eyes closed.

She did not answer. Instead she stood up and leaned over him, placing her lips against his forehead to kiss him softly. Then she put her fingers on his mouth and traced the shape of it before kissing him again. She was shocked at his strength as he pushed her hand aside.

'Don't,' he said. 'Don't pity me now, because I'm a cripple. Don't make me even less of a man by feeling sorry for me, because I have an ugly stump instead of a leg. Because I'm burnt and scarred. Don't do this. Just leave me. For God's sake, go.'

'It's not about pity,' she said. 'Your burns will heal. The doctors will graft new skin on to the damaged places, and they'll heal up just fine. I know about this, because I met so many people recovering from burns when my face was cut. And you will be able to walk, Anthony. It will take time and practice, but you will do it.'

She heard a sound and at first she could not believe the source of it, a howling noise that started deep down in his belly and poured from his lips in a long, uninterrupted wail. His arms thrashed on the bed as he wept and moaned and cried. The door burst open and the nurses were suddenly there, soothing him, talking to him in kind but firm voices. Camilla stood in the furthest corner of the room, trembling as the terrible sound faded and died away. But after a few minutes he cried out again, almost screaming, insisting that his leg was on fire, that he could not bear the agony of it. Finally he raised himself up, thrashing against the soothing hold of the nurses, directing his pain at Camilla, shouting at her that he wanted to die, that she should stop torturing him and leave him, and never come back. She fled from the room, sick and shaken, and waited outside in the corridor, leaning against the wall with her arms wrapped around her body.

'Was it something that I did?' Camilla was outside the door when Nurse Thorpe emerged.

'No, my dear. I'm afraid there are moments when he can't control everything. When it all rushes up into his mind.'

'But what about the pain in his leg? Can't something be done about that?'

'That's a difficult problem. It's called phantom pain. It doesn't exist at all, except in the mind. Almost all amputees suffer from it at one time or another.'

Amputees. The word hit her hard, knocking away her resolve. She made a high, bird-like sound of distress and spun away, running headlong through the corridor to the waiting room, flinging herself into the arms of her friends. Her sisters. The only real family she had, her only source of courage and comfort. They sat together as she described his anger and fear, and the desolation in the sounds he had made.

'He thinks I'm here out of pity. He told me to leave. Not to come back. I've just made it worse for him,' Camilla said, rocking to and fro in her distress. 'I've no idea how to comfort him, what to say or do. Oh God, I thought I could help him, and instead I've caused him nothing but pain and grief. I don't know how to do this at all.'

'Camilla.' Sarah took hold of her shoulders. 'Camilla, what is it you want to do?'

'I want to help him.'

'Why?' Sarah demanded. 'Tell me why.'

Camilla shook her head. She stood up and walked to the window, not looking at either of her friends.

'Listen to me, Camilla. Don't fail him now. If you love this man, then tell him now that you love him, because you may never get another chance. I never had enough chances to tell Piet how much I loved and needed him. Hannah didn't put her arms around him, on that morning, when he left us for the last time. She didn't let him know, one more time, that she loved him too. And she never said goodbye to poor Janni, nor he to her. You've lost Marina, and you weren't able to tell your father that he was a good man.'

'There's no certainty in any of this,' Camilla said. 'I can't be sure of a future.'

'All love is a risk,' Sarah said. 'But if we don't take that chance, our moment may be gone for ever. I had to take that leap with Rabindrah, and I'm grateful that I did. So if you love Anthony, then go back in there, Camilla. Go and tell him you love him. Stay with him, no matter what he says. Make up your mind that you will never run away again, that you will never pass up a single moment when you can tell him what he means to you. Because you don't know if you will be given another day, or even another hour, that you can share.'

There were tears on her face now. On all their faces. Sarah stepped back to stand beside Hannah. Then she reached out and gave Camilla a small push, and they watched her walk away down the corridor, keeping her in their sights until she raised her hand to knock and enter Anthony's room.

Glossary

Afrikaner:	person of Boer origin, from South Africa
asante:	thank you
askari:	policeman or guard
ayah:	child's nurse
banda:	bungalow or small cottage
bhang:	marijuana
bibi:	woman, wife
boma:	a fenced-in enclosure for dwellings and livestock
bundu:	bushland
bushbaby:	a nocturnal animal, one of the smallest primates
bwana:	title of respect to a white man, or boss
dawa:	medicine
debbi:	metal container for liquid
domkop:	idiot, or fool
duka wallah:	a shopkeeper
fisi:	hyena
gari:	vehicle, car
hapana:	no
haraka:	hurry up
harambee:	everyone pull together
hodi:	hello, anyone home?
Iko simu:	There is a telephone call

jambo:	greetings, hello
kaffir:	derogatory term for a black man
kali:	fierce, cross, sharp
kanga:	brightly coloured cloth, worn by women
karibu:	welcome, come in
Kirinyaga:	Kikuyu god, believed to live on Mount Kirinyaga or Mount Kenya
kitenge:	a length of brightly coloured cloth
kopje:	a rocky outcrop
kuni:	firewood
lekker:	wonderful, fantastic
lugga:	a dried-out river bed
mahindi or mealie:	a corn cob
manyatta:	traditional dwelling of Maasai and Samburu tribes
Mau Mau:	violent uprising by the Kikuyu tribe, initially against white settlers
memsahib:	title of respect towards a white woman
mpishi:	cook
munt:	derogatory term for an African
mzee:	a title of respect towards an old person
the Mzee:	title given to Jomo Kenyatta, who became president of Kenya
mzungu:	foreigner (usually white)
ndio:	yes
ngalawa:	dugout canoe
ngombe:	cow
nguvu:	vigour or gumption
nkosi:	boss, sir
nyoka:	snake
panga:	large flat-bladed knife, like a machete
pole:	slowly, or sorry
pole sana:	very slowly, or very sorry

posho:	ground maize meal, used as a staple food
rafiki ya ʒamani:	an old friend
rondavel:	round house
rungu:	large stick
salaams:	greetings – as in hello
salwar kameeʒ:	type of tunic and trousers
samahani:	sorry
sasa hivi:	right now, immediately
shamba:	smallholding, a garden
shauri:	a problem or argument or matter of disagreement
Shifta:	Somali bandits
shitani:	devil, evil spirit
shuka:	traditional red blanket worn by Maasai and Samburu warriors
sijui:	I don't know
sukuma:	push
terrs:	Rhodesian slang for 'terrorists'
toto:	child (short for *mtoto*)
Uhuru:	freedom, the political term for Independence
veldt:	grassy plain
watu:	men, labourers
waʒungu:	white people
yaapie:	term for a person of Afrikaans origin

www.vintage-books.co.uk